ELEGY OF THE DREAMER

BOOK THREE OF A DREAMER'S MISFORTUNE

C.A. FARRAN

ELEGY
of the
DREAMER

C. A. FARRAN

Copyright © 2025 by C.A. Farran

All rights reserved.

Sylvan Ink Press LLC

This edition published in 2026

Edited by Friel Black from Grey Moth Editing @greymothediting

Map created with Inkarnate

Cover design: Franziska Stern @coverdungeonrabbit

Artwork "Another Life, Another Night in the Tavern" by @koijix

ISBN 9798994604403 (paperback)

ISBN 9798994604410 (hardcover) | ISBN 9798994604427 (ebook)

No AI was used in the writing, editing, creating, or design of this book. All em dashes are included by humans who love them dearly.

For anyone with an entire world living in your head. We need your stories.

PROLOGUE

The rope was cool against the burning skin of his neck. Memories of her lifeless body, dragged and deposited at their master's feet, made bile rise in his throat.

She'd been waiting for him.

He hadn't made it in time.

Her roughly torn clothing had revealed no wounds. No explanation for how the brightest light of this world had been snuffed out.

He twisted in his bindings, staring up at the gnarled branches of the yew tree. The place where they used to meet in secret. Where he explored every curve of her body. Swore his heart and his fealty to her beyond death.

How fitting to find himself here again.

"It's a shame you threw it all away." The master's voice was angry, accusing. As if he was the one betrayed. "You had less than a decade left to your contract."

Only an entitled bastard who'd never served anyone but himself would regard a decade of servitude as a drop in a bucket. Not to mention, masters always found ways to extend contracts far beyond their length. Charging for room and board, as if they weren't all relegated to cold storage rooms beneath the ground.

But even that he could have withstood for whatever time he had to, were it not for Lark. The moment he had set eyes on her, he knew he'd do anything to get her out of that place. The way she tended to the children born to indentures and trapped in that life. The delicate lilt of her voice when she sang them to sleep. She was a reminder of a different life, one where softness was rewarded with kindness rather than lashings.

The strength of his feelings for her had crept up on him. Had snuck in through nights of listening to her hum the songs he'd been tasked with playing during the master's banquets. He was ensnared by the sound of her laugh, so addicting, he would have done anything to hear it again. And when they had spent countless nights talking in hushed whispers of her plans for life after servitude, he had been besotted. Far and away gone for her, this ray of hope in the dark room of stone.

A harsh wind cut through the aging forest, drying the sweat along his brow.

They were supposed to be long gone by now, he and his Lark. His love. His *wife*. But they hadn't slipped away when they'd had the chance.

A blood-red sky crept overhead as the sun fell behind the horizon. The light of the dwindling day illuminated the guards and their sneers. They would be the last thing he saw. So instead, he closed his eyes, conjuring the visage of her face. Eyes of honey and hair like wildfire. The way her lips curved in a smile meant only for him. The open expression of unyielding love and trust as they spoke their vows, binding themselves to each other for eternity. She would be the image he carried into the void, all the while repeating the words:

Death is not the end. I will find you again.

CHAPTER ONE

AISLINN

*A*islinn gasped, her back arching as the sensation of her soul reentering her body sent ice spearing through her bones. The familiar rush of exhaustion weighed upon her limbs, and her stomach dipped, threatening to empty its contents all over Inerys' floor. She swallowed down the nausea, massaging her temples to relieve the pounding in her head.

She shouldn't have pushed so hard, but she couldn't bear to return with nothing but her failure once again.

Aislinn glanced over at where Lark watched her with bloodshot eyes, her pale hand clutching Gavriel's limp one with such fierce intensity, her arm trembled.

Lark's chest stilled as if she held her breath. Waiting for Aislinn to finally have good news. To have finally been able to communicate with Gavriel the way she'd promised she could weeks ago. That she'd been more than a useless bystander within his dreams. An unwelcome intruder witnessing his intimate moments and memories with no way of making him hear her, no matter how loudly she called his name.

Aislinn cleared her throat, the echoes of how she'd screamed herself hoarse lingering even in the waking world.

Gavriel never heard her.

"I'm sorry, Lark."

Lark nodded, her gaze falling to the floor. Each disappointment seemed to hunch her shoulders in on herself, caving her posture as if she felt the weight of every failure.

But the failure belonged to Aislinn.

She'd been experimenting with projecting her consciousness the way Inerys had instructed. With Lark, it was effortless, like the tether from when the Reaper first led her soul to the afterlife had never been broken. Everyone else took strength and focus.

When she seeped into Gavriel's dream the first time, she'd been so shocked by it, she broke the connection immediately, sprinting out the door to find Lark and tell her the good news.

She should have waited.

Entering his dreams was not the same as communicating with him. So far, she'd witnessed him in countless different forms. As a small child, weeping for his mother as a man with blue eyes held him on the stone steps of a great fortress. As a young man, purging all over the floor after his first kill. An indenture, clutching his violin so tightly the neck snapped when Lark was punished for spilling wine on the lap of a visiting noble.

She'd seen him as a poor farmhand, a thief, a blacksmith's apprentice working the bellows. He'd worn a dozen different faces. Peered out from different sets of eyes, but she always knew it was him. The dreamer.

"What was it this time?" Lark's voice was scratchy and thick, her golden eyes bloodshot from lack of sleep.

"The execution."

Lark kissed his knuckles and rested her cheek against the back of his hand.

Aislinn had seen this memory before. The most frequent of his dreams. When the guards dragged him to an ancient yew, strung him up, and let him swing. Though Gavriel wore an unfamiliar face, the steely glint in his eyes was the same.

She'd witnessed the memory of him finding Lark's form. The way

4

he howled and fell to his knees, bundling her lifeless body to his chest. Sobs wracking his body with such violence.

But he was always quiet at his own execution.

"Next time." Aislinn always made that promise, the one she had no business making.

Lark nodded, her stare never wavering from Gavriel's deathlike face.

CHAPTER TWO

LARK

"*Y*ou're distracted." Daciana's voice penetrated the haze of fatigue clouding Lark's mind.

They were supposed to be sparring, an aspect of Lark's training to keep her ready for a promised fight. Lark had created a shooting course through the woods to practice with her bow, a running path to keep her muscles strong, and a sparring ring.

Lark preferred the quiet of shooting or running, nothing but the sound of her own breathing and the crunch of snow underfoot.

Though she still practiced with the Reaper Blade, a proven advantage against demons and Undesirables, she had incorporated a new sword into the circuit. One with a longer reach. Lark had gone through the motions a thousand times, until every pass of the blade was as instinctive as breathing and she could perform the five-strike series in her sleep. The weapon she wielded was heavier now, a longsword with a leather grip and twin wolves forming the guard.

A gift from Daciana, bartered for with coin she shouldn't have sacrificed.

The sword hung limply in Lark's grasp, its weight barely registering. Her boots had sunk into the freshly fallen snow, and her cloak hung open in the fierce wind, but the bite of cold failed to meet her skin. Her limbs were heavy, and her thoughts couldn't land on one purpose. Instead, they scattered like the dusting of snow in the wind.

"I'm tired." Nights of waiting by Gavriel's side, hoping to see any glimpse of his return. Of hating to sleep because sleeping meant dreaming and dreaming meant forgetting.

But she always remembered. Once reality broke through, cracking the façade of unconscious fantasy, she remembered.

"When was the last time you slept?"

"I sleep."

"It doesn't count if you're sitting in a chair and doze off for a few moments. When was the last time you *slept*?"

Lark rolled her shoulder, irritation tightening the muscles in her neck. "It doesn't matter."

"It *does*. You'll run yourself into the ground." Daciana sheathed her own weapon and strode toward her. With a gentle touch, she lifted her chin, frowning at whatever she saw on Lark's face. "Gavriel will wake. And when he does, we need you ready for what comes next."

Nereida. The fall of the veil. The swarms of Undesirables moving across the land like a plague. It was a destructive sort of chaos, nothing organized or tactical, but one couldn't assume Nereida was done with her plan. That she'd sit back and watch without revealing yet another hidden poison in her arsenal.

Lark swallowed against a tight throat. "Inerys said—"

"I know what she said." Daciana let out a derisive snort. "And I do not accept it."

Lark sheathed her sword and rubbed her burning eyes. With each passing day, her faith that Gavriel would awaken slipped away like water through a sieve. Inerys' doubt was written in the firm set of her jaw and pity-filled eyes. She had once warned Lark that if she were to access all his memories from all his lives, she would need to proceed with caution. That flooding his mind with every life he'd lived as his soul was reborn over and over would break him.

Nereida had taken great pleasure in bestowing that curse on him. But when Aislinn said she could enter his dreams, communicate with him, a fragile hope bloomed in Lark's chest. No, not fragile. It began as a sturdy sort, a hope that fought its way through the mires of doubt. It was only now, weeks later, that it had grown frail and easy to break.

There was nothing quite like an invisible enemy, a foe she had no defense against. So long as there was purpose, Lark could hurtle toward whatever may come. But with no direction to guide her, she was lost.

"We should head into town, pay Alistair and Langford a visit."

Daciana frowned but said nothing to reveal she knew Lark was avoiding the subject.

Langford and Alistair had chosen to stay at the Walden Inn, taking up permanent residence in Mrs. O'Connell's lodgings. They'd claimed Inerys' home was too small to accommodate them all, but already the cottage had expanded, breathing more rooms into existence, a spell Inerys must have cast. Lark suspected there was an alternative reason they elected to stay away. Whenever they came by, there was an edge of desperation between them. Every time Alistair drifted too far from Langford's side, tension hardened Langford's posture and his hands began to shake. There was an unspoken plea, a terror born from the pain of loss. In every touch that lingered for an extra heartbeat. In every searching glance from across the room.

Would she experience this comingling of pain and relief when Gavriel awoke?

If Gavriel awoke.

"Lark—"

"Actually, I wish to run my shooting drills once more." Lark refused to meet what she was sure to be Daciana's pitying stare. She couldn't stomach it. "Alone."

There was a strange comfort in shutting everything out. In muffling the echoes of her worries and fears. Ceto had once accused Lark of burying her head in the sand, what seemed like lifetimes ago.

Perhaps she was right.

For the first time since Lark was remade as human, it was almost easy to deaden the pulses of fear and pain. To shove everything so far below the surface, she became nearly numb. A living ghost.

A Reaper.

Even as the snow crunched underfoot, Daciana's parting words met Lark's ears:

"Wall yourself in, Lark. Whatever helps in this moment. But know you're not alone."

LARK GASPED down another sharp inhale of icy air. It pricked her throat and lungs, somehow searing, as she pulled her bowstring. Sweat curled the fine hairs at her forehead and temples, drying and cooling as instantaneously as it came. She was nearing the end of her shooting course through Emerald Woods. Sprinting between targets, pulling and aiming without thought, the physical toll lent reprieve to her exhausted thoughts.

Her arrow sunk in the edge of the target, a hit but not a very good one. If Hugo were here—

Lark pulled another arrow, a grunt escaping her lips as she released. A center hit.

Now she could move on to the next one.

She fought to free her feet from the snow, one heavy boot in front of the other. Focusing on the way her steps sunk into wet, thick ground. On her pulse pounding in her ears. On the way her chest burned, her side twinged, her back ached.

A twig snapped ten paces to the east. Lark spun, pulling and holding at her anchor point. Her heart battered against her ribs, the impact near painful.

Inerys has warded her home to prevent Undesirables from attacking. She'd extended as far into the woods as she could, and Lark should have set her course within the limits, but she'd needed the solitude. To fall apart free from Daciana's compassionate stare or Aislinn's guilt.

It was worth the risk. Lark had her bow. Her dagger. Her sword.

Let them come.

A figure ducked out from behind a tree, gold hair shimmering against the frozen scenery.

9

Ferryn.

He wore a sheepish expression and rubbed the back of his neck.

With a sigh, Lark lowered her bow.

"In hindsight, sneaking up on someone alone and armed might have been one of my more foolish ideas."

Lark almost smiled. "That's not saying much. You boast a profound sum of foolish ideas."

Ferryn scowled, and the exaggerated expression against the sharp features of his face made him even prettier. "I don't need you to wound my pride. It's already a decrepit creature, limping alongside me."

Lark tucked her unshot arrow into the quiver at her back and slipped her bow over her shoulder. Ferryn rubbed his hands together and tugged his cloak closer. He had only been in her company for a few weeks, adjusting to his newly human body same as she. The same impish grin slashed against the face of Lark's oldest friend. The same casual posture softened the length of his long body. But the hardness of his eyes was new. Whatever had happened when he and Aislinn escaped Lacuna, he'd been changed.

"I would have thought your pride to be as stubborn as you."

It was easy to do this. To keep her words surface level. It was a level of comfort she couldn't quite reach with Daciana lately. Not with her keen focus that missed nothing.

Ferryn smirked but it faded as quickly as it came. "Lark—"

"Not you, too." Lark pushed past him, her shoulder catching his as he tried to block her path.

"You can't do this. Not again."

Lark clenched her fist as heat bloomed along her throat. "I will not discuss this."

Ferryn grabbed her arm and spun her around to face him. "Fine. Don't say a word. Just listen."

"I said I will not—"

"No." Ferryn shook her hard. "You're not going to sink under." His voice was sharp, and his face turned a mottled red. "I won't watch you drown again."

Lark's chest tightened, and her eyes burned.

"I won't tell you how you should feel—"

"How kind of you."

"But I will say this: you have more than you're willing to admit. You have a group of people, ready and willing to die for you. You get that, right? You know we're not just along for the ride. We're *here,* Lark. No matter what comes, no matter what fate brings, you'll never be alone again."

Hadn't Daciana echoed the same sentiment in fewer words? Were her moods drawing the pity of everyone around her?

Something suspiciously close to shame burned in her gut. "Fuck fate."

Ferryn huffed a soft laugh, shaking his head. "Aislinn exhausts herself trying to bring him back to you. Did you know she spends entire days resting after pushing herself too far to reach him?"

Lark hadn't known. Hadn't wanted to know. If she had, she'd never have allowed Aislinn to risk herself again and again.

"She's blameless," Ferryn continued, "and so are you."

Lark swallowed. "That's not what I think."

"Then why do you hide?"

"I'm not hiding."

"You're hiding right now. Standing before me, you posture and lie and shove everything you want to say down. What do you fear? You think I haven't witnessed your least charming self? Let me have it, Lark. I'm not going anywhere."

"Stop trying to manage me."

"Then stop being difficult, and tell me what poisons your thoughts. Tell me you're afraid. Tell me you hate me, you wish to run, you blame us, yourself. Say whatever you think I can't handle hearing before you burst."

Lark lunged, shoving him hard against a frost-covered tree. The air whooshed out of him in a sharp grunt. "Stop acting like you know all. Like you still have keen insight to my psyche as if nothing has changed. You don't know a thing about me. Maybe you never did. You were a half-rate Reaper then, and you're a delusional human now."

Ferryn dug his fingers into the thick fabric of her sleeves. "Is that the best you can do?" He laughed. "Stop holding back. Stop shutting me out."

Lark shoved at him again, loosening his grip on her. He only bundled her tighter against his chest. "Let go of me." She reached for Hugo's knife, heart hammering in her throat.

Steel was pressed against his throat, Lark's mind having gone momentarily blank. She shuddered, staring at where the edge of her blade indented pale skin. Her head pounded, and her eyes burned. What was she doing? What in the void had possessed her? As her anger dimmed, something cold took root. A seeping dread and melancholy. Her numbness and then her anger were far safer to reside in.

Lark let out a stuttered breath, lowering her hand from Ferryn's neck. A red drop squeezed free from the spot where her blade had just been.

"Skies. I'm sorry." Finally, after weeks of unshed tears, a dam ruptured. "Ferryn—I'd never—I didn't—"

"Shh, it's all right." Ferryn pulled her against him, resting his chin on the top of her head. "Hush, little bird. I understand."

Tears rolled down Lark's face, dampening the front of his exposed tunic. Sobs wracked her body as the weight of exhaustion, of fear, of guilt, of overwhelming failure poured out of her.

"It's all my fault," she said, hiccuping. "I goaded her. Handed her everything she needed to burn the world to ash."

Ferryn rubbed soothing circles against her arms, saying nothing.

"She used my pride." Lark sucked in a few mouthfuls of air, matching her breathing to Ferryn's. "I had the weapon. She was right there, and I failed. I failed everyone. Especially Gavriel." Her voice broke on his name, and a fresh wave of tears rolled down her cheeks. "What if I've lost him?"

Ferryn hummed. "You didn't. One can't lose their shadow, can they? You won't be rid of him that easily." His fingers found her jaw, lifting her head to look at him. His brows furrowed when he met her eyes, and he swept his thumbs across her face. "She outplayed us all, Lark. You're not the only one to feel the fool." Something in his expression darkened. Was he thinking of Ceto? "We have to move forward. Gavriel will wake when he's ready. Aislinn is doing every-thing she can to help. But you need to find a purpose, or you'll go mad."

With a gentle shove, he stood her upright, so she was no longer in his embrace. "What would you do next?"

That was an impossible question. One that only reminded Lark of all the other unanswered questions she'd been avoiding.

The matter of the lowered veil. Of monsters and Undesirables roaming with impunity. Were the paragons in Avalon watching the chaos unfold? What was Nereida's next move? Were Reapers even collecting lost souls anymore without Thanar?

Lark's stomach gave a sickening lurch at the thought of his name. Thanar was dead. Gone. Erased from existence. Seasons ago, this would have given her cause for celebration. But now, it only left her feeling like she'd swallowed a mouthful of bread without properly chewing.

"I don't know."

Ferryn nodded as if expecting her answer. "Promise me this, Lark, no matter how heavy the darkness feels, how deep it pulls you under"—he braced a hand on her shoulder—"remember you have something to fight for."

Lark nodded. At his scowl, she added, "I promise."

But she added a promise to herself. To do whatever it took to make the world a worthy place for Gavriel if he awoke.

When he awoke.

CHAPTER THREE

LANGFORD

*L*angford frowned at his satchel, debating the layout of his packing attempt. On the morrow, they were traveling to Stormfair to escort the mead seller and his wares back to Oakbury for Mrs. O'Connell, and Langford wanted to be sure he knew what he was bringing.

The leather bag was stretched as far as possible without ripping the stitching, the front flap unable to reach the fastening toggle. Three more books sat on his and Alistair's bed, taunting him.

He was going to have to be more economical and make a sacrifice of great importance.

Did he need to bring multiple books on the journey?

Tugging the cramped books free from his bag, he examined each one with calculating scrutiny. He immediately placed the dissertation on paragons and the human pursuit of meaning in the keep pile along with the stolen tome of archaic weapons and mythology from the Kovalian library.

Nothing mythical about his findings there.

He placed the romantic adventure novel in the trade pile. It was impractical to make room for leisure reading, something he doubted he'd have much time for anyway. The days were spent helping Mrs.

O'Connell around the inn and tavern for a far too generous payment. But the reprieve from life-threatening excursions to quietly stockpile coin that wasn't earned through stealing, lying, or slaying was sorely needed.

At least until they could discern their next move, a decision that grew more imperative with each passing day. It was likely this would be their last errand for the kind innkeeper.

Travelers came through with talk of monster sightings, and each story was passed along to Kenna—Daciana's hunter. But there hadn't been an attack in these parts for at least a fortnight. Langford suspected Inerys of exerting considerable effort in her protective measures.

Like all the major organs in the human body, each of them had their part to play. After payment for this errand, Langford and Alistair would rejoin the others to plan their next move rather than for a mere passing visit.

Langford turned his attention to the field guide of poisonous plants and their uses, a rare find this side of the Grey Shoal Ocean, and one he was sure Gavriel would enjoy.

Langford froze, a wave of pity washing over him once more. He'd allowed three days to pass since he last checked Gavriel's vitals, assured there was no cause for alarm in his physical state.

Apart from the obvious.

He ran a hand through his untidy hair. He couldn't imagine what Lark was feeling. Not with any real substantial understanding. Gavriel wasn't gone, but he wasn't here. He was lost in this ambiguous in-between that confounded Langford to aggravation. While his body showed no signs of starvation, sickness, or any other malady to cause concern apart from his inability to awaken, Langford could make no further assertions.

Langford couldn't surmise how this was all achieved, and he suspected the answer resided beyond his scope of medical understanding, delving instead into the world of impossible.

It wouldn't be the first time, nor the last.

Memories of Alistair's final strangled breath flooded Langford's mind. How the life left his eyes, and his body fell slack. Alistair had died. His heart had ceased beating, his chest had stilled, and Langford had held his corpse.

Were it not for Daciana…

Langford tried to slow the panicked rate of his breath. It wouldn't do to fall to pieces, not again. It was as though it happened yesterday rather than weeks ago. Even the land had seen it fit to move on, the dregs of autumn having been swept away by the first of many snowfalls. Dead leaves buried beneath layers of snow, forgotten until the next thaw.

If only he could have the same success.

He brought his shaky fist to his mouth, focusing on aiming each exhale against his knuckles.

Alistair was alive.

He'd come back to him.

Some days, it was harder to remember that. But the memory of those moments Langford had lost him—the way his heart had ripped from his chest like a physical wound no pain he'd ever suffered could compete with—those remained perfect in their clarity.

Langford exhaled a sharp breath and moved the romantic adventure novel from the trade pile to the keep pile.

Perhaps a little impractical escapism was exactly what he needed.

***

"PARAGON'S ARSEHOLE, what did you fill these with, rocks?" Alistair shouldered Langford's pack alongside his own. The pair of horses Mrs. O'Connell had stabled for them to ride on such errands were huddled together. The night had brought a bracing cold Langford could only hope would abate in the midday sun.

"You know better than to ask questions to which you already know the answers." Langford reached for the strap, but Alistair batted his hand away.

"Allow me this. You'll be rewarding me for it tonight."

"You already claimed your reward last night. And this morning."

Even as Langford jested, meeting Alistair's desire to openly discuss such things, his cheeks grew hot.

Alistair arched a brow at him and leaned against the stall door. "Aye. And you haven't begun to balance the debt." He tugged him to his chest. "I doubt you will in this lifetime."

Langford laughed even as the implication of his words made his pulse impossible to ignore. "Chivalry dictates a kind gesture need no reward. You make a terrible gentleman."

Alistair's signature smirk tugged at the corner of his mouth. "We both know I'm not a gentleman." He kissed Langford hard on the mouth, silencing any protestation he might have given.

Dazed, Langford broke the kiss, stumbling toward his mount. They were a fine pair of horses, sturdy and large which would serve them well through the snow and ice. More than sixteen hands tall, they were the largest horses Langford had ever ridden. He'd debated taking Lark's beloved horse, but the farmer Mrs. O'Connell shared her with wouldn't allow such a thing. The horse was destined to be spoiled and pampered.

Langford began to saddle the horse when Alistair cut him off.

"You're tired," he said, far too gently. "Sit and stay warm. I'll do this."

Langford tightened his fist, ignoring the strange sensation that came with the loss of his finger. It would be easier to discuss such things if Alistair maintained his flippant demeanor about them.

But there was nothing glib about the times Alistair bundled him in his arms, allowing him to soak his neck with his tears while reassuring him he was fine. He was alive.

"I'm no more tired than you, I'm sure."

Alistair's eyes softened. "Don't worry about me."

It seemed worrying about Alistair was becoming a permanent characteristic of Langford's.

"We should get going."

Alistair nodded, pressed a quick kiss to Langford's forehead, and continued readying their mounts.

"AND DID you know mead was responsible for the term honeymoon?" Huxley shouted from the driver's seat of his wagon.

Huxley was a decent fellow if a bit overenthusiastic about his mead. When they'd first arrived in Stormfair, he'd ushered them in and made them sample each of his fermented honey wines. The sweeter ones were rather enjoyable, Langford had to admit. He'd occupied their time into the wee hours of the morning, detailing his process and bemoaning the temporary shutdown of trade in their village. He'd been unable to afford hiring a protective escort and without their trade market, he'd been stuck sitting on his wares for months.

"I've had these barrels ready since summer, but no one in town felt like celebrating in seasons," he'd said. *"Poor chaps. I never was blessed with children. Or a lady. But I have my bees, and they keep me busy. Probably have a keen sense of what it takes to be a parent looking after those rascals."*

With enough mead in his belly, Alistair had been all too happy to listen to the man wax on about his mead and refer to his dormant bees by name. But in the cold light of an even colder day, and after a night without sleep, he didn't appear to enjoy it so much.

"It was once common to gift the happy couple a moon's cycle worth of mead in both celebration and promotion of good fortune and fertility!" Huxley continued, his boisterous voice echoing in the snowy woods.

Though Alistair was supposed to take the lead and Langford the flank, he'd led his horse to ride alongside Langford to avoid getting an earful of Huxley's fervor.

It hardly helped.

"We're not getting paid enough," Alistair said, rubbing his temple.

Langford stifled a laugh. "You should ask him for another sample." He gestured to the barrels in the back of the wagon cart. "It would make you more agreeable."

"So would gifting the man a muzzle."

"I'm tempted to accuse you of being rude."

18

Alistair grinned. "Wouldn't be the worst thing said of me."

"No doubt."

"You wound me!"

Langford rolled his eyes and reveled in the way some things never changed. No matter what transpired, or how their friendship had evolved into this all-consuming passion he'd never thought possible—no matter the promises Alistair whispered in his ear when his fears manifested as terrible nightmares—they always had this. The comfort of easy banter. Of never worrying his jests—truthful in nature but embellished in delivery—were always met with equal humor.

Because he and Alistair, they understood one another. After all this time, how could they not?

A harsh wind ushered through the trees, drifting fresh snow powder to sting Langford's nose and eyes. He pulled the scarf under his chin back into place over his mouth and nose. Winter in Ardenas was a dreadful affair, marked with chapped knuckles and wind-burnt cheeks.

Perhaps one day, when all this was over, he and Alistair could spend each winter season somewhere warm. Not Koval, as much as Langford longed to visit the library again. Too many enemies. Too many memories. Anquan boasted a mild winter. Kenna spoke of their Feastday celebration, an entire week of fires and dancing and more food than even the finest banquets in Koval. They'd have to bring Lark to such an event.

His heart panged at the thought of her. He'd kept his distance, not because he wished it, but because he couldn't give her the news she so desperately wished to hear. That Gavriel would wake. Langford couldn't know that, and perhaps that made him cruel, his unwillingness to plant hope where he only felt doubt, but he couldn't bring himself to lie.

He did not know when or if Gavriel would wake.

And here he was, still mourning the death of the man he loved though he rode beside him. He could talk to him. Laugh with him. Feel the safety of his touch.

Guilt accompanied his relief. How could it not when Lark suffered so?

It was easier to keep his distance for the time being.

Coward.

"Don't get me started on the bastardization of good fermenting techniques. There's a reason they called mead 'the nectar of the gods' and I won't abide some saddle goose arguing ale's superiority..."

Langford tuned Huxley out as a chill crept up the back of his neck. He bundled the wool layer of his surcoat tighter around him and tugged the hood of his cloak further about his face. Each *clop* of their horses' hooves against the snowy ground was heavy against the silent air.

Too silent, even for a winter-claimed forest.

Langford glanced at Alistair to find his hand already resting on the hilt of his sword.

He sensed something, too.

Paranoia or heightened survival instinct, one couldn't be too careful. Not anymore.

"Shut your gods-cursed mouth for two minutes," Alistair called out, and Huxley's chatter ceased.

They trekked along, and Langford was all too aware of each step. Each rotation of the wheels in the cart and the way Huxley's barrels of mead bumped over every root. He exhaled a wet breath through the damp covering over his mouth, trickles of steam escaping.

"Perhaps it was nothing."

Alistair tossed him a sardonic expression. "We both know we're not lucky enough for that."

A guttural roar tore through the trees, frozen branches snapping. Snarls filled the air, filled Langford's ears, surrounded them with the piercing threat of violence.

A lone howl rang out, both bestial and human, raising the hairs at the back of Langford's neck and along his arms. It chilled him from the inside out, rattled his bones, shook the very earth beneath him. No. That couldn't be. It was his body's response to extreme fear. Langford sucked down a shaky breath, silently willing his muscles not to lock up. His mind not to conjure a more fantastical threat.

He was a man of science and the physical world. He had faced monsters and demons, all the ilk Lark referred to as 'Undesirables'.

This would be no different, and the sooner his intellect acknowledged this, the better. They had experience and skill on their side. One aggressive creature would not be enough to—

Heavy pounding against the ground cut through Langford's thoughts.

Then came the screams.

ANOTHER HOWL from the beast rang through the air. Its thick fur stood on end down the ridgeline of its back. Even hunched, the beast was taller than any man. Langford stared dumbly at the sight, his sword hanging loosely from his hand. Rough snorts and growls filled the air —wet sounds of flesh tearing from muscle and bone.

It was an instant, one moment to the next, but it was as if time stood still.

Alistair leapt from his horse, charging the creature without hesitation.

No. Not again.

Langford broke free from his spell, lunging to follow Alistair into danger.

But the beast made no move to acknowledge them. It was too busy ripping Huxley to shreds.

The wagon jostled under the weight of the struggle. Another scream—cut off by a gurgling, bloody gasp. Huxley slumped over, his unseeing eyes frozen in fright even in death.

Alistair aimed for the creature, and swept his sword in precise strikes, cutting and slashing. The beast howled, raking its claws against his chest.

Langford clambered up the steps to the driving seat, jabbing at the monster's exposed flank. It screeched, the sound sending a shiver down Langford's back, and it stretched to stand tall before him.

Langford had encountered many beasts in his travels since Lark stumbled into their lives, but nothing had prepared him for this.

A wide, gaping maw, filled with jagged teeth. Saliva dripped from its mouth, and its rancid breath blew out vaporous puffs. A grey face, free from the thick fur coating the rest of its body. Yellow eyes full of hunger and malice glared back at him.

The creature howled and leaped high over their heads, disappearing into the trees.

Alistair appeared, dropping his bloody sword and bundling Langford against his chest. His touch was urgent and desperate, as he assessed him with bottle-green eyes full of concern. "Are you hurt? Did it touch you?"

Langford swallowed against the lump in his throat, forcing the panic to settle deep in his gut where he was sure an ulcer was forming. He wanted to yell at Alistair. To scream and shake him for putting himself in harm's way so foolishly again. To force him to swear he'd never take such a risk, and they'd go live a boring and wonderfully long life together.

But this was the job. This was their life. And Langford couldn't be so selfish as that.

Langford tutted and knocked his hand away so he could assess the scratch marks on Alistair's chest. Three angry lines, the flesh torn and agitated where parted. "These are deep," he said, unable to mask his disapproval, "yet you waste time checking me for injury."

Alistair scoffed. "Getting my hands on you in any fashion is never a waste of time."

Out of the corner of Langford's eye, Huxley's body twitched. Langford turned to assess the corpse. Whether it was his own imagination, or merely the last firing of nerves after the brain had already died, it was nothing to worry over.

He busied himself with cleaning the wound, hoping Alistair couldn't see through his forced unpleasantness. "I see you're determined to use up my supplies before we even rendezvous with the others." It was a reminder for himself not to get too comfortable in their break from running headlong into danger.

Danger would forever remain their constant companion. Langford had to get over his terror. His fear that the life Alistair currently led was a precarious balance. That one couldn't call life back into a dead body without far reaching consequences. That even this was a dream he'd awaken from only to find Alistair had never come back to him, never opened his eyes but remained cold and still on the forest floor—

The sound of his short and harsh breaths cut off his thoughts. They were far too quick and shallow. One couldn't get enough oxygen hyperventilating like that. If he swooned, Alistair would never let him live it down. He'd spend his days sidelined while Alistair handled jobs and missions on his own. He'd—

It wasn't his own breathing he was hearing. Langford took a few slow breaths, deep and controlled. He locked eyes with Alistair, confirming they shared the same dread, before he once again turned to assess Huxley's corpse.

Only, Langford wouldn't have classified the man's body as a corpse by the way his chest rose and fell with each desperate breath. The way his ribcage expanded beyond human proportions on every inhale. The rapid pace by which each huff of air was expelled from his lungs, growing louder and faster. The edge of a growl punctuated each breath, a low rasping sound.

It wasn't possible. Huxley had died. And yet...

Huxley's body arched, unnatural and overextending as it contorted the wrong way. The snap and crack of bones filled the air, along with the wet sound of ripping flesh. Where skin parted, black fur sprouted. Huxley's mouth stretched wide, the jaw snapping and hanging open loosely. His teeth elongated, tearing his lips on the journey.

It wasn't possible. It wasn't—

Huxley's face transformed, his nose stretching into a snout, his eyes bleeding yellow across the irises until that same inhuman stare remained.

He was not dead, nor was he a man anymore.

Alistair leapt into action, angling his sword and severing the monstrous head from his still contorting body. A sickening thud against the wagon, and it was silent once more.

How? *How* did the man become a beast? This monstrous form must have been spread almost like a viral infection, Huxley transforming from the bite or the scratch of the monster that attacked them.

Langford glanced at Alistair's chest.

"You—"

"Didn't see a point in waiting for him to attack us. You disagree? Should I have waited for whatever the fuck was happening to conclude?" Alistair sheathed his sword, his agitation sharpening the movement. "You think me unsporting? Pray tell, what did I do wrong this time?"

Where was his anger coming from? Langford hadn't even had the chance to speak his suspicion, and already Alistair was jumping down his throat. He did not begrudge his decision. The ability to act quickly was imperative to survival, as was evidenced by this very moment. He did not judge him for unfreezing quicker than he; quite the opposite.

"Not at all, Alistair. I only..." Langford's voice was barely above a whisper. As if speaking the words would condemn him to his fate.

Alistair's expression softened, and in three strides he was upon him, taking Langford's face in his hands and gently running his thumbs against his cheeks. "Hush. I'm sorry. I just can't handle you looking at me like I'm some sort of monster."

"That isn't—"

Alistair silenced him with a kiss. "I know I'm on borrowed time until you realize you're far too good for me. But please..." He pressed another kiss to his forehead, hard enough for Langford to feel his teeth. "Please don't stop seeing the parts of me no one else sees. Love me, leave me, break me. But don't stop seeing the good. I'm not sure it's even there, but with you, I have hope it is."

Where was this coming from? Langford's chest ached, and his throat burned with unshed tears. This confession, it came out of nowhere, or did it? Had he been so preoccupied with his own terror, he'd failed to see the internal struggle Alistair battled?

There would be time to remedy this. To assure him he wasn't going anywhere, and Alistair was every bit as good and horrible and selfish and selfless as Langford saw. Every bit.

But now there were pressing issues, and if Langford let his fear lock him up, he'd be useless.

"I'm not looking at you like you're a monster. I'm looking at you like I'm bloody worried."

Alistair's posture relaxed. "That's more like it. What worries you now?"

Langford wet his lips. "Your chest, Alistair."

Alistair glanced down at the angry gashes against his skin, frowning as if he'd forgotten all about them. "Don't tell me you have a thing against scars. I happen to know you've quite the penchant for mine. I happen to know your favorite is down—"

"Alistair, you were scratched." Panic seized Langford's throat, and he swallowed it down. Yes, the path of logic connected Huxley's fate to the beast. But one couldn't leap to conclusions before enough evidence was gathered to support them.

No matter how deep his stomach pitted.

Understanding dawned Alistair's face. He rubbed his jaw, his brow furrowing. "Can't you disinfect it?"

Langford dragged him to the steps to the wagon cart and forced him to sit. It would take too long to argue and explain why he wasn't sure if cleaning it was enough to prevent—

No. Not the time to allow his thoughts to follow that thread. He removed the disinfectant tincture and bandages from his pack. The ritual calmed him. He would need to fashion a poultice when they returned, and Alistair would have to rest under his watch to make sure…

His hands took over, and the familiar motions of treating a wound —Alistair's wound—allowed his mind to cleave itself from the reality of the task.

The half-Huxley, half-monster corpse lay silently beside them while Langford did what he did best.

He fixed what he could see.

CHAPTER FOUR

LARK

Lark couldn't bring herself to return to Inerys' cottage. Instead, she trudged the road to The Walden Inn and Tavern. Langford and Alistair had taken up temporary lodging there, and she was overdue to catch up with them. She would have to spend the night at the inn, a calculated maneuver on her part.

She needed the space from the pitying and beseeching stares. The weight of guilt in Aislinn's furtive glances. The assessing and watchful gaze of Daciana. The harsh disapproval of Inerys' judgment.

Snow crunched beneath her feet, and a second pair of footsteps followed closely behind.

Ferryn. He hadn't left her side since their argument, and though he referred to Gavriel as her shadow, the irony was that he'd embodied that role.

The wind blew, and frozen branches tinkled a delicate chime in response. Ice coated their surface, glimmering in the dwindling light. As the woods parted, the open field stretched ahead, and the last of daylight hinted its retreat over the horizon. Pink and pale yellow painted the sky in a wintry landscape.

When the Walden Inn appeared in the distance with its familiar stone cladding and puffing chimney, Lark exhaled a sigh of relief. She tugged her hood tighter, her ears gone numb with bitter cold.

She craved the warmth of Walden's roaring hearth almost as much as she craved a purpose. Everything had gone to shit so quickly, and somehow the lot of them managed to stay stuck. Hidden away in Inerys's cottage. Frozen in time. It was maddening, this idleness.

Uselessness.

Kenna had found an escape. Journeying off hunting, picking off Undesirables one by one, and checking in between each hunt. That Daciana had stayed behind had done nothing to endear the hunter to Lark, and Lark could admit she envied her freedom.

She couldn't leave Gavriel. She couldn't stay and watch his death-like slumber. She couldn't challenge Nereida. She couldn't. She couldn't.

She had failed in every conceivable way and was now forced to remain trapped in her own weakness. It was as if she was back in the Otherworld, unchanging and frozen in time.

"I see your impressive brooding hasn't lost its edge." Ferryn's voice cut through her thoughts. His distraction was abrupt but desperately needed.

Lark bit the inside of her cheek to hide her smile. He, too, had not lost his ability to lighten her dark moods. After he had pushed, exhausting her anger and reaching beneath the depths of her despair, she'd found herself... relieved. Like Ferryn had forced her to feel what she'd desperately tried to numb, and she'd been granted permission to let some of it go.

And somehow, *somehow*, it was easy to fall into the familiar rhythm of their banter once more. Safe, even. "I see your incessant prattling hasn't waned with humanity."

"So moody. Pluck up or I'll eat the last of that pie you're so fond of."

He wouldn't dare.

An impulse came over her, sharp and quick. There was nothing to do but bend down and fill her hand with snow. Her skin wasn't as numb as she'd thought, as the biting cold seared her palm and fingertips. But she rolled it together between her hands, forming a round shape.

"Lark…" Ferryn's voice was a warning.

A true grin stretched her face, tightening her chapped lips, and she lobbed the ball of snow directly at his chest. The impact was a *splat,* white powder exploding across his cloak and landing in the ends of his hair. His face was so serious, all sharp edges and pinched brows, but still he hadn't brushed the snow from his hair, off his chest. There was even a gathering of white powder in his eyelashes.

Lark snorted, clapping cold hands over her mouth. Her shoulders shook, and she laughed behind her hands, tears filling her eyes.

His eyes narrowed, a calculating look crossing his features. "If it's war you want, it's war I shall grant." Ferryn launched himself into the snow, gathering and piling his attack for the battle she'd started.

Lark fell into the snow, not bothering to hide her mirth any longer as she compiled her own armory. She shoved down the guilt creeping through her chest. The notion that she didn't deserve a moment of laughter, of lightness when all seemed destined to remain dark. Was it selfish to want to smile despite the pain? Or were moments like these unable to be earned, their freedom granted without debt or agenda?

Snow flew, blasting them both with its chilled embrace. Their laughter blew each exhale in gasping huffs of vapor. The cold was a living thing, filling her throat, freezing the inside of her mouth, and still she laughed. She laughed until it ached. Until finally spent, she sprawled on the ground beside Ferryn. The snow had begun to melt in her hair, freezing once more until shards of ice hardened the strands. She'd never been so cold in all her life, and when she sighed it was a sound of contentment. Of finding a spare moment of joy and humor in an otherwise shit situation.

Turning her head, she faced her oldest friend.

"I win."

Ferryn eyed her, a soft smile tugging the corner of his mouth. "We'll call it a draw."

HEAT ENVELOPED Lark as the door to the tavern swung closed behind them. The blast of hot air from the lit hearth sent a pricking sensation through her hands and ears as her blood warmed. The dining area was overfilled with patrons, humans eager for a reprieve from the bitter cold. Tankards and half-eaten mince meat pies cluttered the round tables. Chairs and stools were all angled to face the corner of the room where a bard delicately plucked her lute and sang a tale of the coming days. Of the sunrise after the longest night.

A massive man stood, stretching to reveal his broad back and intricate tattoos swirling up the side of his neck.

And for a jolted instant, a fraction of a breath, Lark almost believed it was Hugo. But when the man turned, his unfamiliar face served to prove how foolish she was to believe it could ever be him.

But could it be? Could Hugo return? The veil had fallen. More monsters roamed the human lands than ever before. Could souls travel freely, too?

"Find us a seat. I'll get us some food."

Before Lark could respond, Ferryn had sauntered over to the bar. He had chosen the easier of the two tasks, seeing as there was hardly even standing room. Stepping over outstretched legs, she made her way to the darkened alcove, the corner by the window. Though no part of her wished to sit near a draft, it was the only spot open. Instead of a table, a few barrels rested against the wall. They could use them as makeshift tables and stand while eating.

As her frozen fingers thawed, the overwhelming energy in the room began to take its toll.

The din of laughter, conversation, and merriment was like a weighted hood blocking out all else. The scraping of forks and knives, the shattered *clank* of a plate dropping and the responding laughter. A chair toppled; the heavy thud of a man hit the floor while his companions roared.

Lark couldn't tune anything out. She hadn't found herself in a crowd this densely packed in ages, and the energy of each person seemed to buzz against her skin. It was too much. Her skin was still cold, but her blood was on fire. Ice and flame shuddering over her body and making a cold sweat prick along her sides. A shock of anger jolted through her before it evaporated. Then a surge of giddy excitement floated through her. A fleeting rush, the violence of a wave crashing against the surf and then a retreat. But like sugar melting on her tongue, each feeling left a taste behind.

What was happening?

She placed a hand against the windowpane, the chill sinking into her palm. She focused on that feeling, on the sharp shock of cold, and gradually the noise fell back to a manageable distance. It was strange, how overpowering it was. She hadn't felt the blow of overstimulation like this in months, if ever. It was as if—

No that would be impossible.

She couldn't have access to that deeper level of awareness she once had as a Reaper. She'd been human for the turn of three seasons. The ability to cast her net and pull others into her consciousness was an ability she'd left behind. But it was as if it had returned to her in a torrential flood. As if a dam had ruptured, and everyone's emotions rushed through, only this time she had nothing to stem the tide. She was human and could feel it all in whole measures.

Lark clenched her fists and slowed her breathing. She was tired. Road weary. Chilled to the very marrow. The stress of everything lately had worn her down, and this was her human body's response to it. An overfiring of nerves and the release of long pent-up feelings. It was a human reaction, and nothing more. Nothing out of the ordinary.

Sharp cold pierced through her. Terror. Undiluted fear and panic. Her thoughts came to a screeching halt as her pulse ratcheted up, a steady and frantic pounding in her ears. Her legs went numb, and her breath quickened.

Something was wrong. Terribly, terribly wrong.

Shaky dread climbed up her spine, up her throat. It stole her breath and sent tremors through her. But why? *Why?*

Ferryn appeared with two mugs, and his smile quickly fell. "Lark?"

"Do you... do you feel that?" She could scarcely get the words out, her voice barely above a whisper.

"What is it?" Ferryn slammed the mugs on the barrel, grabbing her by the shoulders. "What's wrong?"

"It's..." Lark's stomach rolled, nausea churning in her gut. "I feel..."

Darkness. A bitter darkness so strong, it was as if the scent, the acrid taste, coated the very air. It was rage. It was hate. It was—

A thread. It was a thread Lark could follow. And there was no reason for her awareness to latch on to the thread of another soul, but it did. It did, and she felt, and knew, and she was.

She'd just formed a tether between herself and another as she had done so many times before. Never in her own body, never as flesh and blood. But a tether she'd forged.

Curiosity, a burning need to *know*, compelled her forward as if by puppet strings.

If she knocked into anyone, she scarcely noticed. If Ferryn followed, she wasn't aware. And when the door slammed shut behind her, and the cold night air enveloped her, the pull of the tether marched her through the snow. The sky had darkened as the winter night laid claim to the land. The stars burned cold and bright against the black canvas sky. A tug. A pull. The faint hint of a lantern's light in the distance. Tucked between buildings in a narrow alley, the flickering glow cut through the shadows. Another tug.

"What in the fucking void are you doing?" Ferryn's hands came down hard and heavy on Lark's shoulders. "Where are you going?"

"You don't feel it?" Lark pulled away from him, her legs carrying her as if in a dream. As if her body was a conduit to something she couldn't quite name. She continued to that light, drawn like a moth to a flame. A beacon calling to her, beseeching her.

She had to know. Was this nothing but a fragile fractured mind? The weight of too much on an admittedly precarious state of being? Or had Nereida done something to her, the way she had Gavriel, and it was only now showing its symptoms?

Voices. There were voices in the distance.

Lark ran, her cloak billowing behind her, the wind whipping

through her. It bit at her neck, her lips, her knuckles. Her eyes watered, and snow fell over the tops of her boots, freezing her ankles.

The voices were closer now.

"I didn't say nothing, I swear!"

"I'll gut you, you lying little shit. You know I will. Venzo told me you had a meeting with Dammar. How much coin did it take to sell me out? After everything I did for you, you selfish maggot?"

"It wasn't me!" The voice broke off in a scream, a cry of anguish. Choking sobs filled the night air.

Lark skidded to the alley, finally greeting the light of that distant lantern. That beacon. That tether.

Dark blood painted the snow, glimmering wet. A small form was curled in on itself, clutching their arm. And on the ground...

A severed hand. Small enough to be a child's.

Lark's breath quickened, and her pulse pounded in her head.

Three men stood over the sobbing child. *Child.* There was no doubt in Lark's mind. Shadows concealed their faces as they turned to look at her.

"Nothing to see here, sweetheart."

"Run along home, afore somethin' bad happens."

The child groaned, another sob breaking free. One of the men, a dark silhouette, took a step closer. The tether snapped into place, almost a solid reminder of what had drawn her to this alley. Lark exhaled, allowing her mind to tentatively reach out. Testing.

A sharp gasp ripped from her chest as the current connected, binding this man's soul to hers. It had only been months since she'd forged such a tether, but it may as well have been lifetimes with how foreign it felt. Discomfort stretched her insides, like she was the outgrown tunic ripping at the seams. She pushed past it, allowing it to settle beneath her skin. Welcoming instead of fighting it.

And just like muscle memory, her awareness trickled his mind into hers.

Lucente. That was the man's name. He was a petty thief, a swindler. He'd trusted the boy, along with the rest of the child laborers in town. They were his network. His eyes and ears in every house and business. They knew the comings and goings of all the merchants and collected information to sell, blackmail, or bribe with. When another thief put a bounty out for whoever could bring him the location of Lucente's home base, his hoard, he'd become paranoid.

A severed hand was a tame punishment compared to what he'd done in the face of his distrust. This boy wasn't the first. He wouldn't be the last.

Anger. Rage. It poured through Lark, lighting her blood on fire. Was it his or hers? It mattered naught. She'd somehow forged a tether, followed the thread, there was only one thing left for her to do.

Reap.

Lark yanked her bow from beneath her cloak, her frozen fingers nocking an arrow and pulling to her anchor point.

In the shadows, she'd never know if he could school his expressions to mask his fear, but she could taste it was there. A thrilling, heady power of knowing she was in his head. In his soul. Filtering through memories like she was flipping through a deck of playing cards.

No one would mourn his loss. Certainly not she.

The tether snapped, a broken thread, and then blissful silence in her mind. It was like shutting the door against a bracing wind, the way the silence suddenly surrounded her. Connection broken, she was free to end him next.

"You—"

She released her arrow, and the satisfying thunk of it landing its mark was music to her ears. He choked, a wet gurgling sound, before he slumped in the snow, his face finally catching the light. His mouth gaped like a fish on land, opening and closing as if the words were desperately trying to escape. Blood pooled from his lips, down the side of his throat, filling the snow.

There would be no one to lead him to the afterlife. And perhaps, that should have frightened her.

"What in the blazing nethers..." Ferryn said.

A shout, and the two men rushed, the shock of their slain friend finally wearing off. Lark nocked another arrow. A pull and release, it landed somewhere in the man's chest. Hugo's knife was already in her hand. It was simple business deflecting sloppy jabs before slicing her blade across his throat. Beside her, Ferryn gave a grunt, yanking his sword free from the last man's stomach. A slow death. A painful death. And yet... her human emotions allowed no room for regret.

Lark leaped over them, landing beside the unconscious child. Freezing snow bit at her knees. She sheathed her bloody blade—there would be time later to clean it—and lifted his body into her arms. Ferryn quickly took the boy, cradling him with ease. His hood fell back to reveal his youthful face, maybe ten winters old, dark brows and pale skin. His mouth hung open, his face slack in merciful slumber. Lark tore a bit of cloth from her cloak and packed it with snow to wrap around his bleeding stump. It seemed the right thing to do... it would be so much easier if Langford were here.

Langford. She'd completely forgotten they'd trekked this way to meet with them. He would fix the boy up. He always knew what to do. First, they needed to get him back to the inn and get him warm. Mrs. O'Connell would tell them what room to head for.

Anything to delay analyzing what just took place.

"Lark..." Ferryn shifted the boy's weight, eying her with unease. "How..."

Lark shook her head as her gut churned. She would need to turn this over in her mind, explore and agonize and assess. Inerys would know its cause, hopefully. But she could not bear to think about it all now, so she told Ferryn the only truth she could. "I have no idea."

CHAPTER FIVE

GAVRIEL

"*A*gain!" Gavriel's shout echoed in the empty courtyard. The other trainees had long retired to the dining hall, the day's end signaling the call to rest and recover. He mopped the sweat from his brow, slowing his breath to unstitch that twinge in his side.

"I'm starving." Emric's arms hung loose and limp at his sides, his posture defeated. His normally spiky blond hair was matted with sweat despite the little effort he'd put into his training. The boy had no discipline since he was yet four years away from graduating apprenticeship.

He was soft. Gavriel had long since learned that the softness of youth was a liability here. A dullness in need of honing. Yet he could not bring himself to sharpen the boy.

When Gavriel was twelve summers old, Master Hamlin caught him touching the fiddle in his office and ordered him to discipline his mind and learn to play the instrument after lessons and training each day. Even now, he'd become accustomed to practicing for an hour before bed each night.

What he once thought a punishment for childish ideals, he now realized was a gift. One never knew when an assignment called for creative tactics or subterfuge. He could playact as a simple minstrel if the mark called for such an occasion. But more importantly, it was yet another lesson learned.

There is no joy in a life such as this. Only weapons to add to one's arsenal.

It was easier that way and kept him focused on his task.

Plan for everything, anticipate failure, improvise an escape route. These were the lessons Gavriel tried to live by so he might prepare for anything. He was on the cusp of his first assignment. His first kill. Finally, he'd earn back the coin spent on his education.

He'd take as many assignments as possible to expedite the balance to his debt. Whatever it took to support his mother and grant her a peaceful life far away from... that place.

'The whorehouse, Pearson. Call it what it is, your mother certainly takes pride in it.'

Connor's voice was seared into his mind, a constant nagging reminder of everything at stake in this cesspool. Gavriel spun his daggers, forcing a lightness to his tone.

"Reset the course once more, and in return I promise you half my rations."

Emric's face lit up, and Gavriel fought the urge to mourn the boy's lost youth. No one at the Guild could afford the luxury of a childhood. He would do well to remember that.

Classes and training covered a vast wealth of knowledge. Poisons, the fighting arts, diplomatic relations, history, architecture, lock-smithing, wound care. These were as vital to learn and master as stealth, agility, and lying. Not lying, necessarily, but the art of persuasion. One must persuade a target into a snare, and if that failed, a swift silence.

Emric reset the targets, the spring-loaded dummies, and retied the rope traps. This was Gavriel's preferred training course. There were multiple levels, varying in height, and the object was to traverse the course quickly, efficiently, and without injury. It relied on speed, antici-pation, quick reflexes. Each time he mastered the course, he'd perform it twenty more times to be certain, then the next time, it would be structured in a different order. It was the easiest place for his body and mind to remain perfectly in sync. One couldn't let their thoughts wander without a swift blow from one of the spring-loaded dummies. Gavriel had bruised his ass enough in the early days to learn this lesson.

Emric hummed as he worked. "Hey, Gav!" he called out, his voice bright. "Do you think Lark is still alive?"

Gavriel's thoughts hit a jarring wall, a cold sweat replacing his previous heat. "What did you just say?"

"I said," Emric grunted as he heaved a large sandbag onto the platform, "do you think they made those honeyed rolls tonight?"

That wasn't what he'd said, was it? Gavriel pinched the bridge of his nose. He was tired, and sore, and dehydrated. There was something on the edge of his thoughts, like a word on the tip of his tongue or a dream just out of memory. It was a nagging sensation—the sense that something important was forgotten. Something worth remembering.

"So do you?"

Gavriel shook his head to clear his thoughts. "Do I what?"

Emric rolled his eyes. "Think they'll have those rolls again? I've dreamed of them every night since Feastday."

It was a kindness on Master Hamlin's part to allow the cooks to serve traditional Kovalian treats for Feastday. Most of the recruits had never even celebrated a true Feastday. A fact Gavriel had been quick to bring to his master's attention. He'd only replied with, *'There are many things they haven't yet experienced, boy.'*

"Doubtful."

"Rats." Emric frowned, leaning against one of the posts. "Can you finish up? My stomach is eating itself."

Gavriel nodded, feeling not at all assured he'd heard him correctly. A good night's rest. That's what he needed. The mind was a funny thing, quick to fill shadows and doubt with monsters and uncertainty.

"I'll make it quick."

It was best not to dwell in the shadows of one's own mind.

CHAPTER SIX

AISLINN

*A*islinn slowed her breath, desperate to settle the racing of her pulse. She rubbed the sore spot at the back of her head. The heavy drop of her soul reentering her body had rattled her teeth and slammed her back against the wall. She hadn't even meant to enter Gavriel's mind this time, content to sit on the floor and observe him. But her soul had drifted as she slept, an accidental passenger in his dreams.

This hadn't happened since she first found the connection with Lark. Since she first discovered her ability to dream walk.

Her body was heavy with exhaustion. Sleep was no longer restful so long as her soul wandered. She couldn't allow this to happen again. It was too unpredictable. Inerys had been teaching her to control it, to follow the steps of lowering her guard and pressing her awareness out so she could control departing the dreamer's mind rather than violent expulsion.

She glanced at Gavriel's unconscious form, frozen in sleep. His chest rose and fell in a steady rhythm. No change. His dream had been a memory, one she'd witnessed a few times now. But when the boy said Lark's name... when Gavriel reacted to the sound of it... that was new.

Aislinn stood, and a wave of nausea sent her vision spinning. She braced a hand on the wall, trying to settle her stomach.

"I don't know why I even bother with you." Inery's voice, sharp with disapproval, called from the doorway. She leaned against the frame, her dark hair hanging in waves over her shoulders, brown eyes lit with fury. "What have I said about pushing too far?" The tight set of her jaw hardened her words.

Her ire was justified, and the shame of it burned in Aislinn's belly.

"I didn't mean to."

"What a relief your foolishness was unintentional. Perhaps you can explain that to your soul when it flickers out from overexertion." Inerys pushed off the door, stalking over to Gavriel. With abrupt hands, she checked his pulse, his breathing, lifted his eyelids one at a time, before unceremoniously lifting his hand only to let it fall to the bed with a *thump*.

"Just as I thought. No change. No reason for you to linger by his bedside, dwindling your strength."

Inerys had told Aislinn the dangers of dream walking. Of how vulnerable she would be if she didn't master it. If her soul was too weakened to find its way back... if something happened to her physical form while she wandered...

"I only sought to observe. I didn't intend to sleep, nor to enter his dream."

"You're somniavi, you can't afford to fall asleep wherever you land." Inerys' eyes softened. "You have to be more careful."

"I know," Aislinn ran a shaky hand through her hair. "And I am sorry, but it wasn't for naught. I discovered something." She aimed for her most winning smile, the grin her mother used to insist could charm a corpse.

Something cold twisted in her gut. She'd give anything to see her mother again.

Inerys rolled her eyes. "It's rather off-putting to punctuate an apology with an addendum. Out with it."

"Gavriel's mind said Lark's name. He's trying to push through. That must mean something."

Inerys had told her how her own family would never recognize her again. How her appearance and even her voice would be forever altered to the humans who grieved her death. How they buried a body, and their human minds would not allow them to see her for who she was ever again.

But when Gavriel's mind pushed through an old memory, insisted the call of Lark's name, that spark of hope had returned. Maybe the human mind was capable of remembering, of seeing past the pain and the hurt and the grief to find the truth.

Inerys hummed thoughtfully. "It could be a sign he's fighting through the layers of memories to return. Could be they're just over-lapping and echoing within one another. Nothing is certain in this."

Disappointment flooded Aislinn. So, it meant nothing. It meant more uncertainty and blindly following the paths of his dreams with no true direction.

There had to be a way. A way to be the map, the lantern, the compass to lead him back. Otherwise, why was she still here? For what purpose was her death delayed? It wasn't to see her family and be reunited once more. It had to be in this. There had to be a reason Aislinn had been spared even after death. She could not abide a world that would rip her away and then spit her back out as if she was spoiled. If she could not deliver Gavriel from his prison with her abili-ties, what was the point?

If Gavriel's mind could not push through to find his way home, what hope was there for her? What hope could she muster for her own mother to find her in the face of a stranger?

Was she trying to save him or herself?

There would always be doubt. The fear of failure. But her mother's words had stayed with her. When she fought against death, when she took the step forward, when she was trapped in the afterlife, and now that she'd returned. Everything was different. She was different, and the fear of what it might mean threatened to swallow her whole.

But her mother's words remained.

Fear is not weakness, it's your compass. When fear beckons, dare to find your strength.

Perhaps there was strength in the final flickers of hope.
She would rest. Recover. Regain her strength.
And try again.

CHAPTER SEVEN

DEMETRIA

*D*emetria had always envied the artists who traveled the world. The ones who painted landscapes of lands she'd never seen. The gallery at the University of Koval was brimming with imagery of worlds and experiences she'd never been privy to. With a stroke of a brush, vibrant autumn came to life on the canvas. But it was winter she'd always longed to see. To feel. The kiss of soft falling snow, frost glimmering like freshly polished silver, branches adorned with ice the way ladies of court dripped with diamonds.

Demetria shivered, tucking her frayed cloak tighter around her body. Her fingers were numb, and she doubted she could hold her charcoal pencil even if she wanted to. Images of Koval, of the hot season, flashed in her mind. Waking up drenched with sweat, the weight of a thin sheet too much to handle. Reports of citizens falling unconscious under the fierce heat of the sun. In the shade, the air was still thick and humid, but she could sketch until the need to cool off was so overwhelming she had no choice but to chase Evander down and force him to break for the day—

Another shiver wracked Demetria's body, and she shoved images of freckles and brassy hair away, turning her mind to the image of that twisted crone. The one who saw far too deep inside her soul.

Blackened teeth mashing behind cracked lips. Her dark tongue slithering out to sense the air. Anything to avoid remembering the way Evander's neck caved under the weight of the axe. The many swings it took to sever his head from his body.

But these were memories best left forgotten, so she focused on the cold. The biting, unrepentant cold chilling her straight to the bone. The way her nose was numb and her eyes watered. Even her cheeks were stiff. The straw beneath her was frozen, too, hard and scratchy through her meager layers. Another night, another abandoned barn.

She was a long way from the warmth of her plush bed, the fragrant scent of hyacinths floating through open doors and windows. She sniffed, her clogged nose failing to prevent the trickle of wetness from chilling her lip. With her sleeve bundled over her hand, she wiped it away.

"Was it a nightmare?" Balan's voice called out in the dark.

Demetria cleared her throat, afraid her voice would give her away. "Why would you think that?"

"You are weeping," he said, the hint of a growl at the edge of his voice.

Demetria wiped her cheeks, and sure enough, her tears were halfway frozen against her skin. "Can you call it a nightmare if you're awake?"

Balan's laugh was a harsh scrape. "Oh, yes. I'm quite familiar with that particular brand of cruelty." A squeaking turn of a key, and a small flame erupted behind the lantern's glass. The abandoned barn they'd taken shelter in came into view, along with the former demon's tired expression.

Demetria's gaze fell to the crudely broken horns on his head, where two black forms jutted from his skin, their edges jagged and rough. Dark circles were etched beneath his silver eyes, highlighting his otherness even more as he stared down at her over the strong line of his nose. But she was not afraid, never of him. He'd arrived broken and beaten, when first Daciana, Kenna, and she had found him. And though there was a complicated history there, one she still didn't know in its entirety, she trusted him. Far more than the others.

Bitterness coated her tongue at the thought. Of how they used her connections to break into her home and steal her family heirloom for a weapon they needed. Demetria was happy and willing to grant them this; it held sentimental value but paled in comparison to the threat they insisted was imminent. Langford even promised to hold up his end of the bargain by aiding her in seizing the throne from her brother, a far more immediate threat, and it was a lie. All of them lied. Whatever it took to meet their goal's end, and she was cannon fodder.

Ruslan. Her friend and mentor. The closest thing she had to a father and the last of whom she considered family. He aided them in their pursuit, in their ill-formed plan to steal the dragon stone from her castle. They knew the dangers. Demetria had warned them of her brother's brutality, his disregard for others, the lengths at which he would go to achieve his ends.

Ruslan paid the price.

His death was on their hands. Lark's hands. And they didn't have the decency to tell her. They were just as bad as her brother, so when she had the chance, she ran. They couldn't use her for any more of their schemes, and she couldn't rely on them to help her.

It was easier to trust a demon.

"Here." Balan tossed her the last of the bread. It was cold and stale. "We'll need to hit the market again. It would be easier to persuade the woman who brought you here to transport us."

Demetria took another bite, her jaw aching. "No. She'll tell them."

Balan nodded, running a hand down his face.

He wasn't wrong. Demetria had no doubt Captain Ingemar would transport her without asking for a single coin. But she couldn't be sure where the captain would bring her or whom she would tell. Ingemar trusted Langford and Alistair, told Demetria to trust them as well, and look where that had gotten her.

No. They would find their own way without any connections back to those people. It meant learning to pickpocket, how to slash a coin purse in a crowd, and taking the odd job. Anything to save up enough for passage and keeping their expenses low. Sleeping in abandoned huts with holes in the roof and the scurrying sound of rats in the rafters.

Old bread marked down from market price, rationed to last. It meant her shoes were falling apart and her belly was perpetually hungry. It was the sort of life she'd read about in stories, where the hero or heroine rose from humble beginnings to ascend to great power. Everyone rallied behind an underdog, did they not?

Demetria once worried she'd be recognized as the Princess of Koval, but she didn't need a looking glass to know there was no chance of that now. Her hair was a tangled mess, she practically wore rags, and the lack of food had her clothes fitting looser and looser.

She took another bite of that nasty bread before passing it back to Balan. She'd fallen so far from her place as that girl with servants and tutors and a cushy bed with fresh sweet rolls each day. She was little more than the rats above her head with the *pitter-patter* of their tiny feet that eventually sounded like rain. She was the raggedy heroine of her story.

They almost had enough to afford passage on one of the less savory "cargo" transports. Lucky for them, passage to Koval was cheaper than passage to Ardenas. Probably because it was easy to sell them to the highest bidder upon arrival. Balan would never let it come to that. And if they had to, they'd abandon ship when they were close enough and before anyone could notice.

"One more job."

Balan's mouth curved in an indulgent smile. "Right. One more job."

She would be the rat who snuck back into her home, her little steps ignored as they had always been. She would scurry behind Zaire's back, until she became little more than the quiet sound of inconvenient weather.

And when the time was right, she would rain down his ruin.

CHAPTER EIGHT

LANGFORD

*I*n all his years as a healer, Langford had never encountered an injury he couldn't diagnose. He could determine the likelihood of survival with a glance. Recovery time with little prodding. Granted, he wasn't infallible, there had certainly been times his estimates were off, but not by much. The steady and consistent reliance he maintained on his education and experience was grounding, a comfort.

Now... he had no bloody idea how to treat Alistair's wound. He applied his antiseptic to the area—nothing. One of his strongest poultices—no change. He brewed an anti-inflammatory tea, and Alistair purged it. *Purged* it! The same man who once chased a horn of mead with his own questionable homebrew, topping it off with rum, and still maintained his stomach's contents.

Langford's chest ached at the thought, and he glanced at Alistair where he rode beside him in the wagon, his head jostling with the movement.

Alistair's complexion held a sickly pallor, appearing pale even with his darker skin tone. His eyes were glassy, his movements slowed and burdened. Fever made his skin hot to the touch, and even without Langford's training, it was clear something was terribly wrong.

The memory of the mead seller's corpse flooded Langford's mind.

How it twisted and contorted, bones snapping to reform in monstrous ways—

No. That would not be Alistair's fate. The very idea of it was mad. There was, however, the very real threat of infection.

"See something you like?" Alistair's normally smooth delivery was heavy and stilted. Still, he raised a brow like the cad he was, openly appraising Langford in a suggestive fashion. Langford couldn't even find comfort in Alistair's commitment to his scoundrel ways. The man would flirt even on his deathbed. The whole effect was ruined when Alistair broke into a violent coughing fit.

If Langford couldn't properly heal him… if Alistair went septic… if Huxley's fate was a glimpse into Alistair's future…

No. It couldn't be. He almost lost him once; he wouldn't lose him again. But what could be done? How does one heal what they don't understand?

Langford ran a hand through his hair, tugging on the ends. He needed to remain calm. There was no use in losing his head, not when so much was at stake. If he could make Alistair understand, if he could persuade him to take it easy while he assessed the situation, just so his condition wouldn't worsen before he could find a solution—

"I'm fine."

"You're getting worse."

Alistair scoffed. "You worry over nothing. Really, I'm fine."

"You're not fine." His infection was worsening, his fever was climbing, his respiratory system was compromised, and Langford didn't know how to fix any of it.

Alistair fell silent, and the sound of horses' hooves clopping over frozen ground filled the air.

"I've had worse. Remember the time I nearly lost my arm on the Fairbanks job? Were it not for you, I would have had to learn how to do that thing you love with only one hand."

An unwilling smile curved the corner of Langford's mouth. The Fairbanks job was one of the first missions he took part in. Back when Alistair had first found him, penniless, even shoeless (a terribly long and embarrassing story) and took him in. The job was meant to be a simple extraction. Bickering lords concerned with who inherited what from a dead uncle. Halward swore the Medizza painting was bequeathed to him, even though his cousin, Kenzington, kept it locked in his basement. Langford had only been in Ardenas a month when he'd counted himself among Alistair's crew of accomplished thieves and swords for hire. It was also when he learned firsthand the finer point of Ardenian law. Law and order were determined within individual towns and city provinces. There was no official guard to arrest them… but there was Kenzington's paid security, and punishment was an off-the-records sort of affair.

Alistair's wound had been deep, and the man whined for the duration of his recovery time, but it was the first instance when Langford was given leave to treat him. To clean and disinfect his wounds, check his dressings, and fuss over him.

"You were so dramatic. Your arm was in no danger of amputation."

Alistair grinned and rolled his shoulder. "Took that axe deep, no? I'd have taken it deeper if I knew it meant I'd get the most enticing healer in the land to put his hands on me."

Langford's cheeks burned and a pleasant warmth bloomed in his belly. "You didn't think of me in that way back then." It was true. Alistair had been excruciatingly vocal about his *type*. Namely, professionals who had the expertise to keep up with him without forming pesky attachments. It wasn't until ages later Langford even learned that preference included men. Sure, Alistair flirted nonstop. With anyone and everyone, even Hugo who never so much as flinched. But it was madness to think Alistair saw him as anything other than the starving and frightened Kovalian healer, lost in a foreign country.

"Look at me." Alistair's cold hand tipped Langford's chin, forcing their eyes to meet. Instead of glassy and unfocused, they burned with a passionate clarity. "I've always seen you for what you are."

Langford snorted, despite Alistair holding him firmly in his thrall, and slowed the horse to halt their wagon's movement. "And what am I?"

Alistair's fierce green gaze softened. "You're brilliant. Stronger than anyone I've ever known. You're devastatingly gorgeous and command more honor than any man to walk this earth. You're my hope for everything good, because you are far too noble for the world I've known and far too good for me."

Langford's breath caught in his throat, and Alistair quirked a dark brow. "Lucky for us, I don't possess such nobility to insist you find a man who deserves you, and I have no issue claiming you for myself."

"Don't say that." Langford exhaled a laugh at Alistair's befuddled expression. "Stop saying you don't deserve me." He leaned into his touch, allowing his fear of everything, of what he almost lost, what he still might lose, drift off to give way for the truth of this moment. Finally speaking the words he should have said long ago. "You are more than whatever you've been told. I'll never understand why you think so little of yourself when I see proof every day of how extraordinary you are. Your mistakes don't define you. Your past doesn't define you. Your heart, your courage to protect the ones you love... You are everything worth fighting for."

Alistair blinked, his eyes filling with tears. "Ah. Don't—" He cleared his throat, dropping Langford's chin to rub his eyes. He let out a labored laugh, like his chest was too tight to release it easily. Shaking his head, he grabbed Langford by the collar. "Fucking come here."

An exhale of hot breath, and their mouths met in a dizzying kiss. Sparks shot through Langford's veins and across his skin. He deepened the kiss, sinking into the heat of Alistair's body. Langford distantly remembered they were stopped in the middle of the road with a dead man's mead supply, but the liquid slide of Alistair's tongue wiped the thought from his mind.

They were here. This was real. And never, in all Langford's life, had he imagined he could love like this. Drown in it. It was terrifying and invigorating, defying all logic in the best way. It was the only thing he accepted he didn't need to understand. To examine and analyze until all angles were exposed and a hypothesis was formed. It could just be. He could just be.

And he never felt freer.

Alistair wrenched his mouth away, choking on a wet cough that wracked his entire body. Langford's stomach sank as he rubbed his back soothingly, all warmth from the previous moment icing over to a bone-chilling reminder.

He had no bloody clue how to fix this.

WHEN THEY FINALLY CROSSED THE threshold of the Walden inn, tracking snow underfoot, the fiery warmth from the hearth blasted Langford in the face. Alistair staggered in behind him. He needed to get their frozen clothes hung above the fire. Maybe call for a bath to be drawn. Clean towels, the rest of his medical supplies. With a few hours of silence, he could sort out what needed to be done for Alistair, and then—

A body slammed into him, nearly knocking him off his feet. Small arms were wrapped tightly around his waist, crushing his ribs in a bear hug. Before he could shove the offending party away, a familiar red strand of hair pressed against his face.

Lark.

Langford wrapped his arms around her, nearly sagging under the weight of his relief.

"Thank the skies you're here," her muffled voice rang out.

"I could say the same about you." Langford rubbed her back, resting his cheek against the top of her head.

"And what about me?" Alistair nudged them. "Where's your enthusiasm for my presence?"

Lark tore herself away—and before Langford could warn her—had Alistair in her vicelike grip.

"Ah! Mercy!" Alistair groaned.

Langford tugged her away. "He's wounded."

Lark's honey-colored eyes widened, and she held her hands up as if in surrender. "Skies, I had no idea. What's happened to you?" Without waiting for an answer, she began ripping at his cloak, trying to get a look at his injury.

"Easy. Only Langford has leave to disrobe me so violently. Take it slow and allow me to enjoy this."

Cad. The utter cad.

"We'll explain everything, but perhaps we should first retire to a more private location."

Lark nodded, grabbing Langford's hand and dragging him through the nearly empty tavern. Not even Mrs. O'Connell was in sight, a mercy since he hadn't the energy to explain what had happened to Huxley. Or Alistair. Or any of it.

"What's the rush?" Alistair called out from behind them, shuffling to keep up. Langford really needed to see to his chest, maybe consult his books for any answer, a hint of an answer, something to help him understand.

Lark quickened her pace. "He's already lost so much blood."

"Who?" Was it Gavriel? Had he awakened? Or maybe he was attacked while he was still in his deathlike sleep. But hadn't Inerys set a plethora of protective spells and laurels to prevent such a thing? Why would they have moved him? Where was everyone and why was Lark being so strange?

Lark opened the door to Langford's room—Mrs. O'Connell must have told her where he set his lodgings—and rushed them to the bedside.

Mrs. O'Connell stood by the bed, a bloodied rag in her hand. Tears trailed over her rounded cheeks as she gazed down at whoever lay in the bed. The fair-haired Reaper, Ferryn, sat blocking the patient's face from view. He eyed Lark with an expression Langford didn't understand. Was it awe? Fear?

Langford rounded the bed, giving a nod to Ferryn. Ferryn stepped out of the way, giving Langford the chance to see what, or whom, he was actually dealing with.

It was a child. A small boy. Maybe nine or ten, eleven if he was small for his age. His forehead was dotted with sweat, eyes clamped shut as he writhed in pain. Mrs. O'Connell reached for his right arm—

Langford's gaze fell to the bloodied stump where his hand should be.

"What happened?"

Lark ran a hand through her hair, her mouth tight. "Can you help him?"

She was hiding something. Not the nature of the boy's injury. Just glancing at it, Langford could ascertain it was a clean cut from a blade. Something about the circumstances of his wound, perhaps in the receiving of it, she wasn't ready to share.

Langford rolled up his sleeves. He'd get answers after.

CHAPTER NINE

LARK

*W*atching Langford work was a thing of beauty. He rolled his sleeves to his elbows, ushered Mrs. O'Connell out of the way, and unwrapped the boy's bandaged wrist. Not even a flicker of emotion crossed his face, his pinched brow of concentration firmly in place. So many times, Lark had heard how she wore her thoughts and feelings in every expression. But Langford… he kept his locked behind a mask of careful neutrality. It was madness to think he ever suspected himself weak. He assessed the brutal wound without a shred of discomfort, his confidence settling over the room and easing the lingering tension.

Langford placed a gentle hand against the boy's forehead and whispered something Lark could only assume was comfort. With a determined stride, Langford approached his worktable, gathering supplies with a fluid efficiency.

"It's rather crowded. Mrs. O'Connell, I'll require your assistance, but the rest of you clear out." Langford's command rang out, and Lark hesitated.

"Oh, but that domineering tone does things to me." Alistair shivered before placing an arm around Lark's shoulders. "Off we pop."

"But what about—"

"Later. You too, Blondie," Alistair called over his shoulder.

Ferryn's shuffling steps followed them down the stairs to the empty tavern. Empty apart from Mrs. O'Connell's newest hire, a burly man whom everyone called Grim. A dark beard with bits of gray along his hairline. His large frame and intimidating stare made him seem severe.

"Lark, you look ready to keel over," he ground out in his deep voice. "Sit. I saved some of the boss' pie."

In truth, Grim was absurdly kindhearted.

"I couldn't possibly—"

He slid a large slice of apple pie in front of Lark, the buttered crust shining in the candlelight. The scent of cinnamon and nutmeg wafted from the plate.

"Well, if you insist." Lark dug in, plopping a large slice of sugared apple in her mouth. "Alistair, you want any?"

"Already grabbing my late-night snack," Alistair said with a groan as he reached for the highest shelf of spirits behind the bar. How did he sneak back there without her noticing? Grim took pity on him, reaching over his head to grab the most expensive rum Mrs. O'Connell carried.

"What about you?" Lark glanced over at Ferryn.

His face was pinched in a decidedly discomfited expression. "Not everyone favors apples the way you do, Lark."

Fair enough.

Lark continued devouring the pie, trying her best to keep her thoughts firmly planted on the food in front of her. It never failed to amaze her, the ability to smell and taste and experience food this way. She doubted she ever would, and part of her worried whatever happened in that alley, whatever formed that tether between her soul and another's, was a sign that all this would be ripped away. That she'd awaken and find this was all a long and strange dream.

As the last bite of pie hit her stomach, and she was filled with a contented fullness, the image of Gavriel drifted into mind. How he could appear so serious and hard until a smile lit up his face making him appear almost boyish and youthful. A pang of longing swept through her, fierce and unrestrained. It was enough to tighten her chest and make that previous full-bellied sensation more akin to a stone in her gut.

Good news. Her human emotions were in no danger of disappearing.

"We need to talk about what happened." Ferryn's voice broke through her thoughts.

Lark hummed thoughtfully as if his reminder didn't spear a jolt of ice through her heart. "Somber doesn't suit your bone structure."

"Dammit, Lark." Ferryn lowered his voice. "Now is the time for your over-analytical ruminating. You forged a tether. Don't waste your breath by denying it, I know what I saw." He shook his head. "What I don't know is what it means."

If only he knew the dizzying spiral of thoughts and fears Lark had already spun through in search of that answer. It could mean anything.

And that was a terrifying thought.

"Let's take care of what's in front of us before we climb that hill, yes?" Langford was already exhausted and road weary while he patched up the boy upstairs, and there was still the matter of Alistair's medical needs. Was it too much to ask the world to stop hurling so much shit in the same direction for a night or two?

"You're starting to sound like me." Alistair plopped in the stool beside her, yanking the cork out of his bottle with his teeth. "I quite like rubbing off on you."

Lark ignored his suggestive tone. "Are you sure that's a good idea right now?" She nodded at the bottle.

Alistair's expression flattened. "In all our time together, have you learned nothing?" Rolling his eyes, he took a long pull.

She should interfere, Langford would likely give him an earful for this, but instead she turned to Ferryn, his hardened face a worrisome thing.

The last time Ferryn was gravely worried for her, he'd known something she hadn't. Something dangerous. It had resulted in Thanar's punishment—the catalyst that set off a thousand different twists and turns, each more explosive than the last. All ending in a fate written eons ago.

Why did it always feel as if someone was toying with her?

Leaning in, she whispered, "You really didn't feel it? Any pull?"

Ferryn's brow pinched, and he shook his head.

Well, shit.

<hr />

THE SHARP SCENT of blood filled the room, and Mrs. O'Connell had long since retired to her bed for the evening, promising them all sorts of confectionary magic on the morn despite the way she swayed on her exhausted feet. She had done much for them, always had. And without a whisper of recompense.

Langford washed the blood off his hands with a calm assurance. Red bloomed in the wash basin, disbursing until the water was faintly tinged with violence.

The last Lark knew was that the boy, Fendrel—that was what Mrs. O'Connell called him—remained unconscious, but his breathing had seemed stronger, steadier. His wrist had been wrapped tightly with clean bandages. Grim had carried him to a room closer to the kitchens, the promise of the servants aiding in his recovery was enough for Langford to allow his patient to leave. His bedding had been stripped and replaced with new blankets.

Lark leaned against the wall, her head falling back with a soft thud.

Langford chuckled. "Long night?"

"Not as long as yours, I'm sure."

Langford wiped his hands and placed the rag in the corner with the soiled bedsheets. "I need to check on Alistair. Maybe apply a fresh poultice." He strode past Lark, aiming for the room across the hall where she and Ferryn had planned to stay.

Ripples of moonlight spilled across the floor and over the bed Alistair occupied. An icy wind fluttered the curtains where the window had been left ajar. He was already fast asleep above the covers, shirtless, and softly snoring. The gashes along his chest appeared little more than dark shadows. Ferryn silently slumbered in the chair against the wall.

His chin pressed against his chest, his shoulders rising and falling with every breath.

"Can it wait?" Lark whispered. "Can Alistair rest for a spell?"

The visible half of Langford's mouth frowned. "I don't know."

"How can you not—"

A sharp cut of Langford's hand through the air silenced her question. He was already at the window. He shoved the curtains out of the way and gripped the handle.

"Don't." Ferryn's voice was groggy from sleep. "He said it was too hot to sleep with the window closed."

Langford relented and pressed the back of his hand to Alistair's forehead before hissing out a curse. "His fever is climbing, but his body isn't fighting it." With a hitched breath, he swept out of the room, back to his worktable across the hall, and Lark tripped over her feet trying to keep up with him.

"Wait—"

"There's no time. If his fever elevates much higher, we're talking about permanent damage." Langford furiously shoved items into his bag. There was a desperation, not only to his movements but in the very air surrounding him. Lark could feel it. Could taste his panic. Her own pulse ratcheted in response. No. No. She couldn't forge a tether *now*.

Lark gripped Langford's forearm, forcing him to halt.

"Stop. Explain. You wouldn't have waited to treat an infection, and I know the way you pack your bags. You had supplies on the road. What's happening to him?"

Langford sighed and ran both hands into his dark hair, leaving it even messier than before. He sank on to the empty bed, his posture defeated. "It's going to sound mad."

Lark claimed the spot beside him, the bed pressing in beneath her. She leaned her head against his shoulder, a familiar and comforting contact. "Madder than a Reaper who became human and befriended a werewolf only for the witch-queen of the Netherworld to destroy the veil protecting the human realm and allow even more monsters and demons to roam free?" Skies above. When spoken aloud like that, it

57

was a wonder any human could retain this influx of information without losing their head.

Langford laughed, a choked sound. "Compared to that, it will sound positively sane."

"What a relief! I feel more than equipped to hear your tale."

He let out a groan and rested his head against hers. "We were escorting the mead seller from Stormfair when we were attacked."

Lark lifted her head, shifting her position to face him fully.

"At first, it seemed like a typical Undesirable. Some sort of beast. But nothing about it was typical... a wolflike creature who stood tall like a man."

That sounded suspiciously close to a Cursed Wolven. Differing far from the likes of Daciana, and her ability to shift with the moon. The Cursed Wolven were beasts forged in punishment. When a werewolf committed ghastly atrocities in their lifespan, they became trapped between phases in the afterlife. Neither man nor wolf, all malice and rage. And pain. So much pain.

"What happened?"

"The creature killed the mead seller and ran off. It seemed a grave misfortune, but quickly over. It wasn't until his corpse began to exhibit signs of life that I knew something was terribly wrong." Langford met her gaze, his blue-grey eyes wide with fear. "He died, Lark. There was no pulse, his chest was in ribbons. I'd have bloody seen a heartbeat with how exposed his chest cavity was. He died, and then he came back. But he was all wrong."

"Wrong how?" Lark's heart thundered in her chest.

"Somehow... it was like he *became* the creature that killed him. Like it was a virus infecting the next host. I can't explain it. We cut him down, and Alistair... he sustained an injury I haven't the faintest clue how to treat. All signs point to infection, but his body refuses to respond to treatment. And what if he—" Langford broke off, pressing a finger to his lips. As if halting his words would spare Alistair of the fate he feared.

Lark's thoughts spun. How could a Cursed Wolven pass on their curse? It made no sense. Undesirables were forged in the afterlife based on decisions made in this life and the journey back to the human realm. Or that was her understanding… could everything she had learned have been a lie? Without the veil, shouldn't the creation of more monsters be impossible? And how could a human, not a were-wolf, even exist as a Cursed Wolven in the afterlife?

She had no answers, but she wrapped her arms around Langford, offering the only thing she could.

"I can't lose him again, Lark. I can't."

The memory of Langford broken and sobbing over Alistair's life-less body fluttered into mind. How he fought to keep breath in his lungs when Thanar choked the life out of him on Nereida's command. How Langford begged, pleaded Daciana to save him, whatever the cost.

Lark squeezed him tighter. "You won't." It was a promise no one could make, not in this life or any other, and yet she did because she too, would fight against fate, the skies, the apathetic paragons, anything, to keep her dear friend from losing so much again.

"How fast was the transformation? The mead seller, I mean."

Langford sniffed. "Almost instantaneous. I'd call it astounding were it not so terrifying."

Lark pulled back to look at him.

His eyes were red and glassy. "Were I not so worried for Alistair, I'd have liked to study Huxley further. Anything to understand what in the blazing nethers is happening."

Of course, he would. Ever the scholar.

"So, the fact that he hasn't changed already must mean something."

"I've missed your optimism." Langford wiped his nose on his sleeve. "I thought of that. Perhaps death accelerates the change, and while Alistair breathes, it's a slower transformation. Or maybe the infection will kill him." A silent tear trailed down his cheek.

Lark wiped it away. "We'll figure it out. We'll find a way. If anyone can, it's you."

Langford's mouth curved, and he exhaled a weighty sigh. "Some-times, I think—"

A sharp scream cut through the night air, sending a spear of ice down Lark's spine and halting Langford's response. A heavy stillness filled the room, sharpening the silence. The only sound was Lark's heartbeat, pulsing in her ears as a sense of dread washed over her, thick as fog.

More screams. Shouts.

Lark and Langford ran to the window and shoved it open.

Where darkness once greeted them, a silent black sky glimmering with stars, now violent brush strokes of colors and sounds had stolen the night.

Villagers ran, tripping over themselves as they fled in terror. Flames erupted, coiling tendrils of fire reaching high into the sky. Chaos. Madness. Destruction.

But why?

A howl rang out, a long-sustained call in the night. The union of melancholy and malice.

A call for blood.

"Langford!" Ferryn's panicked voice called from across the hall. "Something's wrong with Alistair."

Langford rushed past Lark, nearly colliding with Ferryn as he crossed the threshold. Lark raced after him. Alistair had to be all right, she just promised he would be fine. He was sleeping not moments ago—

Alistair's back arched off the bed, his head shaking back and forth. His body began to shake, tremors making the bed frame rattle against the wall and floor.

"No! No!" Langford flung himself to the bed, nimble hands turning Alistair onto his side.

More screams. Angry snarls. The shrill cry of an infant. The *crash* of a window breaking.

Should she help them? Should she stay? She needed to do *something*.

Alistair stilled, his breath returning to normal. Langford pinched his wrist, his stare never leaving his face as he monitored his pulse. When he exhaled a sigh of relief, Lark almost sagged to the floor the way the tension in her body lifted.

Through the window, a bloody scene was painted in the snow. Bodies ripped to shreds, dark drag marks staining the ground. Some of the bodies were already twisting, arching and contorting.

Transforming.

"Go. I've got him." Langford's voice was firm, resolute.

It was a clear directive. And a message. He knew as well as she did that no one could promise life. Promise to stay the hand of loss.

But they could delay death.

Lark snatched up her bow, her quiver, her blade. Hugo's knife remained where she always kept it on her belt. She might not have control of fate, of Gavriel's condition or Alistair's, but she could stand before the monsters, both magical and mundane, and fight 'til the last of her strength fled her mortal body.

It was simple, the way fear and determination could coexist in the same mind. Same muscles. Same blood and bone and sinew.

Lark strode to the hall, and Ferryn followed close behind.

Down the stairs. Through the dark tavern. To the doors—

Grim stood at the ready, a thick club in his large hands. And Mrs. O'Connell, a crossbow already loaded with a bolt.

Absolutely not. Alistair would kill her if she let the woman fight.

"Go back to your room, bar the door, and for skies' sake, do not come out 'til morning."

"Now, listen here"—Mrs. O'Connell lifted her chin, eyes blazing— "I've never let cowardice guide my hand, and I'm not about to start today." She tightened her grip on her crossbow. "There are good people out there. *Our* people. I sure as shit won't hide while they fight."

"We need you to stay here. Protect the others, Langford and Alistair are still upstairs. What if something gets through? What if—"

"Oh, child." Mrs. O'Connell lowered her weapon, and cupped Lark's face. "You think to carry your burdens alone. Don't argue. I'm an observant woman and I've watched you all these months. Each time you came home. That's what this is, you know? This is your home. It's mine and yours and those besotted fools' upstairs, too. It's home to anyone who ever felt lost and alone but found a warm bed and a compassionate ear for a night or two. Whatever battle is out there, I'm fighting it with you. With them. Because that's how it works. That's how all of this, all this pain in the world, all this destruction... that's how we make it through."

And that was what Lark had longed for, as a Reaper. That passion. That clarity. That undying hope.

It was human.

It was everything.

Lark nodded and squeezed Mrs. O'Connell's hand before lowering it from her face.

If she wished to fight... Lark would just have to make sure she brought her through this alive and well.

Grim swung the door open, and orange light blinded Lark.

Heat. Flames.

Lark nocked an arrow, holding her bowstring loose but ready. A woman ran by, screaming, and a man tackled her to the snow.

Not a man.

The creature still wore the ripped remnants of a tunic, but its hands had elongated into giant claws. The woman held her arms taut, keeping it from reaching her face.

"Help me!"

Lark pulled and released, the arrow sinking into its back. It howled a pained sound of agony. She nocked another arrow, pulled, and released, a hit through the back of the neck. The beast fell dead, trapping the woman under its body. She shrieked and flailed, kicking out her skirts beneath the weight of the beast.

Another body, a woman, lied contorting in the snow. Her back arched, revealing the thick wounds to her gut where her intestines peeked out. Already her teeth were growing longer, sharper, too large for her mouth. Soft snarls broke through, her eyes flashing like a flame through a frosted window. Pain and anger radiated off her. Lark leapt to her side, Hugo's knife already in hand. Stabbing deep in her neck, straight through the spine, Lark twisted the knife before pulling it free. The woman stilled, her transformation stalling.

None of it made sense. Why was this happening? Lark stood and brushed her hair out of her face, leaving a wet trail of what must have been blood across her forehead. She shouted back to the others over the cacophony of pain and suffering.

"Aim for the top of the spine." Why? Why was that the killing shot? Would any vital areas breathe death into these beasts? She didn't know. She didn't know and it was worse that way. Panic clutched at her chest, a coiling tension pulled tight, and then the floodgates opened.

Everyone's fear. Everyone's panic. Everyone's pain flooded her. The weight of dozens of souls collided with her own, and it ripped through her defenses like a knife through hot butter.

Lark fell to her knees, desperately trying to rebuild her mental walls brick by brick. Whatever it took to quiet the screaming in her mind.

Along the edge of the panic. The pain. The suffering. A wildness rattled. It shook and it howled, and it was primal instinct.

Her awareness had touched the soul of a beast.

Shaky hope gripped her, and Lark searched for more. For chaos. For rage. For hunger. She searched and she collected, and she pulled. Each frenzied soul tasted like earth and fire. She tied herself to them. To each one she could find, and she tethered them so tightly, a deep tremble bellowed through her.

She had them. She had them. And it was only natural to connect to their racing hearts and push. Push them higher, pump them faster, and how it burned in her chest.

Lark's vision darkened, unconsciousness threatening to take her under, but she pressed even harder. It was too much. It thrummed in her veins. In her soul. Until—

A *crack*. Like lightning searing down her spine. The clap of thunder in her very marrow as all the tethers snapped, and the weight of a dozen souls broke.

Lark fell back, the sudden quiet ushering in the sound of the wind once more. The crackle of fire as someone's home still burned. The quiet sobs of those who survived. The thrum of blood rushing in her ears.

Heavy crunching over the snow, a heart galloping.

63

A snarl. A deep baritone growl.

Something was coming.

Lark lifted her knife—

Her arm fell uselessly back to the ground. Already the freezing cold was seeping through her clothes, numbing her legs, her back, her head. Every muscle in her body was spent, darkness threatening her vision.

She had no fight left in her.

The snarling came closer. Footfalls rushing closer and closer still—

A metallic thud, and something heavy landed beside her. Lark turned, her temple resting against the frozen ground. The open maw of a beast, bloodied jagged teeth, yellow eyes forever open in death. The large body was stretched beside her, a small iron ball, outfitted with spikes, driven into the back of its head. A chain rustled—it was attached to the iron ball.

Lark groaned, rolling to her back and blinking against her blurring vision.

"Huh. Niall was right. This is handy."

Lark knew that voice. She couldn't place it, her vision was spinning, a dizzying array of colors and shapes flashing in front of her. The voice laughed, bright and unrestrained.

"What in the blazing nethers did you do?"

A pale face came into view. Lark blinked, desperately trying to focus on who stood over her. Dark eyes, delicately shaped. Freckles dusted across the bridge of a nose. Long black hair blowing from beneath a red hood. Wisps of her fringe hanging in uneven lengths.

Kenna.

Lark sighed, relief flooding her weary body.

Kenna grinned and shook her head. "This is what happens when regular folk try to do my job."

CHAPTER TEN

KENNA

Sargon's flaming pucker hole, some people never learned.

The last time Kenna followed a beast to Oakbury, she'd saved a foolish boy trying to fight a wraith with rusty farm equipment. She could appreciate the courage it took to go toe-to-toe with a monster, armed with nothing but a pitchfork and wet breeches, but blazing nethers, send word for a hunter.

Even that bout of foolishness couldn't have prepared her for this.

She had been tracking this lycanthrope for days when it veered in a new direction. When it broke its pattern. It wasn't until she stumbled upon the bloody site, bits and pieces of some poor sod left over in the snow, and the traces of blood from a second person, that she realized what had happened.

Lycanthropes, not the lineage of Daciana's people, hunters didn't have a word for that, but the typical lycanthrope loved nothing more than the thrill of a hunt. The first kill had too much blood, there was no way he'd survived.

But the second.

There were tracks where the lycanthrope fled the scene, but not to flee, to wait. To follow. To bide its time.

Sometimes, a monster was hungry. Other times it was bored. Kenna could relate to that. Not the toying with a person until finally being ready to eat it bit, but the boredom. Waiting for word from the other hunters lent her more than her share of time to fill. Hunting had become a monotonous affair. Find a problem, assess the threat, slay the beast. A bit repetitive. Probably because she was using hunting as a distraction. Daciana—

Nope. Now was not a good time to analyze that particular situation, not when there was an actual hunt. Best left for the wee hours of the morn when sleep was most needed and furthest from her reach. That was her pattern, at least. Her intrusive thoughts made for glorious company.

Dac insisted on such arbitrary boundaries, as if limiting contact would make anything easier. Kenna was sure, after everything that went down in the Emerald Woods, Daciana would pull her head out of her ass and finally admit her self-imposed distance was a needless punishment for them both.

No such luck.

Sure, she *permitted* Kenna's presence. Such a *generous* lass in that. And she even initiated physical contact to a degree. She wasn't ready for more than a stolen kiss or two.

Kenna didn't mind that. There was no use in pretending she wasn't a physical person and she wasn't dying to strip Daciana down and taste every inch of her skin once more. But it wasn't about that. She'd spend the rest of her days living off memories of their heated passion, so long as Dac let her guard down in every other respect. They'd been through enough, pushed each other, pulled away, came out the other side, and for what?

Daciana's impressive walls were rebuilt with ease. And Kenna couldn't stomach watching Dac's shared vulnerability with Lark. Not when she found herself at arm's length.

Why hadn't she just sailed to Anquan to find more hunters herself? What was keeping her anchored to this continent? It wasn't like she was wanted. Even now, what good did she really achieve, arriving late to the lycanthrope's feast?

Kenna blew her fringe out of her eyes, she needed to trim that soon, and surveyed the aftermath.

So many sodding bodies. How did one lycanthrope manage to cause this much destruction?

And why was she not surprised to find Lark in the center of it all?

Kenna was beginning to think that girl was more trouble than she was worth. That was a bit unfair. It wasn't Lark's fault she attracted all matter of danger and... wait, no. It was her fault. The tears in the veil, the increase in monster activity? Lark's doing. Every choice the former Reaper had made had caused the worst sort of ripple effect. The kind that made more work for Kenna. But work was lucrative, so she supposed that was a favor if one squinted real hard—

"Kenna," Lark breathed.

"The one and only." Kenna grabbed her hand and yanked her up, but Lark uselessly flopped back to the snow. "Aren't you cold? Get up and help me count the bodies. I don't know how you did whatever that was but I'm sure you have a long and complicated explanation. Why aren't you getting up?"

"Can't move."

"Shit, really? You hurt?" There was no discernible wound. No blood beneath her.

"I'm... fine." Lark's throat bobbed while she kept lying there. "Just... depleted."

"Ah, gotcha." Whatever strangeness that meant. "Guess you need me to carry you?" Without waiting for an answer, Kenna hoisted her over her shoulder, bracing her hands in a very respectable location south of her backside. Lark's top half dangled down Kenna's back, arms limp and swinging. "Shit, you're heavier than you look."

"Lark? What's happened to her?" A panicked voice called out. The voice's owner came into view.

And of course, it was him. The light-haired Reaper Kenna had zero interest in strolling down memory lane with.

Dying wasn't something one forgot. No matter how hard she tried.

Memories of that day, when Daciana's people found her and Nahnah. When they strapped her nahnah to a spit, slowly roasting her.

Tied Kenna to a stake and made her *watch*. The pain wasn't important. The way they cut and sliced and clawed, bleeding her out with slow and precise wounds. Mutilating her with finesse. It was the sound of her nahnah's voice. Nahnah tried not to scream. The strongest woman Kenna ever knew. The woman who raised her and taught her everything about what it meant to be a hunter. How her father before her was a hunter, and her nahnah before him. How to brew sepsis oil and coat her blades when hunting the right prey. Who told her bedtime stories of the monsters the mortals fear, and Kenna's place standing between them. All of it, every memory was ruined with the sound of her screams as they cooked her alive.

How even when Kenna's soul left her body, those screams followed her. They followed her alongside the Reaper who tried to guide her to the afterlife. His obnoxiously pitying stare hounding her as she accepted her fate.

Even though her soul was called back into her body, and she awoke in Dac's arms, his face was a reminder of everything she'd lost. Unease coiled low in her gut, the same feeling she experienced every time she looked at him. It was a twisting, squirming sensation. Discomfort threatening to build into something more. Something painful.

Physical pain was easier to feel than anything that would lead her back to thoughts of her nahnah. But that was too dreary a thought, wasn't it? That Ferryn's face was enough to incite such a reaction? Better to focus on how pretty he'd look all done up for Fire Feast, her favored winter festival she hadn't been home to enjoy in years.

Maybe it was time to hop a boat back to Anquan.

"She's fine. Where do I put her? In case you haven't noticed, there's an assload of bodies to deal with." And the matter of figuring out what happened, but one thing at a time.

"Kenna?" The Reaper, well, he wasn't a Reaper anymore, was he? He gingerly took Lark from her, cradling her in his arms.

Why everyone was determined to treat the most destructive girl she'd ever met as if she was made of glass, Kenna would never understand.

"I'll make the rounds. Why don't you wrap this one in a blanket and pour her a steaming cup of cider. I'm sure that will be a worthwhile use of your time." Without waiting for a response, Kenna stomped off.

She was most assuredly not bitter about any of this.

CHAPTER ELEVEN

LARK

*T*he ground moved beneath her. Or she floated above it. Rocking. A swell like a wave. A jolt stopping her short. Swirling stars burned behind her eyes. Hissing. Hot breath in her ear. Lark shivered and opened her eyes. Blackness engulfed her vision, pulsing between images. They faded too quickly for her to latch on to anything. A clenched jaw. A drop of blood swelling before it fell. A flash of blinding light.

Lark's head spun, nausea churning her gut. The voice came again, a heated whisper of breath fanning the shell of her ear. "What?"

"I didn't know you could hear me." Someone shifted her, and the ground kept moving. "I said, what in the fucking void was that?"

Ferryn. He was hissing in her ear as he carried her through the snow. Above his brow, a nasty cut wept blood down the side of his face.

"You're hurt."

He scoffed. "Don't worry about me."

Lark's tongue felt like it was twisting in her mouth. "Gonna be sick."

Ferryn lowered her to the ground, turning her and holding her steady so she didn't land face first into her vomit. Her stomach heaved but nothing came up. Already, her fingers were beginning to tingle. Lark flexed her hand. Her strength was returning in slow drips. Calmness, a charged stillness promised the coming of snow. Air chilled by the northern wind and winter's grasp. She took a deep breath of bracing cold air. It flooded her throat, her chest, soothing the ragged edges of pain from pushing herself too far.

Lark still didn't have an explanation for it. For how she accessed that power again. How she forged tethers to those creatures and followed each thread to their hearts, making them burst in their chests.

"I'm not trying to be a tyrant, Lark." Ferryn's voice held a desperate edge. "But I have to know…"

"I don't understand it myself." Lark exhaled, her breath a cloud of vapor in front of her face.

"You did it again, didn't you? You connected with all of them."

Another inhale, her stomach less precarious with each slow breath she took. She'd pulled them all into her, tethered her soul to theirs, and cut them down. They'd been mortal minutes, seconds, before. And now they were all dead. "How many were there?"

"I counted thirteen. Fourteen including the one Kenna took down."

Kenna. Lark had nearly forgotten the hunter had arrived in the nick of time. Did that mean she was coming back? Did Daciana know?

The thought of her friend made the space between Lark's ribs ache. The last time they spoke, she was a right shit to her. Thanks to Kenna, Lark could apologize to Dac for that.

Her arms felt more solid, and she tested their strength by pressing her hands against the ground.

She didn't falter.

Slowly she shifted so she was sitting upright beside Ferryn. Something in the pained expression on his face, the deep lines between his brow and the downturn of his mouth…

"Was anyone else hurt?" Many were hurt, wounded. But he had to know what she meant. She'd allowed two untrained fighters to join the skirmish. Left Alistair and Langford unprotected.

His gaze fell. "By you? No."

Lark's heart hammered in her throat. "That's not what I asked."

Ferryn met her stare. Soft pity reflected in his eyes. "Lark." His voice was gentle. Too gentle. Achingly cautious.

Her stomach turned again. "What happened?"

"Grim. I saw him fall."

He was a good man, decent and kind. It was strange, knowing there was no one to guide him. Where would his soul go?

"And"—Ferryn wet his lips—"that woman... Mrs. O'Connell..."

"Did she make it?"

Silence. The air was swathed in the aching silence. The falling of snowflakes did nothing to soften the sharp truth ringing in the skies forsaken silence.

Finally, he shook his head.

And the silence only grew.

CHAPTER TWELVE

LANGFORD

*G*ods above, hear my plea. Guide me through the darkest shadows. Steel me against the wickedness of this fallen world. Cleanse me in my suffering, for only your wisdom can—

Langford's thoughts abruptly cut short, and the dwindling candle on the bedside shifted into focus. The flickering flame, now taller than the melted wax it sprung from, taunted him for his wandering mind. It was a familiar canticle. The chant his mother had him recite whenever he was afraid. The words had taken shape now in the face of his fear.

And it was foolish. With everything he saw, he learned, he *knew*, these prayers had become a distant memory of childish naïveté. The comfort he'd once found in the familiar words, in the chant that made him feel closer to his mother, was gone. And in its place, a cold realization had taken root.

No one was listening.

It had been ages since Langford prayed to the gods. Even that day in the Emerald Woods, when he witnessed the last breath leave Alistair's body, it wasn't the gods he begged, it was Daciana.

For good measure, maybe he should send a prayer her way.

Daciana, please here my cry. Langford snorted, rubbing his nose and blinking the sting from his eyes. He fixed covers over Alistair, wool scratching his palm.

Alistair's condition was erratic at best, volatile at worst. One moment, his breathing would regulate, pain smoothing from his face, and a calm quiet settling over him. The next, his body would contort, his breathing would quicken, and the sounds he made…

If agony bore a sound, it would be the way Alistair groaned and snarled. It was a pain of rage, and Langford didn't know what to do. Nothing in his examinations nor his experience in the field had prepared him for this. It bore a terrifying similarity to Gavriel's condition—in Lanford's ignorance to it. Unidentifiable. Inexplainable. An affliction no earthly text would classify.

And Langford was useless. Worthless. *Stupid, so stupid.*

Alistair groaned, a softer sound. Langford pressed a fresh cool cloth to his forehead and rubbed circles against the top of his hand with his thumb.

The screams outside had died down. It would be a lie to say Langford had been tempted to help the others. In reality, he wouldn't have left Alistair's side unless he was dragged out, honor or no.

He had an obligation to assess the wounded. To help wherever he could. Gods knew they needed a healer now more than ever. Yet here he sat. A useless presence beside the man he loved. Love really was a selfish affliction, and it masqueraded better than any of the snakes back in Koval. Right now, it bore the mask of fear. A deep burrowing fear that spread like an infection of the blood. It was a sort of paralysis, his inability to take his eyes off Alistair for even a moment.

Apart from the ritualistic habits of his upbringing, Langford was a man of logic, and he could rationalize his way through his fear. It made sense he would pose symptoms of this stress, especially now. Especially after everything. He'd completed a rotation at University, treating individuals exhibiting signs of life-inhibiting fear. It almost always came after a traumatic incident, dominating the individual in a game of mental chess, and Langford had to think three moves ahead to avoid triggering their paralysis.

Langford was never very good at chess, and that particular area of study was his weakest.

Really, wherever Alistair was concerned, Langford was his weakest.

"Was wondering who made my job harder."

Langford snapped his head up. Kenna leaned against the open doorway, arms crossed. Her deep red cloak was fastened around her neck but pushed back from her shoulders to show her outfit of black fighting leathers, daggers and blades tucked into every conceivable holding. A thick chain ran the length of her torso, crisscrossing over her chest and wrapping around her waist, where it ended on a silver ball, spiked and soaked with blood at her hip.

That one was new.

"How did I manage that?"

Kenna grinned, a dimple creasing her pale cheek. "Not you. Him." She crossed the room in languid strides, like she had all the time and not a care in the world. "Huh. He looks like shit."

The aching truth of her assessment clenched in Langford's gut. "He's not responding to treatment."

"Obviously not."

Langford could appreciate her straightforwardness. It saved time. At least that's what he told himself as he gritted his teeth against her callous reaction to the love of his life in turmoil.

Kenna pulled a small satchel from her pocket, dumping its contents into her hand. "I'll admit, I'm glad it was you," she said affectionately to Alistair's unconscious form. "Anyone else, and I'd up my price for the kill." She frowned. "Damn. I have to split the commission with Lark, don't I? That's a slippery slope. Word gets out that hunters will share their bounty with folk who help take down the beast, and more people will get killed, or worse, get in the way of my job. On the other hand, if I don't share, I'm perpetuating the misconception that hunters are greedy and immoral, little better than the monsters they hunt." She shook her head, waving her closed fist full of gods knew what around. "You'd want fair compensation for hunting things that want to kill you, wouldn't you? I can't slay monsters if I can't buy food or gear or pay for a blazing roof over my head, now, can I?"

Langford massaged his temples, a headache taking root behind his eyes. He was not at capacity to follow her mental detours. "Can you help him?"

"Of course, I can." She glanced around the room, holding her closed fist carefully so as not to spill. "Right. Need a little bowl and grinding tool. You got those, yeah? I travel light these days."

Langford could scarcely process her words, but he nodded. On numb legs, he collected his mortar and pestle and handed them off to the hunter carrying the last thread of his sanity. He swayed on his feet as she dumped dried herbs—aconite if he could trust his blurry vision. Gods he needed sleep.

After Alistair opened his eyes and he had the chance to scold him.

Wait. Aconite? But that would kill him.

"That's aconite! Why would you poison him?"

"Don't question my methods. I've had enough of people stepping on my toes lately." Kenna pulled out a waterskin, and holding the bloody spikes over the mortar, dumped water along the edges, washing the blood into the mixture.

"What is your process?" Langford tried to keep his voice steady and curious so as not to alarm her of the very real panic he was experiencing. Aconite was highly poisonous, causing cardiac distress in its victims. Alistair was having difficulty regulating his own heartrate as it was; what would this do to him?

Kenna laughed. "I'm not going to kill him. You know that, right?"

"Please." It was all he could do not to jump up and knock the mixture out of her hand. Logically, he knew she was a hunter with vast knowledge of monsters—the existence of which he'd only recently come to terms with. He also knew Alistair's injury, subsequent symptoms, and nonreaction to healing methods were nothing he could explain.

But he could not rationalize the use of poison. Not without understanding.

"The wolfsbane is for the curse. Blood of the original beast who scratched him. And finally"—she pulled out a small notebook no larger than her palm and flipped to a page with pressed flowers, holding a pink petal between her fingers—"evening primrose." With a smirk, she popped it into her mouth, chewing and watching Langford with a challenge in her eyes.

Langford fought the urge to cringe, knowing what she was about to do. She spit the chewed-up petal into the mortar, grinding it down. Blood and saliva created the binding paste in her mixture.

The pestle was right there. Why would she rely on such unhygienic methods? It took every ounce of Langford's diminishing strength not to gag. Kenna merely appeared amused.

"Want to do the rest? It's basically just layering it over his injury and feeding a small portion into his mouth." She laughed, and Langford realized his expression had betrayed him. "Yeah, I know. But sometimes the old ways are best."

Langford was going to be sick. "And… he'll be all right?"

Kenna nodded, but it was slow. Hesitant. "Probably. I really think so. We'll know for sure by morning." She leaned over Alistair's unconscious body, waiting for Langford to interject.

"Yes. No. I'll do it. I'll do it." He snatched the mortar away and forced his gaze down at Alistair.

Alistair's dark skin was made even darker by the fever, blood pooling in his cheeks. His jawline was dusted with dark hair, thicker than usual without his upkeep. He shivered, his teeth chattering with the movement. And yet, his eyes never opened due to that infernal slumber.

Langford wished he would just wake up and tell him to get on with it. To actually coat his open wound with poison. To feed him poison. He had to do it. Kenna wouldn't lie about this, and he trusted her knowledge, or at least, Daciana trusted her knowledge. But the very idea of purposely poisoning him was a sin against everything Langford had ever known. The safety of a life he had once trusted above all. That even when he was lost and alone, when no one wanted him, not even his own father, his knowledge was his firm grasp on reality. And no one could take that away from him.

With a deep breath, Langford spread the concoction over Alistair's chest. His hands were numb, fear causing his nervous system to accelerate into overdrive, but they were steady, as always.

And when he gently pressed his thumb against Alistair's chin and spooned the rest into his mouth, relief lightened the weight in his chest.

He might be afraid. Challenging knowledge he always took comfort in. But he was about to have his answer to the question that plagued him the entire ride over. The question that had hounded him since the day Alistair's breath stopped, his heart ceased, his life ended... and began again.

Was Alistair really on borrowed time? Was death a transcendent of all the knowledge Langford had come to rely on? Would Alistair slip through his fingers once more, proving without a doubt, that Langford was destined to be alone?

He scooted his chair closer to the bed, sitting beside Alistair and claiming his hand.

Together, they would wait for the sun to rise.

LANGFORD GROANED, wakefulness blending with sleep to create the space in between. Images dissolved, instantly erasing themselves from his mind. Darkness bled away, and spears of light shot through the haze. He blinked, the sudden spill of light burning his eyes.

Soft fingers carded through his hair. A soothing touch, chasing away the last dregs of a dream. The edges of which had already been smoothed to a round and shapeless memory. Almost as if—

Langford shot up, cognizance jolting through him. The night had passed. He'd fallen asleep, and now it was morning. Someone had been running their hand through his hair right before he'd awakened. A fact that could only mean...

Langford blinked again, his vision sharpening. Alistair's gorgeous face came into view. A broad grin stretched across his mouth, always a wild edge of mischief playing on his lips, and his bottle green eyes were bright. His dark hair was a mess, and his jaw had never been so overtaken by the beginnings of a beard. He was upright, propped against a pillow, looking smug of all things.

"Alistair," Langford croaked.

"The one and only." Alistair's grin turned salacious. "I can think of at least six more desirable ways I could have selected to wake my favorite healer, but the way you had me trapped with your head on my lap... oh, I just thought of a seventh way. We'll put a pin in that for next time."

Langford laughed or sobbed, he couldn't be sure which, and placed his hands on either side of Alistair's face. "You"—he punctuated with a kiss—"utter"—another—"reprobate." He didn't even care that he could taste blood and herbs on Alistair's mouth, and when those lips curved into his favorite smirk, the tears finally spilled down Langford's cheeks.

"Aye." Alistair dragged Langford onto his lap, alarmingly strong for a man waking from his sickbed, and placed a heavy hand on the back of Langford's neck. "And you're an utter marvel." He pressed his forehead to his, a weighty silence unfurling between them. "You saved me. Again."

Langford exhaled. "It wasn't me. It was Kenna. She—"

"No." Alistair shook him, only enough to get his attention. "It's you. Always been you."

Langford's throat tightened. There was a lot to unpack with that statement. And more still to assess. Just because Alistair's fever had broken, and his body appeared to be in working order, didn't mean there was no lingering danger. They should gather the materials and ingredients Kenna used. Though, their effectiveness still confounded him, the proof was sitting before him. Langford needed to examine Alistair, assess his vitals, study his response to nourishment and differing stimulants to determine an accurate prognosis. All of which would be easier achieved if Langford had his own space to work rather than a traveling saddlebag with all his tools and books. And if that wasn't enough, there was still the matter of any lasting effects of ingesting aconite—

"Langford," Alistair whispered, squeezing the back of Langford's neck and rubbing deep circles with his thumb. "My darling. Stop thinking so loudly and kiss me."

Langford's body responded before his mind could catch up. Thanks to Kenna, and even Daciana for being the link to the hunter, there would be time enough to cover every base of his mental trajectory.

CHAPTER THIRTEEN

DACIANA

*T*he last of the dying flame flickered, and Daciana continued her meditation beside her nearly spent candle.

It was an exercise from her youth, to meditate the lifespan of a candle.

Closer to her shift, she lacked the ability to master her patience. But in the days after a turn, when the restlessness of her body had given way to balance, it was an old comfort.

The days were short. The nights were long. Inerys and Aislinn worked about the cottage. Tending herbs and checking on Gavriel. Reaching into his mind. Traveling his memories.

And alone, Daciana waited.

Langford and Alistair had a job to wrap up before they returned, Lark and Ferryn had gone—likely because she pushed her too far, and Kenna...

Kenna had taken off weeks before. Too impatient to wait. To understand. To learn. To *listen*.

Daciana knew the value of patience. It was instilled in her from years of tutelage under her mother, followed by mastering the hunt with her father. Impulsiveness, impetuousness, the greed of immediate gratification. The urgency of demanding the *now* when patience would yield far greater boons.

She should have known Kenna wouldn't understand. The hunter was rash and reckless. A force of nature barreling into every situation with the subtlety of a battering ram. She was fire and passion and everything Daciana wanted from the moment she first saw her.

But time to lament her mistakes had carved Daciana a new path, and with that, she hoped, a wisdom in her patience.

They had come a long way since those years spent apart, and then the months side by side with every touch withheld and every word left unsaid.

But it wasn't enough. It would never be enough for Kenna, the girl who burned hotter than any fire.

The last time Daciana saw her, there was a desperation, a pleading in her eyes. She did not beg, but it was clear. How could it not be? Daciana knew the beat of her heart. The thoughts telegraphed in every expression. Every time she bit her lip against words threatening to spill. Each time her hair fell forward to cover her eyes, as if that would hide what was shining bright as a beacon in them.

Her hope had dimmed to scorn. And Daciana didn't know how to repair the damage.

Kenna wanted Daciana's trust, but she failed to realize, it wasn't her she could not trust.

Everything that had come to fruition was Daciana's fault. She would never regret saving Alistair. Bringing him back when the light left his eyes and Langford's broken sobs filled the forest. She would never regret pulling, taking whatever she needed to stitch his soul back into his body.

But the veil did fall.

She did that. To pretend otherwise was to shroud oneself in comforting ignorance, and Daciana knew the dangers of growing too comfortable.

Kenna felt spurned by her, that much was obvious. Not in such base terms as physical intimacy, but she could sense the distance. The caution. Of course, she could. Kenna was the hunter, and Daciana her prey. Or was it the other way around?

Daciana shifted, bringing her focus back into her body. Into the feel of the cushion beneath her knees. The stretch of her leathers. The soft caress of cotton against her skin.

She let her mind wander, knowing where it would lead.

Freckles across a delicate nose. Dark eyes glinting with mischief. Black hair hanging over pale skin. The soft arch of a shoulder. The delicate notch of her collarbone. Images shifted. Hurt shining in her eyes. In the furrow of her brow.

There was no keeping Kenna from her thoughts. Not with how they'd left things.

Kenna pushed. She always pushed. She'd been insistent Daciana start training with Inerys to master her power, but there were more pressing matters like Gavriel's recovery and Aislinn's education. There were monsters roaming free, innocents dying. Demetria had gone skies knew where with Balan in tow. The idea of studying and practicing and mastering her power was a selfish indulgence, a way to keep from beginning the true work of fixing things.

But Kenna knew her excuses were all horseshit, an evasion, a maneuver to hide the true reason she kept putting off training.

Daciana wanted nothing to do with that power again. And the more Kenna pushed, the more she withdrew.

"You said you would try,"

Daciana sighed. "No, you said I would."

"You think I don't see what's happening? You might have the others fooled, but you can't pull that shit on me." Kenna shook her head, uneven fringe falling in her eyes. "You're tucking everything away again, Dac, when has that ever helped?"

"You don't know what you're talking about."

"It's so easy for you to coax vulnerability out of the others, isn't it? You spout such pretty words to Lark. So understanding. So supportive. All that 'we're in this together' shit you love to recite. But it's all a lie." Kenna invaded Daciana's space, until her shoulders were nearly crushed against Inerys' overfilled shelf, vines threatening to spill over

her shoulder. She could have overpowered Kenna easily, but the anger she so rarely showed stole the breath from Daciana's lungs.

Kenna's gaze dipped to Daciana's mouth, and despite everything between them, every broken and lost thing, she wanted nothing more than to taste her. To give in to the madness and crush the last of her defenses to a fine powder.

"You say so many things, and none of them are true. You say you'll master your power so it doesn't rule you. You say we're together, we have each others' backs, no one fights alone. You say," Kenna gave a humorless laugh, and her sweet breath blew against Daciana's face, setting her blood on fire, "that you love me. You lie, and you lie so well, but I see through all of it. You are alone, aren't you, Dac? No matter how close I get, I can never quite reach you. Because you are determined to be alone."

Daciana blinked into the darkness, her candle finally spent. Her skin hummed, her blood a molten ore, but a permanent ache pulsed with every heartbeat.

Kenna was right about one thing.

She was alone.

CHAPTER FOURTEEN

DEMETRIA

"Out of my barn, afore I call the city guard."

Demetria groaned, stretching her achingly stiff arms. A harsh blast of cold erupted against her skin, and a violent shiver wracked her body. She rubbed her eyes. The dull pale light of a frozen morning leaked through the open door. The man frowned down at her, his woolen layers topped with a thick knit cap making Demetria want to weep from envy.

Winter was a season best experienced in the way of appreciating a painting.

"You heard me. Out."

"For fuck's sake," Balan's voice, even harsher from sleep, called out. He sat up, clutching his thin cloak. Straw stuck out from his white hair in all directions, the jagged remains of his horns on full display.

"What..." The man backed away, his eyes widening in fear. "What are you?"

"Please. We mean no harm." Demetria's words were tight behind her chapped lips. "We only sought shelter."

The man shook his head. "You have a monster." He grabbed a pitchfork from off the wall, brandishing it as a weapon.

Though Demetria's heart sank, his fear was a founded reaction. In the weeks since they'd parted ways with the others, monsters had roamed the land. Balan was always adept at sensing their arrival and hiding them away until danger passed.

"You are sentencing us to death," Balan's voice scraped out. "The nearest shelter isn't for miles."

The man waved his pitchfork. "Not my problem. Leave. Now."

Balan's silver eyes glinted dangerously, and he tilted his head as he examined the simple farmer. "Or what?"

"Balan, no." Balan ignored her, and Demetria's panic only grew. She trusted the demon far above the others, but she was no fool. Her mother had told her stories of demons, tricksters, with immense power and corruption. But their wickedness was a reflection of the person bargaining with them. They would twist intent until the true nature of human's folly was laid out for all to see, and by then, it was too late.

Balan was nothing like the demons in her mother's stories. Nor was he the monster Lark and her people claimed him to be.

But even in his diminished state, it was foolish to assume him harmless. Right now, his harm was in how quickly anger found him. His strength was a memory. And Demetria had learned the hard way, the mistake of angering the wrong person.

Balan stood, his fists clenched at his sides. The tremors of cold were still evident in the shakes he tried to hide. "You are but a mere insect beneath my boot, and you dare to threaten me?"

Demetria rolled her eyes. "Enough of this." She stood, too, her knees buckling. In a flash, Balan was beside her, clutching her elbow.

"Little fool," he hissed. "I almost had him."

She leaned into him for support. "Apologies for ruining a most convincing performance. I'd hate to interfere with your craft, so please, continue."

The corner of Balan's mouth twitched. It was the closest he'd come to a smile, apart from the malicious smirks and humorless laughs he doled out to seem cruel. "The effect is now diminished by your chatter."

Up close, his features, though disconcerting with their obvious *otherness*, were quite striking. The remains of his horns and his eyes were the most obvious signs of his demonic nature. Eyes that reminded Demetria of the liquid steel in Felix's forge. But the rest of his face held a beautiful sort of symmetry. Notably, his mouth was far fuller than he made it appear with all his derisive expressions. His chin, a touch too sharp on its own, but balanced with the rest of his face. And his nose was a hard angle, almost regal in its shape. Demetria longed to draw him, and the one time she foolishly voiced this wish aloud, he'd let out a most unbecoming snort and ignored the request.

The farmer lowered his pitchfork, an apprehensive look flattening his features. "Aye. Times are hard these days. Harder still when folks refuse basic decency." He eyed them carefully and hung his tool back on its hook. "Come, warm yourselves by the fire while I muster up something to eat. It won't be any of that fancy stuff at the tavern, but it'll stick to your ribs." He glanced at Demetria disapprovingly. "Something you sorely need."

The temptation to tell the man off for judging her when she was damn near *starving* danced upon her tongue. Also, the notion that anything sold in an Ardenian tavern could be considered fancy had her worried about what he'd serve them. But the memory returned—a conversation she'd had with Ruslan what seemed like ages ago.

"You shouldn't have said that to him."

"But he was wrong, and it made him sound stupid. Was I supposed to let him go on sounding stupid? I helped him."

"A queen knows how to educate without shaming, Princess. And doesn't let pride prevent her from educating herself before speaking."

Demetria stuck her tongue out at him. Ruslan was still her favorite, but he was cluttering up their lessons with boring advice. And receiving a scolding from him made her stomach hurt. "But I already know more than Prince Edvard, I don't need more educating. He said women weren't allowed to fight because they were weaker in combat and better served as nurturers."

"He said that, huh? Change of plan. Today's lesson is how to inflict pain with easy to miss hand movements. A quick strike in the right place, no one's the wiser. Easily done at a banquet, or during a ball. Ready?"

Demetria bowed her head to the farmer. "Thank you for recognizing our needs and responding with kindness. I shall never forget it."

※━━━━━❀━━━━━※

A GENTLE SNOW had begun to fall, thick flakes drifting just beyond the window. The edges of the glass were clouded and frozen, framing the soft wintry landscape. Demetria took another bite of what the farmer had called pottage. It wasn't entirely pleasant, but her hunger was sated and her muscles had finally begun to unlock by the heat of the roaring fire. Balan scrunched his nose as he took another bite of his meal, and she giggled.

Silver eyes darted to hers, narrowing as if challenging her to ridicule him.

Demetria addressed the farmer instead, dusting off her finest manners. "Your hospitality is most refreshing. I'd have your name to properly thank you."

Balan snorted, and the farmer gave her a bashful smile.

"William." He cleared his throat, his soot-covered hand leaving a black streak against his forehead.

"Thank you, William." Demetria allowed her most beatific smile to spread across her face, ignoring another snort from her demon companion.

William appeared younger than she originally thought without fear and anger etching his face into severity. Younger than Ruslan, by her assessment, but old enough to have fathered children or whatever peasants did to fill their lives in this freezing climate.

That was cruel. Unnecessary. Demetria could practically hear Ruslan's voice again, echoing in her mind.

"Don't let your title change you, Princess. There are many qualities you possess, but your nobility is the least interesting thing about you."

"What's my most?" she had asked, eager to be showered with praise.

"Your room for improvement. Now, ready your stance; we haven't got all day."

Demetria's throat thickened. She'd never hear his gruff, chiding voice again. Never awaken to find him tossing her sword and fighting leathers onto her bed for an early training session. Never tell him how much he meant to her. How he was right, their titles meant nothing. How when all was lost, and she felt alone in that great castle, he was a father to her.

"Hope you like the pottage; it's a family recipe."

Demetria forced the last bite into her mouth despite the protesting gurgle in her belly. "It's"—she swallowed—"hearty."

William laughed. "Probably not what you're used to."

There was something about his assumption that she couldn't decipher as insult or not.

"Forgive me," William quickly added. "But you don't sound Ardenian."

"Well-spotted." Demetria shoved the question of what type of gray meat he'd added to the mixture out of her mind. "I hail from—"

"Anquan, Vallemer, a summer or two spent in Koval," Balan had cut in. "Everywhere and nowhere." He eyed her meaningfully. He'd stressed the importance of keeping her identity a secret, but it wasn't as if William was going to guess she was the run-away Princess of Koval based on a foreign accent.

Honestly, demon or no, Balan might have been the biggest worry-wart she'd ever met. Second only to... Evander. Her heart lurched at the name. Now was not the time to recall his boyish freckles or the way the sun set his red hair on fire.

"Balan speaks for himself. But I'm from Koval. This is my first time travelling, can you believe that?" Demetria laughed, even as Balan glared daggers at her. "Rotten luck on my part. Might have saved my grand adventure for another time, had I known the dangers ahead."

William nodded solemnly. "Aye. It's been the harshest winter we've ever seen in these parts. And I don't mean the cold."

Monsters. Beasts. Demons, if the stories were to be trusted. The only demon Demetria had seen was choking down the last of his break-fast. But once the veil fell, or whatever happened when Daciana brought Alistair back from the dead, everything had changed.

"Koval is a long journey away," William continued. "What brought you to Ardenas?"

"Oh, this and that." Demetria waved her hand along with her words.

"Describe the *this*. Describe the *that*."

She laughed, but it was a forced sound. "It's not very interesting."

"I see." William crossed his arms. "You runnin' from something?"

Demetria's legs went numb, cold panic shooting through her limbs. It was an offhand question, a vague prod at conversation. There was nothing to fear from his line of questioning.

And yet.

Balan had gone still, a dangerous glint in his eye. His jaw tight-ened, nostrils flaring. And for the first time since they had gone off on their own, traveling and scraping coin together without the others, he appeared every bit the dangerous entity Lark always swore he was.

"Aren't we all running from something? Or to something, if you're lucky."

William huffed a laugh, a soft smile curving his mouth. "Let's talk about luck. I've never been a firm believer in luck, but Paragon's balls, these past months have shown me the truth." He pulled out a chair, scraping it against the floor and sitting backward on it. "I was born into this business. Generations of my family have tended these lands from before Ardenas broke away from Koval's rule. You might even call it a legacy. But that's not the business I'm talking about."

William cocked his head to the side, waiting.

"Is this where I interject a prompted response?"

He laughed, and the sound made Demetria's skin crawl. She risked a glance at Balan. He delicately dabbed his mouth with his napkin, his knife absent from the table setting. She took the hint, casually stretching her hand over her knife, ready to swipe it from the table the minute William was distracted.

"Let's just say this farm isn't what lines my pockets."

Demetria's thoughts spun, sweat erupting along the back of her neck. Her head throbbed, and a steady pressure began to build behind her eyes.

"What... what is your business, William?" She didn't know why, but it seemed important to keep repeating his name. It was something her mother had always said in her stories. That sometimes the monster was defeated by simply remembering its humanity.

William grinned, turning to wink at Balan.

Demetria's knife was in her lap before his gaze swept over her once more. She ran her thumb over its edge.

Dulled. Little better than a spoon.

"I wasn't lying, it's been damn hard this winter to keep my supply stocked. I've lost all my handlers, either to the monsters stalking the land or to their own cowardice. Haven't been able to deliver any stock on my own. It's a tricky business, needing an extra set of hands at the very least. But it seems my run of bad luck has changed. I only needed someone, or in this case"—he gestured between them—"a couple o' someones desperate enough. That desperation?" He sucked on his teeth. "That's good for business."

His words echoed inside her mind. Darting this way and that. Never landing long enough for her to understand. "What... what are you saying?"

Demetria's tongue thickened. It filled her mouth with a buzzing sensation. Like words had a taste and a shape too large for her lips. Her vision spun, and her stomach rolled.

She fought to keep her eyes open, her arms suddenly heavy.

"No one taught you to mind food from strangers, huh?"

"You fucking bastard." Balan's words were slow, garbled. Or was it her hearing? He stood, staggering, only his hand on the chair held him upright. "I'll paint the walls with your entrails. You'll wish you were dead when I'm done with you."

Demetria's head fell forward, and she caught herself on the table, dull knife in hand.

William laughed. "That'll be hard to accomplish where you're going. There's a demand for people like you in your home country, you know that, don't you? Couldn't have possibly turned you guys in on my own unless you were so *damn trusting*."

Darkness bled into the edges of Demetria's vision, and the room turned sideways. Distantly, Balan growled, another stream of muddled words, sharp with anger.

Then it all went dark.

CHAPTER FIFTEEN

LARK

"We can stay, you know. We needn't rush back. Not if he needs time." Lark cast a glance in Alistair's direction; his unseeing stare was aimed at the wall, eyes red-rimmed.

"We'll be along shortly. Another day or two at most. You shouldn't tarry, not on our account." Langford squeezed her shoulder, a reassuring touch that spoke of everything they did not say.

Lark needed to return to Gavriel's side and to alert Inerys of her newfound power. But it felt like a betrayal to leave them like this.

After news of Mrs. O'Connell's death had reached Alistair, the man had been inconsolable. Lark had always known Alistair reserved a soft spot for the kind innkeeper, but she hadn't known the strength of his care until witnessing Langford holding him close, gently shushing his sobs.

"Will he be fit for travel?"

Langford frowned. "Physically, yes. Whatever Kenna did…" He trailed off, waving his hand up to the ceiling. "And she's agreed to escort us back, if that is your worry."

"I'm always worried," Lark said and tugged him into a brief embrace. "Be careful. Nowhere feels safe anymore."

The truth of that statement hung in the air, like a suspended blade.

For all their troubles, Oakbury had always been a safe haven for them. The Walden Inn and Mrs. O'Connell, a shared home for their group. And perhaps it had been, or Inerys' protective laurels around town had maintained some level of effect. But that was before. Everything was different now.

"I'm trying to worry less these days. Mad as that sounds." Langford sighed, running a hand through his mussed hair. "Wreaks havoc on the nervous system, or so they say." His boyish grin somehow managed to appear both sheepish and forlorn, pain tucked behind the curve of his mouth.

For someone who once confessed his fear of weakness and uselessness, that day they were trapped in a dark dungeon, he was one of the strongest men Lark had ever known. And though she still battled the urge to wrap him in a blanket and shield him from harm, she knew he could withstand the storm to come.

"Safe travels," Langford said, pressing a quick kiss to the top of her head before returning to Alistair's side. He smoothed a gentle hand along the back of his neck, and Alistair automatically leaned into him.

FOR ONCE, Ferryn remained silent, only the sound of snow crunching under their boots filling the air. Interrupted only by the occasional groan of tree trunks as the wind whipped through barren branches. And when they reached the entrance to Inerys' spelled lands, the frozen lake was a mirror, pale sky reflected in perfect stillness. The first few steps upon solid ice revealed Inerys' cottage. Stone cladding, orange light blooming from behind frosty windows, and garlands of evergreen adorning her door. Her sweet box plants were covered in a dusting of fresh snow, as was the roof, where a brick chimney puffed smoke into the wintry air.

It was as inviting a place as any, yet Lark couldn't shake the panic that grew. The closed throat, claustrophobic feeling of hiding away in a box too small. It wasn't that she didn't wish to return to Gavriel's side, every fiber of her being screamed to be near him, but to be walled in with her own helplessness… It transported her back to that cage of idleness. Of remaining in the Otherworld, waiting for Leysa to beckon with word of a chance to return to the mortal world.

The falsity of the comparison made Lark's stomach burn, and yet…

How selfish did that make her?

"You will tell her," Ferryn said, the first words he'd spoken the entire hike back, "won't you?"

There was no mistaking his meaning, not when every glance shouted his concern. He'd been worried before she'd forged the tethers to the Cursed Wolven, and when she'd collapsed in the snow, his panic only sharpened his gaze, his words, even his skies-forsaken breaths were weighty with it.

Lark had to tell Inerys. She had to. And of course, she would. So why did her palms prick with sweat at the thought?

Inerys might have answers. And those answers could be the dread Lark had carried with her all this time. Since she first dragged her naked body, newly mortal and weakened, out from under the ancient yew. That this was all borrowed time or a trick of the senses. Nereida was the one to make her human. What if…

What if she was becoming a Reaper once more?

"I will." Lark's discomfort grew, a coiling weight deep in the pit of her stomach. "Of course, I will."

⁘⁘⁘

"LARK'S POWER HAS RETURNED."

Lark glared at Ferryn, and his impish smile almost broke through the swift heat of her anger.

Almost.

"I *said* I would tell her!" Lark hadn't even finished shaking the snow from her boots when he'd opened his big mouth. He didn't trust her. She meant what she said. She would have told her, in her own time. After she checked on Gavriel, and soaked in a hot bath, maybe found something to fill her belly—

95

Fine. She was going to put it off. For a bit. But it still didn't give him the right to spill her development so carelessly.

Inerys stirred her tea, dark strands of hair hanging in her narrowed eyes. The *clink* of the spoon against her chipped porcelain cup was a judgmental sound. As was the slow, audible sip she took. "So," she began, "care to elaborate? Or am I to play a guessing game?"

Lark would have to select her words with care. To make Inerys understand. To use patience and deliberate wording so as not to alarm the witch.

"I don't know why, but I can feel everyone's emotions sometimes, and I can feel their souls again like I did when I was a Reaper, and I forged tethers twice, and I killed them, but it nearly killed me, I think."

Lark's heart battered in her chest as if trying to break free, her breath shallow and quick from her outburst.

Well... that was almost what she had planned to say.

Inerys' dark eyes were blown wide, an almost comically extreme expression on her face. Lark sucked in a shaky breath and carded her fingers through her hair.

"That's not... I misspoke..." At Inerys' continued silence, Lark continued. "The first time was in the tavern, and it was purely by accident. I felt a tug, much like before, and such terror." The boy. How frightened that boy had been, alone in the snow facing off against that group of men. "And I was able to push past that and select a thread to follow. He did not deserve the mercy I denied him, so I refuse to mourn my choice."

Ferryn scoffed. "Is that what you think this is about?" With agitated movements, he shoved his wet hair back from his face. "Lark, you could torture and mutilate a man in front of me, without offering a whisper of cause, and I wouldn't question you."

"That seems a bit extreme."

"You know what I mean." Ferryn made his way to the hearth, holding his hands over the fire. "I'm not *judging* you, Lark. I'm worried about you."

Of course, he was. He always had been. In his own, immature, silly antics, he'd made himself appear aloof or even oblivious. But Lark had long realized Ferryn had used this to his gain. The ability to appear frivolous and even self-absorbed, all the while closely observing everything around him.

And worrying.

"Can we refocus here?" Inerys set down her tea, motioning for Lark to join her on the settee. "This was the first time, yes? Tell me about the second."

Lark sank into the soft cushion and told her. She told her of the overwhelming fear, of the pain, of being surrounded by panic and all of it flooding her in a torrential wave. How she couldn't keep any of it out long enough to lift her weapon and fight against the creatures attacking Oakbury. How she projected her awareness into those creatures, recognizing the wildness of their lingering souls, and forged a tether so strong, she felled them all by writing the physical effect of panic into their hearts until they all burst.

How she felt the crack in her chest as if her own heart had burst, too.

Inerys listened, an elegantly arched brow raising higher with each revelation, until finally, she interjected. "And you felt the disruption? You said you were almost entirely depleted. So it was you feeding the balance?"

"I guess." When Lark had felt her consciousness dipping, it was like wind testing a flame. A flicker, a distortion, and then darkness.

Inerys nodded, her eyes alight with something closely resembling excitement. "Give me a moment to think. You've proven yourself fascinating rather than burdensome for once."

That may have been the nicest thing the witch had ever said to her.

Inerys paced back and forth, the same creak answering from the third floorboard each time she passed over it. Lark rubbed her cold hands together, warmth seeping through her skin, and awaited her judgment. Whatever it was, it couldn't be so terrible. Inerys would have shown her alarm or at least disappeared to stew over her news. No, there was a determined purpose to her stride, even as she traveled the same length of floor again and again. Analyzing. Weighing. Theorizing. Though she said nothing, her expressions flashed in dizzying succession.

"Have you any news of Gavriel?"

"Obviously not, or I would have told you upon arrival. Now hush!"

It was the answer Lark expected before she asked, before they even stepped through the door, but still her heart sank, as it always did. She hadn't dared give thought to her hopes, but if her power had awakened, perhaps she could reach him through their soulbond.

"You forged these threads in response to high emotional stimuli, yes?"

Lark nodded. It was the only relief in this, to know her human emotions were a guide rather than at risk of vanishing.

"Ah, we'll work on that." Inerys stopped pacing and crossed her arms. "I suspect without the presence of the veil, echoes of old power have no barrier preventing them from returning to their rightful owners."

Lark swallowed and forced her paper-thin words out. "What does that mean?"

"It means," Inerys grinned, the expression odd against her perpetually scowling countenance, "Nereida made a grave miscalculation."

LARK RAN a hand over Gavriel's knuckles, tracing the bone. His slumber could easily be mistaken for death with how pale he appeared. The almost imperceptible rise and dip of his chest. How slow his heart beat. Langford had referred to his body's response as *hibernation mode*.

"You would have enjoyed watching me kill those bandits." The ghost of a smile threatened to curve against her mouth. If there was one thing Lark could count on, it was Gavriel's delight whenever she indulged her ruthless side. Really, any side of her he appreciated. It was a rare thing, being cherished unconditionally. Lark had never known how much she craved it until she had it then lost it.

Gavriel was never disappointed in her. Never wished to alter her.

Being with him was as natural as breathing, as existing. They just... were. It was a beautifully effortless intimacy, and she'd give anything to feel it once more.

If he knew the power once again whispering in her bones, in her very marrow, he'd side with Ferryn in concern. She could already imagine how his scarred mouth would tighten, and his ever-assessing gaze would stay firmly planted on her, watching.

But he remained firmly trapped in the throes of a dream. The misfortune of her own actions atop his head. What she wouldn't give to see a twitch. A spark. Some sign he understood her. That he heard her.

That he knew she was here.

Lark had whispered every secret at his bedside. Every secret she harbored in the dark gloom of a night against a lone candle. She'd confessed every fear, every thought, every hope. And through it all she'd realized something she'd already knew but had been afraid to acknowledge.

It wasn't just the veil, a retrieval of power as Inerys had said.

Lark was more than mortal again.

She didn't know how or what it meant, save for this: She had power. And maybe with the proper focus, she could bring Gavriel back from wherever his mind had gone. Aislinn had been working tirelessly on searching out his dreams, but she had yet to make contact with him.

Perhaps Lark could find a way.

She smoothed the hair back from Gavriel's forehead. It had grown longer, as had the untrimmed beard along his sharp jaw. Gently, she sent her awareness out—

The tether of his soul met hers with ease, as if already waiting for her call. Where with the men brutalizing the boy and the monsters attacking Oakbury, it had felt like an invasion calling them into her connection, with Gavriel it felt like coming home. The rightness sang in her veins, pulsing along with her heartbeat. The soul bond, the one she'd been so quick to condemn, was blessedly still intact in the way their connection entwined.

Relief cracked her chest open wide, and tears trailed down her cheeks. She pressed a bruising kiss to the top of his hand.

He was still here. He was still hers. She would make damn sure she kept it that way.

"He said your name."

Lark jolted, spinning in her rickety chair. Aislinn leaned against the doorway. The girl hugged her waist, eyes shifting about the room. Her long blonde hair had been hastily tied back, strands coming loose to frame her face.

How could Gavriel have said her name? Lark stared down at him, waiting for him to blink his eyes open and apologize profusely for pretending to be cursed. But of course, that was never going to happen. But Aislinn heard her name? From his lips? The girl was overworking herself—the deep circles under her eyes, her unwashed hair and filthy apron, the way she could hardly stand upright without leaning against something. She imagined it. Or dreamed it. Or—

"Sorry, that came out wrong." Aislinn ran a hand down the side of her face. "His mind said your name."

"Hasn't it done so before?" Lark recalled Aislinn telling her of Gavriel's memories. Some of them included her, some didn't. What was different about this time?

"It wasn't..." Aislinn waved her hands before her as if searching for the words. "It was during a memory you shouldn't have been in."

Confusion, exhaustion, and frustration fought for dominance in Lark's overcrowded mind. "What does that mean?"

Aislinn took cautious steps, pacing her way to Lark's side, where she dropped to her knees right on the floor. "I think it means his mind is fighting to wake up."

Fresh relief, so staggering it *hurt* rushed through Lark before she even had the chance to catch up. "What if he's just dreaming of me?"

Aislinn shook her head. "It's not like that. His dreams are his memories. I've seen the same memories a few times, and each time, he's adding things that weren't there before." She gave her a watery smile. "His mind is reminding him of whom he has waiting on the other side. He'll get here, just give him time."

Lark placed her hand in Aislinn's, the girl she'd guided to the after-life what felt like lifetimes ago. Lark had wondered why Aislinn's soul never moved on, or what she'd done to destroy what should have been her peaceful journey. But that was before Lark learned precisely how fickle fate could be. That someone, a name she still didn't have, was pulling strings, rewriting threads of fate to suit a picture too large for her to imagine.

And maybe it was fate that kept Aislinn from moving on. That placed her squarely in the right place at the right time.

Or maybe fate was fucking with all of them.

In any case, Aislinn, the somniavi, the last dream walker by history's measure, was exactly what they needed.

"Thank you," Lark whispered. Aislinn squeezed her hand back.

CHAPTER SIXTEEN

DACIANA

aciana shouldered her pack, adjusting the strap. All around her, the trees swayed in a harsh wind, ice laden branches clinking together like chiming bells. The sky was a muted gray, heavy with the promise of another snowfall, and the air was a living thing.

There was something different about the cold season. About becoming the wolf when the air was ice suspended. It had jolted through her, an ebullient joy in her freedom. And when she had awakened naked and shivering in fresh powdery snow, she'd ventured further west, further than she'd planned, seeking solitude in the frozen forest. Chasing the answer to a question she hadn't realized she'd been asking.

At the edge of the Emerald Woods, a bracing gust of sea air skirted through the trees. Daciana ignored the discomfort at leaving tracks in the snow and pushed forward toward the rumbling of the surf. The snow thinned, and frozen ground gave way to hardened black sand. Not sand exactly. Black pebbles. A dark sea appeared, whitecaps rushing in a steady current of waves. Daciana sat, hugging her knees, allowing the chill to seep into her bones.

Sitting here now, glimmering waves dragging against the black, it was easy to pinpoint where she'd gone wrong. With Kenna. With herself.

She'd been running for so long, hounded by the invisible specter of her past, that she'd forgotten how to stop.

Kenna once called her a coward. No, not once, many times, and damn it all to the blazing Netherworld, she was right. Daciana was afraid of everything she was capable of. How effortlessly death followed her every move. When it was done by her own hands or claws or teeth, it was within her control. Death should leave a stain. A taste. A mark on a person. And she feared that she could not carry the death her power had wrought.

But fear did not keep Daciana safe. It didn't keep her from harming anyone at all. It only formed the bars of her cage.

She looked out over the roiling waves, the crashing surf and harsh wind deafening. The ocean was a great and terrible force, capable of causing immense harm. Daciana had known of ships dragged to the depths of the deep, lost forever. A storm could rile its anger, coax its destruction.

And yet as she sat at the cusp of the sea, sky and water before her, echoes of an angry ocean bellowing against the wind—

There was only peace. Clarity. The answer to that unasked question.

She would return to Inerys, beseech her to give her the tools to master her own power, and then she would go. Find Kenna. Unite the hunters. Travel to the ends of the world in search of the aid they desperately needed. And she would be honest about all that she wanted. About all she could do.

Daciana was through with running. Unless it was in the body of her rawest form, ripples of moonlight streaming down her back and painting her path, her days of running were over.

WHEN INERYS' cottage came into view, it wasn't the small structure that caught Daciana's attention. It was the three figures hiking ahead of her that stopped her in her tracks.

One figure. One shape that stole the breath from her lungs.

The wind howled, that familiar red cloak billowing in its wake.

"Kenna!"

The name spilled forth, a cry, a plea, a desperate apology, and Kenna stilled. But Daciana could not wait, and she hurried across the frozen lake, to where she'd left her heart years ago. She was here, and damn it all, Daciana was downright giddy to see her. To tell her everything she'd held back for the sake of her blasted fear.

Kenna's pale face twisted in a scowl, a deep furrow between her brows at Daciana's approach. But not even her apprehension, nay, her anger could dim Daciana's excitement.

Seeing her standing there, red cloak, anger alight in her eyes, was like seeing the sun for the first time. Every fiber of Daciana's being came to life, stuttering awake as every nerve in her body heightened. Painfully aware of the beautiful hunter.

Moments or lifetimes since they last saw each other, and suddenly, none of it mattered. Every well-thought-out reason. Every scrape of logic in a sound mind. Every reason for caution, it all vanished. Evaporated.

It took every shred of Daciana's control not to march up to Kenna and drag her away, ripping every piece of clothing and armor between them off until all that remained was the aching, heavy truth.

Daciana loved her more than she feared herself.

It was only when Daciana reached her, less than an arm's length away, that she finally paused.

The stilted silence hung between them. The moment rife with tension and significance. The first words she spoke to Kenna had to carry the distance she'd created. Had to mend all that she'd broken.

"Dac!" Lark's voice broke the silence, calling from Inerys' open door. Without a cloak, the fool, she sprinted onto the ice, auburn hair flying in every direction as she flung herself into Daciana's arms in a crushing hug. Daciana hugged her back, relief lessening some of the tension in her shoulders.

Langford, Alistair. They stood at Kenna's side. How had she failed to notice? Alistair wore a knowing smirk, which was ridiculous because the man knew half of what he pretended to, and Langford... his mouth was in a thin line as he darted glances between them. Whatever he found fault with would have to wait. They were back. They were safe.

Daciana squeezed Lark tighter. "You could have left a note."

Lark laughed, the sound muffled by the way she pressed her face into Daciana's neck. "It was mostly accidental. I had every intention of returning the same day."

"Your intentions are as effective as ever." Daciana's gaze dipped to the others, and the expression on Kenna's face made her chest hollow out. Along the edges of her anger, a glimmer of pain had snuck in.

"Don't forget me, you gorgeous creature." Alistair swiftly stepped between them, tugging Daciana into a one-armed embrace. "Unless you're planning a group frolic with your lovely hunter and our darling Reaper," he hissed in her ear, "I suggest you cut down the enthusiasm in your greetings."

"That's ridiculous," Daciana hissed back. It was maddening, the idea that her friendship should be examined with such scrutiny, but Alistair was already pulling away, that obnoxiously smug smirk on his face.

"Pity for me. I enjoy a good spectator sport."

"Behave." Langford elbowed him in the ribs and clasped Daciana's hand. His expression softened. "I've missed you."

"And I you. The voice of reason has been sorely lacking in these parts for some time."

"That is wildly untrue!"

"Oh, hush." Alistair pulled Lark into a headlock, walking her toward the cottage while she laughed and stumbled along. Langford gave a long-suffering sigh, though its effect was lost in his wistful smile. With a shake of his head, he followed them into the house.

Finally, Daciana and Kenna were alone.

The air fell quiet, dusk swallowing them whole.

Kenna lowered her chin, black fringe falling in her face. She kicked at the ice, an action Daciana had come to know was a mask for her discomfort. Her freckle-dusted nose had turned red from the cold, and the chill had bloomed across her cheeks in a comely blush. She still wouldn't meet Daciana's gaze.

A soft *sniff*. Was she crying?

"Kenna," Daciana tipped her chin.

"Ugh. Bloody cold." Kenna wiped her nose, sniffing again. "If we'd gone to Anquan like we said, we'd be prepping for Feastday instead of freezing our asses off in a frozen wasteland."

Anquan was notorious for its mild winter and scorching summer heat. Kenna had always spoken of her Feastday celebrations with frantic excitement. A fortnight of presents and fire ceremonies. More food than an entire village could eat. Dancing and drinking and games.

But she was here, and that had to mean something.

"So why didn't you?"

Kenna scowled, knocking Daciana's hand away and starting for the cottage. "Don't ask stupid questions."

"I'm not." Daciana followed, catching up with ease. "Why didn't you go? You said you would." She'd said a lot of things the last time they spoke. "You were going to leave me to clean up my own mess. That's what you said. Yet, here you are, fixing what you didn't even break."

Kenna scoffed, her steps quickening. "Some things are determined to stay broken, yeah?" She reached for the door, and Daciana snatched her hand away, tugging her with enough force she almost regretted it.

But Kenna was stronger than she looked. Stronger than any of them.

Daciana spun them until she had Kenna pressed against the stone cladding of Inerys' home, hidden by shadows. This close her scent was dizzying, intoxicating. Daciana leaned closer, pressing her nose against her fluttering pulse point.

Kenna shivered, her hands tightening in Daciana's cloak. "What are you doing?" Her voice wavered.

"You were right." Daciana exhaled against soft skin, her lips gently caressing with every word spoken. "About me. About us. You were right, and I'm so sorry it took me this long to admit it."

Kenna squirmed, the heat radiating off her igniting Daciana's blood. "Be more specific."

Daciana huffed a laugh, drawing another shiver from Kenna. She dragged her hands down the firm line of her waist. "I was afraid. But I don't want to be anymore." She wanted to be... happy. A terrifying thought, but once it was given life, given shape, the truth of it was impossible to ignore. Daciana wanted to allow herself this.

Soft hands tilted Daciana's face. Kenna's mouth had pulled into her favorite smile, dark eyes glimmering. "Say it again."

"You were right?"

Kenna groaned, an exaggerated sound meant to amuse rather than arouse, yet it sent sparks through Daciana's blood. "Gods. Those might be the most beautiful words ever spoken. Say it again, this time slower."

Daciana laughed. "Will you shut up and kiss me already?"

Kenna's grin only broadened. "Fucking finally."

And she was there. Soft lips, cold and chapped, met Daciana's, and warmth flooded her body. It seeped and pooled until madness took over, and their mouths turned frantic. A messy slide of a kiss. It was desperate, perhaps even angry, but oh, it was right. Real and right and long overdue. They'd exchanged kisses, short and sweet, only weeks ago. But they were careful. *Guarded.*

There was nothing cautious about the way Daciana devoured Kenna's mouth. About the inferno igniting beneath her skin.

Daciana stepped between her firm thighs, slotting their legs to give Kenna something to grind against. And when she did, Daciana couldn't help the moan that left her lips, quickly swallowed by another pass of Kenna's tongue. It was everything, and skies, it had been far too long. Buckles were unfastened as she tugged wildly at layers keeping her from feeling Kenna's skin against her own. The heat coming off them was enough to melt the snow—

Daciana slowed, the realization that they were outside in the *snow* lessening the urgency enough to think.

"We should——"

Kenna cut her off with another kiss. "No thinking. It only gets you in trouble."

"We should at least find a private location *indoors*."

"Don't be such a spoilsport. Where's your sense of adventure?" Kenna angled her hips, hoisting her leg higher and sending stars across Daciana's vision. "It wouldn't be the first time."

She wasn't wrong. Back when she first fell under Kenna's spell, it was perfectly natural to press her against a tree, strip her down, and taste her until she was screaming and tangling her hands in Daciana's hair.

But that was before. And this was now. And she wanted to take her time relearning every curve of her body. Not shove her over the edge for a quick finish.

The creak of a door opening interrupted her thoughts.

"Dac?" Lark's voice wavered with amusement. "Sorry to interrupt, but Inerys threatened to cast an amplifying spell if you don't come in. Alistair was on board, but I figured you'd prefer some privacy."

Daciana groaned and Kenna laughed, lowering her leg. It was the douse of cold reality they needed, but the added humiliation was unnecessary.

"Be right there," she called back.

"We just need to put our sexual apparatus away. You wouldn't believe the craftsmanship! Koval really is known for their sword smithing if you know what I mean…"

"Kenna!" Daciana hissed. But at Kenna's grin, she laughed and shook her head. Sure, her cheeks heated with embarrassment, but it was welcome alongside the warmth in her chest.

She had her hunter back in her arms. Whatever the world threw her way, she could die happy in the knowledge that she hadn't been too late to fix what she'd broken.

CHAPTER SEVENTEEN

LARK

*L*ark rubbed her blurring vision and shook out her hands. She'd seen humans slap themselves in the face to refocus, should she try that?

"Again, Lark. Make it a good one," Inerys called out from the comfort of her campfire. She held her hands over the flames, admiring the long mittens she'd knitted while Lark toiled away in the snow. They'd been training, or rather, Lark had been training while Inerys barked orders at her.

The goal was to locate the threshold, the maximum power expenditure before collapse. Her practice included tethering her soul to Inerys', writing in thoughts, memories, and sensations, and then untethering.

For hours.

Lark trembled, a bead of sweat rolling down her temple. She squinted into the low light of day's end. Hunger gripped her stomach, and her knees threatened to buckle.

They'd spent the last three days like this, and the temptation to brandish her bow and bring an irreparable end to these lessons was hard to ignore. But firing arrows at the one sheltering them seemed like piss poor manners.

"Give her a fun one," Alistair called out, carrying wood for Inerys' fire. "Show her how you make Gavriel shriek like a girl."

Inerys' face twisted in disgust.

Lark laughed, despite her exhaustion. So far, she'd given her the taste of Mrs. O'Connell's apple pie, the feel of her bow in her hands, the first time she sat under the rain of a summer storm, and countless other moments she could recall in vivid memory. No, she would not share any of her private and intimate encounters with Gavriel, not even to strike back at the witch for *starving* her.

Lark's stomach growled in response.

"Ugh. If I wanted the clumsy experience of a man's flesh sword, I'd have taken any of the villagers pretty enough to catch my eye."

"Flesh sword! I quite like that. I love Langford's flesh sword."

Lark braced her hands on her knees, allowing exhaustion and the absurdity of this conversation to send her into a fit of laughter. "I can't concentrate like this."

"Have we found your threshold for the day?" Inerys stoked the fire, embers falling into the fresh snow. "That didn't take long."

It was one of Inerys' more obvious attempts at goading her. But Lark was spent, and there were more pressing matters at hand.

Like eating the cooked apples spiced to perfection Langford had fried. The aroma taunted her while Inerys denied her the decency of a meal.

"I've proven my word. What more do you need to assess what's happening to me?"

Inerys hummed. "Nothing, really. This was more of a test to see if my idea would work."

Lark had little patience for mind games at this juncture. "Speak plainly... please." She tacked on that last word so the witch wouldn't withhold her answers out of spite.

Inerys stretched, arching her back. "Inside. I could do with a hot cup of tea, and this matter concerns another, too."

"I chopped all this for nothing?" Alistair dropped the stack of wood, letting it land in a heap.

"We always need more firewood. And I needed to observe any

aftereffects of your ailment along with Kenna's antidote." Inerys stood, lifting her skirts so they didn't drag in the snow. "It is rare for a nonhunter to survive the strength of the tonics they mix. Langford was quite surprised she hadn't warned him of this risk."

Surprised was putting it mildly. He had berated Kenna, his pale skin flushing bright red, while an impressive stream of curses tumbled from his mouth. Inerys had informed them all how Alistair's body should have been too weak to handle the mixture. That hunters had been conditioned to tolerate such decoctions from infancy, and giving one to Alistair, though the only remedy for his affliction, was just as likely to kill him.

It was only Daciana's gentle reminder that Alistair stood safe and sound before him that calmed Langford down after that.

Alistair's face fell. He rubbed the back of his neck, gazing at the cottage. "Aye... it isn't fair he keeps needing to make such decisions on my behalf."

What if Kenna promised a way to wake Gavriel from Nereida's curse? Would Lark make the same tough call as Langford? Risk his life for the sake of hope?

Of course, she would.

"Fairness doesn't seem a factor in these things, does it?"

Alistair's smile failed to reach his eyes. "No, I suppose not."

The weight of their mutual silence was only interrupted by the sound of their footfalls in the snow. And when the cottage door swung open, the enticing smell of apples and spices, mulled wine with notes of citrus, and the warmth of freshly baked bread spilled out, enveloping Lark and making her mouth water.

"Ah," Alistair said. "Langford is stress-baking again."

Lark toed off her boots, eager to get her hands on Langford's cooking. "Does he do that often?"

"Aye. Whenever I hid his books and pages to try to force him to rest. He picked up a new hobby to occupy his time and justify leaving our bed in the ungodly hours of morn. He'd sneak out and use Mrs. O'Connell's kitchen in exchange for giving her whatever he made to serve on the menu. She always said—" Alistair's voice cut off in a sharp breath. His brow furrowed, and he shook his head as if clearing his thoughts. "She always said his talents were wasted in Ardenas. That he could open a fine bakery in Koval and shower in the riches of the upper crust. A terrible joke, one she always laughed at no matter how many times she repeated it." He ran a hand over his face and let out a tight laugh. "Fuck. The world is a shite place sometimes, no?"

Lark placed a gentle hand on his shoulder. It was easy to forget how hard the loss of Mrs. O'Connell had hit him. Lark hadn't understood how much the inn keeper meant to him until Langford had explained. How she was the closest thing to family for Alistair when he first came to Ardenas. Over a decade he'd counted on her to offer him home whenever he blew through town. There was safety in that. In keeping the ones you loved far from the heat of the flame.

But it didn't save her.

Alistair placed his hand over hers, giving a short squeeze before shrugging away. "Langford!" He called, the sudden change in his tone jarring. "Did you make that drizzle I love? The one I poured on your—"

"Silence, you bloody fool." Langford appeared in the doorway, flour coating his tunic and breeches. "Don't say another word unless you wish to sleep outside tonight."

Alistair placed a hand over his heart. "You tease me with empty threats. I didn't hear a *no* in your response which means I know exactly where I'll be." He sauntered up to Langford, placing a firm kiss to his lips, which only deepened the bloom of red on his cheeks. "Licking the honey off your—"

Langford clamped a hand over Alistair's mouth, glaring at him. "Not. Another. Word."

Lark snagged a plate of fried apple slices as she snuck away, eager to escape. She shook the feeling back into her numb hands and claimed the spot in front of the hearth. The fire crackled, heat blazing her nose and cheeks as she plopped the first bite of apple in her mouth. Cinnamon and nutmeg exploded on her tongue, and she shoved another piece in.

How did Gavriel's body sustain itself without food? Her stomach soured at her turn in thoughts, and the next bite had lost its flavor.

How could she enjoy anything while he was still lost to the void of Nereida's making? It wasn't right that she sat here, eating and laughing while he was trapped. She'd give anything to trade their places, to free him as she once did when his death was all but assured—

The plate fell from Lark's hand, and it hit the floor with a rattling thud.

Why couldn't she save him as she once had? If Nereida could brew a transference spell, surely, Inerys could as well.

Lark leapt to her feet, tracking apples across the floor as she slid to the kitchen.

Inerys wiped down the butcher block, muttering under her breath about ungrateful guests overstaying their welcome. Langford and Alistair were nowhere in sight. Neither was the honey drizzle Langford had supposedly made.

Lark pushed the thought from her mind and made her way across the kitchen.

"Can you concoct a transference tonic?"

Inerys stilled and slowly lifted her head. Her dark eyes peered out from her warm umber face. "Lark, no."

"It can work!" She could free him. Inerys' rigid posture gave her away. She knew how to brew it, and it would free him. "Why have you not suggested this?"

Inerys tossed the rag into the sink, and the wind it created made the plants teeming the windowsill shudder. "Have you gone mad? What good would it serve to trap you in his stead? Especially now that your power has reawakened. I always knew you to be impulsive, but I never knew how dreadfully *senseless* you were."

"I've done it before. When Gavriel was poisoned, and his death was written by fate, I transferred his injury to me, and I was fine." Lark had held his head in her lap, his beautiful, bloody smile aimed up at her, and her unbeating heart had lurched.

"Right, right," Inerys continued, "and was this before or after you were made human?"

"It doesn't matter."

"Of course, it matters!" Inerys' shout shook the windows. The cottage fell silent for a few heartbeats, her anger stealing the air from the room. She took a deep breath, the exhale harsh. "I know it's hard but you must set aside your penchant for foolish whims." She tucked a tendril of her chestnut hair behind her ear, softening her voice. "You are on the cusp of greatness. The answer to every problem this world faces. Between you, Daciana, and Aislinn, we have the makings of a most formidable weapon."

"I don't want to be a weapon. I want—" Lark's voice strangled in her throat. *Selfish. Foolish. Shortsighted.* She was all these things in disturbing measure. Even now, acknowledging such weaknesses, her heart raged against acceptance. She wanted to sacrifice it all to bring Gavriel back.

But what sort of world would he return to? A life of hiding and fighting until the inevitability of death claimed him? If they had a way to undo Nereida's damage, to turn the world back to rights... she had to stay the course.

A hot tear slid down her cheek, hopelessness hollowing out her stomach. It felt an awful lot like giving up.

Inerys reached out a hand as if to comfort, and with stilted movement, gave uneven pats to Lark's shoulder. "Hold on a little longer. Just, today. Take today to be strong in this. And then tomorrow? You can take that day, too. One at a time until we reach the summit. We have not forgotten him. But let's give him a worthy homecoming, yes?"

Lark nodded, stomach still heavy with the weight of disappointment.

"Besides," Inerys said with a smile, "I haven't had the chance to explain my plan for you and the wolf."

CHAPTER EIGHTEEN

GAVRIEL

"*A*nother round, Pearson?"

Gavriel stared into his tankard, empty, because he'd discretely discarded the shitty ale through the open window. Everyone was celebrating. They'd earned it. His year of recruits had successfully completed their marks, passing the final test.

The test was death, and whether they had the stomach to deliver it or not.

So, yes. He'd finished his mark. He'd killed the man. Kept it quick and clean as Hamlin always said. Some languished in their missions, taking their time to prolong it. But that was sloppy and unnecessary. Efficiency was a far more valuable quality over cruelty.

Gavriel had passed. He'd crept into his mark's room in the dead of night and silenced him forever. It was easier than he'd thought it would be. He'd always assumed his first kill would weigh him down, make the blade heavier, slow his reflexes, anything to indicate the magnitude of his actions.

But it was easy, anticlimactic. His muscles did all the work before his mind could catch up, and when it did—

No. He would not think on it. On how the man's face, though foreign, had seemed so familiar. How he hadn't given him the chance to react, because even Gavriel hadn't the chance to do so. To think. To wait. To consider.

Efficient. That's what he was. Efficient. And the man got what he deserved. A sentence carried out by Gavriel's hand. The blazing poetry of that was not lost on him.

But he never told the man who he was. Why he was there. Who he had taken from him. He offered no words of condemnation or explanation. It was as quick as blowing out a candle. One moment he lived, the next he was a wisp, the ghost of a flame.

Yes, Gavriel had passed. He was a full-fledged Crow.

But there was nothing to celebrate.

"Hello?" Hazel snapped her fingers in front of his face.

"What?" Annoyance flared in his gut. Hazel was little more than a pest with a big ego. Sure, she had the skill to back it up, but listening to someone boast of their prowess was less impressive than simply witnessing it. Why she insisted on disturbing him was beyond his comprehension. Connor would have preened under her undivided attention. And she would have the comfort of joining his band of sycophants.

Yet here she was, grabbing the seat Gavriel hadn't offered.

"You don't strike me as someone who just passed their final exam." Hazel cocked her head to the side, pursing her lips and examining him. "You threw up, didn't you? You look like a puker." She heaved, making exaggerated gagging sounds.

"No. I did not purge."

"Did your mark shit their pants? They do that sometimes." Hazel had a far more colorful background than he. Rumor had it, Hamlin had found Hazel and Gregoire in the forest as feral children. Blood on their hands and around their mouths. That their experience doling out death far exceeded any other recruit prior to initiation. Hazel's cavalier attitude toward death could be evidence of such—or it could be bravado.

Either way, she was a pain in the ass.

Gavriel sighed and pinched the bridge of his nose.

"I see. It was *you* who soiled his pants. There's no shame in that,

Pearson. Bodily functions are a universal inconvenience." She took a swig of her tankard, pale-blue eyes shining with mirth.

"Where's your brother?" Hazel never went anywhere without Gregoir following in her shadow. While she relied on blades and daggers, Gregoir was the best archer Gavriel had ever witnessed. His patience and subterfuge made him damn near impossible to track when he latched on to a target, and his accuracy was precise and deadly.

Hazel grimaced. "He hasn't returned yet."

So that's why she was here, forcing her company onto him. She was waiting for her brother to finish his assignment. *Worried* for him. A shame, but she picked the wrong distraction.

"Maybe he failed. Dead in a ditch somewhere."

Hazel's eyes flashed, a muscle twitching in her jaw. "I'll let that one go, because you're grieving, but don't fucking talk about my brother like that."

Even at the sting of her words, Gavriel's stomach sank in shame. It was a low blow, and undeserved. Truth was, this should have been a celebration. The first step toward building a life for his mother. But instead of paying off his debt and saving coin to build her savings, he was planning her funeral.

He'd have to debrief with Hamlin when he returned. As it stood, he'd checked in with Master Eldridge, the superior who signed off on his change in mark to begin with. But Gavriel didn't fall under his jurisdiction, so it was a conversation he'd have to have again.

Only Master Hamlin always knew when Gavriel was bullshitting him.

Why was there no satisfaction in killing the man who took her from this world? Gavriel was sure he'd feel something. Some sense of justice or at the very least, resolution.

All he felt was empty. An aching, crushing void.

"We could distract each other tonight." Hazel rolled the bottom of her tankard against the table, eying him with clinical scrutiny. She would not play the coquettish courtier with him, even though he'd seen her do just that to get her way. She was direct, unflinching. There was much to respect in that.

"Connor can distract you." Gavriel gestured across the tavern where the loudest peals of laughter rang out. Grating and nasally.

Hazel groaned. "I'd rather fuck a tree branch than listen to him talk out of his ass."

Gavriel laughed, a rusty croak of a laugh, but still it came.

Maybe Hazel wasn't as bad as he thought.

GAVRIEL SAT UP, cold sweat trickling down his stinging back. A hand reached out for him, the owner still hidden beneath the covers.

Hazel.

A moment of weakness, one she'd be more than happy to exploit were he ever interested in pursuing her again.

He pushed himself away, grabbing his breeches and tugging them on. His stomach rolled like the time he drank too much ale, and his head was pounding. The unfamiliar room was dark, too dark. Like the hearth had gone out hours ago. He needed to get back to the Guild. Needed to bury himself in assignments.

His eyes adjusted, and the sky came into view. Thick twisted branches reached up to the stars. A round medallion moon slid out from behind the clouds, casting pale light to illuminate the floor.

The forest floor. Gnarled roots and moss softened ground. Stray leaves and bracken.

Why wasn't he at the inn?

There were no walls. No hearth. No bed.

He'd awakened in the dark forest, and he wasn't alone.

Gavriel rubbed his temples, cycling through his memory. Where was he? What happened? Who—

A groan came from beneath what he thought were covers but was really an old cloak. With a tentative hand, he tugged the shroud down, slowly revealing waves of deep-auburn hair. Her face came into view, and his heart stopped.

Long lashes framed her eyes that were still closed off to the world. A light dusting of freckles painted her delicate nose. Her mouth was a perfect bow, parting as she yawned and stretched, arching her back to reveal the rest of her perfect form. Her naked curves were painted in the silvery moonlight, making her appear more paragon than human.

Gavriel's cheeks burned, and he fought valiantly to keep his stare trained north of her throat.

She rubbed her face, a white thread tied around her third finger, and finally, she opened her eyes.

Gavriel sank to his knees.

Even in the dark, they burned brightly. A warm golden hue, like honeyed ripples of a lake during sunrise. She was the most beautiful creature he'd ever laid eyes on, but it was the affection, the joy in her gaze as she watched him unravel that stole the breath from his lungs.

"Hello, Husband," she said, her voice thick from sleep with the edge of a rasp. A voice that could command him to do anything, and he'd obey. A siren, she was a siren like the stories tales of old and—

Husband? He was her husband? That made her—

"You're my wife." It was as if the earth righted, the sky tilting to balance above the horizon. Everything fell into place.

The lash wounds upon his back.

The apple she slipped to him when he almost fainted from hunger.

The punishment he endured for daring to defend her against a handsy noble.

Her sweet voice as she sang from her shackled perch.

Playing the fiddle 'til his fingers bled to give her something beautiful.

Months he spent dreaming of her face.

Their first kiss.

Whispered promises.

Stolen moments in the wine cellar. Against the garden wall. In the cell they starved in as punishment.

The string he tied upon her finger.

The oaths they swore.

Their yielding bodies beneath the yew tree.

Lark. His love. His life. His wife.

But only in their hearts. They hadn't the freedom to swear such vows. To hold any claim over themselves or another. Their master held the reins until their debt was balanced. A hope forever destined to remain out of reach with the way he tallied additional sums.

But this. He could not take this moment from them. Not in this life. Not even in death. The memory of how it felt to hold her. To breathe her in and thank the stars he found her even in the darkness.

She was his. And he was hers.

Lark's soft touch found his cheek, tracing along his scars and over his lips. "Gideon, you seem far away. Where did you go?"

Gideon.

His name was Gideon.

Layers of memories bled together. Blending and weaving and bleeding. Gideon. Gavriel. He was one in the same. And Lark... oh, she was everything.

He bundled her close, pressing a shaky kiss against her hair. She smelled of sunlight. Of everything good in a world of injustices. "I'm right here, darling."

Lark laced their fingers, and he realized he, too, bore a string around his third finger. "We'll have to hide these," she said, "for now."

For now.

The promise of more, of a life free of their master. Free of his walls, and off his lands. Even now, they risked exposure if anyone was patrolling the grounds. Even with sky overhead and earth beneath, they were trapped within the walls of their master's bastion. And with no weapons or fighting skills to boast of, they could not fight their way free even if they managed to scale the outer wall.

It was foolish to meet as they did, where anyone could stumble upon them.

But they couldn't stay away.

"We must return before they notice we're gone." He loathed the words, and the thought of letting her go, even in the face of survival, filled him with dread. Like this was their last chance to run. Run and never look back.

"It won't be like this forever," she said, nuzzling his neck. "I have a plan."

Despite himself, his mouth curved. "A dangerous thing coming from you."

"Hush or I shan't tell you what the kitchen maid told me about Lord Dawson."

"Cruel woman. You know I can't stand not knowing fresh gossip."

Lark laughed, tugged herself free of his hold, and dressed with practiced speed. "I'll tell all... if you can catch me." She darted off, once again initiating one of their games. Games. Distractions. Anything to mask the truth of their situation.

But how he reveled in every moment spent by her side.

He huffed a laugh, chasing after her.

He'd chase that little demon to the ends of the earth.

CHAPTER NINETEEN

AISLINN

*A*islinn tiptoed about the silent cottage. She would be a fool to assume Inerys couldn't sense her movements, but she knew the witch well enough to trust she would let her choose her own mistakes.

Not that this was a mistake.

Gavriel's memories echoed in the back of her mind. Scratched against her skull. Pounded along her veins.

Lessons with Inerys had yielded more questions than answers. The witch had told her of somniavi with the ability to infiltrate even the strongest of minds either awake or asleep. To bring paragons to their knees. But she was a long way off from mastering such strength and had no interest in such a thing.

If she couldn't use her ability to help people, to help Gavriel, what was the point?

Aislinn wound a scarf around her neck, positioning it against her mouth. She needed to escape the crushing weight of her disappointment. If only for a few hours, skies willing. Beneath her layers of cloaks and skirts and wool stockings, her skin grew overheated. She tugged on her fur-lined boots, secured her long mittens, and grabbed the lantern by the door.

The first blast of cool air was a relief. She winced when the hinges groaned, but no other sound rang out as she slipped through the door into the wintry night. Thankfully, it was a windless evening, darkness and quiet enveloping the land. Above the frozen lake, the stars shone against the black sky, and she marched on. Once she hit the cover of the trees, she turned the lantern key, illuminating the snowy forest with its flame.

Why did she not wait for daybreak? Why did she sneak around darkened rooms, gathering supplies for a journey she'd told no one of?

They would insist on accompanying her.

Lark. Ferryn. Even Daciana. Someone would take issue with her traveling alone. It was funny, death was meant to be a lonely journey, and though it was, she hadn't had a moment's peace since her demise. Her life had once been filled with moments of solitude, of running to the river to sit with her thoughts and lupines dotting the bank.

Aislinn waited for a surge of anger, a flash of heated rage at the memory of the last time she ventured to that riverbank. Of when *he* took all that he could, including her life.

But it didn't come.

It never came.

Why couldn't she find anger? All she was left with was an aching disappointment.

Lark had guided her. She'd promised to ensure Corwyn never hurt another soul again. And at the time, it was enough. What choice had she had? Death had already claimed her spirit, and the only way was forward.

But then she hit a wall. She was trapped in a bitter plane of loneliness and solitude. Whatever it was, it wasn't peace. It was a numbing cold, like when her hand fell asleep and felt almost separate from her body.

And when Ferryn came, she had a companion. A friend. Someone to talk to. She told him... everything. Her most precious memories to the pain of her last moments. It was catharsis amidst the numbness, and Aislinn was sure her next steps would again be forward. Toward something. Anything to grant meaning to all that had happened.

And in a sick twist of fate, she'd gone round in a circle only to land here.

Only here wasn't home. Here was strange and lonely, even surrounded by people.

It seemed a predestined fate, her inability to move on like she was supposed to. Inerys spoke in such awe and reverence when relaying the history of her... abilities.

Somniavi. Dream walker. In life, Aislinn had always loved the safety of her mind. Of spending hours in the forest dreaming and wishing and living entire lives based off her imagination alone. Her father had always called her his little dreamer. Had always said she must have lived many lives before this one, and they were all fighting for space in her memory.

Like all things she loved, he was gone. It wasn't fair. She was supposed to be reunited with him. Lark had promised her—

Wait. She hadn't promised her a thing. She'd been honest in her ignorance, and Aislinn's mind had conjured this hope, this unspoken promise.

Perhaps the dreamer's misfortune was in waking. In finding the truth of the world.

Gavriel's memories beckoned, beseeching a closer inspection. His mind had shifted, blending his dreams, his lives, over a century apart.

Hazel. Aislinn remembered her. She hadn't known of Gavriel and Hazel's history together, but there had to be some reason why his mind had focused on that night in the tavern.

And Lark.

Aislinn had witnessed Gavriel's execution a dozen times, but this was the first happy memory from that life she'd ever been privy to. A stolen moment between souls who could never be free. It was downright cruel for Gavriel to be trapped the way he was now, after everything.

Aislinn shivered and bundled her cloak tighter. Dawn must have been further off than she thought, for darkness still shrouded the forest even as the moon fell through the trees, nothing but her lantern light to guide the way. Frost crunched beneath her feet, diverting from her path to avoid the places where snow piled higher than the tops of her boots.

She ventured deeper into the Emerald Woods, further than she'd ever dared before. Without a map or travel supplies, there was no use in trekking much longer. She could head to the Walden Inn for a change of scenery, but what was the point? The only place she truly longed for was home.

And home was destined to remain out of reach. Map or no.

It was a cruel fate, this second life without living. Here she stood, flesh and blood, or so it would seem, but Inerys swore her own mother would never recognize her face. That anyone who had known her, had mourned her, would never see her for who she was. That death had a way of changing a heart until the eyes could not see that which stood right before them.

Another wish stolen.

She could travel to Meadow Hedge. But she could never go home.

Aislinn ran the top of her long mitten over her eyes, clearing away the burning threat of tears. It could be worse. If there was one thing she'd learned in her short life, it was that things could always be worse.

First light hinted its arrival in the orange glow low in the distance. It would be wise to turn back, follow her footsteps, and resume her existence. Alone while never knowing peace. Chasing a solution to Gavriel's condition.

Never changing.

Never growing.

Never wishing.

But if she spared one last wish, *one last chance*, she would not squander it on youthful ideals. On fairy stories and impetuous whims.

No, she'd wish for one thing:

Something new to shake her existence to the very foundation. Something to remind her that she was *alive* and not the result of fate's cruelty—of death's failure.

A *snap* of a twig sharpened her senses. It was probably an animal, but still, Aislinn's ears pricked, alertness flooding her body with the steady thrum of her pulse. Her breath came in plumes of vapor.

Crunch. Crunch. Crunch.

The steady sound of footfalls in the snow. Slow. Assured.

Not an animal.

She spun around, seeking the source of the sound. She'd ventured too far. Inerys' protective barrier had ended paces ago. But how many? Aislinn couldn't remember. Why had she been so foolish? She should have paid attention. She should have waited for dawn. She should have—

Aislinn took off, refusing to chase the thought of what she hadn't done. The steps followed after, faster, hunting.

The only way was forward.

She leapt over ice-crusted branches, hung low under the weight of snow. She veered, following her steps and their indirect path. She could make it back. She *would* make it back. And instead of wallowing in self-pity, she would demand to be more useful. To have leave to travel and aid in their endeavor. She would not waste this life waiting for it to begin. She'd died once, heart full of regrets, and by the skies, she would not allow that to happen again.

Her foot caught an unyielding pile of ice, and she stumbled to the ground. Her lantern shattered, glass glimmering against the snow as her little flame flickered out.

Lark was right. One couldn't trust fate or wishes or hopes or dreams. One had to carve out their own space, their own life in a world destined to knock them to the ground.

Fear climbed Aislinn's throat, strangling her cry for help. But her mother's words remained.

She would dare to find her strength.

A hand gripped her arm, yanking her hard enough her head snapped forward.

"You're much harder to track than I gave you credit for." A voice. Low and smooth.

His grasp was firm, unyielding, and an echo of panic rang out in Aislinn's mind. Her vision spotted, the edges growing fuzzy as her heart climbed top her throat. Memories of that day by the riverbank clawed along her skin, gooseflesh erupting in their wake. Corwyn had grabbed her when she tried to turn away. He'd held firm until he shoved her to the ground, suffocating her beneath his weight.

Tears burned behind her eyes, her breaths coming harsh and quick, a rising terror threatening to consume her—

Whoever he was, he was not Corwyn. She still hadn't allowed herself to look upon the face of her hunter, but he was not the man who stole her life from her. This was not that day, and she was not that girl discarded by the river.

Fear was her compass, and she would use it to fight her way free.

Aislinn balled up her fist and spun, hurling every ounce of strength behind her punch. Her blow landed, connecting with the rough skin of a jaw, the rest of his face hidden beneath a shroud. Pain burst along her hand, through her wrist. She clawed at his face, nails raking across his still-hidden cheek.

A low growl rumbled in his chest, and he clamped his other hand over her arm, holding her tight enough to bruise and too far to catch his vulnerable flesh again.

In the scuffle, his hood had blown back, revealing his face.

He towered over her, glaring down at her with dark eyes. His black hair reached past his shoulders, half-knotted back while a few pieces fell free. His nostrils flared in his strong, angular nose, and a bruise was already forming along his sharp jaw. Bloody scratches ran the length of his cheek, and beneath the hint of a beard, his mouth tightened.

"Unless you enjoy pain, do not do that again." His voice thundered through her, vibrating along her bones and making her stomach flip.

"Let. Me. Go," Aislinn said through her teeth. Her fear had dissolved into something else entirely. Her body tensed, anger heating the blood beneath her skin, scorching and consuming and demanding.

His mouth curved in a snarl. "You cannot command me, little dreamer."

His words jolted through her, numbing the fight from her muscles.

He knew what she was.

CHAPTER TWENTY

MERIKH

Merikh wasn't sure what he'd been expecting when the assignment of dispatching the last somniavi in centuries fell upon his head, but the little spitfire in his grasp wasn't it. After receiving his orders in the war room, he'd set off to achieve his goal quickly. It should have been a simple matter, finding the new soul capable of Avalon's destruction before it realized what a threat it was. Without training, a dream walker's abilities were little more than a party trick.

But with training? With the slightest level of control?

Calamitous.

She was bundled in an absurd number of layers, bulky and shapeless as she fought against his hold. He was far stronger—that wasn't exactly surprising—but when her hood fell back and her golden hair tumbled free, her face was finally revealed. And it was the fire in her eyes that gave him pause.

The dream walker trembled in his arms, her fear keen and visceral, but the hate in her round green eyes lit him from the inside out. Mortal fear was nothing new. But the sheer rage worn on such a lovely face made him falter. Study her.

It was madness to hesitate, his assignment should have been

completed weeks ago, but she'd always eluded him. There would be glimpses of her presence. A whisper of power slipping through planes of reality, only to evaporate before he could zero in on her. And he'd spent ages searching every inch, every shrub, every fucking branch of this useless forest in search of her. Finding nothing.

Until now.

She twisted against his hold, a breathy snarl breaking free from her full lips. Achar's words echoed in the back of his memory. Stories of humans and their *fervent* prayers and praise. Hours Achar spent languishing in the mortal realm, debasing himself among the lesser. It was disgusting. Disgraceful.

And yet. Something about the way this girl's lips parted, her breath escaping in little wisps of steam, the willful anger burning bright in her impossibly green eyes. Merikh could see the temptation in such an act.

Shame burned in his gut at the thought. Here, this mortal girl likely didn't even know what she was or what she was capable of. All she knew was instinctive fear and shaky survival. And his lecherous gaze was his repulsive response. It was time to stop playing with his kill and finish it. It did not matter if she was innocent, for innocence could not exist in such a deadly weapon.

Deadliest against his kind.

Just grant her the quickest death. Why was he hesitating? Snap her neck. End her life. Cease the danger posed to all of Avalon.

She stared up at him, eyes widening, anger softening into a quiet contemplation in her stare. His heart faltered, and his throat tightened. His hands went numb, and he loosened his grip ever so slightly. She was such a delicate thing. It would be easier if—

A violent tug, and she slipped free, her form much smaller beneath her layers of clothing. Her hands shot out to latch on to his temples. Fire lanced through his head, burning its way into his mind. Merikh fell to his knees, the snow biting even through the haze of flashing pain.

It was like peeling away layers of flesh, all nerves and vulnerability exposed to the raw air. His teeth chattered against the vibrations buzzing in his skull.

To walk the mortal plane and search for her, he'd had to assume physical form. It was the only way to ensure the life left her body by his hands, but it lessened his abilities. Made him weaker than his true form.

That weakness would be his undoing.

His arms fell slack at his sides, and his vision darkened. All that remained was the blurred edges around a cruel and beautiful face.

And when sleep came, it was not gentle.

MERIKH GASPED, jolting awake in the snow. Sharp pain pulsed along his skull, waves of tension squeezing in a steady rhythm. He placed a shaky hand to his head and staggered to his feet. A mottled gray sky hung in the air, taunting him with the question of how many hours had passed. He glanced at the snow; her tracks were still fresh.

Head pounding and stomach churning, he followed them.

He was a fool to have thought her innocent. The girl had far more skill than his superiors had realized. Than he had realized. She must have been trained, prepared for his arrival. But next time, he wouldn't hesitate. He wouldn't underestimate her. He would show no mercy.

Her tracks vanished, ending with a sudden jarring stop. There was no evidence of her covering them or veering off course or taking the trees. They just... stopped.

Merikh groaned, rubbing his head.

The dream walker had a witch's aid. This was going to be harder than he thought. Along the edges of his frustration, a wild excitement took root.

It had been ages since he'd had a worthy hunt. And this little somniavi was going to be quite the prize.

CHAPTER TWENTY-ONE

DACIANA

They began training at dawn, forgoing breakfast in favor of getting a jumpstart on their session.

Neither Lark nor Daciana were pleased with this decision.

"Again!"

Daciana gritted her teeth against the flare of annoyance that seemed to permeate her entire being every time Inerys spoke. It was unfair; the witch was quite helpful but also quick to push beyond their limits— hers and Lark's. Ever since Daciana had asked Inerys to help her master her power, Inerys had been determined to combine Lark and Daciana's abilities. She claimed it was due to fatigue at having to help everyone, but Daciana knew better.

Inerys had realized something, something she had yet to share with them. Daciana didn't appreciate being left in the dark but shoved aside her discomfort.

She owed that, at the very least, to Kenna.

For now, Inerys was content to have Lark practice connecting with Daciana and herself, forming a balanced tether between two souls. While Daciana pulled from Lark to produce minor spells.

Lifting a rock.

Conjuring a gust of wind.

Lighting a fire.

It left Daciana sore and depleted each night, and Lark hadn't fared much better. Her current task was to boil a pot of water without using fire.

"We're not getting any younger!"

With a snarl, Daciana pulled, harder than she normally let herself. The water began to bubble, hissing steam. Triumphant, she glanced up. Inerys scowled, hands on her hips. What could she possibly find fault with? She'd done as she asked, the water was boiling, and—

Lark sank to her knees in the snow.

Daciana caught her before she pitched forward, hoisting her arm around her shoulder to keep her upright. A thin trickle of blood ran from Lark's nose and over her lips.

"You didn't feed the tether," Inerys said, crossing her arms.

"Can't imagine why you think that." Lark grinned, a feeble and wavery, blood-coated smile. "Maybe if you fed me, I wouldn't make silly mistakes."

"If you thought with your mind instead of your stomach, you'd be all the stronger."

"Come now," Daciana said, fed up with the witch's criticisms. "We've been at this for hours now. Since before sunrise. We could all do with some food and rest."

Inerys scoffed and rolled her eyes. "Fine, fine. But don't come crying to me when the both of you lack the necessary discipline to conjure a simple spell without falling unconscious. In my day, we spent days, *days,* practicing our craft without complaint. And do you think we broke for food or water or sleep or 'just one more bathroom break, please?' We dug deeper than the edge of our fortitude to see it done. Generations of softness have weakened your resolve, it would seem."

Lark's mouth hung open, her eyes squinting as if in disbelief. "I'm quite sure I'm older than you. I am, aren't I?"

"A lady never reveals her age. Only her wisdom."

Lark laughed, leaning into Daciana. Daciana supported her weight with a firm hand. "You're really old, then, aren't you? You're just an ancient hag with a pretty face."

"Watch your words, Reaper, lest you find yourself without a teacher."

Lark leaned in, whispering loud enough for Inerys to hear, "I just realized what she is. She's a cantankerous grandmother, isn't she?"

Daciana laughed. "If I have to endure another story about how her generation was stronger, we might have to make a drinking game."

Inerys glared at them, balling her hands into fists. It was all too easy to rile her up. It wouldn't even be the first time they'd set her off. She'd cancel lessons, storm off in a huff, and after a few hours of well-earned rest and recovery, she'd reappear and demand they pick up where they'd left off.

"You ungrateful little—"

Aislinn came crashing through the trees, tripping on her own feet and gasping for air. Her cheeks and nose were red from the cold, her eyes bright with terror. "Someone... he—" She panted, coughing. "Someone's out there."

"You ventured past my protective spell," Inerys said, reaching down to help her up. "What did you see?"

"A man," Aislinn gasped, "but he was no ordinary man. He knew, Inerys." She grabbed on to the witch's shoulders, shaking her. "He knew what I am."

Inerys' eyes widened, and for the first time since Daciana had known her, she scented her fear. The witch eyed each of them, alarm sharpening her voice.

"That's enough training. We're out of time."

⁕⁕⁕

INERYS BUNDLED HER HERBS, tying them off and wrapping them in cheesecloth. She stomped across her kitchen, the force making her potted plants tremble in her wake as she grabbed her rucksack and thrust her wrapped herbs inside.

Daciana tossed a wordless glance in Lark's direction, receiving a shrug in response.

After Inerys' vague declaration, she'd taken to packing seemingly random items from her home. A hardened edge to her focus as she ignored them in favor of stomping around her kitchen.

"What's happening?" Daciana asked, unease weaving its way into her chest. But Inerys continued packing with a frantic pace, muttering frantically.

Aislinn leaned against the doorframe, hugging herself. The witch was frightening the poor girl, and without the decency of an explanation.

"Inerys, stop," Lark said, attempting to block her from packing more herbs and vials into her bag.

Inerys huffed and knocked her hand out of the way. "There isn't time!"

"Well, make time!" Lark snatched the bag away, holding it out of reach. "The others are still out hunting. Are they in danger?"

Kenna, Alistair, and Langford had ventured off on their own. Though Langford seemed determined to keep his distance from Kenna, all things considered, Alistair hadn't allowed his anger to fester and had insisted on the *bonding* endeavor. Daciana knew firsthand how stubborn Alistair could be when he set his mind to something. If only Langford knew how insistent Alistair had been when they first found him wandering the road, alone, under clothed, and starving. She and Hugo had, of course, been willing to help him, but Alistair saw the value in recruiting him even when they'd voiced their disagreement.

If Alistair was determined to adopt someone into his trusted circle, there was no stopping him.

"Well? Are they?"

If Lark understood how lethal Kenna was, she wouldn't worry after them. It was the only reason Daciana wasn't sprinting into the woods in search of them.

"No." Inerys braced her hands on her butcher block. "I doubt he'll cross paths with them."

"Who?" Daciana asked, tired of vague answers. "Who's out there? Who are we running from?"

Inerys sighed. "What are the odds you'll heed my advice and defer explanation for a better time?"

"Unlikely." Lark stole the word right out of Daciana's mouth.

"Fine." Inerys glared at her before allowing her gaze to fall onto Aislinn and soften. "Did you all really think the first somniavi in centuries wouldn't attract attention? She poses the greatest threat to the paragons and warriors of Avalon. Once trained, she can enter their dreams and unravel their minds with the effort it takes to draw water from a well. Untrained? She can hurt them. But it's all unbridled chaos."

"It's true," Aislinn said. "I hurt him. I don't really know how I knew what to do, but I sought his pain and he fell." She bit her lip, fighting a smile. "I'm sorry. I know this is still a great danger. But I took him down. *Me.*"

Inerys huffed. "This is what I've been telling you. Perhaps now you'll believe me." Her mouth twisted to the side. "How did it feel?"

Aislinn shook her head. "Like he won't stay down for long."

Lark nodded, her stare unfocused as she absorbed the information. "All right. We have a Reaper Blade and a somniavi." She lifted her chin, meeting Daciana's eye. "And we have us. Let him come. I've been itching to see how far this power extends."

"Reckless fool!" Inerys spat. "And will you welcome Aislinn's death? Has she no use to you since she hasn't pulled your man from his slumber?"

"Of course, not!" Lark's cheeks bloomed scarlet, and Aislinn's gaze remained trained on the floor. "But what choice do we have? Run? Won't he find us?"

"She makes a good point," Daciana cut in. "If your protection spell won't keep her safe, where is she to find sanctuary from a god bent on her destruction?"

"It matters naught." Inerys wrung her hands. "He is here. It's only a matter of time until he finds a way through." She turned to Aislinn. "Did he tell you his name? Knowing which self-righteous prick we're dealing with might help narrow down our defense tactics."

"He did not tell me his name," Aislinn said, "but that doesn't mean I didn't learn it." She unfolded her arms. "Merikh. That was the name I pulled from his mind."

"Merikh." Inerys hummed thoughtfully. "He's a warrior best known for the War Against the Blight. He doesn't draw much attention and keeps a wide berth between himself and his followers. Unlike some of the others." Her voice held a derisive edge.

"The War Against the Blight is yet another instance when fools favored pissing matches to compete for power. The catalyst being the Netherworld's challenging of Avalon's rule. It was a bloody affair, and more humans died from the tactics of both sides than anyone else. The aftermath accomplished little more than the Otherworld becoming the neutral party between the two planes, serving to keep the Netherworld in check and maintain order.

It was a self-serving war of egotistical gods, and Sargon's a reminder to never cross him."

A pattern was emerging, the more Daciana learned of these higher powers. What hope was there for peace in the afterlife when the ones in charge were petty and conniving?

Daciana clenched her fists, forcing down the useless anger heightening her pulse. Anger was best utilized with direct focus.

Lark was the first to speak. "All right, how old are you exactly?"

Inerys grinned. "I'll never tell. But we have one small mercy. Merikh isn't impetuous, nor is he unnecessarily cruel. Oh, don't give me that look, he's a right prig, but it could have been worse. We can wait until morning for you all to depart."

"And go where?" Daciana asked.

"That is… that is for you to decide." Inerys' gaze dropped, and her jaw tightened.

She didn't know. For a witch that seemed to know everything, that must have been downright terrifying.

Daciana had no qualms with protecting Aislinn against whoever this Merikh was. But it was foolish to assume he wouldn't follow. Where would they have the greatest advantage against a paragon?

"What about Gavriel? I'm not leaving him." Lark's voice rang out, fear and anger tightening her tone.

"I'll protect him. With everything I have, I swear it. But I can't strengthen my protective spell, train the lot of you, and fight a paragon. Leave and trust I will keep him safe until you return."

"I won't leave him to die." Lark shoved the burlap sack back into Inerys' hands. "There will be no debate on this matter. I will stay, and I will fight."

"Then you will die," Inerys said. "To a paragon, I am but a green witch living my quiet life in the forest. Gavriel is my sick patient. But you," her voice dropped, "you are a threat. A stain to the natural order of things, and Merikh will scent you a mile away. Aislinn may be his target, but mark my words, you will be a fringe casualty in this."

Daciana stiffened at Inerys' words. Lark had to see reason, as painful as it was. Gavriel would be safer without her serving as an antagonist to this Merikh. It was a risk, leaving him with nothing but Inerys for protection, but the witch had proven time and time again how strong and capable she was. Blazes, they were all relying on her for protection and safe harbor; imagine how fierce her shield would be on a narrower focus.

"Gods. Witch-queens. Paragons. They're all the same," Lark ground out through a clenched jaw. "They punch down because they think us frightened, weak. They need us to fear them, it's what grants their power. Well, I am not afraid, and I will not run. I'm tired of waiting for them to declare war. Nereida. Merikh. They want us to cower and flee, to await their command. They wish for war?" Lark brought her fist down against the wooden surface of the butcher block, rattling the stack of mismatched teacups. "We bring the war to them."

***

"I DON'T LIKE IT," Kenna said, reaching onto her tiptoes for a dusty bottle of what appeared to be an aged Anquan wine. "It's rather uncomfortable agreeing with Lark."

When the others had returned, Lark and Inerys had set to work trying to sway them to their side of the argument. And when the last of day's light had fallen into shadow, they were at a stalemate.

Daciana hadn't pressed, hadn't confronted Lark with the truth of

Inerys' claims. Lark was reacting in anger, in fear, in despair at the idea of leaving Gavriel behind. And no one would fault her for that. But Inerys hadn't lived so long, seen as much as she had, to send them astray.

Daciana reached for the bottle, examining it. A good year. "You only agree with Lark out of misplaced pride."

Kenna scoffed. "Since when is my pride an issue. I think we can safely say I dropped any semblance of pride long ago. Probably around the time you first brought me to my knees."

"Are you suggesting you debased yourself for me?" Daciana glanced up to find Kenna's cheeks flushed.

"Not at all." She laughed. "Just that I'd crawl on my belly over broken glass for your favor." She rolled her eyes, dismissing the sting of truth. "In any case, a fight delayed is not much of a strategy."

Daciana took the hint to change topics, for now. "No, but the strategy lies in gathering strength and forcing him onto the offensive. Here, we're just waiting for him to find Aislinn." And without the proper tactic to defeat him.

Inerys had stressed the importance of Daciana and Lark learning to combine their powers. How chaos had overtaken the balance and given Lark unstable power. Inerys had hypothesized that Lark might be strong enough to work with Daciana as the anchor to her power so long as she didn't use too much. Hence, the training. But as the witch had said, they were out of time. A true paragon, a warrior of Avalon, had descended to the mortal realm. Aislinn as his target.

If there was ever doubt in her lack of piety, it was now nonexistent.

Aislinn was the key, the weapon against such a being. But she'd spent all her time tending to Gavriel and seeking his remedy, that sending her out against such a foe was essentially throwing her to the wolves.

Daciana scrunched her nose at the thought. She'd always hated that expression.

"Feels an awful lot like running away," Kenna said, climbing higher to reach another bottle. The lean line of her body led to the swell of her backside, and Daciana admired her fill.

"I don't think this is what Inerys meant by packing provisions."

"She won't miss these. Think Alistair could do with some Valle-merian mead? I can't stand the stuff, but he liked that home brew they brought back with them."

Kenna and Alistair had bonded, just as Daciana had known they would. "He'll like anything that wreaks havoc on his liver."

"Noted. Better grab the Kovalian wine for Langford. Where they're headed, he'll need it."

Daciana had persuaded Kenna to chart their destination for Anquan. To finally seek out the hunters, as she'd promised. Aislinn would come, too; they'd get her as far from this Merikh as possible and surround her with fighters capable of battling threats that transcended the mortal realm. And the only way to ensure her safety was if the others had no knowledge of their destination, a fact that didn't sit right with Daciana, but a necessary one. If the paragon returned and demanded answers, there would be none to give. Aislinn had been quiet about this solution but showed no signs of refusing.

Alistair and Langford, however, hadn't indicated what they planned to do.

"What do you know that I do not?" Daciana asked.

Kenna turned, leaning an elbow against the top shelf. "A little of this, a little of that."

"Fine, keep your secrets."

Kenna slid down the ladder to land before her. "Alistair is planning to convince Langford to head to Vallemer. His wish is to speak to the chieftains and hire their berserkers to fight on Ardenian soil against whatever attack Nereida will launch. Because you know she will. This? This trickle of ilk we've seen lately? This is *nothing*. She has to have a plan, and he recognizes this fact."

"You seem quite taken with the man who made you guess the color of his smallclothes upon first meeting."

Kenna laughed. "I like him. He's honest in a way some of us are too afraid to be."

Silence filled the cellar. They always came back to this. Back to the edge of raw truth. It was a game they'd played for far too long. A hint. An implication. Then a retreat.

Daciana was done retreating.

"You're right," she said. "Perhaps we should all take a page from his book and speak plainly." She stepped closer, trailing her finger along the line of Kenna's collarbone. "I wish for things I haven't felt in many moons. I wish..."

Kenna's breath hitched, and she held absolutely still. Daciana unfastened Kenna's cloak, slowly, letting the scarlet fabric pool on the floor at their feet. There was no mistaking her intentions, but she would grant her this courage to speak aloud the thoughts she'd kept quiet for so long.

Kenna deserved to know how loved she was.

"Let me bare you and take everything you claim is mine."

Kenna gasped, eyes widening as she nodded frantically.

It was the trust Daciana needed. The last piece of their unspoken truth falling into place. Heat unfurled deep in her belly—her head grew heavy with it—and she couldn't stop herself now even should she want to.

With a groan, Daciana sealed her mouth over Kenna's, moaning at the burst of her sharp and sweet taste. She dug her hands into Kenna's tunic, pulling, ripping, shredding, anything to reveal her soft skin. Daciana deepened the kiss, wanting to weep, as finally, *finally,* her hands met the soft curves of the woman she craved. The one who drove her to madness. Her hunter. Her solace. Her lament.

Daciana sank to her knees, dragging Kenna's smallclothes and breeches with her. A hard tug, and those, too, along with her boots were freed from her perfect form. Hands caressed Daciana's jaw, her ears, ran along her lips, and she was sure she would lose herself to this. Lose herself to the hunger.

Daciana cast her gaze up, finding Kenna watching her with heavy lidded eyes. Like she, too, was falling into a trance. Kenna thrust one hand to brace herself against the shelf, and glass bottles *clinked.* Daciana ran her hands along smooth thighs, chasing her touch with her mouth, her tongue, her teeth. She bit down, and Kenna moaned, the sound shooting straight through Daciana and setting her blood on fire.

It was heady. Dizzying. Intoxicating. Kenna's pale thighs parted to reveal the glistening space she craved most. Daciana leaned in and swiped her tongue through her slick, and she groaned. Kenna was just as addictive as ever. How they'd ever survived this long pretending their souls didn't call to one another, scream for the rightness of their union, was one of life's greatest mysteries.

Daciana traced every curve, every shadow, reaching her tongue deeper still as she sucked on the spot that always drove Kenna wild.

A bottle shattered, spraying droplets of ruined wine against the side of Daciana's face.

"Oops," Kenna whispered, her voice thin and breathy.

Daciana didn't slow, didn't pause her eager pursuit, devouring the gorgeous woman before her. Her beauty was her heart. Her soul. Her fire. It burned everything around her in a cleansing flame, and Daciana wanted to burn with her.

Hands pulled at her hair, and Daciana lifted her gaze to find Kenna's face. Her perfect breasts heaved, a pretty blush staining her pale skin. Her mouth hung open, dark eyes hazy as she stared down at her. Daciana took another slow, thorough taste. Lingering whenever Kenna's thighs twitched in response. She could spend eternity like this, die happy with the taste of Kenna's desire coating her tongue. She slowed down her movements, wishing to draw out her exploration.

"Dac," Kenna gasped. "Fuck…"

With slow and deliberate care, Daciana coaxed her closer, closer still, before shifting her focus to keep her from falling over the edge. Kenna let out a frustrated whimper, her grip tightening in Daciana's hair.

And suddenly, nothing else mattered more than bringing this woman the ecstasy she craved. Daciana added her fingers, pressing deep and curling just so, doubling down with the soft movements of her mouth in just the right place. Kenna cried out, gripping the shelf behind her. Her thighs trembled, and she panted through the climb.

Another twist of Daciana's fingers, another circle of her tongue, and Kenna cried out, her body clenching and trembling while Daciana worked her through every movement. And when Kenna sagged, gently shoving Daciana's face away, she caught her in her arms, slowly bringing her down to lie upon her cloak and discarded clothes.

Their mouths met in a languid kiss. Slow. Decadent. Sharing the taste of Kenna's arousal between them. Kenna was already running her hands up and down Daciana's body, beginning her search for laces and closures to open. Daciana had half a mind to insist Kenna wait, enjoy the afterglow rather than focus on her, but a tantalizing memory of times they'd done this reminded her of one important element:

Hunter stamina.

"I hope you weren't planning on sleeping tonight," Kenna said, her voice lazy and sated as she sat up and stretched. "Because we have a lot of lost time to make up for."

Daciana's laugh ended in a groan when Kenna teased the spot between her clothed thighs. "Travel will be shit tomorrow if we don't sleep."

Kenna leaned over her, caught the lace of her tunic with her teeth, and tugged it open. "Worth it."

Daciana couldn't agree more.

CHAPTER TWENTY-TWO

DEMETRIA

*T*he world shifted, tilting to one side and then the other. A continuous rise and fall. A pendulum swing. Each movement was answered with a groan, a low *crack* that struck Demetria's ears. She opened her eyes, spinning wooden rafters of the ceiling came into view. She blinked until her vision righted itself.

The space behind her eyes throbbed, and she rubbed her hands down her face, a metallic *clink* echoing.

Where was she?

Where was Balan?

What happened?

Images assaulted her memory. The farmer who'd found them in his barn. The questionable food he'd served. A drug taking effect and stealing her consciousness.

Demetria tried to sit up but was yanked back. Iron manacles encircled her wrists, led by a chain fashioned to the wall. She blinked, disbelief numbing her limbs as the rest of the room came into focus.

Iron bars. The acrid smell of shit and piss. Bodies filling the cramped space.

Not a room. A cell.

Panic strangled her throat, and her eyes blurred with the unfairness of it all. She fought so hard, *so hard,* to escape her brother, the prison of her title only to end here. Would revealing her identity help or hurt? Would they free her or use her as a bargaining chip?

It mattered naught. They'd never believe her.

"You're awake." The rough scrape of a familiar voice made the tears come harder, as relief and despair warred for dominance in the pounding of her heart. A broad back, positioned in front of her as if shielding her from the rest of the prisoners. His white hair, matted and filthy, shone in the low light of the lantern suspended from the wall. Balan turned, a wry smirk upon his lips even as his silvery eyes searched her in assessment. "I trust you're well rested."

Demetria pressed against the side of her head, willing the pressure to cease. "What happened?"

"The man signed his own death warrant by capturing us." Balan's voice was dark and dangerous, a rumble of thunder in a tightly enclosed space. "One thing you humans fail to realize is just how far memory can extend. I shall not forget this." His eyes flashed dangerously. "And he will learn the truest lesson of regret."

Demetria couldn't even find it in her to object to his demand for retribution, even if his voice promised unspeakable cruelty. But it was easy to dismiss while locked in a cell, chained to a wall, with no hope to escape.

"Where are we?"

"Isn't it obvious?" He gestured to the huddled group of terrified faces. Ages ranging from a small child to an elderly man asleep in the corner.

Gods, she hoped he was asleep.

The room rocked, the answering groan of wood as it shifted filled the space.

"We're at sea," Demetria gasped. Of course. How had she forgotten what the farmer had said? How much coin he collected selling unsuspecting travelers to Koval. How easily he manipulated them into thinking he was the vulnerable party, when really, he was the snake in the grass.

Yes. Balan's demand for cruel punishment was a most reasonable response.

"It wasn't the ideal form of passage, but we got what we wanted."

This was not what she wanted. To be hand-delivered to her brother, bound and shackled like chattel. At best, he'd execute her on sight. At worst...

Demetria didn't much like guessing Zaire at his worst. The depths of his darkness were an unanswered question to her even now, and she had no intention of finding out. After Evander. After Ruslan. After everything.

Was there nothing he wouldn't destroy just to see her suffer? They died so she would live, and she'd failed. Failed them. Failed herself. Failed at everything she'd ever touched. There were so many things she hadn't done. So many experiences she hadn't had. She'd escaped and spent her freedom in hiding. And now, it was too late.

Demetria buried her head in her hands, a sob breaking through her chest.

A hand gently patted her back, cautious and stilted in its comfort. She glanced up to find Balan, his arm outstretched, uncertainty etched along his brow.

"It will... be all right," he said carefully.

"How do you know?" She sobbed harder, and his hand flattened against her shoulder, rubbing in small soothing circles.

"I've witnessed the fall of many powerful souls. Broken them myself, actually." A smug sort of pride trickled through his voice. "But you aren't done yet."

Demetria sniffed, searching for the easiest explanation. It was too much to put into words, the keen loss of hope.

"I... what if I die tomorrow?"

"What if you die today?" he asked with a shrug. "Or eighty years from now? Wait until death comes for you to mourn its arrival. You'll waste your life otherwise."

"To die before I've even really lived, knowing others died in my place. It all seems... pointless."

Balan turned to face her fully, sterling silver eyes searching her with a gentleness that softened their sharpness. His mouth, too, had lost its line of tension. Though he was handsome, his features always held a severity. But now, it was smoothed into sincerity. He gripped her shoulder in his large hand. "You worry over wasting your life, and your response is to spend the time you have distressing?" He squeezed her shoulder. "That isn't very strategic."

Demetria huffed a laugh. "No, I suppose not. But you can't know how it feels. You've lived lifetimes. Seen and done so many things. I spent my life caged by my own birthright, and when I was finally free, I still had no agency. You speak with such logic, it's hard to dismiss your wisdom. But I wonder, is it wisdom or ignorance?"

Balan's eyes widened as if in surprise, but she continued.

"You don't know what it's like to live a brief flash of a life, shrouded in what ifs. What if I never escape my brother? What if my kingdom falls to ruin? What if I die before I've ever been kissed?" The last question burst from her lips without warning. Did she really care about such an insignificant thing?

Yes. It wasn't insignificant to want to *live*.

"You're right about one thing," Balan began, "I haven't always known the immediate urgency of mortality, but look at me." He gestured up and down his body. "I am mortal. I wouldn't be so quick to dismiss my insight." He fell silent watching her with a discomfited expression. "And should your death arrive without you experiencing your first kiss"—his throat bobbed, his face tightening—"I will kiss you."

That was... unexpected to say the least. Sure, they'd grown close since traveling on their own, a bond forming between two lost souls searching for—

Well. Demetria wasn't sure what Balan was searching for exactly or why he cared enough to help her reach her own goals. She'd assumed he'd uncovered some sort of protective nature in himself, perhaps an echo of his humanity and she was nothing more than a conduit. But still, she counted him as a friend. That was more than she'd hoped for when she hid on Ingemar's ship, escaping her brother's tyranny.

Balan sat waiting for her response, his face twisting into deeper discomfort the longer she dragged out the silence.

She had to say something. He'd reached out to her with kindness, a promise to soothe one of her unrelenting worries.

"Gross."

Balan's eyes flashed, anger and relief stealing his features. "Not gross. You should be so lucky. Mortals given to my domain begged for my favor."

"Ew!" she shrieked, laughing. "I hope you know I was in no way *asking* you to kiss me. That would be disgusting."

He snorted, an affectionate smile washing the rest of his disquiet away. "Hush, you little fool. Now you have even more reason to avoid your demise."

Demetria leaned into him, reclaiming their easy comfort with one another. "True. Dodging the threat of your kiss is a much more effective motive for staying alive."

He chuckled, more of a huff of breath against the top of her head. "I'm pleased to serve."

CHAPTER TWENTY-THREE

GAVRIEL

*A*nother sharp snap. The rush of wind forged from violence. And pain. Blistering pain. The severing of nerves, bone deep, soul clawing pain. His shoulders ached from being suspended by chains. He dangled from the iron ring set high in the granite column so the tops of his toes just brushed against the floor. The room blurred, marbled floors and columns becoming shapeless masses. They'd chosen the banquet hall for the ease of whip's range and to avoid staining the carpets.

One had to admire the logic behind the planning of his punishment.

His vision dimmed, darkness blotting out the edges, but nothing numbed the agony.

He and Lark had been seen in the cellar. And once word got to their master, his punishment began. It once was an easy thing, to cleave his mind from his body, he'd done it dozens of times. For far greater infractions than fraternizing with a fellow indentured. What a ruse that word was. They were not hired servants paying off a debt. They were prisoners.

The punishment he'd received for his first failed escape left him unresponsive for three days. No, this was not the worst his body had been subjected to, but for the first time, he was vulnerable.

He could not shut his mind off from the pain since his racing thoughts screamed her name. What were they doing to Lark? Was she suffering? Would the master sell them off, forever separating them?

They'd grown bold, he and Lark, stealing away to claim their bright spots of happiness. Of reveling in the way their souls and bodies called to one another even in the darkness. But they'd been foolish to assume someone wouldn't see. To assume someone wouldn't take the only semblance of power they had left in this life to betray them. He couldn't even fault them for this. Desperation did terrible things to a person's sense of right and wrong. But if Lark was punished? If she suffered the same pain as he?

He'd kill their betrayer with his own hands. Slowly. Painfully. Draw out their agony until all that was left was an inhuman echo of anguish, and only then would he grant them the release of death.

Another lash carved deep, the sting stealing the breath from his lungs.

Yes, he was weaker now than he'd ever been before.

Fear was not weakness. Fear was a survival skill, the instinct of nature. But love? Love had found the gap in his armor. Had carved out a hole in his fortress and allowed weakness to flourish.

He couldn't even bring himself to regret that, nor the pain it brought. For with each trembling thought, each ice-cold terror plaguing his mind, there was warmth. And light and laughter and hope.

A pause. Heavy stilted silence hung in the air, only the sound of Gavriel's labored breath filling the empty hall.

Then footsteps. A shuffling slide, like someone was being dragged.

No. No. No.

A scream.

Lark.

He lifted his head, sweat stinging his eyes. Two guards dragged Lark as she fought to break free of their hold. Her red hair hung loose and wild, flickering like a living flame as she kicked and clawed and screamed.

"What have you done to him?" Her voice was a knife to the heart.

She bore no marks, her clothes still tightly fastened and buttoned, no appearance of bodily harm.

Her punishment would be to watch.

He fought against his chains, as if he could break iron and shield her.

The guards tossed her to the floor, almost within reach. Lark clambered toward him, crawling on her hands and knees, terror and desperation in her honey-colored eyes—

She was dragged back, held far enough away she couldn't touch him.

"No! Please! Let him go!" She kicked and punched at the arm barring her in place, her breaths coming faster. "Don't do this! Please!"

The despair in her words, the anguish, it broke him.

Another crack, and he cried out at the searing pain. This was so much worse. So much worse witnessing the way Lark flinched, broken sobs stuttering from her chest. Tears stained her cheeks, and her face twisted.

"Let him go, please. Please! I beg you!"

Another slash, this time curling against his ribs, blending with the sharp cry of Lark screaming his name.

That sound. His name on her lips, amidst the torture, it set something in him. Something they had tried to break.

He was here with her. And she with him. Sharing the pain as if she'd take his place in a heartbeat. He'd never allow that, not in a thousand lifetimes, but the strength of this woman's heart. The way she still fought, consequences be damned, to reach him. To comfort him. Knowing full well, it wouldn't change a damn thing.

Somehow, it changed everything.

This time, he did not wish to blot out the pain and dissociate. He welcomed it all, staying present and sharp as they slashed deeper into his skin, as Lark screamed and wailed and begged. He would not leave her to face this alone, he would remain a fixed point, bearing all her pain as he bled for her.

And one day, he would see her freed. Even if it was the last image he held on to as his soul ushered in the void. That thought, that promise, gave him more strength than anything else in this life.

Lark was more than just his weakness. She was his salvation.

CHAPTER TWENTY-FOUR

LANGFORD

"It isn't the longest voyage, but shall we make use of having a locked door at sea?" Alistair tugged the book down enough to catch Langford's eye, while Langford dutifully ignored him, reading the same words over and over:

'The folly of man is the neglect of his true nature. The beast resides within us all, and societal pressures have forced us into unnatural roles. If we are to reclaim our rightful place among paragons and warriors of virtue, we must dispense with the antiquated notion that civilization is our default state.'

It was meant to be a rousing speech in the climactic scene where the roguish thief rallies the rabble to rescue the stolen countess. Langford could not focus on the story enough to even care, and he had no desire to indulge in Alistair's flirtations. Not when he was still stewing over the decision to journey to Vallemer. They'd barely recovered from their brush with death in Oakbury. He'd almost lost Alistair *again* and already the man was running headlong into danger. Though Hugo had hailed from Vallemer, he'd been an anomaly if the stories were to be trusted.

Vallemer was a nation of warriors who valued tradition, honor, and justice. They were distrustful of strangers and held their own set of laws and punishments independent of Kovalian or Ardenian influence. Langford hadn't the energy to compare conflicting ideologies, nor the time to classify governmental structures. Though if he had to index them in simple rudimentary measures, he'd identify Vallemer as the last place Alistair should be.

The man ran his mouth, often to disastrous results, and Langford wouldn't have any ability to save him any resulting punishment.

There was also the question of Alistair's condition. After nearly succumbing to his fever, on the brink of turning into a monster, he'd been healed by Kenna. Healed with mixtures his body shouldn't have been able to withstand. Langford was a man of reason and sound logic, of observation and assessment. Of recognizing patterns within causes and their effects. The way Alistair's body had healed was nothing short of miraculous, and logic formed by pattern and experience dictated the shift in balance was going to be disastrous.

Plainly, the other bloody shoe was about to drop.

But sure, they should run to a foreign country where they had no connections to ask for a monumental undertaking the Vallemerians have no stake in. One could not think of a better way to spend the winter months.

"What say you?" Alistair leaned over him and ran a finger along the length of Langford's waistband, just dipping in enough to send a shiver down his spine, damn him. "We both know how much you love being surrounded by the ocean. It's practically an aphrodisiac for you."

Langford closed his book and slapped Alistair's hand away, ignoring the wounded expression he wore. "You dragged me along on a trip I vehemently disagree with. Your libido should be the least of your worries."

Though there was safety at sea, especially with Captain Ingemar at the helm, there was always the danger of disembarking. She had halted her trips to Koval after their last escape. Between aiding the princess in fleeing and assisting active fugitives running from the castle, she'd made a target of herself. Which is how she'd ended up here, transporting goods and travelers between Ardenas and Vallemer.

Yes, the journey was easier than Langford had anticipated. But it didn't make the destination any safer.

"You really think I care about my libido?" Alistair's voice was soft, but at Langford's expression, he laughed. "Fine, maybe I do a little. But it's not about that." His arms came around him, and Langford couldn't help but sink into him. "You worry so much, I only want to make you feel good. I assumed my wily charms would do the trick, but I'm open to other methods. I could read to you?" With a jut of his chin, he gestured to Langford's abandoned book on the tidy end table. "One of your romances? I'll do all the voices, just the way you like it."

Langford fought the smile stretching his mouth. It was true, there was great pleasure in listening to the rumble of Alistair's baritone voice as he recited prose like poetry, sometimes whispering against Langford's temple as he drifted off to sleep. It was something Alistair started one night when Langford had been suffering a three-day headache, tension radiating behind his eyes and down his neck. When he'd tossed his favored book, frustrated and dismayed by his inability to do something as vital as *read,* Alistair had placed a cool cloth over Langford's eyes, lowered him to rest against his chest, and began reading aloud from where he'd left off. Langford had to admit, it was a far more enjoyable experience than forcing himself to follow blurring words on a page amidst the pounding in his skull. Alistair had a voice Langford could spend hours listening to and still crave more. But whenever a lady character spoke on page, his falsetto impression was even better.

"You can't just charm your way out of this."

"Can't I?" Alistair raised one brow in his signature expression of wicked glee.

"No. You're the cause of my vexation, and now you must face it head-on."

"A fitting punishment."

"Not nearly punishment enough."

"I'm open to more creative methods."

Langford forced his amusement aside. It was too easy to melt under the warmth of Alistair's carefree attitude. But the threat remained.

"You did not consult me before making this decision."

Alistair tucked his chin into Langford's shoulder. "Ah. I see. About that—"

"And continued onward despite my protests. You don't get to pass verdicts to determine your future without factoring me in. Not if we're equal partners." Langford clenched his fists. "And I refuse to be anything less." It was as bold a proclamation as he'd ever made, but he'd spent too long facing the danger of losing Alistair for uncertainty to temper his words.

Alistair's face softened, any hint of delight vanishing. "You're right, but you're also wrong. I *did* make this decision with you in mind. You're the very drive behind every decision I make. Surely you must know that by now." He leaned up, still remaining close but not looming over Langford like a cat ready to pounce. "But I've grown too accustomed to forming plans and expecting everyone to fall in line to receive their cut. That can't be how I regard you." His knuckles brushed against Langford's jaw. "Henceforth, you shall have equal, if not more say in our next move. Just trust me on this one."

They were all the right words at the right time Langford needed to hear them. But Alistair had that ability. He could turn the charm on and off, his irreverence landing him in hot water only for his honeyed tongue to douse the flame.

"Listen," Alistair continued. "I'm not leaping into danger for the fun of it. Everything I do has a purpose. And right now? My only purpose is to see you happy and safe. Not just today, but the rest of your days. Our days. Together. I do this to have the future you once saw."

The Forbidden Shrine. The source of shame Langford had carried for so long. He'd loved Alistair long before he'd been willing to admit it, and the magic of The Forbidden Shrine had crafted his heart's deepest wish to trap him. A simple life with Alistair by his side. It had taken some coaxing, a lot of coaxing on Alistair's part, but Langford had finally recounted the vision he'd seen. The life they'd shared. An entire year of memories he'd awoken from, only to realize they'd been planted in his mind.

"I want this for us." Alistair traced Langford's knuckles with a featherlight touch of his lips. "Please. Help me make our dream come true."

If there was any hope of Langford holding on to his anger, Alistair had just decimated it. That fact must have been showing on his face because Alistair grinned his heart-stopping smile and tackled Langford to the bed, peppering him with eager kisses as he tugged at his buttons.

"Fine. Fine. You abominable heathen." Langford laughed, warmth spreading through his body as he dragged his hands through Alistair's hair, making it messier than his own.

"Paragon's twisted balls, I love it when you talk dirty."

"Don't blaspheme. Not when we—"

Alistair swallowed Langford's words with a firm press of his lips and a sweep of his tongue.

And Langford lost himself to the man he loved above all else. The gentle rocking of the sea the only reminder of where they were and what they set out to do. Until that, too, was lost in the haze of passion.

CHAPTER TWENTY-FIVE

AISLINN

*A*islinn's foot slipped, her heart leaping to the bottom of her stomach as she slid across another patch of ice.

Daciana halted her pace ahead, unperturbed by their slick travel conditions, and over Aislinn's shoulder another chuckle sounded from Kenna.

"In Anquan, they have a sport designed to utilize the ice for speed and agility. They apply edges to the bottoms of their shoes to glide over the ice without falling. What say you, Dac? Care to muster up some shin bones while I fashion the poles?"

Daciana snorted and continued their journey. "Maybe when we get there."

Kenna's eyes lit up, and she shook Aislinn. "You heard that, yes? I'm taking that as a promise."

"It wasn't a promise," Daciana's tired voice sounded from ahead. "I said *maybe*."

"Too late!" Kenna kept a soft hand on Aislinn's elbow, helping her along. "I'm fixating. We're going to soar across the frozen lake in a sporting fashion until I best you and win a prize to be determined!"

Daciana's laughter echoed through the woods, along the frozen road Aislinn struggled to travel. They had taken the longer route, less direct than if they'd gone through Oakbury to reach the port but with far more stops along the way. Aislinn had convinced them of this upon her agreement to travel to Anquan, stating it would be harder for Merikh to find her if she accidentally dream walked if she was around other people. A lie. She had no way of knowing if solitude made her presence clearer to him. All she knew was they were one stop away from the town she'd been carefully kept from.

The place of her first steps and final breaths.

Home.

Sure, she could never hide this truth from Lark, the one who guided her soul to that bridge, or Inerys who had spent hours dissecting her human life to determine why a somniavi existed after their supposed extinction. But Daciana had no intricate knowledge of her upbringing and thankfully did not conceive any notion she might employ subterfuge to get her way.

Aislinn fought hard against the guilt weighing in her chest at that.

She took solace in knowing Kenna seemed to be genuinely enjoying their trip, as indirect and drawn out as it was. During their stay at Barker's Pond, a small fishing village, the hunter had even engaged in a drinking contest with the locals, using her slight frame to her advantage, as they'd never suspect she'd actually win. But win she had, and when she'd drunk them all under the table and collected her winnings, she'd openly expressed her joy by pressing Daciana against the wall beside the buoy with the chipped paint.

Yes, Aislinn's protectors were enjoying their journey, and it almost quelled the ball of anxiety that had made a home in her belly to see these two brightly bask in the glow of their joy.

But it didn't.

With each step closer to home, Aislinn's anxiety grew. Inerys had insisted her mother, her sister, anyone who loved her, would not recognize her face. But Aislinn didn't believe that. Or she didn't think it was that simple. How could her mother not recognize her soul even behind an unfamiliar face?

Aislinn's stomach knotted tighter, a quiet voice whispering her doubt.

But she had to know for certain. Had to see them one last time. If a paragon was so bent on her destruction, and her true demise was imminent, the universe owed her this much. And if this was a mistake, a misstep, may fate—

Aislinn's foot slipped again, and she decided not to finish that thought.

"WE HAVE THE SUPPLIES; we should cut the time off our journey by forgoing Meadowhedge and heading straight for the coast."

Aislinn jolted, panic flooding her body. No. No. They were so close. She couldn't fail now. Maybe if she could slip away long enough...

"We follow our marked path as agreed upon." Daciana's hazel eyes found Aislinn's, and something warm shone in them. A sense of *understanding*. "After all," she continued, "there was good reason for charting our course as such, yes?"

Aislinn's mouth went dry. She nodded, the motion like a creaky door hinge.

Daciana smiled. "There you have it. We'll arrive just after dusk and spend the night."

Kenna groaned. "Fine, but we're leaving at first light. This is the most indirect path to anywhere I've ever taken, and it's absurd."

At first light? That meant Aislinn would have to sneak away in the evening to find her mother. Or Yera. She didn't even know if Yera and Frederick even stayed in the village.

What if her mother had moved on?

"Aislinn, help me with this." Daciana held out a small bag, a leather satchel she'd pulled from her pack.

Aislinn hurried ahead to grab it, unsure what Daciana could possibly need help with.

"Open it, and count our coin for me," she said this without pausing, keeping her stare trained up ahead as she traversed the snowy road with ease.

Aislinn began counting. They had plenty for another night or two at an inn, and of course passage to Anquan. Daciana had been meticulous in her planning to ensure this. If she was beginning to doubt the sum of their travel—

"I know why you wished to travel this way."

A silver slipped out of Aislinn's grasp, and she caught it just before it hit the snow. "I told you. It keeps Merikh from—"

"No. No. Not that." Daciana's mouth curved in a soft smile. "I, too, couldn't take the word of a hermit witch without investigating on my own."

Aislinn's cheeks burned. Daciana had known the entire time. Had allowed Aislinn to lie and lead them from their path in her own pursuits. "Inerys told you."

"She didn't have to. I had a hunch." Daciana turned, amusement shining in her eyes. "And I overheard your conversation with Inerys. You all tend to forget how sharp my hearing is."

"Why then? Why allow this? I've added unnecessary time and cost to our trip. You and Kenna are sacrificing everything to keep me safe, and I've answered your kindness with... lies and selfishness. You should just leave me to face what comes. It's what I deserve after everything." Tears pricked at Aislinn's eyes, but she would not let them fall. She'd cried enough to last the rest of her days.

"What you deserve?" Daciana's voice was soft but edged with disbelief. "Kenna and I sacrifice nothing. She's been dying to drag me to her home country for years."

"It's about bloody time!" Kenna called out from behind. Any notion she couldn't hear their conversation fled with the echoes of her response.

"And," Daciana continued, "were I in your stead... if I had died, Kenna, Alistair, Langford, and Lark knowing only of my demise and not of my survival... I would exhaust every effort to find them. To show them." Finally, she stopped, grabbing Aislinn by the shoulder. "You think you deserve misfortune? Whatever for? All I see is the soul of a girl who was forced to suffer and has answered that suffering with kindness and strength and selflessness. You deserve a whole lot more than what you've been dealt, but one task at a time." Daciana nodded at the road ahead. "First, we find your family. Then we get you to safety. Once the world is set to rights, we go from there. But don't ever think for even an instant that any of this is what you deserve."

No one had ever said that to her before. And maybe she'd needed to hear it, because something cracked in her heart at Daciana's words.

"What happened before"—Daciana's voice lowered, a venomous hate filling her tone—"that was not your fault. There was nothing you did wrong. Nothing you should have done differently. You did not deserve it."

The tears Aislinn swore would never fall, the rage she hadn't felt since her death, the truth of what had happened to her, of the pain and suffering—*so much pain*—it rose to the surface, slipping over the edges of a wall she hadn't even known she'd crafted.

It wasn't her fault.

Did she really believe it was? Had that stopped her from grieving the loss of her life?

Corwyn had targeted her. Followed her. Waited until she was alone. And she hadn't been able to fight him off. She'd tried. She'd tried so hard her muscles ached. When he'd gripped her hair to hold her in place, she'd fought so hard the hair ripped from her scalp. And when he'd angled his knife against her bodice, she'd pierced herself against its edge.

That was when the fight had left her body, like all her strength trickled out with her blood. Her last breaths had been with drowning lungs, filled with blood and a sense of failure. That was why she hadn't raged at him. At what he'd done. She'd thought... she'd blamed...

Aislinn's cheeks were hot and cold, tears freezing as they fell.

Why had she thought the blame lay with her?

Arms came around her from behind. Kenna. She had pressed her cheek against Aislinn's shoulder. "We blame ourselves because it feels safer to have that measure of control. If it's something you did, you can do something differently next time around. You can make a promise to yourself, never again. But when it's not your fault... how can you make yourself any promises?"

More tears fell, a choked sob escaping Aislinn's chest. Kenna softly shushed her.

"But you must let the blame go. You did nothing to deserve it. You are not at fault. It's scary, I know, but only then will you heal from it."

Aislinn nodded, unsure if one could heal from their own death. If a second chance at life could even connect back to one's first life. If she even wanted it to.

"It won't be easy, or even linear," Daciana said. "But we'll be there every day to remind you."

"And"—Kenna slung an arm around Aislinn's shoulders into a more casual hold—"we can get pissed at the tavern and come up with a plan of revenge should the bastard's ghost ever show up."

"That isn't helpful," Daciana hissed, but Aislinn laughed, wiping her cheeks. Her eyelashes were starting to freeze.

"Actually," Aislinn said with a wet sniff, "that sounds brilliant." It felt... well, not good, but different to actually feel anger and rage toward him. It was a hot shaky feeling, but it was new. That had to mean something. "And a hunter must know all the secret ways to cause a ghost pain."

Kenna laughed, and they plodded along, the three of them in an awkward embrace that felt anything but awkward. "You have no idea."

AISLINN KNEW this door better than she knew her own face.

Aged wood, the grains seeping through the watery stain of green her father had applied before she was born. The wrapped twig wreath, dried and cracked in some spots, that she'd fashioned with Yera the summer they spent practicing weaving crowns for her wedding the following year. Symbols carved at a child's height from when she thought to signal the storied fae-folk to visit her. The copper doorknob, a greenish verdigris, had rusted, revealing more of its original surface. The surface she had begged her mother to allow her to paint after the traveling merchants came through town, an art gallery part of their display. She had painted every conceivable surface in their house after one of the artists explained to her how to create the effect, and the doorknob was the last to receive her artistic touch.

It was the door to home, to a lifetime of memories and wishes and dreams. All she had to do was knock. Knock and allow her mother to see, to know, she was all right. Though there was loss, there always would be, something else had been found.

Aislinn's fist hung heavy by her side.

"Would you rather try again in the morning?" Daciana's voice, heartbreakingly kind and soft, rang out from behind. "Kenna hadn't realized before, but now that she knows, she would not protest delaying our departure to a more reasonable hour."

Kenna and Daciana had been more than understanding the rest of the trek to her home. Keeping the conversation light when it needed to be and shifting seamlessly to support the weight of whatever dark turn Aislinn's thoughts took. It was easy to see how this group of strange fellows from all different walks of life had become a sort of family—a family Aislinn was starting to consider herself part of. If only Ferryn had agreed to accompany them. She missed his comforting presence more than she'd realized. But he'd chosen to remain at Lark's side, a timeless loyalty Aislinn only hoped Lark appreciated.

But Aislinn had Daciana, a steadying presence of strength and will and kindness. She only couldn't decide if having Daciana beside her on the wrong side of the door was a blessing or a curse. Kenna had been all too happy to remain at the tavern and wait, but Daciana had insisted on accompanying Aislinn to her home.

"I would rather do this alone."

"And so you shall." Daciana's answer came smoothly. "But you will always have backup, should you need it."

That was a roundabout way of saying she wasn't leaving.

"If Inerys is right—"

"Then I'll be right here to help. If she's wrong, I'll go and fetch you on the morn."

The low light of dusk faded between the trees, the road bending and weaving between familiar houses before disappearing into the gloom of the horizon. There weren't many milling about; it was far too cold for that, and Aislinn had been too cowardly to set foot in the tavern for fear she'd come across someone she knew.

The very real threat of what Inerys had promised, her face forever a stranger to her mother's eyes, hung above her like a knife.

"Go back to the tavern. I'll come find you if I need anything." Lark always said Daciana was a master of knowing when to push and when to step back. Aislinn could not agree with that statement at present.

"I will not intrude. But you can stop trying to send me off." Daciana remained firmly planted at Aislinn's back. "I'm not going anywhere. And if this goes south, I'm not giving you the chance to fall into harm's way."

Aislinn opened her mouth to argue—but what was the point? Already, she longed to go running off to the riverbank. To the place that once meant her sanctuary, her refuge. It would be different, in the winter, but that was to be expected no matter the season.

It would never be what it once was.

And if Merikh was tracking her, if he'd realized she'd left the safety of Inerys' protection…

A heavy creak, and the door swung open, bathing them both in light from the hearth. The sharp tip of an arrow aimed in their direction, the familiar curve of her mother's bow filling the doorway. Her blonde hair was tied back in a long braid running over her shoulder.

"Who are you, and what are you doing on my doorstep?" That voice. The same one that filled all Aislinn's memories—every mistake chided, every fear soothed, every ounce of courage stoked by the firm reminder of her strength, had been delivered in that voice. Aislinn thought the riverbank her sanctuary, but no, it was right here, standing before her with an arrow trained in her direction.

Her mama.

CHAPTER TWENTY-SIX

LARK

"*I* see my little brooding bird hasn't permitted mortality to change her. What a comfort."

Lark glanced up from her untouched frumenty, finding Ferryn's gleeful expression peering down at her.

"It's like old times!" He gestured to her bowl with his spoon before sliding into the seat next to her and digging into his own breakfast.

Ferryn had decided to stay, insisted, in fact, and when Lark pressed him to accompany Daciana and Kenna, to keep Aislinn protected from the threat hunting her, he'd accused her of trying to get rid of him. It was unnecessary, having him here. But she couldn't deny the truth of his words even if their context varied.

There was comfort in this. In having him here with her. And it did remind her of the way things were, when it felt like the only people in her corner were Ferryn and Leysa.

Skies. What harm had befallen the gentle seer? Lark had heard nothing of her since her attempt to find Ferryn all those months ago. When Inerys helped her access the edge of the veil in search of his fate. Leysa had helped her then, too, given her the guidance Lark had sorely needed.

Just as she always had.

With Nereida at the helm of the Otherworld, there was no doubt Leysa had been punished for her rebellion. The only question was: To what end?

Ferryn had been banished to Lacuna by Thanar, a swift and cruel punishment for aiding in Lark's escape. Only it wasn't cruel, was it? It was a stall tactic, a way of weeding out potential betrayals within his court without tipping his hand. How lonely it must have been, not knowing who to trust. Was the oath, the threat of total and complete submission, even real? Or had he crafted the lie to strike fear in the hearts of his subjects? A maneuver to protect himself in the face of complete isolation? It was strange to think his title was a punishment, a way of forcing him to suffer the deaths of every human in existence.

Did Thanar feel it? When a human died, did a little piece of him die, too?

It was vastly unnerving how much sympathy Lark felt when she thought of Thanar. Perhaps death had a way of smoothing out the faults of others. One would think Lark an expert of death, but the truth was, everything still felt new. Worthy of exploration and endless questioning. She'd existed for centuries but had only been *alive* for a matter of months.

There was much she didn't know. Too much.

Lark scooped her oats, letting them drip off her spoon. "We never talked about what happened. Not really."

Ferryn froze with his spoon in his mouth, darting his eyes to hers in assessment. "A great many things have happened," he mumbled around his mouthful. "Be more specific."

Lark's spoon clattered against her bowl, and she turned to face him fully. "When you swore the oath to Thanar. Everything that happened before. We've mentioned it, but you never told me everything." And it mattered. Right now, everything mattered more than it ever had before.

Ferryn placed his spoon on the table and slid his bowl away. "What do you wish to know?"

"When you swore the oath... what was it like?"

Ferryn hummed. "I suppose now it doesn't really matter, with him gone and all. I'm curious if the magic still holds..." He gazed across the room, lost in thought. "We'll see what happens, shall we?" He took a deep breath. "It wasn't what we were told."

Ferryn jolted, surprise flashing across his face. "So. the magic really does die with him. The oath was not the stories we were told. But you already suspected as much, or else you wouldn't be asking."

"Tell me."

Ferryn leaned back, crossing one ankle over his thigh. "The oath is a connection, access. It was a show of trust. I granted him access to pop into my head whenever he wished. More like… a line of communication. Though, if he happened to reach in while I was thinking really hard about something…" He winced.

"Did that happen before?"

"He might have opened up a line of communication while I was enjoying some explicit memories of private interactions. Let's just say he knew more about my relationship with Ceto than I was strictly comfortable with."

Ugh. That made two of them.

"Why didn't you tell me?" Lark's fear of the oath was a visceral thing, a living snake coiling in her gut. Even the Forbidden Shrine had reenacted her greatest fear of what suffering the oath would mean. The loss of control. The puppet strings. Thanar had even threatened her with the oath to force her to kill Gavriel. What if she had listened?

"That was the only true compulsion. I couldn't speak the truth of the oath. Not aloud, not in my head, not even in writing. I tried, just out of curiosity, and my thoughts would spin elsewhere, my words would dry up on my tongue, and my hand would freeze, unable to pen a word." Ferryn shook his head. "I suppose it was to protect Thanar's secret."

"Thanar had many secrets."

"True enough." Ferryn ran a hand across his jaw. "He was… strange when it came to you. Obsessive."

A sick crawling feeling tingled along Lark's arms. "I know. And I hated him for it."

"Rightfully so, and it made me wary of anything he might use me for. If it was in service to get to you. He couldn't force me to do anything, but I couldn't control my thoughts enough to prevent his access if he looked at the wrong time."

That day in the forest, after leading Emric's soul to the crossroads. After seeing Gavriel for the first time. It awakened something in Lark —something she'd always felt without knowing she could even feel. And when she tried to speak of it to Ferryn, he'd shut her down. Terror in his eyes, he'd begged her to cease speaking.

Because Thanar could have been listening. Could have seen the thought if he looked into Ferryn's mind at the wrong time.

The only one who hadn't seemed to fear him was Leysa. His seer. The one who witnessed every human death and assigned the Reaper best equipped to guide them. The one who remained suspiciously absent amidst Thanar's fall.

What had he done to her?

"When was the last time you saw Leysa?"

Ferryn's expression darkened. "At my trial. Thanar had announced his plan to dump me into the darkest cell in the deepest pit of our prison. Leave me there to rot and forget about me. But Leysa pressed for a transfer to Lacuna."

Were it not for Ferryn and Aislinn crossing paths, Aislinn would have stayed lost forever. And Ferryn would have been out of Lark's reach. "She saved you then!"

"I'm not so sure. I don't believe Thanar would have really left me there. I think that was a way to keep me from anyone's suspicion. He already knew Ceto and I had a certain connection; he could have placed her as my guard trusting she'd never betray me. And I..." Ferryn sighed. "I'm quite certain he would have sent me to the mortal realm in search of you."

That... that couldn't be...

"Why? You're just conjecturing. You have no way of knowing that."

Ferryn held his hands up in surrender. "True enough. But I know one thing. He cared for you above all else. To his detriment. Someone was betraying his secrets, feeding Nereida information she could use against him. But still, his priority was you. I don't think he was nearly as ruthless as he pretended to be." He shrugged. "As you said, I'm conjecturing about a dead man."

"Right," Lark said, ignoring the gnawing pit in her stomach. "How did you and Aislinn escape Lacuna?"

Ferryn reached for his bowl, digging in before he answered. Clearly more comfortable with this turn in conversation. "I suspected Ceto made a deal for me, but seeing her side with the witch, I'm not so sure."

"Unless that was the deal."

"But why free Aislinn, too?" Ferryn plopped another bite in his mouth, chewing thoughtfully. "Doesn't make sense."

None of it made sense. The truth was so twisted behind lies and manipulations, motivations, and secrets. It seemed for everything Lark thought she knew, three more questions sprung in its place, revealing her ignorance.

Somewhere, hiding in the gnarled roots of these secrets, were the answers to how to wake Gavriel and how to take down Nereida. There were still missing pieces, but Lark would find them, one way or another.

"Brooding bird." Ferryn placed a finger between her brows, a soft smile claiming his mouth.

"Not brooding." Lark slid her bowl back in front of her, spooning a large bite. She would need her strength. "Plotting."

She'd always been accused of running headlong into rash decisions. But Lark was learning the value of information before action.

But there was no mistaking, the call to action was bellowing in the back of her mind. She had not forgotten. No, it was a wicked song of her own making, the music of violence and retribution.

LARK POURED MORE WINE INTO INERYS' cup, topping her off in hopes it would keep her talking. The witch had no chalices to boast of, instead a pair of clay mugs housing their drink. Inerys' warm umber cheeks were flushed, a lazy smile claimed her usually dour expression, and her dark hair was messy with how many times she'd tossed her head back to laugh.

"I've never seen you drunken before. It's a nice change."

"Ha. You've never seen many sides of me I'm sure you would enjoy."

Was Inerys… flirting?

Lark grinned, sipping her wine. Langford had spoken of notes and legs and aftertastes like it held more flavor than a sharp and bitter grape. But the thought of him, of his appreciation for such things, sent a pang through Lark's chest.

"I've heard a story or two about you."

"You have no sources."

"Kenna is quite chatty."

Inerys gave a wistful sigh. "I forgot about our little fling."

Lark leaned forward on the butcher's block, resting her chin on her hand. Ferryn bustled around them, huffing each time they were in his way. He was preparing dinner for the three of them, a task he'd announced with such pride, it was far too easy to tease him.

Especially when he'd asked Inerys if he had to cut the carrots before dropping them into the pot or wait until the stew had softened them.

"Spill your secrets, witch."

Inerys smirked, a coy little smile she quickly hid behind her cup. "Let's just say there's a reason hunters are revered for their stamina."

Had this conversation come sooner, before Kenna and Daciana had patched things up so tightly, Lark might have regretted asking. But there was no shame in having a past that didn't always align with the one you were meant for.

"What about you, Reaper? Can Gavriel boast of any skill? In my experience, men are more likely to blindly feel around until they can thrust their sword home. A quick and unremarkable finish to an awkward fumble."

Lark choked on her wine, and Ferryn sighed in exasperation. "Gavriel doesn't fumble. He's a musician with his hands." And even as the thought hurt somewhere deep, a hazy warmth fluttered around the edges. It felt good to speak of him in the present rather than as a ghost of the past. "He seeks my satisfaction sometimes thrice over before his own."

"Really?" Inerys tilted her head in intrigue. "Good for him. Must be his hero complex."

"If you two don't mind," Ferryn cut in, his face flushed and his blond hair tied back at the nape of his neck, "I could use your help or your absence if you wish dinner to be served tonight."

"We don't mind at all." Inerys lifted her cup in salute and turned back to Lark as if he hadn't spoken. "Now where were we? Oh, yes! Men are hopeless when it comes to female pleasure. Do you think part of him remembers your preferences from before?"

From an entire lifespan Lark could not recall. "It's possible." How many lives was he sifting through as he slumbered under Nereida's curse. Was he aware of Lark? Was he fighting to return to her?

Lark took another sip of her wine, the bitterness only growing on her tongue.

"It takes a lot to adjust to that many memories," Inerys said, patting Lark on the hand. "He'll find his way."

"How do you know so much about everything?" Lark had wondered this many times. How Inerys seemed to possess such ancient knowledge. Always offering the answer they needed, despite it being stricken from history. Skies, she knew more about the Otherworld than Lark.

"I'll tell you a secret." Inerys beckoned with a crook of her finger, leaning close enough to whisper in Lark's ear. "It's the way of my ancestors." Her whisper was anything but quiet, loud enough to drown out the sound of Ferryn stirring the pot of questionable stew. "I'm what they call *historia maga*. Upon my birth, the lives and history of my coven, generations upon generations of memories, were instilled in me. I have memories of lives that aren't mine, and yet they are." Inerys' dark eyes were glassy, and Lark didn't dare interrupt her. "I can recall back as far as the creation of the veil, when the land was darkened by the shadows of monsters and the call of death an echoing cry. I know what it is to wrestle with which memory is my own against someone else's. Gavriel will be fine. If my many years have taught me anything, it's that having something worth fighting for is the greatest upper hand." She settled back, examining her cup with a casual air as if she hadn't just dropped more truth of her origin than ever before.

Inerys was a soul of reincarnation, many times over. Hundreds of times. Perhaps even more.

"What happens when you die?"

Inerys shrugged. "I'm the last of my coven, and I have no intention of breeding. So, I suppose the history will die with me." Her jaw clenched, clarity and anger burning in her eyes. "Do not offer your judgement so quickly, Lark, when you do not know what a burden it is. I will not birth an offspring for the selfish gain of others. Some women should be mothers, and some should not. But don't you dare judge me for my choice."

Her words carved an ache deep within Lark's belly. "I'm not! I would never!" She would never judge another for such a monumental choice. Even she could not claim the desire to mother any children at this time, possibly ever. And what a burden for Inerys to bear. Another layer of complications over an already difficult choice.

Lark glanced over at Ferryn who was studying his stew with more concentration than necessary. Utterly unhelpful.

"It wasn't always this way," Inerys continued. "Back when our numbers were strong, girls volunteered to be the next *historia maga*. It was… a great honor." She choked on the words. "But now…"

"You're the last of your kind." Lark finished for her.

Inerys nodded, a solemn expression stealing across her face.

A terrible burden. To be the beginning and the end.

"Well," Lark said, grabbing the bottle of wine, "let's drink to our pity party! It might make Ferryn's cooking go down easier."

Inerys laughed, holding her cup out, and Ferryn huffed his annoyance.

They turned to lighter subjects, jesting and laughing at one another's expense. Candlelight glimmered, bouncing off glass vials and sending shards of light streaming across the table. In the reflections of their wine. In the frosted windows rattling against the howling wind. There was much to fear, and much to face in the coming days, but for the briefest of moments, they were three mortals sharing a kitchen. A kindred experience both mundane and significant. It was a moment destined to nestle in Lark's memory, a feeling she knew she would chase in the future, but she tried to live as humans do, in the here and now.

For just a while.

AN ICY BREEZE ghosted against Lark's skin, and she jolted upright in her chair. The lacy curtain billowed beside the open window. Gavriel's form was unmoved, perfectly preserved in his cursed slumber. Why would she expect any differently?

Lark ran a hand over her face, wiping away the last clutches of sleep. She shifted her legs to alleviate the tingling sensation of blood returning to her limbs, and her foot knocked against the half-empty plate from her dinner. Exhaustion from sparring with Ferryn and training with Inerys, followed by a dose of heavy drinking, weighed her limbs and clouded her mind. When Ferryn had finished cooking their questionable dinner, burnt rolls and over-salted vegetable stew, she'd brought an extra portion to eat by Gavriel's side, soaking up whatever time she had with him in the silence of his room, ready to share if he awoke.

Just being near him felt better than nothing.

Another forceful breeze made the candle gutter out, only a plume of smoke rising in the darkened room. Lark shivered, rubbing her arm. The hearth was dying down, the last embers glowing in their final farewell. She fetched another log, tossing it atop, and pumping the bellows a few times until it caught.

It made no difference in this icy-cold room. Why had she ever opened the window in the first place?

Lark's blood froze as the thought slammed her still.

She hadn't opened the window.

Ferryn or Inerys might have, but it was unlikely. Not without shaking her awake to scold her for sleeping in the chair.

Hugo's knife was in her hands before she could allow her mind to spin enough logic to calm her suspicions. It seemed these days, the first instinct of fear was the body's quest for survival.

Shadows darkened the hall, only a sliver of moonlight illuminating Lark's steps. She edged quietly along, her heart battering against her ribs. If it was a mindless beast, there would have been sounds of a struggle. It wouldn't have bypassed her and Gavriel.

But a calculated maneuver?

Aislinn wasn't here, but that didn't mean her hunter hadn't come looking.

Lark tiptoed along, grateful for once that Inerys insisted on everyone removing their shoes upon entry. The old floors threatened to creak, and Lark held her breath. If she didn't have the advantage of knowing where the threat was located, she wouldn't grant them the courtesy of knowing where she was.

The door to Ferryn's room sat ajar, a shard of light at the end of the hall. Lark crept along, her pulse pounding in her head. *It was probably nothing. He would be fine.*

She pushed the door open, and the groan of rusted hinges was far too loud in the silent cottage. Ferryn lay on his back, one arm thrown over his head, the other resting on his stomach. His blond hair fanned across his pillow, his face softened by sleep as he quietly snored.

Relief flooded Lark in a staggering current. She was being ridiculous. Existing on what felt like the edge of a blade had done a number on her thoughts. Relaxing earlier, taking a breather and letting her guard down, it had felt like opening the door to all she'd desperately fought to keep out. But it was nothing. Another night like any other.

The echo of shattering glass rang from the kitchen, swiftly proving her wrong.

Inerys.

Ferryn jolted awake, wiping his mouth. "Wha—"

Lark placed a finger against his lips, shaking her head. The Reaper Blade... where was the Reaper Blade? She felt underneath the bed, exhaling a sigh of relief when her fingers closed around it. What a foolish and fortunate hiding place.

Another glass shattered. This time, a cry rang out.

Lark sprinted down the hall, tripping over her feet as she tumbled down the narrow winding stairs.

Bloody footprints led across the floor, and shards of glass glimmered like rubies in each tendril of moonlight spilling through the windows. Lark swept over them, avoiding the worst of it, but a sharp prick in her heel proved she hadn't been careful enough.

The kitchen was in disastrous ruin. Pots and pans across the floor, broken glass and bloody hand and footprints. Vials crushed against the countertops. Dirt strewn about, herbs ripped from the roots.

A gust of wind moaned through the open door, a cacophony of voices crying their lament. Lark sprinted into the night, ignoring the bite of cold against the bottoms of her torn feet. More voices. Of rage. Of pain. They called out from the darkness.

And Lark followed.

Streaks of blood marred the snow, like someone had dragged a wounded animal. Ice and frozen twigs snapped at Lark's bloody steps. She staggered, the pain and numbing cold stealing the breath from her lungs. She should have grabbed her boots, but there was no time to turn back now. Pressing on, each step was more painful than the last. Like sharp blades lined the forest floor.

Like she was taking her first steps as a human, once more.

From a distance, Ferryn called her name. It was a sound of fear, of desperation. Still, she followed the bloody tracks in the snow, adding her own to the mix. And she listened. Listened for any sign of Inerys.

The lone moon shone her light through barren branches, through spindly limbs frozen in winter. In time. The wind blew, and they clawed at the moon as if desperate to reach something, anything, to restore life to their limbs.

The voices grew louder, closer.

Lark winced at the growing pain in her ruined feet and crouched down to get a closer look. Through the bracken, through the naked branches, two figures came into view.

A man, tall and broad, had a hand twisted in Inerys' hair, the other holding her arm behind her back. The bottoms of Inerys' bloody feet glistened in the snow, and she was held immobile on her knees, facing away. He pulled Inerys' head back to look up at him.

"Here marks the edge of your protection spell, witch." His voice was pure venom and malice. "You know what happens if we take a few more steps. Tell me where the girl went."

"Fuck you." Inerys spat in his face.

"You are not what I came for, but I will suffer no regret in your death save for this: It's not your time."

"Stop talking. I'd rather die than be subjected to your platitudes a moment longer."

He sighed, a defeated sound. "Have it your way."

"Wait!" Lark staggered toward them. Rivers of blood trailed down Inerys' face. Her free hand sat mangled and useless cradled against her chest, like he'd crushed the bones to prevent her from casting. "You left the rest of us alive. Why?"

He was unremarkable, for a paragon. An ordinary man standing before her, his face haggard by his weary expression. "Fortunately for you, I am not here to eradicate the humans protecting the somniavi." He glared down at Inerys. "But it's my misfortune I can't locate her unless she uses her abilities. A fact you must have told her."

Inerys laughed, blood coating her teeth. "You'll never find her. She's too smart for you. You bloated, overgrown cow masquerading as a god. You are nothing more than an echo of a fool's hope. And I will dance my joy under the moon when she rains down your destruction."

Lark gritted her teeth. Aislinn's hunter, Merikh, she had called him, had shown his violence already, calling it mercy. He did not deserve respect, but it was easier to tread lightly when one didn't stomp out their angry words. It was unnerving to have the tables turned as such— Inerys in her foolhardy pursuit to anger the paragon, Lark the voice of reason. "Let Inerys go. Show us you mean no harm."

"Lark, no." Inerys cut her a disapproving glare, half hidden by shadow and the other brightly illuminated in silver moonlight.

Did Inerys really think she would give Aislinn up?

"The witch is the reason our discussion has taken an unfortunate turn." The man tightened his hold, pulling a hiss from Inerys' lips. "And your poorly veiled manipulations will not work on me. Tell me where the somniavi went before I lose my patience."

This was him being patient?

"We will never let you have her. But you already knew that." Lark pulled the Reaper Blade from its sheath, reveling in the violent song it sang with a metallic *ring*. "You're welcome to try your negotiation tactics on me."

A muscle feathered in his jaw. "You possess a Reaper Blade, but can you wield it?"

"Come and find out."

As if she weighed nothing, he tossed Inerys several feet, well over the boundary of her protection spell. Her head hit the bottom of a frozen tree trunk with a hard *thunk*, and she didn't move.

"I have not engaged in a duel in many lifetimes," he said as he unfastened his cloak, letting it billow to the snow. "Etiquette dictates we share our names so we might alert loved ones of our opponent's demise." He smiled, a sharp and dangerous thing. "My kin are out of your reach."

"I wouldn't be too sure." Lark swung the blade, wishing she had worn her boots despite Inerys' house rules. "You think I never ventured to Avalon for inability? No one cares for you or your kin anymore, Merikh."

His eyes widened at the use of his name. If Lark could make him feel vulnerable, perhaps he would be.

"What are you?" He pulled a simple looking blade from his belt, small and unassuming. An ancient forge with the head of a raven as the pommel.

"I'm a mere human." Lark couldn't halt the smile that stretched across her mouth at the complicated truth of that statement. "Think you can best me?"

Merikh glared at her. "The hubris of humans will always be their downfall." He struck with such speed, Lark stumbled to block his blow. His strength shook the Reaper Blade in her hands. She spun his sword away, counter-striking with a slash against his thigh. It was a shallow, negligible thing, but a message.

He gaped at her, true shock splashing across his face. "You are... a passenger?" His shock melted into something calculating.

Lark slashed again, quicker, deeper. He was half engaged in their fight, blocking with a distracted look on his face, but she gave him everything she had. Another gash in his chest, he bled like a human. But even preoccupied as he was, his strength was too much for her. Another jab, a slash, his skin parted to reveal vulnerability. She could kill him with this blade, if she pressed hard, pushed him further on defensive, if he would stop blocking the strongest of her attacks. But he met her worst strikes, watching her with an indecisive expression. Like he was sorting out what to do with her.

He'd underestimated her, and she would press that advantage.

Lark spread her awareness out to reach for his soul. A quick rewrite of his strength should do the trick—

She hit a wall of iron. Impenetrable. Unbreachable. Lark tried to retreat, tugging her awareness to her, but another wall hit her back. Her power was trapped within his soul.

Panic flooded her body, making her muscles shake. She could still fight him with half her soul in her body. She raised her trembling blade, the cold biting into her feet with a vengeance. She had nothing to block the pain, to push through it. Sinking to her knees, Lark choked on her breaths, rapid and shallow.

No. It couldn't end like this. Not while Gavriel was still trapped. Not while everything hung in the balance.

"It's interesting." Merikh's voice rang out. "I've never met a human Reaper before. That's what you are, isn't it?" He crouched down, and Lark took another swipe at him, her sword heavy, weighing down her limbs in a way it never had before. "We let the Otherworld conduct their own affairs for too long, to languish with impunity. And chaos has ascended."

Lark's sword was ripped away, and her hands bound behind her back. She kicked, falling sideways in the snow. Cold bit into her temple, and Inerys came into view. The witch slowly blinked awake, rubbing her head. When she caught Lark's eyes, panic transformed her features.

"I don't care what happens to you or to the humans. That's not my fight." Merikh hoisted Lark over his shoulder, and the world spun along with her stomach. "But you might prove useful in hunting my true prey."

"Lark…" Inerys groaned. And somewhere in the distance, Ferryn's voice rang out.

And then darkness.

CHAPTER TWENTY-SEVEN

GAVRIEL

*S*omething strange was happening. Gavriel felt it in his bones. In the blood pulsing through his veins. Something pulled, tugging at him, like that of the sensation of hovering over the rail of a ship, staring down the choppy water as his stomach flipped. He was at the edge of a cliff, the precipice of change. The turning of the season, the first light of a new day.

He was…

Bound.

No, not bound.

Stiff.

Paralyzed.

His muscles were locked in place, frozen and unmoving. He tried to stretch, and only a tingle at the very tips of his toes answered. He opened his mouth to call out—

No sound answered from his dry throat. Even the cough that ripped through his chest was a dusty rush of air.

Where was he? What had happened to his body? Where was Lark?

Gavriel wrestled against heavy, immovable limbs, fighting to free his body from whatever invisible pressure weighed it down. It was like the night terrors Emric used to face, the way his body would remain in a slumber paralysis while his mind carried images of his nightmares to the waking world. Gavriel had found him on more than one occasion, unmoving, his terror shown in the way his throat would try to scream against a sealed mouth. It was horrifying to witness until he'd realized what was happening. That it was as simple as the muscles locked in his body during rest had yet to unlock.

That was what it felt like now. Almost as if his mind had awakened faster than his body—

Awakened.

Memories flooded him in a torrential current. Of Lark's beautiful face above him, tears trailing down her cheeks, and then darkness. Nereida's spell. She'd cursed him with every memory his soul had ever perceived, and his body shut down, protecting his mind as he pieced it all together.

And he had.

Lifetimes of memories. People he had been. He'd lived and died many times before this life. And he remembered *everything.* He remembered searching each life for something he couldn't decipher. A word, a name, a face he couldn't envision.

And it was always her.

Lark.

He'd lost her once, lifetimes ago, and that loss had echoed in every single body he had inhabited. Until now.

Visions of her face, her smile, her laugh, her joy and her sorrow— they flashed in his mind. Flipping to the next too quickly for him to keep up. Gavriel fought against the stiffness running down the length of his spine, searching for the strength to *just fucking move.*

A twitch. A pulse. A ghost of movement, vanishing before taking shape.

Lark was out there, somewhere. Gavriel had to find her.

His words from countless lifetimes ago echoed in the back of his mind.

Death is not the end. I will find you again.

A growl rumbled from his chest as he forced life back into dormant muscles. Nereida's cursed magic must have frozen his body in place, keeping him alive for... how long was he under?

Spit flew from his lips as he pushed against an immovable wall of stone. Sweat broke out along his brow, dripping into his eyes with a spiteful sting, and still he pushed. He pushed past the limits of his body, as he'd learned to again and again.

Slowly, so slowly, he began to rise until he was upright in an unfamiliar bed. Panting, he collapsed against the iron wrought headboard, keeping himself up while resting his body from the onslaught. The narrow spindles dug into his shoulder blades, a grounding reminder that he was finally awake.

The first rays of dawn leaked through the window, an ominous red sky lurking beyond.

Red skies in the morn, sailors be warned.

If a storm was coming, Gavriel would brace himself for it.

As he caught his breath, he took stock of what he knew, or what he thought he knew. The last time he'd seen Lark, they were in the Twisted Woods. Nereida had appeared with Thanar and others Gavriel barely recalled. Thanar had fallen... and so had the veil. Thanar had been the anchor, the tether between worlds, and they'd stepped right into Nereida's trap. She had organized everyone's part as if she were a soothsayer, not like the charlatans at the solstice fairs when he was a child, but a skilled seer into the future of all she manipulated. That her schemes promised to spill all matter of danger into the world.

And Lark had been left to face this without him.

Gavriel grunted, lifting his breeches at each leg and dropping his feet against the icy floor. His toes caught a porcelain plate, sending a blackened piece of bread rolling onto the floor. Was it placed there recently? He staggered into a standing position, nearly tumbling back into the bed. This would be difficult, but it was mind over matter. Hopefully.

His legs were weak, barely able to remain straight without buckling, so he scrabbled against the bedpost, the chair, the walls, the door. Inching and staggering toward the hall. Each step threatened to send him careening to the floor, but he endured. It was similar to the time he ingested Kovalian truffles laced with curare. A toxin designed to paralyze its victims. He'd staggered his way back to his room and vomited the rest out. A lesson learned on sneaking sweets from Master Hamlin's desk.

Ugh. What he wouldn't give for a piece of his dark chocolate right now. His stomach rumbled in response. He would find Lark, ascertain her wellbeing, and then find some sustenance.

With each labored step forward, a sense of optimism bloomed in him. Lark had obviously seen him well-cared for if he'd awoken to such accommodations. She had her crew of trusted allies surrounding her when he'd fallen. Daciana, for one, would never let any harm come to her. He focused on that thought, on the strength of resolve behind it, as he shuffled his weak body forward. Yes, Lark was all right, she had to be, and when he finally laid eyes on her, any fear he harbored would vanish. They could conquer impossible odds against a goddess bent on their destruction so long as they did it together.

Or they would burn in a blaze of fiery glory, still, together.

His optimism wasn't working correctly.

The top of the winding stairs greeted him. Perhaps he could just fling himself down the stairs and aim for the least amount of damage.

No. He could do this. If he could endure monotonous hours of lecture and theory, followed by exhausting his young body with endless drills and training, and still end the day in hours of fiddle practice, he could do this.

Although he wasn't that young recruit anymore. He'd never felt older than he did right now. Perhaps folding every lifetime upon his mind like an accordion made his body feel the ages. Or it was the act of hobbling down these skies-forsaken stairs. One step at a time, slow and steady. He greeted each landing with a treasured thought or memory. Lark singing to the frightened children in the cellar. Lark making him chase her across their master's land. Lark binding her life and soul to his, with nothing more than a string on her finger since indentures couldn't own possessions. Memories he hadn't known he cherished, hadn't known he missed, they were his once more.

But there were more, from this life that he would not squander by looking for what he lost in the past.

Lark in the rain. Lark running into his arms in that ridiculous bard costume. Lark gasping her pleasure in his arms, her knees falling open—

Heat burned through him, traveling south. Well, at least that part was awake.

The final step disappeared from beneath his unsteady feet, and Gavriel wanted to cheer. He'd made it down the stairs.

The space was familiar. Leaves and vines and books overcrowding every surface. Tree trunks growing out of walls, as if the cottage was reverting back to the forest it was always meant to be.

Inerys' home.

Gavriel staggered to the window, reaching for the curtain—

He winced, sharp pain searching through his heel. He glanced down.

Blood and glass covered the floor. Toppled end tables lied precariously on their sides. Scattered pages littered the room, red staining their edges. Someone's blood. Gavriel's pulse jumped, a rushing sound filling his ears.

Where in the fucking void was Lark?

The door burst open, a snow-covered figure half-dragging a bloody Inerys through.

Gavriel hobbled to them, his steps coming easier now.

The man—Ferryn, that was his name—appraised Gavriel with wide eyes. "You're awake."

"Where's Lark?" There was no time for explanations he couldn't give. No time to ask what happened. He would assess the damage after he knew she was safe. Why hadn't he awakened sooner? He could have helped—he could have done something other than hobble around in the aftermath trying to catch up.

Why weren't they answering him?

"Where is she?" Gavriel's voice rose, anger heightening his senses.

"He took her," Inerys rasped out. Dried blood coated her hair, her forehead. She wore a simple shift, and her face contorted in pain.

Clutching her hand close to her chest, her fingers were bent at odd angles. "I couldn't stop him." She coughed, a wet bloody sound.

Gavriel's head spun, the walls closing in. The pounding in his head grew deafening, a steady beat that drowned out whatever Ferryn was saying. Whatever comfort or explanation he thought to give. It didn't matter because he was useless, barely upright while the only person who mattered was gone. Taken.

He didn't let death stop him before. He wouldn't let anything else stand in his way.

Gavriel stumbled back until his legs hit a chair, sinking into it and pinching the bridge of his nose. "Tell me everything. Don't leave a fucking thing out. Who has her, and where is she?"

Deep breaths. He would find her. He'd found her once, and he would do so again. Nothing would keep them apart.

Nothing.

CHAPTER TWENTY-EIGHT

AISLINN

"*W*ell?"

Aislinn's throat had gone dry, her vision blurring. She blinked away her unshed tears, swallowing down the sob that threatened to escape from her chest.

Her mother stood before her, unchanged save for the severe expression she wore. Aislinn had hardly ever been on the receiving end of that look, and never had the lines in her face seemed etched so deep. Her green eyes Aislinn had inherited narrowed in suspicion. Her blonde hair more white than gold. Aislinn always recalled her mother's warrior physique, thick arms and sturdy build, but standing before her now, she appeared smaller. Not frail—Aislinn could never think of her strong, proud mother as such—but just… less of her.

Like grief had eaten away at her, leaving only the ghost of her memory.

"I was hoping you could tell me a little bit about the area," Aislinn spat the words out, unsure what lie she was spinning. Her stomach rolled with the turning of her thoughts. How her mother still held an arrow trained to strike.

How she didn't recognize her at all.

"You waltzed up to a stranger's home after dark to enquire for directions?"

"Not exactly." Aislinn cleared her throat, not daring to glance Daciana's way. Not daring to allow her gaze to leave her mother's face. "I used to live here... some time ago."

Her mother relaxed her stance, barely lowering her bow. "You aren't Aalis' girl, are you? Isabeau?"

Aislinn exhaled a sigh of relief. Isabeau was a few years older than she, a childhood friend. When her mother caught her father with a serving girl from the tavern, she'd whisked her away, only stopping by to bid farewell to Aislinn's mother. Isabeau had cried into Aislinn's shoulder, soaking her nightgown. Aalis promised to visit after things had settled, but they never did return.

Isabeau's father drank himself to death years ago.

"It's been a long time," Aislinn said softly.

"Paragon's tits, get in here!" Her mother dragged her forward, her bow and arrow clattering to the floor, and she pulled Aislinn into a breath stealing hug. Aislinn sank into it, letting her mother's comforting scent, peppermint and devil's claw, envelop her. She used to have Aislinn help her prepare tinctures to alleviate her chronic pain. Did she have anyone to help her now?

"It's good to see you. How's your mama?" Her mother clapped her on the back and stepped aside. "Come in and introduce me to your friend here."

Daciana smoothly took Aislinn's arm, guiding her over the threshold.

"My mother, ah, she doesn't know I'm here." It was true enough.

"Can't say I'm surprised. But so long as she's well?"

"She is, thank you." Aislinn had no idea if Aalis was still alive, and the lie was bitter on her tongue. Her mother was still waiting for her to introduce Daciana, and Aislinn couldn't feel her legs "This is Daciana. She's a bounty collector." Daciana raised a brow in her direction, but they were already lying about too much for Aislinn to consider spinning some sort of tale. Besides, anyone at the tavern who got a good look at Daciana or Kenna would know there was something dangerous about them.

"It's a good thing I didn't do anything to warrant your attention," Aislinn's mother said with a smirk.

"Not that kind of bounty," Daciana said smoothly. "Less exciting than all that. More of odd jobs needing to be done. I like to travel, and the work keeps me busy."

"No doubt. Any town you go, there are never enough hands to get shit done."

Had they fallen on hard times? When Aislinn was last here, Meadowhedge was a bustling source of trade, Frederick's family supplying nearly half the jobs in town. His father owned a string of businesses, all rented out for a fair price, and his uncle owned the farmlands nearby.

But perhaps monsters had found their way here, too.

"Yera would have loved to see you, but she doesn't come this way often."

At the sound of her sister's name, Aislinn's heart hammered in her throat. "Yera! Oh, I wish I'd had the chance to see her." Her throat had gone all scratchy again.

"With the little one on the way, you can't blame her for not traveling. But even still, it's hard for her to come back with... everything that happened. I'll send word of your visit. Maybe another time your paths will cross."

Daciana smiled. "It's our fault. Sorry to surprise you like this."

"Not at all, not at all. Isabeau is always welcome home."

The breath in Aislinn's lungs constricted. Her mother was still speaking, but it was as if she'd been plunged underwater, only muffled hints of her voice breaking through. Her sister was pregnant. She was going to be an aunt. An aunt who'd never know her niece or nephew. So many things taken from her. Her life. Her face. Her home.

Home.

Aislinn would never know home again. Not if her own mother couldn't recognize her. Inerys had warned her of this, how the human heart and mind can only take so much. How grieving the loss of a loved one, especially a child, would forever alter a person. How returning to the mortal realm the way she did wasn't the same as extending her life. Her mother had long since buried and grieved her, her eyes would not allow Aislinn's face to appear, even standing before her.

"Excuse me," Aislinn said, interrupting whatever pleasantries they'd been exchanging. Daciana and her mother turned, a mixture of confusion and alarm on their faces. "I need... the privy. For just a moment."

"Out back." Her mother jutted a thumb over her shoulder. "You remember the way."

Of course she did. Aislinn could traverse this house robbed of sight, sound, and sensation. She knew every floorboard, every hole in the walls she and Yera had made while playing, every twist and turn in a home she once thought cramped—too small to house her dreams. And now?

It was everything.

Memories assaulted her as she crept through the sitting area. Her mother reading to her by the fire, running her hands through her hair. The worn chair that belonged to Father. No one was permitted to sit there. Through the kitchen where she'd caused a fire on more than one occasion trying out recipes. The bucket hanging on the wall that Mother insisted be filled with water whenever Aislinn was cooking after the third fire.

Aislinn stilled, the back door waiting to grant her reprieve from the emotions clogging her throat. Along the frame, notches and notes marred the wood. Extending from knee high to Aislinn's height.

—*Aislinn's seventh summer*

—*Yera's first archery competition*

—*Aislinn's first kiss*

Her mother hadn't been pleased when Yera scratched that one in.

—*Yera's first day of work*

A watery smile spread across Aislinn's face at the memory. How Yera had groaned and groused while their mother made her hold still long enough to mark her first day of serving at the tavern.

—*Yera's last day of work*

A sound somewhere between a laugh and a sob broke free from Aislinn's chest as she stared at the notch directly across from it. Yera had lasted all of one day before mouthing off to a customer. It was the day Frederick saw her. He showed up at their home, a handful of wild-flowers, and asked to see the girl who could eviscerate a man with her words alone. The tongue-lashing Yera served him with did nothing to detract his interest, and by summer, they were pledged to be married.

—*Yera's wedding day*

Aislinn ran her fingertips along the tallest notch in the wood. Her final height marked alongside Yera's.

—*Aislinn on Yera's wedding day*

It was the last day of Aislinn's life. The last day that childish whims could seem so important. The last day her mother and sister ever saw her alive.

The words were carved deeper than the others. Like someone had dug their knife into each letter again and again. Aislinn ran her finger along every letter, tracing the last measurement of her height. The embodiment of her life. The end of it all.

Only it wasn't the end. Not really.

"I assume you heard about Aislinn."

Aislinn jolted, spinning around to face her mother's voice. Her mother leaned against the doorway, arms crossed, mouth downturned. "We got our vengeance on her killer, trust me on that, that boy suffered greatly before he was finally put down." There was no satisfaction in her voice. Only a flat delivery of fact. "It didn't matter though, did it? Didn't bring my little girl back." Her mother ran the back of her hand under her nose, blinking away any evidence of tears. "You remind me a lot of her, you know. You and Aislinn were always so close. Seeing you now, it's like having a piece of her here with me."

Aislinn's breath caught in her chest, a shaky sort of hope blooming. "What if part of her still is here?" Her voice cracked.

Her mother tilted her head to the side, examining her. "How do you mean?"

"What if…" Aislinn took a step toward her. *See me. Please, mama, see me.* "What if she's closer than you think. Close enough to look in on you. To wonder if you're all right."

Her mother's face froze, her body going utterly still.

Aislinn continued, "What if she wondered... if you knew how much she loves you. That she thinks of you every day and wishes more than anything for one more chance to speak to you. To tell you she's fine. That even though she feels her loss, deeper on some days than others, that she's found a way to even smile again. A purpose to strive for. That even though her life was cut short, she lives on in so many other ways."

Her mother's chin trembled, eyes blinking rapidly.

Aislinn's tears trailed down her cheeks as she continued, "What if she wanted to tell you... that you were the best mama in the whole world. And even though she left you too soon, she carries you with her. Always."

"Gods," her mother gasped, a hand coming to rest on her chest while her other one rubbed her eyes. "You trying to make an old crone cry or something?"

"You're not a crone." Aislinn laughed, taking her hand and lacing their fingers. "You're beautiful."

Her mother wiped frantically at her eyes, clearing her throat a few times. She squeezed Aislinn's hand. "I hope my girl isn't lingering around here. I hope she's found peace, so much damn peace she's near forgotten about me. That she has endless time for her books and her daydreams. Spends her days lazing by the riverbank—" Her mother's face shuttered, agony slicing through her expression. "That fucker... he got better than what he deserved." She shook her head, giving Aislinn's hand another squeeze and pressing a brief kiss to her knuckles. "I just want Aislinn to be happy. Happy and carefree. I'll join her and her father someday."

It carved a new wound in Aislinn's chest, hearing her mother's wish, and she abandoned the notion that she might plant the seed of thought. That her mother might sense her here, before her, holding her hand and begging her to see her.

With forced lightness, she said, "You have quite a few years left in you, *Grandma*."

Her mother laughed, dropping her hand, and Aislinn wanted to snatch it back. "I've already started carving the little one's first bow. He or she will be shooting before they're walking if I have anything to say about it."

Aislinn laughed, wiping her face and trying not to feel the way her heart cracked. It was a joy to hear her mother talk of such things, that hope can spring anew after so much darkness. But her joy was etched with fissures of pain. Why did happiness hurt so?

"And you, my dear girl, thank you for coming to see me. My door is always open to you." They started back for the sitting room. "Maybe we can plan a visit sometime. You can come visit Yera with me."

"I'd like that."

Her mother paused, her features tightening as if in concentration. "I just wanted to say one last thing. Will you indulge this old woman who hasn't had occasion to lecture any daughters in some time?" She caught Aislinn's eye, staring right into her as if she could see straight into her soul. "You can never lose your home. Not so long as you have memories and the strength to carry them. Home is a feeling, a sense of safety and belonging. And no matter where life takes you, my dear girl, you will always have a home with me."

Aislinn's knees threatened to buckle as a long-buried conversation rising to the surface of her mind.

It was on the eve of Yera's wedding, and Aislinn had grown weary of being dragged to so many events. She'd begged her mother to let her skip the prelude feast. A feast in honor of a wedding to be held the very next day. It seemed wasteful and unimportant. Aislinn had had enough of forced socializing and had pleaded with her mother to let her disappear for a few hours, just to refill her energy. Her mother had declined, reminding her of how important these festivities were. That her sister was who they were celebrating, and she could set aside her preference of solitude for another few days.

Harsh words were exchanged. One of the last conversations, an argument, they'd ever shared.

"I shouldn't have bothered asking. You wouldn't have noticed my absence anyway."

"That isn't true."

"It is! I barely exist anymore. I could leave tomorrow, run far away from here, and you'd never even realize I was gone."

"Enough, Aislinn."

"No! This isn't even my home anymore. It's a shrine to Yera. Your perfect daughter with her perfect life, marrying the perfect husband, while I'm cast aside. You filled my room with larkspurs and ranunculus!"

"We needed a place to store the bouquets!"

"As soon as I'm able, I'm gone. You won't have to deal with me anymore."

"Listen here"—her mother had gripped her shoulder—*"you can hate me. That's fine. Yell and scream and cry if it makes you feel better. But this is temporary. Yera is leaving us, and the sooner you accept that, the better."*

"That's not what this—"

"I wasn't finished. Your sister loves you, Aislinn. She loves you so much. I know things are changing, and I know it's scary. But you will not lose her, and you certainly will never lose me."

Her mother's words had ripped through her poorly crafted shroud of denial. It was easy to find anger in little tangible things. But what she felt was too big to name or feel without falling apart. And suddenly, her anger was too difficult to maintain. It floated away leaving a cold despair behind. *"What if she forgets us? What if I'm not enough for you? What if she leaves and never comes home?"*

"My darling." Her mother had bundled her into her arms, holding her as if she were still a child. *"No matter where you girls go, following your feet to wherever life takes you, you will never lose each other. Never lose your home. Memories and the strength to carry them are the truest home you'll ever know. Both of you will do great things, and I'm so proud of you. How could you not be enough? Aislinn, you are everything and more."*

Aislinn had wiped frantically at her eyes, smudging the kohl her *sister had drawn to create a dramatic effect. "You don't need to say that. I know how quiet the house will be without Yera." She'd already felt her absence in recent days. The days of wedding and feast planning that tugged her bright and vibrant sister away most hours. The quiet was heavy.*

"What did your father always say?" Her mother carded her fingers through Aislinn's hair, a grounding touch.

Aislinn huffed a wet laugh. "That I have a sky full of stars in me. That the world is waiting for me to spread their light." It had been the way he concluded her favored story, the one about the girl made of stardust.

Yera was the sun and she the stars. No one could see the stars when the sun was out, but it didn't make them any less beautiful.

"That's right," her mother had said, "You are a wondrous person full of so much light. I cannot wait to see all you do with the life you have. But no matter what, you, my dear girl, will always have a home with me."

Aislinn choked back her sob as her mother led the way back to where Daciana was waiting. Her words echoing in her mind, filling all the cracks in her heart.

Somewhere, deep down, her mother must know it was her.

And it was enough.

CHAPTER TWENTY-NINE

LANGFORD

The gentle lapping of waves against the ship filled the small cabin, and the soft whistle of Alistair's snores came into focus. Langford smiled, stretching carefully so as not to disturb him, and glanced over at the man fast asleep in his bed. Alistair was always a thing of beauty, his perfectly chiseled jaw dusted in a rakish hint of a beard. His long dark lashes rested against the slight swell of his bronze cheek, and a lock of black hair had fallen over his forehead.

Langford sighed, taking a moment in the quiet to really observe him. The small scar above his brow. The full pout of his lips softened by sleep. And if he opened his eyes, the bright shade of green, brighter than the bottles of sleeping tonic Langford used to fabricate under the watchful eye of his university professor, would peer back at him. But it wasn't Alistair's face that Langford cherished, nor his body as Alistair liked to tease was his greatest asset.

No, it was Alistair's foolhardy passion for the things that mattered to him. His indelible focus on what one could call selfish pursuits. There was a loyalty that ran deep within the man, deeper than any person Langford had ever known. It made Alistair operate in the greyest shades of morality.

Because his loyalty ran deeper than earthly ideals.

And if that wasn't enough—it was enough, Langford had years of one-sided pining to be certain—Alistair had proven himself to be the most caring individual he'd ever met. That loyalty only fueled his passion and focus on Langford, and the man who'd once spent his days whoring and drinking, now spent his time and energy caring for him. Some of the sharpness of his observational skill had returned to him, and he seemed more the man Langford met that fateful day. The day Langford walked an unknown road, cold and alone, only to be found by the one he'd never known he needed. Alistair had a keen eye where Langford was concerned, sensing every shift in his mood. Sometimes before Langford could even give thought to it.

It was an overwhelming thing, feeling treasured. Like Langford was something special and worthy of protection. Like Alistair was ready to leap in front of a blade at any moment to keep him from harm.

That familiar clutch in his chest answered the thought.

As treasured as Langford felt, it was a drop in the bucket compared to how much Alistair mattered to him. He'd lost him once already, he knew the deep gut ripping wound it carved. And no amount of sutures or tonics or tinctures would remedy such a pain. One would think, having faced the worst pain and fear imaginable, there was nothing left to fear. But for Langford, it meant he knew exactly what to fear.

His stomach balled in a knot, twisting and turning like a corkscrew.

Alistair was alive. *He was alive.* So why did Langford continually battle these thoughts?

A rumble came from Alistair's chest. Without opening his eyes, he reached a hand to run up Langford's side, settling at the back of his neck. "C'mere." He tugged him into the safety of his arms, wrapping his whole body around him as if he could shield him from the turn of his thoughts.

Langford pressed his ear against the firm plane of Alistair's chest, and squeezed his eyes shut, breathing in his familiar scent of vanilla and spices of his favored rum. His breath slowed, a calm settling over him as the fiery warmth of Alistair's body against his own spread through him, shoving the chill away.

"I'm here," Alistair murmured against the top of Langford's head. Even in sleep, he always knew what he needed.

But there were yet unanswered questions. And that familiar itching at the back of Langford's mind took root. Why had the tonic Kenna gave Alistar proven its efficacy? Langford could appreciate the unpredictability of chance as much as the next person... well, perhaps not quite as much, but even in the medical field there were bound to be unexplained happenstances. One worked hard to decipher and distinguish variables to aid in understanding, but nothing was stamped with a perfect guarantee.

But a modicum of understanding would help.

Alistair hadn't responded to any of Langford's remedies, an injury beyond human capability and all that, but Kenna's practices were... there was no earthly reason for her tonic to work while his did not. Everything had an answer, even if it currently eluded rational thinking. So, if it wasn't a logical reason or explanation, it was a fantastical reason or explanation. Ugh. He might as well call it what it was.

Magic.

A headache began to throb behind Langford's eyes.

Langford used to think magic fell into two categories of human understanding: Religious connotations and superstitions of the faithful, or a mere leap in knowledge, the bridge of advancement between current understanding and future endeavors. In any case, absence of fact.

Now he knew better. He'd witnessed impossible feats many times over.

But to observe the human body failing to respond to attempts to cleanse a wound of infection? To witness dozens of humans change into monsters right before his eyes? To rely on a practice unfounded by rational thinking and rooted in traditions of a culture he knew nothing of until mere months ago?

Too many unanswered questions.

Gently, Langford extricated himself from Alistair's arms, snorting at the grumble of protest he received. Through the small window, thick clouds buried the moon. Even concealed as it was, the brightness of its light hinted at its strength.

Had it really been a month?

The stale scent of the cabin, wet sawdust and mildew, made it hard to think. Langford stood and opened the window, only needing to reach a few extra inches in the cramped room. The round window squeaked open, the fresh smell of brine carrying on the wind. The breeze tussled Langford's hair, sending tingles across his scalp, and he inhaled deeply.

It would be all right.

He glanced around the cabin, taking in the limited quarters. The bed was small, but even in a large space, Alistair always wrapped himself around Langford throughout the throes of sleep. The end table and modest desk were secured to the floor, the latter brought on board by Alistair, as well as nailed down by him. He'd insisted Langford needed it for vital research, and Captain Ingemar only threatened him a little.

It was all so familiar. Like they were facing the same trials under different names. One day, they would break the cycle and settle down the way Alistair promised.

Warmth bloomed through Langford at the thought. It was something less rational than worrying but far more significant.

Hope.

Perhaps a little hope is what he'd been missing all along.

Langford bent down to retrieve his book, the one Alistair had whispered scandalous lines from in his ear after he'd fallen asleep, rousing him to wake under his hungry gaze. He closed it with a soft *thud* and placed it gently on the end table.

One day, he'd have a library full of books. His very own study. A workstation for research and experiments and learning new ways to understand this strange world. Alistair would never be caught without Langford's usefulness again and he'd strive to answer all those pesky questions.

There was that hope again.

Maybe he was being a touch greedy with it. But dreams were

meant to be, weren't they? In the dead of night, when all around him slumbered, he could be a voracious dreamer.

A harsh gale blew, whipping through the open window and drowning out the sound of Alistair's snores. The clouds parted, and the full moon shifted into view, bright and beaming, ripples of silvery light flooding the room.

Langford was a man of logic, of rational thought, and his sensible mind did not recognize unearthly signs. There were patterns of behavior and observable outcomes.

But gods, maybe this was a sign that his hope was substantiated.

Another gust of wind skirted through the window. The hinges groaned against the onslaught, and the sea grew choppy below, crashing against the side of the ship with an angered violence.

Movement skirted along the edge of his periphery. A flutter of a coverlet. A flash of skin. Langford turned—

The covers had fallen away from Alistair's body, his muscular torso distended in an unnatural way. His back had arched, an extreme bend to his midsection as if pulled by an invisible string.

The hairs on the back of Langford's neck stood on end, and ice poured through his legs.

Alistair's breath quickened, a rapid rise and fall of his chest. Harsh. Fast. Too fast. A growl edging every exhale. It was as if he—

Crack.

Alistair's back bowed, deeper still, a series of cracks fracturing the silence of the room. He fell back to the bed, arms and legs twisting. A guttural sound reverberated from his chest.

And Langford couldn't move. Couldn't think. Couldn't breathe. Nothing existed outside of his terror. This frozen weight holding him utterly still. There was no scream in his throat. No strength in his muscles to run. Nothing but cold.

Horrible, paralyzing cold.

CHAPTER THIRTY

LANGFORD

*A*listair rolled off the bed, his body juddering against the floor. The hard thud of his head against the wood a constant percussion. Something pulsed beneath his skin. Pressing and stretching, his arms and legs thickening, his lean but muscular build filling out and growing larger, larger still. What was happening? What was happening? What was—

Langford cried out, the first sound finally slipping from his lips, and it broke the spell on his legs. He ran to Alistair's side and sank to his knees.

Langford's hands were steady as he assessed his vitals, feeling for his pulse. It raced beneath his touch, far too quick for a human's heart. Alistair lifted one eyelid, and instead of green, a bright glowing yellow peered back at him.

Langford flinched back, dropping his hands away.

Alistair was… he…

Alistair rolled to his side. Blood and spit flew in droplets as Alistair seized, shaking and growling, *and what the ever-loving fuck was he supposed to do to help him?*

Langford threw himself toward his desk, where his pack sat. He dumped it out, supplies, tinctures, and loose pages spilling across the

200

floor. There was no time. *No time.* He needed to think. To decide. To act. To—

Langford's hand found a small leather satchel. He shoved his finger in, pulling the cord loose. A familiar scent hit his nose. Floral and citrus with a sharp undercurrent.

Hogweed. King's cure-all. More commonly referred to as evening primrose.

And aconite. Wolfsbane.

Kenna's mixture. Langford had wanted to study its properties. To learn from it and assess if it had other uses.

Thank the skies he'd kept it.

Alistair stilled, and the abrupt silence filled the moonlit room. Langford's hand flew to Alistair's pulse, and he exhaled in relief at the steady thrum of his answering heartrate. He pinched the mixture between his fingers, stuffing it into his mouth and spitting it back out to moisten it. Unhygienic. Ghastly, even. The bitter taste lingered, burning against Langford's tongue as he tipped Alistair's mouth open, and shoved it in.

It had to work. It *had* to. Without thought, without time to second-guess, Langford knew what was happening to Alistair.

Those eyes... he'd never forget those eyes.

And if he was wrong... if he was wrong...

A heavy exhale, thick and wet. Another, this time blowing hot breath against Langford's throat as it seeped through the thin material of his tunic. Alistair shifted, slowly blinking his eyes open.

A ring of yellow surrounded his pupils, glowing in the darkness of their room at sea.

Langford swallowed thickly, the action getting stuck in his throat as he waited. Breathless.

Alistair smacked his lips, his face scrunching in disgust. "Why do I taste shit?" He heaved, and a torrent of blood and bile sprang from his lips, splashing onto the floor. He coughed, retching again, a whimper closely following.

What was happening? His body was rejecting it? This wasn't supposed to happen. He wasn't supposed to—

Langford rubbed soothing circles against his back, trying to stifle his own fear. Alistair had not purged the solution back at the inn when Kenna first offered the chance to save him. It had been a peaceful transition, a deep and healing slumber.

Alistair coughed again, wiping his mouth with the back of his hand. "Ugh. Much better." He sat up, eyes still catching the light in a way they never had before. A flash of brightness in the dark. A hint of something... *more*. "Why are you looking at me like that?"

Langford cleared his throat, trying and failing to summon his voice.

Alistair followed his line of sight, landing on the bloody mess on the floor. He paled, his mouth gaping and revealing a smudge of blood lingering in the corner of his lips. "I see," he said, a forced lightness to his tone. "Serves me right for trying to drink the first mate under the table, no?"

Langford's heart clenched, panic heightening his pulse.

It was a lie, and not even a well-crafted one. Alistair had hardly touched his drink, more preoccupied with Langford at dinner. Not to mention the heavy consumption of spirits decidedly did *not* result in a fit of convulsions, exaggerated bodily contortions, nor physical transformations.

And spewing blood. That was a new symptom—a dangerous one at that. In his field of study, there was never a comforting reason for blood's presence in emesis. Could this be credited to Kenna's concoction? Or to Alistair's ailment?

Ailment. Yes. That was something Langford could wrap his head around. That was a problem to fix. To think of it differently was to invite doubt, normally a welcome addition to the practice of diagnosis, but in his own abilities?

It was better to frame this as a problem he could endeavor to fix.

Langford steadied his breathing, focusing on the facts rather than falling prey to the litany of fears scratching against the back of his mind.

"WHAT DID I say when I agreed to ferry you and that asshole against my better judgment?"

Ingemar's beautiful face was twisted in fury, her ruthless reputation as Captain of The Savage Jewel on full display.

Langford sighed. "Technically this is a recent development, not one we intentionally hid from you—"

"I said," she bellowed over him, "don't fuck me in the arse."

Langford winced at her crass assessment of the situation. Though her words verbatim at the time were, *'Don't make me regret this,'* he could see the need for embellishment in the moment. They'd had to ring for help—it wasn't as if they had a mop and bucket in their room to clean the floor—and upon her boatswain's arrival, panic had erupted throughout the crew. Accusations of *plague ship* thrown about without care. Ridiculous. And Langford had said as much, but it hadn't prevented the fear from confining him and Alistair to their room like common criminals.

Well, he supposed they were at that. And it could have been worse. They could have been forced to sleep in the brig. But the walls of their small cabin were ever encroaching. What he once considered a reprieve now felt like a prison sentence.

He'd put the time to good use. Cataloguing everything. Studying Alistair's condition and taking notes. The rings of gold around his pupils remained, prompting Langford to test a working theory regarding his vision in the dark. He'd stuffed their blanket into the window at night, blocking the meager moonlight from illuminating their room, and he'd blown out the candle upon their nightstand. In perfect darkness, so dark it lay heavy against his own unseeing eyes, he'd held his fingers up, instructing Alistair to tell him the sum.

Alistair was right every single time.

It was something. One less question, even if it sprouted three more in its stead. Langford took note of everything significant and insignificant.

But even the satisfaction of time spent discerning Alistair's newfound condition did little to expand the tiny room they found themselves contained in. And as such, sitting now in Ingemar's captain's quarters and enduring her reproach was a relief. In its own way.

Ingemar let out a frustrated groan, running her hands over her face. Sweat coated her forehead, giving her deep-olive complexion a dewy appearance, and her waves of black hair hung in knotted tatters. It was a miracle she hadn't ordered her men to throw the two of them overboard to satisfy her rage.

"Is there anything you wish to tell me, Brenner?" Ingemar's voice was pained, weary with exhaustion and disappointment.

Langford sucked in a deep breath, summoning his courage and ability to summarize. It wouldn't do to waste any time on careful words. "We were attacked on the road about a month ago by a beast I've never seen the likes of before. Alistair sustained grave injuries, a fever taking root I could not combat. Nothing worked, nothing healed his wounds, and he grew sicker and sicker." Just the memory of his own helplessness in the face of Alistair's worsening conditions made his hands shake. "We took sanctuary in an inn, which granted me time to assess him, but the beast found us and began slaughtering the town. Everyone it slayed turned into beasts themselves. That's when I knew, Alistair was turning but very slowly, since the wound hadn't killed him. It wasn't until—"

Ingemar's fist slammed into her desk. "You brought that shit onto *my* ship? Endangered *my* men?"

Langford swallowed down the ire threatening to build. "Do allow me to finish my explanation before offering your judgement."

She waved her hand for him to continue.

"A hunter recognized his injury."

"What kind of hunter?" Her dark eyes flashed.

"The kind who specializes in creatures that shouldn't exist. She brewed some kind of tonic, and when I administered it, he made a full recovery." Langford swallowed. "Or so I thought."

Ingemar leaned back in her seat, kicking her feet atop her desk and crossing them at the ankles. She cast her gaze to the ceiling, a contemplative quiet coming over her.

Her cabin was just as spacious as he'd remembered, large angled windows revealing the first approach of dawn on the horizon. It kept her desk, littered with maps, trade agreements, and smuggling routes, from making the room feel cramped.

"You really didn't know?" Ingemar's voice broke through his thoughts.

"I did not. I wouldn't have planned a voyage at sea, sharing cramped quarters." He also liked to believe he had more honor than that, bringing a dangerous transformative curse aboard a ship without having the manners to disclose such things. He nearly snorted at his own turn of thoughts, but the thought that Alistair still carried this affliction sobered his mood.

Ingemar laughed, reaching down into her desk. "No, I suppose not. Nasty surprise, I'd wager."

Langford hummed. A nasty surprise. That was one way of putting it. He was tempted to say, *'Yes, an existential crisis joined with the horrific fear of losing the man I love was quite surprising.'*

Ingemar dropped two glasses atop her old and stained map, pouring three fingers of amber liquid into each. She nudged a glass toward him, a smirk playing on her full lips. Langford began to protest, but she cut him off. "It's not an occasion for wine; we are not celebrating nor are we socializing. We are coping. Now drink up while I try to spin a story for the crew." She slugged hers back, swiftly pouring another. "I'd hate to have to kill them all and start over again." At Langford's expression, she laughed. "Can't have them spreading word I brought some sort of plague onto my ship."

One would think hindering inhibitions to be the more dangerous state of mind, but Langford drank the bitter liquid, welcoming the burn of aged whiskey down the back of his throat.

It was a plague of sorts, wasn't it? In the way of a contagious disease, febrile and grotesque. Could those turned pass it along? Infect others? Or was it only the original creature?

Gods. More questions.

CHAPTER THIRTY-ONE

DEMETRIA

*I*f Demetria could spend the rest of her days on solid ground, never to ride the dipping waves of the sea, it would be too soon.

The first step onto the dock made her want to weep with joy, until she remembered why they were there. A tug of a chain, and she was propelled forward, tripping on her own feet. Beside her, Balan growled, steadying her with a touch to her elbow.

A fortnight at sea, trapped below deck with other prisoners, enduring the overwhelming smell of unwashed bodies and fear.

Demetria never thought fear could have a smell, but it did.

Guards wearing Kovalian colors of burgundy and gold had been waiting for them. As if this was all business as usual. Surely, they couldn't—

Acid washed over her tongue, coating her thoughts with bitterness. Zaire was capable of anything. Evander had warned her of this. Of course, they knew the circumstances of these captives. Though these were just guards doing their job. How aware were they of the darkness they'd shackled themselves to?

Demetria held up her hands as best she could to shield her eyes from the blinding sun. Merchants lined the streets, shouting their wares for all to hear. A group of children ran past, paying the chained prisoners no mind as they skirted around their legs. She carefully stepped across the mosaic tiling of the center court, a great dragon made of a thousand glittering pieces. A plume of fire billowed from its mouth in a proud statement of Kovalian traditions. It was her favorite feature of the capital, this larger-than-life art piece placed beneath the feet of its citizens. Under guarded supervision, of course, she would climb the stairs to perch atop the tallest building and peer down at that dragon.

Now, she stepped her worn and fraying boots over its great body.

She was home.

But there was nothing welcoming about it.

A sharp whistle rang out from across the square, a crowd gathering around the auction blocks. A small boy, tears streaking his filthy cheeks, stood higher than all the others. Whatever the auctioneer said was lost to the rushing pulse in Demetria's ears.

Another tug, and she walked faster, the boy disappearing from view as she was led behind the curve of an alley.

"We need a plan," she hissed at Balan.

"No speaking." Their handler, another Kovalian guard, shoved her to move faster. Demetria stumbled, knocking into the prisoner in front of her.

Balan kept his eyes trained forward, though his jaw tightened. "We need patience."

They fell silent. There was wisdom in waiting, learning, before acting. It was a lesson Ruslan had tried time and time again to instill in her. But Demetria couldn't help the sinking feeling that only grew with each step. Like they were venturing deeper and deeper into the monster's belly, distinguishing any hope of freedom with each step.

"Right now, they're keeping a close eye on us." Balan's mouth hardly moved as the words hissed their way into Demetria's hearing. "We must keep a low profile and wait until they no longer think us a flight risk. Observe. Even the most insignificant detail could be the key."

"But what if—"

"Silence!" A firm grip seized the back of Demetria's neck,

squeezing panic through her. Her head was wrenched to the side, meeting the narrow-eyed glare from the guard. She searched his features, desperate to find some glimmer of recognition. Something she could use to appeal to his humanity. But she'd never seen this man before. A perfect stranger, adorned in Kovalian colors. Above his breast pocket, a crowded array of medals glimmered. How had a man she'd never seen before amass so much recognition during peacetime?

His dark eyes were situated close together, a nose too small to fill his long face, and a derisive sneer stole across his lips. "I'll cut that pretty tongue from your mouth if you speak out of turn again."

Anger coursed through her at his words. There was honor in this title. She did not recognize him, nor know a single thing about him, but if this was how he treated prisoners, one word, one snap of her fingers and he'd—

Cold realization sank in her stomach. No. She had no power, despite being the princess. Not yet anyway.

"Do your superiors take kindly to lowly pissants damaging their goods?" Balan's voice, smoothly edged like the point of a razor, cut across the alley.

"Shut your mouth, too, freak." The guard grabbed Balan's broken horn, twisting his head to the side.

Everyone stopped. They were holding up the group now, all eyes on them.

So much for keeping a low profile.

"I know plenty of sick fucks who'd love to break a toy like you." The guard smirked, and Balan's nostrils flared, his hands closing into fists. But he held perfectly still.

"Understood." The amount of restraint in three mere syllables was a testament to the demon. Balan had told Demetria stories of his former power. And to feel as if all of that was stripped away, he was nothing more than an insect facing off against a large boot...

Demetria understood that feeling.

The guard shoved him away, and they resumed their journey.

Twists and turns, cutting through the market, through the residential district. The stone temple at the heart of the capital stood tall and proud, blindingly white under the harsh glare of the sun. A group of parishioners gathered outside its walls, some leaning against ornate columns, some bowing their heads in prayer. Demetria kept waiting for someone to make eye contact, to rush over and assess if they needed help, to call out the injustice of dragging chained civilians through the capital.

But no one did.

Another twisting bend of the road, and they met the cramped space of a tight alley, herded together like cattle.

"That," Balan whispered, the roughness of his voice somehow gentle, "did nothing to help our cause."

"I'm sorry."

"Stop it."

She let it drop, too afraid of what would happen if she argued her point and the guard heard. Instead, she let her mind wander to all the little what ifs.

What if someone recognized her? Part of her wished they would, but the wrong person would be a direct death sentence under Zaire's orders. But she had friends, hadn't she? Servants she was good and kind to. Gaspard, her favorite cook—he wouldn't turn her over to her brother, would he?

If only Evander—

Demetria's heart squeezed, her breath too thick for her lungs.

Evander. Ruslan. Those were her friends. Her allies. Her trusted circle. And Zaire had destroyed them.

No doubt he'd destroyed anyone who held any loyalty to her.

The castle grounds came into view, and Demetria's heart bludgeoned in her chest. Why were they here? Did they suspect? Had Zaire been watching the port in case she returned? But why would they bring all of them here? Surely, he didn't want to staff his home with common indentures, so the only reason to bring them here was to what? Make an example? A show of his strength and cruelty?

Her breaths came faster, stuttered and shallow. Her vision went hazy as a lightness claimed her head.

"Do not succumb." Balan's voice grounded her. "You are not done yet, fool."

Demetria nodded, twisting her hand in her chains. Sharp pains were still shooting through her chest like a knife, and her steps faltered.

Balan's hand gripped her arm, hard and bruising. Somehow, the point of contact was comforting.

"I will not let you fall."

The carriage house came into view. It was a minor estate, grand by anyone else's opinion, but one of the smaller buildings on the grounds. There was an attached barn of sorts, large enough to house fifty carriages. It was mostly used for parties and revelries, for travelers to have a place to house their carriages, their drivers waiting to usher them back home. The drivers rarely stayed with the carriages, venturing out onto the grounds to have their own little party.

Once, she and Evander had snuck out of a particularly stuffy party, running around the carriage barn, and pretending to be calling upon a visiting lord and lady, choosing their modes of transport and barking orders in silly accents. Her favorite was a simple phaeton, a plush red velvet interior with a large open top seat. She'd be the lady who could drive herself, a future she insisted to Evander would come to fruition.

"Fall in!" an older guard shouted into the crowd, and they all shuffled into place. If he was expecting the tightness of a soldier's response, perhaps they shouldn't have stolen Ardenian civilians and carted them off like chattel.

Under the roof of the carriage barn, the shadows deepened, obscuring the guard's faces, their silhouettes looming before them. It was easier to focus on everything else. The stale scent of old straw. The rotted wood beams that needed replacing. The abandoned carriage in the corner, cracked wheel leaning against the wall. Demetria knew that carriage. Burgundy walls. The tall, domelike shape. If she opened the door, padded silk in gold hues would greet her. That was their mother's favored carriage, and it lay broken and forgotten in the shadows?

What was Zaire spending his coffers on?

"Listen up. I don't like to repeat myself." The older guard's voice boomed. There was something so familiar about him. If only Demetria had thought to study his face before being shoved into darkness.

Balan was right. She needed to observe. Focus all her energy on taking in every detail of her surroundings rather than wasting her time lamenting the past.

She would not make that mistake again.

"You are fortunate, as you have been chosen." The irony of giving a speech of good fortune to a group of stolen captives was not lost on Demetria. "Based on age approximations and physical builds, you will all be reallocated to the mines."

Dread shot through Demetria, a rapid plunge of ice. *The mines?*

"Hard work will be rewarded, as will efficiency." The man kept spouting his nonsense, as if he hadn't just issued their execution. "There are many minerals to be found deep beneath the earth, and Kovalian land is the richest in all the world. But the real prize—" He held up a small mineral formation, crystals growing around a misshapen lump of stone. Another guard lit a torch, bringing it closer to illuminate the stone. "King Zaire has offered unique incentive. The first to find this rare prize will be granted a boon. A day off from mining and a meal within the very palace."

It was blacker than the ink Demetria used in her sketches. A fathomless black that seemed to suck the light into its depths.

Demetria recognized that stone. Had witnessed the power it yielded in the right hands.

Dragonstone.

Ruslan died so Lark and the others could acquire Demetria's family heirloom—a mirror with one of those stones laid in the handle. It had been forged into a blade, power breathed into it by Daciana's incantation. A weapon fit to kill a monster. A demon. Even a god.

A king.

Heat unfurled in Demetria's veins, the sharp stab of purpose piercing through any fear she'd possessed.

"There will be penalties for failure to comply. Each day, whomever has the least yield of value will be punished. None of you hold a contract of stipulation, so earning your freedom is out of the question.

But show your worth, and you might be able to apply for a job transfer in a year's time."

No way in the fiery pits of the Netherworld was Demetria waiting an entire year. She would find whatever scrap of dragonstone hid beneath the earth, and she would buy her way into her own home.

And Zaire would regret everything he took from her. A thousand times over.

CHAPTER THIRTY-TWO

GAVRIEL

*I*t was impossible to imagine setting a course of action that didn't include immediately following Lark into the abyss. Chasing her trail into the void. Beyond that. Not knowing what harm had befallen her, not knowing if she was safe or warm or scared or cold—

It was suffocating.

But Inerys had sworn there was no way to follow, not with Merikh at the helm. A damn paragon. Less than a year ago, Gavriel's worst concerns were completing his marks in a timely manner and keeping Emric alive.

So much had changed.

But without a goal, a mission, a guide, Gavriel was stuck. Even if Inerys was lying, he had no way to find Lark. No way to traverse to an alternate plane of existence. So, he was expected to let her suffer in whatever prison she'd been dragged to?

Unlikely.

"I see you're still sulking." Inerys' voice floated across the room. Use of her hand had been restored, cuts and bruises had healed, not even a shadow of injury remained, and she'd cleansed her home of any signs of a struggle.

Wiping away the blood didn't erase the memory of it spilling. Nor the danger Lark faced. But because Inerys seemed satisfied with an *out of sight, out of mind* mentality, she flitted about the space without a care in the world.

"You diminish a very real threat—one *you* allowed Lark to be captured by in your stead." Gavriel leaned back, the small stool precarious under his weight. "Which came first, the cowardice or the avoidance? Either way, they seem to go hand in hand where you're concerned."

In his periphery, Gavriel caught a shadow darken the stairs. *Ferryn.* But he made no move to show himself. Eavesdropping like a child.

A flash of pain briefly stole across Inerys' face, and she snarled. "I have opened my home time and time again for you lot. Trained three of your women to handle themselves in arts beyond their understanding. I kept you safe and sent Aislinn searching for a way to bring you back to Lark countless times. Do not insult me within the walls I allow you to hide behind."

Gavriel tightened his fist. He was *not* hiding.

"Did it ever occur to you that my confidence in Lark's survival is a direct result of my knowledge of her capability?" She huffed, striding for the door. "Try believing in the girl who's saved you too many times to count." She slammed the door behind her, leaving Gavriel to stew in her parting words.

It wasn't that he doubted Lark's abilities, certainly not, she'd proved time and time again her strength and fortitude. But the thought did little to ease the hollow ache of his chest. That she was facing this danger alone, it echoed against his skull, a constant reminder of his failure.

He should have been there.

From the stairs, Ferryn cleared their throat.

As if Gavriel needed the announcement to know he'd been listening. The man breathed louder than a wild boar on a hunt.

Ferryn's footsteps padded into the kitchen. He appeared still rumpled from sleep, his hair a mess and a crease on his cheek from his pillow. As if he hadn't a care in the world but to get a full night's rest.

214

He stretched as he reached for the cupboard. "She's right, you know." At Gavriel's responding glower, he merely smirked. "Didn't mean to overhear that. But in a house this small…" He gestured around.

As cramped as it was, the cottage had somehow grown since the last time Gavriel was here. He was certain the stairs led to a single room, and now it was an entire hall of doors. The outer facade hadn't changed, but the space had expanded. Was the witch spelling her home to accommodate her guests?

Only he and Ferryn remained. It was a wasted effort on her part. And yes, she had opened her home to them, granted them safe harbor and kept them hidden away from danger while he was trapped in Nereida's slumber curse.

Inerys wasn't wrong. But neither was he. It was foolish to sit around and hope for the best. Lark had ventured beyond mortal planes to save him; he would do the same.

The only question was how?

"For what it's worth," Ferryn said, studying him carefully, "I agree we should try to find her. Just because she *can* handle things on her own doesn't mean she should have to. It's something I wish I'd realized sooner where Lark is concerned. She'd launch headfirst into a terrible plan, risking all if it were one of us."

Gavriel had heard stories of their friendship. A bond formed in another plane of existence. How Ferryn was the closest thing to family at a time when Lark was hopelessly alone. Shit. He was actually grateful for the pest, wasn't he?

"Amazing. You two really do compliment each other." Ferryn slid in beside him, propping his chin on his hand. "You both have such intense expressions when deep in thought. It's not an insult. You're a handsome man."

Gavriel ignored his flattery. "I can never tell if you're laughing at me."

"I'm always laughing." Ferryn leaned an elbow against the table. "So, what's the plan?"

"The plan?"

"Mmhmm." Ferryn took a bite of Gavriel's abandoned breakfast, chewing and nodding as he dragged the bowl over to him. "Rescue plan," he said around a full mouth. "We're going to pretend to listen to Inerys, and mount a plan of extraction, full Lark mode, are we not?" He took another bite, brows raised in question as he awaited Gavriel's response.

Shit.

He was beginning to like this one.

"Absolutely." If Ferryn could keep Inerys distracted long enough, Gavriel could creep into her cellar where she kept her oldest tomes hidden. If there was a hint of forbidden knowledge, she wouldn't leave it lying about.

"Excellent! First you should probably make sure you're fit to travel." Ferryn perused Gavriel at a leisurely pace. "Everything looks good, but you've been sleeping for quite some time."

"I am fine." In fact, Gavriel didn't feel any loss in strength. Not from slumber nor starvation. Almost as if the witch-queen's spell kept him frozen in time.

"In any case, it wouldn't hurt to be cautious." Ferryn hummed. "We'll start with simple exercises and work our way up to sparring."

"You wish to spar with me?" A ridiculous thought. Ferryn was as lean and lank as they came. Tall and easily knocked over.

"Don't be cocky. I taught Lark everything she knows."

"I seriously doubt that."

Ferryn grinned. "Then what have you got to lose?"

Sanity. Patience. Time. A combination of the three?

"I will not sit idly by while Lark suffers."

Ferryn rolled his eyes. "No one is suggesting that. But without the witch's *compliant* help..."

Understanding dawned on Gavriel. A subterfuge. A duplicity. A spot of deception. A strangely nostalgic notion.

"What do you have in mind?"

"I THINK I'M BLEEDING INTERNALLY."

"Don't be so dramatic," Gavriel hissed. "She'll know you're exaggerating."

"I'm not exaggerating," Ferryn insisted. "You sought to kill me."

Gavriel rolled his eyes, resisting the urge to strangle him. They'd spent the day completing various chores for Inerys. Chopping and stacking wood. Shoveling a path to her greenhouse. All under the guise of checking Gavriel's strength. And when they sparred using blunted staves, Ferryn had gotten 'injured' in the scuffle, needing her attention. Right now, he was lying in the snow, awaiting her return. Gavriel kneeled beside him, cold biting through the cloth of his fighting leathers.

Inerys had just stomped off to collect some willow bark, and once she returned, Gavriel was going to search her cellar.

But Ferryn was going to blow his cover if he kept laying it on too thick.

Gavriel had to admit, it was a relief to stretch his muscles. Even though it was a means to a greater end, it was fortunate his strength hadn't diminished in his cursed sleep.

He hadn't allowed himself to sleep since waking. Just the thought was enough to set his teeth on edge. The threat of closing his eyes, only to be trapped once more.

"Ah! My vital organs!"

"You really need to stop."

"Perish the thought. I give a full-bodied performance or none at all. In my former life I was destined for the stage."

Gavriel paused. Ferryn could remember being mortal and Lark couldn't. She must have felt so lost as a Reaper.

"Were you really?"

"Probably."

Inerys huffed her way back, stomping across the snow with willow bark clamped in her fist. "Do we really need to do this outside?"

Ferryn moaned. "My delicate constitution won't allow movement."

Gavriel pinched the bridge of his nose. The overly theatrical fool was going to ruin everything.

"Fine, hold still." Inerys nudged Gavriel out of the way, and Ferryn let out a sharp cry of pain.

"I'm not listening to this," Gavriel said, trudging away.

"You're not actually leaving me here with this bleating goat, are you?" Inerys called after him.

"Just leave him in the snow, it's good for inflammation." He glanced over his shoulder as he headed for the house, waiting until Inerys turned back to Ferryn to give him a nod of understanding.

Inerys wouldn't really leave him in the snow. Gavriel was almost sure of it.

He headed straight for the spot in the floor that hid the stairs to her cellar. Yanking it open, he slid through, closing it above him. The last time he'd been down here was when Lark sought Inerys' aid in finding Ferryn. How ironic that the man in question was now rolling around the snow, feigning hysterics to buy Gavriel time.

It wasn't the most elegant plan. Or even moderately well-formed. But what was the worst that could happen? Inerys might berate him for searching her things without permission.

Through the narrow hall, past the door to the wine cellar. Deeper and deeper still. Twists and turns and who built this place? The door he'd been searching for came into view. The room he'd ventured into with Lark by his side. When he was the anchor keeping her from being lost to the abyss.

A pang shot through his chest at the thought. He'd failed to keep her safe. He failed to keep her anchored to this plane.

If he couldn't be her anchor, he'd be her sails, catching the wind and being the momentum to carry her home.

The chairs they'd occupied sat forgotten, and the table was still littered with empty vials. A bookcase leaned against the far wall, stuffed and teeming with tomes. Gavriel swept across the room, pulling at random. Most were in dialects he couldn't read, and soon a precarious stack of rejected books had formed atop the center table.

It was madness. This helpless feeling of being utterly useless. He tossed another book atop the pile, rougher than necessary. Lark could be hurt. Starving. Beaten and broken. And here he was, perusing a fucking bookshelf. He couldn't wait. He couldn't act. He was just as stuck as he was in that cursed slumber, dead to the world while entire lifetimes flashed in his mind.

He hadn't dared think on it, been too afraid to wonder after its meaning, but every lifetime he'd lived had two universal constants: He was always searching for Lark, even if he didn't know it, and he always died young.

Gavriel had never seen himself grow into an old man, never seen his hair begin to gray, never seen himself sire children, grow fat and happy. No, he always lived a short and bloody life, searching for her. He'd had many names, but only one purpose.

The first was the life he lived with her, when all they owned were their souls that they greedily pledged to one another. The next was a thief, a cutpurse with a penchant for violence. Then, a soldier. Training until the battle that claimed his life. A farmhand slaughtered by raiding bandits. A mercenary falling by the sword of a trusted ally. A blacksmith run through with one of his own designs when a group of marauders refused to pay. An indenture born into life in the mines, killed when he protected a young girl from the wandering hands of their overseers.

Death. Birth. Repeat.

Darkness. Blood. Rage.

It was a cycle he was destined to live and die by.

Until this life. The life of an assassin, sold to the Guild of Crows, and honed into a weapon. Only she didn't see him as a weapon. When Lark looked at him, she saw life. Gavriel knew it, because the same thought coursed through him at the sight of her beautiful face. He would die as many times as it took knowing he could live to see *her*.

She was... everything.

How was he supposed to keep her safe, if the forces beyond their control were determined to keep them apart?

He was supposed to die, that day in the forest. When the poison coursed through his blood. When Lark bestowed a kiss upon his lips and claimed his death, breathing life into him once more. Was he destined to spend his life losing and searching for the woman he loved as penance for this stolen time?

Gavriel roared, knocking the books off the table with the sweep of his hand. They fell with resounding thuds, scattering across the floor. His heart thundered in his ears, pulsing his failure.

Failure.

Failure.

Failure.

"Are you finished, or do you need more time for your tantrum?" Inerys stood in the doorway, arms crossed, while Ferryn peeked in behind her, his expression sheepish. "I see hero mode didn't work, and now you're resorting to what? Petulance?" A crease formed between her dark brows, and she stalked over to where he'd childishly thrown her books to the floor.

"Don't," he said, reaching over to collect them up. "I'll do that."

"Did you really think I couldn't scent your ridiculous plan from a mile away?" Her dark eyes narrowed sharply. "If I strike you as such an imbecile, it's a wonder any of you have relied on my help."

"It wasn't like that." Gavriel returned the unreadable books to the bookcase, wincing when he noticed the dented corners. "I just can't sit by and wonder if she's hurting." He swallowed against the lump growing in his throat. "Please, Inerys. Help me."

Her eyes slid shut, mouth twisting to the side. "I *hate* it when you people ask nicely." She tossed her head back with a groan. "Ugh. Follow me."

Back down the narrow hall, up the rickety stairs, and when they made it to her sitting room, she turned to face them. "Let me make this perfectly clear. I do not approve of this method. I do not condone it. I think it's foolish and impractical and bound to result in more problems for everyone." Gavriel couldn't shake the familiar feeling of guilt and shame from being scolded like a child. "But I am not your master. You are masters of your own fate, and should you wish to throw your lives in the fire, I will not stop you. I will, however, try to keep you from burning."

It was the way of Inerys' kindness. Some hid their poisons behind the taste of sweetness. She was precisely the opposite. Her venom was the subterfuge shrouding the strength of her care. Gavriel was beginning to see that now.

"What do you have in mind?" She must have had a plan. She spoke as if it was already formed.

"How did Lark find you before? Either of you."

"She tried to find Ferryn with your aid. But she discovered he was—"

Inerys swept her hand through the air impatiently. "Yes, yes. I'm familiar with that story. I had to scrub the floor clean of my vomit after that little errand. What boon did she gain in the Forbidden Shrine, allowing her to find Ferryn, and then you."

The lantern. Skies, how had he forgotten about the lantern?

"Will it work? With the fallen veil, will it still lead us to her? How do we use it?" There wasn't any time to waste. They had a method of finding her. Gavriel itched to run up the stairs in search of the item.

Inerys arched a brow. "Take back what you said about me being a coward. Tell me how you really think I felt watching Merikh drag Lark away." Her eyes flashed, and she took a step toward him. A challenge in her posture. "Tell me you know it *hurt* knowing I was powerless to stop it."

Shame burned in his gut. Behind him, Ferryn sighed. The sound one of regret rather than annoyance. Gavriel should remember the way Inerys looked, half-dead and clinging to Ferryn to stay up right. The redness around Ferryn's eyes from crying. How Inerys' voice broke on the words. But all Gavriel cared about was how it affected him. He was selfish and callous and angry.

A shameful combination.

"I never should have said that." His anger, his fear, they had consumed him. And it had been all too easy to lash out. "That was unworthy of me." The space behind his ribs ached. Like something vital was missing and his body didn't know how to function properly. "I just want her back." Gavriel's voice broke on the last word.

Something glimmered in Inerys' eyes. But those couldn't be tears.

"You are not the only person who cares about her. As obnoxious and determined to die as she is."

Gavriel nodded, holding back his thanks. It wasn't his place to feel gratitude, even though he did. Her care for Lark was not about him, but a testament to the way Lark warmed even the coldest people around her. Brought them to life and melted the ice away.

She was the sun, and he could not weather the darkness without her.

"Tell me what to do."

CHAPTER THIRTY-THREE

DACIANA

*D*aciana would never tire of waking beside Kenna. Of her silky black hair spilling over her pillow. Of her pale skin peeking out from beneath the covers, tempting her to run her hand across its smooth plane. She'd never even tire of the nasally snores that escaped her adorable mouth, a fact Kenna still refused to believe.

Was this what happiness felt like? Sometimes, Daciana feared closing her eyes. Of falling asleep only to learn this was a mere dream.

But each day she was grateful that she hadn't allowed her fear to win out in the end. For too long, it had held her back from the woman she loved. Kept her hiding in the shadows, afraid to illuminate her past in the light.

And Kenna was luminescent in her joy. If Daciana thought Kenna beautiful before, it was nothing in comparison to Kenna's beauty when she wore her happiness so freely. She was the same she'd always been, playful and clever. A sharp mind and sharper tongue she put to good use. *Very* good use.

Daciana giggled, a sound she wasn't accustomed to making, though it was becoming a frequent occurrence.

One more night at sea, and finally, they'd make it to Anquan. When they stood on dry land, Kenna's kin at their side, then they would assess the danger Merikh posed to Aislinn. It seemed as long as she didn't use her abilities, he couldn't find her. Having her reach into Gavriel's dreams each night must have made her a honing beacon. The more distance between them, the better.

A tightness crept into Daciana's chest at the thought. She hated, *hated,* leaving Lark behind. Leaving her to face danger without the added benefit of her aid. But Lark's decision wasn't made lightly, and Daciana couldn't pretend she wouldn't do the same were it Kenna in Gavriel's stead.

Still, it felt like a line in the sand, a choice between whom to guard against danger. Lark didn't see it that way, of course, but the guilt followed Daciana like a shadow.

Seeing Aislinn find some peace though, that was an unexpected light in the darkness. Daciana hadn't been sure how the visit to her mother would go, and that Aislinn had originally thought to hide her devices was laughable. Of course, Daciana knew what Aislinn sought when she'd rerouted their path to flow through the town she once called home. And when they'd met with her mother, when Aislinn had the chance to say the words she thought died with her, it was a reminder: One didn't always get that chance.

The importance of saying all that needed to be said so death didn't usher in more pain and regret than necessary...

Daciana tugged Kenna closer, pressing her face into her neck and inhaling deeply. Her intoxicating scent of freshly fallen rain and sharp berries filled her senses.

It was the quiet moments that mattered most. The beauty of normalcy that was hard-won. Daciana would never question her heart again.

There just wasn't enough time in this life.

"First, we'll pop in to see Dagna. She'll put us up, I'm sure. Or she'll know who has the room to house us. I'm not staying at Helvard's; he's creepy and bores holes into the walls of his inn so he can peep on his patrons." Kenna yanked her boots on, chattering away. "Do you think anyone would mind if he had a little *accident*? We take him ice fishing, get him drunk, and oh, no! Is the ice thinner here or here? Ah, Helvard's fallen through! Lost to the abyss! No, we can't dive in and save him—he's already slipped too far." Kenna mimed standing over a hole, forcing an invisible head down under the water. "I said, you're too far gone, Helvard. Give in to the sweet release of death."

Kenna had the ability to hold entire conversations on her own and with people who weren't even present in the room.

"You don't think anyone else has already beaten you to it? Ruva, perhaps?"

Kenna grinned, her whole face lighting up. "I'm so bloody excited for you to meet Ruva."

Kenna had told Daciana of Ruva long ago. They were childhood friends, growing up alongside one another, and after Kenna's parents died and Kenna relocated to Ardenas with her grandmother, they'd continued to send one another missives. Kenna and her grandmother would venture back to Anquan each winter season, to celebrate their favored traditions with Kenna's people. Ice gliding and feasting and dancing and Fire Night.

For a group of lethal hunters, they sounded *fun*.

"How long since you've been back?" Daciana should have known. She should have known what a stupid question that was. And the way Kenna fell silent, her eager prattling halted, she had her answer.

It was before Daciana's people changed everything. Before *she* changed everything. Kenna had a way of hiding her grief behind smiles and sarcasm. Of always moving to keep the quiet from settling in. Losing her grandmother had ushered in more loss than she'd been willing to admit aloud. Carving a wound so deep it never saw the sun.

And Daciana had just prodded at it.

"I'm sorry. I didn't—"

"No, no, no! Don't be." Kenna's cheerfulness sounded forced, and she turned to pack her bags, refusing to look at her. "I could have gone back on my own. Nothing was stopping me."

Daciana didn't know what to say, how to smooth the ripple of pain that followed in the wake of their past. She stepped up to Kenna, wrapping her arms around her from behind and pressing her chin into the crook of her neck. Kenna immediately melted into the contact, hands running their way over Daciana's arms, over the back of her neck to hold her in place.

And for a few breaths, they remained still, wrapped in each other as if letting go wasn't an option.

Sometimes, words were the last thing one needed.

Daciana turned her face to press her lips against Kenna's neck, and Kenna squirmed. "Don't you start that unless you plan on letting me finish it."

"When have I ever denied you your finish?"

Kenna laughed, spinning in Daciana's arms to face her. "I've missed this."

Her words carried the meaning of so many things they'd lost. Joy. Laughter. Honesty. Family. Love.

Daciana pressed her forehead to Kenna's.

"Me, too."

THE MOUNTAINS of Anquan were a humbling thing to behold. Kenna had spoken of their beauty, but nothing could have prepared Daciana for this.

In the distance, they stood tall enough to carve into the clouds, capped in white and starkly contrasting with the pale blue and pink sky. The bodies of their slopes were dark and chiseled like one of the sculptures on offer at the artisan's market.

Anquan sat on the coast of the Permafrosts, boasting both mountains and flatlands in its features. But these were the sort of mountains Daciana could see revered as gods in the old days.

Aislinn, too, was shocked into silence, gazing upon the land before them, small puffs of vapor escaping her open mouth. Her long blonde hair had been wrapped beneath her cowl, a green scarf tucked beneath her chin.

Kenna sidled up next to them, the three of them standing at the port. It was far less populated than Emeraude Port, people moved at their own leisure rather than chasing an overpriced fishmonger or the last spot on a departing ship.

"Shall we then?" Kenna was practically bouncing on her heels.

Daciana smiled. She should have brought Kenna home a long time ago.

"Lead the way."

Kenna hurried ahead, the words never ceasing to tumble out of her mouth as she described childhood memories connected to damn near every step they took. That hole in the dock was put there by a boy named Mackinley when she convinced him mermaids hid in the shallows, disappearing whenever they heard the splash of a human. That hut was once rented out to a peddler selling false wares claiming to be magic. Her grandmother ran him out of town. Against that tree was where she had her first kiss.

"First one that counted, obviously."

Obviously.

On and on, Kenna spoke. Excitement at sharing her history fueling her. Daciana shoved down the rising guilt that Kenna had spent so long away from a home that brought her so much joy.

They were here now. That had to count for something.

Daciana glanced over to see if Aislinn was enjoying the tour. The girl looked around, taking in her surroundings with curiosity, but there was a tension about her shoulders. A hardened line in the way she carried herself.

"Are you cold?" Daciana asked softly, not wishing to interrupt Kenna's story about the time she dared her cousin Sayan to stick his tongue against the frozen iron rod holding up a training dummy. The way he shrieked when they tried to pull him off, but it held stuck.

"No," Aislinn said, but she bundled her cloak closer.

Anquan had milder temperatures at the base of the mountain range, a reprieve from the frigid cold of Ardenian winter, but the higher one climbed, the colder it grew.

They'd need better gear if Kenna wished to take them on a journey to the peak. But that wasn't what they were here for, was it? As much as Daciana wished to give Kenna endless time, fill their days with stories and memories, they had a greater aim in coming.

Recruiting the hunters.

Aislinn hadn't used her somniavi ability, hiding herself from the one who hunted her, but they couldn't live in hiding forever. Not with the fallen veil.

Not with Nereida needing to be dealt with.

If they could get the paragon off their backs and form an alliance with the hunters should Nereida gather her forces...

They might stand a chance at surviving this. But that's all it was. A chance.

"I just..." Aislinn trailed off. "I hate not knowing how the others are faring."

"I know." It was so tempting to ask Aislinn to check on them. An immediate communication rather than sending a missive, which would take ages. She was already attuned to Lark, and it would grant Daciana immediate comfort to know she was all right. Aislinn could even attempt to search for Langford or Alistair, though Daciana worried less for those two. Their voyage to Vallemer on Ingemar's ship would keep them safe until they docked, and then it was only a matter of diplomacy to prevent any altercations.

But Daciana could never allow such a risk. Not with Merikh on the hunt.

Kenna turned around, a frown forming on her lovely face. "Were you even listening?"

"Of course, I was," Daciana answered smoothly. "You've always been a sadistic little terror who delighted in the cries of pain from your poor victims."

Kenna beamed, a radiant smile that dimpled her cheeks. "You were listening! Now here is where Ceilon broke his ankle after I convinced him he could fly..."

THE TOWN of Craghill was as idyllic as Kenna described. Once they made it through the port city and ventured deeper into the valley, the first signs of her village had come into view. If Kenna was excited before, she was damn rambunctious now. Snow dusted the tops of dozens of homes, their exaggerated arched roofs quaint and picturesque against the base of the mountain range. Even in the distance, candlelit windows lit up the night, warmth beckoning across the snowy wind-swept valley. Each home was constructed of a similar build, with a tidy fence surrounding its perimeter.

This was more than a town. This was a close-knit community.

Lanterns hung off strings, twinkling lights across the square. Laid and stacked stones formed the borders of the road as the three of them drew nearer to the inviting place, snow crunching beneath boots and cheeks red from the cold. Despite the impending night and the chill in the air, people were out. Not hurrying past as if chasing a unceasing task list but *strolling* by. Like being out in the cold was a choice made for pleasure rather than necessity.

Daciana had grown used to Ardenas. It was referred to as no-man's land, but that wasn't necessarily true. The ones with the deepest purses called the shots, and the rest fought to survive. Koval was a kingdom based on bloodline sovereignty. Kenna had always told her Anquan was more community based. Shared goods and labor. An entire village working together. It had sounded more wish than reality.

"What luck! We haven't missed Feastday!" Kenna pressed a quick kiss to Daciana's cheek, damn near skipping ahead. The Winter Solstice events and traditions were a month-long series of parties and revelries. Feastday being Kenna's favorite.

Lark would have loved it, too.

A few people stopped, eying Kenna with vague familiarity. Like they were trying to place her face.

Skies, it really had been too long since she'd been home.

"Sayan?" Kenna asked, stepping closer to a man three inches shorter than she, a furred cap atop his head and fastened beneath his chin. He had similar eyes to Kenna, dark, deep-set, with a slight upturn to their shape. Instead of a cloak, he wore a robe lined with fur, buttons running the length of the front.

"Kenna?" The disbelief in his voice speared through Daciana's heart. Like he never thought he'd see his cousin again. With a boisterous laugh, he yanked her into his arms, whispering Anquanian against her shoulder. She answered in kind, and though Daciana did not know the dialect save for choice phrases Kenna would whisper in private, their exchanged tones were friendly and disarming.

"You're finally back," he said in common tongue, pulling away to clap a hand on her shoulder and look at her. His gaze drifted past, landing on Daciana and Aislinn. "And you brought friends."

"This is Daciana and Aislinn," Kenna said, smug pride shining in her tone.

"*Daciana?*" His brows shot up, and the way he stretched out the sound of her name set her on edge.

"Well met," Daciana said, not entirely sure the feeling was mutual. But Sayan nodded.

"Indeed." His smile was reassuring, and he offered Aislinn his arm. "My lady?" With a laugh, she accepted, allowing him to guide her ahead while Kenna and Daciana followed behind. "This will be a revelry to remember," he called over his shoulder.

Kenna slipped her gloved hand in Daciana's, lacing their fingers and squeezing.

Yes. It would be.

CHAPTER THIRTY-FOUR

LARK

*L*ark groaned, awareness trickling like a slow drip through her body, each pulse bringing a searing shock to her nerves.

Slowly, she blinked her eyes open, immediately regretting the way the room darkened in and out of focus. Dingy walls. Blackness. A lone table. Blackness. Pale light from a too high window. Blackness.

Lark wet her cracked lips, and her stomach turned. She shifted—

Her arms wouldn't move. She was bound in place, shoulders stretched behind her, ropes cutting into her wrists. She twisted, attempting to free her hands, and the accompanying burn stole the breath from her lungs.

"I wouldn't do that if I were you."

That voice. It called from the corner behind her. Lark turned, her movements limited and her head spinning at the action. But the shadows concealed its speaker.

"Your binds are spelled to inflict pain should you fight. You aren't much of a quick study, are you?"

Lark recalled that voice. She'd heard it in a dream. She was walking alone in the woods. Snow biting at her raw feet. It was dark. She was cold. Wait. She wasn't walking... she was running. Running toward something or someone. The panic, the visceral fear that something terrible had happened—

Inerys.

The paragon torturing Inerys, dragging her by her hair to the edge of her protection spell. Seeking Aislinn by destroying anything in his path to her.

Lark struggled, the pain near suffocating as the sensation of a thousand needles jabbed into her skin, into the muscle, straight to the bone.

"What did I just say?" he rasped, exasperation hardening his tone.

The creak of the floor. Heavy steps. He was drawing closer.

Lark shoved every whisper of fear down to the pit of her belly. She would face whatever he did to her, and revel in the fact that he'd never get anything out of her. He was far from Aislinn. From Inerys. From Gavriel and all the others. He had no threat to level against her now.

"I've never seen a Reaper made human again," he said, crouching before her and revealing himself from the gloom of shadows.

His dark hair hung just past his shoulder. Grey eyes glared down the line of his strong nose. His mouth firming in a line behind his short beard. He looked nothing like a paragon of Virtue. A warrior of Avalon descended from the heavens to inflict righteous judgment.

He was... ordinary.

"I've never seen a paragon in the flesh. So, I guess we're both up for new experiences today."

"You would never survive witnessing my true form."

Lark snorted. "I'm sorry. I'm sure you're very impressive."

The veins in his thick neck bulged, red blooming across his throat. He was angry, but it was such a human reaction.

Lark could almost imagine Langford's expression when she'd tell him. How he'd mumble to himself and stare at the ceiling. And when she reminded him to speak aloud, he'd say the words she heard echoing in her own head.

Very curious.

"You seem very important, so let's not waste your time." Lark wet her lips again, unable to ignore the sore spot in the corner of her mouth. "Why am I here?"

"Glad you asked." He stood, his towering height meant to dominate, to remind her just how vulnerable she was. "You're going to tell me where the somniavi is."

Lark laughed. The absurdity of his declaration demanded such. "No. I'm really not."

Merikh, that was his name, stepped to the table, grabbing the handle of a very familiar knife. Etchings and markings carved into the wood with care. That comforting glint of steel.

Hugo's knife.

"Shall we try that answer again."

Anger. Rage. It was a flash of fire scorching through her. Dizzying in its abrupt wave. He could use her own weapon against her, but she would not tell him anything.

"No."

There were no glib retorts. No sarcastic comments.

Only a shrug as he stepped closer, kneeling before her. His finger found the small hole in her breeches, tugging it wider to reveal the top of her thigh.

"Have it your way."

The first scrape of the blade, of Hugo's blade, against her skin was a lick of agony. It was the shredding of hope. The kiss farewell to any chance she might have had at sanity. Merikh carved, almost lovingly, through her skin. Another cut to her tunic, baring her arm, and he made his marks there. He was an artist weaving poetry against a skin canvas, and Lark gritted her teeth, tears springing to her eyes, trailing down her cheeks. She would not give him the pleasure of screaming.

TIME PASSED.

There was no way of measuring but by the swelling tide of pain. By the ripping, searing agony as her butcher carved his mark into her skin, healing her of any evidence of his handiwork, only to start again.

When Lark's consciousness dimmed, and the dragging temptation of dreaming caressed the back of her mind, it was for a mere blink. A flash of an image. Gavriel's smile. His dark-green eyes flecked with gold. Daciana's laugh. Ferryn tackling her into the snow. Langford wrapped in Alistair's arms. And *Gavriel. Gavriel. Gavriel.*

It was a taste. A tease. A glimpse of what she longed for most. But she could never hold on to the image. It melted away, the dingy walls of her prison coming into view.

Merikh's disappointed face appeared before her. Like she'd failed him in this.

Tears mixed with blood. Despair with hopelessness. And Lark whispered her apology, for she swore she would not give him the satisfaction of the sounds of her pain. That she would not scream.

And scream she did.

A horrible brutal symphony of screams. Her atonal sonata ringing out in the darkness. And Merikh healed her, his threatening overture looming above, before he began again. A vicious conductor. Never tiring. Never ceasing. Never concluding his violent and bloody song.

Time passed.

But the music remained.

CHAPTER THIRTY-FIVE

GAVRIEL

*G*avriel awoke with a shout, his voice dying on his lips. Sweat covered his trembling body, his pillow a soaked mess. His heart thundered in his chest, and his face was wet with tears.

It was Lark.

Someone was *hurting* her. Not just hurting her, brutally torturing her. It was agony, the sounds she made, the markings against her skin, the stain of her blood—

Gavriel leaned over and vomited on the floor. He wiped his mouth with a shaky hand.

A sob broke free, and then another.

It was like his heart was being ripped from his chest.

Lark. His Lark. Bound and butchered like she was a common beast.

"Just a dream." Gavriel pounded his fist against the side of his head, as if he could beat the images from his memory.

His stomach churned, heaving despite its emptiness. It was like looking out of her eyes. He saw her bound to a chair. The bindings wrapped around her arms, her stomach, her legs. Like thorned vines. They squeezed even tighter when she struggled. When that monster brought a blade to her vulnerable flesh and carved into her without remorse. She screamed and twisted and cried, the thorns cutting even deeper in response.

"Just a dream." His voice was shaky and hoarse. But if he'd learned anything over the last year, it was to follow the pull of his instinct. And every fiber of his being screamed to find her.

Gavriel flung the covers back, stepping over his vomit and beginning to dress. He donned his black fighting leathers, slipping his blades into their hiding places.

Inerys had said she would prepare a few protective wards and hex bags for them to bring, an arsenal to have at their disposal. But there wasn't time to spare.

His steps through the hall were silent as was his entry into Ferryn's room. There was no effort in the act; he didn't care if Inerys heard him; he would not be kept from Lark.

Ferryn slept like a child, cocooned in his blankets, even forming a hood with the coverlet wrapped about his head. Gavriel shook him, uncaring if he was too rough.

"What?" Ferryn startled, wiping the corner of his mouth.

"It's time." If Ferryn didn't see it fit to go to her now, he'd leave him behind. He had no use for dead weight.

He was getting Lark out. Whatever the cost.

But Ferryn didn't argue. He didn't demand explanation. He didn't even hesitate.

With a nod, he sat up, tying his hair back. "Gather anything that might seem useful. I know nothing about fighting paragons except that one shouldn't unless they're prepared to die."

"And are you prepared to die?" It wasn't even a question for Gavriel. Death was nothing compared to the pain of losing her. Death had been his business for as long as he could remember, and he'd never shied away from it.

He wouldn't start now.

"For Lark?" Ferryn stood, stretching his arms over his tall frame, and allowing a humorless grin to spread across his mouth. "Always."

"Good."

"DOES IT MATTER WHERE WE GO?" Ferryn hissed.

"What makes you think I know?"

"You *are* the one who snuck into my room all shifty cloak and dagger, ready to race into the fiery pits of the Netherworld."

Gavriel resisted the sigh building in his chest. "I suspect we need to venture outside of the perimeter of Inerys' protective ward."

Ferryn ceased packing his bag. "How do you suppose?"

It was a hunch, really. But Gavriel couldn't say as much. He was used to following his instincts, but that didn't mean Ferryn would follow them.

"The lantern is supposed to be a tether." He held up the lantern. The glass windows were dull in the absence of a flame. But he remembered Lark using that lantern—the azure glow of its light with the turn of a key. "If Inerys' wards are meant to keep others out, it might keep the connection from forming."

Ferryn smiled, reaching over to pinch Gavriel's cheek. "Beauty and brains."

Gavriel slapped his hand away. "Do you think this a game? I saw her, Ferryn. She was…" His voice trailed off, a lump forming in his throat. "You don't understand the pain she suffers. We have to free her."

"And we will." Ferryn's brow furrowed, regret making its home there. "If it seems I don't care, it's only the opposite. I care so much I need to distract from it. Does it not keep fear from joining your anger?"

"Distract yourself." Gavriel double checked his lockpicks were in place, his iron and flint, and a quick count to his small blades. He slid his favored daggers, his stiletto and Ardenian dirk, into place. "You and I are not friends. I do not need your brand of distraction. I do not need you to accompany me at all should you not have the constitution for it."

Ferryn's face flashed dangerously, the edges of his features hardening. "You forget I'm far older than you, and I grasp a better understanding of this world."

Technically, now that Gavriel's lifetimes of memories had been restored, that wasn't strictly true.

"Then find a way to be useful, but your glib remarks are not it." Gavriel snatched the lantern from the counter and made for the door.

There were no signs of Inerys as he opened the door and let a winter moon slip into view. No hint at her knowledge of their decision. She had asked Gavriel to give her enough time to gather all they might need, so it stood a fraction of a chance of being a rescue mission rather than one of suicide.

And he'd had every intention of honoring his promise.

Until he imagined Lark's screams. Her terror, her pain, her anguish.

No. The only promise he could keep was to the woman who stole his heart many lifetimes ago. The one to command the pull of his soul no matter what body possessed it.

I will find you.

The door swung open beneath his touch, wintry air pummeling him in the face and watering his eyes, a harshly whipping wind skirting beneath his hood and freezing the back of his neck. As if the night beseeched him to stay.

Wasn't happening.

He marched with purpose, his stride unfaltering beneath the weight of doubt. Did he truly know how to find her? No. But that wouldn't stop him. His rage and fear would be his guides. And it would be enough. It had to be enough. It brought her back to him after lifetimes of searching.

He only hoped it wouldn't take that long again.

"I'm the one who gave your death to Lark."

Gavriel's rhythm stuttered, surprise interrupting his stride. How had he forgotten Ferryn's involvement? Guilt tore through his belly. Lark had once told him how Ferryn warned her of Gavriel's death. How much he'd been punished for doing so. Perhaps Ferryn was more honorable than he pretended.

"I won it in a card game."

Honorable was a stretch.

Gavriel's guilt dissolved as heat spilled through his blood. "Do most Reapers regard humans as little more than playthings?" he spat. "Because Lark seemed the anomaly."

Ferryn laughed loud enough to set Gavriel on edge. In any situation, it was dangerous to draw attention to oneself. And announcing their presence in a night-filled forest seemed a shitty way to die.

"You judge so harshly from a quick wag of the tongue. Is that true of all assassins, or are you the anomaly?"

Point taken. But his judgment came from more than Ferryn's flippant remark. It was based on multiple experiences. The first being the woman who collected Vana's soul upon her death. When Gavriel silenced the woman who poisoned Emric. First with her lies than with the Waking Nightmare that claimed his life. That Reaper had laughed, taunting him like it was all a game he just didn't know the rules of.

Thanar. The one who tormented Lark, and for what? His unanswered feelings?

They were all insects to them. Demons. Reapers. Paragons. Gods. They regarded human life with an indulgent amusement. They were petty and vengeful and manipulative.

But not Lark. She was a beacon of hope without equal.

"I gave it to her because I'd been harsh with her." Ferryn peeked over at him. "About you."

Lark had not told him of this.

Confusion nearly stopped Gavriel in his tracks, but his body recognized the need to push forward without pausing. "Explain."

"Lark was..." Ferryn huffed a laugh. "Lark *is* headstrong and impulsive. From the moment she first saw you, her curiosity was an untamable beast. Even in the face of certain punishment."

"And you disapproved."

"I didn't—" Ferryn let out a noise of frustration. "It didn't matter if I approved or disapproved. She was being carefully watched by someone far more powerful than us. And I didn't know how harsh or vindictive he would be when he discovered you had actually crossed paths with Lark this time."

That didn't make sense. Gavriel was a mere mortal to them. It wasn't until Nereida revealed their history that anyone even learned of the significance of their connection.

Unless.

"Are you saying Thanar knew what Lark and I were to each other?"

"He knew a mortal such as you existed. And his seer always brought your soul to his attention each time it was born. He was awaiting word of your next appearance. Our orders were to prevent Lark from finding you. Her marks were always set in the corners of the world farthest from you. Because if she stumbled upon you, even without your tether, she would have been drawn to you. Just as she was when we guided Emric."

Anger was something Gavriel had grown up mastering. Honing it to a fine point to wield with control. But the way his blood boiled at his words...

"Did you know? Is that why you gave her my death?"

Ferryn hesitated. "I didn't understand. I knew you were important, and I knew Thanar wanted to keep you two apart, and Leysa insisted I should—"

Gavriel shoved him against a tree, his hands curling into his cloak and pinning him in place. The branches shivered against the violence of his movement, releasing a dusting of snow on their heads.

"You knew... and you didn't fucking tell her."

"I didn't know what I knew," Ferryn spat. "I didn't know how to protect her. I didn't know how much of my mind was easily accessible. You try keeping someone you care for safe, not knowing if the knowledge you possess will sign their death warrant or worse."

Gavriel hated—*hated*—the excuse of lying to someone to protect them. It was a coward's way out of owning their mistakes. Trying to command some noble honor in their betrayal.

"You keep saying you care for her, but I'm not sure you know what it means."

Ferryn's eyes narrowed, face reddening. "I've seen Lark at her worst. At the very depths of her misery and been there for her. Do not accuse me of not caring just because you're angry. Be angry. It's rightfully earned. But don't make the mistake of thinking your anger makes everyone your enemy. You'll need every ally you can get—not only to get her back but to save her from whatever Nereida is planning."

Gavriel exhaled, the tension leaving his body in slow drifts. Damn it. Damn him. He was right. Gavriel reluctantly released Ferryn, and Ferryn smoothed out his traveling cloak.

"Now, where were we? Oh, yes. You were about to express your gratitude in my rebellious decision to give Lark your death."

Gavriel growled, stalking ahead.

Ferryn caught up easily with his long strides. "I will accept you naming your firstborn after me. Ferryn or Ferryna. I'm not picky."

"You never cease prattling."

"I told you before. It soothes me."

Gavriel bit his tongue. Any response would encourage Ferryn to continue.

Unfortunately, he needed little encouragement.

"It pulls Lark out of her broody little moods, too. Usually just for the sake of trying to shut me up. But still. Lending purpose to an over-burdened mind, a distraction from all it bears, can be a most cathartic experience."

Gavriel should not answer. It would be validating the man's exhaustive personality. But he found a small smile tugging at the corner of his mouth as a memory of doing just that came to him. He'd been foolish to tail Daciana and Lark so closely, but something had called to him, demanding he stay near. And when they were caught, when venomous threats to Lark's person were whispered in his ear, when they drugged her and carted them all off, he'd been consumed by rage—by thoughts of every way the human body experiences pain, so he might employ those methods to their captors and anyone who dared touch her. When Lark awoke, and her fear and panic overcame her, it was her tears that broke him. He did whatever it took to lessen her pain.

"It's true," Gavriel finally said. "I might have employed a touch of the same when we were bound in the back of a wagon headed to the indenture's mining camp."

"See?" Ferryn clapped him on the back, and Gavriel resisted the urge to shove him away. "You and I are more alike than you think! We'll most likely end this journey with special nicknames and matching tattoos."

"Absolutely not."

The edge of Inerys' protective ward on her lands came into view. The snow was melted in a perfectly formed perimeter where she must have performed her spell.

"Black salt," Ferryn said. "I asked her out of curiosity. Though she could have been lying. Or confused. She had lost a lot of blood by that point."

Gavriel pulled the lantern from his bag. This was it. The moment of truth.

He had no way of knowing how to navigate the damned thing, but he knew what his purpose was.

He let his mind wander to her. To Lark. To every kiss they'd ever shared, in this life and the one that started it all. Her smile. The touch of her hand. Her scent of sun-ripened apples and spices. Her laugh. Her joy. A dizzying spell weaving through every precious moment he'd ever been lucky enough to call her his. It was warmth. A freshly lit hearth. It was relief. The first plunge into the lake on a hot day. It was everything. The beginning and the end and every moment of significance in between. It enveloped him. Spread through him. Filled him with the sense of hope he'd only ever felt by her side.

Gavriel turned the key, and blue flame erupted behind the glass.

CHAPTER THIRTY-SIX

LARK

lood and sweat coated Lark's skin, each heaving breath its own form of agony.

Merikh stopped, studying her with almost a pitying stare. "I do not enjoy this, I assure you."

A memory flitted just out of reach. *"I assure you, I don't enjoy this."*

It was a lie then. It was a lie now.

Lark wanted to answer. To call him a liar, but she didn't trust her voice. Not with the fire lancing through her skin. Not with the way she trembled from the pain.

"It really would be easier, for both of us, if you just told me. My fight is not with you, but I can't allow my sympathy to hinder my cause."

"How," she bit out, struggling to keep her voice steady. "How fucking noble."

Merikh sighed as if disappointed. As if he'd offered her the last piece of pie and she'd refused. It was a polite sound of dissatisfaction.

"Very well."

He began to carve again, ripping the neck of her tunic this time. He carefully avoided her breastband, but her ribs, her stomach, her chest, he shredded to ribbons. Lark's vision dimmed, the pain beginning to steal her consciousness. Darkness threatening to take over.

"Not to be cruel, but I can heal you and do this as many times as it takes." He lifted her chin with the handle of Hugo's knife. "You being a passenger soul has its advantages. For me, of course. I'd never bring a mere mortal here."

Lark's thoughts caught on that. On the implication. "Where is here?" Her words were weak, barely a whisper of a sound.

His brow furrowed. "Where is the somniavi?"

"I'll tell you if you can guess how many fingers I'm holding up." Lark laughed at her own joke, the sound of her voice thick and slow like the molasses Mrs. O'Connell used to make her gingerbread cookies. She tried to conjure the memory of their scent. Of how the air could thicken with cinnamon and nutmeg and—

Fog overtook Lark's mind as the pain seeped any strength from her. Pain in her sliced nerves. Pain in the never-ending loss.

"You think this means you're strong. And maybe you are, but you're also foolish. I do not speak false. I have no quarrel with you or your people. I only want the somniavi."

Sweat dripped into Lark's eyes, her tongue too big for her mouth. "And I only want that last piece of pie you mentioned."

The expression of sheer confusion he wore was enough to pull another lazy laugh from her mouth.

"Sorry. I got you confused with the thoughts in my head."

"Your human mind is shutting down. You've suffered considerable pain. Grant me the answer I seek, and you needn't feel any more pain."

"You must enjoy the pain. Is that why you choose it?"

Why did it feel like a dream? An image at the murkiest edge of her mind. Whose voice was she hearing?

"Have you ever... felt like something had already happened before? This all feels familiar."

Merikh's next cut ran down the length of her face. He didn't even falter against the slick of sweat upon her skin. Nor did he react to the sound of pain she released.

"Tell me where she is."

Oh. He was angry now.

"No." Lark laughed, the sound quickly melting into a groan. "No! No! No! No! No!" She sang it like a boisterous song, her voice echoing off the filthy walls.

"Where is she?!" His bellow shook the room. The floor. It darkened the shadows. Something in Lark's mind cracked, and thick, all-consuming awareness flooded her.

"Where is she?"

Lark was stretched across a table, arms bound above her head. "I don't know."

"She was your friend. Don't lie to me, you little bitch." His hand flew, a sharp crack against her jaw. "I assure you, I don't enjoy this. But the master demands answers, and I will have them."

But he did enjoy it. Lark sensed the pleasure brewing beneath the surface. The way his eyes raked down her vulnerable position. His mouth open, breathing heavily as he sought whatever spot made her talk.

Enolf was known for his cruelty. An indenture with the longest, bloodiest history with their master. He was overseer of the rest of them, doling out punishments when the master deemed it below his care. Ayn had gone missing, slipped away in the night,

Of course, Lark knew how she escaped. No one thought to question the guard who'd recently been transferred. No one suspected he'd been vying for a change in position since the first time he laid eyes on Ayn. Or that they orchestrated her elaborate escape.

They were halfway to Vallemer by now, forever out of Enolf's reach. It didn't matter how much he brutalized her body. How many ribs he dislocated. How many fingers he broke. Not even when he lifted her skirts and threatened her with the punishment even their master wouldn't approve of.

His indentures were to remain untouched, as their bodies were his instruments, and none were to be tarnished by such base urges.

Enolf was wasting his foul scented breath interrogating her. And the fact that he hadn't used the whip only proved he was operating without the master's blessing.

Lark couldn't help but smile at the thought.

"You must enjoy the pain. Is that why you choose it?"

She clamped her mouth shut, refusing to add fire to the flame of his anger. If she were lucky, it would die out quickly.

"I know ways to inflict pain that leave no mark on the body." He ran his hand possessively across her chest, and nausea rolled in her belly. "Would you like me to show you?"

The bang of a door against the wall startled them both. A guard stomped in. Behind him, a fellow indenture followed. She'd seen him a few times now but never had the chance to speak to him. Not with helping Ayn plan her escape. What was his name again?

"You are summoned," the guard spat, casting a disdainful look upon Enolf and ignoring Lark entirely.

"I'm a bit busy."

"Your time is not your own. A lesson you seem to need revisiting." The threat hung in the air. That Enolf had taken matters into his own hands was an act of rebellion in itself. The master would not abide such measures.

"I only—"

"You will speak when explicitly told to. Now come." The guard hurried him away, leaving Lark bound atop the table in Enolf's room.

When the last of the footfalls fell silent, the indenture rushed toward her.

"I'm sorry I couldn't get here sooner." His voice was deep, a soft rumble of a sound. Lark studied him. The scars running down the side of his face and across his mouth. The deep sorrow in his eyes. He was handsome in a way she hadn't appreciated in a man. Not for many moons. But it was the way he wore his soul in his expressions that drew her in.

"You're the one who plays the fiddle," she said, grinning when his cheeks flushed pink.

"Ah, yes." His eyes met hers, and something tugged in her chest. "You sing the children to sleep."

It was impossible, the way a warm blanket of safety seemed to wrap around her in his presence. This man she did not know. In a place filled with nothing but pain. Perhaps his kindness was just a rare flame in the dark, and she was drawn to the only warmth to be found.

Lark rubbed her wrists, sliding her hand into his, and allowing him to help her to her feet. His palm was warm against hers, a soft touch she hadn't realized she'd missed.

Neither one of them seemed ready to let go.

"Perhaps we can perform a duet sometime."

He smirked, tugging that scar and her heart with it. "That seems a terrible idea."

"Lucky for us," she said, leaning in close to conspiratorially whisper, "I'm rather fond of terrible ideas."

Lark snapped back into her body. Into her mind. Into her awareness.

Tears flowed freely now, as the first laugh broke free and then another.

Her memories.

Her life.

Gavriel.

His face was not the same, nor his name. But it was him. It was him, and she'd recognize him anywhere, in any life, on any plane.

She remembered. She remembered it all.

"Why are you laughing?"

She ignored Merikh, reveling in her pain and joy and *oh! She remembered!*

Something else was different. Her body still suffered the pain of Merikh's torture, but her mind possessed a greater clarity than before. Like she'd been operating without sleep, and suddenly her energy was restored.

Following a hunch, she spread her awareness out.

She'd freed her power from Merikh's control. Yanked the remnants of her soul back into her body.

Memory was power, and she'd lived too long without hers.

Lark smiled, enjoying the confused flash of fear on the foolish paragon's face.

She had been restored.

CHAPTER THIRTY-SEVEN

LARK

*E*choes of pain remained, the memory still fresh like the lingering taste of an apple upon her tongue. Lark braced herself for the onslaught, for Merikh to drive her further from herself. For him to finally find that one place, the place that held the last shreds of her humanity.

But it never came.

She blinked her eyes open.

Merikh stood with his back to her, examining his blade. His posture was relaxed, but that meant nothing of comfort. He was dispassionate in his torture, and there was no pleasure or satisfaction or even anger as he cut through her vulnerable flesh. It was calculating. Clinical. Cold.

"This isn't working." His low voice, the first words he'd spoken to her in ages, shattered the heavy silence of the room.

Lark was giving him nothing, and he must have exhausted his patience. She held no further use to him, which only meant one thing. "You're to kill me now?"

Merikh sighed. "To take life is wasteful. Especially one as fascinating as yours."

Lark's head spun. He didn't mean to kill her, but to spend what felt like an eternity torturing her, that was more humane? "Your moral compass is faulty."

"Morality is a human construct. We're above that." He turned, leaning against the table. The bloody instruments he'd whittled her skin with gleamed behind him. "I have one aim—to find the somniavi. My efforts are in pursuit of that, not something as base as vengeance. My tactics have not worked, so we're trying a new strategy."

He snapped his fingers, and the spelled bindings fell away. Lark didn't move. If this was a trap, she needed to sort it out before she walked straight into it. There were weapons on the table behind him, but none that would harm him.

She needed the Reaper Blade.

Merikh caught her line of sight, turning his head to examine the knives. He lifted Hugo's dagger, and Lark's stomach turned.

Her blood still coated its blade, crudely crusted over the finish. A stark reminder that he'd taken something she loved, something that represented everything to her, and brought her immeasurable pain.

One might think there was a lesson in that.

"Want this back?" He waved it at her, before tossing it in her direction.

Lark snatched it from the air, her fingers curling around the all-too-familiar handle. Etched symbols sitting in her palm, taunting her.

"Where's my other one?"

Merikh fought a smile. "That one I'm keeping."

Anger replaced the lingering pain. It spread through Lark's body, hardening every fiber until the memory of his torture was replaced by a scorching need to spill his blood. In his brutality, every piece of herself had returned.

Patience. She needed patience.

"If you aren't going to kill me, what do you want?"

Merikh nodded as if pleased she asked the right question. "Follow me." He straightened, heading toward the wall.

There was no door. No exit. Only a solid and stained wall. Merikh placed a palm against its filthy surface, and it rippled under his touch. An illusion.

"I could have escaped at any time?"

"I never would have allowed it," he said simply. "But no, the walls were solid for as long as I wished them to be."

Lark stood, surprisingly steady. "And how long was that?"

Merikh frowned. "Time does not exist here the way it does in your world. On the mortal plane, we've been gone mere moments. But here…"

He let his meaning fall into silence implying an indeterminate amount of time he'd spent torturing her, only to let her go.

"I have another method of persuasion." He crossed his arms, and Lark had the sudden urge to sink Hugo's knife into his heart. It wouldn't make a difference. It wouldn't damage a paragon, but if he could bleed, maybe his blood would wash away her own.

"What makes you think I'll ever trust you?"

"You don't exactly have a choice," he said. "Besides," a wry smirk pulled at his mouth, an eerie sight since his eyes remained flat and lifeless. It was as if he was attempting to imitate a human expression. "I've spent a lot of time inside your mind. I know you better than you think."

"You don't know a damn thing about me."

He angled his head. "Look down."

Confusion jolted through Lark's senses. "I don't know what game you're playing—"

"Look. Down."

Lark glanced down to find her clothing unmarred by his blades. He'd ripped her tunic and leggings to shreds, leaving her in nothing but her small clothes and the scraps of fabric clinging together, but her clothing had been fully restored.

"You… repaired the fabric when you healed me?"

Merikh tutted. "I never touched you."

How was that possible? He'd cut into her skin over and over. Healing and fraying and peeling away from the muscles, the ligaments, the bone—

Lark caught sight of Hugo's knife still in her hand, the blade cleaned of her blood.

"You didn't really think you're the only one with the ability to write in memories of pain, did you?" He scoffed. "Where do you think Reapers inherited their abilities from?"

Lark's head spun, memories warring with the words he spoke. *It wasn't real?* But she'd felt it. Felt every drag of the knife's edge. Felt the warm wetness of her blood, the searing sting of exposed nerves.

"Come," Merikh said. "Like I said, I know you now. You've a strong mind and even stronger will. But your curiosity is your stoutest drive." He grinned, and this time it was a true expression. "Haven't you always wanted to see Avalon?"

THE WALL RIPPLED like a disturbed lake, bending and flowing until it shattered entirely. Drops of its visage fell like rain, the rest of the room fading away.

Lark turned back to regard Merikh, her breath catching when she saw the vast void behind him.

It was a night without stars, the truest blackness she'd ever seen.

"Eyes forward," Merikh said. "Never look back."

With a deep, bracing breath, Lark turned around, gasping. An ancient doorway stood before her. Open and inviting. Gnarled roots formed its edge, redcaps and luminescent flora framing the open doorway. The scent of freshly overturned earth filled Lark's senses, alongside the rich smell of grass and a bubbling brook on a warm day.

The sound of water rushing over rocks met her ears at the thought, and Lark made to spin around and question Merikh.

His hands grasped her shoulders, hard and bruising. "Eyes front, I said."

"What happens if I look back?"

His answering silence was threat enough. The land beyond the door beckoned. A forest of colors she'd never seen amongst trees in the mortal world awaited. Turquoise leaves, pale pink petals, they undulated atop lean and towering trunks. A soft spongey moss created the forest floor. A clearing marked a path to travel through the forest, and

Lark did not trust how badly her muscles screamed for her to take that step through the door.

"This feels... wrong."

"I highly doubt that," Merikh said behind her. "It calls to you, doesn't it?"

"That's what concerns me." Lark could not reverse into the gaping void at her back. But her instincts warned her of traveling forward. "What lies beyond the door?"

"So many questions. And all of the answers are through there." Merikh crowded her space, getting far too close. "Step forward and learn all the mysteries that have eluded you. I promise I will show you everything they hid from you. Unmask every lie they told you, and your curiosity will be fed like the gluttonous beast that it is."

"You speak like a demon of desire," Lark muttered. "You forget, I once received compensation for killing Undesirables let loose in the mortal world."

Desire demons were a special breed of monster in the Netherworld. The type to play with their victim's mind, using their memories, their desires, their ambitions to trap them. Their magic was much like that of the Forbidden Shrine, carrying the ability to project images, sensations, faces of loved ones to force their victim to do their bidding. Their power was derived from hungry desire; the more one consumed the lies they spun, the more one fell under their spell.

"I have no desire, and yours is a means to an end. I will not lie to you, not when the truth wields far more power and damage."

Well. That was something.

Though the word of a man who just spent an inordinate amount of time torturing her was foolish to take at face value.

He spoke true about one thing though.

Lark had always wondered about Avalon. The stories of grandeur were tempered by the nearly universal disdain her kind held for the paragons. Their arbitrary rules and limits on who received peace in the afterlife. Lark had guided and bonded with enough souls to know there was no such thing as a perfect human. One free from the stain of their mistakes. That joy and love and compassion were not mutually exclusive with malice and rage and vengeance.

It was almost as if the paragons loathed the humans so much, they wished to keep them out.

And when Solana, one of Sargon's most beloved subjects, created Arcadia, she gifted that peace to humans who'd never made it to Avalon. She gave them peace and joy in the afterlife. A second chance to be with their loved ones. And Sargon punished her for it. Condemning her to eternity in the Forbidden Shrine, until she agreed to destroy the sanctuary deep within the pits that she had created.

Only she'd refused. And when Lark found her, she'd wished for her freedom, forever crumbling the Forbidden Shrine to rubble. Hugo's body trapped within.

No, there wasn't much about Avalon or its ruler Sargon that Lark trusted. But what choice had she?

Lark forced her feet to move, shivering when the soft caress of an invisible veil ran along her face. She stepped all the way through, that foreign sensation passing over her entire body, and stilled.

Birdsongs trilled in the sky high above. The damp air softened around her, a fragrant embrace carrying the scent of earth and lavender and verdant leaves. It was like an eternal spring, nothing but *life,* of rebirth and growth surrounding her. It was...

"Magic," Lark said on an exhale. Why had she been so nervous? She could spend hours in this forest. Days. An eternity. She could lie down on that riverbank and dip her fingers into the rushing water, allowing it to wash over her. The sun caught the ripples as the river rushed over pebbles and mossy logs, diamond shards of light refracting along the bank.

Nothing else seemed to matter but the peaceful tranquility of this forest and all its wonders. Lark wanted to seep beneath its roots, lay down her own roots, and fit her lungs to breath with the trees for the rest of her days...

Lark startled, ripping Hugo's blade free from her belt and spinning to aim it at Merikh. Her pulse thundered in her head, every cell in her body on alert.

He'd almost had her. *Almost* trapped her.

Merikh nodded, raising his brows. "I have to hand it to you, Lark. Your will is far stronger than I'd anticipated. Mortals who walk in Avalon forget the life they left in favor of rejoicing in their gift." He frowned. "It wouldn't be paradise if they spent their days whining about loved ones who failed to make the cut."

"You said," Lark ground out, "no lies."

"I'm not lying. I will answer every question you have. I never promised you'd possess the awareness to ask them." He gestured around them. "The first one you never had to ask. Why do the mortals who join Avalon bear no grief against the loss of their loved ones. They don't remember them."

"That is no gift," Lark spat, the point of her weapon still trained on him. "You steal their memories."

"They don't miss what they don't recall."

"Trust me," Lark said. "They do. Even if they aren't sure what's missing, they feel it. In every breath, every sensation, every smile, the ache of what's lost is keenly felt."

"I did not bring you here to debate this matter." Merikh's eyes flashed dangerously. "Time might not move here should I wish it, but that does not mean I will linger when I have a job to complete." He edged a step closer, sighing when Lark matched his movement to maintain distance. "I already told you, I will not harm you. My aim is to educate you on matters you are ignorant on so you'll see why you must help me."

"You've tricked me twice, yet you complain I'm untrusting." Lark flipped the knife in her hold, angling her blade in its silent threat. "Sounds to me like you're the one ignorant on the way the world works."

"Stab me or don't. But you'll never get your answers if you antagonize me." A knowing smile tugged at the corner of his mouth. "Nor will you return to your human lover without my leave. Cooperate. Allow me to show you our ways and what is at stake. If at the end, you still wish to use that precious little needle on me, go for it." With one last look, he strode ahead of her, not even turning back to see if she followed.

Lark glanced around the forest. The hum of its song still vibrated in her bones, threatening to lull her into complacency.

She sheathed her blade and ran to catch up with Merikh.

There was nothing he could say, nothing he could promise to convince her to give up Aislinn. But the more she learned about this place, the better. It might come in handy when it came time to dismantle Nereida's plan.

"Avalon is a living, breathing place. It has memory and evolves with its patrons. Describe what you see."

Lark sighed. She never did enjoy a prettily worded lecture. "Trees. It's a forest. Spare me your theatrics and get to the point."

Merikh scowled. "You are impatient for an immortal. Although, since your lifespan has been drastically reduced, I suppose it makes sense."

"I was always this way. Now get on with it."

Merikh made a noise of disapproval. "What you see is truth without absolutes. Another mortal might walk through Avalon's gate and step upon a sandy beach. A favored tavern. The peak of a mountain overlooking the vastness of the wild. My world bends, it flows, it fluidly shifts to match the energy and needs of each individual."

That sounded dangerously close to mind manipulation. "So, it's all a trick."

"No. It's a gift to the senses. Why shouldn't the souls of the deceased be greeted with the peace that speaks to them? How can one promise a blissful existence to all without factoring in individual desires? If we built a community, shoving humans together and forcing them to spend their eternities coexisting regardless of their preferences, it wouldn't be Avalon at all. It would just be another miserable plane of existence."

Lark bit the inside of her cheek, mulling over her response. "That's an awful lot of words to say, 'we lie to you with false images.' It would be quicker to call Avalon a state of mind." Because that's what it was.

It was the oath she always feared from Thanar. The theft of autonomy and connection to reality. It was another lie.

"You oversimplify. Each soul is given a handcrafted paradise. If you are so arrogant not to appreciate such a gift, the odds of a soul like you even ascending to Avalon are nonexistent."

Oh. Someone struck a nerve. "Your bitterness is showing."

Merikh quickened his pace. "I am not bitter. I do not care what happens to mortals who reject the gift of the afterlife. But I question the strength of your logical reasoning if you insist on misunderstanding me."

Lark fought the urge to smile. "All right. We'll call it a gift." *It most assuredly was not.* "So, Avalon has no true form? If it exists to be recrafted to every soul who passes through."

"Paragons and warriors have the ability to see the true face of Avalon, and I will permit you to bear witness." He glanced down at her, a smug smirk on his mouth. "And we haven't even reached Avalon yet. This is merely the passageway."

Well, shit.

The trees thinned, lush forest giving way to a low valley. Grassy knolls lied beyond, a warm breeze skirting through each blade. Beyond the valley sloped a mountainous range, the dark green of its wooded range. The peaks reached high into the sky, scraping through the thick fog of the clouds.

Merikh stopped, and Lark matched his pause.

"What is it?"

"It's time to show you what's at stake. Why I need you to deliver the somniavi to me." At Lark's expression, he added, "Do not lie. I've flipped through every memory you possess. I know of your tether and connection. I know she's infiltrated your dreams before. And with your newly restored power, it should be effortless to reestablish the connection."

Heat pricked along Lark's neck, spreading with each pulse of her blood. He sifted through her memories. Perused her secrets and intimate moments as if flipping through an open book.

Thank the skies she did not know where Daciana and Kenna took

256

Aislinn. The agreement to keep from sharing the knowledge chafed at first but now served as the protective blessing Lark sorely needed.

Aislinn sorely needed.

"You're angry? Good. That is how it felt when your friend dug her claws into my mind without permission." His dark brows furrowed, and his jaw clenched.

Interesting.

"I thought this wasn't personal."

Surprise softened the anger in his expression. "It isn't. She poses a great danger to my world. To all of humankind if she is not dealt with."

"No," Lark said, tapping her chin. "That's not it. She bested you. *Easily*. Bet to an ancient war general, or whatever the blazes you are, that stings."

Merikh's nostrils flared, and Lark internally triumphed at how human his reactions seemed. It chipped away any intimidation he could impose if Lark could imagine him as yet another man punching down when things didn't go his way.

"I am under strict orders to exterminate the somniavi. My feelings are of no consequence."

"Yes, but you have them. And that's the whole point."

Merikh's eyes darkened, a dangerous storm overtaking his features. Lark stood taller, knowing she had him in this.

He shoved her, hard, and the world spun with the movement as she careened down the hill. Legs over head. Head over feet. Round and round she went. A spiral of green and gray and blue and sky was the ground and *that bastard* was so petty—

Lark skidded to a stop, her vision spinning despite the stilling of her movements. Her head and her stomach were in agreement—that if she'd had anything to eat it would be purged on the ground beneath her.

Lark reached out to press her hand against the ground. It wasn't grass... she wasn't at the foot of a steep hill, deep in a valley.

She was on sand. Warm, soft, yellow sand. She cupped it in her hand, letting the grains spill between her fingers. It wasn't like the sand in the arena, reddish clay with stains of blood. It wasn't like the sand in the Desolates, so hot under the unforgiving sun, it burned the skin. It was a whisper of a caress. A touch of silk. A ribbon slipping between the seams of her fingers.

Lark examined her fingers. Light danced atop her skin, but it wasn't the harsh light of direct sun. It was ripples of quiet light undulating along her hand. As if she was underwater and the sea lessened the strength of the sun, letting the light sigh through calm waters.

A rush of wind skirted through her ear, whistling and sending a pleasant shiver down her spine. Her scalp pricked with the warm air blowing against her hair. Like a gentle exhale of breath. Soft. Intimate. The sound of a crashing surf flitted into her awareness, the steady scrape of a wave against the sand.

A shadow loomed above her, darkening her view and blotting out the sun.

"Up you get, Reaper," Merikh's voice rumbled. A large hand appeared before her, a silent offering. Lark resisted the urge to slap it away, deservedly so since it was his fault she was even flat on her back, but rather than accept his help, she pushed herself up, standing on unsteady feet as her equilibrium fought to return to balance.

Before her, stretched a long shoreline, waves rushing up to meet her. Both the sun and the moon sat large and close in an azure sky, their combined light near blinding to look directly upon. But along the sand, the glimmering ocean, along her skin, her clothing, that same gentle flourish of light danced like it fought its way to the bottom of the shallows. In the distance, upon a tall crag, stood a great castle of white stone. Its intricate shape boasted countless vestibules and rooms. Golden spires twisted high in the sky, and matching battlements glittered beneath the sun and moon.

"This is Avalon?" Lark's words escaped her chest with the force of a whisper. Thanar's creations in the Otherworld were always pale imitations, lacking depth and life. But this...

It was as if the paragons had claimed all the life from the human realm, flooding their world with it.

"This is just a piece." Merikh lifted his chin. "Prepare your questions and tighten your jaw. I have no desire to explain to the others why I'm parading a slack-mouthed Reaper through our lands."

It was meant to be an insult, or at the very least, a prodding of her pride. The satisfaction he took in her awe. But all Lark heard was a detail he may not have intended to share.

"Does bringing me here make you look ineffective and weak?"

"My commander knows I am neither of those things."

"Usually, but things don't seem to be going according to plan."

His face darkened. "I cannot control what I am ordered to do to you should you use our arrangement against me. *If* Sargon tracks my presence, I will tell him you are a Reaper turned human ally, gathering intelligence against the slippery somniavi. That you have traveled here to bolster your strength against her and force the connection so I can track her on human lands." His voice was hardened, the words he spoke with stilted and over-enunciated. "Because after I sate your curiosity, you *will* seek to help me."

"You know what they say about assuming…"

His hand curled in her collar, tangling tightly. "Do not play games here. You won't enjoy losing."

Lark was used to losing by now. Damn nearly an expert. None of her plans seemed to work out, so that was not the threat he intended. But she needed to stop tipping her hand. There was power in knowledge, and she wanted to acquire as much of it as she could.

And he did not need the knowledge of her thoughts, now that she'd effectively locked him out of her head. She should stop speaking them aloud.

She gritted her teeth and forced herself to say, "Understood."

CHAPTER THIRTY-EIGHT

DEMETRIA

The air was thin deep in the mines. Made thinner by the scent of sweat. Demetria's body warred with her exhaustion. She lifted her trembling pickaxe, the rough wood biting into her bloodied palms. Fluid filled blisters burst and reformed, slicking her grip and stinging her hands. But she'd learned not to pause. Not to rest. Not to show any form of weakness.

The guards preyed on such weakness.

A girl, maybe two summers older than she, had collapsed on the third day. They dragged her limp body away, and she hadn't been seen since. There were whispers of her fate. That she'd been sold to an underground pleasure house. Gifted as a bride to an aging lord from the northern region. Dumped into the sea and washed away.

The most likely of all, that she was dead. A body unfit to work was just another mouth to feed, and they did not suffer costly investments.

Demetria struck the stone, her cry hoarse from thirst. Her head light from hunger.

They were given just enough to keep them alive. A slow death by starvation as they worked themselves to the bone. No one had harvested anything, and she suspected this to be an empty tunnel. But she was determined to find a shard of dragonstone. She had to gain a foothold in the castle. Track down anyone who might still be an ally, and finish what she started. At the very least, seize the chance to take her brother down. Even if it killed her. It would be a necessary sacrifice in ridding the world of that monster. And if the kingdom fell into chaos?

It was already broken. The fact that prisoners were stolen and forced to labor 'til their last breath was proof of that.

Perhaps the kingdom needed to be burned to the ground.

"Here." Balan handed her a canteen, glancing around to be sure no one noticed him.

"Where did you get that?" Demetria hissed, snatching it up and removing the stopper. The water was warm, a murky taste coating her tongue, but it was the most heavenly thing she'd ever consumed.

"While you've been toiling away, *I* have been forging some necessary connections."

Demetria wiped her mouth, assessing his filthy face. His white hair was darkened by soot and dirt, his silver eyes dim and glassy. A bruise had formed in the corner of his mouth. "What does that mean?"

"It means," Balan said, snatching the water back, "even though my physical form has been reduced to this weak state, turns out I've retained some of my necessary abilities to isolate any given human's greatest desire." He gave her a wicked smile. "Mortals easily plied with hopes and wishes are the lowest hanging fruit."

"Speak plainly before we're punished." Demetria lifted her pickaxe, wincing at the burning in her palm, and continued chipping away at her task.

"I have acquired all the names of the guards on duty, along with their greatest wishes." He leaned against the cavern wall, and Demetria glanced around wildly to be sure no one was watching. "Monk has a pretty little wife at home he simply cannot ripen with his seed. Reeve wants Monk's wife to bounce on his pathetic cock. Ivar is itching for a promotion so his father will stop regarding his life choices as failure, and Berric desires a sudden influx of coin to pay off his gambling debts. But he also wants an edge against the gamemaster because he can feel his lucky streak on the edge of the horizon." Balan snorted, a derisive sound. "The only one I can't crack is Knight Captain Einar. But I haven't spent enough time with him." Balan pushed off the wall and shrugged. "Oh well. Can't win them all. But I can pit them against one another long enough for a distraction."

That might work in freeing them, for the moment. But Demetria would still be a fugitive in her own kingdom. And the notion that more guards weren't waiting for them at the exit was a huge assumption. Balan had to know this, so the natural solution would be taking them by surprise and picking them off one by one. A bloody affair. One Demetria wanted no part in. But necessary sacrifices were small when compared to the lives they'd save toppling Zaire's reign, weren't they? There was a difference between the idea of a sacrifice and ending a man's life with one's bare hands.

"Pass, for now," Demetria said. She couldn't afford to draw hard and fast lines in her moral standing, but she could try. "Once I find dragonstone—"

"There is no dragonstone in this cave. This is what we call manipulative torture of promise. Like when I'd tell mortals they could earn freedom from my torment if they could guess my human name. No one was ever clever enough to assume I'd kept my name."

"It will be worth it when I buy my way into the castle."

"And then what?" Balan crowded her space, glaring down his nose at her. "Some sort of suicide mission? We escape. We regroup. We replan. That is how we survive."

Why was he angry? He was free to follow his own escape plan. After she found the dragonstone. "Not yet. If you enact your plan, I will not run, and you will only make my plan harder to achieve." Because who knew what sort of punishment they'd all face after Balan sprung his escape?

He growled, scrunching his nose in disgust. "Fine. Let's hope your vengeance is worth the cost, little fool." With a turn on his heel, he marched off. His stride tall and purposeful as if he owned the place. He was going to get himself killed if he didn't watch it.

And then she would well and truly be alone.

"Did you two have a fight?" A soft voice, thin and wavery, called out from behind.

Demetria jolted and spun, finding the girl who had collapsed and been dragged away. She was neither dead nor sold, unless this was a spirit taking her form. Demetria shook the thought from her head. It was bad enough being down here, there was no need to despair the notion that even death was a cage. The girl's blonde hair was filthy and matted, dirt staining her cheeks. Her brown eyes sparkled with unshed tears, and she turned the handle of her pickaxe over in her hands. "I'm sorry," she added, her gaze dipping to the floor of the cave. "I didn't mean to intrude. I only came over to see if I—would it be—that is to say…"

Spit. It. Out. Already.

Normally Demetria's compassion guided her thoughts. But she was tired and starving and in desperate need of a win.

"Could I dig near you?"

Oh.

Had it really come to this? Was the girl really that frightened to dig near someone? As if some unknown punishment lied in wait just around the darkened corner.

Warmth spread through Demetria's chest. "That's no trouble at all."

The girl smiled, her teeth chipped and beginning to yellow. Demetria did *not* wish to know how her own appearance fared. "I'm Marian," she said.

"Dem—" Balan was right. She was a damn fool, especially if she was willing to blab her true name to some random girl. Why hadn't she remembered the name Langford had given her when they were docked at Emeraude Port? "Demi."

"Well met, Demi."

Demetria nodded, her throat tight. She would get an earful from Balan later for this slip up. She resumed carving into the earth, the sharp resonance of iron against stone filling the silence.

"Where are you from?" Marian's voice came again.

Demetria struck harder. She could lie, pretend to be from anywhere. But she hadn't thought to hide her accent. "Here, actually."

Strike. "I fled to avoid a fate such as this, only to be swindled by a smuggler in the midlands."

"Oh, no," Marian said softly. "That's awfully rotten luck."

You have no idea.

They fell back into the rhythm of mining, careful to avoid the network of pillars keeping the roof above their heads. Though the notion of collapsing the entire mine was growing more tempting by the moment. Each strike against stone ripped open Demetria's palms and reverberated up her arms.

"My mother, sister, and I... we were from Oakbury."

Her sister. Demetria studied the girl and realized the one who'd collapsed looked an awful lot like her, only a handful of years older. Marian's sister was the one they'd dragged away.

Marian continued. "There was a terrible attack... some sort of beast ravaged our village. It turned people I'd known all my life into..." She trailed off, sobs wracking her body. "Forgive me. It's still so fresh."

The monsters Lark let loose on the world. Daciana tore down the veil in her pursuit of bringing Alistair back. Demetria could not fault her, Alistair was... well, Langford didn't deserve to lose him like that. But it all came back to Lark, didn't it? Even the loss of Ruslan. She created this void, and it sucked everything good everyone else held dear into it.

Demetria tightened her grip on her pickaxe, ignoring the sting of splintered wood against her bloody hands.

"Anyway. We ran and took sanctuary in the wrong harbor it would seem."

A similar mistake Demetria had made. "I'm sorry," she said. And she was. It wasn't fair, this world they were forced to survive in. It made everything that once seemed so stark a bit hazy. The extents to which a person would go, could go, to keep their heart beating was tested at every turn.

"I am, too, about you." Marian winced at her awkward wording. "You know, you're the only person who hasn't asked what they did to my sister."

Demetria stiffened. Her pulse raced, the blood rushing in her ears.

She did not need more fuel to keep her fire burning. "It's none of my business."

"They"—Marian hesitated. "I told them all's she needed was rest. A proper chance to recover. They said she wasn't worth the cost—" She covered her mouth, trembling violently as tears poured down her face. Moments passed, and Demetria stood in shocked silence at her admission. Warring with pity and rage.

She would do whatever it took to gain a foothold in that castle. And every guard on Zaire's command, she did not care if they had a family, if they were a fucking saint of the highest order—

They would all burn.

Marian's breaths quieted, leveling out, and she lowered her hand. "I don't know why I told you that." She let out a stuttered exhale. "Just... don't let your body give out. Don't let them see you give up. We're nothing but tools to these lot, and the moment you lack your usefulness..." She resumed carving into the wall with more force than before.

Her words crept inside Demetria's head, taking their place in the growing shadows. She lifted her pickaxe, studying the girl still silently weeping as she struck at the unyielding barrier.

No matter what befalls me, no matter what comes next, I will not fail.

"GODS ABOVE BE PRAISED!" Marian's voice rang out beside her, and Demetria wiped the sweat from her brow.

They'd been mining for hours, side by side. Marian chattering away at times and falling silent at others. Demetria reserved her strength for fighting against the stone, offering almost nothing to the girl's conversation in return.

But that hadn't stopped her.

She'd told Demetria of her home. Of the best apple tarts courtesy of the Walden Inn and Tavern. Of teetering along the low sitting rock walls, stones nestled and laid to forge the perimeter of the road. She spoke of her childhood crush, a boy named Kol who had too many freckles and a smile too big for his face. Demetria loathed the way it made her thoughts turn to Evander. Marian told her of summer thunderstorms in the field—of whispers of a good witch who lived deep in the forest and left protective laurels around their village. She blushed, admitting she'd considered searching for the witch who watched over her village to ask if she performed love spells.

Marian spoke of her life, of her dreams and wishes and hopes. As if it didn't hurt to remember she had a life with a bed and with people who loved her. How she had freedom and options and hadn't had everything stolen away.

And Demetria plotted. She imagined all the different ways she could end Zaire's life. Would she suffer any remorse when the light left his eyes? She doubted it. Not when the image of Evander's neck, splayed opened by the fall of the blade, reminded her of her purpose. Ruslan's death, a farewell she never got to give, answered her question.

What would her parents say if they could see her now? Shame dipped in the pit of her stomach. Her father... he never would have let it get this far. He was always kind and gentle, but hard on Zaire when he needed it. And in his absence, no one had kept Zaire in check. Whatever Demetria did now, was no fault of her own. It was in response to the violence Zaire called for. But her mother... Her mother had always told her stories of misunderstood monsters, weaving compassion in her tales of warning. As if knowing Demetria needed such things.

Marian was chattering again, sobs coming faster as she dropped her axe and started clawing at the stone, scraping her filthy nails around a dark protrusion. The harsh scratching sound setting Demetria's teeth on edge. "I can't believe it! The paragons do answer prayers!"

She struck the rock, laughing hysterically as her prize finally fell free, and held it out for Demetria's inspection.

Within her dirty palm, a shard of crystal clinging to its edge, sat a black stone. It was rough and shapeless, a layer of stone dust marring its surface, but the depths of its darkness could not be mistaken.

Marian had found dragonstone.

She grinned, tears spilling down her cheeks as she stroked it lovingly. A ticket to the palace. A reprieve from the darkness. A desperate hope to cling to when she'd already lost so much.

It was a shame Demetria had to take it.

It was a necessary sacrifice, one Marian would understand if Demetria had the time to explain.

But there was no time.

Voices were already sounding down the tunnel, people had heard a commotion, and they were approaching to inspect. Zaire's voice floated into mind, a memory of words spoken.

Gather your strength and harden your stomach. We can't afford such sentiments.

She hated that he was right. That he'd forced her hand again.

But Demetria was different from him. He never tried diplomacy. Only surged forward, painting his trail with bloody violence. She could find a new way.

"Marian... I need that."

"What?" She didn't understand, and how could she? "I found it."

"I can accomplish more with that than you ever could. Please, just let me take it."

Marian shook her head, her brows drawing together and mouth falling open. "I'm sorry, but no. I need— I need to get out of this tunnel for a night. I swear, I'll die if I don't. We'll work together, find you one next, I promise."

Marian was kind. In a world fit to forge weapons out of silk, she was kind. And that made it all the worse. Why had she asked to work alongside Demetria? That would have been *her* find were it not for this girl she didn't even know forcing her way into her life.

Demetria swallowed against the lump in her throat. The guilt she refused to wallow in. The grief of the final severance of who she once was. It was like the blade, the one that hacked at Evander's neck, messy and brutal as it severed his head from his body.

Demetria's life had become a series of ruthless strikes, uneven, prolonging. But this was the final fall of the blade.

She lifted the butt of her axe, readying her strike.

Marian finally lifted her gaze to meet Demetria's, heartbreaking confusion forming there. "Demi? What are you—"

"I'm sorry." Demetria struck. It had been ages since she'd trained with Ruslan, but whether her muscles remembered, or the necessity of her actions fueled her, her blow landed with a sickening thud. Marian fell to her knees, blood trailing down her temple. Demetria struck again, and the sound of Marian's broken sob broke something in her, too.

Marian lay on the floor of their cramped tunnel, her breathing labored and punctuated by soft cries of pain.

Demetria blinked back the tears as she wrestled Marian's hand open and snatched the stone from her grip.

"W-why?" her pained voice came out. So small. So lost.

"I need it more."

And Demetria could have walked away, she could have left the girl bleeding and crying on the stone. But what would befall her? Marian was in no condition to work, and the threat of her sister's fate loomed in the back of Demetria's mind. She crouched down, whispering in her ear.

"I will free you all."

"No, you won't." Came Marian's response, soft and filled with grief.

CHAPTER THIRTY-NINE

LARK

"Why do you need my help in finding Aislinn? I thought you lot were all-knowing."

Merikh had just finished the abbreviated tour of Avalon. Abbreviated, because the realm was endless, an entire universe of sights no mortal could consume in one lifetime, but also because there were certain places he could not show her lest he risk drawing unwarranted attention.

Namely, he didn't want his master to know she was here.

"I cannot simply snap my fingers and find someone. To travel to the human world, I must bear my human form."

That's right. He'd said his true form was beyond mortal vision.

"And that stops you how?"

Merikh frowned, leaning against a marble pillar. They stood in one of the cities, crafted with the notion of humans and their penchant for socializing. Every building was created with the same artistic hand as the castle upon the cliff he would not take her to. White stone gilded with golden edges and detailing. To any human it would take the façade of a city familiar to them. A home away from home sort of feeling. Or if none came to mind, an idealized version of a city suited to meet their preferences. It was all very strange.

Stranger still were the humans. Lark could *perceive* them, but they weren't fully formed. Like shadows in the corner of her eye, her mind filling in the blanks to create a person. And whenever she'd turn, they were gone. Merikh had explained that everyone who gives themselves over to the peaceful gift of Avalon could see visages of other humans if they wished, but unless they happened to be mutual loved ones, ascended to Avalon together, they would not truly see or notice anyone.

When Lark had asked, *"How does that work for families?"* Merikh had responded in kind, *"If a mother and her daughter ascend to Avalon, and the father fails to meet our criteria, the mother and daughter live their peaceful existence together. No thought to the father or recollection he ever existed."*

The more Lark learned of the so-called paradise of the afterlife, the less rapturous it seemed.

"When you were a Reaper, could you find a human without a tether?"

No. A tether could be a person or a place, but without it, it was searching for a drop in the ocean. It was the echo of pain and death marking Lark's master's home, lifetimes ago. When Thanar was drawn to a place of great suffering and found her. It was only that echo allowing him to return again and again. Now that Lark's memories had been restored, that had come back to her, too. That feeling. The sense of being watched. Of something waiting in the shadows, observing her private moments. And the moment he appeared to her, dragging her away from the only life she'd ever known.

The only love she'd ever known.

Gavriel.

Lark shoved the ache of her longing away. She had to obtain all the answers she sought to have a chance at returning to him.

At her silence, Merikh continued, "I can no more pluck a human from the earth than you can. But whenever a somniavi uses their abilities, it leaves a trail. That, I can follow."

As long as Aislinn kept her soul from wandering, he'd never find her.

"What does your true form appear as? Did you choose this face?"

"My face is an approximation of the embodiment of my soul, nothing more. Any human constructs of beauty are beneath me. And I would only show my true form to my soul's equal." He sneered at her. "And you are certainly not that."

As if that was an insult.

"Why did Sargon banish Thanar?"

Merikh froze, the hardening of his shoulders the only indicator she'd caught him by surprise. "What do you know of this?"

Lark reveled in his reaction. "I know Thanar was one of your own and supposedly had an affinity for the humans, so Sargon punished him by making him the god of death so he could grieve each and every soul passing for all of eternity." *Thank you, Inerys, for your history lessons.* "I also know Sargon punished Solana for creating something beautiful for the humans who weren't good enough for your precious world."

Merikh scoffed. "Oversimplification, again. Thanar and Solana committed treasonous acts, challenging Sargon in his rule. It was foolish of both of them, making such a public statement without proper backing. His punishments were a reflection of what would hurt them most, not his opinion of humans."

The mental footwork of this guy was unparalleled. He was wrapped far too tightly round Sargon's finger to recognize the hypocrisy of his own words.

"So, you do help humans."

"Yes."

"Have you ever answered a human's prayer?" The mortals called to the paragons and warriors. As far as Lark could tell, they all went unanswered.

He hesitated. "I... have not. I do not feel compelled to listen to the pleas of a temporary form. My efforts are better utilized here. A human may send out a prayer, and we all have the ability to answer it. In that case, they are forging the tether and we choose to respond. If they call us by our name, we have no choice but to beseech their prayers."

Interesting. "So, if I called out, '*Merikh! Get your oversized arse down here and help me with the wash.*' You'd have to listen?"

271

"No. That is not my true name. That is the name I am called. My true name is unknown to all but one."

Sargon. He didn't need to say it. He was just as leashed as Lark had been to Thanar. All the boundaries and governances blotting out Merikh's power were becoming increasingly clear. He had only been able to form the connection within her mind because she opened the door. She wouldn't make that mistake again.

If Lark had to guess, she'd say the threat Aislinn posed was a direct challenge to the paragons themselves rather than the realm he claimed to protect.

"All right. So, you separate humans from their families, brainwash them into thinking they don't care, and trap their minds in a false reality to prevent anyone from complaining." Lark crossed her arms, mirroring his posture. "Why should I give a shit what happens to this place?"

Merikh's lip curled, disgust transforming his features. "You are being willfully obtuse." A strange look came over him, a dawning of an idea. Like the last piece of an enigmatic puzzle had just fallen into his lap. "I have something to show you." He started off, not waiting to see if Lark followed.

She growled in annoyance and begrudgingly trailed behind. The city gave way to a road, vast open fields abutting each side. The sun and moon hung midway in the sky, that same shivery light dancing along Lark's skin. Over the fields of wildflowers. An entire world basking beneath sun-dappled waters. It was strange and beautiful and...

Avalon was not the paradise it was promised to be. Weaving blissful ignorance into the fabric of the souls inhabiting it.

But damn, it was gorgeous.

A thick forest encroached, its trees claiming the fields bit by bit. It swallowed the road up ahead. Something about the features of this world seemed to take shape as one came upon them. Like each region was crafted to keep everyone from searching the horizon for more.

Contentment. Complacency.

Lark pushed aside her gathering dread and followed Merikh into the forest. Birdsongs filled the air, a chorus of sound designed to relax the loud mind. Floral notes, scents Lark had never encountered, wrapped around her. Sweet with a hint of greenery. It blended with the scent of damp earth. The sunlight ripples were less pronounced beneath the verdant leaves above. Glimmering light swayed along the forest floor. The sound of rushing water filled the air, and Merikh parted leaf laden branches to reveal what lay beyond.

It was a turquoise pool, set just beneath a rock ledge. Plants and flowers formed its border, a gentle waterfall rippling its surface. Thick vines with purple flowers hung off branches, dipping into the water.

"Come closer."

Lark leaned over, bracing her hands on the rock and catching her reflection in the pool. Her amber eyes were bright, her red hair hung close to breaking the water's surface. Her skin had paled some, and her freckles had all but disappeared. Ardenian winter was to blame for that, but she'd spent the day in the sun and moon albeit. She expected to see some evidence of that upon her cheeks and nose. Her skin had burned quite easily beneath the Western Desolates' sun.

It was because it was all an illusion. Even now, as Merikh promised transparency. Sometimes a person lived so long in a lie it became their truth.

"There is a human from your memory. The one who gave you that." Merikh gave her treasured knife a gentle tug at her belt, tugging her heart in her chest with it. "You wish to know of his fate."

Hugo. The way he'd left the human world, violently and trapped in the dark, still haunted her. That she'd never had the chance to say goodbye...

Lark's nose stung and her eyes burned, but *damn him*, she nodded.

"Look closer."

Lark focused her attention on the ripples in the pool, allowing her face to fade out of focus. An image of a woman appeared. Petite and blonde. She wore an apron and bustled around a familiar kitchen, dragging a chair over to reach the highest cupboard. Grabbing a bottle from above, she tugged it down, taking a quick sip before pouring some into the pot of some sort of meat and vegetables. She stirred, cooking it down until it became a stew. She cupped her mouth, calling out. A girl appeared. Younger than Lark. A girl on the edge of adulthood, with long black hair and dark eyes.

Lark's breath caught in her throat.

Csilla.

Lena.

Hugo's daughter and his wife. But where was Hugo?

The girl set the table, placing two bowls and two spoons upon it. Laughing at something her mother said.

The image went dark, and Lark hurled herself toward their disappearing forms. Merikh grabbed her before she could make contact with the water, dragging her back.

Rage spread through Lark's body. It burned through her blood, rushed to her head—it made her dizzy and her limbs itchy and *where the fuck was Hugo?*

"Easy," Merikh said, the bastard calm. "Relax. Breathe. I did not show you this to be cruel."

Lark fought against his hold. "Where is he?" How could he not be there with them? The only comfort, *the only fucking comfort* Lark had found in his loss, was that he was reunited with his family.

"Hugo was a good man. But the stain of blood spilled is not to be ignored."

"Fuck you. Fuck Avalon. I hope Aislinn burns it to the ground—"

Merikh clamped a hand over her mouth, silencing her. "Do not behave so rashly. I showed you this to offer you incentive."

Lark ripped his hand away, shoving out of his hold. "I'll never help you. Everything about this place is sickening. Nereida should have warred with you eons ago. I'll let her dismantle you lot before I kill her."

"Still your ceaseless tongue, woman, and listen to me!"

Lark's breaths were heavy and measured. The call for violence humming in her blood. He would pay. It mattered naught if he were blameless in this. He was part of a broken system that punished souls without thought, without reason.

"What if I brought him here?" Merikh watched her curiously. "If I reunited this mortal you seem to hold in such high esteem with his family and granted his afterlife the gift of peace? Would you help me then?"

Indecision warred in Lark. It stole the strength from her rage as well as her muscles. It slackened her grip and made her sway on her feet. Did she want Hugo here? She wanted him out of the Netherworld and where he belonged with his family. Why were souls still barred from here without the veil?

Unless…

The veil was to protect the humans… it was put in place to prevent the monsters from running free from the Netherworld. Avalon had its own veil, its own anchor. If she could find it, or whoever fueled it, she could destroy it. Thanar was the anchor, the tether for the veil. That would make Sargon the most likely choice.

"Well? Your answer?"

She couldn't betray Aislinn. She didn't deserve it. Nor could she lose the one chance at bringing Gavriel back. But to leave Hugo down there… facing whatever torment dreamt up in the Netherworld.

Lark's chest hollowed at the thought. She could not leave him there. Not after everything.

"What would you have me do?"

THE ATRIUM of the great castle of Avalon, home of the paragons and warriors, heroes of the afterlife—it was underwhelming.

Streams of sunlight bathed the hall, illuminating dust motes floating in a swirling dance. Marble floors and gilded filigree on every pillar, great big windows, the lands of Avalon peeking beyond.

But Lark was tired of it all. Tired of the bullshit. Of gods who cared little for the humans they were supposed to protect. This place felt like Thanar's creation. Where Lark once lived as a Reaper.

Empty.

Lifeless.

A void.

Or perhaps she was just numb. Witnessing the horrific truth of Hugo's fate had snapped something in her. Something that had been tested over and over, bending beyond the constraints, only to snap back before it was too late.

But this was the final bend. The exaggerated arch. The last tug on her will.

She was in a losing battle with her fear. Something she'd thought she'd mastered. She feared what punishment Hugo faced in the Netherworld. How had he suffered? What did they do to him? If he was down there, why couldn't he return to the mortal realm when the veil fell?

Merikh held her arm above the elbow, dragging her through the halls, guiding her around every twisting corner of his master's home. And Lark let him. She trudged on heavy feet, resigned her fate as a betrayer.

Was she so sure she could save Gavriel without Aislinn's help? Or that she could survive the knowledge she'd handed her over to be put to death?

There was no mistaking Merikh's meaning. Aislinn would be killed. And Lark was just… giving her over to it?

But… Hugo.

Lark's eyes burned. It wasn't fair. It wasn't fair. Why was there no choice that felt *right*?

She needed Daciana. She'd know what to do. Lark needed her, and she wasn't here, and how was she supposed to make this decision on her own?

Lark ran her hand through one of the cascading streams of sunlight as Merikh led her deeper into the castle. It was motionless, unlike the rippling current of light in the rest of Avalon. Had Sargon spelled it that way? Why in here? So many things about this place didn't make sense. She'd always known not to trust the paragons of Avalon, but to have her disdain confirmed…

A heavy oak door stood before them, and Merikh shoved it open, yanking her violently in, and shutting it with rapid succession.

He really didn't want anyone knowing he brought her here.

A massive table hewn from the trunk of an ancient tree dominated the center space. Painted atop its surface, a map of all the human lands. But why would they need such a thing? Suspended from above without cord or string, the sun and moon and spheres Lark did not recognize spun in a dizzying circle. Rotating around each other.

"What are those—"

"It would take too long to make you understand. First you do this." Merikh dragged her to the table, and Lark gritted her teeth. The shock of Hugo's fate was beginning to dim, clarity and anger taking its place. Why this bastard seemed keen on shoving and pulling her around, she did not know, but she could guess.

He was desperate. His punishment for failing to deliver Aislinn must be severe for him to crack like that. It sent a sobering realization through her.

It was in moments of desperation that grave mistakes were all too easy to make.

A lesson she'd learned many times over yet always needed the reminder. How fickle the nature of her memory could be.

She did not trust Merikh. Did not trust him to have shown her truth about Hugo and his family. Did not trust him to keep his word upon her compliance. Did not trust this blighted plane of existence to even appear as he had shown her.

His desperation fueled him to bargain with her, promising things that were not his to give. Even if she did compromise her code and give him Aislinn, he would never rescue Hugo.

If Hugo even needed rescuing.

Merikh had dipped inside her mind, sifted through her thoughts and fears. Of course, he knew where to strike.

"Right here."

He glanced at the markers upon the map. Lots of little pieces that would typically mean claiming a region or at the very least occupying it. Why were the absent paragons so invested in human lands?

"Reach for her. Call to her. Based on your memories, she'll answer without thought."

Because Merikh had a sense of Aislinn now, thanks to Lark—an understanding of her courage and loyalty, of her sacrifice for those around her even after losing so much. She'd exhausted herself searching for a way to find Gavriel, pushing past her limits. She'd saved Lark that day with the Reaper Blade now hanging by Merikh's side.

Even long before that, Aislinn had saved her. She'd represented something to Lark, something she had nearly forgotten in her time as a Reaper.

Hope.

Lark would never betray the girl in the lavender dress, large green eyes wide with hope as she asked her if Corwyn would hurt another. The one who promised to send Lark a sign after she completed her journey to the afterlife.

Aislinn was her friend, but more importantly, she was more than all the paragons combined.

"Well?" He ran a hand through his dark hair, the movement jerky. "Are you focusing?"

"I am not."

He snapped up his gaze, eyes narrowing. "May I ask why the build in suspense?"

Lark shook her head. "No building of suspense. I'm not helping you."

His hands flexed atop the war table, a ripple of anger tightening through his broad shoulders. "Why?"

She laughed, because it was funny how little this paragon understood of human nature. Of her, even after infiltrating her mind. "Because," she said once her mirth allowed, "I'm not handing Aislinn over for you to slaughter."

"Slaughter?" His brows drew together, and he exhaled a rough noise. "I told you, I take no pleasure from this. It is a means of protecting the greater good. A command given from the highest order—"

"How is it my problem you're Sargon's lapdog?" This was it. The rightness of it sang in her veins, it loosened the last bolt in her chest. She'd always struggled knowing when she was taking the right path.

This was the right path. He had shown his weakness, and now Lark knew better. This was never about Aislinn. This was about him.

"That somniavi has the ability to murder us in our sleep."

"Aislinn wouldn't do that."

Merikh shook his head, baring his teeth. "We do not sit idly by and wait for a threat to eradicate our very way of existence."

Lark rolled her eyes. *Oh, but the dramatics.* "She is no such threat."

"You cannot know—"

"But even if she was"—Lark cut him off, allowing every ounce of venom to spill into her words—"I wouldn't give a shit if she obliterated your entire species." It was the wrong word to use, but it hit the mark.

Merikh's eyes widened, his lips thinning in a firm line. He flexed his hands, balling them into fists. With slow and precise movements, he rose to his full height, towering over her. The muscles in his thick neck bulged, and his throat bobbed.

"Well," he said, voice dangerously calm, "you really are useless, aren't you?"

His hand shot out, gripping Lark's wrist tight enough to cut off the blood to her hand. He twisted, and she cried out at the flare of pain. Clapping his palm in hers, his dark eyes narrowed, holding her gaze in his hateful, vengeful stare.

"You forgot to ask me one vital question."

Lark gasped, as the sensation of fire erupted across her palm, licking through her nerves and searing the skin.

"What do we do with those rejected from Avalon?"

The floor rumbled, a circle of darkness opening at their feet. Shadows curled from its edges like smoke, clawing and reaching as if hungry to catch prey ensnared.

"You will regret your decision." Merikh's nostrils flared. "Mark my words, you will regret this."

Lark struggled against his hold, and he relinquished all but her wrist.

Burned into her palm was a symbol. A brand seared upon her, marking her. The skin was red and glossy, stinging pain lighting up her nerves as the air hit vulnerable ruined flesh. Curves and lines, gnarled like ancient roots, marred her skin. A symbol of the tree's journey beneath the ground.

A promise of where he was sending her.

Lark snarled, fighting against his unyielding grasp on her wrist as he dragged her closer to the shadows eagerly reaching from the floor. Something glimmered at his belt, catching the light. Dark waves etched along steel, the union of light and dark in the sun's touch.

The Reaper Blade.

Merikh angled her over the gaping void in the floor, eying her with a strange mixture of disgust and disdain. "Such a waste."

"Perhaps not." Lark wet her lips, fingers tingling at her side as she allowed him to position her in place. It all came down to waiting for the right moment. Patience. Patience. *Fucking patience.*

Merikh shoved her, and as she fell, she grasped the Reaper Blade at his belt, swiftly ripping it free as the shadows rushed up to grab her. Too quick to catch his expression—to see if he bore his surprise or hadn't registered the action. The blade sang in her grasp, restored to its rightful owner, and Lark smiled even as darkness overcame her.

And she was falling.

Falling.

Falling.

An endless journey of darkness.

Until at last, she reached the bottom of the shadows.

CHAPTER FORTY

LARK

The darkness was a living thing. A whispered breath across her skin. A suffocating embrace. It shoved its way down her throat, twisting her insides, and stretching her skin. It was nothing and everything. A combined punishment of every unsettling sensation she'd ever suffered. It threatened to swallow her whole and plunge itself deep into her very being. Rewriting her veins and filling her very marrow with its shivery voice.

But Lark was once a being of darkness. She had never shied away from the shadows as a Reaper, recognizing their necessity and avoiding losing herself to them.

With this thought, Lark breathed, expanding her lungs and expelling the darkness until the tightness beneath her skin settled and the coiling in her gut smoothed. She was in the shadows. She was not one of them.

Lark blinked, and slowly a dull light appeared. With the strength of a lone candle in a starless night, its modest arc of light was enough. It was enough, and she focused on that light, letting it expand, slowly. So slowly. Until the dimly lit room came into view.

She pushed against the stone floor until she was sitting, braziers lighting along the walls as the shadows slunk away. An archway of stone and a long row of doors in the distance. Each one varying in shape. Rounded, one a perfect circle, one so small she'd have to crawl on her belly to fit.

Where was she?

Her hand burned its painful reminder, and she glanced down at it. It shook, trembling beneath the weight of fragile exposed nerves. Her dominant hand, too, the bastard. Lark ripped the sleeve of her tunic, wrapping it around her hand. She bit her lip against the whimper threatening to break through as she tightened the wrapping, tying it off. Beside her, the Reaper Blade sat. Thank the skies for small mercies. She grabbed it, her strength buckling at the way it bit into her injured palm.

She should have listened when Alistair told her to practice left-handed at least some of the time.

The door at the end of the hall creaked, opening slowly. Lark stood, palming the handle of the Reaper Blade in the wrong hand, her hold awkward and uncomfortable.

The braziers at the end of the hall snuffed out, plunging the doorway into darkness. Footsteps, soft and unhurried. Each set of flames evaporating into darkness, bringing the shadows closer and closer.

Lark's pulse quickened, and she tossed the shortsword to her injured hand. A snarl of pain broke free, and she squeezed. She'd take the pain if it meant fighting her way free. The memory of shooting her bow and reopening her stitches, forcing Langford to work on the same wound again, came into mind. She blinked back the moisture gathering from either pain or that tightness in her chest at the thought of her friends. Her family.

She would see them again.

Another *whoosh* of air as the darkness crept closer. Devouring the light and building the promise of dread deep in her gut.

The last of light died, and she was plunged into true darkness once more. The blood in her ears was deafening, and her heart bludgeoned against her ribs, threatening to break through.

One heartbeat.

Two heartbeats.

An exhale, a caress of breath against her face.

"Larkin?"

A soft voice, too gentle to broach the darkness, called to her. Its familiar embrace sending a jolt through her body.

"Is that truly you?"

The darkness whispered to her in a voice Lark had known for lifetimes. A trusted voice she'd relied on many times. It was the voice of softness and compassion.

Memories from what seemed like lifetimes ago flitted into Lark's mind.

"The future isn't always as stable as you might think. Paths can always change."

"My path seems steadfast."

"I wouldn't be so sure. You acted according to your conscience." She placed a hand over Lark's. *"You have more power over fate than you know."*

Flames erupted along every brazier, blasting the hall with light and temporarily blinding Lark. She blinked it away, her eyes adjusting to find the face she knew would be awaiting.

Large sapphire eyes watching. Cascades of blonde hair spilling over her shoulders. A small knowing smile playing on her mouth.

Leysa.

The Otherworld's seer. One of Thanar's most trusted advisors.

Lark's friend. The one who'd set her on the path, subtly encouraging her rebellion. Gently pushing her to reach further and further.

"Leysa?"

"Larkin." Her smile broadened, crinkling her eyes.

Lark stumbled forward, wrapping her arms around her. "I thought something terrible had happened to you."

Leysa hugged her back, squeezing tightly and sighing. "I'm sorry I couldn't appear to you sooner. I was a bit preoccupied. But none of that matters, because you're here now." She pulled back, pushing Lark's hair from her face. "I can't tell you how grateful I am for the chance to explain."

"Explain what?" Lark was too relieved for words.

When Ceto and Nyx had appeared with Thanar, when Nereida revealed herself as the serpent she was, Leysa had been nowhere in sight. After having helped Lark locate Ferryn in Lacuna, the very real threat she'd been punished had lingered in the back of her mind. But when Thanar appeared to Lark again and again, not as a vengeful force bent on her punishment but as a grieving soul trying to aid her, she'd wondered.

And when Nereida enacted her plan to topple the veil, to crumble it to the ground, once again, Leysa was missing.

"What happened to you? I thought you were—" Dead seemed the wrong term. For she was dead, in a way. All Reapers, even this powerful seer, were once humans who had died. The death of a Reaper was a ceasing of existence. It was—

Thanar. How he reached out to Lark even as he disintegrated. How the once great and mighty god of death, the master of all Reapers, the commander of journeying to the afterlife, had been reduced to ash. Echoes of his power releasing to the wind.

Or did his power reallocate? Nereida had become... so much stronger in an instant. She said it was freedom of her power without the veil, but what if it had been more than that?

Leysa smiled, indulgent patience on her impossibly beautiful face. "You still wear a dizzying array of thoughts plain as day upon your expressions. It's a comfort to know that much hasn't changed."

"Has she hurt you?"

There was no mistaking Lark's meaning. Nereida had claimed both the Otherworld and Netherworld as her own. She would not allow anyone to so much as speak out against her. Balan was proof of that.

"Ah. You worried after me. Such a gentle heart you possess, Larkin."

Lark had been human for the turn of nearly four seasons. She'd become accustomed to the physical responses within her own body. Anger. Desire. Despair. Fear.

And dread. That visceral sensation that something terrible was about to happen. It raised the hairs on the back of her neck and prickled down her spine.

"That is not an answer," Lark said carefully, letting her hand fall to the handle of her Reaper Blade. If this was another trick, an illusion masquerading as her trusted friend, she would need to be swift.

"You never liked when I spoke in circles," Leysa said playfully, her eyes dancing. Her gaze fell to Lark's palm, and her expression turned solemn. "May I see?" Gently, she took Lark's hand from her weapon, turning it over to trace the lines branded upon her skin. "You have seen the ways of Avalon." Her gaze flitted up to meet Lark's. "How did you find your welcome? Is it what you always hoped it to be?"

Lark's hand twitched in her grasp. "It's exactly what I expected based on your teachings. Beautiful and terrible in equal measures. Built for its own paragons and not the humans they pretend to care for."

Leysa grinned, an exaggerated expression Lark had never seen grace her features. "Exactly so. Perhaps now you'll understand."

"As you said"—Lark pulled her hand free, relieved when Leysa relinquished her without a struggle—"I care little for speaking in circles."

"A deal then." Leysa took several strides away, spinning back to face Lark. Her skirts fluttered with the movement, and a strand of snowy-blonde hair blew across her face. "Let us venture somewhere more comfortable than the holding cells. You will not interrupt or case judgment until the very end of my tale. If you speak before I'm finished, I shan't finish, and you'll always wonder." She raised a pale brow. "You always hated to wonder."

This was Leysa all right or a very convincing impersonation. She'd always offered sage counsel for Lark in the past, so whatever she had to say was worth hearing.

Even if she couldn't quell that sense of impending dread pulsing through her veins.

"I'd rather have your explanation here and now." There was no telling how deep into the bowels of the Netherworld they might venture. "I might have a hard time not interjecting." Lark never meant to; it just always seemed to happen.

"I have an easy fix for that! It's harmless, and once our deal is through, all will be as it was. It's just a touch of old magic, nothing to fret over." Leysa stepped closer, and Lark was struck by the fact that Leysa had no scent. She didn't radiate warmth with the nearness of her body. She just... was. "Do we have a deal?"

"Yes."

Fire licked up Lark's throat, coating her tongue. She grabbed at her neck, finding Leysa's face—

She only stared back, watching dispassionately.

Lark opened her mouth to speak—

No sound came out. A rush of air, and nothing.

"It will help you listen, Lark. A deal is a deal."

It was the same helpless feeling from before, when Lark first clawed her way free from the ancient yew, cutting her belly against gnarled roots and bleeding into the earth. It had taken three days for her voice to return. Leysa had not said—Lark had blindly trusted. And now—

"You should be careful when negotiating terms, a fact I thought you'd learned." Leysa's brows pinched, furrowing in disapproval. The downturn of her mouth lifted. "As I said, it's temporary. Now make yourself comfortable, and I will tell you everything."

What choice did Lark have? Until Leysa finished her story, she could not utter a word. It was... surprisingly harsh of Leysa to pull a mean trick like this. But Lark dropped to sit, heavier than strictly necessary, and glared up at her friend, waving her hand to get on with it.

Leysa smiled and let her eyes slip closed. She took a deep breath, and every line of her body seemed to come alive. Like she was a dancer preparing for her last great performance.

"Once upon a time, there was a young girl who wished for love most of all. She would run from her shack in the forgotten part of the woods, chasing away memories of pain from the broken people meant to care for her, and find the wishing pond. It was nothing but an ordinary pond, but to the girl, it was magic. It was hope and dreams in a world that punished dreamers. And every day she would wish for someone to love. For that love to soothe instead of hurt. And most of all, for someone to love her back.

"As she grew, so did her dreams. But they were no longer filled with love and warmth. When she slept, she suffered horrible visions of death. Strangers she'd never seen. Some were young. Some were old. Some were impending. Some were far on the horizon, years and years until their death would come to pass. She saw death everywhere, in every face, in everything of beauty. Except that pond. For even looking upon her own reflection, she could not see her own demise.

"She thought herself mad. These visions of death that did not come to pass. Until, one night, she dreamt of her father, drinking himself into his nightly stupors and venturing outside after dark, losing his step and falling upon the axe he'd threatened her with earlier that day. She was frightened—never before had she dreamt of her own family. But more than frightened, she was curious. She left the axe out after her chore of splitting wood was through, left it just the way it appeared in her dream. Upon the ground, edged blade held up by a stone. When they found her father's body the next morning—that was when the fear truly set in."

Leysa paused, watching Lark carefully.

Lark couldn't tell what she found in her expression, but the ache in her chest at this sorrowful tale was deep. Leysa had been a seer long before Thanar found her. It made sense when he realized her ability even as a human, that he kept her.

Leysa cleared her throat and continued, "Youth bled into early womanhood. Loneliness became her constant companion. And alongside it, bitterness grew. It grew and grew until it near swallowed her whole. She could not stop the visions. The knowledge. Such knowledge no one should possess. Every day she ran to that wishing pond, begging for someone, anyone to hear her.

"What she did not expect was another young woman, with such strange and ethereal beauty, to answer."

Lark opened her mouth to ask the question that died on her silent tongue.

Who was the woman?

Leysa smiled, nodding as if she understood. "Beneath her wide brim hat, her hair was whiter than freshly fallen snow. Her eyes such deep blue, they were nearly violet. She was... the most enchanting creature she'd ever seen. And when the young woman cried that day, she approached, offering nothing but her presence as comfort. And it was enough. For months they met each day, and for months they grew closer and closer. Until finally, the love she'd always craved, always needed, was finally found."

The dread that had loomed along the edges of Lark's instincts reared, a plunge into ice as her legs went numb.

The woman she described... the woman who offered comfort... the one she loved...

"Nereida was her name, and she was a most talented witch. She taught me to hone my skills rather than fear them. And I mastered my fear with her unyielding love." Leysa's gaze flicked to Lark's, a challenge in them. "But her talents drew unwanted attention, and those who would wield her for their own gain began stalking her shadows. History has proven mortals who draw the attention of gods are never revered. They are punished for their might, their souls erased from existence to prevent their notions of the perfect afterlife from being threatened. And when her death came to me, I begged her to cease her conjuring, to live a quiet life with me, and forget magic. But it was as part of her as her very heart—the one she swore beat for me. And to cut her off from her magic was to rip her soul from her body."

Lark clenched and unclenched her fist atop her thigh. Nereida, the self-proclaimed witch-queen of the Netherworld, the architect of so much destruction, was once a mortal girl with magic who got caught up with powers beyond her?

Nereida's words echoed in Lark's mind, from that day in her throne room when she told Lark the truth of her history.

The truth, and not the truth.

"Once upon a time, long ago, there was a young girl named Larkin Byrne... Her death was known by the fates. Written in blood and foretold by the great seer, Leysa. When she received the mark, something urged her to report this particular mortal to Thanar."

288

Something urged Leysa or *someone*?

"When she was taken, when the god of death himself had a great need of her power, she made a deal. She would craft the veil, the protective barrier between the Netherworld, the Otherworld, and the mortal realm, and he would promise the paragons of Avalon would never get their hands on her or on her lover, for she knew, they would only use that love against her in the cruelest of ways. The father of Reapers agreed, and he betrayed her."

Lark's mind spun, and the loss of her voice was a gift because she never would have kept her questions from spilling forth.

Thanar? Thanar betrayed Nereida? Nereida created the veil? *Nereida practiced Life Magic like Daciana?*

What did it mean? Ugh, skies, what did it all fucking mean?

Leysa tightened her mouth in an impression of a smile. "There's no use speaking in circles at this point, is there? Thanar knew Nereida's life would be forfeit in the creation of the veil. That not even she, the greatest vitas conjurer to ever live, could choose where to pull from in the creation of something so vast. That the only way to build the wall between planes was in sacrifice. What he did not know was her cleverness. As the last of her life bled away, she tied his soul as the anchor, vowing to destroy it, and him, one day. Her lover..."

Leysa sighed and shook her head. "No more circles," she said softly. "I was lost. Cast in the darkness once more. I filled my pockets with stones and waded into our wishing pond, making the last wish of my human life: To be reunited with my love. But Thanar sensed my abilities, and it made the role of Reaper that much more controlled. Balanced. Organized." She said each word with an overenunciation, as if they'd been drilled into her mind over and over. "I could see their fates with time to spare. I could sense their human lives in the scent of their death and select the Reapers who would have the best success rate based on temperament. But Reapers do not venture to the Netherworld, and he did not make Nereida Reaper, too. So, we were separated for" —she took a shuddering breath, placing a hand on her chest—"far too long."

A strange sensation came over Lark. A tickle in her throat that spread until her tongue itched with it. Understanding dawned, Leysa had finished her tale, thus the terms of their deal had been met, and Lark could finally speak the words that dueled for dominance. The thoughts racing to freedom. How could she lie to her? How could she *use* her? Thanar. Nereida. Leysa. They were all the same. Lying, manipulating, controlling, using—

"Well, shit."

Lark did not expect that thought to win the race.

"You *used* me." Much better.

Leysa frowned. "Yes, that is disagreeable, but you can't fault me for it now, can you? Not when I helped you find your way back to your bonded? Not now that you know my story? And certainly"—her eyes darkened—"not when you have seen the corruption in Avalon."

"I concede to you there, but Nereida—"

"Is stronger than Thanar ever was!" Leya's voice boomed, echoing in the dark hall. "He was ruled by weakness. By fear. Nereida suffered for eons because of his selfish cruelty. Do not tell me you still think him innocent, Larkin. Do not tell me you share his weakness. Do not fucking tell me you still don't understand!"

The strength of Leysa's anger made the walls seem to grow, the flames along the walls shrinking as if inviting more shadows to join.

Lark swallowed against a tight throat. "That's not what I'm saying," she said carefully. If what Leysa claimed was true... they faced a far greater foe in Nereida than Lark realized. "Nereida killed my friend—"

"She knew it would force the wolf queen's hand. Next."

Wolf queen? Skies, did Leysa know something about Daciana she didn't?

"She hurt Gavriel." Locked him away in his mind. For her own *enjoyment.* Just to watch Lark suffer. Though her history revealed the nature of her harsh actions, did that really justify her cruelty?

No. It really didn't.

Gavriel was still trapped. No. Leysa didn't get to rewrite Nereida as the hero of this tale.

"You still don't understand suffering, Lark. Your refusal to see the greater plan at play has always been your downfall." The gentle seer, the one Lark had called friend, was gone. Had never existed. She'd played her part, and now the mask was ripped away.

Leysa was a force of vengeance. Of scorn.

"Then tell me!" Lark cried, leaping to her feet. "Tell me the master plan, Leysa. All I see is death and destruction. Humans are dying because Nereida wanted to send a message to Thanar. I'm sorry you were separated from her. I'm sorry it's hardened you both past the point that you can't even muster up an ounce of compassion for the innocents dying by her hands. *Her* hands, Leysa. Nereida's scent is all over this, and you don't get to claim the higher ground when you're using it to punch down."

"Punch down?" Leysa laughed, a cold and brittle sound. "Her aim is a bit higher than that. You're just stupid enough to get in her way."

"Fine! I'm stupid. I'm foolish. I'm shortsighted and impulsive and whatever else you can call me. But I'd never, never justify causing the deaths of countless innocents. So yes, I'm stupid enough to get in her way and it's where I'll always stay. The thorn in her side until I can finally stab that vile bitch through her cold heart—"

The air ripped from Lark's lungs, and her throat closed. She could not gasp. She could not plead. She clawed at her neck, her pulse pounding in her head. Leysa stepped close enough their noses almost touched.

"You are a disappointment, Larkin. And nothing more."

The pressure released, and Lark fell to her knees, rough stone ripping through her breeches. Lark gasped, precious air filling her cramped lungs, and coughed deep enough to rip a gag from her throat. Shaky fear trembled through her hands. She was no match for Leysa. Not on her own.

Leysa glared down at her, disgust and disdain twisting her beautiful face.

"I'd kill you now, you know. And I wouldn't suffer any remorse. Not when you're so determined to be my enemy." Leysa glanced at the shadows along the wall, and they seemed to dance. "But I really don't need to. There are many, *so many*, who would love to sink their shadows in you. Survival is harder than you think when you lack the help of your betters, isn't it?"

Lark stood on unsteady feet. She had one chance in this, one chance. And her odds of success were… well, they were shit.

"You're right," Lark said, tracking the way Leysa's eyes widened only slightly. "I can't do this on my own. I've only survived this long by the grace of friends stronger than me." She edged a step closer, careful to keep her body language relaxed and nonthreatening. "You orchestrated so much of my path. Whispering words of rebellion, coaxing my fears to take shape. I really ought to thank you, because without you, I'd probably still be Thanar's favored, preparing to take over when he stepped down." Lark was close enough now—it was a matter of swift hand maneuvering and maintaining surprise.

Alistair's lessons from so long ago came to mind—tactics in subterfuge to hold an edge over a stronger enemy.

"And I would be trapped. Never knowing the love of the soul I was always meant to be with. I'm sorry I lashed out. It hurts to be separated from him. But that's how you felt, wasn't it?" Lark met Leysa's eyes, and she tried to instill as much pity into her gaze as possible. "How painful that must have been for you. Knowing she was just out of reach. If it had been me…" Lark sighed, her muscles ready to spring. "I don't know what I would have done."

Leysa smiled, relief shining on her inhumanly beautiful face.

It was almost too easy. It should have been harder. Lark's hand should have been weighed down by guilt. Skies, she didn't even think she'd strike quick enough, and the shock on Leysa's face surely matched her own.

The Reaper Blade sat deep in Leysa's belly, the protruding handle in Lark's palm. The pain from her branding given way to a deep and chilling numbness.

CHAPTER FORTY-ONE

LARK

*D*isbelief widened Leysa's eyes as they glimmered in the light of the braziers. "You—" Her voice was a rough exhale.

"I'm sorry." Tears trailed down Lark's cheeks, dripping into the crook of her neck as she glanced down at the sword plunged deep in Leysa's belly. Sorry didn't begin to convey the screeching range of her thoughts. It wasn't fair, this rewritten account of their friendship. This betrayal of all she thought she knew carving deep in her belly like the Reaper Blade in Leysa's. It was a sickening lurch, the slip of a misstep and the following plunge.

But she'd had to silence her. *Had* to end the life of someone who knew too much. Who whispered secrets in her enemy's ear. Who had betrayed her with every word since the moment they met. She *had* to kill her.

Hadn't she?

Lark pulled the Reaper Blade free, and Leysa crumpled to the ground. There was no blood upon its edge, and none upon the stone floor as the ancient seer lay dying. Only the soft trickle of her essence, her life, her memories—vast and archaic—seeping from her wound. It wasn't what Lark could see but a keen sense of understanding. She had ended Leysa's existence, and her power had to go somewhere. The only question was, where?

If Nereida found out... if she knew...

Lark pushed the thought away, instead watching one of her oldest friends fade away. It was surely madness, this compulsion that overcame her, but Lark sank to her knees, slipping her hand in Leysa's. And when Leysa weakly squeezed her hand, her heart broke, a crippling agony in her chest at what she'd done. What she'd had to do.

She had to do it.

She had to.

She—

Leysa's final breath whispered its departure, and she disintegrated into ash.

Lark's sobs broke free. It was a shaky and wild desperation, the pain in her ribs as her stuttering breaths fought against the clutches of her lungs. It wasn't fair. None of this was fair.

What had she done? What had she done? Was it necessity or cruelty that commanded her hand?

The shadows moved, silencing Lark's spinning thoughts. They danced and stretched along the walls, reaching ever closer to where she still kneeled in the ashes of Leysa's end. Voices hissing, angry and gleeful. Hungry.

Lark stood, wiped her face, and fell into a defensive stance. The rush of impending danger heightened her senses, burning away her despair. Something was coming. Something greater and worse than the shadows creeping toward her. Lark felt it in her bones, vibrating along her very marrow. It was a promise of fear, the instinctive call of survival, the primordial sense of peril.

The darkness deepened, a black void opening amidst the shades, and a familiar form stepped through.

Eyes glinting with malice beneath short and sharp edges of black hair. A twisted grimace of a smile splitting her mouth. She spun a dagger in her hand, the shadows curling around her possessively. Lovingly.

Nyx.

Thanar's former spymaster. Nereida's attack dog. Another ancient Reaper ravenous for Lark's death. She'd made no secret of her hatred before, and the wicked and eager hunger she wore upon her face now proved it hadn't dimmed.

"Larkin," she hissed, her very voice a shadow.

Lark gripped the Reaper Blade tighter. "Nyx." She dipped her chin in acknowledgment. "Have you come to see me out?" Foolish? Certainly. But Lark was too weary of this unceasing torment to care.

Nyx's smile only widened. Darkness curled around the braziers, threatening to snuff their flames.

Her shadows erupted.

Lark was thrown back, landing hard against the stone, the breath punched from her lungs. She coughed, struggling to find her rhythm, and an invisible weight pressed down on her chest.

Nyx's shadows.

There were always whispers of Nyx's history before becoming a Reaper and Thanar's spymaster. But they were nothing compared to the rumors of her shadow power. That each shadow she commanded was a soul she refused to guide, claiming them as her own instead of marching them across the bridge to the afterlife. That her shadows whispered to her, equally enthralled and enraged by her command of their fate. And since she kept them locked to her soul, she skirted the loophole to prevent altering the balance.

A cunning and dangerous creature, Nyx was.

Lark struggled against her shadows, panic hardening her muscles to stone.

"Fight me fairly!"

Nyx laughed, a scrape of claws against iron. "There is no matter of fairness between us. You are outmatched."

Lark fought against their hold, fear threatening to close her throat. She could not move; she could not fight. Not if Nyx wielded her shadows like this, and it was only a matter of time until the spymaster sliced her blade across Lark's throat, bleeding her human heart dry. Would she become one of her shadows? Would she have consciousness of who she once was? Or would she be a mindless vessel of anger and despair and—

"You'll never get this chance again! Fight me on your own so you might experience the satisfaction of ending Thanar's favored pet." The words were ash on Lark's tongue, yet she forced more out. "I sacrificed nothing for his regard, rebelled at every turn, and he'd *thank* me for it and go on worshipping the ground I walked upon. How many times did you heel at his boot, begging for scraps while I dined at his table? Perhaps you cannot defeat me without employing your shadows to do your dirty work!" Lark's voice shook. "That's what it is, isn't it? Thanar recognized your weakness. Even now you hide behind them when facing a mere mortal. You are nothing but a—"

The pressure dissolved, but a blow to Lark's ribs sucked the breath from her lungs once more.

"You are no match, Larkin," Nyx spat. "Without or without my shadows."

"Prove it." Lark's voice was weak, rasping against what she was sure was another broken rib. She staggered to her feet, and Nyx rushed, too swift to block.

Her slices were rapid and deep, making ribbons of Lark's thighs. A searing scrape against her cheek. A cut down her arm. Blood dripped over Lark's hand, pooling upon the floor in a steady, *drip, drip, drip.*

With a shout, Lark caught the next blow, spinning Nyx's blade away. The Reaper Blade was light in her hand, but Lark lacked Nyx's speed. It was worse than facing two opponents in the arena. It was fighting against the very dark, blocking and slashing against someone who'd already leapt out of the way.

"I know what comes for you. Nereida's plans are wicked indeed. You should *thank* me for killing you."

Nyx's blade ripped down Lark's back, and agony erupted like fire across her spin. She sank to her knees, and a forceful kick knocked her flat on her back. Nyx wound up, slamming her boot into Lark's side. Her face. Her back. The sounds she made were animalistic rage, perhaps centuries built up, as she bashed against every part she could reach.

Lark's vision dimmed, the Reaper Blade falling slack in her grasp.

"She gathers her forces; there is no stopping her. And she has something special planned for each one of your friends."

It was a mistake to goad Nyx. To invite her hurt and anger to fight alongside her. She would not make it quick or easy, seeming keen to beat the life from Lark's failing body.

"Their suffering will be eternal. And you have no one to blame but yourself."

Lark curled in on herself, bracing against ceaseless blows, and trying to protect herself as best she could. If she fell unconscious? Would Nyx be satisfied? Or would she continue reigning down her punishing strikes. She fought against the heavy pull of sleep, knowing it would be accepting defeat and granting Nyx the power to command her soul to her shadows' prison.

But it would be so easy.

A hush of a breeze skirted against Lark, and the pain smoothed to just this side of numb. Nyx still growled and kicked and screamed and spat, but it was muffled like Lark was underwater. Warmth radiated at her side—not fire, but comfort. A soft but strong presence letting her know she wasn't alone. And the last of Nyx's rage, her violence, it faded away.

Skies. Was this a Reaper? Here to guide her? Perhaps it would be better that way—to allow herself to be led to the afterlife. But Gavriel. Lark's heart clenched. She would never be permitted into Avalon, nor the Otherworld under Nereida's command. She would be sent to the Netherworld, where all matter of beasts awaited her eternity of torment. And would Gavriel descend when he fell? Would he search for her, only to find his own punishing and infinite existence?

Perhaps it was better he remained in his own dreams. Safer that way. She could slip away and he'd never face the pain of losing her.

"You're not really giving up, are you?"

That voice. A deep brogue. A familiar sound of warmth, of care, of safety and home.

"Because that sure as shit's not how I trained you to fight."

Lark fought to open her swollen and bruised eyes, the blood

already rushing to where Nyx abused her face. And before her mind could even catch up, shuddering sobs wracked her body. Tears spilling down her filthy and bloody face.

Hugo.

His dark eyes watched her with that familiar protective strength. His dark hair, shaved on the sides, still peppered in gray, and the fire from the braziers danced in his eyes. A thick mustache and beard obscured his face, but the twitch of his mouth hinted at the smile fighting to break free. His tattoos wrapped around his neck, down his arms, across his hands. He was whole and hale and here and how—

"Hugo," Lark croaked. "Is that really you?"

His eyes crinkled, those little lines forming at their edges. "It's good to see you, kid."

CHAPTER FORTY-TWO

LARK

*L*ark wasn't sure this wasn't another trick. Another trap. Her mind conjuring a comforting face to usher in the darkness. But she studied Hugo, his unchanged appearance.

"How—"

"We'll get to that," he said, a frown of disapproval forming on his face. "But for now, take care of this."

Awareness rushed into Lark's body, and along with it, the pain and sounds of Nyx shrieking.

Lark's body flooded with the overfiring of her nerves, alertness tightening the tension in her muscles. She blocked the next blow, grabbed Nyx's boot, and twisted. Nyx fell to the stone with a heavy thud, a sound of shock interrupting her tirade. Lark snatched the Reaper Blade from the floor and drove it down to meet Nyx's throat. A metallic *clang,* and Nyx crossed two daggers, halting Lark's pass.

Muscles trembling, Lark pressed with all her might. Even as the dull pain of her bruised and broken body pulsed with each heartbeat. Even as sweat and blood dripped into her eyes. She blinked her vision clear and pressed harder. Her strength was flagging, and Nyx had hardly begun. It was only a matter of losing her hold, and the spymaster would be upon her. Swift and deadly, lethal and strong while

Lark was fading, the temporary thrill of the fight dissipating into her injuries once more.

Nyx was right. Lark could not hold her own in a fight one-on-one like this. Nyx would always be faster, stronger; she wouldn't suffer fatigue like a mortal; she could fight forever. And Lark would never last. She would fall, and Nyx would claim her victory and tether her soul to hers—

Lark seeped her awareness into Nyx, surprise splashing across the spymaster's face, and Lark forged the weakest of tethers, just enough to send her pain into Nyx's body. Nyx's arms shook, the weight of Lark's injuries written into her body.

Lark pressed harder, flooded her mind with pain and weakness and fatigue and—

Nyx's hands slipped, and Lark unraveled the tether, slamming the Reaper Blade through her pale throat.

The last of Lark's strength fled her body, and she toppled sideways, landing upon the stone. The edges of her vision dimmed, and she blinked the darkness away. Her pulse battered against her throat. She turned, pressing her temple against the stone floor. Nyx's body was crumpled beside her, disintegrating into ash and drifting away.

Relief coursed through her useless limbs, and sleep threatened its hold on her consciousness.

Strong arms lifted Lark, warmth surrounding her as the familiar scent of Hugo's pipe tobacco filled her senses.

"I got you, kid. You did good."

Lark's mouth stretched in a smile, her lips stinging with the action. Her vision blurred, and she blinked away the haze.

"How are you—" The pain stole the words from her mouth, a groan taking their place. She shut her eyes, her stomach rolling with the dizziness in her head. The way her skin bulged in spots, blood pooling at the surface, she'd suffered a formidable amount of internal bleeding.

Her head fell back, hanging over Hugo's thick arm as the ground moved beneath her feet.

"It hurts," she whimpered. The clatter of the Reaper Blade against the stone shaking her free from her dimming consciousness. "I need that!"

"Got it. What's this sodding thing made of?" Hugo's low grunt would have made Lark laugh were it not for the threat of vomiting. "How'd a scrawny thing like you wield such a heavy weapon?"

"Not scrawny," Lark murmured.

Hugo's deep chuckle was the last thing she heard.

———

LARK SAT UP, wincing when her muscles screamed. She wasn't in that dank, dark hall anymore. The one with the shadows and many doors. She was in a darkened room, curtains drawn over the windows.

"Easy." Hugo's voice sent a wave of relief through her, and she sagged against the pillows. Pillows?

"Where am I?" And why was it so dark? And why was she on a bed? And what was happening?

"Hang on." His heavy footfalls thudded across the room. Fluttering curtains were drawn, and the room flooded with blinding light.

Lark hid, throwing the blanket over her head.

"Sorry. Thought you might have some bruising in your head after that walloping. Was told to keep the light out until your eyes could handle it." Another rustle of fabric, and through the fibers of the blanket, the light dimmed. "Better?"

Slowly Lark lowered her makeshift shield, the room coming into view.

Hand-carved furniture dominated the space. A few furs strategically placed to provide comfort and cozy atmosphere. Whittled figures filled a shelf, their artist's touch evident in each rendering. Bears and foxes. A series of cats ranging in size. Even a recurve bow mounted upon the wall.

Hugo sat on the foot of the bed and scratched his neck. "Csilla loves cats for some reason. And the bow..." He trailed off, glancing over at Lark with a resigned expression. "Old habits."

"It's really you." Lark's eyes burned, her vision blurring behind unshed tears. "I thought…" Her words caught in her throat, a shaky sob breaking free. Hugo was here. He was real. So many words she hadn't spoken. So many moments she'd wished for him. And somehow, he was here.

It was too much, and the very real threat of awakening, of discovering this was only a dream, cast a harsh glare over the joy spilling into her chest.

Hugo's expression softened in understanding. "I've missed you, too."

How Lark had hoped, dreamed of seeing him again, and the shock left her unable to voice anything of meaning. Her head spun, and she shoved the covers off revealing a white shift and bare feet. "Why did you dress me?"

Hugo coughed. "I did not. That was Lana. Something about blood staining the sheets."

Lark ran her hands into her hair, tightening her grip and pulling just enough the edge of discomfort was grounding. Her body—

It was sore, there was no mistaking that. But bandages wrapped about her ribs kept the worst of the pain from answering every breath, and the cuts she sustained had been treated with some sort of numbing balm.

"So… confused. So…" Lark's stomach growled, its empty state shouting at her.

"Hungry?" Hugo reached over to a bowl beside him and tossed her a round shape.

Lark caught it, the smooth surface of a bright red apple in her hands. How was any of this possible? Was she dead? No. She couldn't be. The only bright form of paradise was Avalon and Merikh already made it abundantly clear she would not be welcome, nor would she find Hugo there.

"Where are we? How is your family here? Did I die? Did you actually survive? Why do you have apples?"

Hugo frowned and rubbed his jaw, the harsh sound of his palm against the bristles of his beard filling the silence. "Maybe eat first. Or while I explain." He waited patiently.

Lark sat back on the bed, taking a bite and chewing.

"Answers, in order: Arcadia. They came here after they died, too. No. No. Because you like them." He raised his brows. "Satisfied?"

Not even a little bit. This was Arcadia? Lark thought—

Solana never destroyed Arcadia. When Lark set her free, she never returned to Avalon or else she would have been destroyed or forced to eradicate the peaceful afterlife she'd crafted for the souls who failed to ascend to Avalon. The ones who were good but didn't fit the arbitrary standards of Sargon's rule.

But how were Lana and Csilla here?

"I thought... I thought you were separated from your family. That they ascended to Avalon, and you were trapped in the pits."

Hugo's expression darkened. "That was the case. Impossible to know how long. But a woman found me. She saved me from my fate and brought me here. Said she owed you a favor." He lifted his chin, something akin to pride shining in his eyes. "Said any friend of Lark's deserves the wish she gave away. So, I wished for my family to join me."

Solana. All this time, Lark thought she'd abandoned her. Taken her freedom and ran. But she was here. She was here and she had saved Hugo and delivered his family to him.

He leaned over and grabbed Lark's free hand. "Thank you for what you did, kid." He squeezed. "I never would have gotten my girls back were it not for you."

Lark's throat tightened, and she bit into her apple, filling her cheeks with too much fruit. "You're welcome." Her muffled words rang out. But her thoughts caught on something he'd said. "Your wish... why didn't you wish to live again? You could have wished for all three of you to return to the human realm."

Hugo frowned. "Would have if I could. You know that."

There were limits, even to Solana's power. But if Daciana could bring Kenna and Alistair back, maybe she could—

Hugo clapped her on the top of her hand, interrupting her thoughts. He stood, his massive frame filling the room.

"Well," he said. "I'd give you the tour. But you have shit to do topside."

Lark stood too, jabbing a finger into his chest. "And why didn't you return? When the veil fell, and the barriers protecting the human world were lifted, why didn't you come see us?" It was selfish to complain of this. But hadn't he missed them? Hadn't he sensed the force of their grief? It threatened to swallow Lark whole some days. "Didn't you want to?"

"Aw, kid." Hugo pulled Lark into his arms, and she sank into his embrace. "Of course, I wanted to see you. Wanted to kick Gavriel's ass once or twice. Take Langford and Alistair out for a celebratory drink when they finally pulled their heads out of their asses. Tell Daciana it was all right to be afraid of loving someone so hard." He pulled back, smiling down at her. "Wanted to tell you how fucking proud I am of you." He gave her shoulder a gentle shake. "But I couldn't. Not without risking my life here. There was no guarantee I could find my way back."

Sympathy shone in his eyes. Of course, the fallen veil gave souls in the afterlife leave to depart, but it wasn't as if the living accidentally stumbled upon the Netherworld. It would be resigning himself to an eternity of wandering. Of leaving his family, his peace, behind.

There was no choice.

Death wasn't the end but a new beginning. Hugo had a life here. Well-earned and hard fought. Lark wouldn't wish him to give it up for anything.

"I'm always with you, Lark." He cleared his throat, hardening his stare. "But I don't want to see you here for a long, long time. I'm talking decrepit with age, damn near senile, and incontinent."

"So, around your age?"

"Watch it." He chucked her on the chin. "But when you do join us, at least eighty years from now, you better make sure you've kept up with your drills. Afterlife is no excuse for sloppy training techniques, and I'll expect you to keep up with me on our daily runs. Got it?"

Lark smiled, even as her chin trembled. Even as Hugo's face

blurred behind the tears hazing her vision. It was an achy joy, uplifting even as her voice wavered. "Got it."

"Now pack up. You have a lot of work to do."

Her blades were tucked in the corner, alongside her clothing. Cleaned and repaired with expert needlework. Lark grabbed her tunic and breeches, disappearing behind a privacy screen in the corner to dress.

"I noticed you didn't have your bow," Hugo said from across the room. "Getting soft on me?"

Lark laughed. "I didn't have time to pack when one of Avalon's finest stole me from the mortal realm."

Hugo grunted, and a scraping sound followed.

Lark reappeared, buckling her weapons into place. And at the door, Hugo stood holding a recurve, the wall where it had been mounted gapingly bare.

"Here," he said, shoving the bow into her hands. "Take this and these." A leather-sewn quiver, outfitted with near thirty arrows.

Lark smoothed her hands over the grooves in the wood. Over the delicate markings and shapes to create a hold. A perfect fit for her hand.

"I've upped the pull weight on your string. So, make sure you're building your strength and eating properly."

Lark slung the quiver and bow over her shoulder, gazing up at her dear friend. Her mentor. The closest thing to a father she'd ever had, even with her memories returned. It was humbling and awe-inspiring, the many ways that mortals could love. The space within one's heart for so many people.

"Thank you, Hugo." She leaned up on tiptoes, pressing a kiss to his cheek.

"Sure thing, kid."

That familiar tightness crept up her throat. This was her last chance. No regrets. No withholding. How often did one get a second chance at parting words?

Lark wet her lips. "Hugo, before I leave, there are things I need to say."

Hugo crossed his massive arms, canting his head to the side with a thoughtful frown behind his beard. "I'm listening."

She cleared her throat. "Life isn't the same without you. You were the closest thing I've ever known to a father. You were family when I had nothing. I don't wish for you to worry after me, or feel any guilt that you've found peace. But part of me, all of me really, still needed you. I needed you and you were gone." Her voice cracked on the word, the first tear rolling free. "I'll always love you, even if I can only speak to you by whispering to the stars."

Hugo's face shuttered, devastation crumpling his features before he tightened his mouth and nodded. "I love you, too, kid. Always have. Always will." He leaned in, and placed a chaste kiss to her forehead. "I'm always listening."

Something fractured in Lark's chest at that, even as warmth filled her at his words.

It wasn't undoing the loss, the hurt, the grief of it all. But it was enough.

Hugo wrenched the door open, and blinding light filled the room.

The tightness in Lark's chest wasn't a sorrowful thing, nor was it regret. It was the ache of a bittersweet farewell. Only instead of farewell it whispered, *"Until our paths cross again."*

CHAPTER FORTY-THREE

GAVRIEL

"*D*id you do it right?" Ferryn's narrow face wore a pinched expression.

Gavriel exhaled slowly and glared at him. "How exactly does one do it wrong?"

"I don't know, but I'm sure you could find a way. You seem creative in your failures."

"Do you wish to try?"

"Yes! Give it here."

"Don't touch that!" Slapping Ferryn's hand away, Gavriel glanced around.

He'd followed the path of the lantern, searching for Lark. But its intent was to take them in circles, changing course at will as if chasing an overzealous firefly in the dark.

Lark. Where are you?

Gavriel would spend all his days searching for her if that's what it took. But any sign that they were headed in the right direction, any hint that he was in fact drawing closer rather than leading them deeper into the dark, would be greatly appreciated.

They had just reached another corridor. A narrow walkway

bracketed by barred cells. Perfect. Another dungeon. Had they dragged Lark to every bleeding holding in the afterlife?

"Oh, shit. I recognize this place."

"So do I," Gavriel muttered. "Prisons all look the same after a while."

"No, I mean this one in particular." Ferryn darted his gaze around wildly. "We need to go, turn the little key and think harder."

"Give me a moment to concentrate."

"You're taking too long. Give it here." Ferryn tugged, and Gavriel held tightly. No way in the blazing abyss was he handing off his only way to find Lark to someone as inept as him. They struggled pulling back and forth, and Ferryn stumbled, ripping the lantern free from Gavriel's hands.

It all happened so slowly, yet quick enough Gavriel could do nothing but watch in horror as the lantern fell to the stone floor, shattering upon impact. Its blue flame evaporated, dull glass of the broken artifact littering the floor. Any hope at finding her, shattered alongside it.

Shock splashed across Ferryn's face, casting his expression into that of a child who just broke someone else's toy.

"You *fucking* imbecile." Rage tumbled deep in Gavriel's stomach. A harsh and brutal force hardening his tone. "You just killed her."

"Wait," Ferryn said. "It's not an ordinary lantern. We can just—"

Gavriel shoved him. Harder than he intended. Ferryn flew back, and the metallic sound of his body colliding with the bars of the closest cell rang through the dank room.

Ferryn's mouth hung open, his gaze wide with disbelief before he rolled his eyes. He straightened his cloak and tunic, adopting far too casual a demeanor. "That was uncalled for."

Gavriel's hands tightened into fists as the overwhelming urge to strangle the man before him threatened to take over. He exhaled a sharp breath through his nose, focusing on the calm he needed. "Uncalled for? Do you remain willfully ignorant of our current plight, or are you simply that stupid?"

Ferryn made a show of appearing deep in thought, going so far as to rub his chin as he studied the ceiling. "This feels like a trap. I'm not supposed to answer that, am I?"

"You approach everything as if in jest; nothing really matters so long as you're laughing." Gavriel's voice was sharp. "I wonder if you even have a heart."

Ferryn's brow furrowed, his mouth thinning into a firm line. "Perhaps I've had centuries to learn mastery of my reactions. A lesson you'd do well in learning yourself. You never know when your own weakness will be turned against you. So why show your hand?"

But Gavriel had learned this lesson, hadn't he? Years of training, of honing both body and mind, of withstanding life at the Guild. Biting his tongue until the tang of blood filled his mouth. These were all lessons in control, in patience, in fortitude. One wrong move, one subtle reaction before a mark, was an assured failure. He had mastered such things. There were moments when he'd been pushed beyond the limits of his patience, he was human after all, and those moments were occurring more frequently. Could he still claim control of his emotions anymore?

No. Not since he'd found someone worth losing control for. Not since Lark reawakened him. He could not bring himself to regret that. She was worth all the pain of endless lifetimes. But without her, without the knowledge of her wellbeing, his anger was a blade honed for cruelty.

"If we fail to find her, if Lark remains out of reach, the blame is yours."

Ferryn's eyes darkened, his lip curling in a snarl. But for once, he remained silent.

"No glib retort?" Gavriel fanned his arms wide. "Where are your jests now?" The blood rushed in his head, his chest aching with every bludgeon of his heart. Rage bloomed in him, searing and scorching. A laugh, his laugh, rang in his ears. A bitter bark of a sound holding no warmth or humor. "Will you laugh over her corpse? Spit on her memory with ill-timed remarks and thoughtless quips?" His stomach burned, bile rising in his throat even as he spewed the words.

What was wrong with him? The pressure in his head throbbed. It was as if—

"You fucking bastard!" Ferryn's fist collided with Gavriel's jaw, and the salty taste of blood filled his mouth.

He caught the next blow, delivering sharp and efficient jabs in return. The air *whooshed* from Ferryn's mouth, a grunt of pain following. But the madness had taken hold. Gavriel's fists were possessed as he pummeled the man, heat and rage and chaos filling his head with a loud buzzing drone.

"Stop," Ferryn coughed out weakly.

The edges of Gavriel's vision darkened, a red haze filling his sight. There was no thought, no logic, just the primal need to bash the man's skull in.

"Gavriel, stop!" Ferryn's hands flew wildly in a defensive maneuver. "Fuck! It's in your head. Fucking listen to me! It's not you!"

His words barely registered. Gavriel grabbed Ferryn's head, holding it caught between his hands. He'd bash it against the floor, crack his skull open, and see how far the blood would spread.

"Lark," Ferryn cried. "Lark… will never forgive you." His words were muddled, spoken through a mouthful of blood.

The sound of her name jolted through Gavriel, quieting his mind just enough to realize what he was doing. Ferryn was sprawled beneath him, Gavriel's weight holding him in place. One of his eyes was swollen shut, his face covered the with beginnings of mottled bruising. Blood tinged his mouth, and his blond hair was wound through Gavriel's fists as he held his head ready for the killing blow.

Fuck. Fuck. Fuck. Gavriel leapt back, shaking his head. His rage had been temporarily stunned into calm, but it was steadily building once more.

"What's… happening?" he panted.

Ferryn groaned, holding his ribs as he struggled to stand. "End of the hall." He winced. "I suspect they have a"—another sharp breath—"wrath demon. Aeshma."

Wrath demon.

Kenna's bestiary and all its pages flipped open in Gavriel's mind.

There was no drawing, but the words appeared to him as if he had the book in hand.

Wrath demons. A physical embodiment of rage, wrath, and fury. They feed on their victims' rage, fanning the flame of anger until the binding is complete. A human who releases the soul of another through death binds their own to the wrath demon, their rage burning them alive until nothing remains but an echo of pain.

The buzzing was beginning to fill his head once more, his rage building like a fire with too much kindling. But it wasn't real. His anger, his fear, that was true. But this mindless need? It wasn't his to claim. He shoved it down, forced it away, and the pressure in his head subsided.

Gavriel tore down the corridor, scanning each cell until he found the only inhabited cell. Tendrils of light from the brazier's flame danced across wall where a lone man sat, his knees pulled close to his chest. Dark hair, moon-white skin, and not a stitch of clothing on his pale, lean body. He was unremarkable. A wisp of a person.

The man lifted his chin, revealing the fathomless depths of his dark eyes and reminding Gavriel of the indisputable truth: This was no man, but a wrath demon. It was madness to recall how he once thought Lark a similar creature. That he once questioned her own humanity. How the name 'demon' had once been Gavriel's cruel way of reminding her so.

The answering pang of shame at the memory only served to sharpen his need to find her.

Gavriel tucked the thought away, refocusing on the lone being in the cell.

The demon's answering smile sliced across his face. "A shame you ended our game early. It was the most diversion I've had since they tossed me down here." The firelight danced along his cell, the silhouette of two horns atop his head casting their visage against the wall. Despite his commonplace appearance, he could not hide his truth from the shadows.

Kenna's bestiary detailed the nature of the demon, but not the method of slaying it. There were instructions for relinquishing its hold on a human host and banishing it back to the Netherworld. But to eliminate it in the flesh…

Did demons truly have flesh? Balan was impervious to wounding in his original form, as Gavriel had painfully learned firsthand when the demon dragged him to the Netherworld in a bid to lure Lark into a trap. And the demons they fought after Hazel's summoning required the Reaper Blade, the arcane weapon forged by Daciana and the weaponsmith. The weapon they all bled for.

The one lost to him now.

"How do I kill it?" Gavriel ground out, and as Ferryn hobbled over to them, his face losing its angular form to the swelling of his bruises. He'd hurt him, dammit, nearly killed him.

"No need. The cell will hold." Ferryn gestured to the bars. "His greatest punishment is his boredom, and now that you know of his tricks, you shan't fall for them again." He eyed Gavriel meaningfully, arching a bloodied brow. "Right?"

Gavriel shook his head. "I'm in control. Forgive me…" He trailed off, unwilling to finish that sentence.

"For trying to kill me?" Ferryn huffed a laugh though it quickly melted into a groan of pain. "You wouldn't be the first. I'm flattered you held out this long before an assassination attempt."

He was deflecting, but Gavriel was beginning to understand the way Ferryn processed things. Especially the harder things. And it was unworthy of him to suggest fault with that.

"And now I'm bored again." The wrath demon let his head fall back to rest against the wall of his cell.

It didn't seem right, leaving a dangerous entity alive after nearly killing Ferryn. In fact, if Gavriel were a betting man, he'd bet this decision would return to bite him in the ass. But there were more pressing matters at hand. Like escaping without the lantern's guide and finding Lark.

"I feel better. This is bonding." Ferryn pressed a thumb to his nostril and huffed a splatter of blood against the floor.

The sound of armored footsteps echoed down the hall, and the flames of the braziers flickered as if answering back.

Shit.

Someone was coming.

"Now we can put our differences aside—"

Gavriel clamped a hand over Ferryn's mouth, ignoring the slide of blood against his palm. "Shut up. Someone is coming, and now we're stuck. Get in the cell and hide. Keep to the shadows."

Ferryn tugged his hand away and whispered, "We should try to relight the lantern. Just because the glass is broken, doesn't mean the key—"

"After. For now, just hide!" Gavriel shoved him toward an empty cell and backed away to another, slipping through without touching the door and creeping into the farthest corner. There was no way to prepare for an unknown threat. The footsteps were closer now, heavy with intent. As if they wanted to alert them of their presence. He slowed his breath, forcing silence to shroud him. As long as Ferryn didn't do anything stupid—

A wet sneeze sounded from across the cell.

And Gavriel fought the urge to groan in defeat.

The footsteps stopped, the careful sound of glass shifting against stone. "I know you're there," a woman's voice called.

"Where else would I be?" The sound of the wrath demon's voice jolted through Gavriel. If the creature thought to help them for a favor returned, it was sorely mistaken.

"You are to speak when spoken to, lest I cut your tongue out myself." The woman's voice thundered through the dungeon, rupturing the quiet. "Intruder, come out at once."

If Ferryn stepped into view before Gavriel could form a plan...

The woman spoke again. "You didn't think I forgot our little games."

Her voice and words were unnervingly fond. Almost as if she already knew who hid in the shadows with intimate familiarity.

"Of course, not. You love your games. Even when you're the only one who knows they're playing." Ferryn's voice called back, sharp and biting. The sound of his footsteps leaving his cell swiftly followed. "Ceto."

Gavriel should have killed him when he had the chance.

"That's rich coming from the man who chased another woman right into the mortal realm. Don't play the injured party when you're equally culpable."

Oh no. Oh skies, why?

"You know it was never like that. Don't play the jilted lover now."

"You flatter yourself, Ferryn. You were nothing more than a body beneath me and a pretty face. That you chose the wrong side to hitch your ambitions to is no fault of mine."

Was there anything worse than listening to a pair of scorned lovers bicker while keeping one's presence unknown?

Probably. But Gavriel failed to come up with anything.

"You used me. You knew how I felt about you, and you wielded it to serve your purpose." Ferryn let out a shaky breath. "Accuse me of being unfaithful if it makes you feel better. Weave your imaginary web of lies, but here's the inconvenient truth of it all. I fell for your lies. I *loved* you, Ceto. As infuriating and distant as you are, I loved you. Now I'm the fool and you're the victor. Let us all applaud your cunning deceit." His voice was harsh, brittle. A far cry from the façade of humor and deflection he always wore.

"And what of your deceit?" Ceto shouted back. "You swore the oath to Thanar, and you never even told me. Do you think I ever wanted him to know who I cared for after—" Her words abruptly stopped.

"You never cared for me. So, what difference does it make?"

"I could have. I…" Silence. Gavriel shifted uncomfortably, wishing he could sink into the floor and sneak away. Listening in on private conversations was part of the job, a necessary task when gathering intel on a mark. But this felt like an intrusion. "I could have, Ferryn. Do you not understand what that means for me?"

"It doesn't matter anymore, does it?"

A resigned sigh. Ceto didn't sound as if she was about to call the guards and drag them away, so Gavriel crept out from the safety of the shadows, stepping toward the entrance to his cell.

The woman stood half a hand taller than Ferryn. Her black hair was short and cropped close to the scalp. She watched Ferryn with a mixture of anger and regret. Not the best combination for a potential aid, but it was better than a straight shot to murder.

She glanced over, noticing Gavriel for the first time, and her expression darkened. "I see you brought a friend."

"I'm looking for Lark." Gavriel didn't care if that angered her. If that was the line she drew between friend and foe. He wasn't here for her master nor for anything other than finding the woman he loved.

Ceto nodded. "Of course, you are. And you're foolish enough to think I'll help you?" She bared her teeth, turning back to Ferryn. "You think if you play the lovesick fool I'll take pity on you and be your guide? I helped you once against my better judgment. Thinking you truly were loyal to me, that you'd use your freedom to fight your way to my side. But no, you chose your side, and it wasn't mine."

"Ceto." Ferryn grabbed her by the arms, and though she appeared strong enough to break the man in half, she let him. "It was never a choice between you and Lark. I can never and will never choose that snake you serve. Tell me you don't regret it. That your honor doesn't condemn you to rue your decision. I know you, Ceto, even though I fell for your lies—I know your truth enough to recognize you are not like her."

Ceto grimaced, shoving him away. "It doesn't matter. There's no stopping what's coming. I cannot—I cannot undo my choices."

"I'm not asking you to do that." Ferryn hesitantly reached out to cup her jaw.

Gavriel should not bear witness to their intimate conversation, but he was just as trapped as Ferryn was. He only hoped the man knew what he was doing.

"Help me make things right." Ferryn's voice was soft, beseeching. "That's all I've ever wanted to do. You know me inside and out. I play the fool so well no one takes notice, and I fuck up more often than not, but all I wish is to do the right thing. I do not want to break what is fragile in pursuit of righteous anger. Just help me... we can stop her, together."

Ceto shook her head, breaking free from his hold. "I cannot."

Ferryn's hand fell limp at his side. His shoulders caving in, making him appear small.

"But," she said, "I can tell you this. Lark is no longer here. Nyx was dispatched to deal with her and"—her mouth curved in a wry smirk—"Larkin still refuses to die."

"Where did she go?" Gavriel pushed the door open, the metallic creak of rusted hinges answering the movement. "How do I find her?"

"She's returned to your lands." Ceto frowned at the broken lantern. "You'll need a foothold to step back through."

"She is my soul's bonded." It felt like triumph to say the words aloud. To know written into the very fiber of his being that it was true. To have lived ages and ages with half his soul missing and the joy of reuniting the pieces. "Need more of a foothold than that?"

Ceto scoffed. "It'll do. I'll open the door, you think of her, and step through. I can't promise how close you'll land, but the two of you are nauseatingly driven to one another. I'm sure you'll find her eventually." She jutted her chin to a door, its appearance new and out of place in the dungeon. Spiderwebs of ice encased its façade, spreading and connecting as if cold was claiming the door as its own. "Head on through and close it behind you. Wouldn't want anything to follow."

"Thank you." And Gavriel meant it. Maybe it was foolish or downright selfish. But if this Reaper did anything horrible in her existence, he didn't care so long as she sent him to Lark.

Ferryn hesitated. "Ceto…"

"Go. Leave. Before I change my mind and lock you in a cell."

Something about the knowing smiles they exchanged hinted at another one of their games. Not anything Gavriel needed to speculate upon.

"Come with us." Ferryn gathered her hands in his. "It isn't too late."

"It is, though." Ceto freed her hands and took a step back, putting distance between them. "For me, it's far too late."

CHAPTER FORTY-FOUR

LARK

Something about this road was familiar. In the way it bent and curved between trees, boughs now laden with snow instead of leaves. In the drop from the road's edge sat a gorge that was all too easy to roll into. It reminded Lark of another time. Another day. Another journey. Of narrowly escaping Adler's estate clad in a bard's costume and trudging down the road. Thick flakes of snow began to fall, somehow both softening and sharpening the air. A soft peach painted the sky, brushstrokes of color in the cold. Lark inhaled a deep breath of wintry air, reveling in the way it pricked in her lungs.

It was a quiet moment, almost like a dream, after so much had happened in a span of… days? What even was time anymore?

Realization clawed at her calm. She hadn't any idea where she was or in which direction Inerys' cottage resided.

After Hugo had sent Lark through, she had appeared here. Wherever here was. Judging by the climate and familiar slopes and trees, she was somewhere in Ardenas. Same continent as Gavriel, so that was fortunate. But how long would it be until she reached the next town? It wasn't as if she carried camping provisions. And even if she had escaped the clutches of Avalon and defeated two of the most ancient

Reapers in the Otherworld, the very real threat of exposure could spell her death.

How anticlimactic after all that.

But she was alive. She was alive, and Hugo was fine, and Gavriel likely still slumbered in his protective sleep—

Unless Nereida knew what Lark had done. The lengths that witch would venture to sate her revenge were unfathomable. Gavriel could be in true danger with Lark's impulsive action. If Nereida found him, if Inerys' protective wards failed—

Lark broke into a sprint, the cold whipping through her hair. She hadn't the faintest clue if this was even the right way, but still she ran. Her feet carried her faster, pounding into the ice crusted road, jolting through her thighs. Reckless. She was reckless. And foolish and—

Two men walked ahead at the brow of the hill.

She squinted, trying to make out their shapes through the thick snow drifting across her field of view. A tall man, his blond hair tied at the back of his neck. A dark gray riding cloak ending at the knee. As if it were too short for him. As if it were intended for someone else.

Beside him, a lean, defined man. Clad in black fighting leathers perfectly formed to his body, his broad shoulders, his—

No. It couldn't be. It couldn't. He was... he was...

"Wait!" she called, ignoring the way her boots slid on freshly fallen snow. The icy air swallowed her voice, flakes hushing the sound. Her eyes burned from the wind she created in her wake, her hair catching more flakes as she sprinted. It was impossible, unfeasible, and yet every nerve in her body screamed its truth. Her heart most of all. "Gavriel!"

In the distance, he froze, halting in the middle of the road. He turned to face her. His first step was a stumble, a misstep, a staggering approach, but his next was assured, and stronger and swifter. He tore down the road, racing to her.

Lark's heart faltered, the pressure in her chest mounting. Her steps were like flying as she hardly noticed the ground, not when that incessant tug pulled her, called to her, propelled her.

She slammed into him, uncaring that her teeth clacked at the jolted stop. He wrapped his arms around her, and a sob broke free from her chest. Was this real? Was he real? Her shaky hands felt around his chest, his neck, reaching for his face. She blinked the tears away, his face coming into view.

Gavriel's dark green eyes speckled with gold peered down her at, glassy with emotion. Snowflakes dusted his lashes, and landed upon the scar along his cheek, melting upon impact.

Lark reached up, tracing his scarred mouth. "How…"

"We will always find one another." The rumble of his deep voice nestled something deep in her chest. A resonance of longing she'd suffered for too long. "Always." He cupped her jaw, running his thumb along her cheek, his eyes filled with wonder and adoration. "Skies but look at you. I thought I remembered what the sight of you did to me."

Lark leaned into Gavriel's touch, her heart breaking and reforming at his tenderness. At the rightness of his hand upon her skin.

He pressed his forehead against hers, breathing her in, before his mouth descended. His kiss was soft, gentle, exploring as if relearning and remapping her lips, her mouth, her tongue.

Her heart.

It was overwhelming. The feeling of closeness and the sense it wasn't nearly enough. Not by leagues. It burned in places she forgot existed within her.

Lark deepened the kiss, strengthening the force behind it, and Gavriel's hand fisted in her hair, all notion of gentleness lost. She scraped her teeth along his lip, and a low groan vibrated against her mouth. It was everything. His touch, his taste, the strength of his arms. It was everything she'd ached for in all her existence, and this was the first kiss she'd felt the echoes of their ancient past. The desperate longing between two souls bound to never know freedom. The violent strength of their love despite the harsh realities of their world. It was then and now colliding on that road. Their first of many first kisses whispering along her skin.

Their breaths quickened, and her grip on him tightened. Pulling him closer still. As if they could sink into each other and never resurface.

"No need to greet me with the same enthusiasm." Ferryn's voice broke through the haze of their kiss. "Might be a touch awkward."

Lark pulled back, regretting the distance immediately. But the way Gavriel's eyes blazed—all unspoken desire pooling in them—had heat flushing her body even as the snow fell upon her cheeks. She forced her gaze to Ferryn, and she might have laughed at the expression on his face—it was one of both amusement and mild disgust, but for the bruising along his eye. The swelling along the side of his face all the way to the jaw. The foreign angle of his normally straight nose.

"Ferryn... what happened to you?"

He smiled, a ghastly sight with the way the blood pooled beneath his skin. "Hello, little bird."

Ferryn looked as if he'd been bludgeoned repeatedly. It wasn't the type of bruising one might encounter in a mere scuffle. No, it was more akin to a severe reaction, like the boy she'd reaped who lost his life when he'd taken a stick to a beehive. His face had swelled, hiding his features, just as Ferryn's did now. Though the bruising...

"Who did this to you?"

Ferryn's gaze dipped past her shoulder to where Gavriel stood, and a strange, quiet tension snapped into place.

Gavriel's hand found the middle of her back. "Lark... I can explain."

"It was a wrath demon." Ferryn shrugged, letting his hands smack against his thighs. "You know how they can be. Timing is"—he reached up to twist his nose back into place, a sickening *pop* answering the action—"everything."

A wrath demon. They were known to play into mortal emotions. To feed their rage until it consumed them, and a tether had been formed. They were considered a blight even in the Otherworld, disrupting the balance and creating more work for Reapers alike. They were easy to fall prey to, especially when they remained hidden, allowing a mortal's own anger to push them past the brink.

"I would have killed him." Gavriel's voice was steady, matter of fact. "I wanted to."

Though there was no emotion in his voice, Lark could feel what went unspoken. The regret. She leaned back into his chest, allowing his arms to come around her. A wrath demon was no easy feat, and that he broke free spoke volumes of his inner strength. His will.

Words of comfort she would save for private.

"But now he loves me." Ferryn grinned. Was he missing teeth?

Lark stepped out of Gavriel's reach, wrapping her arms around her oldest friend. Ferryn sighed, resting his head against her hair and hugging her back. "I'm glad you're safe."

"I'm glad Gavriel has more control than most."

Ferryn snorted against her hair.

"Is it strange? The pain?" Ferryn was still newly human, and in most ways untried and untested. Lark recalled her first foray with pain, and how alive it made her feel. Alive and overwhelmed in equal measures.

"Not really. We had different experiences in the Otherworld, after all." Ferryn's voice was gentle as if softening the reminder. "Your man may have unwittingly jumpstarted a new preference where pleasure is concerned." He theatrically winked, appearing utterly ridiculous since his eye was already nearly swollen shut.

"I pity your next bedmate," Gavriel said, humor tempering his voice.

"Don't tell me you two have never experimented with the boundaries of pain and pleasure." Ferryn's swollen expression turned gleeful as Lark's cheeks burned.

Gavriel scowled. "*That* is none of your business."

It was fascinating watching the two of them bicker. Lark almost wanted to stand back to afford herself a better view.

No wonder the wrath demon targeted poor Gavriel, with the joy Ferryn took in setting him off.

Gavriel's hand found hers, and he gently tugged her back to him. At Ferryn's affronted expression, he smirked. "You understand," he said calmly. "I just got my hands on her again, I'm not ready to let go."

Ferryn scoffed. "One might accuse you of codependency."

"I really don't care." Gavriel turned Lark back to face him, taking hold of her chin. "Unless you wish me to let go."

She wrapped her arms around his neck, sinking into another kiss. "Never."

***

FINDING the next town took longer than strictly necessary with how many times Gavriel stopped to kiss Lark, to hold her, to whisper heated promises in her ear.

But finally, they'd arrived in Mirefield, and after soaking in a bath until the sensation of all the filth subjected to her skin was finally forgotten, Lark nestled atop the bed, yanking Gavriel to her. He'd insisted on helping her bathe, even joining her in the large basin of water and taking his time thoroughly scrubbing. But they hadn't ventured further than lingering kisses and wandering hands.

That simply wouldn't do.

Lark tugged him so his weight fell on her and began untying his tunic. A waste of time that he put it back on in the first place. His hands found her wrists, slowing her movements.

"Wait," he whispered along the seam of her lips, leisurely exploring. "We need to speak."

Lark stilled, watching him carefully. "Is it about Ferryn? I understand, you know. It isn't easy to realize a demon's compulsion, nor is breaking free. But you did, Gavriel. If anyone understands, it's me and Ferryn." She ran her fingers along his jaw, peering into his green eyes. "And if you ever fear there might be a limit, a line you could cross that would lose me"—she leaned up and kissed him softly—"remember I will never think you anything less than extraordinary."

Gavriel sighed, leaning into her touch. For a few heartbeats, they lay there, foreheads pressed together. Finally, he spoke. "It isn't about that, though I thank every fucking star in the sky for you." Something in his voice hinted at pain.

"What's the matter?"

Gavriel dropped his weight to the side, lying next to her and propping himself on his elbow. "I felt it—when he took you. It's what finally pulled me from the past. From reliving... everything."

When Merikh spirited her away to Avalon. When he locked part of her soul up, leaving her vulnerable and defenseless while Gavriel still slumbered in Inerys' house. She should have been there. She shouldn't have been taken so easily.

"I'm sorry I couldn't protect you."

Gavriel's eyes widened, shock splashing across his face. "You're sorry? I'm the one who failed you. Had I been awake, I could have—"

"Don't do that. There a million possible outcomes that could have transpired. But I'm here now. You're here now. We're finally together. Why do you still suffer?"

Gavriel buried his face in the crook of her neck, inhaling deeply. His breath sent a shiver down her spine, and her legs twitched, reminding her she hadn't put her smallclothes back on and she was clad in a mere towel.

"I felt what he did to you. How you suffered. You ask why I suffer but it was you who bore the pain, more pain than anyone should. And I didn't know how to find you. I searched with that fucking lantern, but it kept leading me astray. And you—" Gavriel's fiery gaze met hers, anger and terror reflected in their depths. "Whatever you need from me, it is yours."

Lark slowly sat up, holding his stare. This man she'd loved with the very depths of her soul. "He did hurt me, and he tried to break me."

Gavriel's jaw tightened.

"But," Lark continued, "something returned to me. Something I'd lost long ago. And while Merikh will get the reckoning he deserves, all I want from you... all I need from you"—Lark wet her lips—"is to know you're not the only one who remembers. I have loved you for years beyond counting, and I will love you until the world ceases— beyond that still. I will love you further than the stretches of time. So, what do I need?" She reached for him, cupping his jaw. "Love me the same."

"Oh, Lark." Gavriel leaned into her touch. "In any day of any life. In any existence or deep in the pits of the Netherworld. Behind any face, I will love you fiercely with every breath I take." He claimed her mouth in a searing kiss, and fire erupted in her blood. He slid between her thighs, pressing against where she ached most.

"Skies, but you're more than beautiful, Lark. You're everything my soul craves."

He tugged off his tunic, revealing the body she knew by heart. Every scar, every muscle, every dip and curve. And when he pulled the edges of her covering away, he sighed. "My dreams did not do you justice." His mouth found the sensitive spot on her neck, and he worked his way down. Little sounds of pleasure ghosting against her skin.

Lark squirmed beneath him. That slippery heat pooling in her stomach and lower.

Gavriel's lips traced the line of her stomach, his teeth and tongue leaving fire in their wake. "I missed you," he breathed against her hip.

"I missed you," she nearly sobbed. His hands hooked around the backs of her thighs, tugging them apart. Cool air hit her warm heat, and her head spun with dizzying want.

"I've dreamt of having you beneath me again." The first touch of his fingers, and Lark gasped. "Of having you writhe under me, the way you feel, the way you taste." With a groan, he followed his words with the barest caress of his tongue, teasing and tasting. Lark cried out, clamping her hand over her mouth. "Of the sweet noises you make." His fingers pressed in, sinking with aching slowness, curling right where she needed him most. "Don't do that." He pulled her hand away from her mouth. "Let me make you sing."

"Please." Her voice was a pathetic, needy thing. "Gavriel."

"Oh, I've missed that, too." His breath between her thighs, fingers sunk deep, were nearly enough to send her over the edge. "Look at me."

Lark forced her gaze down, to wear he lay between her legs, his face peering up at her. Eyes darkened and glittering.

He kissed her inner thigh. "Forever isn't nearly enough with you."

At his quiet admission, Lark's chest tightened. No measurement of time would ever be enough, not by the half of it. She was forever undone by this man, forever her heart would answer his call, and it killed her to think there was ever a time she could not remember her need of him.

His mouth descended, greedy and desperate. Tasting, savoring, devouring. Tingly heat spread through her body, and Lark's eyes fell closed. But no. She wanted to see, and she forced them open once more, finding Gavriel's eyes, dark with lust as the ravenous movements of his mouth twisted something deep in her belly. He groaned against her wet heat, his fingers moving in time with his mouth, his tongue, his lips. It was too much, too much, and it turned to sharp pleasure. Deep, so deep—

The final thread of tension snapped, sending waves of pleasure trembling down her legs, through her body. Gavriel gripped her hip tighter, chasing her shuddering end with languid movements of his wet mouth. Until finally she pushed him away, the pleasure starting to almost hurt.

Gavriel slid up her body, and Lark claimed his mouth, tasting herself in his kiss.

"My little demon," he murmured against her lips, playfully nipping at her when she frowned. "You've always been mine."

Lark tightened her arms around his neck as he lined himself up with her entrance. "Do you remember the first time?"

Gavriel hummed, sinking in the barest of inches. "Mm… you lifted your skirt and sank upon me, claiming my virtue and my heart like the siren you are."

Lark giggled, but it turned to a moan when he sank a touch deeper. "That is not… how it happened."

"It was." He plunged in deeper, the exquisite stretch making her hiss. "I was entirely innocent."

"This was after you snuck us out to the gardens and—*ah*—used your wicked tongue. There was nothing innocent about you."

Gavriel laughed, raining kisses all over her face as he waited for her to adjust to him. "Is it strange that though I cherish the memories I have of you, in any life, this one feels the most true?"

Lark considered his words. Though the memories of her human life were achingly precious, a gift stolen when Thanar dragged her to the

Otherworld, they were marred by pain. By pain of their circumstance. Their separation. Even death. And the man she loved then, Gideon, though his soul was kindred to Gavriel's deepest truth, he wasn't exactly the same. He didn't have a fierce love of dark chocolate, a biting sense of humor, an affinity for tight leather pants. He didn't know his way through any lock, leap from tall heights, procure a disturbingly in-depth knowledge of poisons. He didn't fight to find the light after all the destruction his own two hands had wrought. He was Gavriel, and yet he wasn't.

Gavriel was right. This was their life together. The past was important, but it did not define them.

"That's not strange," she said. "I fell in love with the mortal fighting his way through grief."

Gavriel smiled, the boyish expression that never failed to make her heart race. "I fell in love with the dangerous and beautiful demon." He kissed her in a slow, lingering caress. "My heart is forever yours." He sank all the way in, ripping the breath from her lungs and starting a fire deep in her belly. With each thrust, he kissed her, a devastating devotion on his lips.

She met each of his movements, swearing her own vows in every cant of her hips. She would love him far beyond death. His touch was pure life. Her heart and soul were his eternally.

Gavriel's touch found the intimate space between her thighs, and he sent her careening over the edge. A fluttering, aching pleasure that stole the strength from her body.

His movements turned stuttered, his brow furrowed as if in pain, and when he found his own end, it was with her name upon his lips. He yanked her against him, their racing hearts meeting chest-to-chest, and he kissed every part of her he could reach.

If Lark knew nothing more of humanity than love, it was worth every sacrifice.

CHAPTER FORTY-FIVE

DACIANA

"*I* hate not knowing." Aislinn used her fork to rearrange the food on her plate, balancing it on her lap and pushing the honeyed pear slices around without lifting it to taste. "What if Merikh returned to Inerys' lands?"

It was a fair concern. One Daciana shared. But the fact remained, if Aislinn used her power, even just to check in with Lark or Gavriel, Merikh had a way to find her. Which they could not allow.

"Inerys is a powerful witch. Her protective wards will hold."

"But what if they don't?"

"Trust me." Kenna strode across the room, carrying sharpened shin bones from a fallen wolf. The irony of gliding upon the bones of wolves was not lost on Daciana. "Inerys has more than a few surprises. If they faced off, I'd pity the paragon."

"That's right," Daciana said, arching her brows. "You know the witch rather *intimately.*"

"That is not—" Kenna's voice cracked, and she cleared her throat. "That is neither here nor there."

Daciana gave a good-natured roll of her eyes in Aislinn's direction, and Aislinn smiled, resuming her task of shifting her food instead of tasting it.

Food was prepared in Elder Muirgel's banquet hall and distributed among the people. There was always the option to eat at the long tables in the hall, or to retire to one's home. Kenna hadn't pushed for them to spend any meals other than dinner in the hall, which made for quieter breaks in the day. Quieter and... somewhat cramped.

Kenna's people had kept her grandmother's home, a caravan outfitted with a large plush bed and plum-colored curtains shielding the intricate glass windows. It was warm and cozy, the bed sleeping the three of them easily, but it meant they'd been living in close quarters.

Very close quarters.

Aislinn cleared her throat. "I don't see the harm in making a quick connection with Lark. Just long enough to ascertain their wellbeing and update them on our progress."

"What progress?" The question slipped from Daciana's mouth before she could halt it.

Kenna pursed her lips and busied herself with packing for their planned adventure. Each time Daciana had gently brought up meeting with Elder Muirgel to request the hunters' aid, Kenna had found a reason to stall. She credited wanting to prove they were honoring her people's traditions before asking a favor. And her enthusiasm for showing Daciana her old stomping grounds.

The day before, she had taken her to a frozen waterfall. She professed it was where she always came to make wishes. It was nearly as breathtaking as the sight of Kenna taking in the splendor. Kenna instructed Daciana to make a wish, and instead of wishing, Daciana pressed Kenna against a tree and made her gasp and writhe and pant out her pleasure. What use were wishes when one could reach out and grasp their greatest desire?

Today they had planned to go ice gliding, another one of Kenna's favored pastimes. And Daciana couldn't bring herself to say no.

But soon, whether Kenna liked it or not, they would have to face the reality of what brought them there.

KENNA FINISHED FASTENING the ice blades to the bottoms of Daciana's boots, her eagerness morphing into something else entirely. Something entirely at odds with Kenna's nature.

"Remember to keep a generous bend in your knees."

"All right."

"And always look in the direction you want to go."

"That seems self-explanatory but noted."

"And if you need to slow down, you sort of turn your toes in like a duck."

"Ducks don't have toes." Daciana fought the grin threatening to break her deadpanned expression.

Kenna huffed out a breath, and her uneven fringe fluttered in response. "Turn your toes like a duck's feet."

"Duck feet don't turn inward."

"Paragon's tits, Daciana. Turn your blazing toes in to slow down!"

Finally, Daciana broke, a laugh slipping through.

Kenna was worried. Needlessly so. Daciana may not have ever ice glided, but she was a quick study in most respects. And it wasn't as if it was dangerous. The worst that could happen was she received a few bumps and bruises.

She was so used to Kenna's chaos paired with her inability to take anything seriously, that her sudden shift into responsible and caring partner made something ache in her chest. It was warmth with a twinge, the threat of pain from loving something so much.

Daciana stood from the carved seat deliberately built by the frozen pond. She took Kenna's hands, kissing each one. "This is supposed to be fun."

"And it will be. After we get you more padding."

Daciana laughed again. "Stop." She tugged her back into her arms, kissing her on the tip of her freezing cold nose. "I will be fine. And I'll have you to ice any sore spots later, won't I?"

Kenna's expression transformed into one of gleeful mischief. "I can think of a few places that will need my attention."

They'd spent the last week exploring Kenna's home and practicing each and every one of her favored traditions. Mulled cider, fire dancing, they'd even sung solstice chants. Kenna's rationale was that ingratiating themselves into their traditions and establishing connection was a show of respect. After that, they could ask the Muirgel for aid. They'd request an audience with her, and with any luck, the time they spent there would yield fruition.

And if not... Daciana couldn't deny the joy it brought her witnessing Kenna's excitement. Sharing in these ancient practices with her. It made it easy to pretend there wasn't a world of danger awaiting them.

Keeping Aislinn safe was the top priority. Then recruiting the hunters. Last could be sharing Kenna's traditions.

Daciana was having a hard time keeping those priorities in order, apart from keeping Aislinn safe. So long as Aislinn didn't dream walk, she was invisible to the paragon hunting her. But she'd declined joining their outing, and last night she was withdrawn, blaming a headache.

She should check on her. Make sure she wasn't grieving the visit to her mother. That girl bore so much and without complaint. It was often the ones who hid their hurts well who needed help the most.

"I won't let go of you. So, if you fall, I fall." Kenna tugged on Daciana's sleeve, her nose and cheeks bright red from the cold and utterly adorable.

"I appreciate the sacrifice," Daciana said. "But I will be fine."

"Yeah, she will!" a third voice chimed in, and the smile on Daciana's face turned forced.

Ruva.

Her long black hair hung in a thick curtain down her back. Atop her head sat a vibrant toque, unevenly knitted in an array of random color. Her shawl had been buttoned and fitted to hug her shoulders without hindering any movement, and her fur lined boots appeared to have been resewn many times, as if she'd added material as she grew instead of scrapping them for a larger pair. And somehow, every mismatched piece cohesively blended beautifully. Ruva was exactly herself. She was friendly and beautiful and kind and funny.

Kenna's childhood friend and the one person Daciana had no desire to spend unnecessary time with.

For all of her admirable qualities, and Kenna had spoken well enough of her there were many, she was unbearably cold toward Daciana. She had a way of angling her body to block Daciana when speaking to Kenna. At first, she thought it the result of Kenna sharing their romantic woes over the years and a protective friend asserting their place. That was respectable. But it quickly became clear the girl harbored an implacable mistrust for her.

And an utter infatuation with Kenna.

Kenna couldn't see it, so blinded by her nostalgia, but Daciana had no such blinders. That girl longed for Kenna. When they passed around the mulled cider, Ruva hung off her, slurring strangely intimate comments.

"Kenna smells so damn good, doesn't she? Like berries. Does she taste as good as she smells?"

Kenna had laughed it off and blamed the cider, but Daciana caught Ruva's lingering looks.

When Kenna taught Daciana how to fire dance, Ruva took it upon herself to demonstrate with Kenna, her hands lingering in places they shouldn't. Her head bowed a hair too close to Kenna's.

And even now, when Kenna was taking Daciana ice gliding, here she was again, pale skin flushed a bright pink, the striking blue of her eyes even brighter as the sun beat down upon the snow. Ruva tied her own ice blades on deftly, standing and striding for the frozen pond.

"Let's race! Last one to the end has to buy the caudle!"

Daciana did not care for that particular beverage. Spiced wine was pleasurable, but the moment one found themselves adding bread-crumbs and egg yolk, she was no longer interested.

"No racing. It's Dac's first time on the ice." Kenna slipped a hand down to the small of Daciana's back, fingertips threatening to travel lower. "Gotta make sure she stays on her feet. For now, at least." The last part she whispered against Daciana's ear, coaxing a shiver out of her.

Daciana laughed. "I told you, I'm fine. You needn't coddle me."

Even if it did fill her belly with butterflies. When was the last time anyone took care of her?

"See? She's fine. Get into position or I'm ordering one of everything out of your own pocket!"

Kenna hesitated, indecision warring on her lovely face. Daciana pressed a quick kiss to her cheek, too chaste to consider it sending Ruva a message. Even if it did please Daciana to see the way she looked away pretending to find her boots incredibly interesting.

"You're sure?" Kenna searched Daciana's face. "You don't mind?"

"Off you go. I'll likely catch up and win anyway."

Kenna grinned, the force of the sun in her smile. "Wouldn't that be something?"

"Would it?" Daciana stepped closer, and Kenna's breath hitched. "Would I win some sort of reward?"

"Yes," Kenna breathed, eyes widening. She was so responsive, even after the time they'd shared reacquainting themselves with every inch of each other's bodies.

"How far might I extend this reward?" Daciana lifted Kenna's chin, a ripple of pleasure shuddering down her spine when Kenna submitted eagerly.

"Anything you—"

"Go!" Ruva shouted, taking off gliding down the pond.

Kenna whined, her brows lifting in silent question.

"Go." Daciana laughed, and Kenna raced ahead, disappearing around the corner. The pond was long, with bends and curves through the trees. Heavy boughs glimmering with snow framed the space, forming an almost ethereal fairyland of ice crystals. She waded through the snow, balancing on her ice blades. It really wasn't that hard. Kenna had no reason to worry she couldn't handle—

Her foot slipped out from under her, the first step upon solid ice knocking her flat on her back. The air rushed from her lungs in an abrupt *whoosh!* Coughing and laughing, Daciana pushed herself up to sit.

It was harder than it looked, and a bruise was beginning to ache on her ass. She smiled. Kenna did promise her thorough attentions later, especially if she were sore. Daciana stood, angling her blades the way Kenna instructed, and taking small, cautious strides.

It was awkward and slow going. But the rhythmic scraping of sharpened bone on ice was strangely calming. Daciana set her own pace, lengthening her strides as she gained confidence. The sounds of laughter around the bend grew louder. Kenna and Ruva must have reached the end of their race. Daciana would have to congratulate the winner. Was she considered the losing party? She'd buy the caudle, but she sure as shit wasn't drinking it.

She rounded the corner and froze, heart in her throat.

Kenna was flat on her back on the ice, laughing so hard she couldn't breathe—

And Ruva, painfully lovely Ruva, lay atop her, legs slotted and leaning over her with a smile so big it looked damn near hurting. Her vibrant blue eyes darted up, catching Daciana watching. And she leaned even closer to Kenna.

Kenna did not shy away. Did not tell her to get up. Didn't shout, *'I'm not interested! I have my own lover who could rip the life from your body and stitch it back in should she feel so inclined.'* No. She just lay there. Waiting.

Daciana could leave. Kenna was so wrapped up in this moment with her *friend*, she'd hardly notice. And wouldn't that be the ironic punctuation to their tortured history. Kenna and Daciana. Fought against honor and death, clawing their way back to each other, only for something as insignificant as another person vying for her affections to leverage them apart.

Sure. She could go. Let Kenna decide whether it was worth mentioning. But Daciana was done running away from the things that hurt. And she would not give Ruva the satisfaction.

"Hard to tell whose won when you're both horizontal."

Kenna jolted, shame coloring her face scarlet as she shoved Ruva off. Ruva fell to the ice with a thud, and Kenna paid her no mind, only having eyes for Daciana. Pleading, beseeching eyes.

Somehow, that was worse. If she'd seemed entirely unbothered,

Daciana could accept the notion that Kenna still didn't realize Ruva's intentions. But her guilt.

It only confirmed it.

"I don't feel like gliding today. I'm heading back to check on Aislinn." Daciana might have been impressed by the way she kept her voice steady, steadier than her balance had been on those fucking blades.

"I'll come with you." Kenna glided toward her, a thousand words painted in the hopeful ache of her expression.

"No need." Daciana did not want a single soothing word explaining it away. Her instincts were sharp, sharp enough she'd relied on them all this time. They'd just shared a moment rife with tension. The prolonged breath before a kiss. Kenna needed to sort her shit out. There were more important things at stake than something as inconsequential as Daciana's heart.

It was time she rearranged her priorities.

"I'm coming with you." Kenna threaded her arm through Daciana's, and Daciana ripped hers away.

She did not want to touch her. Not right now.

They glided in silence. The scrape of bone upon ice now an accusing sound. Daciana had wasted time here. Of course, Kenna wanted the fellow hunter. Her life would be infinitely easier.

Loving her would be infinitely easier.

They unfastened their blades, and the silence only followed them. Kenna was not known for her silence, only her inability to maintain it. So, when she sucked in a loud breath baring the promise of finally rupturing the tension between them—

"It wasn't what it looked like."

That was... not a strong start. "What do I think it looked like?"

Kenna reached for Daciana's hand, and she slapped it away. "It looked like we were about to kiss."

"And were you?"

"Yes."

Credit where it was due—Kenna always was honest to a fault.

"But not because I wanted it."

Maybe not so honest.

Daciana nodded. Sure. Easy lie. It was a lie told to oneself, the most dangerous kind. Daciana had fed herself lie after lie for so long, it had become damn near impossible to distinguish truth from fiction. It was wrapping oneself in delusion so thick, it obscured even the light from the sun.

Daciana's boots sank deeper into the snow as they'd forgone the path and taken a long and winding way along the mountain instead. Though she loathed the idea of adding time to their journey alone listening to Kenna spin her stories, it meant they avoided crossing paths with anyone. A stark preference where Daciana was concerned.

"I was just... it's hard to explain."

Sure. It was hard. Daciana understood that. It must have been hard realizing she'd fought for love for so long when love was supposed to be easy. Is that why Kenna wished to stay? Not to share in her traditions and her upbringing, not to bring the two of them closer, but to be certain of whom she wanted before finalizing her decision?

"Dac, fucking stop." Kenna grabbed her elbow, spinning her around to face her. "Stop and listen so I can explain. Ruva is, *was*, my best friend."

Daciana pulled free of her grasp and crossed her arms. She had no words of encouragement to offer, and she couldn't afford to say something she couldn't take back. So instead, she nodded.

"We've always been close. More like sisters."

Daciana scrunched up her nose as disgust hit her. *That* did not appear a familial sort of affection.

Kenna waved her hand. "I know, I know. So, we've always had this closeness... like you and Lark."

"That is not—" If she dared to compare that to her friendship with Lark, or seek to justify it in any way—

"Listen!" Kenna grabbed her shoulders, shaking her slightly. "I'm saying, affection and closeness has always come easy to us and it never seemed off. Until now."

This was torture. Kenna normally spat the words out faster than her mind could make sense of them, and now, with this, she was going to draw out her meaning? "Speak. Plainly."

Kenna sucked in a deep breath and unleashed the full power of her lungs. "Ruva's been so weird ever since we got here. You've noticed that, haven't you? I thought it was just me. I thought I was reading into things. And I didn't want to ruin our friendship over me being paranoid. I justified it by saying I just wasn't used to her affection anymore, or that having yours made me hyper aware of others in a way I never had been before. So, I ignored it, and I shut it away, hoping it would all level itself out. But the tension was there. She was being *so weird*. And when she knocked me down and landed on top of me, my gut was practically screaming at me. But I know Ruva, and she hates being confronted. So, if I said anything and I was right, I'd never know it, because she would try to cover it up. But if I was wrong, again, I'd have no way of knowing for sure, and I hate not knowing! I hate it! So, I thought if I waited, if I let her follow that impulse through, she couldn't lie to me. She couldn't make me feel paranoid, and then I could shut that shit down without any doubt, because you, Daciana, are the only person I'll ever want to kiss for the rest of my fucking life."

Daciana shut her eyes, processing the rapid stream of words spitting from Kenna's panicked mouth. "Ruva loves you, Kenna. Surely, you must see this."

Kenna shook her head. "I don't love her like that. Never have, never will." She stepped into Daciana's space, arms wrapping around her waist to pull her close. "*You* are the love of my life. Nothing even serves as temptation away from that."

Another twinge. Daciana couldn't decide if it was warmth or pain this time. "I have not been... easy to love."

Kenna inched closer, their mouths nearly touching. "You're wrong. Surviving life without you was the hardest thing I've ever had to do. But loving you? Dac, that was too easy. I fell for you without even trying, and even when I did try to forget, to put you out of my mind, it was impossible. Loving you is easier than breathing. It's what my heart was made for. So, stop pushing me away and accept my apology."

Daciana's breath caught, her heart squeezing in her chest. "Did you apologize?"

Kenna huffed a laugh against her lips. "I'm sorry, I'm sorry, I'm so damn sorry." She punctuated her words with a harsh kiss, melding into the next, until their hungry mouths searched one another for any taste of lingering lies or distance.

There were none.

But there were yet unspoken words needing to be given breath.

"Being here... you're happy." It was an oversimplification and an adjacent observation to Daciana's true meaning.

"I've wanted to return. Wanted to relive some of my favorite childhood experiences." Kenna spread her arms, gesturing around them. "This was my home. This... this is where I feel connected to my parents. To Nahnah." Her voice strangled on her endearment for her grandmother.

Daciana wrapped her arms around her, holding her tight as if she could protect her from the past. "I know," she murmured. "I know."

"But it's not the same. I keep trying. I keep pushing to make this place feel the way it used to. And it almost worked. Having you here helped. Showing you this piece of my history made it all seem possible. But—" Kenna's face tightened.

Understanding flooded Daciana, filling the cracks and soothing the edges, though a glimmer of melancholy remained. "But... it isn't home anymore, is it?"

Kenna nodded, pain etched in the resignation of her expression. "And it's been nice to pretend, you know? Pretend this could be our life."

"It could be our life after—"

"No." Kenna laughed humorlessly. "It couldn't. Not when it doesn't feel quite right. Not when your family is on another continent."

It always came back to Lark and the others. Kenna was right, they were her family, and until she knew they were safe, there would be no settling down anywhere.

"You are my family, too. Bidding them goodbye is not the same as forever. We could make a life here. They could visit and we could—"

"I've never asked you to choose!" Kenna's voice echoed through the trees. "I've never wanted you to choose between them and me. I've never wanted to come between you and them, and that's where you always put me. As if you cannot have both. As if I won't allow it. That couldn't be further from the truth. I only wanted—" She swallowed. "I only wanted to be considered part of that family for you."

"Oh, Kenna." How had she let her believe these things for so long? How had she isolated her into thinking she wasn't one of them. "You are my family. You and the others are my family. If you're telling me you wish to make a life close to the people I love, why is it so strange I want to offer you the same?"

Kenna kicked at the snow, her dark fringe falling into her face. "It isn't. And I have enjoyed being back, but... this isn't my home anymore. And I'm not the person they remember." A sad smile curved against her mouth. "So... let's go speak to Elder Muirgel and get the hunters' aid." Some of her vibrance seemed to return. "Lark's going to need all the help she can get, isn't she?"

"You are sure?" Daciana could not accept taking more than she deserved. Though they needed the hunters' help, Kenna was under no obligation to return to Ardenas, nor to stay in Ardenas after everything.

"Yeah, I'm sure." She grabbed Daciana's hand, swinging their arms. "Let's go home, Dac."

CHAPTER FORTY-SIX

LANGFORD

*D*eep in the heart of Vallemerian country, Langford could almost feel the pressure of his headaches subside. With open sky above and solid ground below, Langford could finally exhale his relief.

There was still the matter of Alistair's condition and how to handle his monthly *ailment*. That was Langford's hypothesis, at least—a monthly recurrence. They would know for sure the next time the moon was full. That gave him weeks to prepare. Though factoring in the journey home, it was certain he would be facing another turn aboard the ship, a thought that spiked Langford's heart rate and pricked his lower back with sweat.

Understandable, surely.

Langford had spoken with some of Ingemar's crew, gathering information about the region and its hierarchy to help him understand how to even go about approaching one of their chieftains for support.

Vallemer was divided into four major cities, with scattered towns in between. Their major cities were under the protection of their chieftains, or their jarls, commanding their own fleet convoy of Vallemerian warriors. Hugo had long ago belonged to the western region, deep in the mountain pass. And if they had all the time in the world, they'd venture far enough to speak with their chieftain, see if Hugo's name carried any weight to their cause.

But that had been decades ago, and the history between the other regions and their southern border was complicated.

They were less than a day's journey from the largest city, Skjald-vik, the center of Vallemerian society. Alistair was overly confident in their ability to sway them to their cause, and Langford just hoped neither of them ended up behind bars.

Vallemerian justice was harsh and swift. Needfully so. Apparently, the regions were engaged in a sort of stalemate, a challenge both issued and ignored. Some sort of betrayal—Ingemar's crewman didn't know for sure—had made their leaders wary of one another. And the threat of treachery had made them paranoid.

So long as they avoided offending anyone, drawing unwarranted suspicion, and evaded any threats of death and dismemberment, it would be smooth sailing, as it were.

Langford glanced over at Alistair, earning a rakish grin that promised mischief and misfortune.

Alistair was all bluff and bluster. Though his mouth did get him into all sorts of nasty trouble, his aloofness was all a front. Years of traveling along-side the man, witnessing his broken moments, that heart he was determined to hide, and Langford still found himself lost to the tender care he showed. He'd always known there was more to Alistair than he pretended, and he'd loved him long before he ever knew that love was safe to feel.

And it was safe. *He* was safe. His heart, his mind, his sanity, and even his physical person. There was no one Langford trusted above Alistair. Now it was his turn to keep him safe. He could never allow himself to lose Alistair to the monster threatening to take over.

"I wish to run some tests, with your permission." His own admission startled him, and Alistair's brow furrowed in confusion.

"What sort of tests?"

They had spoken at length about how to handle the reality of Alistair's condition. Likely, a lifelong treatment of Kenna's concoction to manage the symptoms. It wasn't a permanent fix nor a solid answer to their problem. But just because the answer didn't exist *yet* didn't mean it was a hopeless venture. Maybe there was something there, maybe not. It was enough to form a question, and Langford was nothing if not dutiful in finding answers.

There were certain properties in the beast's blood Langford desperately needed to isolate. Even back at University, there were studies conducted on the efficacy of building immunity. If the body withstood a particular illness or disease, the rate at which the individual contracted the same illness or disease drastically dropped to a near nonexistent chance. Alistair's body has resisted transitioning twice now. Perhaps he could build his own immunity.

Though this was a bit more complicated than a pox virus.

"Just a working theory. When we get back home, I'll explore it more."

Alistair grinned. "I can't wait to tell Daciana I'm just like her."

Langford sighed and did not correct him. There was wisdom in choosing one's battles.

The trees thinned, giving way to the horizon. At the foot of the white-capped mountain, below the comforting cover of cloud, sat the city of Skjaldvik. A community of thatched houses, chimneys puffing smoke into the winter sky. Tightly laid and woven sticks formed fencing along the road. In the center of it all, a great building, larger than the rest, stretched the length of four homes.

"That's where we're headed first?"

Langford nodded. It wouldn't do to arrive and fail to seek the reigning chieftain for both permission and thanks. Was it a chieftain or a jarl? The title entirely depended on how he received his position. Best to sort that out first before committing an offense. If he turned them away, they could head north to the next city.

Assuming he didn't think them spies and order their execution right where they stood.

Gods. They hadn't thought this through at all.

"Ready?" Alistair slipped his hand in Langford's and tugged him along. Langford let him lead, silently praying for fate's favor.

"YOU WISH to borrow my warriors, take them from their home, and imprison them in your lands?" *Jarl* Gunther's voice boomed in the empty hall. Empty save for the two warriors, broad in body and armored with leathers and furs, bracketing his throne. Rows of low sitting tables lined the space, fur-covered seats tucked underneath. The centerpiece of the room was a firepit, a low and dull flame flickering within the confines of stone. Behind the throne hung three large bear pelts, framing the red-faced jarl with its silent shout of warning. One might be decorative, two a bit overstated, but three? Well, it seemed an inconsequential thing to focus on, but it really drew one's eye to the dais.

Langford took a steadying breath. He would need every lesson in diplomacy and tact he'd ever learned. "Not at all. We only wish—"

"Do you know how many of us have been swindled this way? Promised glory and wealth to return and shower our loved ones with, only for them to disappear? Never to return?" His bulky arms were crossed over his chest, his white beard thick enough to obscure the expression of disgust that Langford was sure accompanied his tone.

"Just saying, maybe they enjoyed their life in Ardenas, which is why they never returned."

Alistair. Langford could kill him. Assuming the jarl didn't first.

"Also," the damned fool continued, "no one is promising you anything. We can't even pay you for this aid. So, it's really not the same at all."

Langford sighed, annoyance replacing his terror. Well, he'd lived a good life. Short and brutal, but there were some bright spots along the way.

A low laugh scraped from the throne, building in power, until the chieftain was nearly toppling out of his seat with laughter. The bewildered warriors added some half-hearted chuckles to the sound.

"It wasn't that funny, was it?" Alistair hissed at Langford.

"He's probably amusing himself with thoughts of our execution."

"That makes more sense."

The jarl sighed, wiping his eyes as his mirth died down. "It's been many moons since someone spoke so freely in my presence."

"I can continue if it helps our cause." Alistair spread his arms wide as if about to take a bow.

"It would not."

"Fair enough."

The jarl eyed them both from beneath the bronze edge of his skullcap helm. "You speak of monsters roaming freely in your lands. What of our lands? Do you not think we have suffered the same fate?"

"Have you?" Langford was compelled to ask. It was something he had wondered. The veil was theoretically everywhere, so when it fell, all the lands should have been affected. Unless Nereida was targeting them with a bottleneck to keep Lark busy.

The jarl growled, refusing to answer the question. "Stay and see for yourself. Earn your place among my people. When you've proven your worth, I'll consider your ask."

An indeterminate amount of time… to prove something so subjective? Now it was Langford's turn to question the man's motives. Respectfully, of course.

"We haven't the time. Our people are dying, and our friends need our help to stem the flow of bloodshed. If you have no intention of aiding our cause, tell us true so we might find others who will, or at the very least, return to the ones who need us."

"Aye," the jarl said. "I hear you, little one."

Langford's neck burned beneath his collar. That was unnecessary.

"Trust is not handed out freely these days. One cannot know friend from foe this way until too late. We have suffered many losses from those we sought to trust. But I hear you. I hear your need." Jarl Gunther stood, groaning with the effort. "Spend one week earning my trust. Seek to prove you are both men of honor, and I swear to you, you'll have a small contingency of my warriors. I cannot spare them all, because yes, we have suffered the monsters you speak of."

Langford nearly choked on his next breath. Did the jarl actually answer him? And with a determinate timeline?

Jarl Gunther strode off the dais, his warriors following closely

343

behind. The door remained open from their departure, a silent bid for them to see themselves out.

Langford and Alistair exchanged glances of disbelief.

"Did he just…" Langford scratched his jaw and stared at the wood beams running the length of the ceiling. Why did that feel far too easy?

"No, love." Alistair tugged him into his arms. "*You* just. You spoke your sincerity and your passion aloud, and he heard it." He grinned. "I knew you'd get us Vallemer. I just knew it."

Warmth spread through his chest at Alistair's words. Why was he so quick to assume nefarious intent rather than trust his own ability of persuasion? Alistair had a way of reminding him to believe in himself every now and then.

Maybe this trip wasn't doomed to fail.

CHAPTER FORTY-SEVEN

AISLINN

*T*hrough frosted panes of glass, shadows crept across frost-bitten ground. Though Anquan was milder than Ardenas, winter months holding less of a bite and more of a kiss of ice, the cold had seeped into Aislinn's bones, into her very marrow. A constant ache refusing to bate.

It was neither dark of night nor winter winds that set the chill beneath her skin.

Time was a strange thing. It felt like it had been ages since Aislinn fled Inerys' home. Since she led danger to her doorstep then promptly fled. It was a poor thanks for her kindness, her tutelage, her protection. And Kenna expected Aislinn to just accept her ignorance in knowing if they were all right. If Merikh had returned—

A ripple of fear stole down her spine and raised gooseflesh along her arms. Aislinn yanked the curtains closed, hiding the night from her gaze. She'd handled him well enough considering the shock of his arrival, let alone his existence, but she had felt his power.

He was a storm contained to a fragile vessel. Beneath the surface of skin and bone, the forced vulnerability of a human form...

He was a paragon. A god. A warrior with the might of a raucous sea. And when she sank into his thoughts, into his essence, into his soul, she tasted his fear. He was afraid of *her*. So why did they send her away? If she was such a threat to him, why did they hide her away like a bird with a broken wing evading the ravenous cat?

How would the others stand against him? Without the power she wielded?

Wielded was a strong word. An exaggeration.

She still hardly understood her power or what she was capable of. And it was this truth, this fear, that nestled beneath her collar and froze the space in her chest. Had she left them to die in her stead, when all the while she could have been their shield against harm? Or was she as fragile as they seemed to think?

She brought a paragon to his knees, there was no disputing that. She had to be powerful. So how did her ignorance benefit anyone?

Her absence, fleeing the country to follow Daciana and Kenna, only meant leaving the others unprotected. It was her he wanted, not them. And she was the only one who knew how to handle him.

That's big talk for a girl who failed the simplest task.

Gavriel. She swore to Lark she could reach him, and at times, it seemed she really could. But each attempt was only met with failure. How could she defeat a god when she couldn't even wake a mortal from his cursed dreams?

The urge to try again, just for a moment, whispered in the back of her mind. She'd slipped into Gavriel's dreams so many times, she didn't even need to think about it anymore. It was like navigating one's own room in the dark. She didn't need to see. She knew where everything was kept. Which corners of darkness to avoid. It would be too easy...

Another wave of nausea came over her. It had been happening more frequently.

Ever since she stopped dream walking.

She didn't tell Dac about it, for what could she do? If she suffered some sort of sickness from neglecting her power, it altered naught. Dream walking would draw Merikh to her. Let him know how to find her.

But if she could plan it. If she could be ready for him—

And what if she wasn't? What if he killed her, or worse, what if he killed Daciana and Kenna for protecting her? What if he burned Kenna's village to the ground out of spite?

She would have to wait until she and Lark were together, Reaper Blade in hand. So, when he followed her trail, they could cut him down. Lark wouldn't make her hide. Lark would understand the necessity of the risk. That waiting around while everyone else stood in harm's way, especially in the name of keeping her safe, was no way to live. Lark would—

Another cramp clutched her belly.

Aislinn missed Lark. She missed Inerys. She missed *Ferryn*. Yes, him most of all. She hadn't realized how much she missed him until just the thought of his name ripped the breath from her lungs. For so long, it had been just the two of them. And now that the world was wide open again...

He'd all but forgotten her.

Aislinn grimaced at her uneaten pears from breakfast. She hadn't bothered attending luncheon knowing she'd waste more food. Supper was after nightfall, and the promise of a revelry permeated the air. It was to be another feast. But it was wasted on her and her uneasy stomach. She planned to insist Daciana and Kenna attend without her, but they had not yet returned. They'd been gone since midmorning, and now the cloak of dusk was beginning to cover the land. The sun had departed, abandoning Aislinn for another night. It was lonely, the way the sky darkened, with her having nothing to show for her day spent waiting.

And maybe it was her loneliness talking, or simply boredom, but what if Merikh only sensed her power while he was actively looking? She spent months chasing Lark's dreams, and he never appeared to her. Weeks on end searching Gavriel's, too, and he'd only appeared after prolonged use.

Perhaps the paragons had turned their backs on the mortals for so long, they could scarcely see them anymore.

Before she could talk her way out of it, Aislinn slipped her eyes closed and reached. The pull of her soul was immediate relief, a warmth spreading low in her belly, like when she'd lie in the sun by the riverbank. She searched, calling out to Gavriel's dreams and their familiar song—

And no one answered.

Aislinn snapped her power back in, tremors wracking her body.

If he wasn't in his dreams...

Had Gavriel fallen?

She had to find Lark. Had to warn her. What if Nereida had spirited him away where Aislinn could not follow? Once more she channeled her power, coaxing the distance between souls to shorten. Crafting a bridge over the divide, and seeking the familiar glimmer of Lark's mind.

It was a veil. A part in the curtain. Aislinn slipped through, and her soul walked into the dreamer's domain.

Lark sat atop a white blanket, beneath a great and leafy yew tree. A warm breeze rushed over Aislinn, setting her heart soaring from the sensation. It was... vivid. More vivid than entering Gavriel's dreams. Perhaps because she and Lark had always been connected.

Gavriel's head lay in Lark's lap, and he gazed up at her with stars in his eyes.

"What happened next?" His deep voice rumbled. "After they escaped and fled their master's lands. Where did they live out their days?"

Lark hummed, her golden eyes lifting to study the sky. "They didn't set course to one destination. That would be boring. The end was the beginning of their adventure. Traveling to distant lands and experiencing every spark of life within their grasps." She leaned down to kiss his nose. "Where would you have them explore first?"

His hand swept up the back of her neck, holding her in place as he aimed her mouth to land atop his. "Anywhere he could halt the world to taste her lips. No more urgency. No more running. They savored every flavor of their adventures together."

Lark smiled against his lips. "Yes. They lived freely and slowly for the rest of their days."

Gavriel angled his head, deepening the kiss and shifting them so she fell back against the blanket. He climbed over her, his hand skimming up the length of her thigh—

"Oh, gods!" Aislinn covered her eyes. It was foolish, coming here. She had never made true contact before, not with Lark and not with Gavriel. Lark had once told her she sensed her presence but not enough to communicate, and here she was, watching a private and intimate vision.

"Aislinn?"

Aislinn opened her eyes to find Lark sitting up and watching her curiously. It was then Aislinn realized what Lark wore. Instead of her leather breeches and tunic, she wore a cotton dress with a simple bodice. Beside her, Gavriel wore linen breeches and an oversized tunic, untucked and rumpled. Aislinn knew these clothes, she'd seen them in Gavriel's dreams, in one of his past lives. The first life he lived and lost. But his face was the one she knew as the assassin. The Gavriel that slumbered without waking.

"You're not part of my dream, are you?" Lark studied her curiously, gold eyes flitting up and down her person. "There's something about you that seems... misplaced."

Misplaced. The word stung. Accurate in describing her state, but brutal in its honesty.

"I came to speak with you." She glanced over at Gavriel, a mere figment of Lark's dream, but the wry grin he wore felt all too real.

"What's the matter?" Lark's voice immediately sharpened, worry hardening her tone. "Are you all right? Is Daciana in trouble?"

"I'm fine. We're fine. I just—" Aislinn bit her lip. "I can't find Gavriel."

"I'm right here." He gave a little wave.

"No, I mean... I wanted to make sure you all were safe. That Merikh hadn't... and when I tried to slip into Gavriel's dreams... Lark, he wasn't there."

"Of course, he wasn't there." Lark smiled at her, shaking her head. "Gavriel's awake. He's keeping watch right now while I get some sleep."

"Which Gavriel do you like better, him or me?" Lark's dream version of the assassin asked, tracing her shoulder with his finger.

"Him. Obviously."

"Rude."

Aislinn held up her hands. *"Gavriel is awake? But how?"* Was her constant meddling keeping him under? It was strange that as soon as she broke away, unable to slip into his mind, that he miraculously awoke.

Lark's mouth tightened. *"It's a long story..."*

"I have nowhere to be." That wasn't strictly true, as she'd promised Daciana she wouldn't do this, and she needed to leave before Merikh found her. But any understanding to how Gavriel freed himself from his dreams was worth the added time.

Lark nodded, and bit by bit, dream Gavriel faded. *"Dreams always pale in comparison to the real thing,"* she said sheepishly. *"But it's good to dream of him knowing when I wake, he'll still be there."*

"I'm so happy to hear that," Aislinn said. But she was dying to know how.

"Merikh came looking for you—"

"I knew it! I told Daciana we shouldn't leave. Did he hurt you? Is Inerys all right?" Foolish. Reckless. Selfish.

Lark held up her hands in surrender. *"Everyone is fine. Merikh... well he sought to coax the answers from Inerys. But I stopped him. And when I taunted him, he spotted the Reaper Blade."*

"Did he take it?"

Lark twisted her mouth to the side. *"He... took me. I thought I could enter his mind and dominate his will. He locked part of me away and took me to Avalon."*

Aislinn's stomach sank. *"Did he... hurt you?"*

"Yes." Lark's expression held no remorse, no regret. Just a statement of fact. *"He did. But he made his mistakes, too."*

Aislinn clenched her hands into fists. How had she allowed someone else to suffer in her stead. She wasn't even supposed to exist anymore. Her end had already happened, and here they were sacrificing themselves to protect a ghost.

Lark studied her, a softness in her gold-colored eyes that wasn't quite pity but made Aislinn's throat thicken the same. Something about the Reaper's stare had always made her feel far too perceived. Like Lark was reading every horrible thought and suffering alongside her. "He thought he had the upper hand, Aislinn. But I learned his weaknesses in my time there. Weaknesses we can exploit."

Aislinn didn't much like the thought of revenge. It was messy, a surefire way to end in regret. But this paragon hunted her. Threatened her very being. He threatened her friends, and he hurt Lark.

No, this wasn't vengeance. This was justice.

"Tell me all you know."

AISLINN SAT ALONE in Kenna's gran's caravan. The shadows loomed along the wall. A lone candle flickered in the night. She'd fled Lark's dream with just enough time to intercept Kenna and Daciana. An explanation of stomach pain, and a few well-timed moans, and they were all too willing to accept her lie, promising to bring her remedies from the local healer when they attended the revelry.

It gave Aislinn time to think. To stew. To plan.

Lark said there was a way to command a paragon to one's side. Praying to them and begging for their presence. That using Merikh's name would deliver her prayer to him and forge the tether between them.

But a prayer using his true name…

That would offer her power over him. The ability to command anything of him and he would have to obey. It was too tempting, the power to command a god. And Lark had been disappointed she couldn't learn his name, a secret he buried so deep, only he and Sargon knew it.

Aislinn never told anyone the depths of his mind that she'd reached. How easily she slipped past the walls of iron he'd built, as if they were made of spider silk.

Aislinn knew his true name. The one he kept buried. The name that would compel him to do her bidding. All she had to do was call to him.

To what end? Call him to heel, seep into his mind, and what, kill him?

She could. Aislinn could. Everyone was so worried about her. Oh, poor Aislinn. Her own mother doesn't recognize her face. Poor Aislinn. The way she died left a stain upon her soul. Poor Aislinn. Hide her away; she's too weak to face that which hunts her.

But she wasn't weak. And she wasn't stained. And she wasn't lost.

And she was not afraid.

It was such a simple thing. To be that lone candle, that tiny flickering flame in a world of darkness, unassuming and small while the shadows grew tall.

She was more. *She was more.*

Aislinn took a deep breath, exhaling the last of her anger. She would not do this in anger. This was a calm and necessary tactic. Protecting her friends. Protecting herself.

She could do this.

Aislinn let her eyes slip closed and called to him.

"Merikh, I need you to come to me now." She sucked in another breath, bracing herself against her heart bludgeoning against her ribs. "I call you by your true name, Miro. Come to me."

CHAPTER FORTY-EIGHT

MERIKH

"*H*ow is it you still haven't delivered me that somniavi?"

There were a number of failings Merikh could cite in reference to that question. None of which would please his commander. "She is… stronger than we thought. Someone has trained her in evasion." Or he'd been so distracted by her he failed to deliver a killing blow before she slipped into his mind. She must have left a splinter behind, because he had yet to dispel her fully from the turn of his thoughts.

Reaching into Lark's consciousness had only made it worse. He did not need to feed his curiosity about the dreamwalker with the power to destroy him and his land. He did not wish to know more of her, but when he filtered through Lark's memories, the girl was a repeated image, burned into his mind. Lark loved her, that much was obvious, and it was likely her affection coloring his appreciation of the creature.

She was a mortal. Useless and weak. Only she wasn't weak, was she? She was far stronger than him, wild and chaotic, but strong. And useless…

She could topple empires with that power. The power he was tasked with snuffing out like a candle's flame.

353

And yet… it was all the small moments he'd examined in Lark's mind, tricking him into thinking… into feeling…

She was a means to an end. A stubborn one at that.

"Everyone has a weakness. What is hers?"

Merikh hesitated. Why did it feel like a betrayal to answer? "Her friends. She'll sacrifice herself to keep them safe." Foolish to form such attachments, but that was a common side effect of mortality. The ease with which mortals threw their lives away.

"Fine. We extend an invitation for peace talks. If she's stupid enough to tag along, kill her. If not, hold her friends until she delivers herself into our custody. Done. Honestly, Merikh. Even a child could have accomplished this sooner than you."

It would be a wondrous thing to behold the strange dreamer sink her claws into Sargon's mind. Would he run his mouth so freely then?

"By your leave, Commander." Merikh strode to the door, leaving the war room and Sargon's judgment behind.

"And, Merikh," he called out. "I've been merciful thus far. Fail me in this, and you will learn the lengths of my wrath."

Merikh forced himself to nod. "Understood."

He maintained a steady pace, his stride even. It was foolish to attempt diplomacy with Lark after peering into her own mind and witnessing the depths of her loyalty. But her love for the man in the Netherworld ran deep—deep enough he'd counted on a trick of the mind to sway her. He could have killed her, he probably should have, but in that moment, he'd wanted her to suffer. A blinking out of existence was quick, painless, the easy way out. But delivering her to the pits was a lengthier sentence. Eternity.

Though she'd stolen the Reaper Blade on the way down.

And why hadn't he told Sargon of this? That a weapon fit to slay even his own kind was now in the hands of the witch of the Netherworld.

Because it meant admitting another failure. A risk taken without permission. And it had yielded nothing of any consequence. It hardly mattered now. Not when one somniavi could appear in his realm at will. With a snap of her fingers, decimate the Commander of Avalon.

No wonder Sargon was scared. They should all be fucking terrified.

But she hadn't wielded her power. Hadn't retaliated when he stole away her friend. Unless Lark's care was one-sided, but he very much doubted that. Not when every memory she carried of the girl was tinged with warm admiration.

So why hadn't the dream walker come to punish him? Unless she didn't know how to enter Avalon. She really was untrained. Yet so powerful even in her ignorance.

She was knowledgeable enough to know to avoid using her power. That without the trace of her magic, he was unable to find her.

Was he mad that part of him was relieved? He'd gone head-to-head with the girl once and fallen to her influence easily. He needed time to bolster his strength, reenforce his mental walls, train against influential magic to learn how to keep her out.

Though there was no amount of training that would prevent her from entering his dreams. Paragons slumbered for ages. Years. Centuries. When they awoke, they spent eons awake, epochs of time for when they slumbered, an ancient magic held them in their sleep. It was how they restored their power and maintained the power fueling Avalon's creations. For every warrior or paragon slumbering, one had to arise. It was a perfect balance.

But if she learned of this, she could enter the dreams of every sleeping paragon. Destroy them or control them or simply play. Her power was absolute in the dreams of the gods.

And no matter how beloved, or kind, or compelling, or alluring she was… she was just too dangerous. He would take no pleasure in killing her, for there was nothing pleasurable about death. Life. Death. It just was. It was a state of being. The endless cyclical nature of things. And her death was a necessary event in pursuit of the greater good. A shame her soul had to be erased from existence, but from the echo of her falling, something new could take root. It was generous, noble, even. And if he was the one who—

A tug pulled deep in his belly. Insistent. Commanding.

"Merikh, I need you to come to me now."

That voice. No… but it couldn't be.

"I call you by your true name, Miro. Come to me."

A violent yank from within his chest, and he was falling. *No.* Impossible. His true name was known to none other than Sargon. The wielding of names was an ancient and powerful magic. Not even the paragons were trusted with such knowledge of one another.

His form crumpled in on itself, reforming in his human likeness. The sinking in his belly made his head spin. His body was weightless, suspended, but the rush of the ground reaching up to meet him—

He slammed upon the earth, his body and soul falling in tandem. Vision spinning, he braced his hands against the floor, swallowing down the strange squeezing feeling in his gut. It rose to his throat, a threat of pressure. He pushed himself up to sit, cursing the way his head spun.

There she sat. The lethal beauty he'd hunted. He'd fallen to. She sat upon a bed, her golden-blonde hair hanging in waves over her shoulders. Large green eyes wide with shock as she regarded him. Her small hands clasped her knee where she'd slung it across her thigh. Without all those layers, her slight frame was revealed in a pair of fitted breeches tucked into ratty old boots. Her tunic untied and hinting the pale skin of her throat.

She was... she was...

"Good of you to join me, Miro." Her voice was music. A melody in a minor key. Haunting and beautiful.

"Why have you summoned me?" How did she know his name? Did she intend to kill him? It was no more than he deserved.

"We need to talk."

CHAPTER FORTY-NINE

AISLINN

*L*ark had been very specific in her explanations. How Avalon functioned. The truth about the supposed paradise of the afterlife. That the only true freedom existed in the sanctuary located in the Netherworld.

That everything Aislinn had ever learned from her village elders had been lies.

But when Lark explained prayer, that any paragon could answer the call of desperate mortals, that was when Aislinn realized the true extent of their apathy. She knew not the names of lesser gods, only the great Sargon. And when she cried out for help that day on the riverbank.

Nobody came.

Nobody listened.

Nobody answered.

Only one being: A Reaper. The embodiment of death in the eyes of mortals, she had come and stayed with Aislinn when she took her last breath. A kindness born of compassion from the shadows mortals feared.

And the paragons, the warriors, defenders of all mankind, they were silent in their absence.

Aislinn stared down at Merikh, at Miro, at the god at her feet, helplessly awaiting her judgment. His eyes were steel, a hard grey with glints of sunlight upon a blade. But they were widened in fear, was that fear? Could she really command fear in the heart of a god?

"Arise."

He stood without hesitation, like he was yanked to his feet. Aislinn stood, too, unwilling to sit beneath his towering height, but even upon her feet, he was a full head taller, an imposing presence in the small caravan.

This was the man who tortured her friend. Who wrote agony upon her mind so she'd bear it upon her skin. He subjected her to wave after wave of pain and suffering. And though Lark was quick to dismiss it, too pleased with the notion that she'd finally unlocked memories long buried, Aislinn knew better. She knew how easy it was to shove the malicious actions of others aside, namely when they were committed upon oneself. It was easy to condemn the ones who hurt others, but when that hurt was directed upon oneself, excuses, dismissals, justifications, validations, they were all lies fed to the mirror to avoid facing the pain of reality.

Well. Aislinn would face that pain for Lark, as Lark had done for her once upon a time.

"Why do you hunt me?"

Merikh's jaw clenched, a ripple forming where he held back his words. "I hunt you because I have been commanded to." His voice, thick and dark, nearly sent a shiver through her.

Nearly.

But his answer was a lie wrapped in truth.

"Why have you been commanded to hunt me?"

He shut the glimmering steel of his eyes, his expression one of restraint. "Because you will be Avalon's undoing."

Aislinn's patience was wearing thin. While he skirted the line between information and withholding, Daciana and Kenna could return at any time. She grabbed his chin, yanking him closer, and the massive warrior bent to her will as if there was no other option. As if he was almost relieved to relinquish control to her.

"Tell me the threat I pose to you, Miro."

He shivered as if the sound of his name sent a spell across his skin. "You are somniavi. You walk the dreams of others. Avalon is built on dreams as are its guardians. In our slumber, you could decimate all that we've built. Even Sargon himself is no match for you in the vulnerable recesses of his mind."

"Has it ever occurred to you"—she tightened her grip—"that I want nothing to do with you or your realm. That all I wanted was to live my life in peace—peace you have denied me." She shoved his face away, heated rage tingling along her fingertips. "Your fear of me is based on a lot of hypothetical threats I have not once made."

"You are somniavi," he said as if it explained everything. It was the first unprompted response he'd offered. "No one should have that power."

"And what of you? You wielded the strength of your power against Lark, or is that justified since by your hand you trust?" Aislinn shoved into his space, reveling in the way he bowed his head to her in submission. "You fear power you cannot control. This is not about me. This is about the cowardice in your heart. It festers and grows until you can rationalize all the horrors you're willing to commit. Every pain you inflict on others. As if you have the right to take what you want and leave them choking on their own blood—" Aislinn's voice broke on a sob, a trembling ache stretching her chest.

Why her thoughts saw it fit to travel the road long passed was unknown. She steadied her breath, putting her anger aside.

Merikh's head remained bowed, a tight expression evident along the side of his face.

As if she were something to fear.

Maybe she was.

"Sit."

Merikh dropped to the floor with a heavy thud.

"Stand."

He arose in a fluid motion, finding his feet without pause.

Aislinn pulled the small weapon from her belt. "Take this knife."

His large hand engulfed the handle, nearly obscuring the entire weapon from view. His head was still bowed.

"Show me your eyes."

His gaze met hers, dark and storming, a tempest of regret shining back at her. It stole the breath from her lungs, the strength of his pain. She struggled to swallow against the tight space in her throat.

"Press the tip into your hand."

There was no hesitation. He pressed the blade point into his palm, the first drop of blood growing and fattening against his skin. Red. Mortal. But he was no mortal.

"Drag the blade."

Merikh didn't even flinch, he showed no signs of pain as he ripped through his palm. Blood wept through his fingertips, dripping on the floor.

Aislinn's stomach turned. "Again," she forced out.

He held her stare, his brows furrowed not in pain but in shame, as he carved into his palm again and again.

Her eyes burned, and the pressure on her chest grew.

"Again," she sobbed, taking in the bloody mess of his hand. And when he dragged the blade once more, she grabbed his hand, ripping the knife from his grasp, and tossing it on the floor. This was supposed to feel like justice. She was supposed to be the commander of his fear, but all she felt was the same sickening drop in her stomach she experienced whenever she thought of Corwyn.

She dragged him to the corner, and Merikh followed as if walking on numb legs, stumbling and staggering while his eyes remained fixed to her face. She snatched a clean cloth from the pile of freshly folded laundry and pressed it into his palm. This was stupid. *So foolish.* She could not stomach torturing someone no matter how deserved. Her anger did not make her a new person. She was the same she'd ever been. Too soft. Too weak. Too—

A gentle touch against her cheek pulled her from her thoughts.

Merikh's uninjured hand was raised, his thumb wiping a tear she hadn't realized had fallen. A strange look of wonder had come over his expression, as if he couldn't believe her eyes were leaking.

"I'm sorry."

Why was he apologizing? She was the one who'd made him carve up his hand. Deservedly, yes. But it didn't take away from the fact that this was all happening in a strange sequence of events.

"What for?"

Merikh's eyes searched hers, their intensity searing as his gaze flitted back and forth, assessing and studying like she was worth figuring out. "You are crying. I... I do not like it."

"Mortals cry. Strengthen your stomach for this next revelation: Your people have probably caused the mass bulk of the tears wept." Unanswered prayers were silent echoes of broken hearts.

"No." He sighed. "I understand that. But I caused *you* distress."

Confusion stole any other emotion Aislinn was struggling with. "That's a strange response coming from the man sent to kill me."

"I agree." He lowered his hand. "As is rushing to treat the wound of a man sent to kill you."

Aislinn almost laughed. Almost. "Maybe I'm simply kinder than my intelligence dictates. In fact—" She glanced down and startled. His hand was fully healed, no signs of any injury apart from the stained red upon his skin. "Guess that was useless of me. Now I'll have to wash this again." She went to chuck the soiled cloth toward the door, but he caught her wrist.

"Not... useless. Confusing."

Where he touched Aislinn's skin, it burned. Not painfully, but enough she ripped her hand away. "Speak truth. Commanding your name, can I compel you to kill yourself?"

"Yes."

"Can I compel you to kill Sargon?"

His mouth clamped shut, fighting against him. "Yes."

"When you leave my side, are you still under my control?"

Merikh hesitated. "Unless you issue a direct command upon my leaving, I will be free of your influence."

"But you'd have to carry out my command?"

His eyes slid shut, brows knitting together. "Yes."

It was... more power than anyone should rightfully possess, this control over another living thing. And even now it was tempting to experiment with the lengths she could extend that power.

But Aislinn knew what it felt to be powerless against someone. To feel them use your body to their own twisted whims.

She could not justify doing the same.

"Well," she said, only slightly enjoying the panicked expression he wore, "it's a good thing I have no such machinations."

Merikh blinked, staring at her with that confounded expression of intrigue. The one that felt alarmingly similar to the way Langford studied ancient texts he was particularly excited about. "Sargon plans to trick you."

He was not compelled to divulge such information. Which meant he was either volunteering it or lying. "How?"

"He wants to extend an invitation to your group. Peace talks, he'll call them. If you attend, he will have you killed. If you do not, he will imprison your friends until you concede." Merikh wet his lips, his eyes bright. "Do not accept his invitation. Do not trust any offer he extends. Your death is all that matters to him."

"Why are you telling me this?"

"I—" He gave his head a shake as if the question hadn't even occurred to him. "I do not know."

Perhaps it was penance for proving she would not kill him. Or an attempt to sway her favor. Or any other countless selfish reasons.

"Do not tell anyone I know your true name, Miro."

Another ripple of a shudder spread through him, making him arch his back. "I shall not."

"Will you still hunt me?"

Merikh's mouth twitched. "Always."

Aislinn couldn't even find it in herself to be angry. Of course, he would hunt the one who posed a threat to his existence. It would be smarter to kill him now. To command him to do it for her.

But she would not.

"Are you trying to trick me?"

Merikh's expression hardened, and he stepped closer, invading her space. And why did every nerve in her body alight at his proximity. Aislinn swallowed down the sound of surprise that rushed up her throat.

"I will not trick you, Aislinn." It was the first time he'd used her name, and something about the sound of it in his rough voice made her stomach flutter. "If I am victorious, and you submit to me in defeat, it will not be through deception. It will be you and me. Eyes wide open. No lies. No tricks. I swear this to you."

A strange energy crackled, tension pulling taut. Like an invisible thread connected them, binding and strong. Aislinn's exhale was stuttered, a shaky rush of air, and she stepped back putting much needed space between them.

She needed him gone. She needed to think. She needed—

"Leave me now, Miro. Do not come back to me unless I call."

Merikh's eyes tightened, as if he braced himself against an invisible force. He pushed a step closer, slow and labored, his gaze searching hers for something. With a growl, he vanished.

Aislinn's uneven breathing filled her ears, the sudden quiet abrupt and deafening in the stillness of the night.

CHAPTER FIFTY

LANGFORD

"*Y*ou sure you got that, lad?"

"I'm stronger than I look." Langford heaved the axe over his shoulder, allowing the momentum of his swing to do most of the work. The wood split beneath the blade, a satisfying *crack* filling the air. Wisps of vapor escaped his mouth, and he grinned at his own handiwork.

The fresh air and purposeful use of his body had renewed his energy. Though his nights were still spent bent over his books and pages, studying anything that could offer him insight on Alistair's condition.

Skjaldvik had a library full of books Langford had never encountered. Translations and original Vallemerian written word. He'd found a text on sensory stimuli, outlining the use of different familiar scents and sounds to calm victims of trauma. It was worth looking into for Alistair's sake. If he could forge an association between sensory triggers, Alistair could control his violent urges if he ever shifted.

Theoretically.

Three days spent helping out around the village and three nights spent researching until Alistair yanked him away from his work and worshipped every inch of him until he was a panting, writhing mess.

Langford could think of worse ways to spend his time.

The question of whether they were doing enough to earn Jarl Gunther's trust still hung in the air, but the sense of productivity, of working toward an answer rather than blindly feeling for it, was enough for now.

"Paragon's flaming knickers, but it does things to me to see you like this." Alistair's swagger was on full display as he approached, his leather vest unbuttoned to reveal the top of his golden chest, his boots unlaced in that artless, careless way he always wore them. A crooked grin tugged at his mouth as his eyes roved up and down Langford's body.

Langford ignored the way his face heated. "I could say the same. Watching you parade around offering nothing to our cause certainly merits a reaction. Just not the reaction you hope for."

"Oh, but you're wrong on both counts. I love riling you up." Alistair grasped Langford from behind, earning a cry in outrage as he was still holding a sharp axe. "And I've signed us up for the perfect *chore* to earn our aid." He said the word as if it were a curse. "Much more suited to our skills. I see no reason to punish ourselves needlessly in the name of martyrdom."

"You helped with the wash. Once."

"Once was too many."

Langford rested the axe against the chopping block, a thick tree stump, and turned to face him fully. "What will you do when we finally settle down in that little cottage you keep promising. I hope you don't anticipate *I* will do the bulk of the chores on my own."

Alistair scoffed. "Certainly not. Your job will be to read every book you can get your greedy hands on while I maintain the homestead. Washing your knickers is not the same as being dragged out to the frontlines of laundry duty for an entire village." He shuddered.

"Oh, please. You came back bright with excitement and eager to share all matter of secrets you gathered."

"I do love a good jangling session." Alistair pressed a quick kiss to Langford's nose. "And it served us well, because I learned something that led me to ask the right question, thus serving our strategy to win Gunther's trust square in my lap."

Of course, he had. While Langford chopped wood, repaired fences, and caught one of the escaped pigs—escaped because of that blasted fence—Alistair used his penchant for idle talk to yield a greater outcome.

"Let's hear it."

"The jarl did not tell us the entire truth. The reason behind his inability to relinquish any warriors."

"He did, though. He said—"

"Let me draw out the suspense, darling." Alistair tsked. "He did not see it fit to inform us of a mysterious creature hounding their lands."

Interesting. Langford knew better than to interrupt again. It would result in a most impressive pout.

"Three of their men have died over the last two moons, and they have spent each night forming a hunting pack to look for the creature." Alistair shook his head. "To no avail."

"That's where we come in?"

"But, of course. Who better to find their monster than two accomplished monster hunters?"

That was a stretch. "The last time we fought a beast, it did not end in our favor." Alistair had been nearly lost and now forever changed. Bearing the burden of his dual nature.

"This is different. We have a retinue of armed fighters, we have the foresight to expect a creature, thus our guards will remain up, and"— he wagged his brows—"we have the gift of your mind on the case. I have no doubt you'll find something of note."

Langford glanced at the pile of stacked wood. His palms did ache, and this was more akin to their type of job as of late. And the call of yet another question in need of answering was impossible to ignore...

"Fine. I'm in."

"Of course, you are, my brilliant, dazzling, strapping young scholar!"

"I'm not that much younger than you."

"No, but when you run your body into the ground like me, you gain extra miles to your wheel's rotations."

"That... barely made sense."

Alistair slung an arm around Langford's shoulder. "Ah. The blissful ignorance of youth." He silenced Langford's protests by pressing his mouth against his neck and blowing a wet, vibrating sound against his skin. Langford laughed, swatting him away as he began his mental list of villagers to interview.

"TELL ME MORE ABOUT HAAKON."

Anya, a young barmaid with flaxen hair and pale-blue eyes shook her head, sighing. "He was so lost after his Pa's passing. The pneumonia took his lungs and never really gave them back. Everyone expected he'd make his intentions to me known..." Her eyes glassed over. "But he wasn't ever the same."

Haakon was the third victim supposedly fallen to the invisible monster. It wasn't that Langford didn't believe them, it was that he was missing a piece of vital information. Three men of varying age and health were found with very human looking cuts and slices upon their skin. He'd studied the coroner's reports, and their wounds were clean and precise.

And no eyewitnesses.

Curious.

"I'm so sorry for your loss."

Anya nodded, sniffing. "It was the whole village's loss, not just mine. I pray to the gods his spirit finds rest. He deserves it after everything he's suffered. But they aren't listening, are they?"

"What do you mean?" The notion that gods and paragons had turned their backs on even the faithful was not a revelation of any sort. But the way she spoke didn't sound metaphorical.

"I see him," she whispered. "When I'm walking home after a late shift. He's so sad and so alone. Always reaching out a hand to me. Everyone thinks it's my grief, that I'm seeing things, but I know the truth." Her eyes burned like the blue of a flame. "His spirit is lost, and he needs help."

The lingering spirit of a violent death wasn't impossible. Frankly, nothing was impossible these days. But something felt off about her assessment. It was neat and tidy, characteristics Langford normally admired, but in this it was too... easy.

"Why do you think he only appears to you?" She'd said everyone claimed she'd imagined it, so she must be the only one to have witnessed it.

"Because I loved him." Her brows knitted together. "I still do... but not like this." She rubbed a hand against her shoulder as if a sudden chill had come over her.

Langford scribbled his quill across his parchment, keeping his expression carefully composed. "Where does he appear to you?"

"Always by the graveyard. He just stands there, waiting. Lifting a hand to me." Anya shuddered. "It's not the way of things. We live, we die, we ascend to the afterlife. To the Folvjar in Avalon, as promised to us."

Ah. Yes. The favored circle of Avalon reserved for the most honorable. Langford had read about that when he studied the theological differences in the reigning beliefs in Vallemer. They took a far more inclusive approach to the afterlife.

"Do me a favor, *do not* venture even a step closer to Haakon's spirit. Don't even look at him. If he appears again, you keep your head down and travel straight home."

"I don't understand," she said. "He would never hurt me."

"Like you said, it's not the way of things. If he's stuck, you don't want to risk the same fate, do you?" Was it cruel to turn her own fear on her in the name of keeping her safe? Until Langford understood what was happening, perhaps cruelty was justified.

Anya's eyes widened, and she shook her head violently, strands of pale hair falling in her face.

"Good. Thank you for speaking to me about him. I know it wasn't easy."

Her hands grasped Langford's, her bony fingers squeezing tight.

"Find the creature who did this to him. Maybe then his soul will find peace."

Langford nodded. "I'll do everything I can." It was truer than promising what he could not deliver, and he wasn't convinced the deaths of their villagers was a monster in the strictest sense.

He'd need to examine his notes.

"Think we have time to break away?" Alistair's breath was hot in his ear. "They'll never notice our absence. We'll be back in less time than it takes Lyndurgh to sharpen his blade."

Langford snorted. "Your speedy sexual prowess is not the boast you think it is."

"Sometimes we must rely on efficiency. So long as the job gets done, no need to judge the speed with which it's concluded." Alistair glared at him. "Say I never leave you unsatisfied."

They'd gathered outside The Gull and Mountain Tavern with three of Jarl Gunther's warriors. Lyndurgh, the oldest of the group with his white and braided beard, Huvik the youngest and newest recruit with the same abundance of energy as an untrained pup, and Kyall the stoic man with the hardest countenance. Huvik sat atop a barrel someone had forgotten to store in the cellar, flipping through his deck of Paragons and Sinners cards while Lyndurgh smirked over his shoulder. Kyall kept his dark gaze trained to the sky as if waiting for something to appear.

"I see nothing wrong with my cards." Huvik frowned, flipping a Warrior face card over and examining it closer.

"S'not the cards, boy," Lyndurgh said with a snicker.

A fine group to go patrolling in the half-moon's light.

Langford had pored over his notes he'd gathered earlier in the day, failing to find anything truly connecting the victims save for the injuries and one common detail:

Each victim has lost someone in unrelated circumstances.

Heeghan, his brother drowned two summers past. Guinn, his young daughter fell from a tree and broke her neck a decade ago. Haakon, his father to complications from pneumonia.

Everyone had lost someone. One couldn't throw a stone without hitting someone affected by loss these days, so it was hardly noteworthy.

And yet, Langford took note of it.

"Have any of you seen the creature?" The sooner they focused on the task at hand, the better.

"What's that?" Lyndurgh raised a shaggy brow at him. "No, but we've seen enough to be wary."

A universal sentiment.

"How do we normally start? I wish to follow your procedures." It was meant to be a show of respect. That Langford didn't plan to waltz in and treat them like he was the expert.

Even though Alistair assured them they were.

"Easy, lad. No need to flatter me so. If you're fixin for a good fuckin, all you need to do is ask."

Langford's face burned and his stomach rolled. What a disgustingly crass fellow. He had half a mind to point out his glaring flaws. Like the bits of crispbread clinging to his beard or the thick odor that followed him. But that would be no way to ensure the man had their backs against whatever stalked their village. Surely, they could afford to ignore a few ill-worded quips in favor of cooperation.

"Don't you ever fucking talk to him that way."

Alistair had no such reservations. His hand shot out to grip the man's throat, and he poised his blade above his eye, silver glinting in the moonlight. Kenna's blades were deadly sharp and lightweight. A wisp of an edge, which must have been how Alistair unsheathed it with such speed. "Apologize."

"I didn't mean anythin' by it. We all take the piss out of each other. It's no harm."

"I find it *very* harmful. I don't give a shit how you talk to each other. But when you talk to him, you'll show him respect."

Langford darted his stare between Alistair and Lyndurgh, a dull pressure building behind his eyes. It was unnecessary, Alistair's threat. Even if the man's comment had made Langford uncomfortable. They were supposed to earn the Jarl's trust, not antagonize his fighters.

"It's all—"

"Do *not* say it's all right, Langford." Alistair didn't so much as glance at him. "Apologize," he repeated.

Lyndurgh tightened his mouth, eyes narrowing in silent challenge.

Huvik nearly bounced on his feet, nervous energy practically radiating off him. He opened his mouth, and promptly closed it, flitting his wide-eyed stare between them all.

"Swallow your pride," Kyall said—the first words he'd spoken. "He's honor bound to protect what's his. You'll not lose a thing by respecting that."

Lyndurgh's eyes widened. "Ah. Apologies. I knew not you were attached."

"Why does that make a difference?" Alistair pressed in harder. "Were he unattached, he'd not merit your apology?"

"Peace." Kyall stepped closer to grip Alistair's arm. "He speaks out of turn because the old fool is too proud to accept his shame. Isn't that right?"

Lyndurgh decidedly did not appear ashamed so much as angry, but he gave the barest of nods in agreement.

Alistair released him with a snarl, and the tension between the two men snapped tight. A fight delayed, it would seem.

Langford exhaled the tightness trapped in his chest and cleared his throat. "Right, well. Glad we cleared that up. I only meant if you had a circuitous movement in your patrol. I've gathered enough evidence to have some thoughts to share on that front."

"Aye. I knew what you meant." Lyndurgh hadn't broken his death stare with Alistair.

Perhaps another night, or another group would be preferable.

"We don't have a set path." Kyall's even voice came again. "Patterns are easy to memorize and exploit." He stepped toward Langford, his face void of any emotion. Even his eyes... they were flattened. Lifeless. "Where would you have us start?"

"The graveyard. There seems to be frequent activity reported in that area. We could—"

Kyall winced, the first flare of emotion passing on his face, but he quickly suppressed it. "Fine." He stalked off, not waiting for Langford's explanation.

Langford watched his departure.

"Kyall lost his wife last spring." Huvik's voice, softened by pity, interrupted Langford's thoughts. "He hasn't walked past her resting place since the funeral."

Ah. That made sense.

Lyndurgh huffed a thick breath. "He was… inconsolable. He only started patrolling again last moon." He shook his head, finally stepping away from Alistair. "We best be sure he's all right." He strode after Kyall, Huvik bounding after him.

They really did care for one another. And when Lyndurgh made his disgusting comment, he probably did mean no harm by it. Langford glanced over at Alistair, and if he thought he'd find a modicum of regret, he was sorely mistaken.

Alistair spun the silver blade in his hand. "So… about that break we were going to take."

"You're unbelievable." Langford spun on his heel, following the warriors before they disappeared into the dark.

Alistair kept pace easily. "You seem vexed."

"You escalated an already uncomfortable situation. There was no need to turn it so hostile."

"Nope." Alistair tugged Langford to halt, shaking his head wildly. "No. We're not doing that. We're not pretending the way you're treated doesn't matter. I don't care what happens to these people, you get that, right? I don't give a damn if I hurt some old creep's feelings. We're here to gather fighters to make sure at the end of all this, after we're done saving the world, we get to have our life. Our time." He cupped Langford's jaw. "Stop diminishing your importance—"

"I'm not!" Langford threaded their fingers, pulling his hands away. "But you said yourself, our directive is to acquire aid in this fight. Not create more enemies."

Alistair pursed his lips. "Don't turn my words around and make them sound all pretty and suited to your purpose."

Langford snorted, his amusement cutting through his disapproval. "Thank you for defending my honor. Now stop being a thorn in my side so we can complete the goal of coming here." He dragged him along, footfalls coming swifter to catch up with the others.

Alistair let out a theatrical groan, letting him lead. "Fine. Fine. But I stand by my right to react however I deem appropriate in response to anyone disrespecting you."

"You don't even know what appropriate means."

"It means I get violent when someone is crass to you. Someone other than me, of course."

"Hush." They'd almost caught up with the others, and Langford had no desire to make things worse. But the fact that Alistair was once again his normal self, exchanging barbs with speed and amusement, was a relief.

Lyndurgh and Huvik stood with their backs to them, frozen in place in the middle of the field. Up ahead, Kyall gripped the stone wall framing the graveyard, a strange rippling tension in the air. Langford stepped around to see him better, glancing over to find bewildered expressions on their faces.

"What is it?"

Huvik shook his head, his eyes wide.

"This was a mistake," Lyndurgh said. "He wasn't ready."

Langford followed his gaze to where Kyall muttered to himself. "How did she die?"

"Does it matter?" The sharpness of Lyndurgh's tone drew Alistair's attention, but Langford wave him off.

"No. I don't think it does. I was only curious." Asking for details surrounding death was a tricky business. Some found it a natural curiosity. Others deemed it disrespectful. One never really knew until they received their response.

"Childbirth."

Ah. That was... well, fuck.

"And the child?" Langford already knew the answer.

Lyndurgh's slow shake of his head confirmed it.

Kyall's voice grew louder. Louder yet broken, his sobs reaching Langford where he stood several paces behind. It was meant to be a respectful distance. But Kyall's cries, his... answers... his responses...

He wasn't muttering to himself; he was conversing with someone.

The empty graveyard stood before him. Only his voice and the wind carried his cries.

"Who's he talking to?" Alistair angled his head, studying the man. "Huh. Rather chatty when he wants to be."

"Show some compassion," Lyndurgh growled, but Langford's thoughts raced.

Anya was the only one who saw Haakon's spirit. Could Kyall be communicating with his deceased wife?

But no, that would be unlikely. Two different spirits haunting the same ground and only appearing to two different people, the ones who loved and lost them?

Gods above. Gods and skies and what the blazes. Paragon's flaming knickers.

"Alistair," Langford said cautiously. "Kenna's blade."

Without pause or request of explanation, Alistair yanked it from its sheathe, the dagger silent in its movement. With a shared look and a nod, they crept forward.

A large hand clamped onto Langford's collar.

"Let him have a moment," Lyndurgh gritted in his ear.

"What did I fucking tell you about him." Alistair was on Lyndurgh before Langford could protest.

Kyall took a staggering step toward the gate, as if pulled by compulsion.

"No!" Langford ran toward him, footsteps hounding his.

"What are you doing?" Huvik hissed.

"Trying to save his life!" Langford bent down, grasping the snow. Dirt would have been better, easier, and wouldn't have speared ice through his palm. He reached Kyall and tossed it before them.

It landed upon a shape. A figure. Outlining a rounded creature, hunched low.

Alistair and Lyndurgh fell silent. Huvik let out a gasp. A stilted silence claimed the night.

The creature moved, and Kyall fell to his knees. Blood wept down his chest. A shallow cut, but Langford had seen the coroner's reports. This was the first of many this creature would attack him with.

He tossed more snow, giving its outline more shape. "Alistair, now!"

Alistair sprinted and landed in front of Langford, brandishing Kenna's silver blade with his razor-sharp reflexes, slashing quick and sure, until the creature fell upon the snow, its form finally revealed.

It was an ancient hag, bones attached to its back like a cloak. Mottled grey skin covered its body, the rest of it naked. A crude blade, a bone sharpened to a fine edged point, hung loose in its grasp.

Kyall let out a stuttering breath, another sob breaking free. "It wore her face. It… it carried my child."

Langford rested his hand on his shoulder, rummaging through his pack for his antiseptic salve. "I know," he said. "I know."

"ANOTHER DRINK for the lads who saved our hides!" Lyndurgh's voice carried in the tavern, the soft beginnings of slurred speech hinting its approach. After Langford had treated Kyall's wound, Kyall had retired for the night, too shook up to take Lyndurgh's offer of celebratory drinks.

The man had warmed considerably to Alistair, and he to him, as they traded stories and laughs over multiple pints.

Langford smiled over his honey wine, notes of elderberry sharpening its flavor. The same wine he'd been sipping all night. It wasn't that he didn't wish to celebrate; it was that celebrating to him looked more like taking this wine up to his room and poring over his texts. Maybe even examining Kenna's bestiary he'd copied to get a sense of what creature they'd just killed.

His understanding was that it waited in the graveyard, taking the shape of deceased loved ones and only appearing to the ones who mourned them. The bones it wore were dug from the very graves of the ones they impersonated. Something about the bones must have given it the power to take new shapes. It was unclear whether the creature needed a silver blade, but when Kenna had given Alistair one, she'd said *'Never hurts to be cautious.'*

Surely they'd gain the jarl's trust now?

The scrape of a chair, and Langford jolted. A strange woman slid into the seat across from him. The seat he was saving for Alistair, even though the man would have refused and sat beside him. As soon as he was done telling Lyndurgh about the time he'd escaped a dungeon using nothing but a shoe and comb.

"Have we met?" Langford took a polite sip of his wine, assessing the likelihood she had approached him for company he could not, *would not,* offer, or merely conversation. Or something else entirely.

"Not officially, but I have heard of you." She had dark hair and even darker eyes. "Gunther has been more than pleased with your presence here."

Curious. Smelled like a proposition was on the horizon. "I'm flattered but confused as to why you are privy to such sentiments while I am not."

She smirked. "Probably because he spoke of you in a meeting you were not important enough to attend." She dipped her head. "Sorry."

"Who are you again?" There was no offense to be found in her words, not on Langford's part. But she hadn't said her name, which was no accident.

"Moirin, but don't let my men hear you address me so informally. They don't like it."

A group of five unfamiliar warriors filled the corner. Their gazes found Langford's table, a dizzying array of concern and suspicion in their expressions.

"They also don't like you talking to me." Langford set his wine carefully atop the table.

"You are Gunther's newest prize." Moirin shrugged. "We cannot trust you."

"There's an awful lot of that going around." A headache was beginning to bloom behind Langford's eyes. He had no interest in getting caught up in whatever schemes this Moirin woman was planning. Especially not when they were so close to recruiting their fighters. He made to stand, and her hand clamped around his wrist.

"Don't." She shook her head. "Listen."

Panic thickened Langford's chest, and across the room, Alistair noticed. He strode toward them, purposeful and agitated—

Langford could not allow Alistair's increasingly impulsive nature to cast a pall over the evening. He shook his head and sat back down, taking a pointed sip of his wine. Alistair inclined his head in silent question, as if to say, '*Are you certain?*'

Langford nodded, and Alistair's stare lingered, a promise that he'd be paying attention.

"It would seem I am not the only one with protection this night." Moirin's eyes danced.

Alistair was always protective of him, but not like this. He'd weave himself into conversations, charming anyone within hearing and diffusing the situation. Now, he was the combustion. A side effect of his condition?

Gods. Perish the thought. They'd never be able to go anywhere without violence following if this were to be a permanent addition to Alistair's quirks.

"No, and I'd really rather not end the night in bloodshed. So, if there's something you wish to say, speak plainly. I've had a long night."

"Fair enough. Be wary of Gunther." Her mouth tightened. "He is not to be trusted."

More of this. It was a wonder these villages hadn't burned themselves to the ground with all this in-fighting.

"I operate on facts and evidence. Not vague warnings. I said speak plainly."

Moirin sighed. "My husband, Anders, was the chieftain of Grøndal. He was a cruel and horrible man. A drunkard and whoremonger even on the eve of our wedding. And when the drinks ran out and there was no more pleasurable company"—her eyes hardened—"he used his fists upon an easy and near target."

There was much unspoken in that statement. In the way she curled her hands into fists. In the tightness of her breath.

"He sounds horrible."

She relaxed. "He was. But he was the chieftain. I needed expressed permission from one of the jarls to dissolve the marriage." She took a long sip from her tankard. "None would agree to it. Said it wasn't their place to interfere in a marriage. But I know it was Anders. I know he got to them. Threatened them. Whatever it took to prevent me from escaping. I couldn't run. I ran twice, and each time, I was caught, and he left me near dead. So, I did the only thing I could." She took another sip of her ale. "I begged Gunther to help me. He promised he would. Said I was family to him. Even helped me have opportunity to escape my husband. He held a revel, plying him with enough drink to fell a bear. Gave me his dagger. I killed my husband, but Gunther was just as culpable in its planning. Imagine my surprise when he alerted his warriors and my husband's men that someone had stolen his dagger."

"He set me up and only covered my crime to leverage it for his purpose. He demanded I accept his betrothal and combine our lands. As jarl, his claim on his land is his birthright, dictated by the gods. But to extend his reach, he must bind himself in legal measures or sworn oaths. And he must do so before a new chieftain is assigned." She shook her head. "Gunther speaks of honor, but only when it suits him. His honor is a pliable thing, bending to his whims. He is using you, Langford. Making you and Alistair dance while he sits back and laughs. He promised you warriors? You will never get them."

Langford tightened his grip on his wine. "And will you marry him?"

Moirin laughed. "What choice have I? My lands suffer. He lets me attend these meetings as chieftain regent, but we both know I'm powerless to him. Were I a jarl's wife, there would be protection in place. But as a chieftain's wife, my influence died with Anders. When Gunther announces our betrothal, I will be forced to accept. Unless I run."

"Then run!" Langford startled at his own volume. "Come with us and bring your loyal fighters. We don't need Gunther or his back-alley deals. Let us leave with our heads held high."

Moirin shook her head. "You don't get it. So long as he is jarl, my people are in danger. What's to stop him from raiding my lands? Pillaging my village? He had shown his penchant for lies and manipulations, in fabricating his schemes to support his ambition. He has me caught in his web, and I am trapped." She blinked, her eyes glassy. "But you... it's not too late. He has nothing of value of yours to hold against you. Take your man and run."

Something cold took root in the pit of his stomach, like the threat of an intestinal virus. There was wisdom in her counsel, but what if her words were another play? All the leaders had an issue with trust. And to come all this way and leave empty handed...

"I'll think on it. You've given me much to consider." Langford stood, and Moirin stood, too.

"I hope you do."

He walked away, leaving the woman and her warnings behind. Alistair watched him with a wary expression. Langford joined him where he leaned against a wooden post, and Alistair angled his body to block him from view, brushing Langford's hair from his forehead. "Something wrong?"

"A headache; it will pass." And new information to analyze. "The woman told me much, and my mind is overworked as it is."

"Poor thing." Alistair squeezed the back of his neck. "If it's any consolation, they say she's a snake. Killed her first husband in her own bed for her ambitions to rise to marry even higher."

That was one version of it.

"There are always two sides of a story."

"Don't I know it." Alistair kissed him, lingering. "Shall we retire for the night? You look ready to keel over."

Langford snorted, winding his arms around Alistair's neck. "I have some reading to do."

Alistair groaned.

"None of that!" Langford laughed, but the sound was tight. His breath was tight. Much had been revealed, and none of it with any certainty. But he would not let it ruin the night. "Stay. Enjoy yourself. Come up in an hour, and if you're of sound enough mind, I'll tell you everything I heard."

"Ooh?" Alistair tugged him closer. "Now who's the king of gossip?" He kissed him again. "Are you sure I can't join you?"

"You can. In one hour. I need to concentrate." He swatted Alistair's eager hands away as they snuck for places they had no business reaching in public. "One hour."

"One hour." Alistair parroted back, stealing another kiss. "Unless I get bored."

"One hour!" Langford laughed as he backed away, heading for the door. A little time relaxing with sensory stimulus notes and theory would set his mind to rights.

MIDMORNING SUN STREAMED through the window, blinding Langford. He groaned and sat up, still in his clothes and seated at his desk. A paper was stuck to the side of his face, and he ripped it off, smacking his dry lips. He must have nodded off last night. He could already hear Alistair's teasing—

Langford shot up, banging his knee against the desk. Why hadn't Alistair taken him to bed? Even piss drunk, the man insisted on cuddling every night before sleeping. That Langford hadn't woken curled up in his arms was...

He glanced at the untouched bed.

Alistair had never come back.

CHAPTER FIFTY-ONE

GAVRIEL

*I*f Gavriel had known when he was that grieving recruit, young, scared, and alone, that one day he'd have Lark, he'd have the warmth of her care, of her impossibly bright soul alongside his, the nights would have been easier to bear.

Lark walked by his side, her nose bright red from the cold and her amber eyes alight. She warmed the chill from his bones with her heated smiles, feigning innocence the moment Ferryn glanced over. Once or twice, he'd snuck her behind a tree, prolonging their journey while he tasted all that he'd missed when they were separated by his slumber.

But on the edge of his joy sat a bitterness. A fear that permeated every moment of joy. Lark had told him what she faced. What Nyx had promised, a violent and bloody end to them all by Nereida's hand. That while they battled the threats immediately before them, she gathered her forces, capable of great destruction.

If they fell, if Lark fell... there was no comfort in the afterlife. It wasn't an option. They needed more fighters. To bolster their strength so they could sever the source of it all.

The answer danced before him, whispering for release. But the risk...

Lark laughed, high and bright as she launched a ball of snow at Ferryn, causing him to fall when he leapt out of the way.

She was worth the risk.

***

WHEN THE FORK in the road left him no room to delay, Gavriel spoke.

"I'm not going to Inerys. Not yet, anyway."

Lark stilled, whipping her head to face him. Her expression was a mixture of vulnerability and accusation. "What do you mean?"

"I can't sit idly by. And I won't." Not again. He'd spent the autumn months searching for his new purpose after the loss of his, well, occupation didn't quite cover it, did it? But when he was expelled from the Guild of Crows, a bounty placed upon his head, he'd lost his sense of purpose. Of direction. It wasn't perfect, far from it, but it was his. And Lark... he'd follow her to the ends of the earth, but he couldn't watch her fall while he did nothing to stop it.

When he killed Hamlin—when Hamlin forced his hand in the arena —it was the final severing of his old life. But it left him lost. And trapped in his dreams, witnessing his lifespans, always ending so young, he'd been lost for a long time.

But Lark. She was everything. She was everything he'd wished and hoped for.

He knew his purpose. And there was strength in that.

"I'm going to the Guild."

"What?" Pain flashed across Lark's face. If she only knew how much it killed him to leave her. "Why?"

"Because we need the numbers. And I think I can get them." Optimistic or foolish? It was always a fine line.

"That doesn't make any sense." Lark shook her head. "How could you recruit them?"

"Because it's his right." Ferryn's voice broke through, pity softening his sharp features. "You're the next Guild Master, aren't you?"

Lark glared at him as if he'd just betrayed her by voicing Gavriel's thoughts aloud.

Gavriel nodded, and Lark's brows knitted together. It wasn't as if he'd killed Hamlin in a true challenge. Guild members were always welcome to challenge the masters in pursuit of master title. It was suicide to do so, but it didn't stop some of their members from trying and failing.

Hamlin fell to Gavriel's sword. He had inherited the title. A fact he never wished to examine or acknowledge. But here it was, unwilling to be ignored. He had the authority to conscript the assassins in the war against Nereida.

Gavriel had been selfish long enough, burying himself in both the grief and joy he found with Lark. It was time to be more than that. To be worthy of her, the way Hugo made him promise he would be.

"Why didn't you tell me?"

Skies, but that punched a hole in his chest. The way her voice sounded so small.

Gavriel gathered her hands in his, blowing against her cold fingers. "I didn't want to face it myself. But we need the numbers. I can't send you into harm's way knowing I stood by and did nothing to ensure you came back to me."

"But why do you speak as if you're going alone. We'll come with you."

"It's too dangerous."

Anger flashed in her eyes. "You wish to go where it's too dangerous for me to follow." Her nostrils flared. "Not happening."

"I think this will go the way I hope. I do." Gavriel kissed her palm. "But if not, if I'm wrong... Lark I can't even breathe knowing what they'd do to you." Torture methods taught to recruits as young as thirteen were brutal and unforgiving. Maximizing pain and prolonging life. Quick and efficient deaths were their mercy, drawn out agony their punishment. He did not trust they would find mercy if he fell.

"I'm stronger now. They can't hurt me!"

"Yes. They can." Gavriel's heart was damn near splitting in two as she blinked away tears of anger, staring up at him as if he'd just stolen something precious from her. "They can, and they will, and I won't be able to stop them. Please."

She opened her mouth to argue.

"*Please*," he repeated. "I am begging you. I need to know you are safe. Give me something to return to."

Tears rolled down her cheeks, and fuck, he was a bastard for doing that to her. "That isn't fair."

"No, it isn't. But I need you to promise me this. Promise me you will not follow me. You will continue to Inerys, and tell her everything she needs to know to prepare. We haven't the time to waste." Gavriel exhaled a stuttered breath. "I can't lose you, Lark."

"We're stronger together. How many times must we prove this?"

"Once more." Gavriel tucked her hair behind her ear. "Once more, and I promise I'm never leaving your side again."

Lark shook her head, ripping her hands free from his. "This is a mistake. You're forcing my hand, and you're wrong." She wiped her nose. "You can't stop me from following you."

"You're right, I can't." Gavriel reached for her, throat tightening when she put distance between them. "That's why I'm asking. I'm asking you to trust me. My heart and soul are yours. Forever. Just give me your trust."

Lark's face crumpled, and the pain of that look, of being the one to put it there, stabbed through Gavriel as sure as a blade.

"This feels wrong."

"That's because anything that takes me from your side feels wrong." Gavriel gently tugged her to him, and he sighed in relief when she allowed him. "I promise to return, with a small army at your disposal. I just need some time."

Lark sniffed. "If you can promise that so easily, why do you fear my joining you?"

Minx.

"Because I can't show them any weakness. Anything they could exploit." That was what they learned best. Manipulating weaknesses. Assassins were not trained to be the strongest. Or the toughest. It was about identifying weaknesses, pressure cracks, and exploiting them. Adapting to one's opponent and finishing them by any means necessary.

Gavriel was sure to have enemies within the ranks. Some he could guess, and others he wouldn't know until their strike. But he would not risk Lark.

"Right. Right. Because love is weakness."

Gavriel smiled against her hair as she spat the words back at him, words he'd spoken to her when he was nothing more than a disgraced assassin trying desperately not to fall for the beautiful demon he feared.

"You are my weakness." He kissed her forehead. "And my strength." Her nose. "And my hope. I will come back to you. I swore it once, lifetimes ago, I'm swearing it again."

Lark nodded, the barest of movements, and he crashed his mouth against hers. She poured all her anger and hurt into the kiss, stealing the breath from his lungs. They never had a chance to say goodbye, and this was all their goodbyes melded into one, because deep in Gavriel's bones he knew this was the last time they would ever say goodbye. Once he completed his mission, he'd never leave her side.

She bit down on his lip, and he moaned into her mouth. Hating himself for doing this to them.

But it was necessary.

They broke apart in a daze, her cheeks still wet and lips reddened. He kissed her again, softly. Once. Twice.

In that moment, time stood still. The cold wasn't as biting. It was almost as if—

A throat cleared, reminding Gavriel of Ferryn's presence.

"Rather than face the same passionate goodbye I'm sure I've earned"—Ferryn rocked on his heels, hands behind his back—"I wish to offer you both a suitable solution. I will accompany Gavriel to the guild. I can assure you, I have his back should he face any manner of peril. And since I'm of no great loss to him, I can't be used against him. It all works out, yes?"

No. Absolutely not. That was the worst idea anyone had ever had. Ferryn? He was likely to run his mouth and anger the wrong person. Then he'd have the displeasure of explaining to Lark how he let her friend die—

"What if he stays nearby, an extra hand should you need it?" Lark eyed Ferryn meaningfully. "No unnecessary risks."

"Deal." Ferryn marched over, yanking Lark out of Gavriel's arms, and offering her a tight hug. "Safe travels, little bird. I'll keep your assassin safe."

They spoke as if he wasn't even here. "I don't think—"

"It's the only way I agree not to follow you," Lark said, the hint of a smile playing on her mouth.

Gavriel traced that smile, grateful for even the ghost of her joy. "Then I can't argue with that now, can I?"

Lark grabbed his hand, pressing it to her face. "You really promise to be safe?"

Gavriel nodded, running his fingers into the hair at the nape of her neck. "I swear it, Lark."

She snagged a thread from his cloak, winding it around her finger. His chest ached, swelling with affection for this woman. Memories filtered over the present, of Lark winding a string around her finger to represent their promise to one another lifetimes ago.

The words got lost somewhere in his throat, and he claimed her mouth once more.

It was an oath and a reminder.

They would always find each other.

WITH EACH STEP further from that fork in the road, where he and Lark parted, the air grew colder. The sky was a muted gray, gloom curling through barren branches above, and the air carried the bite of impending snow.

"So... wish to hear embarrassing stories about Lark?" Ferryn's chipper demeanor only faltered once or twice in all their acquaintance, so it was no surprise that the former Reaper maintained it in the face of Gavriel's ruminating.

"I would hear anything you have to say of Lark, so long as it's true."

"Don't give me too much freedom. You'll regret it."

Gavriel almost laughed. But the reality of the situation was sinking in. He had every intention of claiming his title as Guild Master and rallying more fighters in the fight against Nereida. But without any guild witnesses to back his story, how would he prove he'd earned the title?

Damn. Even just thinking of it as something he *earned* was disgusting. His mentor/apprentice relationship with Hamlin was... complicated. He'd been his master, so the power dynamic of that was always strange to navigate, but he'd also been his friend and mentor. He had delivered every letter his mother sent. Most recruits failed to receive messages until their apprenticeship ended. But Hamlin never kept Gavriel's letters from him. He had given Gavriel a head start before issuing the bounty, granting him a chance to survive. It was a major infraction on Hamlin's part, and if Master Eldrige had learned of this, Hamlin would have faced a tribunal.

And then he risked his life by coming to the arena when the Den of Lions had Gavriel imprisoned, forcing him to fight.

And after...

"We should camp for the night. I know I'm not Lark, but I have enough body heat to share."

Gavriel's relief at the distraction was swift and fierce. "Steady on. We're only a few hours walk from the next town."

"Fine, but if we share a bed, I'm a blanket hog."

Gavriel sighed. "I don't like that we let Lark travel the rest of the way on her own."

"She'll be fine. What's the worst that could happen?" Ferryn's face went blank as Gavriel was sure he imagined some of the worst scenarios that could happen. The same ones that plagued his mind. She could encounter monsters on her own. Merikh the sadistic paragon could snatch her away again. Perhaps Nereida found her and sought to punish her after killing the spymaster and the seer. Skies, the possibilities were endlessly churning in his mind.

Ferryn cleared his throat. "I'm sure she'll be fine."

Perhaps it was better if they didn't speak.

WHEN THE FIRE burned high enough in the sky to take the immediate chill from the air, Gavriel stretched his legs, watching the embers float to the trees and their skeletal branches. A deep longing pulled at him, the desire to have a certain someone curled in his lap, basking in the warmth of the fire. But it was better this way. Safer. He regretted her tears, but he couldn't regret sending her away. Not when it meant keeping her safe. Not when it meant delivering the fighters she needed to win the war against Nereida.

A shadow darted in his periphery. A whisper of movement. A flutter of darkness.

Gavriel was not the sort to mistake ordinary shadows for the keen sense that someone was watching. Following.

Across the fire, Ferryn was none the wiser. He sat holding a stick with an apple shoved onto it over the fire, frowning at it as it burned. "Lark swears by this particular delicacy, but it looks like shit."

"You're cooking it wrong." Gavriel stretched, hyperaware of his peripheral vision while keeping his stare fixed on Ferryn's burnt apple. "You're supposed to cut it first and cook it over the fire. Not light a damn pyre and torture the thing."

"That's just sad. Now I feel bad for the little thing." Ferryn pulled his blackened apple from the flames, examining it with care. "Think it's salvageable?"

"Doubt it. Give it here." Gavriel reached for the stick, carefully bringing it closer to his side. The shadow flickered, a heightened sense of being watched pricked at the back of his neck. He made a show of looking it over, turning it in his hand. "Utterly ruined. Lark will be most displeased you wasted an apple." With a flick of his wrist, he sent the burning mass straight into the trees behind him. A yelp cried out in response.

Gavriel was on his feet running toward the sound without thought. A slight figure sprinted ahead of him, seeking escape. He tackled them to the ground, their breath knocked from their lungs with a distinct *whoosh*. Turning them over, he grabbed their wrists, bracketing a squirming body between his knees as they struggled to escape.

Familiar eyes, cold and pale, glared up at him. Black hair spilling against the white snow.

Fucking Hazel.

"Fancy seeing you here, Pearson. Don't think Lark would much like our position though."

Gavriel leapt to his feet, dragging her up with him. He shoved her against a tree, her eyes rolling back from the impact. "Why are you spying on us?"

"Ugh. Spying. I wasn't spying, you child."

Gavriel shook her again, and she groaned.

"Gods, stop. You're going to make me sick."

"Answer me. And if I catch one hint of your lies, Hazel, one fucking hint, I'll kill you where you stand. I won't risk you betraying us again."

"I'm here to help you!"

Gavriel shoved out of her space, dropping her wrists in favor of palming his daggers. "Why would I want or even trust your help."

"I know you're the new Guild Master by rights. Bet you're headed there now, aren't you? How do you plan to claim your title without a proper witness?" She gestured to herself. "I'll be your witness, if you promise to take me to Lark after."

"Absolutely not." He wasn't letting this snake within a ten-foot radius of Lark ever again. "You used her. You lied to us. You killed someone for your own selfish gain." Daciana and Kenna had made a new contact, a girl by the name of Amara. She had a… well, Gavriel wasn't sure the nature of the relationship between the girl and the man they found lying in a pool of his own blood, but the way she wailed her grief would forever be imprinted in his memories. And Lark. She'd been so determined to find the good in Hazel. They'd bonded in their time together, and Lark counted her as friend.

Hazel hurt her when she betrayed them all. He'd never let her hurt Lark again.

"Please."

Hazel never said please. Never asked for anything with sincerity.

"I need to make amends with Lark, I know. And there are things I couldn't explain. Things I want to open up about, I do. Lark will understand, she'll hear me out and she'll get it. But—" Her lip quivered and oh skies, no. Hazel never cried. "I need her help, Gav."

"Don't call me that."

They hadn't been so familiar in nearly fifteen years. Now was not the time to pretend they were close.

"I helped Lark save you! She never would have found you were it not for me."

Gavriel narrowed his eyes. "You're resorting to desperation. That doesn't work with me."

Hazel ran her hands into her hair. "I know. I know, I'm sorry. I just —I need Lark, and I'm willing to do anything to speak to her again. Please."

It was a big ask coming from the girl who only looked out for herself. The girl who'd sell you to the highest bidder just to line her own pockets. But there was something in her expression. In the hallowed look of her gaunt features. Her sunken in eyes.

"Where's Gregoir?"

Hazel's face crumpled, and she wiped her nose on her sleeve. "I need Lark. I promise to be your witness. I'll back you at the Guild, even though it puts me at risk for being found guilty of desertion. I'll do whatever it takes if you just give me your word that you'll ask Lark to see me."

Skies, but he was growing soft. Lark's doing, no doubt.

"My contract is broken. I don't know how, but I know it. I feel it." Hazel shook her head. "No one is pulling the strings. I'm a free agent. But Gregoire..."

"Shit. Fine. Fine, dammit." He didn't know what the rutting skies she meant by *feeling* her contract break, but he needed a witness at the guild. Even an unreliable one.

"Thank you!" Hazel reached out to hug him, and he knocked her hands away.

"I still don't trust you. You know that right? Give me one reason, one shadow of doubt, and I'll slit your throat and save myself the hassle of watching my back for the knife you're likely to stab there."

"No lies. No betrayals. No disappearing acts." She crossed her finger over her heart. "Put in a good word for me with Lark. Let me prove this to you."

This was a mistake. And if she betrayed him, it would spell his own ruin.

CHAPTER FIFTY-TWO

DEMETRIA

*D*emetria knew every inch of her castle. Every crack. Every notch she'd scraped into hidden places to leave her mark, proof of her existence in a structure built to last longer than her memory. Walking its halls, she ached. Deep and sharply, she ached. A sorrow for all that was lost.

This was meant to be her home, and yet she was a stranger.

She'd been washed, combed, perfumed, and outfitted in an ill-fitting and out-of-style gown. The material felt strange against her skin. Too smooth. She ran her hands down her bodice, her hands a stark contrast against the pale blue silk. None of the handmaids who helped were her original staff. Had Zaire simply dismissed them from the castle? Or worse?

This was the moment when Balan would have reminded her to have courage. To offer perspective—one-sided and deliberately obtuse at times—but perspective none the less. And imagining his words was lonelier than the silence.

But Balan was still in the mines with the others.

Soon enough, she'd free him along with everyone else trapped in the dark. It was strange how much she'd come to rely on the demon. He was supposed to be a vessel of evil, was he not?

Right now, he was the only soul she could trust.

Demetria kept her eyes trained in front, as she was escorted down the hall by an unfamiliar guard. She passed beneath gilded archways, the echoes of her footfalls harsh and unforgiving in the silence. There once was chatter in these halls, excited whispers of conversation between servants and visiting nobles and even guards trekking to their posts. This castle was once teeming with life, and now it was as silent as the grave.

The dining room was just ahead. Her gaze dipped to the alcove leading to the library, and her stomach clenched.

She'd dragged Evander into the castle many times, sneaking him around because he was too ashamed to be seen in his stained groundskeeper's clothes. Once they hid behind that pillar in the corner because he heard someone coming. Their silent laughter had shaken them both, Demetria's stomach aching from holding it in, and she'd clapped her hand over his mouth, his breath warm against her palm.

They reached door at the end of the hall, and it swung open, smooth and soundless like Zaire had finally ordered someone to oil the hinges. Demetria swept into the room, a feast fit for a queen upon the table. Her stomach growled, gnawing on itself. Roasted duck, glistening and adorned with slices of orange, platters overfilled with grapes and loquats and pomegranate, crusty breads waiting to be sliced, cheese by the block, she had to keep herself from launching toward the table. With measured steps, she approached, waiting for her seat to be pulled for her.

The guard stood by the door, offering no such display of manners.

She yanked out her own chair, lowering to sit, and began piling her plate.

"You must wait for the king."

Demetria crushed the bread in her hand, the pattering of crumbs hitting her plate. "What?"

"You must wait for the king. You are not permitted to eat until he takes the first bite."

"I see." She drummed her fingers against the table. She hadn't realized she'd be dining with Zaire. It made her plan both easier and harder. Easier because she needn't search for him. Harder if he spotted and recognized her in the presence of his guard. In any case, if she fainted from starvation, she would not get another chance. "When will he join us?"

The guard shrugged. "He's still on a hunt. Might not even make it home tonight."

Her hand knocked a glass chalice on its side.

She was given one night, *one night,* in this castle. She wasn't permitted to eat until he arrived, and he might not even arrive?

It was just the sort of game Zaire would play. Making up rules while skirting every loophole.

The time to adapt the plan was nigh.

Demetria leaned over, allowing the low neckline of her unfashionable gown hint at her curves. The guard's stare dipped, pausing for inspection. She was seventeen summers old, and this man appeared to have seen thrice as many. But it all served her benefit. It disgusted and elated her in equal measures, because it made what she must do next that much easier to stomach.

"What's your name?"

"Edvard." The guard offered her a grin. That's right. To him, she appeared nothing more than an indenture lucky enough to get cleaned up. She was no one for him to respect. He had no care for how she received his thorough and probing stare.

"I'm rather bored, Edvard." Demetria neatly folded her napkin on her lap, carefully dragging and hiding the carving knife beneath it. "What shall we do while we wait for the king?"

His grin turned salacious. "I can think of a few things."

Demetria stood, carrying her napkin as she slowly walked to him. She'd spent years perfecting the different masks she was expected to wear, even if her mother indulged her wildness in some capacity. But she'd never donned this mask.

One of Ruslan's lessons sprang to mind.

'You won't always have the advantage of strength, princess. Sometimes you must rely on cunning. They will underestimate you. It's up to you how far off their calculation is.'

Demetria's heart hammered in her throat, threatening to stall the air from her lungs. "Shall we close the door?"

Edvard nodded, turning his back to quickly grant them privacy.

It was now or never.

As soon as the door silently closed, her hand clapped over his mouth, and she pressed the sharpened carving knife against the sensitive skin of his throat. "Shh... Edvard. I don't have much to lose by killing you, do I?"

Little pieces of her soul. But she was beginning to learn the price for peace was steep.

Edvard reached for his sword, and she pressed the knife closer, the first hint of blood rising to his skin.

"I'll be borrowing this." She slowly removed her trembling hand from his mouth, running it down to his sword. "I have no idea what your story is, but I do know this. You will have to answer to me when all this is done. So don't even *think* about doing anything stupid." False bravado, she was finding, was easier to conjure the higher the stakes. She would not return to those mines. She would *not*.

"You'll never get away with this. You think the mines are bad? Pretty girls like you are sold for sport. Passed around even in the barracks."

Anger coursed through her at his admission. Between clenched teeth, she bit out, "You don't glance around much do you? How long have you been employed in the castle?"

"Three months."

"And in three whole months, you never once examined the portraits of the royal family?"

Edvard stiffened in her hold, turning his head toward the family portrait hanging above the fireplace. Demetria was twelve in this painting. But even now, with starvation stealing the softness of her face, the hardened edge to her eyes, the resemblance was unmistakable.

Edvard gasped. "Your Highness, I never would have—"

"Of course, not. You only prey on the weak. On the vulnerable." Rage heightened in her blood, rising like an angry ocean. "I changed my mind, Edvard. You answer to me now." Demetria dragged her knife deep through his throat, soft skin parting beneath the sharp blade like that infernal roasted duck she was not permitted to eat.

She let his body drop to the floor, her stomach dropping with him.

He deserved it. He deserved it. How many girls had he hurt? How young had they been?

She'd never killed anyone before. Why wasn't it... harder? Shouldn't it have been? Or now, shouldn't she feel something?

Maybe that part of her was broken. Maybe Zaire broke it long ago, and she hadn't even realized.

Good. That was good, wasn't it? If she hadn't the stomach to kill a worthless stranger, how would she kill her own brother? Even if he was a monster?

Demetria wiped the blood from her hand with her napkin, a numbing detachedness spreading through her body. Like her hands were separate from the rest of her. She took the seat at the head of the table, spread out the bloody napkin on her lap, and stuck her fingers into the duck. Pulling and prying pieces of greasy meat from its carcass. She stuffed the pieces in her mouth, aware of the slimy texture, but tasting nothing.

Her gaze flitted to the body in the corner. The blood soaking into the floor.

If anyone happened upon them, she'd be executed without so much as a chance of even seeing her brother. She chewed, thoughts racing. She had no allies in the castle anymore. No plan beyond her anger. Had she been foolish? Chasing the path of her revenge without care?

Balan's plan never would have worked. It only would have brought them freedom.

And that was never going to be enough.

She pushed her chair out, its legs scuffing against the floor. It was no small mercy this room was uncarpeted. The blood could be wiped away.

She gripped each of the man's legs, dragging him to the curtains and leaving behind a painter's brushstroke of blood. Once he was safely tucked away, she tackled the floor. Evander had taught her a trick that would come in handy now. But the tablecloth was too long, ten feet in length. She used her carving knife, cutting through the fabric in three places to create smaller squares. She grabbed them one at a time, tugging with one hard and clean pull—

Each pulled free without disturbing the table setting. Only the water danced in the glass pitcher.

She scrubbed at the floor, splashing it with water to wipe it away clean.

Had Evander's stain been removed from the carpet in the throne room? Had Zaire ordered the carpet replaced? Or had he simply left it there as a reminder not to speak out against him even in hushed whispers?

Demetria's eyes burned, her stomach churning as blood stained her hands and her dress. When the floor was finally washed clean of her crime, she stood on shaky feet. Her stomach heaved, and she caught the large decorative urn just in time for the contents of her stomach to splash into the bottom.

She wiped her mouth, the corners of her eyes wet. Her hands were once again stained red with blood. On numb legs, she approached the silver pitcher of water. She dipped her hands in, letting the water darken with the stains of her choices, and slowly lifted them out. Beads of tinged water, a faint pink, rolled down her palms and dripped from her fingertips. Gems the color of morganite formed and fell away as she stared at her hands, before wiping them down the front of her gown.

Demetria could not lose her nerve now. She could not. This was nothing to fall apart over. She'd taken a necessary step in her plan. Nothing more. It would have been harder if the guard had been kind; she should be grateful for that. Because she would have done it anyway. She would have killed anyone that stood in her way, good or no, because sometimes the end has to justify the means—

Footsteps.

It was enough to jolt her out of her numbing contemplation.

Demetria tucked herself into the corner behind the door, clutching the carving knife.

A voice. The voice she knew so well. One that laughed and played with her in childhood. That deepened and roughed and hardened as he grew into the monster who plagued her darkest thoughts.

Her brother had returned.

The door swung open, hiding her, and his voice followed.

"I wish not to be disturbed. When I retire for the evening, send someone to clean it up. But I won't have you standing there watching me." Zaire's heavy footsteps strode into the room.

Demetria steadied her shaky breath, peeking through the crack in the door.

He wore his hunting ensemble. Pristine boots that hadn't seen mud or puddles. A riding cloak hanging from one shoulder while his shirt remained cleanly tucked behind the high-buttoned waist of his trousers. His face had not changed much. Some of the lines of his features were more pronounced. His deep-golden skin and dark eyes, so much like their father and yet so other. He almost didn't look real.

Fashionable. Untouched. Preserved. Like he was nothing more than a painted portrait.

"You're sure, Your Highness?" Demetria nearly jumped out of her skin. The second voice was so close, separated from her by only the door.

Zaire's eyes narrowed, a dangerous glint. "Are you questioning me?"

"No, Your Majesty."

Zaire took a measured step toward him, a dark and silent threat. "Good. Dismissed."

The guard tripped over his feet in his retreat, swinging the door shut and bringing Demetria into view.

But Zaire had already turned away, rubbing his temples.

It was now or never.

Demetria crept toward him. Silent in her silk slippers. The carving knife shook in her hand, and she grasped her wrist to steady it.

Zaire turned, his eyes widening in surprise and his stance faltering. "You—" He shook his head and took her in, analyzing her appearance with a measure of contempt only a brother can. "I imagined you dead."

She tightened her hold on the knife. "Imagined or hoped?"

"Both." At her startled expression, he held out his hands. "Did you expect me to lie?"

Anger surged through her, hot and swift. It was a welcome balm to any hesitancy she'd held. "I expected you to regret your actions when facing the answering knife point."

Zaire laughed, slow and sustained. His face was all wrong. His smile too sharp. His eyes too empty. "Should I be cowering in fear? Should I beg for mercy?"

A memory flitted through her mind, buried beneath layers of grief.

"Ah! Have mercy!" Zaire held up his hands in surrender, all gangly limbs.

"Never!" Demetria stood proud, measuring half his height and wielding a stick like a sword. Zaire had hidden in the woods, leaping out at her and Evander to frighten them. Evander had fallen, landing in the muck and biting down on his lip as he tried not to cry. Zaire had laughed, far too amused with his own joke to care.

Demetria whipped at his knees with her stick, only dragging more laughter from her older brother. It was always a game to him. Even if he was the only one laughing.

"I don't want you to beg." Demetria shook her head. "That would only make what I'm going to do even harder."

"Please," he scoffed. He turned his back on her, waltzed to the untouched wine, and poured himself a glass.

He did not think she could do it. He thought her weak and useless. A parasite. A silly, foolish little girl who couldn't possibly understand what it meant to get her hands filthy.

Zaire had no idea who she had become. What she had become.

Demetria strode across the room, angling her knife. Each step was like justice, the answer to Evander's death, to Ruslan's, to countless others she had never even known of. He thought her too sentimental to be a threat. That the bonds of family ran too deep, but he'd severed those bonds the moment he ordered Evander's head to be severed from his neck.

Zaire tipped his head back, savoring his wine and even smacking his lips.

Demetria clapped a hand on his shoulder and sank her blade into his side. He stiffened, a garbled cry and wine spilling from his lips. She yanked it out and plunged it in again. And again.

He crumpled to the floor, blood pooling beneath him.

She wouldn't clean this mess up.

Zaire's eyes flashed, their hardness softening. "Demi?" He seemed so surprised. As if he hadn't known she was there. "Demi, you're..." He coughed, blood and wine staining his lips. "You're all grown up."

Stillness. All the anger fueling her calmed into a damning stillness.

What was happening? Why was he looking upon her as if he hadn't seen her face in years?

"Zaire?"

"Gods, I've missed you. What's happening to me? Why am I so cold?" He glanced around wildly, searching. "Call for father. I think... I think I'm..." His eyes started to lose focus.

He wished her to call for Father? Their parents died years ago.

Ice spread through her veins as tiny pin pricks of terror flooded her body. And for the first time in years, her brother had returned. Not the stranger who bore his features. Not the cold, ruthless king he'd become. Not even the brat who always teased Evander mercilessly. But the brother who held her hand through their parents' farewell memorial, the one who'd fixed her hair when she collapsed on her bed sobbing but still had to appear before their kingdom to mourn collectively.

Zaire. "Where were you?" Demetria wasn't even sure what she was asking, just that there was truth in her question.

Zaire ignored her words, or maybe he didn't hear them. His eyes appeared to shift in and out of focus. Here and then suddenly far away. "It doesn't hurt so much anymore. It hurt for so long."

Demetria fell to her knees, slipping in his blood. "Zaire?" she repeated his name on a sob. "What did I... how..."

Zaire smiled softly up at her, regarding her in a way he hadn't in many years. Then his smile slipped, his eyes freezing out of focus just past her shoulder.

Demetria wiped her nose, smearing his blood across her face. He was a monster. He was cruel and heartless. So, why did he seem like an entirely different person? Why now of all moments?

A shaky breath left her body, vibrating from her chest in a violent tremor. Even her hands shook, an uneasy panic climbing up the tight expanse of her throat.

This was wrong.

Wrong. Wrong. Wrong.

Demetria pounded her fist against the floor, pain shooting through her hand. She bit her knuckles, muffling the sounds ripping from her mouth. It hurt. Why did it hurt so much? It was a knife in the chest, twisting and digging. It was another loss carved from the pit of her stomach. It was too much. Too much and she was not enough to carry it all.

"Oh, dear, what have we here?" A sultry voice. One Demetria knew. The shock of it numbed her agony and sent a shiver down her spine.

She turned to find the woman standing over her. Thick waves of snowy-white hair spilled over her shoulders. A black dress fitted like a glove and formed to her every ample curve. Her lips painted a red so dark it was almost black.

Demetria had seen this woman before. She had taunted them with knowledge she should not possess. She saw deep into their souls, breathing life to their weaknesses that day in the forest when Lark screamed for mercy. When Alistair died... and returned. When Balan shielded her as if this was the greatest monster he'd ever faced.

Nereida.

The witch-queen of the Netherworld.

"Why... why are you here?"

"Oh, you poor sweet thing." She tutted and angled her head to peer past Demetria—at her brother's body. "I'm here to offer you negotiations for your new contract."

"C-contract?" Nothing made sense. The bloody floor threatened to swallow her whole.

"Yes." Nereida smiled. "The one you just inherited along with that fancy title." She bent in a mocking bow. "Your Majesty."

CHAPTER FIFTY-THREE

LANGFORD

*L*angford tripped over his feet, staggering out of the guest quarters of one of the jarl's many homes. The tavern was a short walk through the village, but the time it took could have been an eternity.

Alistair had never come back to their room. He'd stayed out all night. What could he possibly—

Langford took slow and measured breaths. He would make a list of possibilities ranging from innocuous to grievous scenarios. The reason Alistair stayed out all night: He'd fallen asleep at the tavern after too much drinking. It had happened before, though not recently, and Langford thought those days were behind them, but there it was. He was... occupied with another. Langford snorted. Absolutely not. Not in a million years. He shelved that particular thought under impossible. Someone needed help, and there was no time to come and collect Langford. This one worried him, because if there was an accident or someone had gotten hurt, Langford would be the first person he'd retrieve. And that he hadn't come home would mean he was caught up in something...

The worst-case scenario whispered in the back of Langford's mind, begging to take shape.

Something had happened to him.

It wouldn't do to invent hypotheticals. Langford needed answers, and he needed them now. He kicked the tavern door open, it seemed apropos in the moment and melodramatic in the immediate aftermath, but he stomped his way to the barkeep who had begun to open his business, taking chairs down from their tabletops.

The barkeep was a stout man by the name of Jon. He was no-nonsense, direct, and firm with his patrons. But loyalty ran deep in these parts, and they were still the outsiders. If it meant protecting his own, he'd withhold information Langford needed.

Langford opened his mouth to spew the rant he'd prepared—

"Aye. I know where your man is."

Oh. Well, that was easier than expected.

"Where is he?"

Jon sighed, heaving another chair to the floor. "The holding cell."

"The what?"

"He got mouthy with some of the boys last night." Jon rubbed his chin, his fingers brushing against his short beard. "I've seen my fair share of drunken brawls, but I'd never seen this. Not in my tavern."

Dread filled Langford's stomach, weighing it down like a bout of intestinal distress. Had Alistair turned? But the moon hadn't completed its cycle. They had another week's time before Langford should need to administer Kenna's herbs again. Unless Alistair wasn't bound to the same moon cycle as Daciana. Langford had assumed, especially with his first turn aligning with the fullness of the moon, but what if that was a mere catalyst? What if his turns were unpredictable? What if the effects, once fully realized, were permanent? What if—

"I'm sorry," Langford said breathlessly. "Could you be more specific?"

"He damn near took Lyndurgh's eye out with the broken shard of a bottle. I'm not saying he didn't deserve it, but sometimes you need to know when to ignore the drunken ramblings of an aging warrior. They're not built like you or I."

Whatever that meant. Alistair had been provoked, a violent reaction following the stimulus. It wasn't unheard of where he was concerned, especially not of late. But relief lightened the heavy tension in Langford's legs at the knowledge Alistair had not lost himself.

Not yet.

"Is it like the city drunkard cells?" In major towns and cities in Koval, drunken brawls and public disturbances usually resulted in a night locked up and a slap on the wrist. Major infractions yielded harsher punishments.

"It depends on Lyndurgh."

"How is that?" Was there no law of the land? Vallemer's structure of power suggested there was.

"Offending party submits to the victim's justice." Jon shrugged. "Usually closely resembling eye-for-an-eye punishments. Sometimes worse. Depends on the person."

"That's—" Langford almost said barbaric, but it wouldn't do to insult any locals. "How are there no abuses of this rule?" If it came down to the whims of the injured party, they could level far harsher punishments than warranted or even seek to provoke someone into this position out of spite.

"I never said there weren't."

Panic jolted through Langford's body like a charged current. Helpless fear threatened to crawl up his throat. He shoved it back down. He might not believe in much these days, and the last three seasons had challenged every preconceived notion he'd ever held, but damn any gods or higher power or magical tree or whatever fucking nonsense determined to see them punished.

He would get Alistair out of this, unscathed, and they would return to Ardenas. With or without the aid of Vallemerian warriors.

He spun on his heel and marched straight for the holding cells.

An A-frame structure, built to hold only a handful of criminals behind bars, sat on the far side of the village. Beyond the timber crafted gate, where the forest began to thicken, the building sat behind a crumbling stone wall. There was no door, nothing to keep the frigid mountain air from battering through the cells and between iron bars. Langford crept closer, glancing about the forest and listening for the sounds of footsteps. Only the low groan of the wind answered back.

He stepped through, and rows of unoccupied cells greeted him. At the end of the narrow room, a blessedly empty set of stocks and pillory device hinted at the types of punishments they employed. Restraint and humiliation.

What would Lyndurgh demand of Alistair's penance? Langford tightened his fist at his side, the sensation of his shortened finger nearly a familiar comfort.

It mattered not what his punishment was. He would not face it.

A shadow dipped along the wall, and Langford once again cursed his foolishness for not allowing Alistair to retire alongside him last night. He wouldn't be sneaking into a prison in search for him, nor facing a potential foe absent a weapon at this very moment.

Langford made to turn, when his stare trained on a figure in a darkened cell. The only cell shrouded in more shadow than light from the open doorway.

Alistair.

He was alone in his cell, slumped in on himself with his elbows resting upon his knees and head hanging low. His clothing was rumpled, and a thicker dusting of bristles covered his jaw, but he had no identifiable injury from what Langford could see. He exhaled a sigh of relief despite himself. Even if the guard threw him out, Langford could rest easy knowing Alistair was unharmed for the moment.

He would set him free before the status of his wellbeing could be altered.

Langford focused on the guard, and a familiar face greeted him. Huvik. Once again checking his deck of cards for the secret to good bluffing when engaged in a game. He glanced up, meeting Langford's eyes, and sympathy dawned in his expression with a soft downturn of his mouth. It quickly tightened into a smile, as Huvik stepped into Langford's way.

"I'm sorry," Huvik said, the sincerity in his words grating.

"You can't be serious." The boy was blameless, but he was in the way just the same. "Let me pass."

"You need permission from the jarl." Huvik winced as he said the words. "I cannot."

Fury unlike anything Langford had ever felt rushed through him. It wasn't Huvik's fault, but the urge to wring the boy's neck made him tighten his hands into fists. Alistair was in there, mere paces from where Langford stood, and he was helpless to reach him.

For the moment.

"Fine." The word slipped through Langford's clenched teeth. "I won't be long." He turned on his heel and stomped away.

Skies and fates and whatever else be damned, he was getting Alistair out of this.

⊱ ⋆ ⊰

LANGFORD RAN a hand through his untidy hair as he waited for Gunther to grant him an audience. Alistair had once said he'd go bald fiddling with his hair as he did. And when Langford had feigned offense at such a proclamation, Alistair had whispered all matter of indecent thoughts as reassurance that he'd still find him irresistible.

And why did the thought of that conversation send a pang through his chest?

They'd been in worse predicaments than this. But unease settled in his gut like a poorly digested meal. Langford had no one to fall back on. If he couldn't make the jarl see reason, if Alistair could not receive some sort of pardon... he'd cross that bridge when he came to it. He'd do anything in his power to see Alistair freed. And what if it wasn't enough? What if *he* wasn't enough?

Langford pulled his hand free of his messy hair and shoved the thought away.

It was a fool's hope to expect Gunther to grant Alistair mercy unreciprocated, so Langford didn't dare hope for it. He'd need a convincing argument. To offer all appearances of negotiation. Langford didn't enjoy lying or even the intention to lie. But he knew he would resort to subterfuge to avoid risking his position as the only chance at breaking Alistair out of a Vallemerian prison.

Langford smoothed his hand over the rough wool of his over tunic,

406

all under the watchful eye of Kyall. While they waited for the jarl to make his appearance, a charged silence of mutual discomfort filled the air. Discomfort for Kyall, surely, for the events that transpired only last eve. The man looked worse for wear, which was to be expected after witnessing the ghost of his dead wife and child only to discover it was a monstrous hag luring him to his death.

Langford broke the silence. "How's the chest?" He drew a line across his own to indicate the injury he'd sustained. It was an easy conversation to have, despite the circumstances. It was always easy to focus on the wounds of others.

"Still a bit sore." Kyall frowned.

"I have a salve for that." Langford patted down his pockets, finding a small tin he'd meant to give to Kyall anyway. "Twice a day, even after it's healed. Unless you wish it to scar, in which case, just until the skin seals."

Kyall regarded him with a thorough, searching stare and quickly tucked the salve away when shuffling steps sounded outside the hut.

Gunther appeared, his jaw clenched and steel gaze sharper than before. "Langford," he said. "I can guess why you asked to see me."

"Yes, Your Grace." Langford wasn't sure how they addressed jarls apart from title, but perhaps some Kovalian manners would soften his words. "I understand you've had Alistair imprisoned and denied him visitors. Whatever your reasons—"

"I'm quite aware of his misdeeds." Gunther sat upon his throne with a grunt. "The question is, are you?"

Langford wet his lips, unprepared for the interruption. "He got in a tavern brawl. Things got out of hand."

"Out of hand." Gunther chuckled, a slow dark laugh. "He broke Lyndurgh's arm and nearly removed his eye. Over a jest."

Beside the jarl, Kyall stiffened.

Gods give him strength. Langford had known the man long enough to know him capable of brutality, but violence wasn't the sort of thing Alistair engaged in without cause. Unless a threat had been leveled against someone he cared for, felt responsible for. The memory of Alistair's old crew catching up to them in Koval floated to the surface of Langford's mind. How Alistair maintained his carefree snark, feigning disregard for Langford in an attempt to sway their focus, until they threatened to commit unspeakable acts of cruelty upon him.

Langford tightened his grip, the sensation of his missing finger a stark reminder of that day.

"What did Lyndurgh do?"

Gunther eyed Langford with false pity. It was a smug and superior form of sympathy. Langford had seen it a thousand times at court in Koval, well-wishers who were all too delighted at his mother's passing, offering barbed insults cloaked in comforting words.

"It matters naught. Lyndurgh's offense was his tongue, and Alistair was the one who escalated the situation."

Langford's hand found his hair again as the back of his neck burned. "It matters to me."

Gunther nodded, his smile sharpening as he ignored his words. "I'm sure it's no surprise to you that we cannot aid you in your plight, not since your partner chose to sever any trust we'd been building."

That was unsurprising, and yet a sick realization leadened Langford's limbs. Moirin had warned Langford of Gunther's manipulations. That he was never going to send his warriors. That he enjoyed offering help in the form of a trap. Had Lyndurgh been the snare?

Gunther continued, "The fact remains, Lyndurgh offered him one of two recompenses. Alistair chose his time in prison." He folded his hands in his lap. "If you've come to sway his sentence, my hands are tied. The ways of our clan are finite. Alistair chose his punishment. It's not my place to alter the law. I merely uphold it."

When it suits you.

"What was Lyndurgh's alternate choice?" And why hadn't Alistair taken it?

"He would drop his charge against Alistair if given one night with you."

All the air rushed out of Langford's lungs. *What the actual fuck?* His vision blurred as anger burned against the back of his neck. "And you see that as a viable option? Selling someone else's body? You would stand by that?"

Gunther scowled. "Alistair overstepped, you being the subject of their altercation. Lyndurgh chose a solution that would represent Alistair's contrition or a year of his life to reflect on his choices. It was within his right to extend these punishments."

"And if Alistair had accepted?" He would never. Not in a thousand lifetimes. But there was something fundamentally broken about this law. "I would be expected to honor a bargain struck utilizing my body without my consent?"

"You would have the choice to honor it or force Alistair to adhere to his sentence." Gunther bristled. "Your quarrel is not with me, but with your man who cannot control his impulses."

Langford laughed, a cold, brittle sound. The jarl had no idea how dangerous Alistair's impulses could be. They were fortunate it hadn't been a full moon, assuming that was still the pull of his shift.

"I find it only prudent to inform you, you are welcome to stay so long as you continue to earn your keep." Gunther leaned back in his throne, watching Langford for his reaction.

Langford nodded even as he bit his own tongue hard enough to bleed. Alistair was imprisoned for a year, Langford, was walking a fine line dangerously close to the likes of indentured servitude in Koval, and they would receive no aid even if they were released. He wouldn't have trusted a single one of Gunther's fighters anyway.

Langford turned and stalked out of the jarl's receiving hall.

He'd heard enough.

LANGFORD STORMED through the doorway to the guarded cells, nearly knocking Huvik off his feet.

Alistair's head snapped up, and he scrambled to the bars.

Huvik chased after him, adjusting his helm and tripping over his own spear. "I'm really not supposed to!"

There wasn't enough patience in Langford's entire lifetime for this.

He glared at the young warrior, hardly recognizing his own voice as he said, "Let me pass, or I'll tell Anya you switched patrol schedules to watch her during her shift."

Huvik's ears turned red, confirming Langford's suspicions. Huvik always watched Anya with a pitiful mix of admiration and desperation in his eyes, while she appeared ignorant of his devices.

Huvik bit his lip as he considered. "Don't tell anyone I let you in."

"They might mistake you for compassionate. Perish the thought." Langford shoved him out of the way, heading for outstretched hands he knew by heart. Alistair's reach had slipped between the bars, and as soon as Langford was close enough, he grabbed him by the back of the neck.

"There you are," Alistair breathed. His unkempt jawline was darkened by a shave missed, and dark purple circles had formed beneath his eyes. Their vibrant green had been dulled by inflamed blood vessels. But thankfully he was otherwise unharmed. "Langford, I'm so sorry."

Langford leaned into his touch, heart swelling at the contact. "Don't apologize yet. We need to get you out."

"Didn't you hear?" Alistair's signature smirk failed to reach his eyes. "I've been given time to examine my actions and really learn from them. They'll release me in a year."

A harsh punishment for a fight fueled by drink and an overfiring of the sympathetic nervous system. "Absolutely not. I'm getting you out, today. And we're leaving. Even if we have to swim for it."

Alistair's eyes softened as his thumb stroked the back of Langford's neck.

"I'll figure it out." Langford already knew there was nothing he could do to sway Gunther. Submitting to Lyndurgh was not an option. Alistair would kill the man immediately upon release, and then where would they be? Not that Langford could ever stomach that choice. And he had nothing of value to promise Gunther in exchange for mercy. It wasn't as if they had any lands or holdings. Langford had a fine collection of books, but somehow, he doubted that would mean much.

"Love," Alistair said softly. "There's no talking our way out of this one."

Deep down, Langford had already recognized this truth. They were at the edge of the world, away from their friends or any influence they could garner.

No, this would have to be a jailbreak. An extraction. A job.

"Forget words." Langford lifted his chin, determination burning away the last of his unease. "I think I'm ready for my first solo mission."

*　　＊　　*

SPEAKING in hidden truths was easier than Langford had anticipated. It helped when one had spent every day for the past five years with a person. Alistair could reference obscure memories and allude to his meaning without giving his thoughts shape. And Langford caught every word.

"The way you fuss and drag your feet always makes me wish I'd gotten you that cat. The one that always basked in the sun by that book vendor." Alistair grinned, reaching through the bars to grab Langford's knee. "Such a temperamental, spoiled little thing."

To Huvik, this must have sounded like random musings. But Langford knew better.

The DuPointe job was one of his favorites, simply because it granted him the chance to play the part of a disgruntled book collector, haggling the price of a poorly translated story he'd already known by heart anyway. The book didn't matter. The price didn't matter. The bloody cat didn't matter. No, the factor was him. *His* insistence. *His* displeasure with the price. It was enough to keep the vendor busy while Alistair snuck into the man's home across the lane and pilfered his wife's favored heirlooms. The ones he kept when he kicked her out of their home under the accusation of adultery, which she vehemently denied. Langford might have believed the vendor's claims had he not made a grand show of his preference for professional company each night in the tavern.

The heartbroken husband, indeed.

And when Alistair had reemerged, with more than what the bookseller's wife had hired them to retrieve, Langford had grumbled convincingly and paid full price for the ill-translation. A drop in the bucket compared to what they'd just stolen from the man.

The intent in this instance was clear: Make the jarl think Langford wasn't done with his plight to sway favor to Alistair's release. If he seemed too accepting of Alistair's fate, that would draw suspicion.

"My *fussiness*, as you so lovingly put it, is already an observable trait. One hardly deserving of a cat but noted just the same." Meaning, Langford had already begun that step in his meeting with the jarl. It would be no hardship to continue the ruse.

"Clever minx." Alistar traced Langford's knee through his trousers, and Langford bit back his flush of delight. "And you will maintain your schedule even while I'm here? It lends structure to a day, no?"

He meant guard rotation. Langford nodded his understanding. If Langford was to bring Alistair his set of lockpicks, he couldn't risk prying eyes. Certain guards were more focused than others. Including poor Huvik, who now seemed jumpy and on edge every time Langford stopped by to visit.

"A year isn't so long," Alistair continued. "It does make one reflect on the contrast between need and want. I doubt half of my belongings will matter much to me by the time I'm out. They could all sink to the deepest part of the ocean or tumble down a mountainside, and I'd hardly notice."

Langford rubbed his temples, leaning into the appearance of grief. Alistair was telling him to pack light and keep from being obvious about it by moving them out bit by bit to a hiding space so when he freed Alistair, they could head straight for the mountains.

If Ingemar wasn't docked, they'd have to keep moving, cover their tracks, and bide their time until she returned.

One thing at a time.

Alistair traced his finger up Langford's chest until he reached his chin. Gently tipping it up, he leaned closer, frowning when the bars prevented him from pressing his forehead to his. "I love you." His voice was rough. "Thank you for staying by my side when it would have been easier to cast me off."

Langford's throat squeezed, his heart thudding painfully against his chest. Alistair's words dug into him, carving an ache so keenly felt, it stole his breath.

He was telling him to leave him behind.

As if Langford would ever listen to such madness.

LANGFORD CREPT back toward the village. He had stashed all their belongings bit by bit up in the tree with the trunk shaped like a woman, which was Alistair's observation, not his, something having to do with two strategically placed knots. Now it was time to enact part two.

Huvik had been relieved of his shift, and Tyire was almost finished with his. It was late, a too-small moon high in the sky and a hush settling over the land. Lough was next, and he had an affinity for puff pastries, a fact Anya had been eager to share with Langford. It didn't take long for Langford to convince her to let him teach her the Ardenian way of dough folding. It was a simple thing to fold copious amounts of valerian into his pastry.

Langford snuck to the entrance of the holding cells, bribe in hand, lockpicks in pocket. All he needed was—

"Figured you'd show."

Langford cringed and turned to face none other than Lyndurgh. His arm was wrapped and supported in a shoulder sling, his eyes narrowed in malice. A deep gash beneath one of those eyes had been gouged down his cheek. This was the first time Langford had crossed paths with the warrior since Alistair's imprisonment. His presence and the threat of his lewd comments and suggestions should have sent terror running down Langford's spine. And yet, all he could think was how poor his woundcare was. It appeared on the verge of infection, red rimming the cut as it puffed out with the hint of pressure beneath the skin.

Langford adjusted his cloak, painfully aware that he hadn't brought a weapon. It was harder to stash on his person without notice. "Why are you here? Isn't it a conflict of interest to allow you to guard Alistair?"

"I could ask the same." Lyndurgh glance at the pastry. "You bring that for him or me?"

"Lough. It was a bargaining chip to allow me to speak to Alistair." Folding truth in with the lie. It was easier than outright lying.

"Is that right?" Lyndurgh's smile crept across his face. "You could sit a spell with me instead."

People like him were all the same. It wasn't about desire, it was possession. Power. Langford could likely be anyone, but the fact that Alistair reacted so strongly and *shamed* him, bruising the fragile ego of the man, that was the driving force behind his relentless taunting. Langford had seen it dozens of times amongst the nobles in Koval.

Didn't matter what continent one found themselves on, there would always be people who craved the rush of power and control.

"Not interested." Langford made to pass, but a large hand gripped him by his cloak, hauling him back.

"Now, now," Lyndurgh said, the stench of sour ale on his breath making Langford gag. "Don't be like that."

Langford pushed with all his strength, fighting to break free of his hold. But he might as well have been shoving a boulder for all it did.

"Don't tire yourself out." Lyndurgh's voice was harsh in his ear. "Not yet, anyway."

Langford aimed his knee for Lyndurgh's groin, earning a grunt of pain, and he twisted free of his greedy hands, stumbling back.

Lyndurgh gripped himself, a groan of pain leaving his lips. "You're gonna pay for that."

Langford dodged, running headlong into the holding cells. His foot snagged on the uneven floor, nearly dropping him to the ground. His stomach dipped, and he staggered with the effort of remaining upright. He was so close. *So bloody close.*

Alistair's cell came into view, and he was already gripping the bars, worry etching his brow. "What's going on?"

Langford's hands shook as he reached into his pocket, his blood rushing in his ears. Alistair's lockpick set caught on the frayed seams of his old trousers. "Come on. Come on," he muttered to himself, tears pricking his eyes.

"Give it here, love." Alistair's voice was jarringly calm against the tumultuous panic barraging Langford's nerves.

Langford reached out, placing the set in Alistair's outstretched hand. Their fingers brushed, lingering for the barest moment. Alistair would make quick work of it. He was always—

A large body barreled into him, knocking him sideways and rattling a few teeth as he hit the ground. The room spun, and nausea churned in Langford's belly as the wind was knocked from his lungs. Sharp pains speared through his chest. He struggled to breathe, hands flailing as Lyndurgh fought to grasp him by the wrists.

"Don't you fucking touch him!" Alistair's voice shook.

Langford blinked back tears as Lyndurgh's massive body crushed him into the floor. *What was taking Alistair so long?* He'd had locks picked in record time. Langford tilted his head, only to find Alistair's lockpick set on the floor, out of reach of his cell.

Lyndurgh spat at Alistair and turned his attention back to Langford. "You're not much of a fighter, are you, boy?" He laughed, leaning into him. Langford wheezed, and a sharp, blistering pain lit up his side.

His ribs. At least two of them had been forced out of place.

"You're killing him! Get the fuck off him!" The hysteria edging Alistair's voice was more terrifying than the pain—than the reality of being crushed by the massive warrior.

Langford opened his mouth to speak, only emitting a few pained garbles.

"Whasat?" Lyndurgh leered down at him. "Wish to reconsider my offer?" He shifted his weight just enough for air, glorious air, to fill Langford's chest once more.

Langford gasped as his breathing finally regained its tempo, but Lyndurgh squeezed his wrists tighter. The dots blurring his vision began to clear with each unsteady breath, but he was rapidly losing the battle of strength against the hulking warrior crushing him to the ground. He would not stop fighting until his muscles gave out. Until he could no longer move, he would claw and fight and Alistair had to get that door open—

Langford twisted beneath him, angling his knees to wedge beneath his chest. Lyndurgh laughed, a rough guttural sound of cruelty. As if this was proof of Langford submitting. As if he'd won. As if Langford couldn't possibly have any hope of escape.

If there was one thing Langford and Alistair had learned after years of misreading one another, it was how to communicate without words. Langford slid his gaze to Alistair's cell, where Alistair stood, baring his teeth and gripping the bars as if he could bend steel with anger alone. Out of reach. Too far to render any aid. Trapped.

Alistair's gaze burned brightly, finding Langford's eyes, and swearing his unspoken promise. A dip of his chin in the barest of nods. *Understood.*

Langford pushed his knees into Lyndurgh's chest as hard as he could, a sickening pop in his ligaments the least of his worries. Lyndurgh flew back, shock smoothing the malice from his features as his body shifted back from where Langford lied on the filthy ground.

Alistair's hands flashed through the bars, gripping Lyndurgh by the hair and throat. A metallic *thud* of his head hitting the bars rang out. Another. Another. The wet squelch of exposed skull resonated against those bars. Over. And over. The noises Alistair made were hardly human. Animalistic rage transformed his features. Lyndurgh went limp, only making little choking sounds in short jolts. But Alistair clawed his hands to the warrior's face, his fingers dipping into his eye-sockets and ripping.

Horrible. Brutal. Monstrous.

Langford wanted to weep. Not out of fear of Alistair's rage, but out of gut-churning guilt.

Alistair didn't deserve the violence of this moment. He'd done enough in this life to protect the ones he loved.

The light of a waxing gibbous moon spilled onto the floor, illuminating Lyndurgh's destroyed face. The blood pooling at the back of his head. Trails of connective tissue spilling from his eye-sockets.

Langford trembled. He reached over to grab the dropped

lockpicks, wincing at the pain in his ribs and knees. Slowly rising to his feet, he shuffled the remaining steps to Alistair's cell. Alistair's bloody hands found Langford's, achingly gentle as he removed the lockpicks from his grasp. When the hinges creaked, signaling Alistair's freedom, Langford couldn't find any words. The silence was deafening.

"Langford?" Alistair's voice was so unsure.

Langford lifted his head, meeting his eyes. Praying to the gods that Alistair could see he harbored no fear of him, no judgment. Alistair's face crumpled, pain finally etching itself in his features, and he bundled Langford in his arms, letting out a shaky breath. Langford leaned into him, pressing his face into his neck as he held him tight.

"I'm here," Alistair breathed into the crook of his shoulder. "I'll never let anything happen to you."

The last knot in Langford's chest loosened, because he knew this to be truth.

***

"BRENNER, NEED A WORD." Ingemar turned on her heel and marched out of their quarters, a silent command to follow.

Langford sighed and wiped at the ink dried between his fingers from extensive notetaking. He only had the equivalent to three moons' worth of Kenna's elixir left. And since one of the main components was the blood of the beast who'd attacked Alistair, this posed a grave problem for supply accumulation.

He ran a filthy hand into his hair, trying his best to keep his panic at bay. Once they ran out, what then? He hadn't thought that far in advance until he'd noticed the moon over the sea last eve. It would soon be full, which meant another cycle of keeping the beast firmly locked within Alistair. He had to find a way to replicate the elixir, but how?

He tripped over his feet in the narrow hall, rubbing his bleary eyes as he approached the stairs to the deck. Ingemar's private cabin was situated at the stern of the ship behind an ornate door. He and Alistair hadn't caused any issues this time around. He was prepared for Alistair's turn this time. What could she want?

Her door was left open letting warm light spill out. Langford pushed his way through, stretching his cramped neck from hours of poring over notes.

"I got an interesting missive," Ingemar said as she kicked her feet to rest upon her massive desk.

The stunning captain was coy as ever, and though they hadn't dined together, a sense of camaraderie permeated the room whenever she entered. Perhaps it was due to their history. Or how quickly she set sail no questions asked when he and Alistair rushed the ship after escaping Vallemer. It could be they'd settled into an easy trust, something she hadn't shared with Alistair in a long time. Maybe it was Langford's unfiltered honesty when she asked what had happened to the princess. Or maybe it was that she'd been successful at restocking her reserves with her favored wine. Whatever the cause, it made a previously sharp sensation in Langford's chest soften.

"Oh?" He claimed the chair opposite her. "And why do I care?"

Ingemar grinned. "It was addressed to you."

What had he just been thinking about trust?

Langford wet his lips as he prepared his most measured voice. "You read a message intended for me prior to my knowledge of it?" He leaned back, massaging his temples. "I don't suppose I might have the courtesy of an explanation alongside my private letter?"

Ingemar laughed and reached into her desk. "You're more fun than Alistair. So polite even whilst you imagine strangling me."

"Don't tempt me," Langford grumbled, almost amused. Almost.

She tossed a scroll, wax seal broken, naturally, in his direction. "I read everything that travels through my hands. Not because I don't trust you, but because I'll never be blindly complicit to anyone ever again."

Heavy implication weighed down her words, and Langford almost asked for the story behind it.

"But!" Ingemar's grin had returned, and she topped her wavy curtain of dark hair with her tricorn captain's hat, slightly askew, and winked at him. "This message, I approve of." She lowered her feet to the floor, and leaned across her desk. "You have good news for a change."

Langford unrolled the parchment, heart hammering in his chest. He scanned the scrawled penmanship, the words hastily scratched into being. And when his eyes caught on the name *Kyall*, a smile broke across his face.

Moirin's name and insignia concluded the message.

Ingemar was right about one thing. This was *very* good news.

CHAPTER FIFTY-FOUR

GAVRIEL

G avriel stood before the great double doors to the Guild of Crows. His home for over twenty years. It was strange coming back here, somehow the tower seemed smaller.

"Must we knock or…" Ferryn glanced between Gavriel and Hazel. "Are we sneaking in? What's the plan?"

There was no point in drawing it out with subterfuge. Gavriel was here, before the ancient fortress, to address the remaining masters. There would be no question of sneaking. No duplicity involved. He would enter the unyielding tower of stone and claim the title he'd earned when Hamlin forced his hand in the arena.

"There's no use in sneaking," Hazel said, mirroring Gavriel's thoughts and staring up at the tower. Was she remembering the same moment as he? Or was another memory snaking through her mind?

"They already know we're here. Likely knew the moment we hit The Wastes," Gavriel said. The Guild trained their assassins to remain undetected and vigil when the occasion called for it. And three uninvited guests in the aftermath of Master Hamlin's death were occasion enough to warrant their special attention.

With a deep breath, Gavriel pushed the doors open.

The entryway was silent—dark save for the flickering torches along the stone walls. The masonry was uneven, crumbling in weak spots. Gavriel frowned. That was new. It wasn't as if the fortress had been attacked or seen any sort of battle. The ballista they kept in the assault tower had never been loaded in all his time at the Guild.

So why was the fortress in such a state?

The winding staircase led to the battlements, and across the way sat the upper barracks, a tempting route to take since it meant paying a visit to Hamlin's private office, but Gavriel was short on time. Masters Derwin and Eldridge had to have already been alerted of his presence.

He followed the long corridor to the receiving hall. He'd rather put on a spectacle than be dragged to the dungeons for a quiet and private death.

He'd earned his freedom, his title, built upon the blood of his master. They could not deny him.

The receiving hall was hardly grand. There was no room for vanity in the guild. A large stone room, a sparring circle painted upon the floor, and the raised dais, seating three Master Assassins.

Two of the chairs were filled, Masters Derwin and Eldridge calmly awaited his approach, while Master Hamlin's chair stood empty. As it had since that day in the arena.

"Gavriel Pearson," Eldridge's voice, sharp with disdain, rang out. Where Hamlin was a master of technique, of historical weaponry and technical skill, Eldridge was a master of poisons. Both poisonous words and substances, he excelled at the art of toxic pursuit. There were many ways to poison a man, whether it be his body or his mind, and Eldridge was a most venomous snake. His famed poisonous blades were said to be hidden all over his person, but it was his chained flail, spikes coated in a noxious substance, that he always had visible at his side. A silent threat. His long gray hair hung over his shoulders, a stark contrast against the black of his robes. Two dark eyes narrowed at Gavriel's approach, and the poisons master wrinkled his angular nose, glaring down at him with swift familiarity and disgust. "You've come to face your reckoning."

"Not exactly." Gavriel did not permit his steps to falter, Hazel and Ferryn at his flank. "I'm here to claim my title."

"Oh?" Eldridge raised a graying brow, shooting Derwin a smirk that creased his weathered face. "And what title might that be? Father Slayer? Bastard born? Walking corpse? You have returned to face your death for the crimes written against your name."

"I have returned to claim my place as Master Assassin."

The two masters fell silent, a weighty pause filling the room. Before their laughter echoed against the stone.

"Impossible!" Derwin laughed heartily, leaning over his great belly with mirth. His red beard was streaked with gray, his hair also hinting at his age. Derwin was the deadliest axe wielder Gavriel had ever seen. Even after outdrinking assassins in their prime, he could take a man down with three swings. Sometimes he even employed dual axes, one in each hand, and struck with such force it was said to vibrate the very earth. He was a master of power and might. Of all the masters at the Guild, Derwin seemed the warmest. His laugh was boisterous, even his joy revealing the strength of his force. But his temper was a wicked beast.

"You waste our time with such stories of grandeur." Eldridge sneered while Derwin wiped the corners of his eyes. "There can only be three masters, and you are not one of them."

Gavriel bit back his anger that they claimed not to know the circumstances of Hamlin's death. He'd assumed they would have called him a liar, but to feign complete ignorance as to why he was here?

Unless Yuri never sent word.

"I am."

Ferryn shifted, and Hazel glanced around.

Eldridge's eyes flashed. "On what grounds? Enlighten me, Pearson, what gives you the right to claim this title?"

Gavriel gathered his calm, willing his racing heartbeat to slow. *Patience. Unyielding patience.* "Master Hamlin fell to my sword in the sands of the Western Desolates arena, under the eye of the Den of Lions master, Yuri." Gavriel had trusted the rival guild master, on the grounds that Hamlin trusted him. Not enough to leave his drinks unattended or ever fully turn his back, but enough for limited dealings with the man. Gavriel had been twelve the first time Hamlin brought him on an extraction job, trading prisoners with Yuri. The Den of Lions had a particular way of recruiting their assassins— many had been stolen from neighboring countries, imprisoned, and sold on the indentured market. Yuri took his pick, offering them a better life than anything Koval would offer them, and recruited them for the guild. When he came across a lost cause, he'd offer them to Hamlin before disposing of them, a way to manipulate a return on investment.

Because Hamlin couldn't resist adopting the strays.

Gavriel never suspected Yuri to be the snake he was, but he should have. He should have known he'd leverage Gavriel's position to lure Hamlin to the arena.

Hamlin's sacrifice... it was no victory of Gavriel's. But he wouldn't let these bastards prevent him from claiming the gift Hamlin gave him. "By way of our code, Hamlin's seat is mine."

Derwin's eyed widened, shock splashing across his features.

Eldridge's face grew red. "You lie," he hissed.

"He speaks true." Hazel stepped forward. "I was there. I saw Master Hamlin fall. Gavriel's blade took his life, and by rights, he is the new Guild Master."

"Another deceitful serpent," Eldridge spat. "You are complicit to his crimes and will face the same punishment as he. I don't trust either of you to stay put. We'll deal with this now." He stood, his chained weapon dragging on the ground beside him.

"This is madness." Gavriel eyed the master's blade. He was known to coat its edge with Waking Nightmare, so his cuts needn't be fatal nor deep. So long as he met blood, his opponents met their ends. "I swear on my mother's grave, on the death of my father by my hands, I killed Hamlin. I bled the life from this throat and bore witness as his blood painted the sands!" He should have known they'd avoid a true trial. They wanted him dealt with quickly and quietly. But he would not go quietly. "I am the third master."

Derwin shook his head, running a hand over his beard. "How can that be true, when Hamlin yet lives."

Had they not thought to question his former master's absence? Gavriel clenched his hands into fists. He had killed him. He *had*. There was no mistaking. And here they sat, ignorant to Hamlin's demise.

They were useless. Utterly useless. They'd sat on their asses for too long and grown lazy in their positions. Perhaps a complete shift in power was necessary.

The creak of the hall doors cut through his thoughts. Slow measured steps echoed through the silent hall. He turned—

Gavriel's knees threatened to buckle, and his stomach sank like a stone. It wasn't possible. It wasn't possible. No one had stopped him. No one had saved him. Hamlin's corpse had grown cold in the bloodied sands of the arena, and *it was not possible*.

Hamlin calmly approached, his gray hair tied back, his hands tucked behind his back. He stopped before Gavriel, giving him a wink.

"What's the matter?" The familiar voice of his mentor knocked the wind out of him. "You look as if you've seen a ghost."

"Your favored pupil was just informing us that he killed you." Eldridge smoothed a hand down his robes, preening with that smug superiority he always wore. "And he's earned your title."

"Is that so?" Hamlin's blue eyes crinkled. "How unfortunate for me." He made a show of inspecting himself. "Everything appears in order. A mistake, perhaps?"

Gavriel's muscles locked in place. He had seen him die. *He had.* Gavriel had fallen to his knees and watched the life leave his former master's body. Grieved yet another soul lost to the void by his own hand. Hamlin had died. He'd died. How was he here?

Death wasn't truly the end, was it? All Gavriel's life, the inevitability of the end was his life's duty. He was the final mark on the last page of a man's life. The farewell. The elegy. And yet everything in the last year proved how wrong he was in that philosophy.

"How…"

"Whatever do you mean?" Hamlin tilted his head in mock confusion. "The stress of life on the road has gotten to you, and your memory has failed."

"No!" Hazel cried out. "No. You died. I saw you! I watched you die. You do not get to treat us like we imagined it. Explain yourself!"

Gavriel shushed her, barring her with his arm as she lunged for their former master. Any of them—Eldridge, Derwin, Hamlin—were far more dangerous than any assassin of their age. These masters had trained them. Knew all their weaknesses and how to exploit them. They would get their answers but not by antagonizing them.

"When did Hamlin arrive?" Ferryn's voice broke through.

"Who in the blazes is this?" Derwin gestured with a wave of his hand. "You are not a crow."

"Thank the pits for that." Ferryn scoffed. "But my question remains. This Hamlin fellow. When did he arrive? I assume he disappeared for an extended journey. Perhaps in pursuit of someone?"

Hamlin snarled, his eyes flashing. "We needn't entertain this preposterous line of questioning." He lunged for Ferryn, and Gavriel shifted to block his former master. Something in his eyes… they were his, but they weren't quite right. It was in the way they caught the light, almost reflecting it back.

"Let him speak. If we're all to die for my *failing memory*, the least you could do is let the man talk." Gavriel nodded to Ferryn, hoping he got the hint. *Speak wisely.*

"Your… Graces," Ferryn sketched a bow, and Gavriel bit back a groan of frustration. "I merely aim to understand the confusion. Your wit and intellect are far beyond a man as simple as I. But did your third master take a trip?"

"He did…" Derwin glanced around uneasily.

"And did he return around say"—Ferryn counted on his fingers—"two months ago?"

Eldridge, relaxed the hold on his chain, casting a furtive glance in Hamlin's direction. "That's right."

Ferryn's face lit up. "And did his return make things… better? Did little conveniences start popping up? Almost as if silent wishes were being granted?" He waved his hands, staring up at the ceiling. "I don't know. A lost supply wagon showing up on your doorstep with the exact vintage of wine you'd just been thinking about? Or extremely high paying marks falling into your laps after an extended dry spell?"

Where was he going with this?

Derwin's mouth fell open, and Eldridge narrowed his eyes. "You've been spying on us."

"Ah. Just as I suspected." Ferryn ignored Eldridge's remark and swept his hands over his tunic as if dusting himself off before squaring his shoulders. "That's not your Guild Master." His nose curled in disgust as he examined Hamlin. "That's a desire demon."

"A what?" Derwin's voice echoed, harsh and sharp, through the hall.

"*A desire demon.*" Ferryn spoke as if educating a child. "It explains everything. See, two months ago, the veil fell, allowing all sorts of monsters and beasties a foothold in your world. Desire demons are cunning little things. They take the form of whatever will fool their victims. Be it, a beautiful woman, beautiful man, I once knew a desire demon take the shape of a cake. Figure that one out. Desire takes many forms, not merely the fun ones. Sometimes desire is a wish to rewrite a choice once made. It seems in this instance, your demon has borrowed the face of a trusted colleague. They feed off energy, reveling in the chaos they spin. The more time you spend with them, the more you let them in, the stronger their foothold in your mind." Ferryn winced. "Now it does bear questioning, have you had any mishaps with new recruits? Unexplained deaths, illnesses, disappearances, unlikely accidents?"

Derwin's horrified expression confirmed Ferryn's questions and formed a weight in Gavriel's stomach.

So. This demon wore the face of his master, plagued the halls of the Guild of Crows, and murdered new recruits?

Gavriel thumbed his daggers, searching his memory for Kenna's bestiary. Had she ever written of desire demons?

Shit. She had not.

Hopefully they fell to steel.

"Right," Ferryn continued. "Well, this all tracks. So... there you have it! Not a ghost. Not a lie on Gavriel's part. Just good old fashioned illusion magic."

"You cannot," Hamlin's voice called out, "expect us to buy this horseshit." He edged toward the dais, addressing the other masters. "Clearly they've been spying on us and collecting enough information to spin this outlandish story." He turned back. "But we are not the fools you took us for."

Derwin still appeared unconvinced, but Eldridge wore his expression of accusation like a favored cloak. "More lies?"

"I really can't with you people." Ferryn sighed, placing his hands on his hips. "We'll just have to prove it, won't we?" He turned to Gavriel. "Ask him a question. Wearing Hamlin's face does not equate to acquiring his memories. Go on."

Gavriel searched his mind for something the other masters would know and confirm. "What instrument did you force me to play."

Hamlin scoffed. "The fiddle. Did you keep up with it, or have you lost your discipline?"

Shit. Hamlin had a fiddle in his private study. Gavriel should have known better than to ask such an easy question.

"Ask another," Ferryn said.

"Who was my first kill?"

Hamlin smirked. "That's an easy one. Father Slayer."

Of course, that nickname followed Gavriel, and even an imposter would have heard it had his name ever come up.

"I've had enough of this." Eldridge descended the steps. "No more of this farce."

"Wait!" Gavriel held up a hand. "One more. Please."

Eldridge stilled, waving Gavriel to get on with it.

Gavriel swallowed. He couldn't fuck this one up. He had to select a question Derwin and Eldridge knew the answer to, but something that wouldn't have come up in the two months this demon had worn Hamlin's face.

"What was my mother's name?"

Hamlin's smile faded, his brow furrowing.

He had him. All the masters knew his mother's name. It was even rumored they'd visited her in… that place. Promising to aid Gavriel's training in exchange for a free night. Hamlin never partook, but he knew her name. He knew it and spoke it every time Gavriel hid in the corner of his study trying not to cry as a scared little boy. He spoke her name, because Gavriel needed to hear it. He needed to remember he had a life outside these walls. Memories worth holding on to, and a future worth fighting for.

Sabina. His mother's name was Sabina, and she didn't deserve the death fate had forced upon her. She didn't deserve to die in that shit-hole, and she didn't deserve to have the disappointment of him as a son.

"Her name." Gavriel pulled the dagger from his belt. "Say it."

Hamlin shook his head, turning to the other masters. "This is ridiculous."

"You know her name, Hamlin," Derwin said. "Just say it."

Hamlin studied each of their faces, his laugh tight and restrained.

"Well," he said. "This was fun while it lasted."

A flash of blinding light, and a deafening *boom* greater than thunder shook the room. Where Hamlin once stood, a monster had taken his place. Its likeness was a woman with gray skin, black horns curling from her head. Her eyes kept switching colors. Black to gold to gray to green to blue. Her teeth were feline, long fangs jutting from both the top and bottom. She hissed, a forked tongue snaking between her teeth.

She lunged, appearing before Derwin. Her shape shifted, horns melting into long dark hair and a pair of fighting leathers sprouting over her skin.

"Tyanna?" he whispered, his axe lowering.

She looked like the woman in the painted portrait above Derwin's desk. The one he always stared at when he'd had the right combination of mead and despair. When Gavriel was a new recruit, he'd learned the tradition of trying to guess the identity of the woman in the portrait.

"It's me, darling." She ran a hand down his face, and his eyes rolled back. Her mouth descended upon the aging master's in a forceful kiss.

"Don't listen to her!" Eldridge whipped his chain toward her, and without breaking the kiss, she caught it. When she turned, Derwin collapsed on the floor, convulsing.

"Oh, I almost forgot! It's important you don't let the desire demon kiss you," Ferryn said.

Hazel whipped out her daggers. "What's happening to him?"

"I'm a Reaper, not a healer. But I'm guessing she just stole enough of his life that his body is shutting down."

The desire demon shifted, taking the form of a young man with long dark hair, the side of his scalp shaved. Eldridge stumbled back. The man swept his hands out in front of him.

"Aren't you happy to see me, Father?"

"You... you are not Kimo. Kimo died."

"Because you left him to rot." The desire demon wearing his son's face laughed, stepping closer. "You imagine his face every day. His memory perfectly preserved in the corner of your thoughts. But you don't wish to think of the day you found him, do you? How Summoner's Dust eats the body from the inside out. He begged you for help, and you turned your back on him."

Summoner's Dust was a low-grade poison that caused hallucinations in its victims. Some people even used it recreationally, for its mild flood of joy in small doses. Highly addictive. Prolonged use decayed the body. Eldridge's son had died a slow and agonizing death from the poison, and Eldridge had always blamed himself. A fact Gavriel only learned when he was hiding in Hamlin's office one night and Eldridge came to lament on the anniversary of his son's death.

Gavriel lunged, tackling the demon to the floor before it could grab Eldridge in his stunned stupor. Gavriel sliced into its flesh, a scream erupting from its mouth.

"Gavriel, stop! It hurts!" Lark's voice echoed back. And Gavriel stilled. Beneath him, the demon shifted, searching for her likeness.

"Do it, Gavriel!" Ferryn shouted. "Do it now!"

Lark's golden eyes stared up at him, filled with tears. "Why do you hurt me?" Her voice broke, and Gavriel's muscles locked up.

It wasn't her. He'd watched the demon shift and reform into different faces. But how did it know what she looked like? What she sounded like?

Lark's face smirked up at him, her hands running up his forearms, trailing to his wrists. "You sent her off alone. Did you really think one of us wouldn't find her? That we weren't looking for a soul as sweet and... warm as hers?"

Gavriel's blood thundered in his ears, tremors shaking his hands. What if they had captured her? What if they'd dragged her to the Netherworld? Tortured her again? Why had he sent her away? He should have listened. She told him it was a mistake. She told him not to abandon her. She told him—

"Gavriel, now!"

Ferryn's voice broke him out of his paralysis, and he plunged the blade of his dirk deep into her throat. Gold eyes widened in pain, blood spurting from her mouth. Those eyes shifted. Brown. Black. Green. Blue. A thousand faces flashing beneath him before the demon landed on its own and fell still.

Gavriel stood on shaky feet, turning back to the dais. Eldridge kneeled over Derwin, inspecting him. Hazel ran over to offer assistance. But the force of Ferryn's stare pulled him from the sight. The former Reaper stood, hands clenched into fists, rage contorting his features.

"You utter fool," Ferryn spat. "Have you any idea what Lark would have done to me had you fallen? And to something as base as a desire demon?" He was shaking. "After everything she's suffered, and I promised—I *swore*—I'd bring you back alive. And you just—just—"

Gavriel reached out, gripping Ferryn's shoulder. "Thank you," he said. "Thank you, brother."

Shock splashed across Ferryn's face, chasing away any lingering anger.

Derwin finally sat up with a grunt, holding his hand over his heart.

The strong bastard was still alive, and Gavriel almost laughed in his relief. Eldridge glanced up at Gavriel, offering a nod.

It was enough. It was everything.

As Master Assassin, Gavriel had the authority to command the assassins to abandon their marks and fight against Nereida's army. And after this altercation with a demon, the other masters would back him on this.

He'd gotten Lark her fighters.

CHAPTER FIFTY-FIVE

KENNA

"*We* need to talk."

Ruva glanced up from her tome, the dissertation of cross-species hybrids open beside her. Her familiar scrawl of tidy notes beside her mug of tea. She lowered her quill with a smirk. "That sounds ominous."

Craghill's library was once one of Kenna's beloved spots. Not for the sake of sitting by the rounded picture window, peering out at the frost-covered ground. Not even for the shelves of books carved into the very walls. Nor being surrounded by knowledge, the history of Hunters, beasties, and demons.

No, it was the rafters where she used to hang upside-down until all the blood traveled down to her face and her head threatened to explode. She did her best thinking that way. Would Ruva mind if she climbed up there for this conversation?

Kenna sighed and dropped in the seat across from Ruva. A far more practical position. "You almost kissed me."

Ruva laughed, tossing her black hair over her shoulder. Kenna hated that it made her think of the elderberries Nahnah used to make into tea whenever Kenna had a cold. "We both know *almost* only counts in horseshoe and alchemical combustion bombs."

Kenna tightened her fists, bracing herself against the shite conversation she was about to have. It was worth it—of course, it was. She never wished to see that expression of hurt and betrayal cross Daciana's face. Not only would Kenna never so much as glance at another woman that way again, but Dac sure as shit didn't deserve even a whisper of disloyalty. So, if losing Ruva's friendship was the path to keeping Daciana assured of her feelings... well, then that was on Ruva.

"I love Daciana."

Ruva still wore that infuriating smirk, crossing her arms and nodding. "Mmhmm. The wolf who betrayed you and let you wander the world alone and lovesick for the better part of ten years." She shrugged. "Sounds like a healthy relationship."

"I told you things in confidence," Kenna hissed. "And you twist my words. Why? Why now?"

Ruva turned her attention to the window, refusing to look at her. "Why did you even come back? It sure as shit wasn't for me. It wasn't to stay either. I can feel it. In every laugh. In every meal we share. In every word you speak." She frowned. "And do not speak. You're here to say goodbye."

Kenna drummed her fingers on the table and bounced her knees beneath it. Ruva wasn't wrong. From the moment Kenna set foot on this island, she knew what this trip was. Yes, of course, they were protecting Aislinn. Obviously. But it was a chance to reconnect with Daciana, to show her the roots her Nahnah had instilled in her. It wasn't to sway her to stay, the way Dac assumed she'd meant, and it wasn't because she was achingly homesick.

This was a chance for Daciana to get to know a piece of Kenna's history. One that wasn't marred by bloodshed. But that's all it was. History. History best left in the past.

"I'm here because my request for hunters' aid has been ignored. We have an immediate threat we're facing. And we cannot afford for the bulk of our hunters to hide here and pretend it doesn't affect them. We have a duty—"

"You think I don't know that?" Ruva slammed her hand down on the table, jostling her tea. "We've lost so many, *so many*, in our travels. When Elder Muirgel decided to temporarily suspend our voyages in favor of rebuilding our numbers, I was relieved." She slid her hand across the table, threading her fingers with Kenna's. "You were supposed to come home. Most of us did. But not you—"

"I was not raised to retreat with my tail tucked between my legs."

"Is that what you think we did?" Ruva's eyes glimmered. "Did losing Nahnah mean nothing to you? She died, and not so you can traipse about the continent searching for the monster who will finally send you to her."

Kenna ripped her hand away as if it burned. "Don't speak of her. Don't speak of things you do not know. I am not the only hunter who sees it fit to continue our cause, even in the face of hardships."

"Hardships?" Ruva laughed humorlessly. "Is that what you call the death of your entire family?"

Unfair.

Ruva lived this sheltered life, protected by a community of hunters and watchers. Only venturing out to fight monsters in a supervised, educational setting. That was not the way of a hunter.

"You've lived too long in this world of theory." Kenna shoved Ruva's tome. "The real monsters, they don't care that you're tired or wish to switch your schedule to accommodate a day of rest. They sure as shit don't care when you've lost everything to your name, surviving each day with the unyielding thought that *there has to be more. The sun must rise again.* No, there is no reprieve. There is no planning. And there are people out there"—Kenna pointed out the window— "who haven't got a fucking clue how to defend themselves against these monsters. We are duty-bound to protect them."

"Are we duty-bound to die for them?" Ruva's eyes glimmered, red blooming high on her cheeks.

"If it comes to that, yes."

And that was the crux of their conflicting ideologies as hunters. Nahnah had taught Kenna in the old ways of the hunter. Elder Muirgel perpetuated a new way, one that left room for cowardice.

"I did not come here to argue with you over this." Kenna's words were softer now. "I came to tell you I've only ever loved you as a sister. And that is how I will always see you."

Ruva wiped her nose, offering a weak laugh. "Because of the wolf."

"No." Kenna's tone hardened. Ruva's refusal to call Daciana by her name was really quite irksome. "*Daciana* is the reason I will never even think to touch another again. But were she gone, I still would only see you as sister."

"Right, well." Ruva smiled, and it was a weak and brittle thing. "Can't blame a girl for trying." She ran her finger along the page of her forgotten tome, her mouth quirking this way and that, as if practicing the words she spoke next. "I only wanted to make sure the wolf—Daciana—was worthy of you. Willing to fight for you and all."

Kenna laughed far too loudly in the quiet library. It was absurd, the way such a passing remark still stung. They had crossed that bridge, built that foundation or whatever phrase fit best, hadn't they? The notion of Daciana giving up on her, on them, was a healed wound, but the scar was annoyingly sensitive.

Maybe 'healed' was a touch premature.

Kenna pushed the thought away. "Daciana would destroy the world if it meant keeping me safe." And despite any lingering hurt, any unresolved pain that would only heal with time, Kenna felt the truth in those words. For better or worse, it was the way of things where Daciana was concerned. "And just because you can't goad her into a reaction, doesn't mean she didn't make her claim on me perfectly clear." Kenna grinned remembering just how *thorough* Dac was in that regard.

The memory alone was enough to give Kenna that jittery feeling where her leathers suddenly were too restrictive. She bounced her knee and silently calculated the likelihood of stealing a private moment, or hour, with Dac after this. Kenna had made up her mind to speak with Elder Muirgel today, but if she cut down the vendor lane to where Dac was helping Korik with his roof, she could tell him his wife needed him down by the quarry—

Ruva ran a hand through her hair, the movement interrupting

Kenna's thoughts. She'd nearly forgotten she was sitting across from her, having this painfully vulnerable conversation.

Kenna shifted in her seat, guilt forming a slippery feeling in her gut. "She loves me better than anyone else could. And I, her."

Ruva's eyes glimmered, and her chin gave the slightest tremble. "That's all I want in the person lucky enough to hold your heart."

Kenna's chest grew tight. Though it was true, she'd never harbored feelings other than familial for Ruva, she hated hurting her this way.

"Besides," Ruva continued, "I've decided my next conquest will be shaped like a virile goddess." She poked Kenna in the chest, a silent taunt at her lack of *womanly assets.*

Daciana sure as shit didn't mind. Kenna's mouth curved at the thought. But she recognized a diffusion of discomfort. Blazes, she was practically fluent in diffusion and evasion. If Ruva was willing to put this behind them and return to their good-natured jesting, who was she to deny them that comfort?

"Come with us to Ardenas. They boast many a buxom woman, unattached, not blood-related, or otherwise." In Craghill, it was nearly impossible to find someone who hadn't married into your family, didn't share a common ancestor, or hadn't already pursued a failed romantic entanglement with you or someone close to you. Tiny pond. Not enough fish. Anquan was a vast enough island of a country, with each town spaced enough to lend the feeling of adventure when traveling. But years had a way of shrinking the corners of the world.

"I'll think about it." Ruva closed her book. "What are your plans for the rest of the day?"

It was as close to a resolution as they were going to get, and when Ruva kicked Kenna under the table, her easy smile returning to banish the maudlin mood, Kenna felt her own ease loosen her shoulders.

Kenna stretched, exaggerating the motion. "Now that this uncomfortable conversation is concluded, I figured I'd have another."

"Elder Muirgel?" Ruva's brows lifted. "Good luck. She's in a right mood today. Someone ate the last of the honey cakes, and we aren't due for another shipment of her favored almond flour for at least a week."

"Someone... hmm?"

Ruva grinned, some of her light returning to her face. "I admit nothing."

Was that... sugared honey in the corner of her mouth?

STANDING before Elder Muirgel's home, Kenna felt small. Obnoxiously so. Like she'd just been caught stealing the blackberries from her bush, and Nahnah was forcing her to apologize in person.

That had only happened three times.

Elder Muirgel's home was one of the permanent structures in Craghill. While Nahnah preferred the caravan, for ease of travel, Muirgel always kept her timber-framed structure. The windows were clouded with frost, and it was too early for the lantern above her door to be lit. The roof had a slant to allow snow to easily skid to the ground, and a fresh dusting coated the stack of wooden crates by the door.

With a deep breath, Kenna knocked.

The door opened before she'd even finished knocking, Muirgel's face appeared, sporting a single lens eyeglass. Her white hair hung in two thick braids over her shoulders, woven fabrics of red and brown peeking between the plaits. It was a symbol of wisdom and respect, weaving cloth into one's hair. It was a sign of strength and courage and resilience. A practice long held by Kenna's people.

In the study of slaying monsters, Hunters found conduits of their own strength by handing down threads and fabrics worn by their ancestors. Kenna's nahnah had made her a quilt of all the fabrics of their ancestors, using the same threads from her childhood keepsake to fashion her red cloak.

Wearing that cloak, even if it was bright enough to call attention to her presence, a spot of blood against white snow, always made Kenna... fearless.

She should have worn it today.

"Kenna." Elder Muirgel's voice was a blanket of comfort. "What can I do for you?"

"Am I interrupting anything? It's more of a, *let me in and feed me while I talk,* sort of situation." Talking without saying anything was easy. It was when it came time to cut to the quick and delve into the heart of the matter that made Kenna's palms sweat.

Muirgel held up a book, her thumb keeping it open to her current page. A crudely drawn man stood, his chest bare while he hiked up the skirt of a curvy woman in his arms. "A bit of light reading."

"They come with pictures now?"

Anquan was home to one of the greatest writers. Literature bearing no name. Kenna had spent most of her life trying to sort out who the author was, since they never revealed their name. Only handwrote their tales, bound them in wood and leather, and left them in odd places. It was one of the greatest mysteries of her homeland and made for interesting theories when the drinks were flowing.

"They do now." Muirgel examined the page with great interest.

Kenna would have to see about borrowing one of these for Langford.

"You mentioned food. Are you hungry, child?"

No. But Kenna needed something to do with her hands while she essentially accused Elder Muirgel of ignoring the threat in Ardenas.

Kenna wiped her hands against her trousers.

Elder Muirgel was so old, no one in town remembered a time she wasn't the elder. With the title came responsibility. Her word wasn't law, but people respected the piss out of it as if it were. The only person with the stones to challenger her was..

Well...

"You remind me so much of Kiannor," Muirgel said, ushering her in. "That same glint of mischief and bottomless pit of a stomach."

Kenna's nahnah was a bit of a legend here. Kenna had grown up hearing stories of her, like she was this larger-than-life hero. Nahnah had summoned her first demon to slay by age ten, and by the time she'd had her first child and second husband, she was just as respected as the late Elder Nuala, Muirgel's predecessor. Kenna was always so damn proud to have such a strong, fierce woman as her namesake. And she'd spent a lifetime trying to live up to the honor.

"You know Nahnah, never met an adventure too large or plate too full."

Muirgel smiled, gesturing to the seat at the table where a stack of unnamed books sat tall and precarious. "Perhaps you'll pick one for your journey home."

"Aren't I home now?" Kenna slid a dark-green book in front of her, flipping to find how graphic these drawings were. Oh. Quite graphic. *Better put that in the keep pile.*

Muirgel placed a plate with frosted cinnamon rolls in front of her. "This hasn't been your home for a long time, but you knew that already."

Kenna's stomach growled. She swiped the roll with the most frosting and took a large bite, chewing slowly. "You never answered my letters." It was a statement of fact and an unspoken accusation. Kenna hadn't really been wanted back.

"My lack of response was my answer."

Kenna wasn't hungry. The roll, though deliciously decadent, a thick flavor of cinnamon and cardamom, all topped with a coating of vanilla, sat in her belly like she'd swallowed a rock. "People need us."

"Kiannor thought so, too." Muirgel nodded solemnly. "And how did that turn out for her?"

The urge to chuck the frosted roll at the wall came over her so suddenly. With great difficulty, Kenna lowered it back to the plate. "She died refusing to abandon me." Dac's father had come to their campsite, demanding Kenna. It was she they sought. No one else. They had even offered Nahnah freedom in exchange for the one their ascending wolf was meant to hunt.

Dac.

Kenna still didn't know if all that was bullshit or not. If Daciana's father really sensed that the hunt had chosen Kenna, or if he'd found out about her and Daciana and found an easy solution to dispose of her. All she knew, was Nahnah's death was her fault. They were supposed to leave the day before, but Kenna begged for delay to give Daciana a chance to tie up her loose ends before running away with them. Dac even told her to depart without her, said she'd catch up. But the truth of it all was that Kenna was afraid Dac would change her mind.

So, they'd stayed. For her selfishness. For her weakness. And in the darkest moments of the longest nights, Kenna wrestled with that choice.

Blazes. She still struggled with it. She could never regret Daciana, but could things have turned out differently without sacrifice?

"I was the one who fucked up. You want to know how it turned out for her? Pretty shitty, being roasted alive like the fucking main course of a feast. But she died with her principles intact." Kenna crossed her arms, tucking her shaking hands against her body. "If you died today, could you say the same?"

Muirgel's eyes flashed, anger stealing their pitying expression. "I understand your grief, child. But it doesn't give you leave to disrespect with impunity. Rise above your pain, as we all have, and acknowledge the truth you are so quick to dismiss. I am the reason our hunters' numbers have not dwindled into extinction. Your nahnah was brave, there is no disputing that. But when your parents died, when her *son died*, she had the chance to raise you right. To keep you from harm instead of teaching you to run into fire. Her failing does not reflect—"

"She didn't fail at anything!" Anger burned bright and hot beneath Kenna's skin. "The only failure here is you. Without Nahnah to challenge you, you've become lazy and cowardly. What would she say if she were here right now? What would she think of what you've let us become? A few of us nomads remain, traveling the continents to carry on our legacy, our duty to protect people from monsters while you hide the rest away like rats on a sinking ship!"

Muirgel's nostrils flared, her stare dangerously dark. "Well," she said, "we'll never know what she'd say, because she's the one who's dead."

Never in all of Kenna's life had she ever been so... disappointed. And worst of it is, she hadn't expected any different. Muirgel was the same coward she'd always been. A few fond memories weren't enough to change her opinion of the old fool. "I take it you won't lift a finger to help us."

"Stay here if you wish. Bring all you've grown to love and care for. They will all be welcomed with open arms." Muirgel shook her head. "But no, we will not sacrifice what's left of us chasing your cause."

Kenna snatched the green book. She was taking it to Langford, dammit, and the old crone could just deal with it. With the back of her hand, she slapped the rest of the books, and they tumbled, spilling across the table in a jumbled heap.

Childish? Perhaps. But Kenna stomped her way out of there like the child she was.

CHAPTER FIFTY-SIX

LARK

$\mathcal{I}$t was a foolish thing, the way Lark's heart ached when Gavriel sent her away. And had she told him why she wanted to spend every last moment with him, before what was coming, he'd have found a way to stop her.

Nyx had spoken of Nereida's plans. Of the forces she'd gathered. The strength she'd accumulated. Lark had barely, *barely,* survived her altercation with Nyx. It was by the grace of the goddess Solana and Hugo—her heart clenched—that she lived. But that fight had shown Lark something, something she could wield against Nereida. Something Nereida did not yet know she possessed.

Her ability to swiftly forge a tether. But she'd never have the time to sever the tether to Nereida. It would have to be an instantaneous decision. A reflex. The span of a heartbeat.

And while chaos erupted, when Nereida fell, Daciana would have to be the one to rebuild the veil—same way Nereida had eons ago. And when she did, she'd need the anchor.

Lark could think of no greater purpose her death would serve, felling their enemy and reinstating the veil to protect the mortal world from the Undesirables seeking to burn it.

She had yet to broach the subject with anyone, and this was all on the basis of theory, needing more substance to carry its weight. Langford and Inerys, maybe even Amara could help with that, provided she'd even be willing to speak to them. But the fact remained that this was their best plan. This was how they would defeat Nereida. Every time Lark stood against her, she fell, because survival was always part of the equation. She'd fought hard to earn her life, her mortal existence once more; she'd be a fool to throw it away.

And she would be the fool if it meant keeping the ones she loved safe. If it meant ending the threat of destruction. There was still the matter of Sargon and his attack dog hunting Aislinn, and Lark had yet to uncover the solution to that particular problem.

But each day, each hour, felt significant. Vital. Like she was counting down to the last, and she'd wanted nothing more than to spend it with Gavriel. After lifetimes apart, it was all she wanted. All she craved. They had stolen moments here and there, but fate seemed determined to crash them together only to separate them again. The pull of the tide against waves crashing against the surf. Their connection was the union of pain and beauty, and all she wanted was time. Time with him. Time to love him.

But how could she lament these things now? How could she retreat to the darkest corners of her mind, penning the elegy of their tragic connection, as if nothing else mattered? As if there weren't things bigger than her and her selfish heart?

Selfish. So selfish.

"Well, well. What have we here?"

Lark froze. A beautiful woman, bared even in the snow, slinked out from behind a tree. Inerys' protective wards were deeper in the Emerald Woods, and Lark stood unprotected.

"All those unspoken desires." The woman arched her back, exaggerating the curve of her spine and thrusting her chest into the air. Her black hair skimmed the curve of her backside, endless smooth skin on full display. "Hasn't anyone told you it's bad for your health?"

"I've heard that somewhere." Lark hovered her fingers above the handle of her Reaper Blade. "I'd ask if anyone taught you the differing seasons, but we both know you can't feel the cold."

A Desire Drinker. Kenna had written the word *Vrykolaka* into her bestiary under a crude drawing to its likeness. They were monsters sustained on blood but specifically drawn to the blood of one fighting their desires. There was a particular taste of torment, a flavor distilled in the suppression of desires withheld.

"You smell..." The beast behind the impossibly beautiful face took a deep inhale. "You smell like... *more.* What are you?"

If Lark had a silver for every time that question was posed to her. "You have more pressing matters to fret over." She pulled the Reaper Blade from its sheath. Coils of dragonstone embedded in the blade like black snakes. Like Nyx's shadows.

The desire drinker smiled, her jaw threatening to snap open, hinting at the danger lurking beneath the façade. "I've been known to play with my food before eating. You might even enjoy it."

Compared to Nereida, this creature was nothing. An insect. A pest. Knowing that Lark faced a far greater foe, any whisper of fear dissipated, leaving only vague annoyance in its wake.

"Well, then. Come and play."

The desire drinker grinned, her mouth splitting like torn seams all the way to her ears. Rows of large jagged teeth peeked out from her gaping maw, and she pounced.

Lark angled the Reaper Blade, allowing the thrill of a fight to spread through her veins, and lunged.

WINTER WAS BEAUTIFUL. A hushed sort of magic coating the land. Blankets of snow and crystals, both soft and hard, the dichotomy of human nature and its fickle ways. But the fact that Lark had to travel the entirety of the woods, vrykolaka blood coating her skin and hair and clothes, made this season decidedly her least favorite. Gone were the days of dipping in streams and rivers, of cleansing the blood from an unexpected skirmish. No, she carried the remains of her fight, the scent of death wafting with each shallow breath.

And it was cold. Cold and stiff and—Lark shivered.

Fighting the creature had been... well it was a relief, actually. She'd stretched her awareness, weaving a tether between her and the desire drinker, forging memories of pain before unraveling the tether. An exercise of her will, and an experiment to how swiftly she could forge and sever. It wasn't too long ago that Lark's fear at facing such foes had been impossible to ignore. But now, she welcomed it. Reveled in it. She'd send each of Nereida's minions back to the blazing pits of the Netherworld piece by bloody piece.

And her blade would reap their deaths. Already, the coils upon the steel had grown, as if feeding on each kill and strengthening the blade. It was a myth she'd heard long ago, that the strength of a sword forged by death, or in this case, by life, would grow with each felled foe.

If it was true... Lark would seek more enemies in pursuit of whetting her blade for Nereida. For Sargon. For every monster who threatened their existence.

But first... a bath.

Inerys' cottage came into view, the familiar stonework a stark contrast against the white of the snowy forest. The frozen lake was solid beneath Lark's feet as she slid across its surface. Her body ached, weary and road worn, and her skin stung from the numbing cold, but when that puffing chimney came into view, along with Inerys' plant covered home, Lark smiled, shuffling faster.

Gavriel would return soon. Ferryn would make sure of it. And they would have their time together. They would plan and strategize and spend each night curled up in one another. Perhaps if she thought it hard enough, it would come true.

Inerys' door opened, the witch appearing on her step, her dark hair blowing in the wind. She gathered her skirts and sprinted down her steps.

Lark laughed. *Inerys was safe.* She slid across the ice, skidding to a halt when Inerys met her there.

Inerys scowled, her dark brows pinched, eyes narrowed and mouth tight. "You—" Her tone was accusatory. Angry. "You... imbecile."

That was not the greeting Lark expected, but it was in fact very Inerys of her. "Good to see you, too."

"Don't you ever, *ever*—" Inerys shook her head, tossing her arms around Lark's filthy body and pulling her into a tight embrace.

Lark hugged her back, laughing softly. "I'm sorry I worried you."

"As you should be," Inerys muttered. "Next time, have the decency to die in front of me so I don't wonder."

Lark pulled back. Biting her lip to keep from laughing again. "I promise when I die to ensure you witness the spectacle."

Inerys led her by the elbow. "Don't even think of sitting anywhere until you wash. I can't even identify the layers of filth and grime you're sporting."

"Hm. Some of its monster blood. Probably some shit rolled in there. Death is a messy business."

"Hush." Inerys gently pushed her inside, the warmth of her home enveloping Lark like the surprising embrace she'd just given her. "I'll make tea and prepare myself for whatever earth-shattering news you have to share."

"You know me so well."

CHAPTER FIFTY-SEVEN

MERIKH

*D*ays and nights bled together. Time was meaningless. And even in this knowledge, the slow drip of time confounded him. For in each moment, his thoughts turned only to her.

The strange somniavi. The enigmatic soul capable of fathomless destruction.

But she wasn't capable, was she? Not in spirit. Not in action. Merikh didn't know why, but he trusted her when she said she only wanted her peace. Her words rang of truth and sincerity, something he'd hardly encountered in all his days. Sargon, his master and commander, was adept at wielding the truth. It was a simple matter of omission, and anyone could speak false truth.

But this dream walker.

Aislinn.

Something about her drew him in. It whispered promises of an existence worth having.

And he hadn't the faintest idea why.

It would be easier if this was his season of slumber. He could close his eyes and lose himself in dreams. Entirely miss the short lifespan of the strange dreamer. But his time was now, and he could not hide away in his dreams without disrupting the balance. Without risking her falling to Sargon's schemes.

And why should that matter?

There was… one option. The hall of mirrors. It was forbidden, of course, but were he to venture through its doors, he'd have his answers. But sometimes the truth was the far greater punishment. The light, harsher than the dark.

It was said that for a paragon to look upon their true form, face the cruelest parts of themselves, and still find the courage to ask for answers, they would be granted with divine knowledge. Divine truth. Sargon had forbidden any from entering on the grounds that too many paragons had lost themselves in the hall of mirrors.

But what if it was more than that.

What if…

Treasonous thoughts. Treacherous and dangerous. It was not his place to question. His only duty was to kill the somniavi and report back to Sargon. Eventually her face would fade from his memory, as they all did, and when his slumber came, perhaps even his dreams would be kind enough not to remind him of the incessant pull he suffered in her presence.

Large green eyes filled his mind. They plagued his thoughts with the truth of her stare. The unbridled honesty of her soul. Even after everything she'd suffered…

Memories of Lark's returned to him. The details of Aislinn's death. Of the monster who tortured her in her final moments. Merikh snatched a quill from his desk, quickly scribbling out his command. When he was through, he held the parchment up, watching the flames devour it from the edges as he sent it through. The Netherworld and Avalon were not strictly in accord, but he had some pull with a few select entities down below. It was nothing to warrant their *special attention* for a man already in their domain, was it?

The mortals were the ones who tacked the notion of virtue to the name of paragon, not he.

It was foolish of him to care. To get involved. It was none of his business what her life had wrought, and only her death, her wiping from existence, concerned him.

The thought speared a jolt of pain through his chest for reasons he could not name.

He was a good soldier. Following orders was second nature. He'd never questioned, never wished to. Everything had run smoothly, from the first existence of Avalon when Sargon lit the first flame of creation and breathed life into the universe, to the first time Merikh opened his eyes to behold the gift of life bestowed upon him.

The mortals were their own breed, created from the sins of the Netherworld. From greed and malice and passion and pride. They were seeds of selfish impulse, spread far and wide. That Sargon even allowed some of them the gift of his paradise...

But when did this all start to sound like bullshit?

Merikh growled, pushing out of his chair and stomping to the door.

Visiting the hall of mirrors might be a mistake, in fact he was sure of it, but to sit idly by and convince himself that killing Aislinn without question was his divine calling was...

Well, more bullshit.

CHAPTER FIFTY-EIGHT

DACIANA

"$\mathcal{W}$e didn't need the hunters anyway."

Kenna glared at Daciana, as she had just violated the agreed upon understanding of not mentioning the other hunters ever again.

But it was true.

Though it would have been helpful, really they needed to sort out a plan to kill Nereida. Battling the monsters and demons from the Netherworld, that was secondary. Until they could stem the flow of ilk into the mortal world, it was like placing a bandage over a gaping wound.

The hunters would have bought them some time, time they sorely needed, but without winning the war, it was a lifetime of never-ending battles. Destroying Nereida was vital to their cause. Only then could they hope to rebuild.

The Emerald Woods was beginning the first stages of the thaw as spring teased its approach. They wended through the trees, the earth peeking through melting snow. They were on the cusp of growth. Rebirth. Life. Daciana felt it in her bones, the promise of change in the wind. Even the air was warmer. Winter's chill still clawed at the edges, but a blooming warmth had hinted its call. Birdsong filled the forest, and the steady drips of snow melting from branches softened the sounds of their footsteps.

Aislinn trudged along beside them, awfully quiet. Ever since they'd left Anquan, she'd hardly said two words to them. When Daciana offered to swing by for her to see her mother again, she'd shook her head, insisting they take the shortest path back to Inerys. Her appetite seemed to have returned though, which was a relief.

"Stupid, stubborn, shitebag," Kenna muttered. She'd been brooding ever since they left Anquan. Her conversation with Elder Muirgel hadn't gone according to plan, but that likely wasn't the main issue.

"You miss Ruva?" Daciana hated putting Kenna in a position to strain her friendship. Though her discomfort was warranted and even confirmed based on what Kenna had shared, she hadn't wanted her to leave on unfriendly terms. Hadn't wanted the last threads of family to be snipped in their departure. Kenna had already lost so much, she didn't deserve to lose any more.

Kenna snorted. "No. I miss frosted rolls dusted in cinnamon and endless caves and alcoves to steal you away into."

Daciana sighed. She missed those, too. Spending time in Anquan was a bit like taking a break from reality. With so many hunters in a close vicinity, she hadn't needed to be so on guard. If they tumbled into bed while Aislinn was out, or if they snuck away to wish upon the frozen waterfall, she needn't worry about the others. Someone was always around to help, always around to fight, and Daciana could be...

Selfish seemed both fitting and unfair, but there it was. Daciana could be selfish with her time. And once Ruva was no longer a pressure point between them, Anquan became everything Kenna promised it to be.

"Waste of a trip."

"I wouldn't say that." Daciana leaned into Kenna, whispering for only her hearing. "I rather enjoyed having you all to myself."

Kenna grinned, flashing Daciana's favorite dimples. "I concede that. But you weren't planning to board up shop between your thighs just because we're back in the land of doom and gloom, were you?"

Daciana cringed. "*Never* say that to me again."

"I mean it." Kenna tugged on her, shaking her with the impatience of a child. "It's hardly romantic, the impending end of the world, and you're making it sound like we won't find any privacy again!"

Aboard the ship returning home, they hadn't. They'd shared a cabin with Aislinn, and though she spent much of her time above deck, they hadn't had the chance for intimacy.

"That's not what I'm saying. I'm merely relaying how much I enjoyed our time visiting your home."

"You implied it. There was much in your subtext."

"I implied nothing!"

Aislinn called back to them. "If you wish, I could make myself scarce for a few moments. Just up ahead. If you need some time, that is."

Kenna's swift and immediate interest in that suggestion almost made Daciana laugh.

"Thank you, but no. We really should—"

"Return to Lark. Blah, blah, blah," Kenna smirked, belying her irritation. "I agree. Let's hurry home."

Home.

Damn. Daciana liked the sound of that. That home could be wherever their destination was so long as they were together. That home didn't mean sacrificing all else. Home could be here in Ardenas, across the sea in Anquan, blazes, they could make a home in Vallemer should they wish to.

The thought of Langford and Alistair made Daciana's chest tight. She missed them fiercely. They had a much greater task of recruitment. Kenna at least had her connections, even if they didn't help in the matter. Alistair and Langford were heading in with nothing. And based on the way Hugo departed Vallemer, they couldn't exactly use him as a character testament.

Hugo.

When would it stop hurting to think of him?

The first step onto the frozen lake revealed Inerys' cottage. Daciana took careful, easy steps. Unless the witch spelled it to remain solid, the first of the thaw could mean weakness in the ice. It wouldn't do to fall through and drown.

The door to Inerys' cottage opened, a silhouette of a woman bathed in golden light appearing in the doorway.

She leapt down, red hair wildly bouncing as she sprinted toward them.

Lark.

Daciana's heart lifted, joy spreading through her warm and swift. Lark was safe. The one who hunted Aislinn hadn't hurt her.

"Oh, go on." Kenna rolled her eyes. "Go run to her. You know you want to."

Daciana pressed a quick kiss to Kenna's cheek and sprinted over the ice, uncaring if it groaned beneath her steps. Lark jumped into her arms, hugging her tightly while a mixture of a laugh and sob broke through.

"Skies, I missed you."

Daciana laughed. "Missed you, too. Hasn't been that long, has it?"

"Feels like ages." Lark squeezed her one more time before pulling back, her amber eyes swimming and her smile too big for her face. "I have so much to tell you."

When she caught sight of Aislinn and Kenna, she grabbed for them, too, pulling Aislinn into her arms first and whispering something the girl nodded at. And when she got to Kenna, Kenna flashed Daciana a knowing smirk and allowed herself to be pulled into a one-sided embrace.

Kenna laughed as Lark shook her, encouraging her to hug her back. And finally, Kenna wrapped her arms around her, shaking her head and grinning.

Kenna would get used to Lark's affections. And Daciana was just grateful for the fact that there would be time for such a thing.

CHAPTER FIFTY-NINE

LARK

*M*ortal instincts were such a beautiful, overwhelming, and fickle thing. Lark felt it in her bones, this sense of impending arrival. But each time she glanced out the window, only a mixture of mud and snow greeted her.

No Ferryn.

No Gavriel.

Skies, how long would it take him to return?

He'd promised, *promised* her he would. Was she so foolish to believe in promises against death?

But he did not promise her an avoidance of death. No, he promised to find his way back to her. Which they had both done. Many times. Spanning lifetimes and crossing the divide of death and rebirth.

He would come.

He would always come to her.

"No signs of them, huh?" Kenna sat beside her, peering out the window. They'd settled into a comfortable friendship, a fact Lark was most grateful for.

She could voice her longing, she did not suspect Kenna of ridiculing her for feeling it. But it was easier to deflect. "Not yet, but I figured if I wait by the window and watch the horizon, they're bound to appear sooner. That's how it works, isn't it?"

Kenna laughed. "Good luck with that."

Aislinn appeared in the doorway, and Lark lurched from her seat.

"Aislinn," she called. "We need a moment."

Visibly stricken, Aislinn nodded and allowed Lark to drag her into Inerys' private room. The one with the sound deafening spell. There was much to say, much to inquire, but if anyone else heard, it would ruin everything. Lark couldn't be too hasty. She needed a delicate approach, or Aislinn would never agree to it.

She opened her mouth to speak, but the way Aislinn fiddled with a loose thread on her gown gave Lark pause. Aislinn's gaze bounced around the room, focusing on the living tree claiming the wall, the vines draped about the mirror, anywhere but meeting Lark's stare.

Aislinn was hiding something.

Suspicion rose in Lark's belly. "You have something to tell me."

Aislinn shook her head, exhaling a sharp breath. "What? I don't understand. Why would I... what do you even..."

"I told you far more than I should have regarding Merikh considering I was nowhere close to protect you should you do anything rash." Lark pursed her lips. "Did you do anything rash?"

Aislinn's far too innocent expression revealed she indeed had done such a thing.

"Spill. Tell me everything." Lark's plan could spare a moment in favor of unearthing whatever had Aislinn fidgeting worse than Kenna whenever Inerys commanded her silence for a moment.

Aislinn toyed with the sleeve of her gown. "I... Lark I'm so sorry, but I couldn't bring myself to kill him."

Now Lark hadn't the faintest idea what they were talking about. "I need more details to follow your meaning."

"Merikh." Aislinn's voice escaped in the quietest whisper.

Lark's mind stalled. Aislinn had seen Merikh. *Had nearly killed him?* "I... so many questions. What did you do? What happened? Where were Daciana and Kenna. Skies above, how are you alive?" Too many questions racing and dueling for dominance.

"I called him by his true name."

"But you don't know his true name."

Aislinn's silence confirmed she did indeed know his name.

"Ugh." Lark backed away until her knees hit the edge of Inerys' bed, and she sank down upon it. "I won't interrupt. Tell me everything." To be safe, she clapped a hand over her mouth.

Aislinn sucked in a deep breath, her thrumming pulse visible against the delicate skin of her neck. "I learned his true name back when he first found me."

"But—"

At Aislinn's cutting look, Lark squeezed her lips between her fingers in a silent bid to hold her questions.

"I can't explain it," Aislinn continued, pacing the room. The floor gently groaned beneath her steps. "I didn't even have to try. I just slipped in. Like I was always meant to. I saw so many things..." Her voice was breathless like it ached to speak. "When you told me of his crimes against you, I couldn't wait. I couldn't bear to do *nothing*. So, I bided my time until the others were away and distracted—"

"Daciana should have known better." Lark bit down on her tongue too late. It was unfair to blame Dac like that, but the whole point in whisking Aislinn away was to keep her safe. "I'm sorry, go on."

Aislinn inclined her head in acknowledgement. "I call him by his true name, and he bends to my will. I don't know if it's wielding his name or something more, but when I commanded, he cut himself; he had no choice but to obey." She snapped her fingers. "In an instant, without thought. I could command him to do anything."

It took everything in Lark not to interrupt, so she focused on the way Aislinn's fists clenched, the tension in her jaw as she spoke. She was angry, but why?

"I sent him away. Before I could force him to do something really awful."

"I'm sorry, but why did you let him go?" Lark couldn't bite down on her sore tongue an instant longer. "You could have ended him right then and there. *Why* would you let him escape?"

Aislinn ceased her pacing and shook her head. "Lark, I couldn't bring myself to force his hand."

"We can't afford to be sporting these days." Lark tried desperately to keep her voice gentle. But how could Aislinn let him walk away unscathed? They had enemies on all sides, an impossible feat ahead of them. Anything to tip the balance in their favor would have been the *right* thing to do. Now was not the time to cling to the ideals of another life. Now was the time for sacrifice.

"It isn't that." Aislinn sat beside Lark, indenting the bed beneath her weight. "It isn't right, stripping someone of their choice like that. It's…"

"A violation," Lark finished.

Aislinn nodded.

"I understand," Lark said even though her throat constricted on the words. "But what if he comes for you? What if you aren't prepared? It sounds as if you can hold your own against him. But I—" Lark couldn't. Not when she so eagerly rushed into his trap. Perhaps she could stand against his power, but she could not rely on such unstable chances.

So, why risk it? He was too powerful and too dangerous not to use every advantage they possessed. Even if Lark understood never wanting that power or influence over another person. Even if every piece of her soul rebelled against the very thought of controlling someone else. If she had Aislinn's power, she would do whatever it took to protect the ones she loved. To protect the life they fought for. Even if it meant dirtying her own hands and betraying herself.

Maybe Aislinn's ideals were a stark reminder that she'd had to part with her own.

"I trust him, Lark."

"Aislinn…"

"No, listen." Aislinn took Lark's hand. "I know what he did to you, and I hate him for it. I wish nothing but his deserved punishment. In equal measure, no, tenfold!"

Lark squeezed her hand back. "I don't care about that. I care about you, being safe, not falling for his trap the way I did."

Aislinn huffed out a laugh. "But don't you see, it was *my* trap that ensnared him. I saw into his mind. Into his soul. I could just... sense him, you know?"

Lark did know. She'd experienced the sensation of sifting through someone's memories and revealing their true nature. But one could know a person, intimately know them, and still be surprised by their actions. Gavriel, for one, would never suspect what she planned. Guilt burned in her belly. "Sometimes, people don't behave according to their nature. I trust what you saw in him, but I do not trust his decisions."

"I know," Aislinn said. "I know." She studied Lark with a wary look in her eye. "Are you going to tell the others?"

"No." Lark released Aislinn's hand and let herself fall back onto the soft comfort of Inerys' bed. "Not if you don't wish it."

"I don't. Not yet." Aislinn lay back, too, both of them staring up at the ceiling. Crawling vines crept across the rafters, crowned with verdant leaves. Even in the heart of winter, Inerys kept her greenery. It was easy to lose oneself in studying the veins spidering through each leaf. Hundreds, thousands, countless paths to trace.

"There's something I needed to tell you," Lark began. She'd waited long enough to broach the subject she'd originally dragged Aislinn here to discuss. "Something I hope you can show the same amount of discretion I am extending." Was it a manipulation? Likely. But as she'd said, now was not the time to be sporting.

"A secret for a secret. I am familiar." Aislinn turned to lie on her side, bright green eyes narrowed in suspicion. A lock of golden hair fell across her brow. "I promise."

Lark exhaled a tight breath. "I think I have a way to kill Nereida."

Stilted silence.

Aislinn sat up. "Why that's wonderful news! Why wouldn't you wish to tell the others? We should share the plan and start sorting how to best utilize this knowledge—"

"No." Lark rose to face her. "You and me. That's it."

Aislinn's brows furrowed. "I don't understand."

458

"I need to know Nereida has fallen. I can't allow the threats she's made to come to pass."

Nyx's voice echoed in Lark's head.

"She gathers her forces; there is no stopping her. And she has something special planned for each one of your friends. Their suffering will be eternal. And you have no one to blame but yourself."

Lark could leave no stone unturned, for Nereida would extend the same attention. She would never rest until all that Lark loved had burned to the ground, and worse. There was no escape. There was no grace of death where Nereida was concerned. This had to end.

"I found a way to kill Nyx, a Reaper far more powerful than I. When I forged a tether, I was able to link us." But it had been close, and Nyx had been right. Lark was outmatched. She'd have no hope to overpower Nereida. The element of surprise, however…

A misdirection.

An instantaneous calculation.

"And then what?"

"I severed the link in time to cut her down." Lark couldn't count on being that lucky again. It was a one-shot chance, no room for failure. And she had failed. Many times. Every time she went head-to-head with Nereida.

No. Failure was not an option. Not this time.

"All right." Aislinn frowned, her voice was careful. "This is the plan with Nereida?"

"Almost." And this was the hardest part. "I will forge the tether, and before she knows what I've done… I need you to kill me."

Aislinn blinked, her expression blank. For a heartbeat or two, they sat in the weighted silence of Lark's declaration.

Aislinn choked out her words. "No. No that's—you're panicking! There's a lot at stake, and you aren't thinking clearly—"

"I'm not panicking." This was the calmest Lark had felt in ages. This was clarity. "You use the Reaper Blade on me while I'm linked to Nereida. Nereida's death will release the power needed to rebuild the veil. I need you to tell Daciana that we have a plan to cut Nereida down, since you and I are the only ones who can wield the Reaper Blade—"

"And Ferryn."

"He'll never agree to it." Lark wouldn't dare reveal this plan to him. She couldn't risk his opposition. "We tell Daciana to be ready. That we have a plan, and to prepare to draw from Nereida to put the veil back in place." She swallowed. "No more Nereida. No more monsters roaming freely. Everyone gets their happy ending."

Aislinn chewed her lip. "Only if Daciana brings you back the way she did Alistair."

"Yes. Then Daciana can bring me back." The lie fell smoothly from Lark's lips. The truth was... Thanar had been the anchor for the veil. Though Nereida's release of power could fuel its creation, without a soul to tether it to, it was incomplete. But for now, she could let Aislinn believe they would all make it out unscathed.

Lark might even let herself believe it for a moment or two.

LARK TOSSED and turned in her bed. The hour was late, the candle long spent, but she couldn't shake her unease. Gavriel should have arrived. What was delaying him?

After her conversation with Aislinn, the finality of everything seemed so imminent. And each day that passed without sign of him was another day lost.

A strong breeze groaned through her room, billowing the curtains. When had she opened the window? Shivering, Lark slid out from beneath her covers, bouncing on the balls of her feet as she rubbed her arms. Skies above, if spring was due, why was it so cold?

She lowered the window, locking it. A strange sort of tension pulled taut. The mortal instinct of sensing someone else's presence. Her knife was under her pillow, she only needed—

A hand clapped over her mouth, a strong arm winding around her waist and dragging her back.

"Hello, Demon."

That voice, skies above, that voice.

Lark sobbed against Gavriel's hand, spinning to throw her arms around his neck. Sweat slicked his skin and seeped into her own as she pressed herself as close to him as their bodies would allow.

Gavriel lifted her, carrying her to the bed. "Did you miss me?"

"Terribly." Lark tugged at his clothes, ripping the neck of his tunic wide enough to lift over his head.

"Don't you wish to know why I snuck through your window like a common thief?"

"No." Lark claimed his mouth, swallowing his laugh. She couldn't get their clothes off fast enough. Needed to feel his skin against hers. It was a needy, desperate, overwhelming pull. There wasn't enough time. There never would be. All they had was this—

"Wait, Lark." Gavriel's gentle voice made her chest tighten, and she stilled beneath his touch. "Let me look at you." He reached over and turned the key to his lantern, illuminating the concern in his eyes. "You're shaking."

"Am I?" Was she? "Must be the cold."

Gavriel didn't appear convinced, but he pressed his brow to hers. "I've thought of nothing but you since we parted." He lifted his head, gazing into her eyes with that fire she'd come to love. The same fire that burned the first time she saw the mortal cursing the name of death as his friend faded away. His touch found the thread tied to her finger, tracing it. "Never again. Never again will we separate. I swear it."

Lark kissed him, yanking him close so he couldn't see the truth in her eyes.

When he sank in deep, claiming every part of her, she buried her face in his neck, her tears falling against his skin.

She could not speak falsely. She could not promise him this.

"AGAIN!" Inerys' voice rang out through the clearing.

Lark glared at her, mopping the sweat from her brow. "Let us rest a moment."

"You can rest when you're dead."

Daciana laughed, covering it with a cough when Lark turned her glare on her.

They'd been at it for hours.

Daciana was training under Inerys' watchful eye to direct the pull of her power. Her aim? Lark. And Lark was expected to forge a tether and return her strength and life back into her own body. Repeatedly.

Daciana hadn't even broken a sweat, meanwhile Lark was a panting mess.

She had to admit. They were gaining skill.

The first day, Daciana had nearly drained Lark to the point of unconsciousness. The next day, her head swam, and her nose bled. But bit by bit, they felt the natural pull of their powers. The union they'd created. It was like finding the anchor point, once Daciana and Lark found the threshold, they matched each other's strength, so no one was pulled too far the wrong way.

Speaking of anchor point, Lark needed to practice with Hugo's new bow. When she'd told Daciana of seeing him, of learning his fate and his peace, it was like a final weight had been lifted from Daciana's chest, relieving her of an invisible burden.

Across the way, Gavriel and Ferryn sparred. Their easy banter echoed through the space, and Lark smiled despite herself.

It was almost like old times.

"How do we think Langford and Alistair fared?"

Daciana snorted, drinking from her waterskin and passing it to Lark. "I think they're having the easiest time of anyone and are fighting the desire to extend their trip." A sly grin spread across her mouth. "Do you think Ingemar finally tied Alistair to the figurehead for the duration of the trip like she always threatened?"

Lark coughed, dribbling water down her chin. The image of Alistair, shout-singing his bawdiest songs while tied to the snarling lion at the head of Ingemar's ship was too much.

"Skies, I hope so."

CHAPTER SIXTY

LANGFORD

*L*angford couldn't breathe, and he'd never been happier for it.

Daciana had pulled him into a rib-crushing hug, and Lark had come up from behind to hold him tightly, too. It was being surrounded by true warmth and love and acceptance. Something Langford once thought he'd never find. And that he'd found this family across the ocean, all from different walks of life, from different planes of existence even, was the most remarkable thing of all.

"What about me? Daciana, you and I are practically the same person now." Alistair tapped his foot, waiting for his turn.

"You are not." Langford snorted even if the implication of Alistair's condition was a painful reminder. He needed to speak privately with Kenna, voice his concerns, and formulate a plan. But somehow, being here with Daciana and Lark and Alistair, all of them reunited once more, made it all seem possible.

Lark reached up on tiptoes to kiss Alistair's cheek, which only resulted in him lifting the former Reaper high into the air until she was gasping with laughter and begging to be put down. Daciana pulled Alistair into an embrace and whispered something to him, and Alistair nodded, burying his face in her neck.

Langford's heart swelled at the sight. It was good to be home.

"So, after I saved an entire village from the tyranny of Gunther, they agreed to fight alongside us."

Langford rolled his eyes at Alistair's embellished account of their time away. "That is *not* how it happened." In fact, it was Kyall of all people who had been instrumental in their success at securing Vallemerian aid. The warrior had contacted Moirin while Langford and Alistair planned their escape, pledged his loyalty to her, and been the one to end Gunther's hold on the land. And she in turn offered a contingency of her men to their cause. It wasn't nearly as many fighters as they'd aimed for, but when faced with the imminent threat of walking, nay, running away empty-handed, it was a blooming success.

Of course, they hadn't known this when they departed port, but a missive for Langford had been waiting at the next port, and when Ingemar's messenger had retrieved the message, she'd gleefully shared the good news with Langford.

Aboard her ship, Langford had taken the time to study the ingredients of Kenna's elixir, alongside neurological triggers to attempt to prevent Alistair's turn under the moon's call. Langford was able to delay Alistair's symptoms through scent triggers such as his favored lavender-based soap. Ultimately, he'd had to implement the concoction, but still the efficacy of breathwork and sensory grounding was worth noting.

Two more moon's turns. That was all he had left to find a solution. He would grant them one more night of peace, they'd earned it, but first thing on the morrow, Kenna and he would sit down and figure this out. They had to.

He refused to lose Alistair.

They all sat around a large bonfire, the heat of the flame reaching Langford's nose and cheeks. The log he sat atop was still damp from melted snow, and the wet reminder seeped into the back of his trousers.

Lark whispered something to Daciana, and the two of them erupted into a fit of giggles. Alistair stretched his legs out, tucking his hands behind his head as he watched Langford with a heated look. Ferryn and Aislinn sat close, sharing a cup of Ingemar's mulled wine. Occasionally he reached over to Lark, knocking the back of his hand against her thigh as if reminding her he was there. Inerys had retired for the night, claiming there were far too many faces within the vicinity for her to relax, and Kenna watched Daciana with an awestruck expression. Gavriel tuned the pegs of his new fiddle. He'd said he procured it from his former master's office.

His office, now.

Master Assassin. That Gavriel recruited The Guild of Crows to join their forces was news worth celebrating.

Gavriel fiddled, running his bow along the strings and coaxing Lark to dance. Her answering smile spoke of thoughts best left for privacy, until she seemed to realize she needed a partner to dance with, one that wasn't the assassin serenading her with his fiddle. She peered around until her eyes landed on Langford. With a crook of her finger, she rose, beckoning him to dance.

Oh, fine.

Langford took her in his arms, spinning her round and round and they danced about the fire. They'd always had a natural rhythm together, a similar height and instinctive steps. It was why Alistair had insisted on their covers as Lord and Lady Brenner not once but twice in rather disastrous missions.

But this. Dancing. Langford almost believed he and Lark were meant to dance with one another. A kindred friendship he'd treasure for the rest of his days.

And it almost seemed safe to hope for such a thing.

"I've been thinking about Alistair." Her voice broke him out of his trance. He'd been watching Daciana and Alistair badly stomp their way through a dance. Once Alistair allowed Daciana to lead, their movements became smoother. "What if the veil is the reason he still fights the turn?"

Curious, but a theory without evidence was nothing more than a passing thought. "Explain."

"The veil is what prevents the clashing of planes. When Daciana rebuilds it... what if it helps Alistair master the beast? Lock it away? Would he wish to do such a thing?"

Langford glanced over at where Alistair was pretending to bite Daciana's neck. She held him back with one hand, their dance forgotten, as she laughed until tears ran down her cheeks.

"I don't know."

"It's something to think about."

"You have enough on your mind. You needn't worry about us, too." That she had was enough to tighten Langford's throat with gratitude.

Lark laughed, leaning her head against his shoulder. "Don't be silly. I'll always worry about all of you and do whatever it takes to keep you safe."

It was a sentiment they all shared, both spoken and unspoken. But something in her words... It was almost like a confession.

"Besides," Lark continued, lifting her head once more, "you never gave up on Gavriel when he was lost in slumber. Why do you think you don't deserve the same?"

Langford's eyes blurred, and he spun her again, pulling her close. There were many things to say. Things needing voice and words and all the vulnerabilities that come alongside the act of baring one's heart on their sleeves. Yet somehow it seemed like chancing something terrible to say them all now. Like... admitting defeat and bidding farewell. They all faced a greater threat than any in all of history, and it seemed vital to keep these moments protected. Safe. Hopeful. So instead, he settled on, "I've missed you."

Lark grinned. "Skies, I've missed you. I've had so much to talk about and no one to share it with."

"That can't be true." Inerys had demanded a full briefing on Avalon. Kenna wished to know how easy it was for Lark to kill a Vrykolaka with her newly restored powers. Daciana requested the details of Hugo's appearance several times over. And Gavriel would listen to that girl spout off about anything with stars in his eyes.

"I discovered a most curious thing." Lark practically radiated excitement. "Something I think you'll find most intriguing."

"Out with it, woman."

Lark laughed, tossing her head back. "Have you ever heard of the plant Paragon's Whisper?"

Langford frowned. The name didn't ring a bell. Though, he supposed, etymology could be a regional thing. "I have not."

"Nor have I," Lark said, lifting her chin. "But apparently it's a form of truth serum. It sort of, breaks down mental defenses, making influence easier."

"What a vile, appalling discovery you've made. No one should have this power. I'm outraged it exists. You must draw me a diagram and identify its natural growing state and location."

Lark grinned. "But of course, husband."

Langford laughed, spinning her faster. Any advantage they could claim, any at all, was not anything he'd turn his nose up at.

As the fire grew taller, and the drink flowed faster, the sense of rightness settled deep within.

They had this, and it was more than enough.

Aislinn tucked her hair behind her ear, her eyes widening as Ferryn held out his hand, and she appeared to consider, before nodding and letting him lead her into a dance.

"Mind if I cut in?" Alistair's voice sent a thrill through Langford.

"He's all yours." Lark scampered away, landing before Gavriel on her knees. Something she said made his face bloom bright red, and he missed the next note, screeching his sharp mistake.

"How is your night?" Alistair slowed their movements, holding him around the waist with his hand in his, swaying more than dancing. It settled Langford into calmness, Alistair's touch. It was a balm more powerful than anything Langford could create, and he leaned into him.

"Better than some." Langford angled his head in Inerys' direction where the witch had reemerged, a sour expression puckering her face.

Alistair laughed. "That woman needs a good lay."

"Don't be crass."

"She needs a sweet and romantic entanglement that lasts anywhere from an hour to a full night and sates all her needs." Alistair arched a dark brow. "Better?"

"You're incorrigible."

"And you are utterly breathtaking." Alistair ran his thumb against Langford's hand, and Langford rested his head against his shoulder. For all the time they'd had together thus far, he was utterly grateful. And yet, something about this moment sharpened a sense of longing. A fear of missing something sorely needed.

Before everything changed.

"We never got to do this at the ball."

"No. A shame, too. You always look so dashing in finery." Alistair's voice rumbled against Langford's ear.

All around, the air was permeated with a sense of revelry. Everyone continued to laugh and chatter after Gavriel had lowered his fiddle to swing Lark into his arms. Kenna and Daciana sat with their heads close, whispering against each other's lips. Aislinn was now showing Ferryn a game where she placed small objects in his hands and forced him to guess without looking at what he held. Their friends, old and new, all around the fire as if there was no grave threat looming.

"I wonder how Demetria is," Langford finally said. "She disappeared without a word. I... I regret the way things happened."

"She has the demon, apparently." Alistair's tone made it clear exactly how fondly he regarded Balan. "She's smart. Sees more than she lets on, and she put up with all of us without running away screaming." He grinned. "Don't fret about her. I'm sure she's fine, wherever she is."

"Right," Langford said, allowing Alistair to spin him and press a distracting kiss to his lips.

CHAPTER SIXTY-ONE

DEMETRIA

*D*emetria remembered the flowers her mother had always kept in crystal vases. Bright blooms soaking in water, sunlight catching each facet of carved glass, the full spectrum of color dancing across the room. But she'd always wondered why her mother insisted on cutting these blooms from their roots, stripping away pieces of her garden, flower by flower. They never lasted long, and wilted flowers were not permitted. So, they cut more and more. A constant stream of nature's last kiss before tossing them in the rubbish. It was needless and wasteful. The gardens outside held hundreds of flowers, one need only step through the door. But now Demetria understood.

Her mother just wanted to bring a little bit of life inside these walls.

Already the weight of death, of so many deaths, constricted the very air within the castle, like the strangling vines Evander always had to snip away from her mother's roses.

Demetria sat upon the throne she'd never wanted. The throne built upon the blood of her people. Built upon the deal her great-great grandfather made so long ago. That their kingdom would mine for every last mineral of dragonstone and leave it for Nereida's agents to claim. That they would sacrifice so many to see it done, whatever the cost. And in return, their kingdom would forever prosper, and Nereida would extend immunity in the coming days. Whatever destruction the world had wrought.

"I don't understand."

"Oh, sweet thing. You will."

Dragonstone had never been the source of the kingdom's riches, had it? No, it was by the blood sworn along the bottom line of that gods-forsaken contract. The one now etched with Demetria's name. Her blood.

Demetria's head throbbed, and she lifted the crown from her hair, turning it over between her hands to catch the light. It was a simple enough diadem, weighty and solid in gold with a lone ruby at its center. The light of the braziers burned a blinding reflection along the plaits and knots etched into its surface. Already Demetria's neck had begun to ache wearing the damn thing. Perhaps that was why Zaire forwent wearing the crown.

Perhaps, living under the weight of it had driven him mad.

Demetria swallowed down the lump in her throat and placed the crown back where it belonged atop her head.

It shouldn't have been so easy.

Killing her brother.

Seizing his kingdom.

Signing her name upon Nereida's scroll.

Demetria's face crumpled as tears filled her eyes. Zaire had been… a casualty in a bargain struck long before his time. Nereida had shown her the contract sealing their fate.

Koval was a protected nation. Wealthy, prosperous. Untouched by the monsters in her mother's stories. But that was no accident. The terms of their deal were to harvest dragonstone in exchange for their kingdom to flourish. Failure to do so resulted in nullifying the contract, to the whims of the holder.

Nereida.

When Demetria's parents shut down the mining operation, stopping the retrieval of dragonstone, their deaths were the result of their failure. And when the crown passed to Zaire, darkness bloomed in his heart like black ink on a wet page. The wording of the contract specifically targeted male heirs. It created a loophole for Demetria's escape, yet she came running back.

Now she was expected to carry on in Zaire's place.

Demetria had signed her name, and in an instant, the title of Queen was hers. No pesky rebellion necessary, no tribunal. She'd murdered her brother, and they celebrated in the streets. His blood painted the floor, and they planned her coronation. It was like half waking mid nightmare, knowing how wrong it all was, but not being able to shake fully awake to escape.

Demetria had shut down the mines, freeing the indentures still in there, granting the foreigners leave to travel home, and when she searched for the girl she'd broken to finalize her plan. The one who'd shown her kindness in the darkness of the mine, the girl was gone. No one seemed to know or remember her. So many had been lost.

It wasn't enough, not by half measures, but it was a start. An end to the bloody reign under Nereida's boot. It was only a matter of time until she came to collect.

And what would come of Demetria's kingdom, then?

The doors opened, familiar footfalls echoing through the space, and despite herself, Demetria almost sighed in relief at his presence.

Balan. He'd washed and been outfitted in only the finest clothes. Black leathers, his preference, with silver threading. He tugged his cap from his head, the one he wore so as not to alarm her subjects, and fanned himself with it. Even with his broken horns, he appeared every bit the fearsome demon he'd claimed to be.

Despite the softness in his silver eyes, there was concern in his gaze as he studied her face.

"Why do you hide in here when there are countless nobles vying for your favor?" Balan sat on the arm of the throne, lounging close enough they touched. It was easy, being close to him. They'd spent all that time huddled together, trying not to freeze to death or worse. Having him here was the only comfort she found.

But even that wasn't enough.

"How is this hiding? It's the throne room, the most obvious

choice." Were she to hide, she'd like to think she was a little cleverer than that.

"You achieved your aim." The rough scrape of his voice was befuddled. "Yet you brood. You should host a revelry. A ball. Something to compensate for everything it took getting you here."

Killing her brother. Maiming an innocent girl. Discovering just how easy it all was.

That was the worst part. It should have been difficult. What did it say about her that it wasn't?

"And why are you still here?" Demetria's voice had a bite not meant for Balan. "Do you enjoy playing human?" She didn't mean it. She didn't mean it and she couldn't seem to stop. "You spoke of yourself as the sort of beast to strike fear in the hearts of your victims. A force to be reckoned with. And now you laze about, asking after my *feelings*?" Her fists shook, and she wished her tongue would fall off. "When did you become so weak?"

Her mother's stories of monsters always held compassion for the creatures. That they were the result of pain and torment.

But Demetria was not prepared for the monster to be her.

Balan stilled, a tense silence falling between them. She'd never been so cruel to him. And he'd done everything she'd asked. He'd stayed as her advisor. Spoke to the people on her behalf. Held her in silence while she wept over murdering her brother. Why was she lashing out at him? Why couldn't she say what she meant? Was it the contract? Was it a condition of Nereida's deal?

The time Zaire struck her, so long ago when she was still a princess asking her brother to see reason, he'd seemed almost surprised by his own action.

Would her actions become those of a stranger's, too? Shame dipped in her belly as the image of Marian and her accusing stare filled her mind. *They already were.*

"You tremble." Balan's brow furrowed, and he clamped a hand on her upper arm, crushing the fine velvet of her dress. "Why are you afraid?"

"I-I'm not afraid. I'm angry to be surrounded by useless—"

"No." Balan yanked her up, turning her to face him fully. He sat on the throne with her sideways on his lap. He studied her face, searching. "What are you not telling me?"

"Nothing." She fought against him, and he held firm.

"No. You cannot fool me." He stood, holding her upright so she didn't fall. Grabbing her face with both hands he peered intently into her eyes.

Something flipped in her stomach as his gaze penetrated hers so forcefully.

"Has anyone questioned your right to rule?"

"No." She exhaled. "Not aloud at least."

"Do you regret your actions. Killing Zaire—do you wish you'd spared him?"

Demetria's eyes started to slip closed, but Balan shook her, jolting them open. "No." Even if he'd been a prisoner to this insipid contract, he would have killed her. He would have killed her and carried on his reign of terror. His death had been necessary.

It was a shame it was also his saving grace.

Pain speared through her belly at the thought. At the memory of the way he looked at her, *really saw her,* before his eyes dimmed to nothing.

Balan's brows knitted together, frustration stealing across his face. "Did… someone visit you?"

Demetria's heart began to race. She opened her mouth to speak—

Nothing came out.

Nereida's contract. It inhibited her from speaking anything of it. Silencing her in her suffering.

Demetria nodded.

"Can you speak of it?"

Demetria shook her head, pressuring building behind her eyes.

Balan's eyes widened, fury claiming the concern in his gaze. "You made a deal?"

Tears slipped down her cheeks as she nodded.

"Fuck!" He snarled as he tore away from her. "How could you be so stupid? I've told you of the dangers of taking deals from demons.

Why would you throw your life, your soul away for shortsighted gratification?"

Demetria shook her head. That wasn't fair. It wasn't like that. The contract was already in place. She had no real choice in the matter. Let her kingdom burn, which Nereida had more than enough power to do, or sign to the predetermined terms.

But she could not say any of this. Could she write it?

Demetria staggered to the table where a scroll sat bearing the news of her coronation. She flipped it over and grabbed a quill, scrawling out the truth of Nereida's visit.

It was as if her hand belonged to someone else. She couldn't control its path, and a series of meaningless lines and scribbles took form. Balan stood behind her, watching over her shoulder.

"Was it a demon?" His question was soft against her neck.

She shook her head. Waving her hands around. *More.*

Balan grabbed her by the shoulders, turning her to face him. "Was it Nereida?"

Demetria's neck locked, she could not move to indicate, but her expression must have confirmed it, because a preternatural stillness came over him. Darkness stormed across his eyes, and for the first time, the echoing clutches of fear tightened Demetria's chest at the demon before her.

It was easy to forget. To overlook. To allow her personal feelings of trust and safety to negate the fact. But there was no dismissing it now. Balan was a demon forged in the bellows of the Netherworld.

His voice was both soft and harsh, ghosting a chill down Demetria's spine. "I won't let her use you."

And there it was. He could be a creature of violence and malice. Of pain and suffering. But at the end of the day, he was the only one left who gave a damn about her.

"How can you promise such a thing?" Demetria's voice had returned, weak and thin. "What power have you over her? She—" Her voice cut off again. Unable to discuss the details of the contract.

Balan's eyes darkened. "Because I am the thorn in her side. The one she had to banish to prevent from poisoning others against her." He lifted her chin. "I will not let her have you."

Demetria choked back a sob, the sound getting lodged in her throat as her vision blurred with tears. She threw herself into the arms of a demon, of her only friend. His arms immediately came around her, forgoing their usual hesitance at her affection.

He seemed so sure. So steadfast.

She almost believed him.

CHAPTER SIXTY-TWO

AISLINN

*L*oneliness wore many faces.

Aislinn hugged her knees, peering out the window. More snow had given way to the forest floor, allowing the sun to warm the earth once more. In two moons, it would be an entire year since her death. Since her life was stolen by the river in Ferus Woods. And while she'd grown close with these people, with Lark's vast array of friends, Aislinn felt well and truly alone. She was the only one Lark was so certain would go along with her plan, the one that meant Lark's death, albeit temporarily.

The guilt burned in her belly, driving her to avoid the others as much as possible. To the point of her own seclusion.

That loneliness drove her to asinine urges.

Merikh's name whispered at the back of her mind. His true name. Begging her to call for him.

To what end? To see if he'd try to kill her? To exert her power over him?

Or maybe it was because he was the only one who didn't see her as this fragile little bird in need of protecting.

A soft knock at the door pulled her from her thoughts.

"Come in."

Gavriel appeared, a sheepish smile on his face. He was handsome in a boyish way when he wasn't scowling. Not like Merikh who was more... rugged.

Aislinn's cheeks burned at the thought, and a puzzled expression claimed Gavriel's face.

"I wished to speak with you," he said, suddenly uncomfortable. "It will only take a moment."

"I should hope so, I have many pressing appointments today."

Not even a hint of a smile. Perhaps assassins failed to recognize sarcasm.

"I wanted to say thank you." He crossed the room, sitting beside her on the bench. "I can't begin to balance the debt I owe."

"Debt?" She hadn't done a thing to help. She'd tried, skies, had she ever tried. But it wasn't enough.

Gavriel's eyes, dark green and serious, gained intensity as he spoke. "You gave Lark hope when I could not. You sought a way to free me, and I know it was out of love for her. I am forever grateful to you."

Aislinn shifted. He would not thank her if he knew what his Lark intended. If he knew she had sworn to aid her in her sacrificial pursuit. "It was nothing." Daciana would bring Lark back, and the sickening sensation of guilt ripping apart her stomach would cease.

"No, Aislinn. It was everything." He stood, hesitating. "If there's anything I can do, name it. It's done."

As he retreated, the words demanded release. She had to tell him. Had to give him a chance to talk Lark out of it. What if Daciana couldn't bring her back, and Aislinn let Lark die?

"Gavriel?"

He stilled, his hand on the door.

Tell him.

"Can you teach me to fight?" The wrong words left her lips.

Coward.

He lifted a brow. "You mean with a sword?"

"Sword, dagger, axe, whatever." She should tell him to spend every waking moment at Lark's side, just in case.

If he noted the misery in her voice, he said nothing to it.

Gavriel appeared to consider before saying, "I have a few ideas. Do you have appropriate clothing?"

Aislinn glanced down at her pale green gown, the one with the delicate ribbons along the bodice. She'd dug this hole, might as well jump into it. "I can change."

"Good. Meet me out in the training yard as soon as you're ready."

The training yard? Inerys was not going to be pleased he'd renamed her garden.

———※———

"FIRM YOUR WRIST. There'll be no limp blocking on my watch." Ferryn squeezed Aislinn's wrist in emphasis. "Pretend I'm actually a threat."

Easier done if he wasn't making strange faces at her each time he lunged his 'attack.' The last face appeared as if he'd frozen mid-sneeze, sending Aislinn into a fit of laughter that earned the both of them a stern look of warning from Gavriel.

"He takes this very seriously," Ferryn whispered, pointing in the newly titled Master Assassin's direction. "Don't let him see you having fun."

Gavriel had agreed to teach Aislinn to fight, showing her basic blocks and maneuvers to feel more confident holding a sword. He'd enlisted Ferryn's help in her practice, a fact she was most delighted in since they hadn't had a chance to speak in far too long.

What Aislinn hadn't accounted for was how much enjoyment she'd find in these quiet moments. They were nearly chased away by a rising wave of guilt each time her thoughts turned too completely from the dilemma she faced, but Ferryn was the embodiment of chaos. Always distracting her from her darkest thoughts.

"Remember to follow the natural line of your body—"

"I know, I know." Aislinn gritted her teeth, moving through the awkward motions. It wasn't the instruction or even the series she was attempting to master, it was that she couldn't turn her mind from Lark's request.

Her very secret, catastrophic plan.

And each kind word from Gavriel, each smile from Ferryn, only served to hammer in her shame.

She was betraying them by allowing Lark this. And they would never forgive her.

She would never forgive herself.

"You're deep in thought." Ferryn parried the sword from her hand, catching it lightly before returning it to her. "Share."

"I'm merely concentrating."

"No, you're not." He scowled. "Don't insult my intelligence, Aislinn."

Of course, he'd see right through her. They'd spent months alone together, no one but one another for company. Watching the world pass without them.

But she couldn't betray Lark's trust. Not like this. Aislinn would come up with a plan to prevent Lark's unnecessary self-sacrifice.

The thought brought her mind to a screeching halt. Resolve strengthened, a warmth spread through Aislinn as she reveled in her decision. She would prevent Lark's death. She would pretend to go along with her plan for the moment, but she would find a way to stop her—she'd find an alternative way to kill Nereida and restore the veil. She'd employ Merikh if she had to. Yes! He must know something. How foolish she was to not have thought of this sooner...

Ferryn stood watching, a silent and unyielding sentry awaiting her answer. She couldn't very well tell him Lark's plan—that would drive him to impulsive action out of desperation before Aislinn had the chance to gain insight from Merikh. No, she needed to throw Ferryn off the trail.

"I did something. Something I shouldn't have."

Ferryn's brows lifted. "Continue."

Lying by telling the truth. That was... a manipulation she was not well-versed in.

And yet, the words fell easily from her lips.

"I have feelings for someone I shouldn't. I don't even know the nature of these feelings, only that they shouldn't exist. And... I'm confused. I'm confused and irritated to suffer feelings I cannot name for someone I should not be thinking of."

There. That was vague enough to cover her tracks. He could analyze her nonanswer all he wanted without—

"Oh no." Ferryn's expression melted into one of pity. "Aislinn... you can't. It's—" He glanced over at where Gavriel was engaging in some sort of duel with Alistair. Staged for practice as they kept halting to argue swordplay methods. "I understand it's hard not to mistake intimate knowledge of a person as intimacy." His hand fell to her shoulder, and Aislinn glanced at it, perplexed. "But Gavriel will never see you that way. He'll never see anyone that way. He and Lark... well, it's obnoxious and nauseating at times, but they're actually really sweet and perfect for each other. Were that not enough, their soul bond poses a problem to any interested parties. What you're experiencing is something I myself have felt many times as an unseasoned Reaper. When you know so much about a person, about their life and their thoughts, it's easy to build them up in your mind and cast them in a role they are not fit for. Do you understand me?"

Aislinn's mind stuttered, several sentences attempting to take shape. "Wha—why are you talking about Gavriel?"

Ferryn's pity melted into confusion. "Your feelings. You harbor feelings for someone you shouldn't..."

"No! No!" Aislinn waved her hands wildly, drawing the curious attention of Alistair and Gavriel. "I do *not* have feelings for Gavriel."

"Oh." His brow furrowed. "Daciana?"

"Forget it!" Aislinn stomped away. She should have known better than to say anything. Just let him think she was hiding something, which she was, but it didn't need sharing in any fashion.

It wasn't as if she'd ever tell him her thoughts had an annoying habit of turning to Merikh, the paragon she definitely should have killed when given the chance.

Ferryn caught her by the arm, spinning her back to face him. They stood far enough away the trees obscured Alistair and Gavriel's sparring match. A breeze whistled through the forest, and gooseflesh erupted along her skin.

"Stop, I'm sorry." His voice was soft, and he was standing awfully close. "Sometimes I'm utter shit at picking up hints."

Hints? *What hints?*

"If you—" He wet his lips. "If I were—" His mouth tightened. "You are my friend, and I treasure you. Right now, that's all I can handle. But maybe one day…" His teal gaze bore into hers, offering promises he couldn't possibly give. Aislinn had always known his love for Ceto ran deep, a twisted gnarled sort of fixation. She had no interest in getting caught up in that.

Not that he wasn't handsome or kind—not that he didn't make her laugh when simply breathing didn't seem feasible. Ferryn was special. The brightest light in the darkness.

And maybe she could see herself wondering what it would be like to kiss him. One day. But not today.

Ferryn searched her stare as if begging to find her answer there. What could she say?

Aislinn gave him the barest of nods, and he sighed in relief. His lips found her forehead, cold and soft, a caress of a kiss before it vanished entirely, and he pulled back to face her.

"All right then. What say we quit early and go pester Lark? I owe her a battle of snow before the last of it melts, and with you on my side, her defeat is imminent."

Aislinn laughed, shaking her head and letting him pull her back to Inerys' cottage.

⁂

AISLINN STARED at the cracks in the ceiling. Spiderwebbing in horsehair plaster. Each crack diverged into a forked path, running like a river destined to carve its own route.

So many little choices. All defining the path.

Watching Ferryn laugh and jest with Lark only sent a thousand more cracks through Aislinn's chest. Fissures of decisions. Of mistakes.

She couldn't shake the feeling that she was on the cusp of something. That her path was diverting into a thousand little rivers, and the pressure to choose the right one...

There was one person compulsion-bound to speak truth to her. But was wielding that power an abuse? Lark spoke of necessary evil, but Aislinn could not decipher what was necessary anymore or what was simply the wrong river followed.

And Merikh—

Her heart squeezed at the thought of his name. Her pulse echoing in time with it.

Merikh. Merikh. Merikh.

A flutter of a breeze. A whisper of movement.

His imposing form was beside her, sitting curled toward her as if he'd always been there. Dark hair loose against the tops of his shoulders. Gray eyes searching, beseeching.

"Why did you call for me?"

"Why did you answer?" Aislinn sat up, ignoring the way butterflies erupted in her stomach at how close he was. "I didn't use your true name. You were under no obligation to answer."

His brow furrowed and he ran a large hand into his hair. "I came because you called."

That wasn't an answer so much as a statement of fact. But by the bewildered expression he wore, she could guess it was as much a mystery to him as it was to her.

"How goes Sargon's plan to destroy me?"

He scoffed. "I told him I relayed the invitation to his peace talks to the witch. That she seemed tempted by the idea of pawning you off to continue her life in solitude. That she hadn't agreed but the wheels were in motion." Merikh turned his intense gaze on her, his jaw tightening. "I lied."

"Why are you doing this?"

Merikh's hands flexed into fists, the slightest tremor wracking his body. "I have been to the hall of mirrors. I cannot ignore what I've learned."

Why was he so angry? And why was he so ready to help them now?

"What hall of mirrors?"

His brow furrowed. "It is a forbidden place. But I had to know the truth, and now that I do…" The sheer agony in his eyes made Aislinn's throat constrict.

She fought to keep her voice steady. "What have you learned?" If it could aid them in this fight, save Lark from her foolish endeavor of martyrdom—but would he speak true? Or was this a trick? Aislinn could pull the truth from him, use his true name and command him…

"Sargon is not what he seems." Merikh's voice was a ripple of thunder. "Nor am I." He stood, pacing the room with an agitated gait. The floor groaned under his steps. "I am unable to kill you, Aislinn. I will not. Not now, not ever. There will never be a plane of time or existence where I could kill you."

Her mind spun with dizzying thoughts. "Why? Why not?" Wasn't that his mission? His purpose? What had he learned of Sargon to change his course so?

Merikh stopped, glancing over at her with a pained expression. "You… you are so much more than I can… I can't articulate it, but the mirrors do not lie. You are something special, and it would be a tragedy to have any hand in your ruin." He dropped to sit on the bed, bouncing her with his weight. "In all my years, I've never thought much of the humans. But if they were more like you, they'd be worth saving."

How dare he? *How dare he?*

"There are countless humans, all worth saving." Aislinn stood, her head light with the heated anger coursing through her. "If you weren't stuck in the clouds, your arrogant head up your own arse, you'd know this. Calling me special and the only human worth saving isn't a compliment but proof you are a vile, arrogant, self-important—"

Merikh stood, looming over her. And even as Aislinn's words were ripped from her tongue, even as she glared up at him, there was no fear, no panic. Only anger and fire and—

His hand found her jaw, thumb smoothing over her skin. Aislinn gasped, as a wholly new sensation flooded her. A pull. A tug.

He leaned in, the warmth of his mouth so close to her own. Her eyes fluttered shut, and she forced them open again. Wanting to see. To know.

Merikh dropped his hand and stepped back, stricken. The abrupt rush of cold almost sent Aislinn staggering, the tension ripped from her chest with the sudden distance.

"I'm sorry." He shook his head. "I'm so sorry. That was... I'd never think to... That will never happen again." He stood on the opposite end of the room now, wall to his back. "I merely admire your passion and... kindness. If only I possessed such things... I should not think of you this way."

Aislinn's pulse hammered in her head. "What way?"

Merikh's gaze, tormented with heat and longing, speared through her. "Like... I wish to know the passions humans are capable of beneath your touch. To learn—" He shook his head again. "I know not of what I speak. Only that I should not regard you so."

Too many thoughts warring for release. He was ancient, and he did not know passionate touch? He wanted to learn with *her*? "Why do you keep saying that? That you shouldn't think of me in this way?"

His gaze fell, heat giving way to cold. "I—you—" he let out a soft noise, clamping his mouth shut. Finally, he met her stare. "You are *more*, Aislinn. That you even exist..." He shook his head. "Avalon does not interfere in the lives of mortals. Any human notions of miracles are just wishful thinking, but you"—his eyes burned into hers—"*you*, Aislinn, are beyond anything I've ever seen in all my years. Beyond the heavens and the earth, and I do not deserve to even breathe the same air as you."

Shock evaporated any lingering warmth in Aislinn's body—stole the air from her lungs and the words from her throat. He continued.

"And I saw it in Lark's mind, your demise. That you suffered so—" His words fell away again, and his expression tightened. "I have sent word to the Netherworld that any demon to spend extra time with their creative torments upon that mortal will receive a favor from Avalon."

"That's a dangerous thing to promise." Aislinn finally found her ability to speak once more and chose to ignore his original confession.

"It isn't nearly enough. Not by half." His voice was darkened by anger.

Aislinn exhaled a slow breath and shook her head. "I do not wish to command you, but your explanations confound me further." It was as close to acknowledging what she suspected he meant.

"I know." He stood, towering over her once more. "I want to tell you all. To make you understand. All I can say is I will never allow any harm to come of you. I am yours to command, and I will not allow my personal feelings to cloud my judgement."

None of that made any sense. One thing was clear though. They were both playing a very dangerous game. Aislinn hardened her stomach and her words. "I won't pretend to understand this newfound devotion you have for me."

His expression faltered, and she continued.

"You tried to kill me. You tortured my friend, even now you're on the side set to destroy her and allow the mortals to fall to ruin." It was a good reminder. For them both.

"My place is by your side. At your feet. In your shadow," Merikh snarled. "I will follow you to the edge of the void if it means keeping you safe. You have my word."

Aislinn's heart climbed up her throat, fluttering her quickened pulse. This was what she wanted, wasn't it? A chance to wield him against Nereida without forcing his compliance.

But it all felt wrong. Like decay was just beneath the surface, the initial rot in the root cellar. The thought of trusting him was tempting, too tempting. An almost nervous buzz of energy hummed along her skin. She wanted nothing more than to believe him. But Aislinn had learned the hard way how easy it was to fall for the facade. How dangerous it was to trust the wrong person.

No, she would command his actions, using his true name and betraying the corner of her soul so desperately wishing to remain good and soft in a world set upon destruction. She would break her own heart if it meant protecting everyone.

"I wish that was good enough." The words were ash on her tongue.

Merikh's gaze lifted, pinning her in place. He surveyed her, head to toe, greedy in his exploration, his gaze once again landing on her face. "Me, too, Stella Somniavi. Me, too."

With a whisper of a breeze, Aislinn was once again alone in her room with her thoughts. Unable to demand what he meant by that name. No closer to any answers. She was an enemy of Avalon, but why? Because of some ability she shouldn't even possess? Was that why she hadn't moved onto the afterlife?

No one spoke of it, the pall cast over her current state.

She was supposed to be dead, but instead she was an abomination. A danger to the supposed paradise of the afterlife.

Candlelight danced, casting shadows' movements along the walls. She, too, was a shadow, an absence of light, the silhouette against a wall, a void.

She could be more than that. She would be more than that.

Her heart climbed up her throat as she paced to her door. It opened beneath her touch, and she ventured down the hall. A sliver of light shown along the bottom of Daciana's door. She hardly felt the door beneath her knuckles as she lightly knocked. And when Daciana appeared, concern wrinkling her brow, Aislinn knew her determination must have shown upon her face.

"Dac," she said. "We need to talk."

CHAPTER SIXTY-THREE

LANGFORD

*L*angford frowned at the table overflowing with breads, flaky pastries, and assorted hand pies.

He had been *stress baking* as Alistair liked to call it, and Inerys was going to be furious at how much he'd raided her larder, but he'd needed the distraction. Kenna was due to rise any moment. The others were all fast asleep save for Gavriel, who'd found sleep harder to come by after his prolonged state of unconsciousness. Langford could not fault him for that, but Gavriel remained in the room he shared with Lark, lending privacy to the impending conversation in desperate need of having.

Langford needed to pick Kenna's brain for a plan, any plan, to prevent Alistair's turn once the mixture ran out. Kenna was known to wake before the others, a habit of hers, and pace the perimeter of Inerys' warding spell. Langford sought to intercept the hunter and finally share all of his concerns and fears.

She'd know what to do, surely.

He'd overestimated his ability to wait for the dawn's approach, so anticipatory he was, and spent the night in Inerys' kitchen. He wiped leftover flour from the table's surface, and neatly stacked his creations, carefully hiding his failed attempt at a braided loaf. Lark would no doubt claim the apple pie for herself. There was enough food here to feed a small army.

Yes. Inerys would be vexed indeed. Especially after she'd aided him in his endeavors to extract the remnants of the beast's blood in Kenna's concoction. He'd only had enough left for one moon's turn. One last dose. One last chance. And here he was about to squander it.

No. He couldn't think that way. This had to work. It had to! Even if the witch was skeptical. If he could accept he needed magical interference to aid his process, she could afford to extend the same level of faith to his own process.

Langford ripped a piece off the nearest loaf of crusty bread, popping it into his mouth and chewing.

The rest of the ingredients to Kenna's concoction were attainable. Aconite. Evening primrose. The mixture had proven its efficacy, but without access to more of the wolf beast's blood, he was relying on sand in an hourglass.

But if there was a chance he could eliminate the virus rather than manage it, it was worth it to try, wasn't it? He'd start with small doses of the beast's blood, slowly work his way up, and pray to the gods Alistair developed immunity.

The shuffling of sleepy footfalls sounded at the top of the stairs, a slow drag of each descending step following. Kenna appeared in the doorway, black hair mussed from sleep and pale cheek imprinted with the lines of her pillow. She opened her mouth in a wide gaping yawn, stretching like a cat. Her tunic lifted enough to show a glimpse of a silvery scar running along her midsection. Kenna scratched at it absently, before breaking off her yawn with a grin.

"You made breakfast?" Her voice was scratchy. She glanced at the overabundance of breads and confections. "Are we expecting company?"

"Not exactly." Langford gestured for her to sit and handed her a flaky sweet roll.

Kenna's dark eyes narrowed, suspicion alighting her features, before she slid into her seat and took a giant bite out of the roll, claiming half of it in one go. "A'right, L'ngford." She mumbled around her inhumanly large bite of food. "You have my attention."

Kenna wasn't one to mince words or dance around the truth. She was direct and open in a way Langford admired.

"Alistair is still bound by the moon." Langford was nearly proud of himself for meeting her candor with equal frankness. "And your remedy is a temporary fix for a long-term problem."

Kenna nodded, her tongue poking into the side of her mouth. "I heard something about that. I suppose this display of domestic hospitality is in pursuit of my help?" She shoved the rest into her mouth, cheeks bulging, and waved for him to hand her another. After swallowing it down, she said, "It's pointless for you to bribe me. One, because I'd help for free, and two, because I have no fucking clue what to do about it."

Langford's stomach twisted as cold ran the length of his body. "You're the expert, but I was hoping you'd hear me out on my theory."

"Let's have it then."

He pulled the vial out from his pocket, the one he had every intention of injecting bit by bit into Alistair. "I want to cure him once and for all. If we treat his symptoms like a viral infection, maybe we can build up immunity to the curse."

Kenna chewed, her face scrunching up. "I don't think it works that way."

"You would claim defeat before we even try?" Heat bloomed across the back of Langford's neck, and he tucked the vial back into his pocket lest he break the glass in his fist. "The whole lot of you are so quick to trust your ancient folklore and traditions." He held his hands out. "Even I have accepted I do not know all in the way the world works. That there are things I cannot explain. But that doesn't mean my knowledge is useless."

Kenna dropped her second roll onto the table, dusting off her hands, and bracing her elbows atop the table. "Langford." Her voice was so gentle, too gentle, and the crease between her brows only made her pity more unbearable. "No one was prepared for this. What happened back in the village… I've never seen anything like that in my entire life. I don't know, it could be the loss of the veil, but this is new territory for me." She reached across the table, placing her hand over his. "I'm not saying it won't work, just that I doubt it. If it does, great. If it doesn't, we'll figure it out. But—"

Langford ripped his hand free of hers. No. This was all wrong. He was a healer, and that's what he did. He healed. He fixed what was broken. To live in a world where his abilities were canceled out by powers beyond mortal capability meant he had no guard against the dangers lurking outside these walls. What if this failed? What if Alistair succumbed to the curse? What if he lost Alistair for good, this time? What if the man he loved disappeared behind the snarling face of a beast? Huxley's corpse appeared in Langford's mind. Twisting and turning and the *snap* of bones breaking as they reformed into something else. The image flickered until it was Alistair's face elongating into a monstrous snout, bloodlust replacing the tender affection in his gaze.

He couldn't lose him. Not again. The last time damn near killed him, too.

Memories of Alistair gasping for breath, his face turning purple as his lungs refused to fill with air, assaulted Langford's mind. Of the life leaving his bloodshot eyes and his body going far too still. He couldn't save him. Not against wounds not of this world. He couldn't save him.

But no. Daciana had been there. She'd stitched his soul back into his body. Alistair was safe. He was alive. He was here. He was—

Langford pressed his fist against his mouth until his teeth hurt. Until the waking nightmare abated to the edges of his thoughts, lingering with a dull throb of a poorly healed bruise. He dug his fingers into the woodgrain of the table hard enough for sharp spots of pain to light along his nailbeds. His chest tightened, and the edges of his vision blurred.

"Are you all right?"

Kenna's voice broke through the deafening throb of his pulse in his ears.

Langford's head ached, tremendous pressure building behind his eyes. Pain. It was too painful. He took an unsteady breath, the shaky sound of his exhale far away. Another, deep and slow even as it shuddered, exhale of a shivery breath.

Warm hands found the back of his neck. Hands he'd know anywhere. Langford sagged against the relief of Alistair's grounding touch.

"I'm here." His voice was a balm. "I'm here, love."

Langford nodded, focusing on his breathing as Alistair massaged the back of his neck in the familiar way only he could. Just the right pressure to alleviate the pain behind his eyes.

Inhale. He was capable. There were things he could control.

Exhale. His panic was a response to stimuli, not a sign of weakness.

Inhale. If Kenna thought the fallen veil was to blame…

Exhale. All the more reason to see it restored.

Calmness dragged over Langford like a weighty blanket. The exhaustion from lack of sleep, from spending the night baking, from his body's reaction, it all pummeled into him like a battering ram.

With great effort, he lifted his head to find Alistair watching him with softness in his vibrant green eyes. Not pity, never pity, but a knowing fondness the man reserved just for him.

He'd want an explanation, surely, but Langford wasn't sure he could offer one. Not in this moment, when the words thickened his tongue and choked in his throat. Not when it meant admitting his doubts that he could save him. Somehow saying the thoughts aloud gave them power, and Langford was sick of feeling powerless to his spiraling thoughts.

As if sensing the inner turmoil in his head, Alistair pressed a kiss to Langford's sweaty temple. "Tomorrow," he whispered. "But now, we return to bed."

Without waiting for an answer, without even asking after the pile of forgotten breads, the reason for his mental state, the hushed whispers shared in the beginning hints of a quiet morning, Alistair led Langford up the stairs, down the hall, and back into their private room.

Distantly, the door snicked shut behind them, and Langford collapsed atop their bed, the cool pillow hitting his cheek. His eyes dragged closed as Alistair's arms came around him. Langford didn't even have it in him to ask if Kenna was still at the table, reeling from his sudden and swift decline.

Langford offered no resistance to the pull of sleep as Alistair whispered against his ear, "I've got you, love. Now sleep."

LAST EVE'S conversation with Kenna had been...

Well, it had gone to utter shit. Langford hated to use the word, but there it was. He'd gone into it with a specific outcome in mind, a hope for a plan at the very least, and walked out with an attack of his anxiety and a headache.

But as he lay in Alistair's arms, the rightness of his touch soothing his overworked mind, Langford had found his clarity. He would simply ensure the veil was reinstated and refuse to accept defeat. It was the type of plan Alistair would thoroughly approve of. Simple. Elegant. Lacking in finer details.

Langford didn't need details to know he wasn't giving up on Alistair without a fight. And if the love of his life turned into a beast...

Then he'd love the beast.

That thought didn't sit right. *He'd love the beast whilst searching for a cure to the end of his days,* he amended.

Staring into the mirror, Langford gave up on fixing his hair in favor of retying the neck of his tunic.

"You've been awfully quiet." Alistair rested his chin on Langford's shoulder and wrapped his arms around him from behind, pulling his hands away from where he was trying to refasten his belt after yet another attempt gone awry.

Not that Langford was complaining this time.

"That must be strange as you know I enjoy filling the air with incessant chatter." Langford frowned at his reflection. Was he deflecting? Obviously. But what good would it do to spew every turn of his thoughts when he'd already made up his mind that it didn't matter? His resolve was steadfast; he needn't dwell on the panic he'd only just managed to assuage.

Alistair turned his face into the vulnerable skin of Langford's neck, rubbing his unkempt facial hair vigorously enough to startle a shriek out of him. "Tell me what holds your tongue, lest you wish me to put it to better use."

"Alistair!" Langford's stomach flipped in that warm, pleasant way only Alistair could coax out of him.

"*Gods,* but the way you say my name."

Langford rolled his eyes even as his cheeks burned. "You've become a most bothersome item of study. First you fail to respond to proper stimulus—"

"Langford, you stimulate me most properly." Alistair grinned, sliding his hands up to untie Langford's tunic. Dammit he'd just tied that!

Langford batted his hands away. "There was once a time a tree vaguely shaped as a woman would stimulate you."

"Are you... sassing me? Langford Brenner, I'm rubbing off on you."

"Yes, well. Perhaps we need more friends."

"Undoubtedly."

"Will you cease trying to undress me?"

"Never."

It was a familiar song and dance. Alistair had many ways of showing his care, and one was in the form of his insatiable appetite. And Langford was tempted, *so tempted,* to lose himself in it. But there was much to be done, and though the fall of the world should have been the strongest driving force, the sudden and immediate threat of losing Alistair to the beast was his greatest motivator.

Selfish? Most assuredly. But if this was the end of days, Langford had earned the right to be selfish.

But one thing at a time. And right now, his task was to escape his room without spilling his thoughts to a most persuasive man currently tugging at his breeches.

"*And* now you become an utterly indecorous beast even without shifting." Langford sniffed. "How am I ever supposed to work under these circumstances?"

Alistair stilled, understanding dawning his expression. "You worry after me."

Why had he said that? It was more than enough for Alistair to follow the thread of his thoughts. Langford inhaled deeply, exhaling with precision. "I always worry after you." It was foolish to even attempt to keep his fears to himself. But old habits and all.

"And you spoke with Kenna." All notes of teasing swiftly fled Alistair's tone, leaving his voice somber and contemplative. "Is there no hope then?"

Langford spun to face him, anger licking up the back of his neck like fire. "There's always hope." There had to be. He grabbed the trousers he'd hung over the back of the chair and gently pulled the vial from his pocket. Red blood gleamed behind the glass. "Do you trust me?"

"With my life," Alistair swore.

Langford set the blood down, reaching for his pack. He'd need to sterilize the needle again before administering. "And if this doesn't work, we'll find another way." He lifted his gaze to ensure he was still listening.

"And if there is no other way?" Alistair's jaw tightened. "If I do not remain myself..." His eyes blazed, unspoken pain reflected in their depths. "I won't allow you to tie yourself to a monster. To a life full of pain. I know you, Langford. I know you better than anyone. You would condemn yourself to an existence of studies and experiments, all the while failing to *live*. If I'm to be a beast, you will move on from me. You will find your happiness and forget I ever stole your heart for a short while—"

"Alistair." Langford's heart pounded in his chest. Anger and panic thudded painfully together with each pulse. "Do not even *think* of finishing that sentence." He gripped Alistair's chin, forcing his eyes to remain fixed on his. "I love you, you bloody fool. In any form. In any life. I love you. I'm not giving up on us. Not for anything. Nothing will come between us. Not even death. So, save your breath. I'm not going anywhere."

Alistair's brow furrowed, and he grabbed Langford's wrist, pulling him against his chest with one violent tug and crashing their lips together. His hands were greedy, desperate in their pursuit, as he ripped Langford's tunic open, unbuckled his belt, and led him backward to the bed.

How could Alistair ever think he would agree to separating?

"I love you so much, sometimes it's hard to breathe." Alistair's voice was a growl against Langford's skin, and he shivered. "One day," Alistair continued, panting between hungry kisses, "I'll buy us a house and build you a library, so you never need to trade your books again. You'll have a study and workbench, and you can run every fucking test and experiment you want on me."

"And we'll make sure"—Langford exhaled as Alistair bit into the sensitive skin in the crook of his neck—"we have a spacious yard so you can run around and a rule about cleaning your teeth before entering the house. I don't want any of your victims' blood, chickens and the like, to stain my floors." It was just the sort of thing Alistair would say, another deflection from the harsh reality they faced. But Langford believed his own words, could even imagine the life they would have together, should this be Alistair's fate.

Because beast or no, Langford would forever remain his.

Alistair laughed against Langford's skin. "Paragon's tits, love."

"Don't blaspheme."

Alistair jammed his fingers into Langford's ribs, pulling a breathless peal of laughter from his chest.

Only Alistair could wring such lightness and joy even on the darkest of days. His hands were ravenous in their exploration, revealing more and more skin as he tossed the rest of Langford's clothing to the floor. He ripped his own tunic over his head, new and old scars, both familiar and intimately known to Langford, stretching across his dark-olive skin.

Langford would never tire of this feeling. Not when they were old and soft and rounder in places. Not when the days were filled with mundane problems of a secure life. Alistair would always be this larger-than-life soul, misunderstood by most, but kindred to the deepest parts of Langford's soul. His touch, his heart, his fire alone would always be Langford's hope. His belief that something good can grow even in the harshest truths of life.

Alistair's mouth trailed over Langford, worshipping every part of him with a heartbreaking fervor that lit his nerves on fire and sent tears pricking his eyes. It was overwhelming, the way Alistair consumed him. The way he always had.

When their mouths met once more, Alistair's gentleness, his knowledge of every inch of Langford's body as they joined, sent lightning down his spine. And when Alistair reached that deepest part of Langford, he groaned against his lips, a sound of both pleasure and agony.

"You deserve more than my heart," Alistair whispered, pressing his sweat-slicked forehead against Langford's. "You deserve everything."

Langford turned his head to steal a kiss, harsh and brutal and unforgiving, before it melded into a softness he knew Alistair needed. "Alistair," he whispered his name, a soft caress of breath that he knew drove him mad, "you are everything."

Alistair's hand clamped on the back of Langford's neck as he claimed his mouth. He once more moved within him, possessive yet tender in his strokes, his eyes never leaving Langford's.

And when they were spent, wrapped in each other and fighting for air, Alistair pressed his face into Langford's neck, whispering promises of forever against his skin.

SOMETHING WAS AMISS. Langford could feel it. Well, not *feel* it so much as observe and draw conclusions.

Daciana and Lark had commenced their training with Inerys, a practice that usually filled the air with camaraderie and laughter.

But there was nothing friendly about this exchange.

Daciana was stiff, cold. Her demeanor closed off and abrupt. He'd never seen her regard Lark in this way, not in all their time together. Only Alistair earned this side of Dac, and he had the ability to thaw her chilly manner almost immediately upon arrival.

Something had happened between them.

And Langford was terribly curious.

Lark seemed just as curious as he, with the way she tossed puzzled looks Daciana's way, tried to coax her out from behind the wall she'd erected between them, even the hitch in her shoulders at her failure to do so.

Hmm… a one-sided grievance it would seem.

"I'm done for the day." Daciana turned to leave.

"Wait!" Lark called after her, catching her by the arm. Whatever she said next was too low for Langford to hear, but across the way, Alistair was inching closer, a determined expression on his face.

Good. He'd find out and tell him later.

"Everyone heard you and Alistair this morning."

He turned to face Kenna, the glimmer of mischief already crinkling her eyes.

"No shame. Only Inerys seemed annoyed by it. I'm surprised she hasn't spelled your room yet with a silencing ward. Maybe she will now. Dac and I certainly put ours to good use."

No. They were not going to bond over this.

"I have no interest in discussing this."

Kenna grinned. "I think it's great, actually. Heard some of what you said through the walls. You'll really stay with him if he's a monster, won't you?"

Langford bit down on his tongue. She of all people should know better than to prod. It was only last night that she'd nearly dashed his hopes of her having another cure in their gambit. He'd still administered the blood last eve and this morning. Another dose tonight, steadily building Alistair's immunity before his own blood could burn it off.

But standing here now, listening to Kenna make light of the situation, it set his teeth on edge.

"We're done talking about this." Langford shoved away, storming deeper into the woods to escape her merciless taunting.

"Wait!" Kenna jogged alongside him, keeping pace without losing the steady measure of her voice. "I'm not trying to be an ass here. I mean it! You're better than most because you don't shy away from the hard bits, yeah?"

Langford stalled in his tracks. "The hard bits?" he repeated. "Alistair faces the very real possibility of losing himself entirely, and you want to what? Pat me on the back? Rub salt in the wound while praising my loyalty?"

"All I'm saying is you know he won't hurt you." Kenna placed a cautious hand on his shoulder. "Sometimes that's enough to break through, you know?"

It was another glimmer of hope. An unanswered question, which normally vexed him greatly, but in this happenstance, the unknown possibilities were the greater aim. It was when the answers were definite and resolute in their hopelessness he would fall apart. But if he could… if the moon incited Alistair's turn, if he merely coaxed his rational mind to coexist alongside his beast…

"You might be on to something." Langford shook her shoulders, earning another grin.

"Of course, I am." With a satisfied shrug, Kenna sauntered away, heading for where Daciana and Lark were closely whispering to one another. She grabbed Alistair by the neck and steered him away from where he'd been conspicuously eavesdropping.

Langford had one last dose of the cure left, in case it failed. But there was time. Their Vallemerian forces would arrive in a week's time, as would the assassins Gavriel had recruited. If he just spent the next few days working with Alistair and really focusing on narrowing down the grounding techniques he'd attempt to employ, he might—

"Langford!" Lark's voice called out, panicked and on the edge of hysterical. The rest of her words were a garbled mess.

Langford shook his head, cupping his ear to signal he hadn't heard.

Her eyes widened, and she sprinted toward him.

Whatever her issue was, he was quite certain it wasn't an emergency. In fact—

Hot piercing pain lanced through him. His back... it was burning. A fire had erupted across his skin. No... not fire. Searing cold.

Alistair bellowed, his eyes glowing bright as he launched himself across the clearing.

Langford stumbled, his legs giving out. Wetness bloomed across the back of his tunic, the union of fire and ice upon his skin. Gods. It hurt. Why did it hurt?

The world toppled sideways, and the image of Alistair, his visceral fear as it melted into rage, was the last thing Langford saw.

CHAPTER SIXTY-FOUR

DACIANA

"*T*hat is not the point!" Daciana bit back the instinct to snarl as Lark's golden eyes glared right back at her.

Langford gave them a nervous glance. He knew not of what they spoke, Daciana was sure of it. Nobody knew apart from them.

Aislinn had told her everything. Lark's request for secrecy. Her asinine plan. Her fucking *death wish*. Daciana could understand the passing thought, the urge to follow what seemed the easiest plan, but to outright plan to die right under their noses, to scheme with innocent, hapless Aislinn and pressure her to keep such a horrific secret...

It was as if Lark held no faith, no trust in any of them. As if all those months spent together, seasons and moons passing as time spun on, meant *nothing*. They were all dispensable, the whole lot of them. Too insignificant to warrant a conversation.

Rage burned in Daciana's gut. Rage and... hurt. How could Lark think so little of them? How could she—

It didn't matter. She would not let her die. Not for the sake of whatever misguided quest for sacrifice she clung to. It was abhorrent. Nonsensical. And the fact that she'd use the very weapon Daciana forged...

What the fuck were they training for? Why pretend and play along with Inerys, working alongside Daciana to feed each other's energy into sustainable use, if she'd planned all along to cut her life short?

And she hadn't so much as whispered a word to her about any of it.

"It is, Dac. I've seen what you can do. I *know* what you're capable of. I trust you."

Daciana laughed, the sound a bitter bark of pain. "Trust. That's really funny, Lark." Trust would imply she'd confided in her, extended the truth in its rawest form. But no, she'd hidden her plan, endeavoring to make them all unwitting accomplices to her death.

"You brought Alistair back." Lark had lowered her voice, glancing around the melting garden where the others were training. Her gaze snagged on Gavriel, her brow furrowing.

Interesting. Daciana followed her gaze to examine the assassin. His grin and ease of laughter as he and Alistair circled each other confirmed what she already knew: He had no knowledge of this plan, and Lark intended to keep it that way.

"I don't know what it will cost to bring you back or if I even can again. Don't you get it? I haven't been practicing necromancy."

"Don't call it that."

"You would be dead, Lark! Don't you get that?"

Lark's gaze dropped, her mouth firming in a thin line, and understanding washed over Daciana like a bucket of ice water. "You never intended for me to bring you back. That's why you didn't tell me. It was only a lie you told Aislinn to get her to agree to it."

Lark exhaled a shuddering breath and ran her hand impatiently through her auburn hair. "I didn't wish to add pressure to an already impossible situation. I thought if you knew what I planned, you'd lose focus and—"

"Do not lie to me." Daciana lowered her voice, clenching her hands into fists as the fury raced through her blood. "Not now. Not after everything. If I ever meant anything to you at all, do not lie to my face thus."

Lark's eyes glimmered, her wet lashes threatening the fall of her tears. "I knew I would die. And I expected nothing but peace in the knowledge that all of you would be safe." She grabbed Daciana's elbow. "You are like a sister to me. I will sacrifice all that I must to see you and the others well and safe from my mistakes."

It hurt. Her words, they *hurt*. They tightened Daciana's throat and clenched in her chest. The ache of loving someone so fiercely, of finally finding her true family, and knowing the end was imminent. She understood, of course, she did. Beneath the anger, the hurt, the betrayal, was the understanding of Lark's nature. It was as she always was. How she always would be. The light so bright it burned. The love of those close to her so strong, she would sacrifice all.

But the wrongness of it all still twisted in Daciana's belly, and her response came out harsher than she intended. "Tell Gavriel, or I will. You owe him that much."

Lark's hand dropped away, a sorrowful expression claiming her delicate features. "I only wish—" Her words cut off abruptly as her eyes widened in panic.

The hairs on the back of Daciana's neck stood on end, and a chill rose through the garden, carried on a harsh breeze. A threat. A warning.

Something was coming.

Lark shook her head and screamed, "Langford!"

Daciana's haladies were in her hands before she even turned.

Langford was crumpled on the ground, blood pooling beneath him. Far. Too far away from them. Across the garden, it might as well have been across the world. A harpy stood over him, baring its teeth and raising its bloody claws, dotting the snow with evidence of his pain.

A growl rumbled from behind, but Daciana ignored the sound and ran to Langford. She leapt over stones partly revealed beneath melted snow. Over a stacked pile of kindling Alistair had left out. Her heart pounded in her ears as she ran, faster than her legs had ever carried her. A shadow fell over Langford's form, blocking the harpy.

A figure crouched over his unconscious body. Another rumbling growl filling the space. It was a protective posture, the way the creature was positioned between Langford and the harpy. It let out a roar loud enough to vibrate Daciana's teeth.

A sudden knowing, a sense of instinct came over her. This creature would not hurt Langford. It swept out its claws, striking the harpy down but made no move to leave Langford.

It couldn't be... Langford had used Kenna's cure on him. He wasn't due to turn for another week, and the midday sun shone bright and insistent upon the bloody snow, but there was no mistaking who this creature was.

Alistair.

His ears elongated to sharp furred points. His jaw extended, razor-sharp teeth slicing through his mouth and cutting his lips on the journey. A heavy exhale, thick and wet.

She could scarcely recognize him. The very bone structure of his features had shifted, his face becoming monstrous. His brow ridge stood stronger, casting a dangerous severity on his expression. His jaw was wider, protruding in an elongated underbite, the tips of his sharp teeth pressing through his bloody lips. His eyes were brighter than the moon but yellow like the center of the chamomile Langford used in his teas.

Alistair had shifted under the harsh light of the sun. Somehow... he'd become what was meant to answer the moon's call. It was wrong. A twisted form of change, neither wolf nor man, but just wrong.

And why... why could he turn at will, while she was still bound to the moon?

A question for another time, and Daciana shoved her bitterness down. The very real danger posed was that he hadn't mastered his shift yet, hadn't learned to keep the man and the beast within.

Daciana slowed her approach, not wishing to alarm Alistair. He would not let any creature harm Langford, but would he see her as a threat?

Lark hadn't noticed, running toward the harpy as it rose once more. She let out a cry, raising her sword high before hacking into the creature. Its black blood coating the ground like an oil slick.

If Alistair attacked Lark...

Daciana's anger toward her was a foolish, childish thing. If her last words spoken were in hurt—

Alistair crouched over Langford's form, making no move to lunge at Lark as she stuck her blade deep into the harpy's belly, twisting and yanking with a sickening squelch.

Shouting. Screeching. All the while, Alistair's beast remained fixed over Langford. That was something. He hadn't attacked Lark despite her proximity. If he perceived her as friend, perhaps more of him remained in control than she feared. They could slowly coax him away, see to Langford's wound, and work on dispensing Kenna's cure to return him to his human form. It was a perfect plan. Calm. Rational. What it lacked in excitement, it made up for in predictability. Just another few steps until she could safely position herself between Alistair and Lark...

The wind rushed through Daciana's hair, carrying the scent of warning.

The clearing erupted, ripples forming in midair. Jagged talons clawed their way into view, a bone-chilling cry of rage searing the air. Antlers pushed through, emaciated bodies of beasts, ribs exposed and flesh hanging in tatters, followed. The incessant beating of wings, torn and ragged, carrying the putrid scent of death.

It was an ambush.

Monsters poured in, appearing as if slipping through a gossamer curtain.

Inerys' protection ward.

Daciana leapt toward the nearest creature, uncaring if she spooked Alistair. She slid her blade beneath the chin of a harpy, pulling free with a bloody finality.

If war was upon them, she would show no mercy.

She lifted her gaze, searching until she found Kenna. Kenna's eyes were blown wide in shock, but when she caught sight of her, she smiled, tossing her a wink before raising her red hood over her head. She let her chain unravel, the metal spiked ball hitting the earth with a thud.

A hunter readying for the kill.

Inhuman sounds of rage, of anguish, of suffering filled the garden.

504

It was as if a dam had ruptured, flooding the land with immeasurable pain. And nothing could stem the tide.

Harpies. Leśniks. Manananggals. Wentikos. Vodníks. Some strange creature dragging a giant rusted axe and a bloody canvas sack. A lone bubak, watching and waiting.

There was no end to them.

"Kenna!" Gavriel bellowed. "Any information would be greatly appreciated!" He cut down a manananggal as he shouted, severing her head from her bisected torso. "Anyone have any salt?"

"On it!" Kenna tossed a cannister to him, and he caught it, sprinkling with care so not to spill it all. "These tree looking bastards and the ones with the antlers are pretty standard. Pointy end of your sword should do it." She grunted as she knocked a harpy back, slashing her silver blade through its throat. "Fire for the one wearing human skin."

"Charming!" Came Ferryns' response.

"Just use silver blades if you have them and keep them busy until one of us can get to you."

It was madness. Chaos.

Lark and Ferryn slipped into a coordinated effort, tossing the Reaper Blade back and forth as needed. Gavriel focused on every manananggal he set his sights on, depositing salt on their bisected pieces as he finished.

Alistair's beast form remained crouched in a defensive stance over Langford. Never yielding.

They needed to get him inside. At least for Inerys to look at him. They could battle these creatures until their muscles gave out, but letting him bleed out in the snow was not an option.

Daciana slowly approached, and Alistair growled, turning his yellow gaze on her. His features were all wrong, too prominent and twisted, but something about his face still felt like... Alistair.

"I won't hurt him, I swear it."

Alistair bared his fangs, a low guttural sound escaping his chest.

"Please, let me help him." Daciana held out her hand, refusing to breathe as Alistair sensed the air.

Tension thickened the short distance between them, but she held utterly still, awaiting his judgment.

Alistair huffed, stepping back enough to reveal Langford. All the color had drained from his face, and a yellowish color stained the snow alongside his blood.

Poisoned talons.

"Fuck." Daciana lifted him into her arms gingerly and offered Alistair a nod. "I've got him. Kill as many of those bastards as you can."

Several heartbeats passed, and Alistair lunged, tackling a wentiko to the ground and ripping out its throat. Daciana rushed to the house, kicking the door open.

"Inerys! Aislinn!" She carried Langford into the kitchen, and Inerys appeared, her hair a mess, and dark circles etched beneath her eyes.

"Wha—"

"No time. He needs help."

Inerys shoved all her pots and pans and teacups off the table, the sound of porcelain shattering filling the room. Daciana laid him upon its surface, turning him on his side for Inerys to see.

If the witch was worried over his wound, she hid it well. Not a flicker of emotion crossed her face. "Hold him down. This will not be pleasant."

But the others were outside fighting...

Daciana stood by his head and gripped Langford's wrists, holding him firm while still keeping his back exposed to Inerys' keen eye.

"I need to draw out the poison, it's already calcifying."

A gasp sounded from the doorway. Aislinn stood, a hand over her mouth.

"Good, you're here. Go to the cellar and fetch me my salve. Once I extract the poison, you take over."

"But I can't—"

"The salve, Aislinn."

Aislinn spun on her heel, disappearing with a flutter of her skirts.

"There are more out there." Daciana did not wish to rush Inerys, but time was of the essence.

"I know. I need to recast the protection wards," she said grimly. "Someone has managed to weaken them. A vital conversation to have later. For now"—she grabbed a thick cylinder of wood and handed it off to Daciana—"slip this between his teeth and be ready."

Daciana peeled back Langford's bloodless lips, her heart lurching in her chest.

Inerys nodded and began scraping her fingers through the deep gashes in his back. Langford's eyes fluttered open, a pained groan muffled behind the wood piece.

Daciana crouched to his eye-level. "Shh. It's all right, I'm here."

Tears rolled down his face, shrieks of pain breaking through. Daciana pressed her forehead to his, a helplessness filling and expanding her chest. If she could take his pain as her own, she would in a heartbeat. "I'm so sorry," she whispered, vision blurring.

Langford trembled, back arching with each pass of Inerys' hand. His eyes rolled back, and he was once again still.

"Inerys..." Daciana could still sense his heartbeat, weak and faint.

"I know." She grabbed a sprig of thyme, rubbing it between her palms before gently coating his back with it. "This is for my own peace of mind."

Aislinn appeared, breathless and cheeks flushed, a small tin in her hand.

"Good, bring it here." Inerys pointed to her spot, stepping out of the way for Aislinn to take her place. "Coat his wounds and repeat the words I told you, yes?"

Aislinn nodded, her throat bobbing.

"You can do this." Inerys grabbed her by the shoulders. "I need to place the wards. Remember to feel the pull, and let go if it goes too deep."

"Yes. Yes, I understand."

Daciana didn't fucking understand. "How do I help?"

"You get back out there, and make sure nothing gets in."

She could do that. Daciana marched to the door, taking her place outside the cottage. Haladie in one hand, she pulled her sword from its sheathe at her back and twisted her wrist in a readying motion. This part was easy. There was no question.

It was everything that came after that would be hard. Alistair... how long did it take for him to shift back? Could he even shift back? When there were no more enemies to slay, would his rage be sated or would he attack one of them? And there was the matter of how these monsters found them. Inerys had said her protective wards had been weakened, but by whom?

A wentiko howled, its voice sending a shudder down Daciana's spine and alerting her nerves. She let out a whistle, and its red eyes clamped on her. She sank into a defensive crouch.

Yes, this part was easy.

CHAPTER SIXTY-FIVE

AISLINN

*A*islinn sagged against the table, her energy spent. Inerys had disappeared into her cellar to reinstate the protective ward.

Someone had tampered with it. Had cut ribbons into its strength.

She glanced over at Langford, his back already mostly healed. Inerys' salves worked well enough on their own, but she'd showed Aislinn how to help them along with transference energy. She was only supposed to speed up the healing process, not close the skin entirely.

But Aislinn did not know what they faced outside these doors, and if she didn't do everything she could to ensure he would stand on his own to face the dawn—

A wave of exhaustion rolled through her, nearly knocking her to the floor. Aislinn braced her hands on the table.

Inerys would not be pleased.

The *crash* of a breaking window sounded, and a screech filled the cottage. Aislinn staggered to the counter, grabbing a carving knife. Pathetic. Useless. It trembled in her weak hand.

Why had she used so much of her energy?

Langford's breaths were steady and even.

Yes, that was why.

A mottled hand reached through the broken window, smearing

blood against the sill. Aislinn's heart climbed up her throat, and she held her knife out in front of her.

Fear is not weakness. Fear is not weakness. Fear is not weakness.

An arm appeared, thick and bound in leathery skin.

Fear is my compass.

Aislinn's breath escaped her chest in rapid gusts, and the room spun.

A large twisted body, stitched together by uneven sutures, pulled itself through. Its mouth was bound and sewn shut, black eyes revealing no malice or mercy. No life. No thought.

Only death.

It stood to its full height, head skimming the ceiling. At its side a large rusted axe rested against the ground. It took a step toward her, scraping the head of its axe against the floor and raising all the hairs on Aislinn's arms.

Dare to find my strength.

Aislinn lunged, positioning herself in front of Langford, and held her knife out. She shook so hard, her teeth chattered.

It took another step, and the big bulging sack stained with blood came into view.

A tear rolled down her cheek.

She could do this. She could do this. She'd brought a very paragon to his knees.

Merikh's face filled her vision. Grey eyes a storming sea. Strong nose leading to a full mouth tightened in pain. *Merikh.*

The creature came closer still, lifting its giant axe high.

Aislinn rushed, stabbing at anything she could reach—but the knife stopped short as if hitting something solid beneath its skin. She cried out, stabbing until her arms gave out. Black blood coated her knuckles as her sobs broke free.

The creature stared down at her, readying its axe for the killing blow.

She could run, she was faster than this creature, but she would not leave Langford unprotected.

Aislinn shut her eyes, preparing for the pain.

A whisper of warmth against her face. The passing of the blade? The wind from its wake?

She opened her eyes to find a large figure standing before her, blocking her from the creature. He stood tall, his hands holding the creature's axe and the collar of its robe. With a twist of his wrist, he shoved the axe through the creature's neck, and its head hit the floor with a heavy thud.

Aislinn's breath had taken a desperate edge, near wheezing. The man turned—

Merikh.

His face was drawn in concern, brows furrowed and mouth tight. "Are you hurt?"

She shook her head, knees finally giving out. He caught her before she hit the floor. There was no reason to sink into his hold, and yet she did. A warm feeling of safety enveloped her, and when she rested her hand on his chest, his heart battered against her palm.

"Aislinn." Her name was a broken whisper on his lips, and he leaned his head closer to hers. Closer still. She let her eyes slip closed. The warmth of his breath upon her mouth— "I thought I had more time, but I must show you something."

Aislinn blinked her eyes open to find an expression of indecision and guilt warring on his face. "What is it?"

"I need you to trust me. I swear to you I'll never hurt you. Not today or any day that follows until time ceases. I will not harm you." He ran his finger down the length of her cheek. "But I need you to command me with my true name. Command the answers that will prove my word."

She shook her head. "I don't understand." She pushed at him, and he gently rose to stand, stepping away and releasing her from his grip. Already she was colder. "What do you need from me?"

"I must show you the hall of mirrors. And you must command me to bring you back unharmed as soon as you've seen their truth." Merikh fell to his knee before her. "Please, Aislinn."

He wanted to take her to Avalon? To the very place where the highest paragon resided and wished her dead? It made no sense. How could he expect her to trust him when he was actively pursuing her death? And she almost let him kiss her. Was he manipulating her feelings—feelings she shouldn't even possess?

"Please, Aislinn. Use my true name. I beg you."

"Miro." Her voice pulled taut, anger hardening its edge. "Why do you wish to take me to Avalon?"

He sagged as if in relief. "I wish to show you the truth."

"Does Sargon know?"

"No." He shook his head vehemently. "Sargon can never know."

Aislinn edged closer, peering down at his sincere expression. "Why does this matter so much to you?"

Merikh took a deep breath. "I've learned much of my knowledge is based on lies. I wish to remedy this, for all of Avalon, but mostly for you."

It was like balancing on a knifepoint. "Why?"

"I care for you. I wish to see you warm and safe. Happy and at peace. I do not understand the nature of this care, nor could I begin to assign it meaning, but all I know is you are my mission." He stood, suddenly far too close and still not close enough. "*You* are the meaning I've been searching for. And I don't know why, but I know the call of my instinct enough to say"—his eyes searched hers—"I will lay down my life in pursuit of your safety. It's but a trifling thing in comparison. I swear to you, I *swear*, I've learned enough to know I'm finally on the right path."

Aislinn exhaled a shaky breath. It was too much. Too much with no basis. He didn't mean he loved her, did he? Or was this a strange power dynamic she'd enacted by using his true name...

"Command me," he whispered. "I'm already yours."

Tears pricked at her eyes as her throat tightened. "I do not wish to command anyone!" She shoved away from him, too many thoughts and feelings conflating her judgment. "You offer this as if it's some great gift, but it's a terrible thing. I do not wish for it!"

"And yet you have it." Merikh's eyes pleaded. "Allow me to show you your truth. Every fiber of my existence demands I follow you!" He crept closer, pain etching his face. "Grant me this, and you'll never have to see me again if you wish it."

"Never?" Her chest panged at the thought. At the notion that she'd never see this strange, enigmatic paragon again. But it was better this way, wasn't it? It was... too much, being near him. "What of my friends?" They still faced untold horrors outside the cottage.

"Your witch is already stabilizing the barrier. And this distraction won't last long. I need to get you there before Sargon can track my whereabouts."

Distraction?

"You did this?"

His eyes widened in alarm. "No!"

"You sent those beasts to our doorstep? You're the only one who knew where we were."

"I swear, Aislinn. I did not. But Sargon is tracking their movements. Your witch will keep him out, but right now is the only time we have to slip into Avalon undetected."

It hurt to do this, Aislinn hated herself for it, but she swallowed down the tightness creeping up her throat. Necessary evil, right?

"Miro, did you have any hand in these attacks."

"None." He didn't even flinch.

"Fine." Aislinn rubbed her eyes. "We can't be gone long..." They'd need her. And if she left Langford unprotected...

"Time is not a fixed point. I'll return you before you can be missed, I swear it." He held out his hand, an offering.

It was no small thing, trusting someone. Even with the ability to command his true name, what if that was a larger scheme orchestrated to fool her into complacency?

She'd trusted the wrong person before. Look where it had gotten her.

But as Merikh searched her gaze with beseeching eyes, begging for her trust, there was something different about this. About him. He was many awful things, righteous and blind to the struggles of others. But there was a sincerity in him, too, even without commanding him. He was ancient and yet new.

Unknown and familiar. In equal measures.

Aislinn placed her hand in his, shivering at the feel of his large hand closing over hers. He pulled her close, bracing an arm around the small of her back.

But why, *why* did it feel so right?

"I've got you," he whispered against her brow.

Then the world fell away.

CHAPTER SIXTY-SIX

DEMETRIA

*D*emons. Monsters. Chaos.

It all erupted through the floor of her throne room, spilling pain and bloodshed into her castle walls.

Demetria was now the Queen of Ruin and Destruction. A fitting title for all that she'd wrought.

It was all her fault. Nereida had warned her what would happen if she failed to uphold her end of the bargain. And when the Reaper called Ceto came to collect, Demetria had refused. Lying between her teeth that all the dragonstone they'd harvested was lost to the depths of the sea. That she'd ordered it put there to prevent whatever plan Nereida had concocted from taking root. Ceto had shaken her head, a pitying expression only just softening the hardness of her features.

"You will fall."

Balan appeared before her, bloodied and eyes bright. "We must go." He knocked back a creature clawing at the dais. "There is no end to them."

Let them come.

"I'm not abandoning my kingdom." Demetria stood, her mortal blade heavy in her grasp. It would fell some of these monsters but not all. It was like trying to fight the sun from rising. Pointless, utterly pointless.

"You must." Balan seethed. "Order a regiment of guards to escort us to a ship."

It was a romantic thought in theory. Escape with a few swords, pack the dragonstone for travel. Maybe even find Daciana and forge more blades.

But none of them could use them.

And what of the rest of her kingdom?

"How much dragonstone have we got?"

"Not much." Enough to make a handful of weapons at best.

Balan turned to one of her guards. "Gather the dragonstone in the vault and assemble a team. We sail for Ardenas." He turned back to level Demetria with a glare. "Harden your stomach, little fool. Your death achieves nothing."

Demetria fisted her hands by her sides. "It is not foolish to recognize a losing battle."

Balan stomped over to her, standing close enough their noses almost touched. "It is foolish to give in before you've lost. Dying now proves nothing. It does not absolve you from whatever guilt you choose to carry."

Rage bubbled in her, boiling her from the inside out. "You know nothing of me!"

"I do!" He grabbed her shoulders, the handle of his sword pressing in hard enough to hurt. "And I recognize a fading light when I see one. Do not give in. Not today."

A sob broke free from her chest. "Balan... I can't."

"You can." He adjusted his position, steering her out of the throne room, stepping around bodies and carcasses. "You and I will ensure that you do. Because you are not done yet."

"Why does it matter?" Why did any of it matter? She'd failed. Failed herself. Failed her kingdom? Why was he so insistent—

"Because"—the word slithered from between clenched teeth—"it just does. Nothing has mattered for a long fucking time. But this does.

516

Do not give up. Stay your course until there is nothing left in you. You have so much fight left, do not let them convince you otherwise."

His words echoed in her ears as they stumbled through the halls. Bloody handprints marred the marble columns, and family portraits were torn to ribbons. A familiar face lay in a pool of his own blood.

Bastien.

Once her favorite guard. The one with the best gossip. The one who whispered in Zaire's ear of her meeting with Evander.

Bastien's eyes were blown wide open in an unseeing stare.

They stepped over his corpse and continued to the vault.

Her favorite window, the one with the colored glass that sent streams of reds, blues, and golds across the carpet in diamond shapes, was shattered. Sparkling glass coating the floor.

A retinue of ten guards awaited them. Demetria couldn't make her gaze focus on their faces. "We shall escape through my family's secret tunnels." Her voice was thick and rusty. "Unless some of you have family you wish to return to. Then I suggest you run."

"Can we—" A small voice broke. "Can we bring them?"

The young face of the guard speaking swam in front of her eyes. His voice though, he was a new recruit. Signed on to send money to his ill father.

"There's no time."

A hitched breath, and the young guard said nothing else.

"We will rebuild." Balan's voice was a steadying presence in her ear as they tripped through the underground halls. "I swear it, Princess."

When the tunnel opened up and sky came into view, it was a hopeless horizon. And when they filed onto the ship, the captain was somber as he readied his crew for travel. There were no stars against the churning sky. No moon to light the way. The choppy sea beckoned, and the scent of brine carried on the wind whipping through Demetria's hair and drowning out the sound of screams as they sailed away from her home.

Leaving her people to face their deaths alone.

CHAPTER SIXTY-SEVEN

AISLINN

There once was a girl made of stardust, whose dreams painted the skies.

Her father's words echoed in her head, a flutter of wings, a gentle whisper. Over and over, they called. *Remember. Remember. Remember.*

The mirror was no mirror at all but a rippling pool. She sank beneath its depths, weightless, bodiless, an untethered soul of energy and star light.

Memories of her life kept nudging their way in, reminding her why she was here. Where she'd come from. Who she was.

But soon that, too, slipped away, and only her father's words remained.

There once was a girl made of stardust, whose dreams painted the skies. And when she got lonely with only the moon as her company, she breathed life into her dreams, crafting an entire world from the pieces of her soul. Scattering them about. And within those dreams, she started to dream, and those dreams started to dream, too.

She was nothing. She was everything. She was infinite.

In those dreams within dreams, life was born. And within the kiss of creation, souls erupted into being, catching whispers of dreams and stardust she'd painted into every corner of the world. These souls grew, taking shape and form, fueled by dreams within dreams until she was no longer alone.

But a soul is a hungry thing, gluttonous for more. More life. More stardust. More dreams. And soon the souls she'd crafted from her very own self ate her whole and spat out the pieces. She trickled down, catching on fallen souls as she floated on the wind. And each time a piece of her grew large enough to take shape, the hungry souls she'd crafted cut her down, stealing her dreams for their own gluttonous whims.

The world changed. It grew and reformed. It shot off in all directions, expanding the vast corners of creation. And those souls twisted, scared and alone without the comfort of her dreams. They grew hateful. Malicious and spiteful at being forgotten and abandoned.

But she never abandoned them. Though she forgot. Though pieces of her soul littered the world, sprouting creation without memory. Life without knowledge. She never abandoned them. How could she when they were the very fabric of her own dreams?

She walked amongst them, for all eternity. Never knowing. And always dreaming.

CHAPTER SIXTY-EIGHT

LARK

*L*ark collapsed to her knees, exhaustion claiming her strength. Ferryn reached a hand beneath her arm, yanking her to stand. They leaned against each other, fighting for air.

"It's a good thing... you kept in shape..." Ferryn's words escaped between each heavy breath.

Lark laughed, a thin huff of air in her taxed lungs. Across the clearing, Gavriel sought her gaze, a shared relief passing over them as he staggered in her direction.

They had not planned for this. They'd grown complacent within the confines of Inerys' spell, taking their safety as granted. But something had let them slip free. Dozens of monsters spoiled the ground, pieces scattered.

The flow had halted, which meant Inerys must have reinstated her wards. But that this happened in the first place...

It was far too close.

Gavriel's arms came around her, tugging her out of Ferryn's grasp, and she sagged in relief.

"Let me look at you." Gavriel's words ghosted against the top of her head as he ran gentle, searching hands over her body. "No injury?"

Lark shook her head, winding her arms around his neck as he pressed his lips to every inch of her filthy face.

They could never be caught unawares like this again. The assassins and the Vallemerian warriors weren't due to arrive for another fortnight. They had to bolster their defenses in the meantime. That no one was hurt—

Langford.

Lark scrambled, panic flooding her body. "Where is he?"

Gavriel's expression melted into worry, and he glanced around.

Alistair's beast stalked the grounds, ripping the throats out of any creature still breathing. Daciana slowly approached him, hands out in a nonthreatening position. "Langford is all right." Her voice was slow and reassuring. "He's just resting."

Lark hadn't realized Alistair had shifted, actually shifted, until Daciana had positioned herself between them. His face was all wrong, monstrous and exaggerated behind a swath of dark fur, but somehow, *somehow,* it was still him. Something in his features hinted at the handsome rogue, but would that familiarity fade in time? Would he ever return to his natural state? How had this happened? What did this mean for him? He appeared himself enough to avoid attacking any of them, but where did his control end?

Lark's head spun from the speed of which her thoughts turned.

Alistair lifted his snout, sensing the air, and let out a sharp howl that made the inside of Lark's ears tremble. He rushed for the house, spitting and snarling.

"Fuck!" Lark pulled away from Gavriel, limping after him. If he attacked Inerys or Aislinn...

The door was left wide, sounds of a struggle echoing from inside.

Gavriel tucked in front of Lark, angling his sword as they slowly approached. Heart in her throat, Lark swallowed down the rising panic. Alistair was still in there. So long as Langford was all right, and Daciana said he was, it would be fine.

Alistair's beast crouched over Langford, sniffing his neck. Langford groaned, tossing and turning beneath him. He opened his eyes, confusion stealing his expression before it melted into panic. His body locked into place, frozen beneath the beast that was Alistair. Until Alistair leaned close and gently touched his snout against Langford's nose. A rush of an exhale, Langford's eyes softened, and indulgent amusement took hold of his features.

Alistair shook, a ripple shooting through his entire body, and his skin pulsed. He let out a whine of pain that shifted into a groan. Fur smoothed into bruised skin. Bones shifted and shortened until his body collapsed back into his true form.

His very human, very naked, straddling Langford, form.

Langford reached up and stroked Alistair's jaw. "It's still you," he said softly. "I have so many questions." He ducked his head. "But firstly, what did I say about cleaning your teeth?"

Alistair grinned and sat up, his ass on full display, *skies,* Lark could only imagine the front view of his posture.

"Oh, look. We're already halfway there. Might as well undress you, too." He peppered Langford's face with kisses, ignoring his protests and playful swats.

"Clean... your... teeth!" Langford laughed shoving him off.

Alistair pressed his forehead to Langford's, whispering something in his ear, Langford nodding in response, before he finally climbed down. He cocked a hip out, unabashedly revealing his naked form to the entire room. "So... now you've seen everything."

"We've already seen you naked literally dozens of times," came Daciana's easy reply. "This was a less painful sight."

Langford grinned, a lightness dawning his face Lark hadn't seen in ages. He sat up with his shirt ripped open. Only a few faint red lines marred the pale skin of his back.

Thank the skies. He was all right.

Lark rushed forward. Langford tucked her into his chest, hugging her fiercely.

"I thought..."

"I know," Langford whispered. "You won't rid of me so easily, *wife.*"

Lark laughed, the tightness in her chest finally abating with the easy reference to their shared joke. "Wouldn't want to let you out of this marriage too soon, husband. 'Til death and all that."

Langford snorted, releasing her and lifting his gaze to assess the room. "Are we all accounted for? Anyone need aid?"

Of course, Langford would awaken from a mortal wound from a poisonous harpy's claws and ask if he could do anything to help.

"Kenna and Ferryn are just rounding up the bodies to burn." Daciana tucked a thumb over her shoulder.

"We should probably talk about Alistair's condition." Lark glanced over at where he was still posing, bare as the day he was born.

"Yes that." Langford hummed thoughtfully. "I have a few theories, and even more still that were thrown out the window by his ability to shift without the moon. Perhaps Kenna's cure granted him a level of mastery. Sort of... when one falls ill and they recover, there will still be traces of the original ailment in their bodies. It forms an almost resilience against catching it again. Perhaps that's what happened here?"

It was a bright spot of good news, one sorely needed. And by the look on Daciana's face, Lark would wager she was already tying threads of hope and understanding to her own wolven nature. As comforting as that turn of events was, there was still the very real danger of betrayal. Of who had led Nereida's monsters to them.

As if sensing her thoughts, Gavriel spoke. "We need to regroup. Figure out what the blazes happened." His voice was harsh, almost accusing.

He wasn't wrong. They'd been betrayed before, by Hazel though. She hardly warranted the trust they'd given. And although Gavriel had shared all that Hazel had done in the name of backing his claim, Lark still felt the fool whenever she thought of her.

The floor entry to the cellar crashed open, and a hand appeared. Lark knelt down and pulled Inerys up. The witch's eyes fluttered, a trickle of blood leading from her nose over her chin. "Aislinn," she gasped. "Aislinn is gone."

"What do you mean... gone?" Lark's blood ran cold. No. No it couldn't be. Aislinn would never... and if someone took her...

"I can't sense her spirit anywhere." Inerys coughed. "She's gone."

CHAPTER SIXTY-NINE

FERRYN

Ferryn glared at his uneaten food alone in his room. Aislinn had up and left. If he'd been able to give her more. If he'd been ready…

But he wasn't ready. He was a fool to long for someone so cold and unattached, where Aislinn was nothing but warmth and comfort. He wanted to want those things. But a certain set of dark eyes, glittering and narrowed with annoyance, filled his mind at every turn.

A flutter of a breeze.

Ceto.

He didn't even turn to acknowledge her presence. He knew it had been her. Who else had access here and reported directly to Nereida? He was once again the fool, played by his own heart and its ruthless owner. When they'd crossed paths in the dungeon, he'd let Gavriel believe it was their goodbye. But really, he felt it when Ceto forged the tether, silently asking permission to come to him. To find him in any corner of the earth. And when she visited and they found their passions in the darkness, he'd been fool enough to believe the lies she spoke against his skin. The promises she whispered. The way she begged for forgiveness between gasps of pleasure.

He'd always been a plaything to her.

"Ferryn," her voice was an unspoken apology, all pity and guilt.

He hated that his heart fell for it.

"I know what you did."

"You do not." Ceto's steps echoed as she came to stand before him and sank to her knees.

Ceto lowered herself to him. No, that was his place. Begging for scraps at her feet—

"Look at me."

Despite himself, he could not ignore the command in her voice. She was just as searingly beautiful as she'd always been. A perfect face of dark skin and inhuman symmetry. Her full lips that teased him with every scrape of her teeth. Dark eyes that seeped deep into his soul until he was a puddle at her feet.

"What more do you want? Have you come to gloat?" Ferryn stood, momentarily reveling in the surprised look on her face. "You relentless bitch, haven't you done enough?"

Ceto snarled, gripping his shirt in her fist, and *fuck* if the shiver of excitement didn't still ignite him head to toe.

"Nereida's oath is not the same as Thanar's." She shoved him back. "I had no choice in the matter."

"I don't believe you."

"Fine!" she spat at him. "Then believe this, I know how to defeat her. She's testing me, granting me access to her plans to see if I betray her. I will have no choice in the matter when she sifts through my thoughts in search of betrayal, so I might as well tell you."

"I don't wish to hear it!" But he did. He wished to hear every lie, as always, one more time.

"Nereida needs to maintain her foothold in the Otherworld to tackle Avalon. Without it, she'll lose the power she's been granted. Your life wielder must recraft the veil using considerable power drawn, and she must bind it to an anchor."

"I don't understand—"

"Thanar was the anchor, Ferryn. The next anchor will take his place." Ceto invaded his space, and it physically hurt not to kiss her. "It is a prison sentence of sorts. Relegated to the Otherworld, bound to watch the death of every human, and responsible for their guidance to the afterlife. Without Leysa, death has become unpredictable. We're losing souls without the right guides to lead them. And until we have a veil and anchor in place, Reapers assigned to deaths are random."

"What do you expect me to do about it?"

"I expect you to rise above your feelings and fight! Or are you not the man I thought you were?"

Ferryn fisted his hands in his hair. "You *broke* that man, Ceto. You used me and twisted me to suit your purpose and discarded me. Over and over and—"

"I did not!"

"I will never compare to Priamos, I know that."

Ceto's face hardened, her beautiful mask slipping back into place.

"But I thought you cared for me, as best you could." How pathetic was he? Still begging for scraps.

Ceto's face crumpled, and she ran a hand down his jaw. "I did care for you. I still do. The best I can." She lowered her hand, and he wanted to grab it again. "You're not the only one who's broken, Ferryn."

That this fierce warrior, stronger than all Reapers in existence, the commander of their forces thought herself broken...

"What more can you tell me of Nereida's plan?" Part of his ruined heart shattered, and he wanted nothing more than to lose himself in her one more time.

Her eyes hardened, fire and anger blazing in equal measures. "Everything."

CHAPTER SEVENTY

LARK

*B*y the window overlooking the thawing lake, Lark sat in wait. Gloom claimed the sky, clouds carrying the threat of rain, and in the distance, the last of day's light stretched its farewell. It would be another starless night.

Unease was a disquieting feeling. Even with Moirin's Vallemerian warriors camped outside and Gavriel's assassins lurking about, including Hazel. *Skies, what a mess.* Lark couldn't shake the sense that they were unprepared for Nereida's wrath. Seemingly aloof and unbothered, she always wielded destruction like a cataclysmic event. But alongside her anger?

Lark had killed not only her spymaster but her lover. That was sure to coax her rage and fan it into an inferno. After the first wave of Nereida's forces and then a resounding quiet on all fronts, Lark was sure they'd only just begun.

"Lark?" A voice came from the shadows in the hall.

"Hazel," she ground out, and the assassin slid out of the darkness. Would it kill her to use a door? "You shouldn't be here."

"I can't seem to catch you alone." Hazel laughed, her blue eyes flat. "And I figured if I knocked, you simply wouldn't answer."

"Astute."

"All right, Gavriel promised to speak to you on my behalf, and obviously he didn't, so I'm here to plead my own case—"

"He did speak to me."

Hazel's gaze sharpened. Gavriel had spoken to Lark, and the truth was, there was too much at stake to deal with Hazel at present.

Hazel sat beside Lark on the bench seat along the wall. "Why have you avoided me then?"

"Because if I help you now, you'll only disappear when we need you most."

Hazel winced. Perhaps Lark was being unfair, but Hazel not only betrayed them to Nereida, tracking them and revealing their movements, she'd killed Aidan. The hurt Amara suffered...

Sometimes Lark still heard her screams.

"That's fair," Hazel said quietly. "My brother... Gregoir has always been a hopeless cause, but he shouldn't have to pay for my choices."

Lark fiddled with a ripped seam in the upholstery. Inerys still slumbered most days in her room, appearing for meals before vanishing again. Rebuilding and maintaining the protective ward around her land was taking more of a toll than she would ever admit.

Lark turned away from the window, facing Hazel fully. "Tell me the whole story, the truth, Hazel, and if I believe you, I swear I'll help Gregoir," she said. "Assuming we survive."

A soft smile curved against Hazel's mouth, a stark contrast to her usual sharp demeanor. "Yes, assuming that." She heaved a sigh. "Where do I begin?"

"Wherever your mind goes when you think of the beginning," Lark said with a smile, recalling the same words spoken to her by Daciana mere months ago. She needed a chance to rebuild what she'd broken in her trust. Lark never should have enlisted Aislinn the way she had, not without telling Daciana.

And Gavriel.

Skies, she needed to tell him.

Hazel sat beside her on the bench and cleared her throat. "My mother died when I was young, and my father racked up considerable debt. He entered indentured servitude with a sum in mind. Once he paid it off, he'd be free. His master was... kind enough, I suppose, to let us live there free from servitude, at a cost. It became harder for my father to pay off his debt when the mere act of Gregoir and I existing added to its sum. He met my stepmother shortly after, and with the master's blessing, they married. Father... well, whether it was loneliness, a misguided attempt to grant us a mother, or a strategic move to pay off his debts faster with their combined earnings, he failed to factor in one important detail." She rolled her eyes. "The woman *despised* us."

Based on Hazel's upbringing, she must have lived in Koval. It had been ages since indentures were recognized in Ardenas.

"Gregoir and I played with the other children. Grew alongside them. There was one boy—" Hazel's mouth downturned. "His master sold him when we were twelve, and I didn't see him again until the arena."

Lark's mind spun. *The arena?* When Gavriel was taken? She wracked her memory searching for a face... "Wait, the one you fought?" Images of their dizzying match, of the heart stopping smile he aimed Hazel's way when he invoked stalemate. He was the one who helped Lark while she was in the cage, before they sent her out onto the sand.

"Leander." The way Hazel said his name was an unhealed wound, but she shook her head. "Gregoir and I overheard our stepmother convince our father to sell us in their stead. That we were younger and would have much life left to live after paying off their debts. That we *owed* it to them. My father argued there was no way they could know what would become of us. That the master could sell us to someone cruel or send us to work in the mines or... worse. My stepmother was insistent, beseeching him to think of their unborn child." Hazel's voice flattened. "My father, the spineless coward, agreed. I hoped he would change his mind. That he'd—" Her voice broke off. "Within a week, new papers were drawn, and we were trapped." She brought her knees to her chest. "You know what happens when you're well and truly trapped, Lark? Do you know what desperation feels like?"

Lark did know. She knew what it felt to be desperate enough for a way out that one sports blinders, unable to see anything but the path to freedom. She nodded. "Mistakes are borne of desperation."

"That's right." Hazel nodded. "We ran. We ran to the forest knowing it made us fugitives, that we'd forfeited any right to buy our freedom. We were... forever lost." She wiped her nose. "That's when she found me. I traded one shackle for another. I couldn't say her name, the contract forbade it, but I knew when it was rendered null and void. It was like a chain snapped."

"Who held your contract?"

"Her name was Leysa, and she promised me freedom. All I wanted was a way out for me and my brother. She said she'd grant it if I owed her a favor to be called upon at a time of her choosing. It was an easy choice, an easy deal. I was a child, and I did not know what I was agreeing to."

Leysa. Leysa was Hazel's contract holder? When Lark killed her, it must have freed her.

"She erased our names, even the memories of our names. When we opened our eyes, we were in an unfamiliar forest on the wrong continent. Hamlin found us and gave us purpose. Meaning. Identities." Hazel shook her head. "The memories came back in slow trickles. But never my name. Not until—"

"Until I killed her," Lark finished.

Hazel scoffed. "I should have known you were the one to ask for help. But I didn't want to owe any more favors. To find myself in more debt. I just—" She hung her head. "I should have asked for help, whatever it cost."

Lark understood. Of course, she understood. "I can't condone your choices, but I can understand them. Just remember something, Hazel. I am not one to tally debts. I do not live by the scale of balance, and so long as you never fuck with us again, I will never hold my help against you."

Hazel's head snapped up. "Do you mean..."

"Yes." Lark nudged her shoulder. "I'll find your brother. Just... let me survive the coming days."

"I'll make bloody sure of it." Hazel nudged her back, a true grin dawning on her face. "And I'm sorry if I ever made it weird with Gavriel..."

"See, that we don't need to bond over."

Hazel laughed, the sound releasing with a sharp breath. The tension hardening her shoulders slacked, like she'd finally felt safe enough to let her guard down. It was equal parts beautiful and heartbreaking.

"If you don't mind my asking," Lark began, "what is your name?"

A soft smile curved the corner of Hazel's mouth. "Kassandra."

"Kassandra," Lark repeated. "That's beautiful."

Hazel shrugged, her eyes downcast as if she found discomfort in the compliment. "It doesn't really feel like mine. But I remember my father telling me it was my mother's choosing. Whether or not that's true..." She shook her head. "It's nice to remember."

An aching sense of understanding jolted through Lark. She and Hazel were far more alike than she'd realized.

A throat cleared. Kenna stepped out from the shadows along the far wall. "Sorry, I... oh, who am I trying to fool? I was obviously listening."

It was rather impressive how silent and undetected Kenna could be when she wanted to.

"How is Dac?"

"Nope." Kenna shook her head. "You two need to figure your shit out, I'm not playing middleman."

It was just as well. Lark needed to speak to Daciana herself. To apologize for... so many mistakes, and for what was to come. She couldn't bear the way they'd left things, and the shame of hurting Daciana roiled in her gut.

Kenna strode over to the window. "Someone approaches." Kenna made a noise of surprise. "Damn. You're never going to believe this."

Lark pushed the churning sense of regret away and turned back to the window. "More of Nereida's forces?"

"Don't think so."

Lark rushed to the door. No... it couldn't be... It swung open under her touch, confirming her limited visibility had been correct.

Demetria stood, decked in military dress robes with a simple gold coronet about her head, one lone ruby in the center. Beside her stood—

"Balan."

"Ah, good of you to remember me, meat sack."

The sudden urge to slam the door in his face nearly overcame her, but why was Demetria here?

"We need to talk," Demetria said as if reading her mind, standing a little taller with her hands clasped behind her back. "Nereida is coming."

"YOU'RE SAYING Koval has been in Nereida's pocket for generations?" Lark grabbed her tea, long gone cold, and took a sip. The chip in the rim was sharp against the corner of her mouth.

"You're acting like that's a surprise," Alistair said, leaning against the counter.

Across the table, Demetria maintained her stoic poise and control. A girl far beyond her years, forced to grow up too quickly. And after everything, after Lark's failure to save Ruslan, her decision to hide his death, here Demetria was offering the few resources she had.

"I offer you enough dragonstone to make a handful of weapons and those who escaped the city."

Lark had counted twenty outfitted guards and ten sailors under Captain Reinhardt. They needed every person they could get.

"I do not think we possess the time to forge those weapons." Felix was the only smithy Lark trusted, and they could not part with Daciana long enough to fashion these blades. Not to mention she'd need people to go with her to draw from...

"Understood. But we wish to aid you in any way we can. Nereida stole my home. I can't let her infest the rest of the world."

Lark glanced in Gavriel's direction. His arms were crossed, but he nodded along, and when he caught Lark's eye, their mutual view of the situation was evident in his gaze.

"We welcome all the help we can get," Lark said. "And... I just want to apologize—"

"No need." Demetria cut her off. "I understand... more. It is not so easy, weighing the cost of things. And I reacted the way I did because I was shielded from these truths for too long." She stood, offering a nod that wasn't quite friendly but maintained a level of respect. "We have greater aims these days."

"Agreed." Lark stood, ignoring the way Alistair was puffing out his chest. "Inerys' home is at full capacity, but you're welcome to camp on site as the others have done." The cottage adapted to meet the witch's needs, granting more bedrooms and space for them. But with how much energy Inerys was exerting maintaining the protective ward, Lark wouldn't risk taxing her further.

Demetria nodded and strode from the room. Every bit the dismissive royal. Balan trailed behind her, pausing to offer Lark a tight-lipped nod. And when only Lark, Gavriel, and Alistair remained, Alistair let out a sigh.

"We stand a chance, don't we? Everyone is so somber, but we've handled things on our own for so long, having help can only be a good thing." He dusted off his tunic. "Though I'd prefer a smaller crew, larger cuts that way..."

"You know there's no payment." Lark gave up on pretending her cold tea was worth examining.

"Not yet, but saving the world tends to make people grateful. Maybe that bard of yours can write of our heroics."

"He's not my bard." Lark hid her chagrin, but Gavriel grinned at her.

"I don't know. He seemed quite taken with his *Songbird*."

Alistair began to hum the tune, and Lark groaned.

Now that song was going to be stuck in her head all day.

NIGHT FELL WITH A GENTLE HUSH, ushering in a balmy breeze more suited to late spring than winter's end. Lark stared at the wall, covers drawn, and wrestled with a guilty conscience.

She still hadn't told Gavriel her plan to take Nereida down. And with everyone's stout confidence in their chances, it was getting harder to ignore. Yes, they might stem the flow of bloodshed in battle, but without cutting the head of their army, it was like trying to fight the current.

Nereida needed to die. A true death. And Lark's way was the only choice.

The bed dipped, and Gavriel's arms came around her. "My demon," he murmured against her ear. "How do you fair, lovely one?"

Lark turned to face him, her heart nearly breaking at the earnestness of his smile.

She had to tell him.

"Gavriel... do you think we'll kill Nereida?"

He leaned over her, running his nose along hers. "Yes. We have the numbers. We have the strength. We have the heart. And we have you." He kissed her. "I've no doubt we'll succeed."

Gavriel's faith in her only twisted the knife. "And how do we kill her?"

His smile faded, sharpness filling his gaze. Assessing, always assessing. "With the Reaper Blade?"

He had to sense something was amiss. The line of tension that snapped into place was too obvious to ignore.

"Mmhmm. And how do we get close enough to use it?"

He sat up, annoyance tugging at his scarred lip. "She liked to talk. Lure her into relaying a longwinded story and cut her down."

Lark shook her head, tears forming behind her eyes.

Gavriel's brows lifted. "No? Do you have a better way?"

She nodded, and the tears slipped free. His thumbs chased them away.

"Why do you cry?" His voice was so soft, a caress of comfort she didn't deserve. "What are you—" Realization dawned his face, and the words strangled to a stop. His eyes darkened. "You cannot be serious."

"Gavriel, wait."

"No."

"Will you at least listen before condemning?"

"I cannot allow you—"

"Allow me?"

Gavriel leapt up from the bed, pacing the room. His bare chest gleamed in the dwindling candlelight, achingly familiar rivers of scars along his skin. "Don't do that. You know what's not what I meant."

Lark rose to her knees atop the bed, her gaze tracking the path of his anger. "It's the only way. If she slips through our fingers again, if next she claims Avalon, there will be nowhere to hide. We must stop her whatever the cost!"

That earned her a look of pure acid.

"Whatever the cost? Tell me, Lark, if it were me coming to you, saying I have a way to kill Nereida, only it involves a hefty dose of martyrdom, what would you say?"

"That isn't fair—"

"No! You're fucking right it's not!" Gavriel braced his hand against the wall, his face bright red with anger. "How—How can you expect me to listen to this without fighting with every ounce of strength I have to stop you?"

Lark reached over to catch his arm and tugged him back. "We must kill her, we must!" Gavriel fought to pull free, but she held firm. "If you truly believe we always find our way back to one another, then we will. You know we will."

"Lark—" His voice broke. "I just got you back." And at his words, her heart broke. Because it was true, for lifetimes of fate, of destiny to be reunited, there was always something cleaving them apart. Perhaps that was their true fate.

But no, Lark couldn't allow doubt and despair into this moment. Into any other moment they shared. They were too precious, too few and far between.

"I know," she whispered, not trusting her voice to carry beyond the distance between them.

Gavriel crushed her to his chest, his lips finding hers as they toppled back to the bed. Clothes were shed with an urgency bordering on anger. Their kisses turned brutal and harsh, and when they joined, it was a rough climb, clinging to one another as if their lives depended on it. It was an unspoken goodbye, whether he admitted it or not, the desperation in their movements, in the way he held her tight enough to bruise. In the way she dug her nails into his skin. It was pain and anger and forever cut short once more. Gavriel whispered impossible things against her skin, promises already broken, and when they broke, it was with tears on their cheeks and Lark's heart in her throat.

Gavriel shuddered under her touch, holding her firm as the last waves of pleasure ebbed.

There was still so much to say. So much she couldn't say. So many lives wasted. And yet—

An alarm sounded. One of the Vallemerian horns of battle.

They were out of time.

CHAPTER SEVENTY-ONE

DACIANA

$\mathcal{K}$enna tossed her a spare blade. Daciana tested the weight. Silver was a lighter metal, easier to manipulate. It worked well against most monsters, but if she were to cross blades with another swordsman, she ran the risk of damaging the sword.

"Just take it, and quit sulking that it isn't Kovalian made."

"I was not sulking."

Kenna smirked and leaned up to press a quick kiss to Daciana's lips. "After we win, I'll buy you a whole new armory."

Daciana caught her by the clasp of her cloak and pulled her in for a deeper kiss. "Deal."

They raced down the winding steps of Inerys' home, heading for the door. Lark and Gavriel followed closely behind, buckling their armor into place. When Lark lifted her head and met Daciana's stare, she gave her a grim nod.

Daciana's stomach sank.

They hadn't had the chance to discuss Lark's asinine plan, but one thing Daciana had made perfectly clear was her refusal to allow such a thing so long as Gavriel was left in the dark. If Lark refused to tell him, she'd lock her in the damn cellar to keep her out of the fight. That

Aislinn was the one to tell her when she approached with a solution of her own—

It mattered naught.

Daciana had assumed Lark would falter, unable to tell Gavriel of her suicide mission, or at the very least he'd react in the same fashion she had.

From the lingering looks and his refusal to create more than an arm's length of distance, Daciana could assume he was panicking internally, perhaps even hoping she'd change her mind or that they'd find another way.

But Lark was as stubborn as they came. And Daciana was left to assess how to move forward, knowing what she knew.

"Are we all ready then?" Alistair appeared, a rakish grin lighting up his face, and Langford trailed behind, tucking his shirt into his trousers and trying to tame his wild hair.

Alistair reached over to smooth a particularly stubborn lock of hair down, but it sprang right back up. He smiled, letting his hand run down to Langford's jaw.

Ferryn ducked his head as he stumbled down the steps, a dazed look on his face.

Lark tugged her boots on. "Here's the plan. Gavriel, you stay with Hazel and the assassins, and try to coordinate their efforts. They should focus on picking off as many Undesirables as they can." Lark turned to Alistair and Langford. "You two stay with the Vallemerians, and try to guide them to into breaking down the horde. Dac, Kenna, Ferryn, and I will aim for Nereida with Demetria and her band."

"Absolutely not." Gavriel angled his body to block the door. "I'm not separating from you. Hazel can handle the assassins, and Ferryn can help her."

Lark's voice carried an edge of frustration. "No, Ferryn stays with me."

"He would be better utilized with the assassins who have no knowledge of these monsters." Gavriel's words were tight between his teeth.

"I'm literally right here," Ferryn said with a groan.

They ignored him.

"Ferryn needs to stay close. Without Aislinn, he's the only one who..." Lark bit her lip.

"Who can what, Lark?" Gavriel's gaze sharpened. The two of them engaged in some sort of stare off, falling silent while communicating a thousand words between them.

Daciana knew why.

Gavriel was likely hoping Aislinn's disappearing act meant Lark's plan was moot. But even if Ferryn refused, she would likely ram the Reaper Blade into her own belly if it meant ending Nereida for good.

Daciana's chest tightened at the thought. There hadn't been enough time to say everything she needed to say. To convince Lark otherwise. To apologize. Any words she could speak now would be rushed, half-formed in panic.

"My, my, this is just like old times, isn't it?" Alistair hung off Langford, grinning at all of them. "Although I'm due for a good-natured argument with the dazzling, effulgent, gorgeous—"

"I hope you mean Dac." Langford grimaced.

"Of course, he does," Lark said with a shake of her head, threading her fingers through Gavriel's and leaning her head on his shoulder. "Who else would he call effulgent?"

Daciana cracked a smile, despite herself. "You did not just call me effulgent." It felt almost good to pretend this was all there was. An exchange of words said in jest. That they were all safe and readying for a night by the fire.

Alistair winked at her. "I wasn't finished. She's also the squanderer of perfectly good wine."

It took a moment for Daciana's thoughts to catch up with her, and when the vivid memory of the wine cellar resurfaced, her cheeks warmed. "Kenna!"

"What? I was bragging about you!"

Everyone broke into a chaotic combination of comments and conversation, apart from Lark and Gavriel, who were still locked in a silent battle of wills. Lark's eyes were pleading, but Gavriel's were tormented, like he already knew this fate to be written.

It wasn't fair. None of this was fair. Lark had barely had the chance to live, and she was throwing it all away.

Throwing them all away.

It was absurdly selfish to think of it as such, but Daciana couldn't help it. It was easier than the anger of wasted time. Of months and weeks spent apart. If she'd known Lark's days were numbered, if she'd had any clue—

That was the trap of mortality, wasn't it?

"All right, that's enough. I'm getting a secondhand headache off of poor Langford." Alistair smoothed out his gambeson, ruby ring glinting with the action. "We go with Lark's plan. It keeps us all evenly spread enough to do some serious damage." Gavriel opened his mouth to argue, and Alistair continued, "You are the Guild Master, Gavriel. You've asked these people to fight on your behalf. Lead them."

Gavriel's expression was murderous. "That isn't fair. You don't know—"

"I'll help the assassins!" Kenna said quickly. She gave Daciana a knowing look.

Daciana had shared Lark's plan with Kenna. Moreso shouted it at her. She was more grateful for the silencing ward than ever as she'd yelled and thrown a bottle or two. And though Kenna had agreed it was foolish, she'd admitted to seeing why Lark was so determined. "Gavriel can go with Lark, Dac, and Ferryn. I'll keep your little stabby bastards in line, you guys can flirt with all the hulking Vallemerians, and we call it a day."

Alistair clapped his hands. "Splendid! And when we all survive— yes, I'm calling it, we're all making it out of this shitstorm—we have a revelry of the ages. I mean bottomless spirits, Gavriel tickling the old horsehairs, a fire large enough to melt the rest of this blasted snow, and there must be dancing." He raised a dark brow. "Lots and lots of dancing."

Silence fell. Daciana glanced at Lark, finding the pained expression she desperately tried to hide behind a watery smile.

"It's a plan," Lark finally said.

"Count me in," Daciana added.

It was an impossible promise, made only worse by the knowledge Lark had already made up her mind that they'd be a head short.

Gavriel threaded his fingers through Lark's, indecision warring on his face. She reached behind him and opened the door.

Darkness greeted them—a night-cloaked forest.

Kenna aimed a wink Daciana's way, and made to leave. Daciana grabbed her by the arm, hauling her in for a thorough and lingering kiss. Warmth erupted against her lips, filled the expanse of her ribs, and left her breathless. Kenna blinked her eyes open, gazing up with her smoldering stare. Daciana breathed her in before relinquishing her grasp.

This was not goodbye.

This was a reminder of what they were fighting for.

CHAPTER SEVENTY-TWO

DEMETRIA

*T*here was nothing glorious about watching a man's innards cut from his body by the swipe of sharp claws, and the light slowly leaving his eyes, too slowly, as the creature feasted on his entrails.

Never had Demetria seen such horrors. If she ever had children, would she trickle the truth of battle into her stories? Or would she gloss over the horror, leaving them cozy and snug in their beds with delusions of honor and grandeur in their heads as her mother had done?

Balan ripped her out of the way just in time as a beast landed where she stood not seconds ago. With a battle cry, he cut it down, blasting them both with the bloody spray of his felled foe.

"Do mind your surroundings a bit more."

"Why would I when I have you to watch them for me?"

He snarled, hiding his grin, Demetria was sure, and continued cutting his path of death ahead. He was a storm of fury, of beauty, and she could see how one could fall under a demon's spell, if only for a moment. How terror and destruction was an artform, honed by years and years of existence.

Would he leave once they'd finished what they'd started? If he could return to the Netherworld, full power again, would he? Would she want him to?

It was strange how moments like this could cause time to halt, or was it that her heart was beating so fast, her perception rapid in its assertion?

For everything she'd lost, everyone she'd lost, Balan was... a true friend. Someone she was grateful for. And to think she'd spent these days lashing out at him. Because he was her safe harbor, strange as it may be, he was. And... he was the only person she did not think she could scare away with her darkness. With the depths of what she was capable of.

She'd never had that before.

After all this was over, she'd tell him. She'd tell him everything she thought of him. How terrifyingly beautiful he was. How she counted him as friend. As family. And if he laughed in her face, that was fine, too. So long as he knew his place in her heart.

"What have we here?" A low scrape of a voice, a baritone rumble, cut through her thoughts. Demetria turned to find a man—no not a man, a demon, standing before her. His hair was blacker than a raven's wing, two long curved horns of silver curling from his head, and his eyes were a milky white, lacerating with his roving gaze. "You're the little human queen we've been tasked with finding." He smiled, and it sent a shiver down her spine. "Nereida is so looking forward to your next appointment."

Demetria's stomach rolled, and she backed away. What would she do to her? Oddly enough, the threat of torture, of pain and dismemberment, wasn't what sent ice spearing through her veins. No, it was the image of Zaire, his eyes finally his own only in death. Would she find herself similarly a stranger? Could Nereida influence her mind to achieve her aim? Twist her into something new and horrible and—

Demetria swung wide with her sword.

The demon chuckled and held out an arm. "Shall we?"

Demetria shook her head, and his smile faded.

All around, the sound of battle waged on, and she was an invisible specter to it all. No one was coming to save her. No one was coming to aid. She couldn't even spot Balan through the throng of violence. Of bloodied limbs both red and black. She couldn't even call to him, for her voice would be lost to the cries of pain.

No. She must save herself.

Ruslan's lessons, what felt like lifetimes ago, floated back into memory.

When facing a stronger foe, make them underestimate you. Stay ever vigilant, for you can't afford a wrong move. Now, show me again, Princess. When strength is unmatched, what will you aim for?

"Pride," Demetria exhaled. She let her sword hang awkwardly in her hand as if it was too heavy and widened her eyes with terror. Allowing her fear to spill across her face was the easiest part; it was what came next she dreaded.

The demon smiled, running a finger down her jaw. Demetria flinched but made no move to attack.

Steady.

"She didn't say what condition you needed to be in. So long as your heart was beating." The demon grabbed her by the chest plate, pulling her violently toward him. It was this proximity she needed. Demetria's head snapped back from the movement, and she shoved closer. Her dagger was in her hand before she could blink, and with a quick bend of her arm, she stabbed it deep into the demon's side. He howled, grabbing her wrist and giving her the opening she needed. Twisting her sword, she struck true, embedding her blade deep in his belly and out through his back.

She'd done it! She'd actually done it! Warmth flooded her hands, her knuckles, as his blood stained her skin. She yanked her blades free, ready to watch the creature bleed out over the snow dotted ground.

The demon pulled his tunic up, revealing his skin as it restitched together.

Horror rocked through her, hardening her muscles and locking her in place. Of course, her mortal blade was not enough. How foolish she was. Bile rose in her mouth, and she swallowed it down. Her gaze darted about, but Balan was nowhere to be seen.

She was going to die. Alone. Forgotten.

The demon bared his teeth at her. "That was terribly foolish."

He yanked her back into his chest, and a scream broke free from her throat. His mouth met her neck, teeth sinking deep into her skin, and a cry choked off into silent agony. Pain, hot and searing, erupted at her pulse point. He chuckled against her skin, pulling back enough his hot breath stung the bloody teeth marks at her neck. "You taste of fear, but there's nothing innocent in your blood."

Demetria's eyes widened as her sword fell slack in her grip, and he licked his lips. He drew back, readying to bite her again, when he was knocked to the side.

Balan stood, rage rolling off him in waves, nostrils flaring as his chest rose and fell with each breath. He drew her to him, keeping her upright even as her knees threatened to buckle. "Don't fucking touch her."

The demon stood, dusting himself off and eying Balan with a hint of amusement. "I remember you." Demetria's blood stained his lips.

"Then you know what I'm capable of." Balan's gaze flicked to Demetria, assessing her. She nodded back, silently confirming she was all right. Her hands clenched into fists, fighting the tremors of fear.

Balan was here. She was all right.

"Perhaps once there was a time," the demon said, "when I wouldn't have crossed your path for fear of retaliation. But you're a pale imitation of what you once were." He grinned. "So, let's have at it, then, shall we?"

Balan sneered, angling his body to block Demetria. "Go, now."

"I'm not leaving you."

"Go, little fool," Balan hissed over his shoulder. "I will find you once the battle is spent, but you must go to Lark." The only one with a weapon capable of killing demons.

"Swear it." It was a childish notion, that promises carried any weight in the face of battle, but she needed to hear it.

Balan sighed. "I promise."

Why hadn't they made more Reaper Blades? Why hadn't she left her kingdom sooner, rejoined Lark and her people and strategized their attack rather than arriving at the eleventh hour?

"Wait," he called out. He turned, bringing a trembling hand to her jaw. His silver eyes searched her face, beseeching. Slowly, he brought his lips to hers, the barest caress of a kiss. A burst of warmth, fleeting and overwhelming. Then it was gone.

He pulled back, and Demetria could hardly stand.

"You were right," he said. "Absolutely disgusting."

Demetria laughed, though it broke into a sob. "Balan…"

"Now, go! I'll find you." His face echoed such a longing pain before he gave her a shove and angled his sword in a fighting stance.

Demetria blinked away tears and ran, her heart breaking with every step.

He'd kept his word. He'd kissed her before she died.

CHAPTER SEVENTY-THREE

LANGFORD

*L*angford swiped his blade across another harpy's throat, only slightly flinching when black ichor sprayed against his mouth.

That was... horrifically unhygienic. He whipped a cloth from his pocket, wiping his face. Beside him, Alistair laughed.

"Darling, you should wear your kills proudly."

"Shall I wear whatever infections I acquire with equal pride?" It wasn't that Langford was squeamish about bodily fluids. As a healer he had a clinical detachment to the sight of blood and pus. But these were largely unstudied creatures. After the cursed wolf debacle, which they still needed to address, the notion of licking harpy blood off his lips seemed too risky.

Alistair hadn't shifted again. A relief, consequently, since they were fighting shoulder to shoulder with Kyall and his contingency of Vallemerian warriors. They were formidable fighters, and strangely comfortable battling monsters. Gunther had said his people faced the same darkness Langford had come to him with, begging for aid. But if Alistair shifted into a beast right before their very eyes, would any of them attack? Would Alistair attack them, failing to recognize them as allies? That he'd shown no hostility to the others was a blessing, but would he show the same restraint for these newcomers?

Too many questions.

"Sargon's flaming knickers, this one is ugly." Alistair's words pulled Langford from his thoughts.

A scarecrow was pitched in the middle of the battle. Hoisted high on a post made from human spines. Its wide brim hat fluttered in the breeze, in the wake of swords swinging nearby. But it remained still, and it hadn't been there a moment ago. A long coat draped over its gnarled shoulders, billowing behind it, and in one gloved hand rested a rusty sickle.

Kenna had sketched this creature in her bestiary, naming it and all of its properties. *Bubak*. She'd told them of the day she and Dac faced one down in an abandoned field. Langford wracked his brain for the memory of its weakness. Silver? No.

A wide swing of a sword slit open the filthy and poorly patched tunic of varying shades of gray. It split apart, raining maggots and grubs to the forest floor. Langford swallowed down the saliva filling his mouth, his body's response as it readied to vomit.

The bubak wore no tunic. It wore pieces of human skin sewn together.

"Fucking blazes," Alistair said beside him.

Blazes! Fire!

"Quick, turn out your pockets. We need flint and steel to start a fire." That was how a bubak fell. Fire. Flame. A special fire oil Kenna would coat her blades with. They had no such oil on them. But Langford was willing to bet Alistair carried a firestarter.

"Brilliant!" Alistair dug in his pockets, pulling out a small corked bottle and handing it to Langford.

Liquid sloshed against the glass, and against his better judgment, Langford popped off the cork and took a whiff. "Why do you carry rum on you into battle?"

Alistair scoffed, producing the flint and steel with a triumphant wave of his hand. "That's a silly question."

A loud screech filled the air, sending a jolt down Langford's spine as he struggled to cover his ears. A plume of black smoke rose from the bubak, the wind carrying it to stretch in their direction.

Not smoke. The beating of wings could not be mistaken. Crows. They launched their attack, piercing cries and sharp beaks and talons surrounding them. Searing pain cut across Langford's hands, his head, the back of his neck. Talons pulled on his hands where they protected his face, wings hitting him in the face as they aimed for his eyes.

"We need to get closer!" he shouted. Hands found his shoulders, shoving him down to the ground as Alistair covered him with his body.

"Fire, yeah?" Alistair panted against the top of his head. "Leave it to me, love." He ripped a piece of cloth from Langford's tunic, binding it around his hands and snatched the bottle of rum back. Lifting it to his lips, he tossed his head back, taking a short draught of the liquid.

With quick movements, he wrapped the cloth around his hand and doused it with more rum. His mouth remained clamped shut as he offered Langford a wink. He struck the flint against steel, lighting his wrapped fist on fire, and stood. Flames engulfed his hand as he stomped over to the bubak, bearing the brunt of the crows' onslaught.

"Mind the eyes!" Langford called out, peeking between his fingers. Black wings surrounded Alistair, one arm and hand bloodied as he fought his way closer to the bubak commanding the birds, the other outstretched as the fire danced before him.

Alistair pushed forward, flinching at each swipe of claws and nip of beak, and when he stood close enough to reach the bubak, he stilled. Langford could have sworn he smiled, before he spit the rest of the rum into its face, and punched his flaming hand into the creature. Flames erupted, lighting the creature up brighter than the sun. The crows dissolved into ash, scattering on the wind, and maggots and grubs poured from the bubak, screeching and popping.

Langford ran to Alistair, using his own cloak to smother the fire against his hand. "There were smarter ways to achieve that end," he muttered as he unwrapped Alistair's hand. Blistering skin greeted him, and Langford held back the urge to further scold him. His dark skin was marred by too many lacerations to count, and Langford would be fighting the man's sepsis on the morrow, he just knew it. But as Alistair smirked at him, his handsome face covered in blood, ash, and dirt, Langford couldn't find it in him to be angry. Relief almost made him smile back at him.

"It was worth it." Alistair's other hand came up to rub the back of Langford's neck. "My favorite healer can patch me up."

Langford shook his head, pressing a firm kiss against his mouth. It was true enough, but one didn't need to go lighting themselves on fire simply because burn salve was available. Despite the very real threat of death, there was something about fighting by Alistair's side. Like they'd already faced so much together over the years, it was all in preparation for this moment. It allowed hope to warm the spot in his chest that used to ache each time Alistair took another bedmate for the night.

Hope. What a strange thought to have in the midst of a battle.

A shout of pain, and Langford spun around to find the voice.

A Vallemerian warrior fell to his knees, a bloodied claw-tipped hand shoved through his back and out from his stomach. Langford recognized the man, but his name eluded him. He'd played a round of Paragons and Sinners with him one night, amidst Alistair, Kyall, and a few others. He was a cheat, but such a poorly concealed cheat no one minded. It was almost endearing, the way his spare cards fell from his sleeve each hand. And now he was silenced by the pain of a brutal and impending death.

A harpy stood over him, wings tucked in tight. Wearing the face of a beautiful woman, it contorted its features in malice, baring its jagged and yellowed teeth. It threw back its head in an infernal shriek to shake the heavens. Intestinal contents, liver bile, seeping liquid waste matter, it all coated its inhuman hand flexing through the poor man's belly. The warrior's mouth opened and closed, gaping like a fish out of water, and his eyes clouded over, but the pain remained twisted on his face.

It was a horrible way to die. He did not deserve it.

Alistair charged, his sword glinting with the movement, and with a flick of his arm, the harpy's hand was severed from the wrist, landing limply into the dirt. Another turn of the blade, and the harpy's head rolled from its shoulders. The warrior pitched sideways, landing in the dirt. The sounds of his pain, gasping exhales of agony, accompanied the twitching of his limbs. Until the twitching stopped and the man was utterly still.

Another scream. It was too much. Too much death. Too much waste. Too much blood soaking into the earth. Langford's ears began to ring, and the sounds of pain and suffering were muffled as he staggered past another fallen warrior. Alistair's voice called out to him distantly, but Langford pressed on until he found the source of the scream.

Demetria. The princess, no, the Queen of Koval. Tears mixed with blood and dirt stained her cheeks, as she held a limp body close to her chest. White hair, the jagged edges of black horns jutting through. The demon's lifeless form was like a ragdoll in her arms. She let out another wail, the anguish in her voice enough to make Langford's head spin.

Balan.

That was his name. The one who left Hugo for dead. The one who joined them and guided Daciana to create the Reaper Blade. And now the soul the last royal of Koval mourned.

Balan's eyes were blown wide, unseeing silvery grey staring up at the sky while Demetria rocked back and forth. "He promised," she whispered. "He promised."

Alistair placed a hand against Langford's shoulder, offering him a short nod. They took their stances, guarding the queen as she fell apart over the loss of her demon.

The gasping of each inhale, the desperate cries strangling from her throat, it was enough to remind Langford of one unforgiving truth: Hope was a dangerous thing.

CHAPTER SEVENTY-FOUR

GAVRIEL

There was no rutting end to these damn beasts.

Gavriel flipped his Ardenian skinner in his hand, a swift flourish of steel against the exposed throat of a manananggal, its moth-colored wings flapping a putrid breeze against his face, before he drove his silver blade through one of its depthless black eyes. He didn't bother wiping his blades clean, even as the blood coated his knuckles, running between his fingers. It was messy work. Inefficient, even. Killing monsters wasn't the same as killing humans. Humans were more predictable. If he studied a mark long enough, he could memorize the man's shitting schedule. He could manipulate their weaknesses, their pride, their fatal flaws. There was an art in keeping death as quick and clean as possible. No need to waste precious energy on cleaning a blood-soaked jerkin.

Gavriel cut down another beast, relying on the silver blade from Kenna rather than the guesswork of his own. His lungs burned from the effort it took to keep moving, keep swinging and hacking and stabbing. It was artless. A lesson in brute strength and unwillingness to die by the hands of a monster.

He wiped the sweat from his brow, smearing something sticky against his skin. Probably blood. Skies, he hoped it was blood.

Lark shouted to Ferryn, tossing him the Reaper Blade. She whipped the bow from her back, firing off as many arrows as she could at the giant tree-like creature stalking toward her. The exhaustion wore on her beautiful face, in the furrow between her brows and the trembling in her hands, as she nocked arrow after arrow.

Gavriel's belly burned and his throat tightened. The urge to toss her over his shoulder and run as fast and as far as his legs could carry him was overwhelming. He kept pushing the thought of her plan from his mind, remaining close enough to intervene the moment he suspected she would enact it.

Her death.

That's what he was truly fighting. Not this endless wave of monsters and demons and that fucking tree Lark was shooting at. But the notion she would willingly part her soul from his again.

He wasn't about to let that happen.

Had they not suffered enough to span endless lifetimes?

When Nereida's curse claimed his mind, his body, and precious time in this life, he'd watched dozens of lifetimes spent searching for Lark. Seeking her warmth. Yearning for her heart. It was madness, the way her absence clawed at him in every life. He'd relived the very moment he found her and lost her. Why was she so ready to cast him aside again?

It was selfish, so damn selfish, to view it as such. But death was a burden borne by the living, and he could not face her loss again. He'd fight his way through the rutting Netherworld to find her if she was so determined to die. But would her soul even travel there? Death once meant certainty, and now, it was a gaping void of unknown.

A root sprang from the ground, wrapping around Lark's leg and yanking. She hit the still frozen earth with a *thud*.

Gavriel saw red. He charged to where Lark was scrambling to hack at her prison. He landed beside her and immediately set to chopping into the thick root. The tree creature screamed, throwing back its head and shaking the long tendrils of what appeared to be moss from its jaw.

"Fucking lesník." Lark gasped as another root wove its way around her stomach. "Can't... breathe..."

Panic flooded Gavriel's body, his hands shaking as he sawed his blade through the root cutting off her air. For each root he severed, the lesník sprouted more from the ground, intent on Lark.

It would not have her.

Gavriel cut through the last one and turned to advance on the creature. Sticky sap coated his hands, and it was enough to renew his determination. If it bleeds, he could kill it.

Silver was too soft a metal to use his sword, and he would not risk losing the only weapon that could kill some of the other creatures. His smaller, concealed blades would have to do.

He leapt at the giant tree, and ripped his stiletto dagger from his sleeve, driving it deep into the tree-trunk torso. Next his dirk through its eye, severing its merciless gaze. On and on he went with weapons more attuned to artful kills behind closed doors. He jabbed and sliced and hacked at anything he could reach until finally, the lesník let out a great roar before collapsing to the earth, its body seeping into the ground.

Gavriel searched for Lark, tightness clutching his chest until he found her, filthy and bloodied but safe. Ferryn had tossed her the Reaper Blade once more, and she cut down a wentiko with impressive speed before lowering the sword and catching her breath.

Gavriel strode to her, wrapping an arm around her waist to check her ribs.

Lark smiled through her labored breath, bracing an arm on his shoulder and leaning into him. *It would be too easy to spirit her away from this madness.*

"Just checking to see if anything's dislocated," he murmured against her ear, scanning the field behind her to see if any creatures noticed their compromised position.

"And here I thought," Lark said between heavy breaths, "you had less honorable intentions for your wandering hands."

Gavriel laughed despite himself. Despite the fact that just existing hurt in places he'd numbed for so long. Because each moment he stood by and watched her fight, was another moment he was tempting fate to rip them apart again. "I'm saving that for later. My reward for surviving this battle."

Lark's beautiful dirt-streaked face fell. Her liquid-amber eyes slid shut, as if he'd just prodded the spot that ached, and her full lips downturned. "Gav..." she said softly.

"Lark!" Ferryn shouted, his mess of golden hair matted with black blood. "The sword!"

Lark sighed, pulling herself free to toss the blade back to the former Reaper. She stepped further away, brandishing her dagger before launching herself into another attack. And Gavriel hated himself for letting her go.

CHAPTER SEVENTY-FIVE

LARK

*C*arnage. That was the only word to describe the landscape. Pure, bloody carnage.

Lark cut her way through the horde, showering black ichor across her face and chest in putrid spurts. She and Ferryn had adopted their cooperative style of trading off the Reaper Blade as needed. Sometimes Gavriel would hold the line long enough to grant Lark time to catch the Reaper Blade and carve her path. It was foolish, but Hugo's dagger felt a more formidable weapon in her hand than the forged blade meant for slaying otherworldly beings.

Human sentimentality was still such a funny thing.

Up ahead, a flash of white hair.

Nereida.

She'd stepped onto the battlefield. Lark marched through the muck, through the muddy puddles mixed with blood. Over severed limbs and silent deaths. To the woman who started it all. The Reaper Blade hung loose in Lark's hand.

Someone called her name, but Lark didn't dare look back. She only had eyes for Nereida, the Witch-Queen of the Netherworld. The one who started it all. And Nereida's eyes lit up when she spotted Lark, a smirk tugging at her black-painted lips. Her form-fitting leather suit hugged and accentuated every curve, and she rested a hand on her hip, amusement dancing in her violet eyes.

"The little Reaper returns." Nereida grinned. "And her shadow not far behind."

Gavriel.

Lark turned to warn him off—

But it wasn't Gavriel, it was Ferryn. He stood by, a muscle feathering in his jaw.

"You have been a naughty boy." Nereida pouted. "But then again, you always were." She clapped her hands. "Ceto come here."

Ceto marched up to her, a pained expression on her face.

"Let's show Ferryn how it works, shall we? Pull out your dagger."

Ceto yanked it from its sheath at her hip.

Nereida rolled her eyes. "What are you waiting for, put it through your hand."

Ceto plunged it through the middle of her palm, her breathing harsh. Ferryn staggered forward as if about to stop her, but Nereida held up a hand. "Uh, uh," she said. "Wait your turn."

"How do you fare without Nyx?" Lark swallowed down the anger climbing her throat, churning in her gut. "And Leysa."

Nereida's eyes flared, a momentary anger stealing across her expression, but she quickly schooled her face into a mask of amusement. "Nyx was never really tamable. Not the way our Ceto is." Nereida ran a hand down Ceto's cheek, and Ferryn looked ready to spew his stomach's contents. "As for Leysa..." Nereida shook her head and stepped closer to Lark.

The Reaper Blade sang in her hand, a wicked song promising death.

"You think you found my weakness, little Reaper." Nereida smiled. "My secret is, I don't have one. I have nothing and no one you can use against me."

"That's a lie." Lark couldn't help it. For the witch to stand here and pretend Leysa meant nothing... "You loved her. Admit it."

"I loved her power." Nereida lifted her chin, her smile failing to reach her eyes. "She was a means to an end, nothing more. Her attachment worked to my benefit. You took away my tools." She angled her head. "What will happen if I take away yours?" She turned to Ceto. "Get your man."

Ceto disappeared, vanishing as if she'd never been, and reappeared behind Ferryn, gripping his cloak.

"Come, dear, hold him tighter."

Ceto's face tightened, and she dragged him to stumble against her.

"Now take out your blade."

"Ceto, stop!" Not Ferryn. *Skies, no, not him.*

Ceto shook her head. "I can't, Lark."

"Wait, wait." She had to think of something. Some way to stall Nereida long enough for Ceto to break whatever compulsion she was under. "I know you created the veil!"

Nereida answered with a razor-sharp smile. "Leysa really was chatty, wasn't she?"

"I know Thanar betrayed you. That you escaped the clutches of Sargon only to end up Thanar's kept pet, relegated to the pits."

Nereida shook her head, the smile falling. "You know nothing, Larkin. My power was life itself. Do you know what happens to a witch cut off from her raw magic? It's existing without a soul. Without dreams." She exhaled a short breath, resuming her nonchalant façade. "But I found a new way, didn't I? And Sargon will never command me again." She turned her glare on Ceto once more. "Kill him."

"No!" Lark ran, her steps weighted down and her heart in her throat. Ceto fought against the compulsion, her arm trembling, blade shaking, and when Lark sank the Reaper Blade into her back, she cried out. Relief painted her features, her arms falling away from Ferryn.

His eyes glimmered, his mouth forming the word, *no*, over and over without any sound escaping. Ceto, sank to her knees, Reaper Blade still sunk in, and she laughed. "Finally," she said, before crumbling into ash.

Lark's throat tightened, and her legs went numb. For all the animosity she'd shared with Ceto, all the poison between them, she'd deserved better than this. Better than falling as a pawn in Nereida's schemes. Ceto was a warrior at heart, and her death should have *meant* something.

The Reaper Blade trembled in Lark's hands, shadow and light glimmering against steel. Regret formed a knot in her gut. If she'd had more time, if she could have found another way to save Ferryn...

"No," Ferryn finally said. The sound a croak. "How... why..."

Nereida clapped. "Bravo, Larkin. Bravo. What a talent you have for destroying everyone around you. But it's my turn. See, funny thing about tethers, you know this, they don't actually disappear in death if the contract holds true." She turned to Ferryn. "Arise."

Ferryn stood in a fluid motion.

Dread filled Lark's stomach.

Nereida laughed, jumping up and down. "Ferryn and Ceto were tethered, romantic little fools. Didn't he tell you how I knew where to find you?"

"Ferryn..."

"I'm sorry, Lark. I'm so sorry." Tears streamed down his face.

"So now his tether is mine, since I owned Ceto." Nereida grinned. "Ferryn, pick up the blade." The Reaper Blade glistened in his hand, dark shadows swirling against steel. Hungry for blood.

It was now or never.

Lark chanced a glance over her shoulder, finding Daciana cutting down a harpy. She shifted her gaze to where Gavriel felled a wentiko, his eyes lifting as soon as he felt her stare. Terror widened his eyes, and he shook his head.

I love you.

Lark crept her awareness out like a rolling fog, slowly, carefully, creeping up to Nereida—

And waiting.

Waiting.

Waiting.

"Kill her."

Lark forged the tether, as quickly and as tightly as she could. She bound their souls and cried out as she seeped into Nereida's memories.

Images of human Leysa, all tinged with lust and affection. A possessive ownership. It shifted to Thanar, his cruelty and selfishness. And pain. So much pain. The pain of being cut off from her own magic —it rivaled the force of Thanar shattering Lark's soul over and over when he tried to weave her memories in. And Nereida's pain was constant. A searing aching reminder of what she'd lost.

Everything.

Ferryn cried out, a vein pulsing in his forehead as he fought against the compulsion.

Lark finished forging the tether with a tug, weaving it into her body, into her soul. The tether she commanded, not Nereida. Not anyone else. Her fate was her own, and now, Nereida's was, too. There was a bright and burning sense of rightness, deep in her gut. All of her doubt vanished, evaporating under the weight of this simple truth: Lark had found a way to master her fate—all of their fates.

She turned to Ferryn, his face ruddy under the effort of fighting the compulsion. Sweat dotted his brow, and the blade trembled in his hands. Coils of dragonstone swirling and bleeding and begging for death.

"Ferryn," Lark whispered, leaning in and pressing a hand to the back of his neck, "it's all right."

Ferryn shook his head no, a tear rolling down his cheek. "Go. Go! I can't hold it any longer!"

"I know." Lark pressed her forehead against his and pushed herself onto the sword. The Reaper Blade sank into Lark's stomach, a deep, burning pain as flesh parted beneath steel and dragonstone. Lark gasped, the pain swallowing her voice. And when she lifted her dimming gaze, Nereida was doubled over in pain, too, clutching her stomach. She fell to her knees in the snow, the revelation of betrayal claiming her features. As if she'd never imagined Lark could outplay her. Could choose death if it meant sharing it with her. The air around her thickened, the winds current surrounding her, and bit by bit. She started to drift away. Her face, and all its dangerous beauty, crumbled into ash. Violet eyes darkened to black, and her nose collapsed. The wind blew once more, scattering her into countless particles like star dust lost to the sky.

It was done.

Joy filled Lark's chest, even as cold took root. It spread through her limbs like ice cracks upon the lake. It seeped within her, chilling her very bones. She fell to the earth, and the numbing cold stole some of the pain. She smiled. Even if this was the end. Even if this was the final note of her life's song, she had lived and loved and died. On her terms.

Someone fell beside her, a heavy thud shaking the ground beneath her.

"*No.* No! Lark!" Gavriel's agony broke his voice, and his strong arms bundled her to his chest. His scent filled her lungs, northern wind and dark chocolate, and it was the greatest parting gift this life could offer.

As the last of Lark's strength slipped from her body, and her mind ushered in the dark, she was not afraid.

CHAPTER SEVENTY-SIX

LARK

*D*eath was once Lark's constant companion. The guide by which she counted her existence. Lark looked upon her own body, at Gavriel cradling her to his chest. At his broken sobs and screams as he held her shell.

And it hurt.

Death wasn't supposed to hurt. She was supposed to find peace in her choices. But watching him break, it clawed at her. Ferryn, too, had fallen to his knees, shock stealing across his face. Daciana had halted her blade, running over to them, and landing beside Gavriel.

"Are you ready?" A voice called out.

Lark turned, and a woman stood, her radiant beauty near blinding. Her rich toned skin, deep brown and full of light, and that lone sunburst tattoo glowing in the middle of her forehead. Large green eyes, crinkled in fondness, and sparkling black hair housing a thousand stars.

Solana.

"How are you here?"

Solana shrugged. "A mutual friend of ours told me to be on the lookout for you."

Hugo.

Lark laughed, the sound tight. "Does that mean I've earned a place in Arcadia?"

Solana hummed. "Not exactly. Let's go for a walk."

The battlefield fell away, and instead the turquoise lake with the wooden bridge took shape. Nestled deep in a forest of lavender and red, purple light painting the ground. The crossroads. The destination to which she'd taken countless souls. It was strange seeing it as her own destination. What once seemed so inviting now felt... unknown. Terrifying.

"Something's changed, Lark. I can feel the fog lifting." Solana turned to her. "I'd forgotten... so many things, but my memories have been restored, and with memory there comes power. Avalon is not what it seems."

"I have no interest in Avalon or anything Sargon crafted." Why hadn't she earned a place in Arcadia? She did not want to ascend to Avalon.

Lark never wanted to forget again.

"Avalon was not created by Sargon," Solana said calmly. "He stole it. Tell me, Lark. Are you familiar with somniavi?"

Aislinn. "Dream walkers? What's happened to her? Did Sargon find her?"

"Peace, Lark. Somniavi are remnants of the old gods, and the true makers of Avalon. They were tricked and destroyed by Sargon, their power an echo of the betrayal he committed during their slumber. Their celestial energy had been recreated in the past, but Sargon always hunted them down, trying his best to erase them from existence."

"Does that mean..." Lark couldn't form the words. Couldn't connect the thoughts enough to understand.

"It means," Solana said, "your friend is no ordinary mortal. She is an echo of the most ancient power, bound in mortal form because Sargon could not destroy her energy. Aislinn is one of the old gods, and she has awakened."

It wasn't possible...

"Where is she?"

Solana let out a soft laugh. "I'm guessing, based on the flood of memories restored to me, that she discovered the truth, and is working on awakening the old gods once more."

It was too much. Aislinn was...

"I don't understand."

"You may never understand." Solana shrugged. "And that's all right. The important thing is..." she let a slow smile creep across her mouth. "This is not your time."

"What do you mean?"

"The fates are changing, Lark. You had a hand in that. You all did." Solana waved her hand, and the fog beyond the bridge dissipated. "The way is clear; you need only follow your feet."

If this was how vague Lark had been to mortals facing the afterlife, she owed each one an apology for being so obnoxious.

"How do I—"

"Follow your feet." Solana gave her a gentle nudge. "I'll be seeing you. Not anytime soon, I hope."

Lark crept to the bridge, confusion spinning her thoughts. Was walking across agreeing to death? But Solana said it wasn't her time. She still needed to unpack the truth of Aislinn's existence.

Just follow my feet. "Great advice, Solana." Lark trudged across the bridge, fear of the unknown mounting in her chest. And when she reached the other side, she took a deep breath and jumped.

CHAPTER SEVENTY-SEVEN

LARK

*L*ark awoke with a gasp, choking as air filled her deflated lungs. Pain and the weight of life flooded her body. Gavriel cried out, holding her close to his chest, his tears soaking her neck.

"Skies, I thought I lost you. I thought I lost you." His sobs echoed in her ears, and Lark clawed at him to get closer, to find his lips. Their kiss was desperate and bruising, teeth clacking hard enough to hurt.

Someone tugged Gavriel away, leaping atop Lark in a rib-crushing embrace. "I'm so sorry, little bird. I'm so sorry."

Ferryn.

Lark hugged him back. "Don't be. We killed her, Ferryn. We did it. Together." She opened her eyes to find Daciana standing over her, too, tears trailing down her cheeks.

"There's still much to be done." Daciana sniffed and wiped her nose on her sleeve. "But without Nereida, Inerys' protective wards are active again." Which meant the flood of Undesirables should have been held at bay. Lark held up a hand, and Daciana hauled her to her feet, crushing her against her chest in a suffocating embrace. "Don't *ever* do that again."

Lark hugged her tighter, uncaring for how bloodied they both were. "I'm sorry, Dac."

Daciana extricated herself from their embrace, stepping back to meet her eyes. "Are you as tired of apologizing as I am?"

A tight laugh broke free from Lark's chest, the edge of relief hinting its approach. They'd done it. Hadn't they? They'd well and truly succeeded. After centuries of failure, of being bound by fate and answering the call of destiny, she had broken free and changed the course of her path.

A wave of dizziness spun through Lark's head, and her vision dimmed. Gavriel was immediately upon her, holding her steady and keeping her close. "I'm fine," she said quickly. "Death is an exhausting business."

"It's far too soon to jest," he growled against her temple. He was right. But the joy of finally, *finally,* succeeding over Nereida filled Lark with a giddy, ebullient energy.

It was too soon to be celebrating so, wasn't it? Langford and Alistair were still fighting with the Vallemerian warriors. They hadn't yet accounted their losses or assessed Demetria's forces and Gavriel's assassins.

The scope of destruction had yet to be measured.

Lark glanced around, searching for what it cost to bring her back, and her gaze fell on Aislinn. She appeared the same mortal girl she'd always known. A simple homespun dress of green bringing out her eyes. But those eyes were different. Fathomless depths Lark had never seen reflected back at her. Solana's words rang in her mind. *'Aislinn is one of the old gods, and she has awakened.'*

Aislinn smiled and reached out her hand. "It's good to have you back."

Lark struggled to approach, uncertainty weighing down her feet. "Y-you..."

"We have much to discuss," Aislinn said. "But first, Daciana has work to do."

The veil. They needed it reinstated to prevent more Undesirables from ravaging the lands. Only a life-wielder could create it.

Daciana nodded. "Tell me what I need to know."

"The echo of your spell, of bringing Lark back, it left a considerable imprint of power. Use that, and if need be, draw from me once more and erect the veil. Do not fear this; we will not falter."

Aislinn had been the power Daciana pulled from. Lark examined the girl. She stood hale and healthy. No signs of fatigue. When Daciana had pulled from Thanar to bring Alistair back, the ancient god of death had crumbled into ash.

How powerful was Aislinn?

"There's more," Ferryn's voice broke through her thoughts. "She needs an anchor, someone to tether to the veil. Someone to take responsibility for the balance and of maintaining order so this never happens again." He took a deep breath. "Choose me."

"What? No." Lark would never let him do such a thing. It was madness, utter madness.

"It's not your choice, Lark." Aislinn's voice was soft but firm. A finality to it.

Helplessness crawled up Lark's chest, tightening her ribs and making it hard to breathe. "So, what, I never see you again?"

Ferryn blinked rapidly. "I wouldn't say that. I could never go that long without spying on you." He smiled, even as his eyes misted over. "The Otherworld needs order, Lark. I will restore the balance." He leaned over and kissed her cheek, whispering in her ear. "You know I'll always watch over you, don't you, little bird?"

Lark's chest expanded, the pain at his words filling the space and stretching enough to burn. It wasn't enough. It was letting go of the remaining pages of a story she could not bear to end. It was allowing memories to become the placeholder of his role in her life. Her oldest friend. The levity she sorely needed some days. The reminder of who she'd once been and who she could be.

Don't go.

Not where I cannot reach you.

But that was a selfish thought, wasn't it?

A tear trailed down Lark's cheek, and she nodded. Ferryn's smile grew, a true dawn of joy lighting up his face as one tear escaped the corner of his eye.

"Ready?" Aislinn called out.

Daciana shook her hands out, letting her eyes slip closed.

Arms wrapped around Lark, pulling her close. She leaned her head back on Gavriel's shoulder, her hand finding Ferryn's.

Nothing would ever be the same.

CHAPTER SEVENTY-EIGHT

DEMETRIA

When she was eight, Demetria asked her mother what happened after death. It was a time of turmoil following the loss of her rabbit, Duchess, and she'd needed to know death wasn't the end. That something greater than life awaited them all. That one day she'd see Duchess again and stroke her impossibly soft fur. Her mother had told her so many wondrous stories, and Demetria had believed them all to be true, so there had to be something more after a body was returned to the earth.

But her mother had said, '*That's the beauty, my darling, no one truly knows.*'

Demetria cried herself to sleep for a week after that.

She ran her fingers through Balan's hair, streaks of blood marking her touch. She hadn't even seen what killed him. What creature felled the only person left in the world who cared about her. The wound in the center of his chest where his heart should be was a gaping hole. Demetria placed a hand over the empty space. He'd bled and suffered and died like a human. And she hadn't been there. Hadn't held his hand when he died. No, she stumbled upon his cold body, silver eyes wide and unseeing. What were his last thoughts? Was it only pain? Did he regret their journey?

He must have felt so alone and forgotten.

Demetria's eyes burned, but no tears remained. She'd wept until her stomach ached with it all. Until her voice grew hoarse and the strength to mourn fled her body. She was a husk, an empty vessel. And despite having nothing left, having exhausted the extent of her pain, it still *hurt*.

Balan had died alone. He died never knowing how much she needed him.

And now she was alone.

"We mustn't tarry," Langford's soft voice washed over her.

Demetria ran a hand over Balan's eyes, slipping them shut. If she ignored the utter stillness of his chest, she could convince herself he was merely sleeping.

"There is still danger." Alistair's voice was harsh, insistent, and someone shushed him. "What? There is. Just because we closed the door, doesn't mean we didn't shut a few nasties in here with us."

Was it true? Could they really have defeated Nereida? It seemed impossible to hope for anything with the way Demetria's chest collapsed in on itself with each breath like the very act of existing was asking too much of her.

"A touch of sensitivity would go a long way," came Langford's voice, this time closer over her shoulder. "She's in shock."

Shock. Such a short and simple word to define her current state. Over the past few months, she'd lost her best friend since childhood, her mentor who was more of a father than anything else, her homeland, and any sense of security. She followed that up with murdering her own brother, condemning her kingdom to ruination, and losing the last person in this world who cared whether she lived or died. All to be summed up in one word spoken in a pitying whisper behind her back.

She wasn't in shock. She was in mourning for the death of everything she'd ever loved. It was only now catching up to her, on a blood-soaked battlefield, in the silence of Balan's chest.

"Death is nothing new, love. Not even to her."

Demetria almost preferred Alistair's callousness to Langford's coddling.

Langford crouched beside her, finally bringing his face into view. Blood and dirt matted the side of his head, his hair even untidier than usual. The pale tone of his skin was a stark contrast to the smudges of black and reddish brown. "We have contingencies sweeping the field, seeking out any lingering monsters. And my companion here could choose his words more delicately." Langford glared up at Alistair, and Demetria followed his gaze. Alistair offered them a roguish grin, the action pulling at a cut down the side of his face. "But," he continued, "he's not wrong. We must clear the forest and get as many of our people to safety as possible."

"Our people?" Demetria's throat cracked, and a fresh wave of tears blurred her vision. Blood and snow and white hair and black shorn horns all blended together. It was an odd thing to say, considering they were little more than allies at this point. The last of *her people* had been slain by the same monsters ravaging her kingdom.

"Of course." Langford gently slipped a hand beneath her arm, helping her to her feet. Demetria stumbled, and another set of hands caught her.

I have no people.

Alistair scoffed. "Could have fooled me, Princess. Why else in Sargon's flaming knickers would we be standing here in the cold, hours after the other have retired to more pleasant endeavors?" He wagged his brows at Langford, earning him a disgusted noise that sounded more amused than actually disgusted.

She must have spoken aloud.

Did he say hours? Demetria scanned the horizon, and sure enough, the sun had given way to the stars, only a glimmer of color remaining low in the distance.

"You should have left me." Demetria tugged her arms free, her knees buckling. Two sets of arms caught her, keeping her upright. "I will not be anyone's anchor." *Not anymore.*

"Anchor? Blazes, Langford, she's worse than Lark."

"I won't hear another word about Lark." Langford sniffed. "I'm still furious with her."

Why would they be angry with Lark? The former Reaper could do no wrong so far as her friends were concerned. No matter how many people died in her wake.

Gut churning nausea spun low in Demetria's belly. She was just like Lark, wasn't she?

"We're all furious with Lark," Alistair said, rolling his eyes. "But you, Princess. Or is it Queen? It doesn't have the same ring to it." He scowled at her. "We aren't leaving you. And yes, you are still one of us. Blood in, blood out, love. 'Fraid you're stuck accepting our help, our meddling, our bad influence." He tucked her in tighter against him, and Demetria wanted to sag in his arms and weep in relief. "We don't abandon our own so easily."

"But I left." Demetria's gaze fell to where Balan still lay in the snow, his handsome face frozen forever. He was like an otherworldly prince in one of her mother's fairy stories. But there was no spell to break, no magical cure.

"And you came back." Langford eased her arm over his shoulder.

The simple act of being held, an almost familial affection between people who should have probably remained strangers, it was enough to thaw the corner of ice in her chest. It was enough to exhale one complete breath. It was enough to not feel entirely alone in the world.

It was enough to find a shred of hope.

"ARE YOU ALL RIGHT?"

Demetria glanced up from the pocked wood of the witch's table to find Lark standing over her, fiddling with the ends of her hair.

"That was a stupid question." Lark slid into the chair across from her, resting her elbows on the table's flat surface. "I heard about Balan, and I only meant—"

"I know what you meant." Demetria traced the woodgrains, allowing her perusal of Lark to remain in her periphery. Lark had bathed, as they all had, thankfully, and wore her red hair loose around her shoulders. Bruises had bloomed along her slender neck, and a few cuts and gashes marred her face. But nothing lasting. Nothing that wouldn't fade easily with time.

Demetria, too, bore minimal markings. Her neck was sore where the demon had bitten her, and with each heartbeat, the pain pulsed alongside it. But she hadn't even needed Langford's stitching or Inerys' poultices. She was unscathed in all the ways that hardly mattered.

"I've spoken with your commander," Lark said, her voice gratingly gentle. "He tells me your men wish to return home."

"Of course, they do," Demetria spat out. They'd lost many of their own, even more back home. It was only natural her men were eager to return to face the wreckage she'd caused. "I don't know which is worse. The idea of facing my own execution or the notion I'll return to nothing but rubble." She didn't mean it. She'd far rather fall than see her kingdom reduced to ash.

Lark stiffened. "Who in their right mind would call for your execution? Who would even have that power? Demetria, you are *queen*. I only shared his thoughts because they keep their distance from you."

Too afraid to tell her himself, she meant. Skies, she really was just like Zaire.

"I only wish—" Demetria's voice cracked. "I only wish I had better news to share." That she hadn't run away like a coward, spelling their doom with nothing to show for it.

"The land is safe once more, Nereida has fallen." There was something tight in Lark's eyes as she said this. "Isn't that the greatest news to deliver?"

"I left them." Demetria wanted nothing more than to return home. To find something, anything, to protect the precious memories of a life that felt eons ago. The waterfall where she and Evander used to play mermaids, the training yard where Ruslan taught her more about life than fighting techniques, and all of the *what ifs* that loomed around every corner of the castle. Every alcove, every whispered shadow. *What if* Balan hadn't fallen. What if he was returning with her. What if they had all the time in the world to heal and grow and maybe, just maybe… find more.

Lark reached across the table, her hand hovering over Demetria's before she finally placed it, warm and reassuring, over her knuckles. "Yes, you left. And now you'll return. You'll return with the hope they desperately need."

Demetria turned her hand to squeeze Lark's hand in return. So many words bubbled up in her throat. So many thoughts and fears and worries. "I don't want to be alone."

Lark's eyes burned, golden and bright like the sun catching on a field before it slid beneath the horizon. "You will never be alone. This I promise. You have friends; you have people in your corner. No matter how far we are, we're here, Demetria."

It was an impossible promise made by the woman who sacrificed someone dear to Demetria. Her words should have been water in a sieve and trickled away as fast as they'd come. But Demetria clung to them, wrapped them tightly in her fist as if she could bring them back across the ocean to Koval with her.

Lark slid her hand free, watching her with a calculating expression. "Have you chosen your advisor?"

The harsh shift in conversation jolted any lingering sentimentality from Demetria. "Balan was… I suppose I'll need to appoint a new one. If there's anyone left."

Lark nodded, an eager grin stretching across her face and crinkling the wrinkles along her nose. "Alistair and Langford would make for perfect emissaries. I'm sure you could coax them to appear a few times a year with lavish balls and parties. But there's someone else, someone who would make frequent trips to your side. Someone who knows the ins and outs of both Kovalian law and its underbelly."

Lark's enthusiasm was nearly infectious. Already the thought of having Alistair and Langford, even just their presences in missives and letters, having people to talk to who knew and understood everything that had happened, lightened a touch of the load bearing on her chest. "Who?" she demanded.

Lark's grin turned wicked, a knowing smile like she was far too pleased with herself. "Captain Ingemar."

CHAPTER SEVENTY-NINE

AISLINN

here once was a girl made of stardust...
Aislinn's father's words echoed, time upon time folded in on itself like an accordion. The Hall of Mirrors revealed much, too much, and though Aislinn would never be the same, could never be the same, parts of her were. The part who picked fights with her mother when her feelings grew too large, who hid by the river to escape the endless noise of too many voices, who was willing to bleed herself dry if it meant proving herself useful.

Aislinn gazed up at the trees, bare branches carrying the promise of spring, of new life again. She had not donned a cloak, despite the chill in the air. She could feel it if she wished, or she could turn it off. Instead, she basked in the way the breeze carried the last of winter's grasp, weaker with each passing day but enough to raise gooseflesh on her bare arms. The hem of her green dress was brown and wet, soaked through by the mud and snow.

Nereida had fallen, just as Lark had planned. And Daciana was able to draw from Aislinn to restore her soul to her body. It was draining, allowing herself to be the conduit to something as strong as transcending death, and the weakness lingered in her bones. And when Daciana restored the veil, anchoring Ferryn as its keeper, Aislinn's

576

vision had spotted from the strain. But she had not told the others of how it taxed her. Could not let them see how much it took from her. She would gather her strength, and they would be none the wiser. It was the least she could do, knowing what she now knew of her power.

Her thoughts turned once more, as they always would, to what she'd learned. Truths unearthed, long buried and forgotten. The power of memory restored, even memories that were not hers. It was too much for a mortal mind to comprehend, but she was no longer mortal, was she? She was scattered pieces of a long-lost power.

Aislinn was not alive, yet she was more alive than she'd ever felt. How was such a thing possible?

Aislinn was the descendant of the Mother of All, the creator no one remembered. Stardust and dreams and creation. Why was her name forgotten? It ached of the deepest loss, the greatest sorrow. The loneliness of the Mother, erased from existence, from memory.

"Are you cold?" Merikh's voice came from beside her, along the ripple of another breeze. He draped his cloak around her shoulders, large hands lingering.

Aislinn leaned into his touch. "Does Sargon know?"

Merikh's hands tightened. "No. And he will not until you are ready. Until you give the order."

It was a funny thing, power. Aislinn had been repulsed at the thought, at the idea that she could command Merikh without his consent. It was an abuse, one she would never use over him. But that was the thing about power. One could choose whether to wield it.

"We have many wrongs to right." Aislinn turned her head to meet Merikh's eyes. A storm brewed in his gaze, and his mouth tightened beneath his beard.

"By your leave, Your Worship."

The title ran through Aislinn's veins like ice. It crawled across her skin like an unwanted touch. She shrugged out of his hold. "Why do you call me that?"

Merikh's eyes widened. "You are the last of the Mother. I owe you my deference."

She couldn't be the last. They'd been so sure all the somniavi were long gone, and yet, here she remained. Their oversight meant there had to be others.

But it wasn't his casual dismissal of other beings existing that had her stomach churning.

"I don't want your deference." Disgust curled in her throat and threatened to prick her eyes with tears. Once a soldier, always a soldier, isn't that what he was? Was nothing between them anything more than a void of power and a need to submit? Was every tension charged moment between them his desire to please her? "Do not tell me words you assume I wish to hear. Do not treat me like the next fragile power to be managed. Give me your truth! Do not hold your thoughts back! Think for yourself for once in your life, Miro, tell me unbridled truth!" His name slipped from her lips without thought.

Merikh shuddered, the power of her influence, the use of his name falling over his broad frame. He stood even taller, expanding under her gaze. A hint of shadows curled about his shoulders, fanning out to form the shape of massive wings. His stormy eyes burned, a glowing flare in their depths as a surge of energy jolted between them.

"My truth." His voice was a dark rumble of crackling energy, the first hints of his true form ever revealed to her. "I wish to worship you in every way. The fervor of mortals is unfamiliar and unknown to me, but I wish to learn by worshipping your flesh. I would sacrifice myself at your altar for all the sins committed against you by my kind and by the humans. I will gladly follow you into oblivion, because you are the true ruler of Avalon and because I trust you to release us from the perdition of Sargon's rule. But I cannot get these images out of my head. I should not imagine you so, but I do. With every breath and every waking moment, I think of you. And when my season of slumber arrives, I will dream of you."

Aislinn trembled, her knees threatening to buckle as warmth spread through her belly at his confession. "Why... why do you feel this way? Is it merely compulsion? A draw to power? Answer me, Miro."

Merikh's eyes rolled back, another shudder through his shoulders as he sank to his knees before her. "I burn for you, Aislinn. I will worship you until the end of my days. You are more than I ever thought could exist in a soul, and I will spend eternity wanting you from afar."

It was too much, this confession she yanked from his soul. And the knowledge that she'd forced it... Aislinn hesitantly reached out, running her fingers through his hair. Merikh groaned and leaned into her touch.

"I will never command you again," she said softly.

Unless....

It was a dark and wicked thought, one she couldn't help but let bloom in her mind. Fire erupted along her skin as images assaulted her. Images of exactly what he'd thought of, of writhing beneath him and allowing his patient and thorough perusal. Of using his name to heighten his pleasure, his anticipation, before unleashing him upon her.

As if sensing her thoughts, Merikh let out a soft noise, and rubbed his face into her belly.

It was too soon, by all accounts, to explore whatever was growing between them. There was too much work to be done to fall prey to distraction. And even now, she could not be sure his feelings were not compulsory in nature.

"Please arise," Aislinn said, forcing the fire from her voice in favor of something softer.

Merikh rolled to his feet, gazing down at her like she had stars in her eyes. She ran a hand up his chest, reaching his neck and angling his head to hers. It would be so easy, *so easy,* to breech the distance. "Can I ask you for something?"

"Anything." Merikh's voice rumbled deep in his chest, the reverence in his tone settling over her and lighting her blood on fire. She canted her head, and he slid his hand along her jaw. There was no fear. No panic. Only a warm sense of peace came over her.

But that's all they could be. This moment upon a precipice, the stilted silence before an exhale. She would take it no further. Not without certainty his actions and feelings were his own.

Aislinn pulled away, and Merikh nodded, as if knowing her

thoughts, relinquishing his grip and allowing the space between them to grow.

"When I call for you, will you come?" No forced compliance. No abuse of his true name. Aislinn did not want to wield him like a sword.

He gazed at her as if the very sight of her face was his greatest joy. "Always."

Now, the true work would begin. Once she said goodbye to the others, her new life would bloom like the early leaves of spring.

Aislinn would restore the memories Sargon had rewritten. She would be the driving force behind Avalon's rebirth.

And if there were any others in existence like her, living or dead, she would find them.

⊰ ⊱

"I SEE your healer has been raiding my larder," Inerys sneered, though the effect was lost as she'd shoved bits of cloth into each nostril. She called the nosebleeds *residual side effects* of her spellwork in containing the battle of the Emerald Woods. Aislinn would see to it the village of Oakbury erected a statue in Inerys' honor for everything she'd done for years to protect them.

"Langford is *our* healer. And don't pretend I didn't catch you inhaling his puff pastries." Daciana laughed as she said it, diminishing any bite her words might have held. Not that they would. Her words were light lately. In fact, her entire being seemed unfettered by worry. Something else about her was different, but Aislinn couldn't put her finger on it. Perhaps it was the way she openly wore her joy.

Daciana's gaze fell to Lark where she leaned her chin atop her folded arms, and some of that carefree joy dimmed to a quiet contemplation.

Aislinn studied Lark. They hadn't had the chance to speak privately, and now that the flutter of activity that was Vallemerian warriors and Kovalian soldiers had died down and they'd all returned home, it was easier to note the downcast air she kept. Was she missing Gavriel? He'd been busy dealing with the aftermath of his newfound underlings. His assassins were due to leave on the morn, extra time and care taken to assign Hazel enough power to keep things afloat while Gavriel kept his distance. But Aislinn was sure if he were to return to the Guild, it would only be with Lark by his side.

"It seemed a waste to let them perish, especially since my own supplies were utilized." Inerys hung her cast iron kettle on the crane over the fire, preparing water for the tea both Aislinn and Lark had turned down.

"Right..." Daciana tossed a knowing smirk Lark's way, and her returning smile was stilted and tight. "You all right?"

Lark slid her arms off the table, forcing herself to sit upright, but the movement was sluggish. "I'm fine. Merely tired." She gave an exaggerated yawn. "Death and all that is a tiresome business." She let a smirk curve against her mouth, and though Daciana's stare remained wary, she did not press.

Dark circles had formed beneath Lark's eyes. Had she not been sleeping? The days had taken a toll on them all, and while exhaustion and grief permeated the air, there was also relief. The slow exhale after a long day's work. But Lark still appeared coiled tight, as if she'd been unwilling to let the breath of relief leave her body.

"Now that my apprentice has far exceeded my teachings, what will she do?" Inerys tilted her head in mock consideration, eying Aislinn with a sharpness that was all teeth and no real bite. Inerys had already shown her hand in the days after the battle by way of random embraces and never-empty cups of tea. She'd worried after Aislinn, after all of them, and though she'd never say it, she showed her care in her own grumpy ways.

"I don't know about that," Aislinn said with a laugh. "I've learned many things, yet I feel more confused than ever."

"I don't believe that for a moment." Inerys said, shaking her head. Her wild dark hair spilled over her slender shoulder, and when she brushed it back, a new scar lined her jaw. "You've always been a witch of instinct, never forget that. Your gut will tell you more than any supposed expert can."

Lark's stomach growled, and Daciana laughed.

"Your gut is telling you to eat," she said, reaching over to grab an apple and pressing it into Lark's palm.

Lark wavered, apple in hand, before she sank her teeth into its flesh with an audible *crunch*. Her chewing slowed, and a thoughtful expression crossed her face. "Things are so unknown now, aren't they?"

Understatement of the century.

"Having seen all I've seen, I know less than when I was blind to it all." For every answer revealed, a shroud of mystery followed its path. Aislinn felt at home in the truth of existence, in what could only have been revealed in death, but any insight it offered was tempered by its historical erasure. How could anyone help her learn what she was, when her very existence had been evaporated from living knowledge.

It was a terrifying thought, that there was no one she could ask.

"Do not give ignorance merit where it is not due," Inerys said with a harrumph. "If you lack answers, get out there and find them."

"I agree," Dacaiana added. "There's a whole world waiting for us out there. And for the first time, we have leave to explore it without agenda. Without pressure. Without fearing the very fall of human existence."

"It's true. You won't find your answers here in my kitchen. You'll find them out there." Inerys nodded toward the window.

It was a simple enough response, but one that reignited Aislinn's determination. She might not know the way, but she would figure it out. As Inerys had said, her instinct had always been her guide, and it would not fail her now.

Kenna poked her head through the entryway, a grin already formed on her face. "Dac, I need you for, um, wine inspection."

Daciana's face lit up, a radiant smile transforming her features. She stood, hesitating where Lark sat, shoulders hunched and apple forgotten. She placed a hand on her arm. "Get some sleep, yeah?"

Lark tightened her mouth in the approximation of a smile. "Yeah, yeah I will. I promise."

Daciana squeezed her arm once more and trailed after Kenna.

Lark's gaze was distant, eyes far away though trained on the table.

Perhaps the journey back into her own body had yielded more pain than she let on.

"Speaking of answers lacked," Lark said, twisting the stem off her apple, "with the veil intact, how will death work now?"

"I'm sure Ferryn has his hands full in the Otherworld." Aislinn frowned. She hadn't had the proper time to bid him farewell, and though she suspected she could find a way to reach him being what she was, it seemed an unnecessary risk for the time being. Passing through the veil, traveling across plane. If the veil needed time to strengthen, it wouldn't do to cause any tears. "I'm sure he'll have it sorted. There were many Reapers who only followed Nereida out of fear. He can rebuild." As would she.

"I mean... can anyone who has already died still reach out to us?"

They fell silent at that. If Lark spoke of echoing souls, the creation of earth-bound spirits, the new veil should have prevented such a thing.

"Souls are not meant to linger," Inerys said, slowly enunciating. "And if they do, they become a problem. Your best bet would be not to engage or give them a foothold to communicate with you."

"That's not—" Lark sputtered. "I'm not saying for *me*. But what about Demetria? Could Balan be living it up in the Netherworld right now? Waiting for the opportune time to appear?" Her words were rushed, nervous. What was she hiding?

"It is my limited understanding," Aislinn began, "that demons, and otherworldly souls... they do not die as mortals do." Though Balan had been reduced to mortal strength and capabilities, he was still a demon that fell. "Though his body remained, his soul should have disintegrated, finding rebirth in other ways." Dustings spread far and wide, in mortals yet to be born, lingering echoes of his soul might be found once more. But this was all still new to Aislinn, and she couldn't be sure of anything.

"Balan does not exist anymore." Inerys' voice was cautious. "Aislinn is right, if he fell, he will never be as himself again. Parts of him will exist in future souls, but Balan, as you knew him, is no more." She narrowed her dark eyes. "Why, do you miss him?"

Lark huffed her hair out of her face with a sharp breath. "This is all hypothetical. I was merely asking what it would mean if Balan were to show up for Demetria in a form only she can see."

Dread pooled in Aislinn's belly, and she did not know why.

"Listen to me very carefully." Inerys leaned toward Lark, and unable to help herself, Aislinn leaned in, too. "If Balan were to appear in a form only Demetria can see, there could only be three causes. He would still be alive, his visage would be a trick, or she would be losing her grasp on reality. But we know he is dead, do we not? And we know she is of sound mind and reason." Her mouth twitched. "For the moment, at least."

Lark nodded, her gaze darting to the far wall and back. "Yes," she finally said. "Yes, of course." She mumbled to herself, but Aislinn could have sworn she'd said, *"Just a trick."*

If Lark was seeing Balan, if he was appearing to her, why not just tell them?

The shrill whistle of Inerys' kettle rang out, and Lark nearly fell out of her chair. She stood, knocking it back hard enough it hit the floor. "Sorry!" She ran her hands through her hair, but Aislinn didn't miss the way they trembled. "Sorry. I think I'll have a lie down."

Lark backed out of the kitchen, leaving Inerys and Aislinn to stare at each other.

"That was strange." It seemed the kindest, least accusatory thing to say.

Inerys gave a little scoff, pouring steaming water into their cups. "Strange is a natural state where our friend is considered." She slid Aislinn's unwanted tea toward her, taking her seat once more. Lifting her cup, Inerys blew gently against the steam, a crease forming between her brows. "Keep a close eye on her."

Aislinn reached for her own cup. She'd already planned on doing just that.

CHAPTER EIGHTY

GAVRIEL

"There you are." Gavriel leaned against the doorway, watching Lark. She sat on their bed, her knees tucked in tight. He regretted the hours they'd spent apart, especially after he'd nearly lost her, but the Guild needed a unified approach. He'd never wanted to uphold the life sentence of being a Guild assassin, but the sanction it required to prevent trained killers from being unleashed to an unsuspecting populace was necessary. Derwin and Eldridge would uphold his claim to the title of Master, but having Hazel as his delegate would be the extra protection required.

It still took far longer than he'd preferred, but it was done.

Lark still hadn't turned, her stare trained on the wall. Gavriel crossed the room, taking a seat beside her on the bed and gently turning her to face him. Panic had been splashed across her features, widening her eyes and stealing the color from her complexion.

"What's wrong? Are you hurt?" Damn it all! Langford must have missed something, a wound, perhaps internal. "I'll call for Inerys—"

"No." Lark grabbed his hand, holding it tight between hers. Her palms were clammy. When had those dark shadows gathered beneath her amber eyes?

"Lark, if you are unwell—"

"That's just it." She squeezed tighter, adjusting her position on the bed so she was practically in his lap. "I'm well, aren't I? I came back to you. I'm here. We won."

"Yes…" Gavriel followed her words, the direction her thoughts must have been traveling. The stress of it all, of all the days, it must have finally caught up with her. And skies knew he'd been having nightmares, memories of her lifeless body in his arms. Of the amount of blood painting the ground, his hands, her clothes. Of how pale she'd been. Pale and so limp. She'd once mentioned the weight of a soul, and in that moment, he could have sworn her body felt lighter in his arms than it ever had before. "You came back. We always come back to one another."

Was the reminder for her benefit or his own?

Lark surged forward, pressing a breathless kiss, harsh and rough, against his mouth, before pulling away far too quickly. "I need to tell you something."

Gavriel braced himself. The line of tension in her body, the abrupt fall of her words. It wouldn't be good. "You can tell me anything."

Lark's face crumpled, and his heart ached at the sight. "I think something's wrong with me." She cast another glance at the empty corner where the walls met and the shadows gathered. "Nereida died, didn't she? She died. I died and she died and it happened. It was real."

Gavriel frowned. Whatever he'd thought she was going to say, that wasn't it. Was she worried none of this had come to pass? That this was all a dream before the final battle? "It was real, Lark." He ghosted his touch along her arm, over her shoulder, until he cupped her jaw. "*This* is real."

Lark searched his eyes, her impossibly beautiful face warring with unspoken thoughts. "I hear her, Gav. I *see* her. She whispers terrible things, and I can't tell what's real anymore." Her eyes filled with tears. "She won't let me sleep. I thought nightmares were keeping me from rest, but it's her, it's *her.* She makes me relive our worst moments. I never saw when they hung you. When they killed you after Thanar took me. But I've watched it countless times now while Nereida slows your speed of death and makes me watch." Lark clawed at his tunic, tugging him closer.

"Darling." Gavriel yanked her against his chest, tucking her head under his chin. "She can't hurt us anymore. Nereida is dead. I watched her fall with my own eyes. Whatever echoes in your head... she cannot hurt us." It felt safer to reassure her with such certainty. "I will *never* let anything pull us apart again."

"I just wish to sleep." Lark's voice cracked. "Sleep and not fear what I might witness. Do you think it's me? Did I fracture my mind when I returned?"

"No, my heart. You are perfect. Should I ask Inerys for a sleeping draught? I'll watch over you so you can rest." He would spend the rest of his days protecting her. Each night she would lie in his arms, and he would guard her and her heart until his stopped beating, and beyond that, too.

"What if it only traps me in a bad dream?"

Gavriel's heart clenched at the vulnerable fear in her voice. He understood better than most the torture of being trapped in dreams. It seemed like forever ago he'd been trapped by Nereida's cursed sleep. But Lark saved him, as she always had.

"Another time. For now, let me watch over you while you sleep. I promise you'll be safe."

Lark lifted her head, jutting her chin toward him in an unmistakable demand for his kiss. "And if I have a nightmare?"

Gavriel pressed his lips to hers. Once. Twice. A third for good measure. "Then I shall wake you and prove it wasn't real. By any means necessary." He allowed a suggestive smirk to curl against his mouth, and she huffed a laugh in response.

"I'll try to sleep." She yawned, her eyes slipping shut in that adorable way he loved. "So tired."

Gavriel gently repositioned himself so they lay on the bed. Lark nuzzled into his neck, her head turning this way and that against his chest until she was comfortable. He pressed a kiss to her brow. "Sleep, my demon."

Lark's answering smile carried her into sleep.

GAVRIEL REMAINED ALERT, even as darkness crept through the open window, drawing a shroud over their room. He inhaled her scent of sun-ripened apples as he carded his fingers through her hair. It would take a long time before either of them really felt normal, wouldn't it? They'd finally gained the life they'd earned, but it came with a sense of impending dread. Of waiting for the other shoe to drop.

Whether it was him or her, it was very likely one of them would always awaken in a cold sweat from a nightmare of horrors past. But he didn't doubt they would find a way through together.

He wrapped a tendril of her hair around his finger. In the darkness, it was hard to see the vibrance of flaming red, but the glimmer of gold caught the moonlight, casting a shimmery glow around his knuckle. It seemed such a superficial thing, being that her very soul and the turn of her always active mind was the claim on his heart, but she really was absurdly beautiful in a way that just didn't exist in this world. The memory of the Reaper who came to collect Vanya, the killer he'd disposed of back before Lark had found him again, came to mind. He'd once thought her inhumanly beautiful, but once Lark had appeared before him, a vial in her hand and bright eyes wide with panic, he was a goner.

Never before had he—

Lark fell slack, the weight of her body lessening in a way that sent a spear of ice through Gavriel's blood. He uncurled her hair from his finger and angled his head down to look at her.

She'd been slumbering peacefully against his chest, the occasional twitch and a steady soft snore of breath between her teeth.

Now she was utterly silent, and far too still.

Gavriel gently nudged her shoulder. "Lark?"

No response, and the stillness of the room only grew.

Heart hammering in his throat hard enough to ache, Gavriel sat up, bringing her up with him. She was limp in his hands, her head lolling to the side.

"Lark!"

She was cold. Why was she cold?

This couldn't be happening. It couldn't be happening. This was his turn to suffer a nightmare. He'd wake up to her smoothing her hand across his brow and—

"Lark! Wake up!" Gavriel shook her, panic locking his muscles and sending his blood in a frenzy. Her chest remained still, not a hint of breath filling her lungs. "Lark!"

The door shoved open hard enough to hit the wall. Aislinn appeared, holding the pitiful flame of a candle upon a pricket. "What's happening?"

"She won't wake up. She's—" He would not say the word. He wouldn't even fucking think it. His eyes burned, and his chest constricted. Bundling her against his chest, he lifted Lark into the air. "Get Daciana! Get someone!"

Aislinn opened her mouth a few times before placing her candle on the bedside table.

"Did you fucking hear me? We need to fix her. What did Daciana do? She'll set her soul back in place and she'll—" Gavriel's voice broke. "She'll be fine. I promised her she'd be fine." Lark would open her eyes, she would stretch and smile up at him, grateful to have finally gotten rest. She would be fine. They would be fine. She was still here. He had her. He had her. He—

"Gavriel, I need you to let me examine her." Aislinn's voice broke through his thoughts. "I need to know what happened."

Gavriel ran a shaky hand down his face. "She… she was tired. And I told her to sleep. I said I'd keep her safe." He couldn't lose her now. By the rutting skies, he would not lose her now.

"Safe from what?" Aislinn's hands were slow and measured as she placed them on Lark's chest, feeling for a heartbeat.

"She said Nereida had been appearing to her." The strength fled Gavriel's body, and he leaned against the bed. He loomed over them, unwilling to put much distance between himself and Lark. "She hasn't been sleeping well."

Aislinn stilled, leveling him with a dark stare. "Nereida? And you didn't think to mention this when she told you?"

"She said she needed sleep! I only wanted to give her what she needed." She'd only just told him, and Gavriel hadn't thought to mention it before giving her the rest she desperately needed. How many of his own ghosts flickered in the corner of his mind's eye, reminding him of his pain? It was a normal thing, to be haunted by one's own memory.

"I... I sense Lark. Her soul is not here, but it's much the same as your sleeping curse."

Sleeping curse?

"What do I do? How do I help her?" Even if she had been dead, Gavriel would have followed her to the afterlife and dragged her back home to him. If there was one thing he'd learned in all his years, it was that he did not except death so easily.

Memories from long, long ago whispered in the back of his mind. Memories of a day—the first time she'd been taken from him.

Death is not the end. I will find you again.

Aislinn sighed, pulling her hands away and rubbing her eyes. "Lark forged a tether to Nereida to kill her. And we pulled Lark back." She lifted her head, eying him with a pained expression. "What if we brought Nereida back, too?"

"Tell me what to do." Daciana stood over Lark, her hands balled into fists.

"First, we let the experts assess the situation." Inerys was not happy to be woken in the dead of night, even less happy that Lark had shared her fears with Gavriel instead of her. "Hero needs to keep back."

That charming nickname she'd reserved for him. Gavriel grit his teeth and made himself release Lark's hand, stepping away to give Aislinn and Inerys the room they needed.

"Langford can stay, the rest of you, out!" Inerys voice left no room for argument. Even Alistair had the good sense to keep his mouth closed as they filed out of the room.

Langford hesitated, placing a comforting pat against Gavriel's shoulder, before he shut the door in their faces.

"So," Alistair began, "this is what it's like to be useless. It's an odd feeling, almost freeing, really."

The man didn't always need to fill the silence.

"It matters naught what they say." Daciana leaned against the wall. "We'll get her back."

"I know we will." Alistair's voice softened. "That girl is unkillable. Hard to believe she's the same creature who stumbled into our camp, tottering like a newborn fawn and unable to speak a word to us." He grinned. "Even in her most weakened state, she sure knows how to bring a man to his knees, huh, Gavriel?"

Gavriel let his head fall back against the wall with a *thud*. Yes, even when he thought of her as the demon who led Emric away, the strength of her pull was impossible to ignore. It was her heart, he was sure, that pulled everyone like a relentless tide.

"Lark needs us. We can swap anecdotes if it offers comfort, but she needs our action, not our warm thoughts." Daciana thumbed the haladies at her belt, her gaze far away despite the cramped space of the hallway they shared.

There was a note of panic in her voice, something Gavriel hadn't noticed before. Not that it was strange to worry, but if anyone should enter the situation with confidence, it was the one who had successfully resurrected thrice in her lifespan.

It was enough to catch Gavriel's attention and ratchet his own fears to new heights. He studied her, the way she kept walking her fingers along the handles of her blades. The tight line of her mouth. The worrying crease between her brows.

"What aren't you saying?"

Daciana stilled, the very picture of the cornered wolf. "I can't feel it."

"Feel what?" *Speak plainly, or so help him—*

"My power," Daciana said on a rough exhale. "I can't feel my power anymore. It always lingered at the edge of my mind, the tips of my fingers. Waiting. Ready. I can't... I can't feel it anymore." She shook her head. "I'm sure it just needs restoring after bringing Lark back and creating the new veil."

Lie. That was the first lie she'd told him. She wasn't even lying convincingly enough to fool herself.

Oddly enough, it did not rattle Gavriel the way he thought it would. It was no question, he was going to bring Lark back one way or another. Barter his damn soul if he had to. That Daciana was not a viable solution only felt... inevitable. It would always come down to him and Lark.

The door hinged open, a loud creak filling the tension-fraught hall. Langford appeared, a hand mussing his hair. "All of her vitals indicate her state is stable. Currently, that is."

"It could change?" Dread dug its hole in Gavriel's stomach. He needed time.

Langford hesitated, his eyes bloodshot. "It could always change. But I believe we've surmised a way." He gave Alistair a meaningful glance.

The healer thought to fill his lover in first? Not happening.

"What's the plan?"

Langford angled his head to gesture to the door. Without waiting another instant, Gavriel forced his way through.

"Tell me what I need to do before I summon a fucking demon and make a deal to bring her back."

Aislinn's eyes widened and Inerys scoffed.

"Calm down, hero. There's still hope you could sacrifice yourself."

Gavriel recognized her jests for what they were, deflections.

"There is still hope," Aislinn interjected, standing and approaching him with clasped hands. "I cannot reach Lark myself. I worry about risking the construct of the new veil. But you"—she pointed at him— "you could reach her, with my help, you could travel to the Nether-world and bring her back."

"Done. What do I do?" Why were they standing around talking? The sooner he got underway, the better.

"There is still a grave risk, and if you push too hard, Lark may lose her footing in this plane."

He would not let that happen.

"And we don't know how much of a threat Nereida still poses." Aislinn glanced back at where Lark lay on the bed, frozen in a deathly slumber. "But we need Lark to sever the thread, and to use the Reaper Blade on what's left of Nereida."

What's left of her? Enough to steal Lark away from her body. "I will endure all to bring her back."

"How romantic," Inerys said dryly. "I fear I may swoon. Aislinn, catch me."

Aislinn ignored her. "Nereida was weakened significantly, which must have been why she needed to isolate Lark from the rest of us to gain a true footing."

The image of Lark's exhausted eyes, the deep-purple shadows from being tortured in her sleep. The break of her voice. Nereida had done that. Had worn her down. Anger tightened Gavriel's hands into fists. "I should have believed her."

"We had every reason to believe Nereida was dead." Aislinn side-stepped his guilt. "And every reason to believe we can still succeed."

As if he needed a pep talk to race into the pits of the Netherworld to bring the love of his life, his soul bonded back. "Get me the blade. I'm bringing Lark home."

CHAPTER EIGHTY-ONE

GAVRIEL

The Reaper Blade weighed heavily against Gavriel's back. How Lark and Ferryn and even Aislinn could swing it without great difficulty was a mystery. With Kenna's silver blade, his many daggers, and the vial of questionable liquid Kenna had insisted he carry, he was ready. He'd even slipped Hugo's blade into his boot with the hope Lark could wield both blades when he found her.

He stepped past the boundary of Inerys' wards, Aislinn close behind. Stars glimmered between the trees, the dark of night cloaking the forest.

He would be going alone.

"You understand," Aislinn said, her voice tight. "I can't tie myself to Lark. My power is still new, and I don't know what Nereida will do with it."

"I understand," Gavriel said, stepping over a felled tree trunk. "And it's not lost on me how much you continue to help us." When it was he who was trapped in his dreams, Aislinn gave Lark hope. Now she gave him a chance to bring her back.

"I will guide you as far as I can," she said, disregarding his words. "After that, it's up to you."

She held out her hand, and Gavriel grasped it in his own. A great wind blew, surrounding them in a tempest unsuited for the season. Her hair whipped around her face, and Gavriel squinted against the onslaught. The forest disappeared behind a wall of gusting force, hiding all from view and caging them.

The churning storm threatened to peel skin from the bone, and the stinging of Gavriel's face was worse than when the Den of Lions had dragged him through The Wastes under the blistering sun. The sound was unlike anything, a banshee wail battering against his ear drums. He tightened his grip on Aislinn's hand and gritted his teeth against the pain.

The wind slowed to a dull roar, and then... nothing. Muffling silence met his ringing ears, and the force against his very skin dulled to a stillness of the air. The cage of wind fell away to reveal a great set of double doors, ancient and gilded in strange markings. A twisted archway encased the edges of the doors, flickers of movement and spinning of dust like it was a living thing. Like the cyclone that had surrounded them, the air spun at a dizzying speed, the moan of the wind a constant undercurrent. A hand pressed free from the churning arch before it was sucked back into the violent vortex. A face appeared, mouth open in a silent scream.

These were twisted souls, trapped and spinning in this whirlwind of suffering, serving as a mere marker for the entry.

Bile rose in Gavriel's throat as another face appeared, agony stretching their exaggerated features.

"I've never seen the entrance to the Netherworld before." Aislinn's whisper ruptured their thick silence. "That's what this is, isn't it?"

Gavriel forced his gaze from the pain of the twisted souls to study the doors. Each marking shone like metal catching the light—inscriptions and runes he could not decipher. When Balan had spirited him away to the Netherworld, he'd bypassed any sort of entrance, materializing within the confines of his prison cell. But this...

A shudder broke across his skin, dread bringing a cold sweat to the back of his neck. There was something terribly wrong about choosing to enter the Netherworld as a living mortal, like signing away his life to resign himself to an eternity of darkness.

But Lark was in there, somewhere. And he would get her back even if it killed him.

"There's no time to waste." He shoved into the great doors, pushing with all his might, until they gave under his touch with a creak. Any fear he still carried, he welcomed. He invited it to spread in his blood like a poison. Fear had always been his survival, and now he rejected any notion of survival instinct. The only instinct he cared for was the one to lead him to her.

The doors finally swung wide, revealing an endless hall with no escape. The hairs raised on his arms, and a sense of wrongness once again came over him, thick and overpowering, like the smoke bombs Emric used to experiment with. It filled his lungs with the threat of panic. Such a strange, unperceivable power.

"Wards?" Gavriel asked, keeping his breathing slow and steady.

"I think so," Aislinn said, her voice shaky. "Gavriel, I don't know if I can enter here. If my presence alerts Nereida…"

"You've done enough." Gavriel gentled his voice. "You've done more than you know. I can take it from here."

Aislinn bit her lip, glancing around the threshold as if searching for a rip in the magic spelled to create such an overwhelming deterrent. She nodded absently, as if answering a question she hadn't asked aloud before grabbing him by the hand. "I'll wait for you both here and try to sense your departure. This isn't… I'm not well-versed in any of this, and I don't know exactly how to beckon Lark's soul to return. But my instinct tells me it's vital you keep this in mind." Her green eyes bore into his, alert and determined. "Memories have great power. Use them however you have to, and break her free."

Gavriel nodded, not quite knowing what she was getting at. Was he supposed to remember something helpful? Aislinn was a kind girl dealt a shit hand and far more powerful than anyone had realized. But she was still just a kid trying to make sense of an impossible situation. It wasn't her fault she didn't know how to save Lark, and he wouldn't put that on her.

Aislinn's eyes widened, true terror rounding their shape. "Someone's coming!" Her breathless gasp yanked Gavriel from his thoughts.

The Reaper Blade was in his hand before he could blink, and the sword bowed in his grasp, too heavy to hold upright without two hands.

Shit. That wouldn't work.

He stuffed it in the sheath at his back, groaning under the weight. Kenna's silver blade and his Ardenian dirk were already poised in his hands as the air before them rippled like a lake under the weight of a rock thrown. The ripples spread, until finally a figure appeared.

He wore a black doublet with gleaming silver buttons all the way to the throat. The billowing sleeves of his black tunic cast him in the role of a roguish yet fanciful pirate. Blond hair tied back at the nape of his neck, and palms rubbing together. "Missed me already, huh?"

Ferryn.

Staggering relief coursed through Gavriel at the sight of the former Reaper.

Ferryn wore a haunted look, and he forced a smile to transform the bottom half of his face. He grabbed Aislinn, tugging her into his arms and whispering against her hair. She nodded, and he released her and clasped Gavriel on the shoulder, hauling him against him in an embrace. Gavriel held his blades a safe distance, embracing him back without skewering him.

"How are you here?" Gavriel pulled away. He knew nothing of the hierarchy of the afterlife, but from what Lark had said, crossing from the Otherworld to the Netherworld was a task shrouded in secrecy. Though as the anchor to the veil, perhaps Ferryn existed in a more fluid state.

"I have every right to check on an unannounced mortal lingering at the Netherworld gates." Ferryn shrugged, but there were shadows in his eyes that hadn't been there before. "As the new Master of Reapers, it falls under my care. At least until I can sort out a governing structure in the Netherworld." His brows furrowed. "Nereida left quite a mess."

"You've taken Thanar's place then?" It was a strange thought. Ferryn of all people in charge of the Otherworld and leading souls to their destiny.

"I already know the lay of the land, so to speak. I'm the physical anchor, and I'm popular amongst my own." His usual biting sarcasm fell flat and emotionless. What had happened to the impish, carefree Reaper?

"Of that, I have no doubt," Aislinn said with a soft smile. "But if your power extends here, why have you not rescued Lark?"

She stole the words right out of Gavriel's mouth and delivered them with a soft blow. How the rutting skies did it slip Ferryn's notice that Lark had been stolen away?

The first true flash of emotion, panic, transformed Ferryn's sharp features. "What do you mean?"

"Nereida still lives and has cast her spell over Lark, rendering her body frozen in time while her soul is trapped in the Netherworld." Gavriel took a deep breath, reaching for the calm he needed. He sheathed his weapons and dragged the Reaper Blade from his back with great difficulty. "Now that you're here, you can carry the damn thing. We're getting her out."

"Of course, we are," Ferryn said quickly as he held the blade like it was little more than a dagger. "I'm just..." He shook his head, a weariness reserved for the old hounding his face. "I thought this was all over."

"You and me both." Gavriel gave Aislinn a nod, and she answered with her own. He would delay no more. "How do we find her? She escaped your notice easily enough. How do we track her?"

"I'm still learning on the job. I don't have it down to a practiced ease quite yet, and Nereida has thousands of years on me. She's more slippery than an eel, but she's also a vain creature. I have no doubt someone down here knows where she's hiding." Ferryn's eyes narrowed, an unfamiliar hardness claiming his features. "We will weed out her remaining allies and force their compliance."

Gavriel doubted Ferryn employed the same tactics of interrogation he'd been forced to master. For an ancient Reaper, he carried a delicate air. But something had shifted in the man, an edge taking shape that hadn't been there before. And a plan was as good as the ones willing to carry it out. Gavriel was willing to take it as far as possible. Further than the limits he thought he possessed, once upon a time.

THE NETHERWORLD WAS the birth of nightmares. Not that Gavriel was any stranger to nightmares, but its shapeless, ever shifting landscape was enough to drive a man mad. The scenery bent to the will of its inhabitants. Gavriel had not realized what a kindness it was that Balan melded hard and fast walls to his perception, shaping a prison out of the realm of nightmares to create something tangible.

Now, Gavriel passed through nightmares; one moment he was traversing a green countryside, the sound of a woman wailing carrying over the moors. The next, he was tripping over someone's dead horse, forgotten and abandoned in the sands of an unforgiving desert. He couldn't make sense of where he was headed, if he was traveling closer to Lark or further away, and as each visage melted into the next, the sense he was growing more and more lost crept across his mind.

Only Ferryn, his steadfast gait and assured stride, kept him from spiraling, That, and the thought of Lark equally lost.

"Why does the path keep changing?" Gavriel couldn't halt his question as he stepped from a blazing hot desert into the muck of a gloomy swamp, instantly transporting him to another unfamiliar location.

"The Netherworld is a mess right now." Ferryn's lip curled in disgust. "Nereida really fucked everything up down here. Probably a security measure to elude capture after slinking from her battle of defeat. In any case, we should be almost through the Suspended Lands."

Gavriel frowned. "Lark's never mentioned such a place." And he'd never witnessed it. But the difference between appearing within the confines of the Netherworld and entering from the outermost gate would explain the discrepancy.

"I love Lark, you know I do, but the girl woefully neglected her studies in favor of mooning over mortals." Ferryn gave Gavriel a once over. "At least she had good taste."

Gavriel fought the urge to smirk at that. It was a comfort to converse of her this way. It distracted from the task at hand while maintaining focus. Skies, he was starting to not only understand Ferryn's coping mechanisms but even agree with them.

"The Suspended Lands is the place where lost souls who do not deserve eternal damnation languish."

"I thought Arcadia was their salvation. Lark saw Hugo, she saw that he—"

"I said *lost* souls, Gavriel. Do keep up." Ferryn held out a branch to give Gavriel room to step between the trees. "Some souls are too... wounded to advance properly. But they at least crossed the bridge to the afterlife, so humanity is maintained." A somber expression stole across his face. "As does their suffering."

Anger welled up in Gavriel, swift and fierce, as the unfairness of it all set it. How little hope mortals had for peace in the afterlife. Avalon was a farce. Arcadia was easy to miss if one suffered in life and died before healing. It was a game rigged for most players to lose. And what would be the point in it all? In any of it? If suffering was rewarded with more suffering, how could anyone justify life? It was all a means to pain upon pain. Unhealed wound layered upon unhealed wound. It was an endless cycle of agony and—

"Fuck. Is there some sort of despair demon nearby?"

Ferryn stilled, his eyes searching Gavriel's face. "It's this place," he finally said, that new edge he'd honed hardening his words. "It feeds upon your pain and draws it to the surface." He placed a hand on Gavriel's shoulder. "You don't think anyone wishes to remain trapped in their pain, do you?"

Gavriel scratched the back of his heated neck. Yet again, he'd proven no mastery of his emotions, something he'd been so sure of a year ago.

"Are we through yet?"

"Nearly." Ferryn lowered his hand and continued on, his boots making sloppy noises in the sludge of the swamp. "I sense another change coming, likely the last one before we enter the next gate."

"The sooner we're through this the better." Gavriel forced his feet to move, ignoring the thick wet mud filling his boots and squishing beneath his feet.

The damp forest dissolved piece by piece until solid walls of wood grew in its stead. Gavriel's next step was upon solid floorboards, a swath of heat from a fiery hearth hitting him square in the face. Heady perfume filled the air, strong and thick, as did the scent of cheap ale. It was a tavern. Echoes of laughter and voices surrounded him, shadows of figures drinking and gambling, but no true shapes took form. It was like trying to remember a dream upon a waking, its image just out of grasp though burned against one's eyelids.

Throaty moans, practiced and overembellished, joined the din of noise, and dread churned in Gavriel's gut as he realized where he was. It had been many years, nearly fifteen years, since he'd set foot in this place. Since he'd forced the nausea and guilt down to the pit of his stomach to plaster on a smile and step through the doors. As if he could be happy seeing her here. As if he didn't know some of the assassins from his guild didn't frequent this infernal place, trading coin for skin without a care as to why some of these people were even selling.

Footsteps down the stairs, the soft sound almost lost amidst the noise, and she appeared. She hadn't changed. Not one freckle. Not one strand of hair dulled from years of stress. Not the circles under her eyes she poorly hid with powder, nor the familiar bruising along her neck.

Fifteen years, and this image of her was easier to conjure in his mind than all the memories he'd tried so desperately to cling to.

Fifteen years since he'd last seen his mother, alive in body but not spirit, behind the confines of this prison.

It was like being dropped into one's most vivid nightmare. The image burned into the back of one's mind, lying in wait, never forgotten, casting a shadow over one's thoughts.

His mother wiped her hands on her ill-fitting dress, careful to avoid the torn seams, and gathered her skirts as if she wore a handsome gown rather than tattered rags littered with stains.

Gavriel swallowed against the increasing tightness of his throat, his gaze surrendering to follow her every move about the tavern. A shadow called out something to her, a suggestive jeer in his voice, and her answering smile was too slow to be natural.

His mother tucked a strand of grayish-brown hair behind her ear, her eyes lifting at the sound of the door. She stared right through him, her green eyes the mirror image of his own, crushing hope in her gaze. Her eyes lowered, shoulders caving in ever so slightly.

She was waiting for him to visit. It was one of the days he couldn't break away after training. One of the days he'd pushed himself too hard. And she waited for a visitor that never came.

The searing ache of it all burned through Gavriel's chest like a scorching blade. How many times had he promised a visit in his letters, only for his own selfishness and pride to stand in his way? He told himself—he *lied* to himself—that his failure was in service of her freedom. That if he trained harder, pushed his body past its limits, took extra work details, he was acting in her best interest. But the ugly truth gripped his stomach. He'd always been ashamed that she sold her body. That his best chance was selling them both, him to the Guild and her to whoever entered that place with lined pockets and a hunger for flesh.

"Easy." Ferryn's voice broke through his thoughts. "Don't get caught in the cycle of torment, Gavriel."

Gavriel could scarcely breathe, his chest was so tight. "That's my mother."

She couldn't see nor hear him. She trudged about the room, feigning coy smiles and suppressing shuddering disgust. And when a group of shadows tugged her to the stairs, she only hesitated a moment, casting one last glance at the door, before allowing herself to be led away.

Gavriel was frozen in place, unable to take another step. It was foolish, downright illogical, but every fiber of his being wished to dash up the stairs after them, drag her away, tell her she needn't do this. He could take care of them both, he would. He would.

The scene flickered, shadows shifting almost in reverse. His mother appeared once more, wiping her hands on her dress, casting her glance to the door with a hopeful stare. The moment had reset, her pain and torment to fulfill a vicious cycle of waiting for her son who never came. To resigning herself to another night spent at the mercy of those who treated her like an object for purchase.

It was the loss of hope. That was her punishment.

Gavriel's eyes burned at he stared at his mother, still beautiful despite the way life had eaten away at her, leaving her frail and bruised.

"We need to go." Ferryn tugged his arm. "We can't afford you to get stuck here. Think of Lark."

Just the sound of her name was enough to douse Gavriel in reality. *Lark.* His hope. His love. His salvation. He would not allow his guilt to keep him trapped, separated from her for an instant longer. But there was one thing he had to do first.

"I'm sorry," he called out to the visage of his mother, his words unheard. "I should have told you how much I love you. I recognize your sacrifice now, and there is no shame." Tears threatened to fall. "The only shame is mine. I should have broken away from the Guild. I should have taken you away from this and not allowed your guilt to keep you trapped here."

His mother's face fell, and she once again allowed herself to be led to the stairs by a group of shadows.

"I won't leave her here," Ferryn said. "I promise. But we need to go now."

Gavriel nodded, watching until his mother disappeared up the stairs. "I know," he said and continued their journey, only letting his eyes slip closed when the tavern melted away to reveal another door, a door smaller than the first entryway to the Netherworld. He took a breath, long and deep, and on his exhale, released the last of his guilt.

It felt wrong to let it go, like the guilt was a piece of her he'd kept safe from time. But the truth was, he was a child back then, and a child did not deserve to bear the weight of his mother's choices. Ferryn would find a way to release her soul, and that was the best he could hope for right now. He could not change the past, but he could honor her sacrifices in the choices he made each day.

He would tell Lark more about her, rather than fear the pain of speaking her name, of remembering his guilt.

Something tugged at him, deep in his chest. A hard tug that almost made him take another step forward. It was a visceral sensation, like a fist had closed around his heart. Gavriel rubbed his chest, relief and joy claiming dominance over any lingering pain. It was insistent, coursing through him like it had always been part of him, nestled deep within his soul.

"We're getting closer."

Ferryn nodded, reaching a hand up to the door. "How can you tell?"

Gavriel rubbed his chest again. *Thank the skies.* "I can feel Lark."

CHAPTER EIGHTY-TWO

LARK

Searing pain dug into the bottoms of her feet like the relentless edge of a blade. Lark opened her mouth to scream and was met with silence. The roots of the ancient yew dug into her vulnerable flesh, carving into her skin the more she thrashed to free herself. She'd never known pain, only mere whispers of sensation ghosting by, and the full-fledged onslaught of physical sensation over-whelmed her. It dug agony from the inside out, weaving fire and ice beneath her skin as the tree tightened its hold on her.

The air was frigid, biting and unforgiving. Another breeze wailed through skeletal branches, the lonely sky a muted grey, darkening with each passing breath.

Lark was alone. She was alone, and she didn't know why. Why was she even here? What was happening to her? As a Reaper, she did not feel pain. She did not feel fear or joy or love or pain. And now... she felt too much. Aching in a way she did not understand as tears rolled down her filthy mud and blood covered cheeks. Her body was naked and trapped beneath an ancient unyielding tree, and she was afraid. It had to be fear. The way her heart quickened, the way each breath got caught in her lungs, panic climbing up her throat. And pain. So much pain. The pain of her body and something deeper. The gnawing loss of something she couldn't remember. Something important had been snatched away, ripped from her, and she did not remember.

She could not cry out, her voice had been taken, too. And she didn't understand. She didn't understand, and why was she alone and afraid and *hurting*?

More silent tears tracked down her face, but Reapers could not cry. They could not cry, and they could not dream, so this was no nightmare. And what if this was what Thanar meant when he threatened to send her to the pits?

Lark pulled against the roots, more of her skin ripping open as fresh blood oozed down her belly and arms.

What had she done to deserve this?

She searched her memory, desperate to find the truth, but her mind kept hitting a wall. She remembered leading the mortal girl—Aislinn was her name—to the crossroads. After that, she punished Corwyn without disrupting the balance; she'd been so careful. Thanar hadn't even minded, she'd barely been scolded for that. He'd dismissed her and then...

Nothing.

Nothing but this unceasing torment.

Why was this happening?

Lark let out another silent scream as she fought against the confines digging into her skin.

But even if she had made a sound, she was well and truly alone in this forgotten forest.

It would be easier to give up. To let the roots swallow her whole. To decay and rot into the first floor until she was the earth and the moss and part of the tree forever.

Lark fought against her prison, agony slicing through her skin at every movement. She would tear herself apart fighting to get free. Because even through the pain, she was here. She was here and whole and had control over her mind. She had not sworn the oath to Thanar, and she never would.

The memory of Thanar punishing her, of forcing his will into her soul, assaulted her. She had been punished. But for what? Not for Corwyn. Not for Aislinn. What had she done?

Lark squeezed her eyes shut, breathing through the pain as she pulled against the roots and pushed against the wall in her mind. Something, there had to be something. An explanation of why she was here, suffering as if in a mortal body—

Lark gasped as a flood of memories poured in. The mortal man, Gavriel. His green eyes burning against the gloom of a darkened room filled with death as he bid farewell to his friend. Of the way his grief cut into her and made her feel things she couldn't feel as a Reaper. How she'd sworn he'd seen her, impossible as it was, and how she'd wanted nothing more than to know what his cheek felt like beneath her palm.

Gavriel.

And she had run her hand against his jaw. Once. Though the sensation was lost to her. And she had kissed his bloodied, poisoned lips. Once. And when the poison cleared his system and his eyes widened with anger and disgust, she'd felt something. Something she wasn't supposed to feel.

Lark was supposed to kill him, to eliminate any threat of disrupting the balance with her fascination, and she'd refused. Was this her penance?

No. No, she'd escaped the dungeon. Ferryn had come to her, and—

Nothing. A hard wall of stone blocked any more memories from trickling through. Exhaustion weighed down her bloody limbs. Exhaustion from fighting and from pushing her mind past whatever held her captive. She rested her temple against the harsh roots, their claws gripping her even tighter, and she let the image of the mortal man, *Gavriel,* linger in her mind.

His green eyes like a pine forest on a misty day. His hard scowl that melted into a boyish grin, a dimple creasing his cheek and whispering promises of easier coming smiles. The scar along his lip. His scent of northern wind, leather, and dark chocolate—

Lark jolted, digging the roots deeper into her skin.

Reapers did not experience the sense of smell, not without a memory fueling it. How could she possibly have the memory of his scent?

The wind groaned again, this time carrying the phantom echo of voices.

There was something vital she needed to remember. Something that would answer every blank spot in her mind and explain why she was here, trapped in torment. Something someone did not want her remembering.

"Lark!" A familiar voice called out again, panic lacing their tone, and Lark's heart leapt in her chest.

Joy. Relief. Painful hope. It all collided in her chest with the force of a battering ram. Someone was coming. Someone knew she was here and had come to find her. Tears pricked her eyes as Lark opened her mouth to yell back.

Silence.

No. No. No.

Lark yanked and tugged, her mouth open in a silent scream as she ripped skin from her arm desperately trying to free one hand. Her hand broke free, blood and muck mixing where her skin had torn open, before the roots closed back in around her, nearly suffocating her with their angry embrace. She dug at her enclosure, balling her hand into a fist and beating into it with every ounce of her dwindling strength.

It was no use. Her blows fell softer, muscles too weak and pain too great.

"Lark!" His voice called out again, and something tugged in Lark's chest.

Hope.

She could not call back to him, but he would find her, whoever he was. And just by his voice alone, Lark knew he would not hurt her.

The man appeared in the distance. The side of his head was covered in blood; it dripped down his jaw. His gait was uneven, favoring one side, and his chest rose and fell in an uneven rhythm. When he caught sight of her, his pace quickened, and a hand shot out to steady him.

Ferryn. Lark would know that head of golden hair anywhere. His face was twisted in a grimace as he ran toward her, aiding the wounded man beside him.

His was the face that punched the breath from her lungs.

It was the face she'd been imagining—the face of the man who'd glared up at her in disgust. The one that haunted her thoughts, clouding her judgment, and sowing desire for *more* than this existence.

Gavriel.

There was no disgust in his expression this time, despite the gruesome scene she was sure he'd just stumbled upon. Only pain and anguish and relief.

He sank to the ground beside her, hands shaking as he brushed them with heartbreaking gentleness across her brow, her lip, her jaw. The care in his touch, touch that should not feel this familiar and safe, pushed the tears to spill down her cheek.

"Lark," he whispered. "I'm here."

Behind him, Ferryn had already begun to cut away at the roots, wielding a strange shortsword with glimmering shadows along the blade. The roots fell away, and cold air bit at her suddenly exposed wounds and nakedness. Gavriel bundled her into his arms, lifting her easily and stepping away from the infernal tree. Lark clung to him, unable to articulate a single word despite the spiral of her thoughts.

How had they found her? Why did he feel so familiar? Why was she even here? What did any of this mean?

Gavriel ripped off his jerkin and then his tunic, gently pulling it over her head and guiding her arms into the sleeves. When he tried to put his leather armor piece on her, she shook her head. It would hurt too much to have anything pressed tightly against her frayed skin. He nodded and tied his cloak around her neck, replacing the jerkin over his bare torso.

Ferryn crouched beside her, placing a gentle touch beneath her chin. "Are you all right?"

Lark could not give an answer she did not know, so she merely stared back.

Ferryn's brow furrowed. "Can you speak?"

Lark shook her head. That she could at least answer.

Gavriel cursed. "Nereida's doing?"

"Assuredly." Ferryn stood, running his hands into his hair.

Nereida. Why was that name so familiar?

Lark darted her gaze between the two men. Was Gavriel a Reaper now? No. He was wounded and Reapers bore no physical marks. She reached up to his temple, and when he flinched she immediately regretted the action.

Gavriel caught her wrist before she could pull away. "What's the last thing you remember?"

That was the question, wasn't it? Lark shrugged and shook her head. Frustration gnawed at her. She could not tell him that she was sure she was missing important pieces of her memories.

Gavriel's eyes widened, and he called back to Ferryn. "Aislinn told me something—said it was important."

Ferryn turned to regard him.

"Memories have great power. Use them however you have to, and break her free." Gavriel angled his head, studying Lark with a contemplative expression. It made her want to take liberties she should not take with a complete stranger.

Though he wasn't a complete stranger, was he? She might not know how, but he was familiar and known to her in a way she could not mistake.

"Lark"—his voice was a deep rumble—"do you remember how you got here?"

Lark shook her head, unable to hide the smile twitching against her lips. It was such a relief to hear them ask the right questions.

"Do you remember me?" The hope in his voice made her chest tighten.

She didn't know how to answer that. She had a recollection of him, but it felt incomplete. She shook her head with a shrug. *Let him make what he can of that.*

Gavriel's lips parted, understanding dawning on his face. "She made you forget… everything?"

Lark nodded, not understanding who *she* or *everything* meant.

"That fucking bitch!" Ferryn's voice called out, and Lark jumped at the sound. "She couldn't just accept defeat, could she? No, she needed one last shot." He huffed out a growl before stalking over to sit beside them. "I'm Ferryn and I'm your favorite person in all of existence."

Lark rolled her eyes, gesturing to him in hopes it communicated she already knew him.

Ferryn blew out a breath. "Thank the skies, all the important parts remain."

Gavriel ignored him, scooting closer to run a hand along her jaw, Lark leaned into his touch, unable to deny the comfort it brought. "You trust me?"

She nodded, keeping her face against his palm.

Gavriel leaned toward her, breathing his words against her lips. "I'm going to kiss you, and you're going to remember how long we've loved each other."

Lark shivered at his words, at the puff of breath released alongside them, and the first press of his lips ignited fire along her skin, along her veins, deep in her blood. Uncaring for her still open wounds, Lark launched herself at him, pressing her mouth firmer against the seam of his. It was life. It was everything. Something tugged deep in her chest, pulling her closer, and she delved into the heat of his mouth.

Gavriel groaned against her kiss, his hands careful on her as he gently pulled her away. "Do you remember?" he panted. She shook her head, leaning in for another of those life-giving kisses, but he halted her. "Wait," he said. "I can't... how do I do this?" His brow creased as if he was in pain, and the sight was enough to douse any lingering heat.

"Memories have great power," Gavriel mused aloud, soft enough Lark couldn't be sure he was talking to her. He leaned his forehead to hers. "You are my soul-bonded. Please, *please,* remember that."

And maybe in the stories mortals told to give themselves the illusion of power over the gods and goddesses who remained ambivalent to their plight, it would have been enough. Skies, Lark wished it was enough. But the wall remained firmly planted in her mind, shutting out anything else from trickling in.

"I admire your spirit," a rich voice called out coyly. Gavriel spun around and Lark angled her head to look past him.

Leaning against a tree, inspecting her nails as if she was bored, was a woman. Her hair was a tattered blanket of snow, uneven and hanging in jagged shards down her back. She flitted her gaze to them, and deep violet eyes rimmed in shadows glared at them. "Unfortunately for you, handsome, I've done a much better job tying the knots in her mind. You won't unravel them so easily."

She spoke of her. *She* was the reason Lark couldn't remember. Why she was trapped here with no explanation. What had she done to earn this woman's ire?

A metallic sound rang out, and Ferryn stood brandishing the strange sword. "You're finished here, Nereida. You think I can't sense you? Your power is lost. You're hanging by a thread. Just look at you." His face twisted in disgust. "It's embarrassing."

So, this was Nereida. A trickle of familiarity glimmered in Lark's mind, but it wasn't enough to crumble the wall down.

"Embarrassing?" Nereida grinned, her smile sharper than a blade.

Gavriel angled his body in front of Lark's, and something about that irritated her. Like he was more fragile than he realized and should be hiding behind her instead. Lark struggled to stand, the pain against the soles of her feet nearly sending her to her knees, but she remained upright. Gavriel's tunic hit her midthigh, her legs dripping her blood into the earth.

"I see your weakness, Ferryn." Her grin was a cruel slash across her inhumanly beautiful face. "I can smell your pain. You finally got what you always wanted, and yet, the victory rings as hollow as your eternal emptiness. You got a taste of living and forgot what a pale imitation the memory of life is."

Ferryn's eyes slid shut, the only sign that her words landed their mark, before he opened them once more to glare at her. "I will undo everything your cursed touch has spoiled."

"Oh, yes." Nereida nodded. "I'm sure you will. And you." She turned her attention to Gavriel. "Haven't you figured it out yet? You will never have her. You are destined to forever chase the love you failed to protect."

Gavriel leaned closer into Lark, as if his proximity was enough to prove her words wrong.

Rage, bitter and dark, bloomed in Lark at the woman's vicious attempts at goading them. There was much she still didn't understand or remember, but her blood heated, muscles trembling in the wake of her words.

"We took out your pathetic stragglers," Ferryn continued. "You hide here behind Lark. You can't possibly think you can win this."

"You're right." She pushed off the tree, and both Gavriel and Ferryn stiffened. "I have no intention of killing Lark, and I know I cannot hope to defeat you all." She bit her lip, eying Ferryn with a suggestive look. "But I don't need to kill you, do I?"

The wind had died down, silence claiming the dead forest where they stood. And something about that, about the utter stillness in the air, set Lark's mortal heart pounding in her chest.

Nereida jabbed a sharp nail in Lark's direction. "*She* took something from me. Balance must be restored."

Lark tried to speak, tried to ask what she'd done—

No sound escaped her silent throat.

Nereida scoffed. "That's more irritating to me than anything." She waved her hand.

Lark choked, gagging on the influx of air stretching her throat. Gavriel's hands found her shoulders, and his face appeared before her, worry tightening his features.

"I'm fine," she said. Realization dawned on her. "My voice…"

"I thought it would be poetic justice," Nereida said, breaking off into a coughing fit. "But without your memory, it just doesn't land."

None of this made any sense. Nereida was toying with her, but why?

"This ends now." Ferryn charged toward her, and Nereida held her hands up in mock surrender.

"You know Lark and I are still tied to one another." When Ferryn froze, she walked her fingers up the blade of his outstretched sword.

"And you have no life wielder to bring her back this time. Sure, perhaps with proper training you could learn to penetrate the veil to give and take life, but you'll never master it in time. And do you really wish to take that path? The same path to Thanar's undoing?" At his horrified expression, she cackled. "You really didn't think this through, did you? How will you ever take Thanar's place if the most basic of critical thinking eludes you?" She knocked the sword away, stomping over to where Gavriel stood poised in front of Lark. Nereida stumbled before finding her footing.

She was weaker than she pretended. It was worth noting.

"And you!" She gripped Gavriel by the jaw, and he pulled his face away. "You're nothing more than cannon fodder. Pity, she won't even remember to mourn you."

Lark's head spun, dizzying thoughts competing and churning. Who was Nereida? How did she have everyone so afraid of her? She must have been very powerful. But something glimmered along the edges of Lark's awareness. She had said they were tethered to one another. Lark gave an experimental tug on their thread, as was her right as a Reaper.

Vile hatred met her. A toxic, poisonous anger that simmered like a cool rage beneath the surface. It was a creeping vine, vengeance and injustices mingling to create these twisted thoughts.

She killed her... I have nothing... Death is too easy... Make her bleed, make her hurt... Slow and lingering... Take her hope... The mortal's death is not near enough...

Lark gasped as Nereida's fantasy for Gavriel filled her mind. His stomach was ripped open, guts and innards spilling across the forest floor, and crows pecked at his remains. She fought to even her breath, letting the panic subside.

Lark did not remember, but her body did. Her body remembered the utter horror she would feel, the grips of despair she would succumb to, if ever Gavriel's death came to pass. And it was enough.

"You're very powerful," she finally said, stepping around Gavriel to address Nereida. "I can sense it in you, your power. I wonder why you remain tethered to me at all." She stepped closer, forcing herself to draw nearer despite her mortal instincts screaming to keep her distance.

"Is it because right now you're gravely weakened? Do you possess enough power to survive on your own?"

Nereida's eyes flashed, and Lark smiled. She gathered her will, preparing to delve into Nereida's soul—

The forest melted away, grey sky darkening to a stone ceiling, onyx floors replacing moss and roots, and the *crackle* of fire in the lit braziers replacing the hum of the wind. A grand throne room stretched before Lark, Nereida seated upon the throne. She braced herself on the arm of the throne, appearing too weak to even sit up.

Lark glanced around. No Ferryn. No Gavriel. She and Nereida were alone in that grand hall.

Frustration raced through Lark in the quickening of her pulse and the heat in her cheeks. "Why do you run?"

Nereida laughed, and the sound choked off into a rasping cough. "I run, because I do not wish to die." She hung over the side of the throne. "Foolhardy as that might be, any chance to extend my life but a moment is worth it. Is it not?" Another wet cough. "We are more alike, Larkin, than you wish to admit."

"Perhaps if I remembered, I could admit much more than you know."

"Ooh." Nereida pushed herself to stand. "I quite like that. Unfortunately for you, your memories are locked up here." She tapped against her temple. "You will not retrieve them with my death, and I am the only one who can release them."

Lie. That was a lie so beautifully spoken, such assured confidence, that Lark almost believed her. But the truth was, Lark had pushed against that impenetrable wall and sought memories tucked away before she'd been locked out once more. And her emotions, her reactions, they remembered Gavriel. Nereida was lying because she was desperate.

"Someone once told me that mistakes are borne of desperation." Another memory hit Lark. Nereida in her study, scroll in hand and sharpened bone in the other. Lark signed her name at the bottom of that contract, sealing her fate, sealing Gavriel's, even Thanar's.

Because Thanar had inherited the debt she bore and set her free.

615

A simple act of transference magic. It was when they stood in this very hall, and Nereida revealed the soul-bond she and Gavriel shared—

Lark staggered as another flood of memories washed over her. Memories of sneaking into his tent, his hand upon her throat. The first time she made him laugh. The desperation of their first kiss in the middle of the road. The night they spent exploring one another at sea. Nights and promises and kisses and whispers, all filling her head and her heart with precious memories. And once they nestled back into place, more followed.

Another life, sneaking away from their master to do the most wondrous and dangerous thing a mortal can do: Dream.

"I remember."

Lark glanced down at her hands, palms torn from roots Nereida had planted in her mind. Because that's what they were. The trap of pain within her own head. It was real, and yet...

With a whisper, the wounds disappeared, skin restitching together as if never parted. Because she wasn't physically here. This was her soul, torn from her body back in the mortal plane, and held captive by her own fears, her own pain, her own doubts.

The life she lived as a mortal was real. This was another illusion, as was the illusion of Nereida's lingering power. They had defeated her, and this was but a mere echo left behind, clawing to live with the same desperation Lark had shown against those roots.

Lark delved into Nereida's mind, unraveling the tether as easily as pulling a thread.

"We are free," Lark said, a watery smile claiming her mouth. She lifted her gaze to where Nereida had sunk to her knees, the air around her rippling. "There's nothing left for you here."

"You think you've won," Nereida gasped through labored breaths, "but you don't understand the power Avalon holds over us all, still. They're—" Her voice broke off, another gasp escaping. "They're the ones who punish us all."

Lark nodded. "I know. Which is why Aislinn is going to tear it down."

Nereida's eyes widened, and for the first time, shock splashed across her face, lending her sultry features an almost innocence. She flickered like the fluttering flame of a candle, guttering in a phantom breeze before she burned away into ash. Silence thickened the air, a true echo of absence.

Nereida was no more.

Lark fell to her knees, without the tether to her soul, weakness weighted her body. She reached out to Gavriel, a sensation only made possible in the planes of the afterlife, and his responding tug was the relief she craved. She pitched forward, content to wait for him to find her, as he always had, as he always would. Physical sensations dulled, as the truth of her distance from her body settled around her and swathed her.

Footsteps scuffed against the floor, her name carried by two voices.

Ferryn appeared, relief washing over his features as he shook his head at her. "Little bird," he whispered. "You pain in the ass."

Lark grinned back, and when Gavriel appeared, she reached up to him, allowing him to hold her, even if she couldn't feel it.

"I remember," she whispered.

"I knew you would," he whispered back. Gavriel stared down at her, almost the mirror opposite of the way she'd held him all those months ago, when she was a Reaper and he a mortal with stars in his eyes.

"Because of fate?" Lark asked, smirking at him. Fate. The bane of her existence and sometimes the last hope. Fate that they were destined to find one another. In any life. In every life. For all eternity.

Gavriel pressed a gentle kiss to her brow. "Fate had nothing to do with it, darling. It was all you."

CHAPTER EIGHTY-THREE

LARK

$\mathcal{D}$ays bled together, pouring into the next, like water in a basin. Without Nereida's torment and isolation, without the shroud of doubt Lark had been trapped in, she could assess the state of things in the aftermath of battle.

Ferryn was gone. Lark knew what he'd said, and there were moments she wondered if he really could step into the mortal world, cloaked from sight, and watch her without a tether. If he'd taken Thanar's mantle of responsibility, he had his work cut out for him in the Otherworld and Netherworld. But with the truth of Aislinn and the other old gods...

Things had changed.

Aislinn kept her designs for Avalon hidden, unwilling to involve them. She would not share any details save for that she would search the mortal plane for any lingering somniavi, and together, they would dismantle Sargon's poisonous kingdom and restore what once was. Merikh stood at her side, the proud soldier, as she relayed her plans to give Avalon back to the dreamers. To allow the old gods to awaken, in whatever form they took, and take their rightful place in Avalon. Where souls who wished for peace could carve out their own oasis and dream.

Arcadia was to remain, a domain run by Solana and granted as an option for those who sought it.

And the Netherworld. Ferryn had had enough of the Netherworld's chaotic imbalance of power and planned to divide it into multiple planes of existence, ranging in severity of punishment. Demons were no longer to be created, forged from the forced cruelty they endured and committed. Punishments of the afterlife were to befit the individual's crimes, not languish in the pleasure of torture. But Lark would not see him in the afterlife. One promise he'd made her, was that she would never be a Reaper again but would know peace when her time came. It was a heartbreaking kindness, one she'd accepted with tears rolling down her face. And in their final embrace, it had been the hardest thing in the world for her to let him go. But she wasn't the only one he made promises to.

Gavriel's mother, for one, would be freed from her eternal torment. As would any who'd been stuck reliving pain they did not deserve.

But even knowing all this, all the good Ferryn sought to achieve, did not alleviate the pain in Lark's chest that her friend was too far from her grasp. Forever out of reach. Perhaps he wished it that way, after Ceto. Another parting gift of his was information about Hazel's brother, Gregoir. He was not in the pits as Leysa had sworn. No, she'd wiped his memory and set him free. Untethered, he was invisible to Ferryn and his Reapers. Unless Gregoir prayed to the gods, he remained unknown to Aislinn as well.

Hazel was determined to find him, one way or another, and though she promised to mind matters of the Guild, the look in her eye said otherwise.

She was going to run. Lark couldn't even blame her for it.

Demetria had returned to Koval to rebuild. And though her gaze bore the age of someone who'd suffered many losses, there was still hope to be found in the remains of her kingdom. Under Captain Ingemar's advisory, Demetria had formed a plan to reshape the very governing structure. To prevent such disparities among her people and their well-being from ever happening again.

Daciana... building the veil damn near killed her. She'd poured every shred of her power into its creation, severing her own tie to her magic in the process. She had confided in Lark the reaching consequences of using that much power. That when she'd awoken, she'd reached for the tendrils of her abilities—

Only to be met with silence.

Nereida had turned vengeful and merciless in the absence of her power. She'd said it was like existing without a soul, without dreams. But Daciana was so much more, had so much more to live for. And each day it was as if an invisible weight was lifting until finally she was free.

Inerys retired indefinitely. Refusing to peddle even the simplest spell. Said she needed her solitude and her return to nature. Lark respected that, admired it, even. And she would endeavor to keep from asking for help for as long as she could.

Though Langford and Alistair accepted their roles of emissaries to Koval with surprising ease, they focused on working tirelessly on their building plans for their home. Books on garden keeping were acquired, and many arguments over keeping animals erupted. It was impossibly comforting to see those two bicker about such normal things. The everyday happenings of life.

And Gavriel. His nightmares had returned. As had Lark's. Most nights, she awoke to his pain, his tossing and turning, protests spilling from his lips. She'd gently wake him and reassure him she was here. She was all right. All was well. And he'd bury his head in her neck, holding tight enough it nearly hurt. Shaking. Sobbing. Lark hated what she'd done to him. The pain she'd caused. But as days turned to weeks, gradually his nightmares softened. He'd still awaken with a jolt and reach out for her. And Lark was always ready to reach back and slide into his arms.

Right where she belonged. For all the days to come.

LANGFORD

*L*angford tilted his head, thoughts warring with indecision. Everything hinged on this, the final precipice of change. If he chose poorly, all would suffer. If he chose correctly—

"Paragon's tits, Langford. Choose a bloody curtain." Alistair smoothed his annoyed tone over with a kiss to Langford's temple.

"Don't rush me. This is an important decision. One that will determine—"

"The rest of our lives, yes. You said the same thing about the chairs, the table, even the box plants outside. You know they die every year, don't you? We'll get another chance soon enough."

"That is not the point." Langford turned away, hiding his smile. "I just want to make this place ours."

"Aye," Alistair said softly. "I know." He wrapped his arms around Langford, resting his chin on his shoulder. "Which one speaks to you?"

Langford leaned back, reveling in his warmth. After the bloody battle against Nereida's forces, he hadn't thought he could ever feel well and truly safe again. There was much to be done in the following days; many lives had been lost, and the changes in the world were undeniable.

Ferryn and Aislinn...

"Which curtains do you imagine throwing closed as I ravage you?"

Langford's cheeks burned. "Don't be crass."

"I'm not!" He turned Langford to face him. "I want you to imagine them in our home. They're parted to allow the sun to lend you ample reading light. I come home from the market, devastatingly handsome after a rousing hunt for bargains, and overcome, you throw yourself at my feet."

"None of this sounds real."

"*Then*," Alistair continued, "you realize your error. The curtains! What if the neighbors see?"

"We don't have any neighbors. Not close enough to peep in our windows."

"But it's too late, you've awakened the beast, and I will have my fill." Alistair growled, scraping his teeth against Langford's neck.

It was a reminder of what Alistair had once become when the veil was still absent. Now, after Daciana restored the veil and anchored Ferryn as its tether, Alistair didn't shift anymore. Last they heard, Kenna was devising a concoction to grant Daciana the mastery to shift at will, but they'd made no proclamation of success. Despite Alistair's cure from the shift entirely, it didn't prevent him from being particu-larly... *rambunctious* each full moon.

Langford suspected it was an excuse, especially since the only time he'd actually become his beast form was under the sun rather than the moon, but he wasn't complaining.

"Come now, love," Alistair rasped in his ear. People were staring now. "Which one do you see desperately pulling shut while I pleasure you within an inch of your sanity?"

Damn that foolish, impertinent lecher.

And damn him for its effects.

"The... blue ones."

"Good choice." Alistair scraped his beard across Langford's neck. "Think we'll have everything ready before Lark's return?"

"Don't ruin it now."

Lark and Gavriel had plans to venture the world, seeing every continent together. A grand adventure before returning to Ardenas once more. The assassins were governed under Hazel's care in his absence, but something told Langford Gavriel wouldn't be returning to the Guild of Crows. Not unless Lark wished it.

Daciana and Kenna also had plans for an extended trip. To travel and seek out any lingering monsters. It was an honorable goal, one they should have sought after as well, but Alistair had put his foot down, saying, *'we've done enough.'*

Langford turned on his heel, fabric in hand, and marched away. Laughing when he spotted Alistair chasing after him.

DACIANA

"*D*on't tell me you're surprised," Daciana said with a laugh, neatly folding and rolling her clothes to fit in her pack.

They should have finished packing hours ago, enjoying their last afternoon and evening before they traveled the world for the better part of a year. But Kenna always found a way to procrastinate, and that usually involved distracting Daciana from her own tasks.

Kenna huffed, tossing her things into her satchel, uncaring of the state they landed in. "I'm annoyed."

"Is that a new feeling in regards to Ruva?"

Ruva and a small band of hunters had arrived... long after the battle. Kenna was still moaning about the *convenience* of their *fortuitous arrival.*

"I'm only saying, send a bloody raven. If she'd arrived a week sooner, I'd be appreciative. But no, she waited until after a lot of people died, people who had no business fighting monsters. I've said it before, and I'll say it again. Don't do a hunter's job without proper training. Although we needed them, so I suppose this was a one-off situation. But it could have been avoided if Ruva had found her spine sooner—"

Daciana silenced her with a kiss. "I know. Believe me, I know."

In the aftermath Daciana was almost... guilty. She'd severed her cursed power, relinquishing it to the veil when she'd erected the new barrier, and she was glad. No more worrying over pulling too much, no more fear of losing control. She just was.

And that was the greatest gift. Second only to her chatty hunter. And when Kenna had seen the envy in Daciana's gaze when Alistair had shifted from an emotional state, not the call of the moon, she'd immediately set to work on making a similar serum.

By the grace of the skies, she'd done it. Daciana maintained full control of her shift, choosing when and how long to run in her wolf form. Out of habit, and to prevent agitation, she shifted under the full moon's watchful eye still. She *reveled* in it, and for the first time since her bloody ascension, she recognized the gift of her bloodline's power. The freedom it granted... it was unparalleled.

Kenna harrumphed, mashing her still-dirty tunic into her bag filled with clean clothes. "I still don't trust it was an accident."

"Perhaps not." Daciana wrinkled her nose as Kenna forced more items into her pack, stretching the seams. A tattered edge of a book peeked out from between a stack of breeches. She inched it free, careful not to disturb the pile. "What's this?"

Kenna stood on tiptoes to peer over Daciana's shoulder. "Oh! Ruva lifted a few more books from Elder Muirgel's house as a peace-offering. Didn't I tell you?"

Daciana flipped through the pages, grinning. "You did not."

"When I find the writer, I'm getting them to sign each one of their works." Kenna chucked another tunic at her pack, knocking the stack of breeches to spill across the bed.

Daciana continued thumbing through Kenna's book, letting page after page flip until she landed on the final page. An elegantly flourished pair of initials glared up at her.

B. R.

One name came to mind...

"Who did you say wrote these?"

"I didn't." Kenna stuffed her spare cloak into her pack. "My home's best kept secret. No one knows who the writer is."

Daciana reached into Kenna's bag, pulling another book free. She flipped to the last page to find those same initials. She grabbed another book and another, each containing B. R. on the last page.

She laughed, unable to contain her mirth. What if it was the bard? The one so affected by his run-in with Lark he penned a ballad in her honor? *Bartrand Rigglesby.* It wouldn't be the strangest thing to happen to them, not by far.

"Why are you laughing?" Kenna's arms came around her, and Daciana leaned into her hold.

"An amusing theory regarding your secret author. If we happen upon him again, I'll find out if I'm right."

They would spend the next year traveling, seeking out any lingering monsters still plaguing the mortal world. It was a goal and plan, both things Daciana appreciated. It granted time and space for she and Kenna to see the world together without the mounting pressure to return swiftly.

Though she would miss Lark.

Watching her fall... watching the life leave her eyes... she still hadn't gotten over it. Even after stitching her back into her body, calling her back to the land of the living, the memory of Gavriel breaking over her lifeless body...

But she came back to them. To her. Lark came back, and they had years and years to look forward to. They would pen letters as they'd done before. Gavriel would take care of Lark, as she would care for him, and Daciana could take some much-needed time with the love of her life. Free from outside pressures and grave threats of mass destruction. Without worrying if Lark and the others were safe.

She inhaled a deep breath, grounding herself in this moment, this truth.

"Do we need this?" Kenna held up another riding cloak, durable fabric and fine detailing. It was likely the most expensive thing Daciana owned. But her own pack was full, and Kenna's was about ready to pop.

"No," Daciana said, allowing the wave of peace to come over her. "I have everything I need."

LARK

*L*ark stared out over the fields of Oakbury. The Walden Inn and Tavern sat at the edge before the forest, the same as it had always been.

Yet somehow smaller.

"Care for some company?" Daciana plopped down beside her, following her line of sight. "Interested in a pie for the road?"

"No," Lark said swallowing. "They don't make them like she did." Mrs. O'Connell's loss was mere months ago, yet somehow it felt like ages since she'd wrapped any of them in one of her flour-covered hugs. So much had changed, and while there was great joy to be found, they'd defeated the witch-queen of the Netherworld, restored order and balance to a world on the brink of destruction, and came out alive.

Most of them.

Daciana regarded Lark, quirking her mouth to the side. Her hazel eyes had narrowed in quiet calculation. "I spoke of my power," she began, "after everything. I confided in you about its loss, but you have yet to share, and I admit I grow impatient. Do you still feel it?"

Lark flexed her hand against her thigh. After recovering from Nereida's invasion, after her soul had returned to her body, she had tried experimentally to forge a tether.

No echoes of her Reaper abilities remained, and Lark couldn't find it within herself to care. She was mortal, through and through. A wish once seemingly so impossible, her reality once more.

Lark let a slow smile dawn on her face as she turned to Daciana. She shook her head, and Daciana's answering smile was as brilliant as the last rays of the day's sun.

They fell into a comfortable silence. Daciana was one of the few people Lark could sit like this with. Without forcing words to take shape. It was true, she didn't grieve the loss of her powers, and there was much to be grateful for. To celebrate. But bitterness tinged her thoughts. A sense of loss.

Ferryn was gone.

Aislinn was also venturing out of reach.

And now Daciana was leaving.

"Would you change things?" Daciana asked.

Would she change things? Lark didn't know how she could. The veil was restored. Nereida was defeated. Aislinn was determined to take control of Avalon.

Lark should say no, she would not change things. She should revel in all that survived the depths of the darkness. "The selfish part of me wishes I could. The rational part knows I cannot without risking greater sacrifice. So, I don't know."

Daciana nodded, slinging an arm around Lark's shoulders. As if she sensed Lark needed that touch. "We never did celebrate the way we planned."

An unwilling grin spread across Lark's face. "You mean the revelry Alistair promised?"

"The very same."

"But you're off so early in the morning." As was she. Gavriel had planned an entire expedition to show Lark every corner of the world. For a Reaper, her whole life had seemed so tight and narrow. Now the vast expanse of the horizon had spread, lending unlimited opportunity. But a sense of fear scratched at the back of her mind. The fear of losing something she'd desperately clung to.

Daciana, Alistair, Langford. Lark did not wish to experience a life without them.

"I don't mind traveling tired or hung over." Daciana stood, yanking Lark up with her. "When we all return next spring, we can compare our journeys. Whatever you don't share in your dutiful letters I'm expecting."

"We will come back, though, right?" It was a fragile hope, shaky and weak within her chest. It tightened her throat and pricked her eyes.

"Oh, Lark." Daciana wrapped her arms around her. "You don't really think any of us wish to part, do you?"

Lark nodded, unsure if she was answering the question correctly.

"You are my family, Lark. My sister. Home is by the fire with you, Langford, and Alistair. This is not goodbye." Daciana pulled back to regard Lark with the warmth of her gaze. "Never goodbye."

Lark wiped her eyes, the clenching in her chest releasing. "Never goodbye," she repeated back. Because they had proven time and time again, not even death was the end. "Let's see if Inerys has anything good in that cellar of hers."

"Oh, I've found *many* delights in that cellar."

Lark laughed as they traipsed back through the woods.

The cadence of her heart settled as the familiar sense of belonging filled her.

This was no elegy. No final page of a book.

This was a new beginning.

EPILOGUE

Spring had beckoned, and the lupines had answers. They swayed in the warm breeze, dotting the riverbank in deep purple. Light glinted off the river, water rushing over rocks and glistening like diamonds. The air was warm, carrying the floral scent of nature's rebirth with every call of the wind.

Dappled sunlight danced across Lark's arms, the verdant leaves above swaying in a hushed gale. Gavriel's hand found her thigh, and she laughed as he squeezed.

"Tell me your thoughts," he said.

It was too big a question. Lark's thoughts were everywhere and nowhere. They followed their friends out of doors and across the sea. They climbed taller than the trees and soared on the airstream. They nestled deep in the forest and clung to the warmth of the riverbank—the warmth of this man, who had spent lifetimes loving her.

They'd spent the better part of a year together, exploring all the regions of the world without fear, without haste. A leisurely pace of adventure and new experiences. They'd bathed in the fresh springs of Koval, rode along the ridges of the Western Desolates, even climbed the frosty peaks of the Permafrosts. They'd spent days and nights mapping out new places to sleep under the stars, relearning the art of living. Living the life that had been stolen from them for so long. Coming back to Ardenas, seeing the life Langford and Alistair had built, only served to expand the bliss Lark had found with Gavriel. The knowledge that life could slow down, be filled with quiet moments by a familiar hearth, and hold the joy of an adventure all the same.

"I'm thinking," Lark said, grinning when he climbed over her and his face filled her view, her favorite scar curving against his mouth. "I rather like this feeling." Sunlight glinted off the simple gold band he wore, the one that matched her own. This life had granted them another chance to pledge their hearts and souls to one another.

He bent his head and kissed her, slow and thorough. "What feeling is that?"

"Like I'm finally where I was always meant to be." No more fighting fate. No more clawing her way out of the trenches. She was here, she was present, she was home. It was the simpler life of mortals she'd always craved. The joy of deep contentment. She'd never wished for more than life. Than living and feeling and loving and experiencing. It was… everything.

"Right here?" He kissed her nose. "Or here." Her neck. "Perhaps a bit south?" He slid down and she laughed, grabbing him by the face and tugging him back up to her.

She gazed up at him, his forest-green eyes speckled with gold. The grin stretching his scarred mouth as he gazed down at her. Even the first hints of freckles along his nose. She leaned up and kissed him. "Right here."

He melted into the kiss, running his hands up and down her back. "We could stay here all day you know," he murmured against her lips.

"Mmhmm."

"But something tells me a certain wolf would be greatly vexed with me if I fail to return you in a timely manner…"

Lark shoved him up. Today was the day? How had she forgotten Daciana's ship was scheduled to dock in a week's time, giving them the chance to rally Alistair and Langford and meet them at the port?

"What are you waiting for? Off me now! Let's ready to journey to the port!"

Gavriel laughed and rolled to the side, resting his head on his hand as he watched her with amusement dancing in his eyes.

"Actually," he said, drawing out the word, "she wrote me a fort-night ago. Said there was a change in plans."

"Oh." Lark sat, disappointment deflating her. That was all right. Plans change. No doubt Daciana was enjoying her journey with Kenna and needed extra time.

"She said she was returning early, that she'd arrive at Langford and Alistair's at about noontime on this very day." Gavriel squinted up at the trees. "Think she's there already?"

"What?!" Lark lunged at him, pinning him to the ground and pressing kisses all over his face. "How could you trick me like that? Come on! Don't dally, Daciana awaits!"

Gavriel laughed as Lark extricated herself, stumbling as she pulled her boots back on. He held her up by her hips so she didn't teeter over.

"One day, you'll show that same level of excitement about me."

"Yes, yes. Now hurry!"

Gavriel shook his head and gathered their things. Hand-in-hand, they scurried through the forest.

Even if Lark knew nothing more of humanity than love—the love of the man beside her, his palm warm and calloused against her own, lifetimes echoing in his eyes; the love of her family, all hailing from opposite corners of the world and brought together by circumstance; the love of contentment, of finding appreciation for the here and now —it was everything worth living for.

AFTERWORD

From the very first sentence in Songs of the Wicked, I knew Aislinn would play a huge part in this story. Though her life ending was the catalyst to this tale, she was always more than that. She was every soul who's ever felt powerless. The ones who weren't saved in time. She was the pain I couldn't put into spoken word, and she became everything. Though Lark is the beating heart of this trilogy, Aislinn is the soul.

She has more story to tell… she and Merikh… so stay tuned for that announcement.

Thank you for embarking on this journey with me!

ACKNOWLEDGMENTS

I wrote a trilogy. Even as I type this, I scarcely can believe it to be true. I have so many people to thank, such a strong support system in place.

Lance. You are the reason I even started writing. You believed in me when I thought my stories were nothing more than daydreams. I love you forever, and you are my inspiration for true love.

My daughters, Wilding and Elfling. You inspire me every single day and bring so much joy and magic to my life. You both taught me what it feels like to love without measure.

Friel Black. My editor. My sister. My writing soulmate. I would have fallen apart without you. This series would exist hidden away on an external hard drive without you. You've been with me from the very beginning. You saw me when I wanted to hide, and I love you to the moon and back for that.

Elle. You are every star in my sky. I see you in every night, and I know you're still with me in some way.

Stella. You are the champion of my courage. You always know exactly how to challenge and encourage me, and you always find me when I lose my way.

Alysha. Your enthusiasm, your support, and our beautifully chaotic musings kept me from losing faith in my work, and kept this book from staying unwritten. I'm so grateful for our friendship.

Everyone who has ever read my trilogy, messaged me to yell at me about Hugo, shared how this story touched you, thank you. From the bottom of my heart, thank you.

ABOUT THE AUTHOR

C. A. Farran is a fantasy author. She's addicted to video games, KitKats, and energy drinks.

Farran grew up by the sea on a steady intake of fairytales, renaissance fairs, and mythology. She's always felt a profound connection to horror and dark fantasy, spending her childhood searching the woods for monsters and magic.

Now, she spends her days photographing nature in Maine with her three cats; Commander, Demon, and River, her husband, and their two wildlings.

To stay up to date on her shenanigans and literary mischief, check out cafarran.com or find her on instagram. She's absurdly friendly, it's rather off-putting.